AIR FORCE WIVES

✦ ─────────────────────── ✦

"There's something I have to tell you," Shelley said. "It may change your mind about marrying me."

"It doesn't matter," Tad said. "Whatever it is, we can work it out."

"I'm afraid that if you find out who my father is, you won't have anything to do with me."

"That's crazy...I don't care who your old man is."

"My father is General Pritchard."

Tad felt as if a fist had hit him in the solar plexus. He left the room, came back, and looked at her for a long time. Finally he smiled. "I wouldn't want to be in your shoes when you tell your father that you're marrying an enlisted man. Maybe we'd better elope and tell him later."

AIR FORCE WIVES

RUTH WALKER

Copyright © 1986 by Ruth Walker

All rights reserved under International and Pan-American Copyright Conventions. Published in the United States by Ballantine Books, a division of Random House, Inc., New York, and simultaneously in Canada by Random House of Canada Limited, Toronto.

Library of Congress Catalog Card Number: 86-90796

ISBN: 0-345-32380-7

Manufactured in the United States of America

BALLANTINE BOOKS • NEW YORK

Library of Congress Catalog Card Number: 86-90936

ISBN 0-345-32380-7

Manufactured in the United States of America

First Edition: November 1986

IN MEMORY OF MY HUSBAND, GEORGE ST. CLAIR WALKER, WHO SERVED HIS COUNTRY AND THE UNITED STATES AIR FORCE WITH HONOR.

ACKNOWLEDGMENTS

Since it would be impossible to acknowledge all the Air Force wives (and Air Force members) who so generously shared with me their hopes and dreams, their problems and everyday frustrations and hardships, their goals, and, most important of all, their pride in being part of the Air Force family, I'll say a hearty "thank you" to all with a special acknowledgment to the following: Linda Murphy, Thayer Thompson, Sandra Wheeler, Karla Wilson, Vicki Horton, Sue Kinnan, Capt. Joseph Nickolas, Paula Bavilacqua, Mary Raber Musson, Capt. J. Kenneth Harkins, Jr., Karen Wren, Candace Faber, Rosemary Redmond, M/Sgt. Bill Brienza, Bette Maisonneuve, Ginny Wilson, Mary Lynn Melleger, Malinda Van Vector, Cheryl Sue Lamoureux, Melanie White, Francine Speziale, T/Sgt. James R. Eddy, Susan Hewitt-Schroeder, Sherry L. Bennett, and Joanne E. Ewing.

I also want to add an especially warm "thank you" to Capt. Eileen Collins, Lt. Patricia A. Louis, Lt. Judy Martini, and Capt. Patricia Ann Randall, who epitomize the fine young women who are making the Air Force their career these days.

CHAPTER
✦ 1 ✦

Tai was riding the curl of the wave. The rest of the world was locked out, and she was aware only of the pressure building beneath her fiberglass surfboard, of the force pushing, pushing, pushing against her body, of the wave that arched above her, enveloped her in a tunnel of ice-blue water.

As she used her arms and feet to keep her body in perfect balance, exhilaration filled her. If she failed, she had only herself to blame, but if she won and reached the shallows without wiping out, then she had conquered, however briefly, the brutal force of the waves and gravity and the treacherous, unpredictable surfboard.

She broke through the end of the tunnel, into the Hawaiian sunlight. Briefly, the swelling sensation beneath her feet intensified, as if she were rising rapidly in an elevator, and then the drop began, the long descent, the sliding, slipping movement that told her *this* time she was going to win and ride the wave all the way to shore.

A few minutes later, her movement slowed as the wave lost its momentum, but the surfboard glided on another few yards, into the shallows a few yards off the beach.

Well satisfied with herself, Tai dropped to her stomach on the fiberglass board and paddled the rest of the way to shore.

She smiled indulgently when she saw that Bobby Jo was still stretched out on her lauhala mat, a scarf protecting her auburn hair, her dark green eyes hidden behind outsized sunglasses, her body well oiled against the Hawaiian sun, looking as if she hadn't moved during the half hour Tai had been surfing.

Although Bobby Jo was her best friend, they were a striking contrast to each other. Frankly indolent, Bobby Jo had never been on a surfboard and in fact seldom went into the water when she came to the beach. Where Tai's skin was the color of ripe apricots, Bobby Jo's was peaches and cream, and her body was all curves with no angles—quite a contrast, Tai thought ruefully, to her own narrow-hipped, small-boned build.

She'd once overheard a teacher at Punahou, the Honolulu prep school from which they'd both graduated three months earlier, describe her as a China doll. Actually, she was *hapa-haole*, what the Hawaiians called those of mixed blood. From her Cajun father, she'd inherited her blue eyes, but her diminutive size, oval-shaped face, and black hair, as glossy as a mynah bird's wing, had come from her Chinese mother.

Tai deposited her surfboard in the sand, squeezed the excess water from the ends of her long hair, then dried herself with the towel she'd left at the edge of the surf. As she squatted on a corner of Bobby Jo's lauhala mat, her friend propped herself up on one elbow and gave her one of the smiles that came so easily to her lips.

Tai didn't smile in response. She and Bobby Jo had been inseparable since their sophomore year at Punahou, and their friendship had never faltered, even though their interests were so different. The question was, . . . would it also survive the next couple of years when they shared an apartment off campus at Colorado College?

"Something new's been added while you were doing your surfing thing," Bobby Jo said sotto-voce. Her eyes danced as she tipped her head toward the sand dunes. For the first time, Tai noticed the motionless form of a man, stretched out on the sand near a patch of sea grapes. He was lean, obviously young; his body was almost as brown as the khaki-colored towel he was using as a headrest. Tai thought he was asleep, but it was hard to tell for sure because of the coconut frond hat, bleached white from the sun, that covered his face.

Bobby Jo sat up, hugging her round knees with her arms. "Crystal's late—and I'm starving. You know what this fresh air does to my appetite." Despite a strong Arkansas twang, her voice was like warm honey. "You think she'd have a tizzie if we went ahead and had a sandwich?"

Tai shook her head. "Why would she? If I know you, you've brought along enough food for a dozen people."

"Right. It's habit—you know, from all those church picnics back in Arkansas. Mom used to pack enough food to feed an army. Lord help the preacher's wife if she didn't have plenty of fried chicken and deviled eggs and potato salad for the bachelors in the congregation."

Tai nodded, bemused by this view of a world that seemed so alien to her. Bobby Jo's father was a chaplain at Hickam Air Force Base, but unlike Tai, who had lived all over the world with her own air force father, Bobby Jo was comparatively new to military life.

She realized Bobby Jo was still talking, and she brought her attention back to her friend. "—so when I told Larry that no way was he going to crash our picnic, because this outing was strictly for females and one last—what was it Crystal called it?"

"'One last hurrah before we scatter in all directions.'"

"Yeah—whatever that means. Half the time I don't know what she's talking about," Bobby Jo said, sighing. "And anyway, it isn't strictly true about us scattering, is it? Crystal will be staying on in the Islands, going to the University of Hawaii, and you and I'll be roommates at Colorado College—are you sure you want me for your roomie, Tai?"

"Why do you ask that?" Tai said.

"Well, it's just that you're so superneat. Honestly, your room gives me the creeps, all the hangers in your closet are turned the same way and no hairs in your comb and a weekly schedule tacked up on your bulletin board. I'll probably drive you out of your gourd."

She paused to give Tai a mock serious look. "Just don't expect me to change. If Mom's nagging didn't do it, yours sure won't."

"Maybe we can trade off. I hate sewing, so I'll pick up after you and you can sew buttons back on my shirts."

"It's a bargain," Bobby Jo said.

"Right—and I think I'll take another run at the waves before Crystal gets here," Tai said, standing up. "If she isn't here soon, we'll start gorging. I wonder what's keeping her? You know how punctual she usually is."

"Maybe she's finally decided to go on Hawaiian time like the rest of us," Bobby Jo said around a yawn.

She was rubbing more oil on her legs when Tai picked up her surfboard and ran toward the water.

The rays of the Hawaiian sun slid through the open window of the aging Toyota as it sped along Farrington Highway, heading toward Makua on the leeward side of Oahu. It lay, as intrusive as an overheated hand, on Shelley's bare arm as she listened to Crystal's smooth, cool voice.

Already Shelley wished that she hadn't agreed to come on this beach picnic with Crystal. Yes, she did admire Bobby Jo and Tai, the classmates they were meeting at Mahuiha Beach. But it was a little late now for anything like real friendship to result from this excursion. In fact, she wondered if Tai and Bobby Jo would welcome her inclusion in the picnic. She wasn't really one of them, and besides, she had her suspicions about Crystal's sudden invitation.

When she'd enrolled at Punahou in the middle of her senior year, Shelley had been flattered by Crystal's friendliness and her throw away compliments that seemed so spontaneous and genuine. But that was before she'd noticed Crystal's manner toward her parents, that mixture of charm and deference, and how she always managed to turn up when Shelley's father was at home. Even then, Shelley had hoped that she was wrong— until her father, who was the current CINPACAF—Commander-In-Chief, Pacific Air Forces—told her he thought her "little friend" was the right sort, that he was willing to recommend Crystal for that job she wanted at PACAF Headquarters.

Well, she should be used to it. Being the daughter of a four-star general laid you wide open for that sort of thing. It also set you up for rejection. In Switzerland, where she had gone to a private school that catered to the daughters of Europe's military and diplomatic community, she had frequently been subjected to a reverse form of snobbery. Some of the other military dependents had been so afraid she would think they were impressed by her father's rank that they'd bent over backward to ignore her.

Or maybe it wasn't her father at all. Perhaps it was something closer to home—such as a lack in her own personality.

It wasn't that she didn't try—but somehow she always came across as cold and distant. Oh, yes, she'd heard them call her the Ice Maiden behind her back. The nickname had something to do with her looks, of course, her white-blond hair and Nordic-blue eyes. Even her high cheekbones gave her a haughty look that was so deceptive because she wasn't any of the things she'd been accused of. She wanted desperately to be liked, to make friends—wasn't *that* the main reason why she'd accepted Crystal's invitation this morning?

Crystal asked a question, and Shelley realized she hadn't been listening. "I beg your pardon?" she said.

"I asked how Hawaiian beaches compare with the ones in southern France."

Crystal was a tall, angular girl with a long, thin face. Her hair, chestnut brown and very thick, was her only claim to real beauty. Her smile, although frequent, never seemed to reach her gray/green eyes—something, Shelley thought, only she seemed to notice.

Crystal took her eyes off the road long enough to give her a sidelong glance, and Shelley realized she was still waiting for an answer. "I love the beaches here—and I love the Islands, too," she said quickly.

"Well, you haven't been here long enough to get rock fever. It must've been neat, going to school in Switzerland."

"The winter sports are great, but I like it here, too."

Crystal's eyebrows rose slightly. "And even if you didn't, you wouldn't say so, right?"

"I'm not just being diplomatic. I mean it."

"Uh-huh. Well, if you ask me, this place is nothing but a tourist trap these days. All those visiting firemen and their fat wives—you can't move without falling over them. Luckily, no one ever comes to this beach where we're meeting Tai and Bobby Jo. Far as I know, it isn't even on the map. Of course, we have to hike in for a quarter of a mile or so after we park the car at the end of the road."

"Sounds great to me. Shouldn't I have brought along some food?"

"No problem. There'll be plenty for four—if Bobby Jo doesn't scarf it all down first. She eats like a beach boy."

"And yet she has that super figure."

"Wait a few years. She'll fill out like a balloon."

Her words made Shelley feel uncomfortable, and she cast around for a safer subject. "The University of Hawaii should be a fun place to go to school. What are you majoring in?"

Crystal was silent for a moment. "I haven't decided yet.

I've got plenty of time to make up my mind since I won't be enrolling until next term," she said. "What about you?"

It was Shelley's turn to hesitate. She didn't really want to talk about her efforts, so far unsuccessful, to talk her parents into sending her to Parsons School of Design in New York instead of to Radcliffe, her mother's alma mater, where she was already enrolled. Not that Crystal would do anything as crass as telling her what a dumb switch that would be. She would probably raise her thinly arched eyebrows and murmur, "How fascinating!"

"I haven't decided yet, either," she said finally.

To her relief, Crystal dropped the subject. "I've always wanted to learn how to ski, but my dad's never been stationed near a ski area. I guess you must be pretty good at it, living in Switzerland all those years."

"I love winter sports," Shelley admitted. "I feel about skiing the way Tai feels about surfing."

"She's really into that scene, isn't she? Well, not for me. Look what all that salt water and sun does to your skin."

"It hasn't hurt Tai's skin."

"So far," Crystal said, shrugging. "She'd better enjoy life while she can. The fun and games will stop once she's married to Steven Henderson and starts trying to make it on a second lieutenant's pay. It'll be years before he gets any decent rank. The promotions are really slow since we pulled out of 'Nam last year."

"What do you suggest? That Tai wait until Steven makes major?" Shelley said lightly.

"Fat chance. The two of them sizzle like a couple of fire-crackers whenever they get close to each other. She'll marry Steven as soon as he graduates from the Academy, and nine months later—give or take a few months—they'll have their first kid. Then she'll either turn into a robot, doing the military wife thing, or she'll start hitting the bottle."

Again, there was a tinge of acid in Crystal's voice. Since Crystal's trademark was her cool, unflappable manner, Shelley wondered what was bugging her today.

"That doesn't have to be true," Shelley said. "Military life is a challenge to some women."

"Maybe. But if I went that route, I'd find myself a husband who was higher up the ladder than a second lieutenant—like a lieutenant colonel or maybe a fast-burner major."

"But look at the age difference—and besides, anyone with that kind of rank would probably already be married," Shelley protested.

Crystal's answer was a shrug. A few minutes later, she steered the car onto a sandy shoulder of the road and killed the motor. "Here we are. Dammit! There's another car parked behind Tai's Simca. Hope that doesn't mean a bunch of kids kicking sand in our faces. If this excursion's a bust, it's on Bobby Jo's head. Right now, she's on an old-friends-never-die kick. It comes from being a chaplain's daughter, I guess."

"She's really great," Shelley said, her voice a little stiff. "I'll never forget how friendly she was when I transferred to Punahou in the middle of the year. I was really feeling out of it until she took me under her wing and introduced me around. No wonder she was elected homecoming queen."

Crystal didn't answer. Too late, Shelley remembered that Crystal had competed against Bobby Jo for homecoming queen—and had lost by a country mile. Was it possible that it still rankled?

Shelley felt a sudden self-disgust with her own speculations. Maybe she was being unfair—it was very possible that this recent suspicion of Crystal was all in her mind. After all, it could've been her father's own idea to recommend Crystal for that job at PACAF Headquarters. Why did she assume the worst of someone who had gone out of her way to be friendly to her?

She slid out of the car, and a minute later, carrying a straw mat and her beach bag, she followed Crystal into a growth of shoulder-high weeds, already turned brown from the summer dry season.

The brown-and-tan weed pods rattled like tiny castanets as the two girls brushed against them in passing, following an overgrown path that wandered among the dunes. Fifteen minutes later, they came out on a pocket-sized beach, sheltered from the wind by dunes and a stand of wind-sculptured Christmas berry shrubs, so old that they had acquired the height and thickness of small trees.

There were two people on the beach. One was Bobby Jo, who was stretched out full length on a lauhala mat, her golden legs glistening with suntan oil. The second was a young man, lying on the sand farther down the beach. He was wearing cut-off jeans, and his bare chest was well muscled, his hips slim. Even in repose, his wide mouth had a humorous look.

Shelley was staring at him when she realized that his eyes were open under the rim of his coconut hat. She met the blazing blue of his gaze and quickly turned her eyes away. After that, she was careful not to look in his direction again.

Bobby Jo waved to them lazily. If she was surprised to see Shelley, it didn't show in her greeting. "I thought you'd never get here. Tai is off on her surfboard and I'm bored, bored, bored."

"You could've brought along something to read—like a confession magazine," Crystal said.

Bobby Jo made a face at her. "Meow, meow. Okay, so I like a good sexy read once in a while. But I prefer girl talk. Which is the reason for this outing. Just think—in another month, we'll all be gone except you. Aren't you going to miss us, Crystal—just a little?"

"Everybody's going to miss you, Bobby Jo—especially the boys." Crystal's voice was flat. She jerked her head toward the supine figure of the man. "Looks like someone else discovered our beach," she added, not bothering to lower her voice.

Bobby Jo gave an infectious half laugh, half giggle. "He's a real hunk, isn't he?" she whispered, rolling her eyes.

"He's a loser."

"How do you figure that?"

"From the military tag on his license plate, dopey. He's an enlisted man. Don't waste your time."

"Oh, I'm not sure it would be a waste—but maybe you're right. I should be saving my energy for all those groovy cadets at the academy."

"Groovy? You *did* say groovy, didn't you?"

"So?"

"So they'll laugh you off campus if you use words like that at Colorado College."

"I yam what I yam," Bobby Jo said, grinning.

Crystal's groan was lost as Tai came running up, her long black hair plastered to her head. She gave Shelley a friendly smile, and suddenly Shelley felt welcome and comfortable about being there.

She wondered, as she had before, what set Tai apart from the other girls at school. Why was it that Tai, so much her own person and so obviously indifferent to personal popularity, was the one who always set the trends that others followed? Why not Crystal, who seemed so much more mature than the rest of them—or Bobby Jo, who'd had seven invitations to the senior prom? It was a mystery she wished she could solve—and maybe that was part of Tai's mystique, that she made others want to know what made her tick. . . .

Shelley dropped down on the sand as Bobby Jo began doling out ham-and-cheese sandwiches and slightly warm cans of Pepsi from a covered basket. As they ate hungrily, they chatted about their plans for the fall, and afterward, lulled by the lazy rhythm of this last day in the sun, about their dreams for the future.

Bobby Jo confessed that she had a secret yen to do something really exciting with her life—she hadn't decided just what yet. And Tai, who was usually so reserved, talked about the problems she anticipated once she was a military wife who wanted both a career as an engineer and a family, since Steven and she, both being only children, had decided to have lots of kids. Even Crystal let down her hair long enough to admit that she had plans—big plans—for the future.

Shelley listened silently, and after a while, her attention wandered—to the man, lying on the sand.

I wonder what his name is? she thought.

And why, when he hadn't moved a muscle in the past ten minutes, was she so sure that he was awake, this his eyes were open under the rim of the hat—and that he was watching *her*, not the other girls?

Tad—his full name was Theodore Adolph Brotski—came to Mahuiha Beach whenever he needed a little space. Although he had found a home in the air force, as the saying went, and was content with his present assignment as a line mechanic at Hickam AFB, he sometimes felt a need to be alone to think over some personal problem or simply to get away from the bull crap that passed for conversation in his barracks.

Not that he didn't get along with the other guys in his outfit. Even his last promotion, to staff sergeant, which had jumped him ahead of older men with more time in grade and which could have caused him a peck of trouble, had been a popular one. He'd made sure of that by downplaying the whole thing—and he'd also bought the whole outfit several rounds of beer at the Airmen's Club. After all, he hadn't survived growing up with six older brothers, all bigger than he, without learning a few things about getting along with other men.

But occasionally he liked to go off alone to this isolated beach on the leeward side of island for a few hours of sun and relaxation. Usually, he was the only one there. Even when he had to share the beach with others, they were always locals, family groups who gave him a wide berth, obviously resenting his presence on their own private corner of Oahu.

He never brought anyone else here, not even one of the girls he dated. His buddies would think he was nuts if they knew how he enjoyed an afternoon of solitude once in a while. They had no such inclinations. Most of them gravitated to the attractions of Hotel Street after payday or, when they weren't so flush, to Waikiki's popular public beaches.

There was a legend among the island's military male population that most women tourists, the young ones, were oversexed, so they cruised the places where the tourists went. They wore aloha shirts, open to the waist, over-faded, skintight swimming trunks, affected Hawaiian drawls, and, if they could get away with it, tried to pass themselves off as beach boys, hoping for an easy score.

Common wisdom also said that there were certain sure-fire ploys for attracting women. You dropped a few island phrases— "No big t'ing, brudder" and "Hello, dere" and talked about things in the past being *pau*, and if you played it real cool, why, the chicks dropped right in your lap, all those repressed schoolteachers from Des Moines or St. Paul or Seattle, who were looking for their own score away from the old folks at home.

Tad never went cruising. He had all the female attention he could handle—civil service workers, sales clerks at the base exchange and waitresses at the base's snack bars, plus the female airmen who worked on the flight line. Since the age of twelve, when he'd been initiated to sex by the sixteen-year-old girl who lived next door, he'd been able to score whenever he felt the urge. Even though he didn't really understand it, he accepted his success with women as one of the few gifts the gods had dropped into his lap.

After all, he didn't have a smooth line like some of the guys in his outfit, nor was he any great shakes when it came to looks. In fact, he considered himself pretty ordinary looking. Okay, a few women had told him that he looked like a dark-haired Paul Newman, but when he looked into his shaving mirror, he saw an ordinary Joe from a Pennsylvania mining town with the map of Poland written all over his face. If he hadn't joined the air force, he'd still be working the mines alongside his father and older brothers.

So he had plenty to be grateful for. He'd joined up as the easiest way out of town after he'd been caught making it with Susan Hardy—the guys called her Susie Hard-ass—who just happened to be the daughter of Tunsten's town marshal. Then, to his surprise, he'd discovered that he'd done the right thing for the wrong reason. Not to get sloppy or anything, but he loved the air force, loved the—what was it called? the camaraderie?—of other men, the chance to see the world while at the same time having the security of a steady job with a decent pension off in the future somewhere.

Although Tad was always careful to bitch about the air force as much as the other guys, he intended to stay the full course and retire with thirty years under his belt. Sure, he could get out in two years when his present hitch was up. He was sure he could walk into a good job with an airline—they were always looking for skilled mechanics—but then he'd be stuck in one place, tied to the same job for the rest of his life. If he did that, he might just as well have stayed back in Tunsten. . . .

When he first reached the beach and realized that it was already occupied by a girl sunbathing on a mat, he had muttered a disgusted "Oh, shit!" under his breath because he'd hoped to have the beach all to himself. Feeling disgruntled, he'd settled himself at the far end of the beach, and it was a few minutes before he realized that the sunbather wasn't alone, that another girl was surfing in the waters off the beach. As he watched the surfer from under the rim of his hat, he hoped she knew what she was doing, going out without a buddy, because he was in no mood today to rescue females in distress. When the girl caught a wave and rode it expertly toward shore, he decided she must be an island girl. Not only did she have what he thought of as a "local" look, but who else could handle a board like that?

He resigned himself to waiting them out and turned over to his back, wriggling his lean hips deeper into the sand, trying to get comfortable. A few minutes later, he was fast asleep.

It was the sound of women's voices on the path that led to the beach that aroused him. He opened his eyes just as two girls came out onto the beach. The one leading the way was tall, very slender; although she was not Tad's type, he knew that men who liked their women lean and a little hungry looking would probably find her attractive.

"I hope this outing isn't a drag for you, Shelley," she was saying. "It was Bobby Jo's idea, you know." She shrugged as if disclaiming all responsibility. "I wonder how she'll get along at Colorado College. I asked her why she didn't choose some livelier school like UCLA, and she said that she wanted to mingle with all those singles at the Air Force Academy! Imagine getting excited over a bunch of cadets, for God's sake. Not at all like those cool Continental types you must be used to."

"I'm not used to any type, cool or otherwise. We managed to meet a few men on the ski slopes, but . . . well, I did go to a girls' school, you know."

The speaker's voice was pleasant, with a subtle accent Tad couldn't place. He slid his hat up an inch higher so he could see her better. She was a couple of inches above medium-height with long, slender legs and a sleek, narrow body. An outsized man's shirt was knotted at her waist, and the bikini she wore barely covered the essentials of decency. Her hair was thick, shoulder length; it looked so alive that he was sure it would cling to his fingers, soft as silk, if he touched it. Even though it was a startling white blond, he was sure the color was natural because no way would *this* girl go for anything phony.

Tad discovered that his heart was playing taps inside his chest, that it was hard to breathe. He wanted to snatch the blond girl up and carry her off to some isolated place where he could make love to her. Conversely, he also wanted to protect her from any jerk, like himself, who might have lustful thoughts about her. In other words, he felt mixed up and confused, all the more so because his gut instincts told him that she was out of his class, that he didn't have a snowball's chance in hell of ever getting to know her.

Then she turned her head to stare at him. It was a minute or so before she must have realized that he was awake and watching her in turn. She looked away quickly, but not before Tad knew, with the instinct that had served him so well in the past, that he had registered, that she was very much aware of him as a man.

Tad relaxed against the sand. There was a chance, after

all—if the breaks fell his way. Avid for information now, he strained his ears, cursing the wind that carried away their voices as they greeted the other girl, and he wondered how the devil he was going to find out who she was.

CHAPTER

✦ 2 ✦

WHEN CRYSTAL ARRIVED WITH THE NEW GIRL FROM SCHOOL in tow, Tai's welcome was friendly, although Shelley wasn't someone she would choose for a close friend. But at least she didn't try to wear her father's rank. Not that rank mattered to Tai. She made her friends where she chose, with the kids of officers or enlisted men or locals. Most of her classmates at Punahou had been the same way.

After they had exchanged greetings, the four girls settled down to eat, and because she had skipped breakfast, Tai was hungry enough to finish off two ham-and-cheese sandwiches even though she preferred the island foods she was used to.

From her Chinese mother, who had come from an old Honolulu family, she had learned to cook the everyday foods of the Islands. Like most of the locals, her mother had adopted the dishes of other island cultures, adapting them to her family's taste. After her mother's death, when Tai was ten, she had continued to cook the same way for her father. If he preferred the Cajun food of his own childhood, he kept it to himself and never complained. That he also never complimented her, no matter how hard she had worked over a dish of fried rice or teriyaki steak, didn't negate the fact that he seemed to prefer her cooking to that of anyone else's.

Would it be the same with Steven? Or, when they were married, would he expect her to cook the way his mother did?

When they were married . . . How good that sounded! So

solid and permanent and—and right. An image floated through Tai's mind, and she closed her eyes, afraid that her friends would guess what she was thinking.

Steven holding her against his strong, nude body, kissing her, touching her, sending her into that erotic state where nothing mattered except the fire in her veins and the explosion building inside.

And wasn't it strange that only when she was surfing did she feel anything close to the way she felt when Steven was making love to her? God, how she did miss him! His leave this summer, those three weeks a year that a cadet could call his own, had been too short, too packed with obligations toward his parents. What she'd really wanted was to go off alone with him so they could take all the time they needed to make love without hurrying. . . .

Bobby Jo's teasing voice penetrated her reverie. "Anyone want to bet she's *not* thinking about Steven?"

"Not me," Crystal drawled. "I only gamble on sure things."

The wind suddenly felt cool against Tai's cheeks, and she knew she was blushing. Which was very strange because blushing wasn't her style. She had sat in on too many poker games with her father's cronies, who never modified their obscenities just because she was there. But then her feelings for Steven were so very private, and she didn't appreciate being teased about him, not even by Bobby Jo, her best friend. . . .

"Oh, let her be," Bobby Jo said, blithely ignoring the fact that she had started the teasing. "Tai has a right to her fantasies. If I had a chance with a fox like Steven, I'd daydream, too—and never come down to earth again."

Shelley gave Tai a tentative smile. "Your fiancé is a cadet, isn't he? Did you choose Colorado College because it's so close to the academy?"

"That's one reason. Also, I got a partial scholarship at CC."

Shelley nodded her understanding. "How did you meet your fiancé, Tai?"

"At Sunset Beach. We were both surfing and—"

"It's a real Cinderella story—the base sergeant major's daughter and the base commander's son." Crystal's voice cut through Tai's answer. "Now *that* should make for an interesting wedding party, don't you think?"

A retort rose to Tai's lips, but Bobby Jo beat her to it. "I think it's a great combination. What would make it really per-

fect is if my father did the honors and married them." She
giggled suddenly. "And your father could provide the champagne, Crystal."

Briefly, Tai caught a flicker of some strong emotion in
Crystal's eyes. Was it anger—or hurt? The idea that Crystal
might be as vulnerable to hurt as other people startled her. She
watched with interest as Crystal came up with a thin smile.

"After my father retired from the air force, he bought part
interest in a liquor store—you know, to keep himself busy,"
Crystal said, addressing her remark to Shelley. "I'm sure he'd
give Tai's father a good deal on champagne."

"Thanks for the offer, but we're going to be married in the
chapel at the academy," Tai said. "Steven's family expects it.
His parents were married at West Point during June week."

"Wow! A traditional military wedding with raised swords
and all the trimmings." Bobby Jo's voice held envy. "I should
be so lucky."

"So catch yourself a cadet—that *is* why you're going to
Colorado College, isn't it?" Crystal said.

"I'm going there to get an education."

"So what about—and I quote—'I wanna mingle with all
those groovy singles at the academy'?"

"Strictly for laughs, *ma cherie*. Naturally, I intend to kick
up my heels—nothing heavy, just some good clean fun. Being
a chaplain's daughter can be a drag, especially when you have
four younger brothers, all panting to tattle on you. But after I
graduate, I'm going to work for a while at something really
exciting, and then look around for some nice, steady guy and
settle down. And it won't be a military man. No moving from
base to base for me. I've had it with military life." Bobby Jo's
lips curved into a smile, showing a dimple high on her right
cheek. "But first I intend to have a good time."

"Better be careful how you 'mingle with the singles,' or you
may have to get married quicker than you plan," Crystal
observed.

Bobby Jo looked hurt, and Tai decided it was time for a
diversion. "So who scarfed down my pickle? Is that a dill seed
I see on your chin, Bobby Jo?"

In the rush of indignant denials, Bobby Jo's attention was
diverted and the subject of the academy was dropped.

They were finishing their lunch when Bobby Jo commented,
"I don't know where the summer went. It doesn't seem possible

that I'll be leaving for the mainland tomorrow morning. Are you still coming to see me off, Tai?"

"I'll be there—complete with plumeria leis," Tai said. "If you weren't taking that side trip to Arkansas to see your grand-parents, we could've traveled together."

"Well, you'll be along in another two weeks—and who else is going to see me off?"

"I'll try to make it—but I can't promise," Crystal said. "How about you, Shelley? When are you leaving for the east?"

"Saturday—two weeks from now. Maybe we'll be on the same plane, Tai."

Bobby Jo smiled at Shelley. "You're really lucky, going to Radcliffe with all those Harvard types so accessible. The hunt-ing should really be super."

"Trust our Bobby Jo to think of that," Crystal said.

Bobby Jo didn't seem to hear her. "Do you realize that it could be years before we all get together again—if we ever do?" she said wistfully. Her face brightened suddenly. "Say, I have a great idea! Why don't we have a reunion in five—no, make that ten years from now?"

"Sounds great to me," Tai said amicably.

"I'll go along with that," said Crystal. "I'd be interested to find out how the rest of you are doing in ten years."

"Am I included?" Shelley asked, her voice small.

"Of course," Tai said. "Should we include husbands and kids?"

"No way. If I end up like my mom, I'll have six kids by then—and all six of them will be boys." Bobby Jo sounded so rueful that everybody laughed.

"Okay, it's settled," Bobby Jo went on. "Ten years from now, the four of us will meet here in Hawaii—and in the meantime, let's not lose touch with each other. Is it a deal?"

"It's a deal," Tai said, just as if she believed that the reunion would take place.

All day, Crystal had been fighting off one of her migraines. It had started as a scintillating veil at the perimeter of her sight, progressed to flashes of jagged light, and had now reached the nausea stage. She had taken medication as soon as she realized what was happening, and while the pills had helped, her pain threshold was so low that she was sensitive to irritants she usually ignored, such as Bobby Jo's juvenile jokes and Tai's

quiet—and unconscious—air of confidence. As she listened
to their bantering conversation, Crystal was careful to conceal
her irritation behind an amused smile. Even so, their comfortable affection for each other was like a burr under her skin,
and several times she'd been goaded into remarks that bordered
on cattiness.

She hadn't protested the choice of this dreary beach for their
outing for the simple reason that when it came to competing
with the other three girls in a bikini, they outclassed her by a
mile. Not that she didn't get her share of attention from men,
even in a bathing suit. But without the concealment of clothing,
her too small breasts and lack of other endowments were all
too apparent—something her mother never missed a chance to
point out.

The thought of Janet sent a fresh stab of pain radiating up
the side of Crystal's face. When she'd left the house—that
tacky house in Pearl City with its single-walled construction
that let in all the neighborhood noise—her mother had been
sprawled out on the koa-wood sofa in the living room, a vodka
and orange juice in one hand, watching her favorite early-
morning talk show.

She'd been wearing a soiled muumuu, the loose kind she
favored, her hair blowsy and her face bare of makeup—and
it really burned Crystal that she still managed to look like a
million dollars. Janet would never see forty again, but she could
easily pass for twenty-five—on a good day. What's more, the
bitch knew it—which was why she was always flaunting the
fact that her husband still lusted after her like a moonstruck
kid.

This morning, Maurice must really have been horny. He'd
eyed Janet at the breakfast table as if she were a juicy slice of
mango. In fact, he hadn't even waited until Crystal was out
the door before he'd had his hand halfway up Janet's thigh.
Right now, they were probably going at it hot and heavy, with
her father panting like a dog after a bitch in heat. Which brought
up an interesting question. Was it a coincidence that he seemed
always to start pawing at Janet before she, Crystal, was out
the door?

Crystal winced, willing the old pain to go away. For as long
as she could remember, she had been jealous of her mother,
but it was only lately that she'd begun to suspect that her father
was at fault, too, that he got a high out of acting horny in front

of his own daughter. Otherwise, why was he always touching Janet, giving her those long hot looks that hinted at secrets shared behind their bedroom door? How many nights had she heard them in there—her mother laughing in that throaty way, her father's voice murmuring, murmuring. . . .

And the other sounds—the moans and sighs and the squealing of bed springs. Oh, yes, she knew what they did in their bedroom, and she thought it was disgusting. Bad enough to act like a bull with a rutting cow when both partners were young, but for two middle-aged losers who had been married for almost twenty years, it was too much. In fact, sex was too much—messy and uncomfortable, the absolute pits.

And she should know because she'd done it with Kimo Kapiolani in the backseat of his dune buggy three times, each experience painful and humiliating. For a long time, she'd held out, letting Kimo do just enough to keep him coming back for more, and when he'd become restless and had started looking at other girls again, she'd helped him get it off without going all the way.

But that hadn't been enough for Kimo. No, he'd wanted to "put it in her," he'd said, and because he was captain of Punahou's football team and she'd been convinced that he could cinch the homecoming queen title for her, she had finally let him go all the way. Of course she'd been smart enough to pretend that his fumblings and lungings really sent her into orbit. Afterward, when he'd asked if it was good for her, too, baby, she had snuggled up against him, trying to ignore the disgusting odor of sweat and sex, and told him he was the best stud in Hawaii.

And it had all been for nothing—*nothing!* He hadn't been able to swing enough votes for her, after all, and Bobby Jo had been elected homecoming queen. . . .

Well, she'd fixed Kimo—but good. On their next date, she'd waited until he was hot and ready, and then she'd told him a few truths about his lack of physical equipment and how he turned her off. He'd lost his cool and slapped her, but she hadn't told anyone. After all, it was a fair trade-off. She'd learned something from the experience—not to mess around with a man's ego when it came to sex.

"You look pale, Crystal." It was Bobby Jo's Arkansas drawl. "You got a headache?"

"I never get headaches. I was thinking you must be pretty

excited, leaving for the mainland tomorrow," Crystal improvised.

"It's exciting all right, although I can't say that I'm looking forward to the cold weather. I do love the sun." Bobby Jo rubbed her upper arms as if she already felt the winter wind off the Rockies. "Colorado would be right down your alley, Shelley. You sure you don't want to sign up at dear ol' CC? You could ski all winter—and Tai and I would be there, so you wouldn't get lonely."

One of Shelley's rare smiles lit up her face. Crystal felt a familiar tightening in her stomach. It was obvious that Shelley had no idea of the impact her looks had on other people. Didn't the little fool ever look in the mirror? If *she* had that hair and those eyes and that figure, she'd hook herself a real winner, someone who wouldn't get bogged down halfway up the promotion ladder like her father who had retired as a stinking major because he'd been passed over for promotion too many times. She'd be a general's lady someday, like Shelley's mother, who had every officer's wife on base catering to her, hanging on her every word.

But since she didn't have Shelley's class or Bobby Jo's looks or Tai's charisma, she would do it the hard way. After all, she was smarter than any of them, including Tai. When she really put her mind to it, she could get anything she wanted.

As for this outing today—all this girl talk and baring of souls was for the birds. It didn't pay to tell people about your private dreams. Better to keep a lid on them. For instance, they all thought she was going to the University of Hawaii next term. What they didn't know was that there wasn't any money for her tuition, not one lousy dime.

Oh, her father had been sorry about that. "Financial upsets," was his explanation. But she knew where the money had gone. It was Janet's drinking and other extravagances that was such a drain on Maurice's retirement pay. And that job he'd taken— she'd told her friends that he owned half interest in the store, but actually he was just a clerk, augmenting the measly retirement check his grateful government sent him every month.

Well, she wasn't going to make the same mistakes Maurice had. The job at PACAF Headquarters that General Pritchard had recommended her for—she had a good chance of being hired even if locals did have the advantage. Once she got that job, she intended to use it as a stepping-stone to something better. Because she certainly didn't intend to be a file clerk/typist, a nobody, all her life. . . .

C H A P T E R

↑ 3 ↑

AFTER CRYSTAL LET SHELLEY OFF IN FRONT OF THE
quarters known to base personnel as Four Star House, Shelley
paused to survey the cars that lined the access driveway and
filled the parking lot next to the service entrance. She searched
her memory, trying to recall if today's affair was a strategy
meeting for one of the charities her mother headed or something
more formal like an afternoon tea at which she would be expected
to make an appearance.

When she drew a blank, she shrugged and headed for the
service entrance in the rear of the building, skirting the high,
neatly groomed hedge that provided privacy for General Pritchard and his family.

Although the sprawling house with its red-tiled roof and
spacious grounds was the largest set of quarters on Hickam
AFB, the one reserved for the Commander-In-Chief of Pacific
Air Forces, it was old-fashioned and inconvenient, something
Shelley's mother pointed out at least once a day. Secretly,
Shelley wondered why the inadequacies of the kitchen and the
haphazard arrangement of the rooms should matter to her mother.
After all, she never lifted a finger to do any of the housework.
Since generals rated a house steward for each star, there were
four young airmen at her mother's beck and call, ready to do
any chore she put them to—including washing out her personal
lingerie by hand. The slots were voluntary; the majority of the
stewards were drawn from men who worked in the food service

field. Under the present occupants, the faces in the kitchen changed so often that Shelley had given up trying to learn their names.

When she came through the kitchen door, two stewards, wearing white serving jackets, were standing at opposite sides of a large enamel work table in the middle of the room, adding last-minute touches to trays of canapes and hors d'oeuvres, while a third was trying to pry a plastic bag filled with crushed ice from the depths of a freezer. No one saw Shelley as she paused in the doorway, waiting for a break in the conversation so she could ask a question.

"—and then the old bitch tells me the punch tastes like stale ice. I kept my mouth shut, but I wanted to say, 'Look, Miz Pritchard, those cubes came from the ice machine at the liquor store, so take it up with the NCO Club if you've got a beef.' God—I don't know how much longer I can hack this job! That woman is always on my back, griping about something."

"That'll learn you to volunteer. You figured you was walking into a nice cushy job, right?"

"Yeah. Better I shoulda stayed in the mess hall, dishing out slop at the steam table and taking the mess sarge's crap."

Shelley retreated into the service room. This time, she slammed the outside door to warn them she was coming. By the time she reentered the kitchen, the three men were silent, ostensibly occupied with their chores.

"What's on the schedule for today?" she asked, looking at the trays of canapes and hors d'oeuvres.

"It's a tea—something to do with the women's auxiliary at Tripler Hospital, miss," the newest steward said, his voice guarded. "Your mother was here a few minutes ago, asking if we'd seen you. She said she expected you to . . . uh, make an appearance soon as you—y'know, changed and all that."

At her involuntary "Dammit," his black eyes brushed the cleavage of her bikini top. Shelley was too busy trying to think of an excuse to get out of what could only be a dreary event to pay any attention. She hated attending her mother's social affairs. Not that she was expected to do more than be polite for a few minutes before she made some excuse and left. In fact, it was de rigueur that she limit the length of her visit because there was always the possibility that if she stayed too long, she might say the wrong thing and reveal that her pose of social ease was only about one cell thick.

"Do you think you could forget you saw me?" she asked, addressing the question to the oldest of the stewards, a good-natured local man twice her age. His name was Sam Kealoha, but everybody called him Portagee.

"Sure thing," Portagee said. "I ain't looked up from these appetizers for the past half hour. A dozen people coulda walked through the kitchen for all I know."

He winked at the other stewards, and they all grinned sheepishly. Already Shelley regretted her words. It would be all over the base by tomorrow that General Pritchard's daughter was avoiding her mother.

"It's just that I forgot about the tea and made other plans," she said quickly. "I'll be going out again in a few minutes."

"Not to worry. Nobody here'll fink on you. You have one good time, okay?"

Shelley gave him a grateful smile before she retreated through the door that led to a center hall. The door swung shut behind her, but not before she heard the steward named Ernie—or was it Arnie?—say, "Man, I'd really like to get into that one's jeans—"

Shelley's cheeks flamed as she hurried down the hall toward the service stairs. Damn his foul mouth—every time she saw him from now on, she would think of that remark.

She locked her bedroom door behind her and flung herself down on the bed, wishing she had stayed at the beach. If she had taken her own car instead of going with Crystal, she could still be there. Maybe she'd get up early tomorrow morning and go back. It would be really cool to spend a day alone without having to make polite conversation or put on an act.

After a while, she rose and went into the bathroom that adjoined the bedroom to strip off her bikini. She dumped it and the man's shirt she'd been using as a beach coat into the clothes hamper, knowing that tomorrow they'd both be back in her closet, washed and dried and ready to wear again. The window louvers were closed, so she didn't bother to put on any clothes after she'd taken a shower to wash the salt water out of her hair. Instead, she stretched out on her back on the bed, letting the air that came between the louvers dry her still damp hair. A sudden image of the new steward's bold eyes made her wince. He'd probably explode if he walked in on her right now. Eat your heart out, Ernie/Arnie, she thought.

But she felt uncomfortable now, so she rose, pulled on tennis shorts and a T-shirt, and tied back her hair with a brown silk scarf. Restlessly, she prowled the room, stopping to study one of her own paintings, an Alpine scene, that she'd brought back from Switzerland. Despite her attempts to put her own mark on the room, it was as impersonal as a hotel and anything but homey. In fact, when she tried to think of a place that fit the word "home," her mind drew a blank.

She had lived in a lot of places in her eighteen years—sometimes government quarters, other times off-base housing that ranged from a villa in France during one of her father's tours with SHAPE to a country place in Virginia when he was stationed at the Pentagon.

Of course, she'd only spent her holidays and summer vacations at those places. Since she was six, she had lived in boarding school dormitories. One question that she had never asked her parents was why she had been sent away to school when she could have lived with them and attended private day schools. It hadn't been for lack of decent housing. Her father had already been a major general when she was born, and there are always adequate quarters for generals' families.

In fact, her parents had been living in a French villa when she'd been sent to that first boarding school in Nice. She had cried her eyes out there—the rooms were so drafty, the discipline so rigid, the teachers so frosty, and everybody had spoken a language she didn't understand. But she had survived the loneliness, the feeling of being abandoned. She had even learned to speak French like a native.

Shelley continued her slow circle of the room, finally stopping in front of the framed portrait of a smiling man who wore colonel's insignia on his air force uniform. Tony—God, she did miss him. Although they saw each other so seldom, she adored her older brother. It didn't even matter that he was their parents' favorite. She loved him because he'd always made room for her in his life those times when both of them had been home at the same time.

Even though Tony was married now and had teenaged stepdaughters, that part hadn't changed. . . . No, that wasn't strictly true. His wife had let Shelley know, not so subtly, that his immediate family came first with Tony. One thing about Gretchen—she wasn't intimidated by her in-laws. In fact, she never let them forget that, as the daughter of a Supreme Court judge, she considered herself a few cuts above anyone in the military—even four-star generals. She also made it clear that she thought Tony was wasting his time and education and intelligence piloting a plane.

A sharp rap at the door made Shelley flinch. When the doorknob began to turn, she knew that she was trapped. Since it was futile to pretend that she was in the bathroom and hadn't heard the knock, she went to unlock the door and admit her mother.

"Didn't the stewards give you my message?" Mrs. Pritchard said sharply by way of greeting. She was tall and narrow and white-haired, as fragile looking as the bride atop a wedding cake, but it was no secret that there was an iron fist inside the white gloves that were her trademark. One of the things that caused a high ulcer rate at Hickam was her control over the base officers' wives, for whom she set high standards of dress and manners and social obligations.

"The stewards were busy when I came in," Shelley said. "I guess they didn't see me."

"Well, I reminded you yesterday about the tea for the Tripler Hospital Auxiliary. I expected you to put in an appearance—"

"I'm sorry, Mother. I went to the beach with Crystal and some of her friends, and since it wasn't my car . . ." Shelley shrugged, hoping her mother would drop the subject. "Was it important that I show up? Those ladies aren't interested in me—"

"Do stop calling them ladies." Mrs. Pritchard's well-bred voice was cross. "It sounds so common. 'Women' is the proper word. And it was only common courtesy to make an appearance."

Her robin's-egg-blue eyes held a chill, and Shelley wondered how much of her mother's disapproval stemmed from an awareness that there was something a little ridiculous about a woman in her early sixties having an eighteen-year old daughter. It must have been quite an item of gossip at Wright-Patterson AFB when General Pritchard's wife, who already had a son at West Point, started wearing maternity clothes. Or had she gone into seclusion before the telltale swelling of her belly had given away her embarrassing predicament?

Shelley had often wanted to ask her mother why she hadn't had an abortion. But of course this was another question she didn't dare ask. Because what if her mother told her that she'd wanted to have one, but that for some medical reason it had been impossible? Maybe she hadn't realized she was pregnant until it was too late—at her age, she could easily have been misled into thinking she was starting an early menopause.

Well, Tony hadn't been embarrassed to have a kid sister twenty years his junior. He'd treated her as if she were a doll—and wasn't it ironic that he and Gretchen hadn't been able to give her father grandsons to continue the family's military tradition? It would be even more ironic if Gretchen got her own way and talked Tony into resigning and going into law.

After one critical look around the room, her mother left. As Shelley changed into a summer shift, she felt a little ashamed of her uncharitable thoughts. In penance, she twisted her hair into a sleek French knot and put on a touch of makeup before she went down to dinner that evening.

There were dinner guests, as always. This time it was two couples. Both men, a major general and colonel, were on her father's staff; their wives could have been interchangeable, although one was a plump brunette, the other a pencil-thin blonde with sharply defined features.

As Shelley listened to the polite exchange of conversation that revealed nothing about the people behind the social smiles, an image of Tai's intelligent face flickered into her mind. Did Tai realize what she was getting into by marrying a cadet? Was she prepared for endless evenings of this kind of sterile socializing? Or, being Tai, would she hold on to her own individuality and rise above it—without, at the same time, jeopardizing Steven's career? Well, Tai was crazy about Steven, and he was crazy about her. Maybe that would make all the difference.

Even before Bobby Jo came fully awake, she knew she had overslept. She lay with her eyes closed, listening to the sound of water rushing through the hot-water pipe that ran through the wall behind her bed. She had missed her turn at the shower—which meant she'd probably have to wash in cold water again this morning. Well, that was an insignificant thing next to the adventure that lay ahead of her. To be totally on her own for the first time in her life—it was almost too much to grasp all at once. In fact, she wasn't sure if she was exhilarated or just plain scared. When she got to Colorado, maybe she'd better just take things one step at a time and sort of ease into her new life.

Her mother's exasperated voice came from the hall. "Bobby

Jo—you'd better start stirring around in there. You know how your father hates it when you're late for breakfast."

Bobby Jo made a face, but she sat up and called back, "I'm waiting to get in the bathroom, Mom."

"Well, it's your own fault you missed your turn. While you're waiting, you'd better give your closet and chest drawers one last check, just to make sure you haven't forgotten something important. Your father said we have to leave here by eight. You know how heavy the traffic is on Kam Highway. . . ."

Her voice diminished as she hurried off down the hall. Bobby Jo stretched, then swung her feet over the side of the bed. She looked around the small, cramped room, feeling a tinge of nostalgia. Once she was gone, it would pass on to Neil, her oldest brother, who hadn't bothered to hide his glee that he'd finally have some privacy. There was something to be said, she thought, for being the only girl with four brothers. At least you got your own room. . . .

A few minutes later, dressed for the trip except for her jacket, she went downstairs to find the whole family already sitting around the table in the dining room. Although she was too excited to be hungry, she knew better than to try to skip breakfast.

Her father, a small, plump man with fussy mannerisms, glanced pointedly at his watch, then gave her a reproving look, but for once he didn't comment on her tardiness.

The boys, as usual, were fighting—not openly, but with sly kicks under the table and exchanges of scowls and insults muttered under their breath. Her mother, plump and harried looking and no longer pretty, bustled back and forth between the kitchen and the table, dispensing cereal and milk and fruit juice. As Bobby Jo took her usual chair and bent her head while her father said grace, she already felt divorced from the family—and also a little guilty. That her whole family would have to sacrifice to supplement the small scholarship their church had provided for her tuition was not something she felt comfortable about.

"You will remember to write at least once a week, won't you?" her mother said now.

"I promise, Mom."

"And watch your expenses. Your allowance will only stretch so far—"

"I'll be careful. I'll write down every penny I spend."

"We expect you to affiliate with the Colorado Springs First Christians United as soon as you get settled." This from her father, who was frowning at her. "Just because you're on your own is no excuse to neglect your spiritual needs."

"I have the address you gave me, and I'll contact the minister as soon as I get settled."

"See that you do." He glanced at his watch again. "It's almost time to go. Finish up, everybody—and Neil, since you've already gulped down your food, you can put your sister's bags in the station wagon—"

An hour later, they were waiting at Honolulu International for the departure call of Bobby Jo's flight. Bobby Jo was a little hurt that Tai hadn't made an appearance, laden with plumeria leis, to see her off. Luckily, so many others had shown up, some from school and others family friends and neighbors, all bearing leis, that she didn't have time to brood about it.

There was a flurry of kisses, of last-minute promises to write, as well as a few tears when the plane began loading. Even after she had shown her pass to the passenger agent, Bobby Jo's father and mother were still giving her advice. Their voices, following her down the canvas tunnel to the plane, were embarrassing, but when she met the smile of the male flight attendant who was welcoming passengers on board, she put them out of her mind, elated by the knowledge that she was finally on her way.

As she edged along the aisle, looking for the seat she'd been assigned, she thought how great it was going to be. No more messy toilet seats because one of her brothers had missed again. No more worrying about someone eavesdropping when she was on the phone with her friends. No more—well, no more recriminations when she missed one of her father's curfews. In fact, no curfews at all.

It wasn't as if she were wild. She was a lot more straitlaced than any girl she knew, but she did like to have fun, to have guys compliment her and make a fuss over her. So what was wrong with that? And now that she was free to do what she wanted, she meant to really live it up. She wouldn't do anything foolish, of course. Having fun was one thing, but getting trapped into a serious relationship with a man was something else. So she meant to be very careful—but oh, she did intend to kick up her heels a bit before she settled down. . . .

Bobby Jo was a little disappointed when she discovered that

her seatmate was another woman. She'd had this fantasy about sitting next to some really groovy—no, *cool* guy. Someone older and into something glamorous like the diplomatic corps. He would fall for her, write her and send her flowers, and all the girls in her dorm would be jealous as hell.

Well, at least the woman was youngish. Probably in her mid-twenties. Good-looking, too, if you liked teased hair and overplucked eyebrows.

After she'd fastened her seat belt, Bobby Jo relaxed, still savoring her new freedom. Not that she meant to abuse it or get into drugs or anything like that. No, that's why she intended to date cadets at first. The academy expected their cadets to act like gentlemen, didn't they? And gentlemen didn't come on too strong or try to push you into anything heavy. Sure, she'd let her dates fool around a little sometimes, but only so far, and then she'd always put a halt to it. She'd never gone all the way with any boy, although this was something only Tai knew. Dating cadets would guarantee that things wouldn't get out of hand, which was why she was really looking forward to the academy hops.

One thing—she wasn't going to fall for some guy and end up getting engaged. She didn't intend to go the same route Tai was taking, marrying just a couple of years out of high school. She also had no intention of being a military wife. Sure, she'd been excited when her dad had been chosen by his church council to be an air force chaplain, but that was different. Being the preacher's daughter in a small town was the pits, and she had welcomed the change. But she also didn't want to live on a military base for the rest of her life, raising her kids on the run, never knowing from one month to the next where she would be living.

What she wanted was a normal life. A successful husband who stayed home nights, a nice house in the suburbs—or, if they lived in a city, a townhouse in a good neighborhood— with enough money to send her kids to decent private schools. Vacations in Hawaii or Bermuda, and maybe a summer cabin in the mountains or on the beach. Yes, that was the life she intended to have someday.

But first she meant to enjoy her freedom without the "preacher's kid" tag hanging around her neck. She might not be the most exciting person when she didn't put forth a special effort to be vivacious and gay, but at least she could be anyone she wanted to be at Colorado College.

A shadow fell across her lap. The male flight attendant at her elbow was wearing a big smile. He was the one with the curly black hair and green eyes who had greeted her at the door.

"Can I get you a drink, miss?" he murmured.

Bobby Jo's fundamentalist religion forbade alcohol, so she automatically started to shake her head. Then, remembering that she was asserting her freedom these days, she changed her mind. "I'll take a—a glass of white wine," she said, saying the first thing that popped into her head.

The woman in the window seat asked for a gin and tonic, and Bobby Jo wished she'd asked for one, too, because it sounded so much more sophisticated than white wine. When her drink came, she took an experimental sip and discovered it had a tartness that made her grimace.

"Something wrong with your drink, miss?" It was the steward again, hovering by her elbow. His gaze was so appraising that she was glad her mother had insisted she wear a blouse that buttoned high in the front.

"It's fine," she said. "It's the—the altitude. I don't want to gulp it down."

"I can see you're an experienced traveler. I wish I had a dollar for everybody we've had to pour off this plane." He hesitated, then asked smoothly, "Are you heading for college on the mainland, miss?"

Bobby Jo felt a little let down as she told him she was going to Colorado College. Was her age so obvious?

"A senior, right?" He didn't wait for her answer. "Say, why don't I put your leis in the cooler? That way, they'll still be fresh when we get to San Francisco."

As Bobby Jo handed them over, he asked, "How long is your layover in California?"

"I have an hour between planes."

"Too bad. That's my turnaround. I thought we might have dinner in San Francisco if you were going to be there overnight."

"I'm sorry, too," she said, smiling.

After the steward went off down the aisle, carrying the leis, Bobby Jo's seatmate commented, "What a line—it really creaks,

doesn't it?" She lit up a cigarette. "Hope you don't mind—
this *is* the smoking area."

"I don't mind," Bobby Jo lied. "Do you know him—the
flight attendant, I mean?"

"I know his kind. I almost laughed out loud when you told
him you only had an hour's layover in San Francisco. That
really took the wind out of his sails."

Bobby Jo felt a pang of disappointment. Had the steward's
invitation just been a line? She had thought he really liked her.
"Have you been vacationing in the Islands?" she asked, wanting
to change the subject.

"My daddy's navy—he's stationed at Pearl. I've been home
on vacation—I teach English lit at Northwestern. But I graduated from Colorado College three years ago. This time of
year, half the passengers on this plane are students, you know."

Bobby Jo looked around, noting for the first time how many
young people there were. "I think you're right," she said.

"See that redheaded girl sitting on the aisle? She was a
freshman the year I graduated. She's doing postgrad work at
CC this year, going for her masters. I guess she stayed too
long at the fair."

"I don't understand."

"You know—she chose CC so she could catch herself a
cadet. But you have to do it quick or suddenly you're too old
for them. Personally, I never dated cadets. Most of them are
pretty dull—and then there's all those restrictions, too, which
is a real downer."

Bobby Jo took another sip of wine to cover up her confusion.
Why was the woman so critical of cadets? What did she mean
about most of them being dull? Maybe she was intellectual—
yes, that was probably it. Were there many like her at CC?
Well, maybe this was a lesson for her to be careful whom she
made friends with at first. Luckily, she wasn't going there
alone. Not that she intended to lean on Tai, but it would be
good to have a friend to sort of break the ice for her.

And in two weeks, when she reported in at CC, it would
all begin. New friends, new experiences—a whole new life.
Here I come, ready or not, she thought as she raised her half-
empty glass of wine in a salute to the future and then took
another sip.

CHAPTER
✦ 4 ✦

TO TAI, THE DAY THAT HAD STARTED OUT SO PLEASANTLY changed subtly after Crystal arrived with Shelley in tow. As she helped her friends police the beach and said her good-byes, then drove off with Bobby Jo sitting beside her in the ten-year-old Simca she had earned with baby-sitting money, she tried to pin down the reason for her sudden uneasiness.

It wasn't because of their unexpected guest. Shelley's father might be the highest-ranking air force general in the Pacific, but she was not a snob, something Tai hadn't realized until the end of the school year. At first, like the other seniors, she had read Shelley completely wrong, and it was only gradually that she'd come to realize Shelley's cool aloofness was really shyness.

Although she herself had never suffered from shyness, she'd had her own share of personal problems. There was that attack of acne when she was twelve which had almost turned her into a hermit—until the doctors had discovered that the hormones in the enormous amounts of milk she drank was the cause. Also she'd been a "late bloomer"—an expression one of her father's friends had used to describe her. While other girls her age were giggling over boys, she'd wanted to be one of the male gang who played kickball in the playground at Maxwell AFB, where her father had been stationed at the time. She hadn't been ready to play the boy/girl games her friends took to so naturally, so she'd often felt like an outsider.

Then, when she was fourteen and long before she was ready for it, the acne had disappeared and suddenly boys started noticing her. With so many girls her own age soaring in height, her petiteness had made her popular with boys still fighting their own insecurities.

But she hadn't encouraged the attention, hadn't wanted it, even after she'd started high school, not until last summer when she'd met Steven. . . .

Only half listening to her companion's chatter, Tai smiled dreamily, her mind playing with images of Steven. As the car sped along the highway between the ocean and the Waianais, the range of low mountains that robbed the leeward coast of Oahu of its share of the island's rains, she relived the day she'd first met Steven.

Very early that morning, she had gone to Sunset Beach, a popular surfing spot on the windward side of Oahu, hoping to get in an hour of surfing before word got out that surf was up. To her chagrin, she found the beach already crowded. To add to her irritation, several of the surfers were novices who not only couldn't handle their boards properly, but obviously didn't know the unwritten rules that governed surfing protocol.

One novice, a tall, rangy man in his early twenties, committed the offense of snatching a wave out of turn, almost running Tai down with his board. She gave him a sizzling look and called him a name not used in polite company, and was doubly furious when he laughed and blew her a kiss. Later, when she was waxing her board on the beach, he sought her out.

Tai would have blistered him with a few truths, except that something very strange happened. As she took in his engaging smile, she was suddenly aware of herself as a woman—and she found herself wondering what this hazel-eyed stranger thought of *hapa-haole* girls with long black hair and blue eyes.

"Sorry about grabbing your wave," the man said, obviously confident that she would accept his apology. His hair was shorter than the island boys, and his flat stomach and lean hips didn't match the strength apparent in his muscular arms and thighs. As she looked him over, the iodine odor of salt water, of healthy, overheated male flesh, made her nostrils flare. For some reason, she thought of a sleek, long-limbed greyhound—and then was furious with herself because she found herself wondering if he was involved with a woman.

"I'm new to surfing—as you can plainly see," he added when she was silent. "After I grabbed your wave, one of the local guys took me aside and told me I was way off base. Peace?"

He held out a lean, brown hand and as she let him shake her hand, Tai felt as if her stomach had suddenly dropped a few inches, and a hot sensation started up along her thighs. Even a late bloomer recognizes the stirrings of sex by the time she's sixteen, and Tai was no exception. But until this moment, her budding sexuality had had no focus. None of the boys she knew had ever affected her the way this stranger did. Was it his strong body, so devoid of fat? Was it the expression in his hazel eyes, as if he were laughing at himself—or was he laughing at her? Did he realize the physical effect he was having on her?

She must have stiffened, because his hand dropped away and the smile faded from his face. "Look, my name is Steven Henderson—and I really am sorry. What else can I say?"

She maintained her silence a few seconds longer before she relented and said, "My name is Tai—Tai MacGarrett."

As always, her unusual name broke the ice, and after she'd explained that Tai was short for Tai-Ching, that her mother's maiden name had been Ching, Steven told her he would be a thirdclassman when he returned to the Air Force Academy in two weeks, a status he described as being one small step for a worm and one giant step for a doolie—a freshman, he explained—before he went on to say that he was home on summer leave to see his parents, who lived at Hickam Air Force Base.

When they discovered that her father, Chief Master Sergeant MacGarrett, worked directly for Steven's father, Colonel Henderson, who was Hickam's base commander, the last barrier dissolved.

"Hey, we're family," Steven joked, and Tai laughed and didn't tell him that her father considered his superior, Colonel Henderson, a "politician"—an epithet he reserved for officers and noncoms who put their own concerns above the welfare of their men.

They made a movie date, and that evening, after they'd left the outdoor theater on Pearl Harbor Channel and walked through the soft warmth of the July night, Tai knew that if Steven wanted sex with her, she would have a hard time refusing him.

As it happened, on their first two dates, he only kissed her good night, but on their third evening together, at a Waimea Bay beach where they'd gone for a night swim, Steven drew her down on the still warm sand behind a tangle of sea grape plants and kissed her throat, then pushed aside the strap of her bikini top and nuzzled the feverish flesh beneath.

Tai knew what he wanted, and because she wanted it, too, she slid her knee between his thighs, pressing against the throbbing hardness that betrayed his need, letting him know that the answer to his unspoken question was yes.

Even then he didn't rush her. For a long time, they kissed, their legs entwined, their bodies pressed together—his blatantly hard and protrusive, hers yielding and pliant. When he stripped off the bit of cloth that covered her breasts, she surrendered completely to voluptuousness. He untied the strings at the sides of her bikini, touching her with an intimacy new to her, and she discovered that her body had the jump on her and was already prepared for what came next.

Tai expected sex to be painful. Other girls had told her not to expect fireworks the first time. But as so often happened with her, she didn't react in a typical way. That night, she experienced not only her first sex, but her first orgasm. Steven realized it, too. Although she found out later that he wasn't nearly as sexually experienced as she'd first believed, he knew what those contractions deep inside her meant, and he was so surprised and maybe so grateful that Tai had another first that night—a proposal, which she promptly accepted.

"We'll have to wait three years until I graduate," Steven warned her. "Cadets can't marry and stay in the corps. Look, it wouldn't do for you to get pregnant, so maybe you'd better start on the pill. Until you do, I'll take—you know, precautions, even though it isn't nearly as good for either of us that way."

Tai agreed with everything he said. She was in love for the first time in her life, and it was she who initiated lovemaking the second time that night, even though it was very late and she knew that she'd have some tall explaining to do when they got home.

It was the engagement announcement that diverted her father's attention from the lateness of the hour. He disapproved—violently. Not only was the whole idea ridiculous because they'd only known each other for three days, he told them, loud and clear, but Tai was much too young to think of "going steady," a phrase that made her wince.

"I want you to stay away from Tai," he said, scowling at Steven. "You'll be going back to the academy in a few days— it's not fair to tie my daughter down at her age. Hell, she's only sixteen, man! No way am I going to let her get mixed up with you."

It was a white-faced Steven who finally left their quarters. Tai was in despair, sure her father had ruined everything. It didn't help when she later learned about the quarrel that had erupted the next morning in the Henderson quarters when Steven told his parents that he intended to marry the daughter of Hickam's base sergeant major.

The airman's wife who did housework for the Hendersons reported the quarrel with relish to her neighbors in Hickam Village, the off-base housing area where she lived. A week later, the tale reached Tai's ears—including Colonel Henderson's remark that "hell, no, you aren't marrying some halfbreed, and that's final!"

His words cut deeply, but Tai didn't make the mistake of blaming Steven for his father's bigotry. After all, her own father was just as prejudiced against the son of an officer he considered to be unfit. Although Tai pointed out that Mac's attitude was as obsolete as the dodo bird, it didn't help. In the end, she stopped talking about Steven at home, not only because it made her father furious, but because it put such a strain on their relationship.

Ever since Tai could remember, Mac had been the focus of her life. Her mother had been a soft-spoken woman with a frail body and a deceptively gentle manner—deceptive because she sometimes had a will of iron, something her wealthy Chinese-American family had discovered when she'd fallen in love with a military man not of their race.

Her marriage to Mac had been her one rebellion. With her husband, she was submissive, never criticizing him in any way, and it was only natural that Tai should grow up with the same attitude toward her father. One hard look or sharp word from Mac, and Tai was crushed, not from fear, but from love, an uncomplicated emotion that had dominated her life until she fell in love with Steven.

It took time, but eventually both families became resigned, if not approving, of the inevitable. When the romance lasted through the next year of separation with no sign of slackening off, both Sergeant MacGarrett and Steven's parents realized that the wedding would take place no matter what they did—but that they would have no part in it if they didn't give in.

So Steven's mother called upon Tai, and since Tai had no mother, Mrs. Henderson (Tai never thought of her by any other name) offered to make all the arrangements for a wedding in the academy chapel the week after Steven graduated.

Tai went along with Mrs. Henderson's plans. She didn't point out that a simple ceremony at the Hickam base chapel would be more appropriate to her father's income. But she made a private vow that once she and Steven were man and wife, they would live their own lives without interference from their parents. Until then, she could afford to be patient—and not make waves.

Today, as she drove past the guard station that flanked the Hickam gate, she waved to the young airmen on duty without slowing down. A few minutes later, she dropped Bobby Jo off in front of the duplex where her friend lived with her chaplain father, her mother, and a brood of younger brothers. As Tai drove along Beard Street, she passed the tall water tower, a landmark that dominated the broad banyon-lined parade grounds that separated "general's row" from "chief master sergeant's row," and she wondered if Steven and she would ever be lucky enough to be stationed at Hickam. If it happened early in his career, they would live off base because there were no quarters available for lower-grade officers and enlisted men.

A few feet past the parade grounds, she pulled into the driveway of the quarters she shared with her father. It was a two-bedroom single unit with thick walls and a red tile roof that dated from the early thirties, and Sergeant MacGarrett liked to boast about the bullet holes in the roof from strafing Japanese planes on Pearl Harbor Day.

Although he could have requisitioned new furniture and appliances from base supply because of his position as base sergeant major, her father followed a policy of never asking for special favors. Tai approved in theory, but she did think it would be nice to have decent living room furniture instead of the overshampooed sofa and chairs with which the quarters had been furnished when they'd moved in. And a new washer—the one they had could qualify as an antique. Was it too much to ask for a washing machine that got the clothes clean?

She left the car in the driveway, then cut across the lawn toward the back of the house. The monkey pod trees that lined the street rose to a height to rival even the African tulip tree in the side yard with its orange blossoms and its tan-and-brown pods that looked like small boats. A multicolored hedge of slow-growing crotons, decades old and shoulder high, lined the driveway, and the thick trunk of a coconut palm cast a graceful shadow against the cement latticework of the carport. In the perpetual shade of the monkeypod trees, only ground ivy would grow, and as Tai cut across the lawn, carrying her tote bag and rubber zoris, the tender ivy was spongy soft under her bare feet.

Tai was humming as she let herself in the back door, passing the despised washing machine with its chipped top and the mismatched dryer that was almost as old. She was getting a glass of water at the kitchen sink when she heard a cough in the living room and knew her father was home early from work. She drank the water, then went through the dining room and into the living room at the front of the house.

Sergeant MacGarrett was sitting on the sofa, staring into space, a glass of amber liquid dangling from his hand. His skin was so gray that he looked as if he'd been sprinkled with ashes, and his eyes—Tai had never seen his eyes so dull and unfocused before, not even when her mother had died.

Her first thought was totally selfish. Something's happened to Steven—oh, God, something awful's happened to Steven. . . .

She touched Mac's shoulder, but he didn't move. Only when she asked, "Is something wrong with Steven?" did he raise dazed eyes to her face.

"Steven? Not that I know of," he said, the words slurred.

It took Tai a minute to refocus her fears. Was her father ill—had he just found out that he had some terrible disease?

"What's wrong, Mac?" she said, using the name she'd called him since she was a toddler because somehow "Daddy" or "Pop" had never seemed right.

"Wrong—yeah, something's wrong when a man gives his life to the air force and then gets kicked in the teeth."

Mac's voice was harsh, grating, and Tai recoiled instinctively, dreading the next question she must ask. "What happened, Mac?" she said. "Are you in some kind of trouble?"

When he didn't answer, she tried a different tack. "Do you need help? Should I call Colonel Henderson?"

Dark red color stained Mac's cheeks, and suddenly his eyes came alive. "You do that. Call the bastard and ask him why the hell he told the provost marshal those lies about me."

Tai tried to make sense from his words. Did this have something to do with the fact that he disliked his superior? Mac had once told Tai that two types of men become base commanders. Either they were youngish men on their way up the promotion ladder who needed the practical experience of dealing with base-level problems, or else they were senior officers who had been passed over and were being pastured out in a "safe" job where they couldn't screw up too much.

In Mac's opinion, Colonel Henderson was a mixture of both kinds, a man still in the running for promotion who was trying to use his job as a springboard to a higher command level. To this end, he toadied to the brass at PACAF Headquarters as well as to those of the tenant commands who also headquartered at Hickam. If he won favor with the generals he dealt with, the next step was up. If he didn't, he would retire as a colonel instead of a general.

"Please, Mac—you're scaring me to death," Tai said. "I'm imagining all kinds of things. Tell me what's wrong."

Mac stared at her as if, for the first time, she really registered. "I'll tell you what's wrong. Your old man is under house arrest. Seems there's some irregularities in the commander's contingency fund." His voice was wooden, devoid of emotion now, and she knew that he was trying to hold his temper in check—and was having a hard time of it.

"What's that?"

"It's the fund set up for the base commander's compulsory social obligations—you know, when some VIP has to be entertained at base level."

Tai nodded understanding, remembering the banquets and receptions and other social affairs Mac had helped set up for visiting politicians and foreign dignitaries. "And something's wrong with it? How does that affect you?"

"I handle the fucking fund." Mac took a long drink from the glass in his hand. The raw odor of bourbon stung Tai's nostrils, and she had to restrain herself from reminding Mac that after his last annual physical, the medics had warned him not to drink.

"I told Colonel Henderson that the liquor order he wanted for the dining-in was excessive. 'Hell, sir, we don't need all that booze,' I said. 'Every guest there would have to drink a gallon of Jim Beam to knock off that much.' But the old man told me to go ahead and put in the order anyway, and after the dining-in, the storeroom was still full of crates of liquor. Now they've been ripped off, and I don't have a clue what happened to them."

"Why do they hold you responsible? Anyone could have broken in—"

"There's no sign of a break-in. Someone used a key—and the only two in existence are mine and the one the colonel has. Hell, they think I ripped off that liquor and sold it to one of the local bars. I told them the truth, but the old man still relieved me of my duties. Can you believe it? Twenty-one years I've given the air force, and they still think I'm a stinking thief."

He looked at her with red-rimmed eyes. "And that crudball Henderson—he said he doesn't remember me telling him the order was too big. Said he told me to order the usual amount. He's covering his own ass—or maybe he set the whole thing up. Maybe he wants something like this to happen. I told you it would cause trouble, you taking up with that frigging colonel's son."

Tai felt as if a heavy weight had settled on her shoulders. She sat down on the sofa, careful not to touch her father. "It has to be some kind of mistake," she said. Even to her own ears her voice sounded hollow, because she'd known all along that Steven's parents didn't want their son to marry the daughter of a sergeant—especially a girl of mixed blood.

"I think you'd better get some legal advice," she said, careful not to sound argumentative. "Aren't you entitled to legal representation?"

"I've already called a lawyer—a civilian, not some stinking shavetail just out of military law school. If it takes every cent I have, I'm going to beat this rap, and then I'm going to hang that brown-nosing bastard—"

As he went on listing his grievances, his words were so slurred that Tai finally realized how drunk he was, something that hadn't been apparent before.

She rose silently and went into the kitchen to put on a pot of coffee, knowing that when Mac was drinking heavily, he was a different man, unreasonable and obdurate. Not that she could blame him for tying one on when the thing he believed in had failed him. She felt a little bruised herself, but of course her pain was a mere shadow of what Mac was going through.

The hardest thing for her to accept was the knowledge that nothing she said, neither her advice nor her sympathy, held much value to him. Her father loved her, she was sure of that, but basically her opinions weren't important to him. The school honors, the swimming and other sport trophies she'd won, and the class offices she'd held were like the tricks of a clever dog, rating only a verbal pat on the head—if that. The truth was that no matter what she did, she couldn't overcome one handicap in Mac's eyes. She was a female, a daughter, and there was no way she could ever be the son Louis MacGarrett had really wanted.

Why having a son had been so important to her father, she didn't know. Why the fact that she was female made her less valuable in Mac's eyes was a mystery, buried in the past he never talked about as if he had been born the day he enlisted in the air force. He had loved her mother so much that after she had died, he'd almost turned into an alcoholic. So Tai was sure it wasn't some latent hatred of women. Maybe it was simply that he was a consummate military man who only valued those who could carry arms and fight for their country. And none of this would really matter right now except that just when she wanted to be of comfort to him, she couldn't reach him.

In the end, she called one of Mac's poker buddies. Within minutes, the house was filled with men's angry voices, all Mac's cronies having rallied behind one of their own who was in a jam. That some of them suspected there might be some truth in the charges brought against Mac, Tai guessed from the things they *didn't* say. She could only hope that Mac didn't realize it, too.

After they were finally gone and the house was quiet again, Mac told her. "They don't believe me, Tai. They figure I did a little midnight requisitioning and forgot to cover my tracks."

"You're wrong," she lied. "Everybody knows you wouldn't even take a one-cent stamp from petty cash that didn't belong to you."

"Hell, didn't you see the way they kept avoiding my eyes? Sure, they all volunteered to be character witnesses if this business comes down to a court-martial, but they've still got their doubts. And it's my own fault. I've been around the barn a few times. I should've insisted the old man sign that liquor order himself. That's where I slipped up. I thought I was safe in the system." He gave a hoarse laugh. "And it's the fucking system that's going to do me in."

He was still muttering to himself as Tai gathered up the glasses and carried them into the kitchen. She put them in the dishwasher and then stood there, staring out the window at a flowering plumeria tree. The past hours seemed unreal. Her father was in the worst trouble of his life, and she felt like a spectator at a play, as if the lights would go on any minute and she could get up and leave.

But it wasn't a play. It was real. And what exactly would all this mean to her engagement to Steven?

She felt an acute longing to talk to Steven, to hear his voice telling her that nothing could change things between them. She started for the phone in the dining room, only to reconsider before she reached it. Trying to contact a cadet at the academy by phone was an involved process. It wasn't as if it were an emergency in his own family. Besides, what could she say? That his father was trying to railroad Mac into prison? That she wanted it to stop?

For one thing, she wasn't even sure it was true. Maybe Colonel Henderson had simply forgotten Mac's warning about the liquor order. Yes, that had to be it. To believe anything else was to borrow even more trouble and to add to her feeling that her whole world was slowly beginning to unravel.

CHAPTER
↑ 5 ↑

To Tai, the next few days were a nightmare that seemed to have no ending. Mac sat around the house in a pair of wrinkled trousers and a soiled T-shirt, even when company came, drinking too much bourbon and refusing to eat or even to take a shower. Before Tai's eyes, he seemed suddenly to be coming apart, bit by bit, reduced to a much smaller man. She had always thought Mac was so strong and invincible, willing to tackle anything that came along, but now he seemed a stranger, a stranger with empty eyes and a brooding expression.

It came to her that her father was acting like a man with a broken heart, and it was then she made a personal decision. Never would she make the mistake of believing in anything— or any person—so totally that if things went sour, the props would be pulled out from under her.

As for friends, it seemed you couldn't really depend upon them, either. At first, the living room was full of Mac's cronies, all indignation because he was being chewed up by the system. But as the days passed, the phone calls and visitors gradually dwindled down until only a couple of his oldest friends still stopped by regularly to see him.

Tai grew to dread these visits because invariably Mac's drinking increased even more, and she was forced to put him to bed after the company was gone. It was also excruciatingly painful, watching him slowly fall apart.

To relieve her own fear, she poured out her concern about

Mac in her letters to Steven. His answering letter seemed guarded, stilted. Although he told her he loved her, that he would be glad when the next two years were over so they could be married, it was the things he didn't say that disappointed her. He referred to Mac's troubles as "that mess Mac is involved in," and not once did he give any indication that he thought her father was innocent. While she couldn't really blame him for taking his own father's side, a small core of resentment took root inside her.

One thing that bothered her was that Steven hadn't yet called. Although it was difficult for her to contact him by phone, he had no restriction during his off hours. But the phone call never came—and his second letter was shorter, concerned mostly with a decision he must make about which subject he wanted to major in. Without the assurances and comfort she craved, she felt alienated from her lover at a time when she needed him most.

Her enrollment day at Colorado College passed. She waited for Mac to mention it, but he didn't seem to notice the red circle she'd drawn around the date on the kitchen calendar. Although Tai went through periods of rebellion when she wanted desperately to leave and escape Mac's disintegration, she knew she couldn't desert him.

At the last minute, she called the registrar at Colorado College to explain that a family emergency would prevent her from enrolling that term. The woman was sympathetic, but she also made it clear that Tai's scholarship depended upon her attendance during the first semester. Otherwise, the scholarship would pass on to the next candidate on the list. Tai thanked her, then hung up, almost sick with disappointment. But she kept her feelings to herself. How could she add to Mac's burden when he was so beset with his own problems?

After all the waiting and the anxiety, Mac's court-martial, in October, seemed almost an anticlimax. Everything, from the first call to order to the reading of the verdict, was dry and businesslike, without drama. Looking pale and wrung out, Mac stated the facts in a wooden voice, but he had nothing to support his contention that Colonel Henderson was responsible for the excessive liquor order for the dining-in. The expensive civilian lawyer he'd hired didn't help. In fact, Tai suspected that it had been a mistake to bring in an outside lawyer, that a "shavetail just out of military law school" might have impressed the five-man jury more than an outsider.

Colonel Henderson gave his testimony, looking very military and, even to Tai's partisan eyes, very convincing as he expressed his regret for having to refute Sgt. MacGarrett's testimony. He was sure that the sergeant hadn't mentioned the size of the liquor order, certainly hadn't voiced any objections. In fact, he himself had assumed that it would be the regular order for a dining-in. As for the disappearance of nine cases of bourbon and Scotch from a locked storage room to which only Sgt. MacGarrett and he had keys—unfortunately, he couldn't even testify that the crates had been stored in that room. If he'd known so much liquor was left over from the dining-in, he would have ordered it to be returned to the base liquor store for a refund.

The whole business saddened him, he added. He'd always had the highest regard for Sgt. MacGarrett's efficiency, and he still wasn't convinced that it wasn't some kind of mix-up, a lapse of memory on the sergeant's part. After all, no one wanted to believe that a veteran with twenty-one years of honorable service would deliberately lie.

The jury believed him. Tai read the belief on the faces of Mac's peers, military men who lived by the book. When she saw how they avoided looking directly at Mac, one of their own who had disgraced them, she knew what the outcome of the court-martial would be.

The verdict, that Mac was guilty as charged, didn't surprise her.

Later, in the hall outside the courtroom, the civilian lawyer shrugged philosophically and told Mac to cheer up, that it could have been worse. He could've been sentenced to ten years at Leavenworth on top of getting a dishonorable discharge and having to pay a big fine. He went on to recommend that Mac file an immediate appeal because the evidence was so flimsy it would never stand up before a federal judge.

Mac watched him with dull, unseeing eyes. He opened his mouth to speak, but the words never came. Instead, an almost comical look of surprise spread over his face. He fell forward, like a tree downed by a bolt of lightning, and only because Tai moved so quickly to support him did he escape a bad fall. As she staggered under his weight, the lawyer jumped forward to help her, but she wouldn't let him touch Mac. She told him to call the medics, that she would take care of her father.

For three days, Mac lay in a coma in the intensive care section of Tripler Army Hospital, looking like a stranger with his face the color of wax, with tubes and paraphernalia attached to his motionless body. On the third day, as Tai sat dozing beside the bed, he opened his eyes to stare at her, but when he called her by her mother's name, she knew it was his dead wife that he saw.

"You shoulda told me to get lost, Mai-Lei," he said as if continuing a conversation he'd started earlier. "You deserved better than a guy like me. But I was crazy about you—I never did take up with another woman, even though people were always telling me that the girl needed a mother. . . . I just went through the motions after you died, trying to get her raised so I could let go. . . . I think it's time to let go. . . ."

He closed his eyes. A few minutes later, he was dead.

There was a crowd at the funeral. Their faces long, their intentions good, most of Mac's friends made an appearance. They said the conventional things, praising Mac for being a great guy—and no one mentioned his court-martial. There'd been a problem about his burial, about whether or not he was entitled to lie in the hallowed ground of the island's national cemetery. In her bitterness, Tai didn't fight it. Instead, she made private arrangements for his burial in a civilian cemetery. Although she knew that she was spending too much money for the funeral, the flowers, the casket, and the burial plot, it was very important to her that Mac be buried with the honor and dignity of which his government had robbed him.

It was a bitter day during which she didn't even have the comfort of Bobby Jo's company. As soon as Bobby Jo heard the news, she called from Colorado Springs, offering to return for the funeral. Although Tai wanted her there, she thought about Bobby Jo's meager personal allowance and told her friend it wasn't necessary, that she wouldn't be alone, not with Mac's friends to help out.

To her surprise, when she reached the base chapel, Shelley was waiting for her, standing near the entrance. She was wearing a dark blue summer suit, and she looked very sober.

She didn't tell Tai, as others had, that it was all for the best, that time would heal her wounds. Instead, she asked, "Is there anything I can do? Anything at all?" and Tai, although caught up in her own private hell, was struck by the sincerity in her voice.

"There's nothing anyone can do," she said, her words ragged.

Shelley hesitated, then asked, "If I were Bobby Jo—what would you want me to do for you?"

Tai stared at her. What would she want from Bobby Jo? Why, to be beside her during the ordeal ahead—and hold her hand. "Will you sit with me in the chapel?" she asked.

"You know I will," Shelley said.

A group of Mac's friends and their wives came up, interrupting them, and when Tai looked around, Shelley was gone. But later, after she'd been ushered to the front row of the chapel, Shelley slipped onto the bench beside her and took her hand. She held it tightly during the brief eulogy, spoken by Bobby Jo's father, and when the ceremony was over, Shelley accompanied her to the cemetery in the hired limousine.

To make conversation, Tai asked Shelley why she was still in Hawaii and if she'd changed her mind about going to Radcliffe as she'd planned. A veil seemed to drop over Shelley's eyes. She hesitated, then said, "I'm not sure what my plans are. I'll call you soon—I have something to tell you."

Before Shelley left, she asked again if there was anything she could do to help, and Tai knew she meant it, which was more than she could be sure about with the others. How strange that while she'd known some of these people for the past three years, had seen them in church, at the NCO Club, and helped Mac entertain them at barbecues in their backyard, she still felt as if she were surrounded by strangers. Was it because they were all air force people—and the air force was suddenly her enemy?

As a final irony, when she returned to the base after the funeral, she found a letter from base housing in the mailbox. It was addressed to Mac, and it informed him that since he was no longer assigned to Hickam Air Force Base, he and his family must vacate their quarters by the end of the month.

Not that eviction mattered to Tai. She couldn't wait to put everything behind her that could remind her of the wrong done to her father. It was later, as she went through Mac's personal papers, that she found the bill from his lawyer. She didn't know whether to laugh or cry when she realized that all of Mac's civilian insurance and his savings would go to pay for the lawyer who had done so little for him. Although the insurance wasn't part of her father's estate and couldn't legally be tapped for his debts, she knew that she would pay the bill. Since the six months' pay gratuity she normally would have drawn as Mac's heir was forfeit because of his dishonorable discharge, she couldn't even depend upon that. In fact, her college fund would just cover the fine levied against Mac by his government, leaving her with only her own small savings account to keep her afloat until she found work.

It wasn't, she told herself, that she wanted Mac's insurance—or anything that came from the air force. No, it was the unfairness that rankled. She felt as if her eyelids had been scalded by the tears she'd shed as she packed Mac's clothing into cardboard boxes and called the Salvation Army to come pick them up.

The next day, she sold Mac's four-year-old Mercury to a neighbor, knowing she was practically giving it away because she needed the money to clear up the last of Mac's debts. She loaded her personal possessions into her own car and left the base without notifying anybody where she was going, dropping the key in the mailbox after she'd locked the door. Besides her own possessions, the only things that she took with her were a few personal mementos—Mac's old-fashioned pocket watch, his Cajun grandmother's bible, written in French, her mother's photo album, which was filled with studio photographs of Chinese relatives she'd never met.

She hadn't bothered to notify the Chings, her mother's family, that Mac had died.

She doubted if they even knew he had returned to Hawaii for another tour of duty at Hickam. After all, why would they care if the husband of the woman they'd disowned had died, leaving his daughter an orphan? No, she was totally on her own now, and she felt as if she'd been cast adrift, cut off from everything familiar to her.

By now, she didn't even have Steven—and that was the thing that cut the deepest.

Steven had finally called her the night of her father's death. When a neighbor, who was answering the phone for Tai, told her it was long distance, she put the receiver to her ear, said a tentative "Hello?" For a moment, she didn't recognize Steven's voice because it sounded so tinny and far away.

"Tai? This is Steven. I just heard about Mac—are you okay?"

It was the concern in his voice that broke through the protective wall Tai had built around herself. Her face convulsed with grief; she lost her voice and couldn't answer him. She knew he was still talking, but it was a few seconds before the meaning of his words sank in.

"Look, Tai, I asked for leave so I could come to your dad's funeral, but it's a no-go. If it were family, there'd be no problem, but as it is—for one thing, I'm in the middle of an interservice tennis tournament, and the team's depending upon me. This wouldn't stop me if I could get leave, but . . . well, it does put on the pressure, I still haven't given it up, but my adviser, Major Downey, doesn't hold out much hope—"

He broke off, as if finally realizing that she still hadn't spoken. When he went on, there was a defensive note in his voice that grated against her nerves. "Look, I know this is a really rough time for you. I've been worried sick about you—Dad said he tried to reach you, but your line's been busy—"

"And of course your parents live too far away to drive over to our quarters," she said, the bitterness inside her erupting into words. "Well, your father is right. The phone hasn't stopped ringing. Everybody's so sorry about Mac—but where were they when he could've used some support? Why should your parents be any different? If your father really wants to help, he can tell the truth and clear Mac's name."

There was a long silence on the line, broken only with tiny electronic blips. A laugh struggled up in Tai's throat, and she put her hand over her mouth to hold it back. Maybe it's the CIA, she thought, on the verge of hysteria. Maybe they've bugged my line to find out if I'm trying to corrupt one of their precious million-dollar cadets.

Her neighbor, a middle-aged woman who was married to a senior master sergeant, came to the door. When she saw Tai was still on the phone, she waved and went away again.

"Are you okay, Tai?" Steven said.

"Oh, sure, I'm just great. Mac is dead because the air force broke his heart, but I'm fine. And how was your day?"

"Look, I realize now that this was the wrong time to call. Why don't I give you a ring later? We'll talk things over and—and decide what to do."

"Do about what?"

"About—you know, our personal plans. Is there any chance you can still enroll at Colorado College? I saw Bobby Jo last night at the fall hop, and she told me you had to forfeit your scholarship—"

"You already knew that. I told you about it in one of my letters."

"Yeah, I guess you did—I've been so snowed under lately that I don't have time to think. My workload is really murder, but if I can get away for a few days around the holidays, maybe we can get together then—"

"I need you now."

"You know I can't get away. Hell, they keep us so busy. I don't have a spare minute."

"But you have time to go to fall hops, don't you? Who did you take? Some little freshman from Colorado College?"

"Look, I explained how the system works. It's the whole-man concept—and going to social affairs is part of it."

"Yes, I remember. The whole-man concept—do they allow you to act like a real human being, or is that against the rules?"

"You're being unreasonable. This isn't the time for—I know you're under a terrible strain, Tai. Why don't I call you after you've had a chance to unwind a little? We have things to talk over, decisions to make, you know."

"I know. Like whether or not to call the whole thing off. Your parents would like that. I'll bet your father's been burning up the phone lines, telling you what to expect if you marry the daughter of a man who got railroaded out of the air force—and a half breed at that."

"That's a hell of a thing to say. My father isn't perfect, but he isn't a bigot—"

"That's the word he used to describe me when you told him we were engaged."

"Where the hell did you hear that?"

"Nothing's a secret around an air base, especially something that juicy. It only took a week to get back to me via the gossip hotline. Is that why your father lied on the stand about Mac? Did he cook up the whole thing to break us up?"

There was a short silence; Steven's voice was cold when he said, "Dad did everything he could to help Mac, but that didn't include lying under oath. Mac should have admitted he made a mistake, that he got careless and left that key lying around, and maybe it would have ended there."

"It was your father who lied," she said hotly. "He was so busy worrying about his own hide that he threw Mac to the wolves. Mac had his number from the first day he reported in. Your father may end up with general's stars, but he'll never be the man Mac was—never in a million years."

"You're talking crazy, Tai—and before we say something that we'll regret, I think I'd better hang up. I'll call you tomorrow."

There was a click in Tai's ear, breaking the connection. She wanted to scream into the receiver, to call Steven a stuffed shirt, a traitor to their love, but it was too late. She took out some of her anger by slamming the phone back on its cradle, and then she went into her bedroom and closed the door. Even though she knew it was all over, the thing between Steven and her that had been so good, she didn't cry long. She had already shed too many tears over Mac.

The next day she left the base with everything she owned piled into her Simca. She rented a one-room efficiency apartment in a shabby apartment building on Beretania Street. Except for some of her clothes, she didn't bother to unpack. The apartment was temporary, necessary shelter while she decided what to do next.

Getting a job came first, of course. Now that she'd paid a month's rent, there was very little money left in her wallet—and why didn't it seem more important that she was almost broke? Something was wrong with her brain—she felt as if she were floating in a gray limbo. So many things that she'd believed in all her life had failed her—and she couldn't seem to get her priorities straight. There wasn't even anyone she wanted to talk to about it. If Bobby Jo were here, it would be different—but Bobby Jo was in Colorado, leading her own life.

For a brief moment, Crystal crossed her mind, but she shook her head. Crystal had called a couple of times, but her words had been so guarded that it was obvious she didn't want to get involved in Tai's trouble. No, Crystal wasn't her friend—why had it taken her so long to realize this? There was Shelley, of course, who had been so kind at Mac's funeral, but they hadn't really been close friends. Even though she knew Shelley's offer to help had been sincere, still it would be unfair to use her as a sounding board.

As for her other friends from Punahou—most of them were

on the Mainland, enrolled in college or working. There wasn't anyone she wanted to see—or was it that she was afraid? Afraid that if she called anyone, they would let her down? And maybe this was her fault. She'd been so busy competing for trophies, or making the honor roll and winning elections, that she'd spread herself too thin. No wonder her friendships had been shallow—except with Bobby Jo.

And wasn't it ironic that all her effort had been a waste? She had done it for Mac, to win his approval, but he hadn't cared, hadn't really noticed. She'd only been an obligation, someone he was duty bound to take care of. If she'd been born a male, would that have made a difference? Would he have called her by name there at the end instead of referring to her as "the girl"?

Late that afternoon, hunger finally drove Tai out of her room. She was standing at the counter of an open-fronted saimin booth on Beretania Street, eating a bowl of noodle soup, when she glanced down at an early edition of the *Honolulu Advertiser* that someone had left on the counter. The words "Air Force Academy" seemed to spring off the page at her, and she picked up the newspaper and read the article, which had a *New York Times* byline.

In a tongue-in-cheek manner, it described the ordeals of a female cadet who had just made it through her first year at the academy, and after Tai had finished reading it through, an idea came to her that made her lose interest in her food.

According to the article, female cadets, admitted for the first time that year to the Air Force Academy, had the same opportunities as men cadets. Whether or not this was true, there was no denying that if they survived four years at the academy, they would graduate with a prestigious engineering degree. After they had fulfilled their obligatory five years of active duty as air force officers, they were free to leave the service and get a job. As the article said, the pickings would be easy for a graduate of one of the best engineering colleges in the country.

What's more, the air force would pay for every last cent of it.

"Wouldn't I love to screw them the way they screwed Mac?" Tai said, speaking out loud and evoking a curious stare from the Japanese counterman.

She paid for her saimin and went back to her room, taking

the newspaper with her. That night she didn't sleep much, but she got in a lot of thinking. The air force had robbed Mac of everything he valued—his faith in the system, his honor and pride and, in the end, his life. And they had robbed her, too—of her belief that the world was a reasonable place where hard work and loyalty were rewarded in the end.

She knew differently now, and it was time she started playing the game by the rules. The thing was—what were the rules? For instance, how could she get any appointment to the Academy? What qualifications did it take—and did she have them?

Her grades at Punahou had been very high—a lofty 3.9 cum. As far as the whole-man concept went, there were the various honors and trophies she'd won, including being valedictorian of her class. However, since life wasn't always logical or fair, it probably took something more than that, some kind of an edge, to qualify as one of the Academy's token women cadets. . . .

She tried to remember what Steven had told her about his own appointment. Although the sons of servicemen on active duty usually went after presidential appointments, those openings were limited and competition for them very high, so Steven had applied for his through a United States congressman, a man who had been Colonel Henderson's classmate at West Point. He had been nominated and accepted after he'd passed competitive exams and tests.

Well, she could play that game, too. She did have an edge, after all—her family ties with a United State senator.

Only Mac and she knew that Walter Ching, the senior senator from Hawaii, was her uncle. It was something they never talked about, even to each other, because Senator Ching was titular head of the family that had disowned her mother and who had never acknowledged Tai's existence.

But if she was going to start playing the game by the rules other people set up, she would just have to swallow her pride. Her uncle could give her the edge she needed—provided she had the guts to go to him and ask him to nominate her for an appointment to the Air Force Academy.

CHAPTER
↑ 6 ↑

TAI PRETENDED NOT TO NOTICE THE CURIOUS GLANCES OF her uncle's secretary, a Chinese woman of indeterminate age, as she sat in the waiting room outside her uncle's office. She wasn't sure what to expect from a meeting with her uncle. Suspicion, surely. Hostility, perhaps. Certainly not any great display of interest. The fact that such a busy man, a United States senator, had granted her half an hour from a schedule that his secretary had let her know was "incredibly busy" seemed at least to indicate curiosity.

What would he think of her? With her Scottish, French, and Chinese heritage, did he expect her to be some weird hybrid? If so, he would be disappointed. In minor ways, she looked like both of her parents, but she could just as easily pass as Hispanic or one of the Mediterranean races. Strangers had assumed she was just about every race—including American Indian.

This elusive quality was both a detriment and an asset, depending upon the circumstances. In Hawaii, with its multi-racial society, she blended in so well that she'd found easy acceptance. But during her father's tour in Germany, she had looked so alien and out of place that she'd had to fight discrimination, something she had treated as a challenge rather than letting it get her down.

And now, in another few minutes, she would face an even bigger challenge. Which was why she had prepared herself mentally for any reaction her uncle might have—including total rejection. Inwardly, she was all geared for battle; the adrenaline was pumping like mad through her veins and her senses were alert, on guard. It was always this way with her, this automatic reaction to any kind of competition or challenge. Did this make her masculine, as she'd been told a few times by disgruntled men she'd bested in fencing or kung fu? Or did it simply mean that she was a competitive person—period?

"Senator Ching will see you now," the secretary told her and Tai rose on legs that were suddenly a little rubbery and followed the woman into an inner office.

She was prepared for luxury because she'd read newspaper and magazine articles about her uncle's famous collections of Chinese antiques and objets d'art. So it wasn't the spacious room, with its teakwood chairs and tables and its cabinets full of ivory and jade collections, that surprised her. What she hadn't expected was the man himself. She had seen pictures of him, of course, but she hadn't realized that Senator Ching was so small, a birdlike man with still ebony hair and sharp black eyes that examined her without expression.

It had been a long time since Tai's mother had drilled her in the proper way to greet an elder relative, so it was instinct that governed her as she folded her hands at her waist and made a deep bow.

A twinkle—or maybe it was simply a reflection off the bronze lamp at his elbow—flickered in her uncle's eyes as he returned the bow, a mere shadow of hers, this one proper for a man of importance greeting an insignificant young niece.

"I see that you still remember your mother's teachings," he observed, waving her toward a chair.

Tai waited until her uncle had seated himself behind his deeply carved teakwood desk before she sank onto the chair. This was going to be a contest of wills, it seemed—and she had a hunch that her uncle held most of the weapons.

But not all of them. No, not all of them. . . .

"I hope you are well, Honorable Uncle," she said, her tone respectful.

"I am—and since you are obviously blooming, I won't ask how you are. You resemble your mother in many ways, you know, although you look more Occidental than Chinese."

"I've been told that I resemble both my parents."

"Since I never met your father, I must accept your word for

that." He was silent a moment, watching her, before he added, "My condolences on the death of your father."

She nodded silently, hoping that her face was as impassive as his. Did he know about Mac's court-martial? If so, was he waiting to see if she would mention it?

"The doctors say that my father died from a stroke, but I think it was from a broken heart," she said finally.

"It's very possible. When one is betrayed by the thing one honors the most, the heart suffers." He reached forward to press a button on an intercom. He spoke into it quietly before he turned back to Tai. "I've ordered tea—you do have time for refreshments, don't you?"

To Tai, there was a hint of cruelty—or was that amusement in his purring voice? As she nodded, she reminded herself that he couldn't possibly guess why she was here. Why borrow trouble? Why not assume that he had granted her these few minutes out of curiosity—and possibly guilt?

A few minutes later, as she sipped pungent green tea, she felt wrung out emotionally, as if she had just been put through an inquisition. Although his courtesy had never faltered, the questions her uncle had asked revealed a knowledge of her personal business that was completely unexpected.

Did she enjoy being back in the Islands—and how did she rate Punahou as a school? How had she adjusted to the constant change and travel of military life? What had she thought of Germany—of Florida and Alabama, of Washington, D.C.? And what did she plan to do with her life now that her father was gone and her engagement to that young cadet had been broken?

It was an ordeal, but because she knew there must be some purpose behind the questions, she answered them truthfully, with as much dignity as she could muster.

"I'm surprised that you know so much about me," she said finally.

"Why shouldn't I take an interest in the daughter of my only sister?"

"But you never came to see me—"

"It wouldn't have been suitable. Your father wanted no part of the Ching family, and of course I was forced to respect his wishes," he said smoothly. "And I believe you came here for a purpose? Perhaps you'd better tell me about it."

It took Tai a moment to reassemble her thoughts and make

changes in the speech she had prepared so carefully. "If you know so much about me," she started out, "maybe you already know that my grades at Punahou were excellent, that I excelled in math. I've always wanted to be an engineer, but unfortunately my father's death"—she paused for a heartbeat of time because this was the first time she'd said those words aloud—"left me without funds for college tuition."

She hesitated, uncertain whether to explain about the lawyer's fees, the funeral expenses, the scholarship at Colorado College that she'd forfeited.

"I still intend to be an engineer," she went on, "only now it will take longer. As you must know, the military academies are now admitting women cadets. I'd like to apply for an appointment to the Air Force Academy. It's too late for this year, but I'm sure I could qualify for the 1978 freshman class, provided I get the opportunity. I'm not afraid of the competition, but unfortunately there are still very few slots for women. That's why I asked for this appointment. I'd like your help."

Her uncle lifted his cup to his lips, his eyes veiled. The porcelain was so thin that she could see the shadow of his hand through its translucence, and it occurred to her that he looked very much like fine porcelain himself—fragile to look at, but durable, with the ability to age well. As Senator Ching sipped his tea, Tai tried to read his face, but it could have been carved from ivory. Was he offended by her bluntness? Should she have approached the subject in an oblique way—the Chinese way? She hadn't planned to sound so formal. Why had she allowed her pride to get the upper hand?

"I see you are a very forceful young woman, which I'm sure you inherited from your father." Her uncle's voice was dry. "However, your visit, although pleasant, was unnecessary. I have already considered the possibility of appointing you to the academy."

"But—but that's impossible. How could you have known? I didn't tell anyone—"

"No one?"

"Only my adviser at Punahou. I called her a couple of days ago to ask if she knew what the requirements are for an appointment to the academy . . ." She paused to frown at him. "Is that how you know so much about me? Have you been getting reports from my adviser? But why? Why would you care about my grades?"

"As head of your mother's family, I've always been concerned about you. You are my sister's daughter, and although she chose to turn her back on her heritage, still there are family ties that must be honored."

"But you've never shown any interest in me—" She stopped as a realization struck her. "But you have, haven't you? Is that how my father was able to send me to Punahou?"

"I have never communicated with your father."

"But someone else did. That partial scholarship Punahou offered me after Mac made inquiries about enrolling me there—he couldn't have afforded to send me to Punahou without it. And the one at Colorado College—did you have something to do with that, too?"

Her uncle stared at her with oblique eyes, and she knew that she would get no answer from him. Not that it was needed. Whatever his reason—guilt or concern for his sister's child—he had intervened in her life. But what she had really needed—a sense of identity, a close relationship with her mother's family—he had denied her. What's more, she bitterly resented the implication that her father couldn't take care of her properly without help. For Mac's sake, if not for her own, it was time that she left.

Carefully, she set down the fragile cup and saucer and rose. "I see I made a mistake, coming here. Thank you for your time. I won't bother you again."

"Sit down, Tai-Ching. You must learn to control your temper. It's unseemly in a woman. I have a proposition—one I want you to consider very carefully. This idea of your about going to a military academy—you do realize the difficulties of such a life for a woman, don't you? You would be subjected to humiliation, badgering, insults, and even open hostility. I realize that it's a different world these days, but why not choose something more practical? I am willing to subsidize your education at any school you choose—including one of the Ivy League colleges. If you prefer to consider it a loan, that's agreeable to me."

When she didn't answer, he added, "You do understand that my neglect wasn't of my own choosing, don't you? My wife and I are childless. After your mother's death, we offered to raise you as our own daughter, but your father rejected my offer. All that has changed now—"

"Nothing has changed," she said through stiff lips. She

hesitated, then said reluctantly, "Thank you for arranging those scholarships, although it wasn't necessary. From now on, I'll handle my own affairs."

She bowed stiffly, then headed for the door, determined not to cry in front of her uncle. The whole thing had been a fiasco—no, worse than that. It cut her deeply, this discovery that her father, who had never corrected her belief that her mother's people had turned their back on her, had been lying by omission all those years.

Well, she had inherited Mac's pride, and she had no intention of accepting any more favors from her uncle—although the opportunity to compete for an appointment to the Air Force Academy didn't really fit into that category. Unfortunately, that channel was closed to her now. Not that she intended to give up. There were other congressmen. She would go ahead with her plans—it would just take a little longer.

The efficiency apartment she'd rented on Beretania Street had been closed up most of the afternoon; the hot air inside reeked of bad plumbing and roach powder and stale cooking odors as she let herself in the door. She opened the windows as far as they would go, then curled up on the sagging couch she used as a bed, too dispirited to cry, even though there was nobody there to see her tears.

The depression was still with her the next day when she awoke, but she dragged herself out of bed, put on a cotton blouse and skirt and her most comfortable sandals and started looking for work. It seemed a good omen that she found a job in a novelty shop in the arcade of a Waikiki hotel, the Royal Hawaiian, on her fourth try. The pay was minimal, the chance for advancement nonexistent, but she was confident she could live on her earnings. There was an added advantage, too. Since it was only part-time work, she would have extra time to correct any deficiencies in her education that might hinder her in applying for an appointment at the academy.

She no longer felt comfortable consulting her adviser at Punahou, so she contacted an air force recruiter and got the information she needed from him. She already knew that her background in the sciences was weak, but after studying the academy brochures, she was sure that her math skills would be competitive with other applicants. Since it was too late to enroll for evening classes at the University of Hawaii, she got permission to monitor two science classes. In addition, she would follow her own private study program.

That weekend she sat down to write Bobby Jo a letter, not only to send her a change of address, but to tell her friend what she planned to do. She didn't contact anyone else. A wide gap had opened between her and the people she knew—and besides, her emotions were still too raw to accept their advice or their pity or even their offers of help.

It was different with Bobby Jo. She might be a featherweight in some ways, as Crystal was always intimating, but her friendship was like a rock—and it would never occur to Bobby Jo to offer advice.

It was four months later, in early February, that Tai came home from work to find a long cream-colored envelope waiting for her in her mailbox. When she saw her uncle's Washington address on the envelope, a tremor started up in her hands, and her uncle's letter rustled slightly as she took it out and read it.

The words Senator Ching had dictated were dry and impersonal. He congratulated her on her appointment to next year's entering class at the Air Force Academy—the graduating class of 1981—and then reminded her that she must still meet rigid physical and academic requirements. He added that she would be contacted shortly by his office for further information and instructions.

CHAPTER
✦ 7 ✦

CRYSTAL KNEW ABOUT SGT. MACGARRETT'S TROUBLE AL-
most as soon as it happened. She had called the base to talk
to one of the few girls she'd bothered to keep in touch with
after graduation. Her ex-schoolmate, the daughter of Hickam's
provost marshal, was full of the news about Sgt. MacGarrett's
house arrest.

Briefly, sympathy for Tai stirred. Tai's troubles were none
of her own doing but stemmed from her father's shortcomings.
Since Crystal had suffered from the deficiencies of her own
parents, she felt a rare if fleeting kinship with Tai. Even so, it
was two days before she called the MacGarrett quarters. It was
her experience that it was best to maintain a certain distance
from people in trouble.

Crystal voiced a few platitudes, said she would keep in
touch, a promise she had no intention of keeping. After all,
she had her own life to lead.

The same day she heard the news about Sgt. MacGarrett,
she did call Shelley, intending to pump her for details, only to
be told by Mrs. Pritchard's fluting voice that her daughter had
left the house early that morning, and no, she had no idea
where she had gone, but she would leave a message for Shelley
to call Crystal when she got home.

Mrs. Pritchard warmed up a bit when Crystal pumped enthusiasm into her voice to tell her how grateful she was for General
Pritchard's recommendation for the job at PACAF Headquarters.

In fact, she even unbent enough to invite Crystal to stop by to see her after Shelley had gone back east to school.

"It's gratifying to know that there are a few young people these days who still appreciate the American work ethic, my dear," said Mrs. Pritchard, who had come from an "old money" New England family and had never earned a day's pay in her life. "It's that deplorable rock music—I blame it for the weakening of moral values. I do believe Shelley only plays it to annoy me."

Crystal murmured something sympathetic, careful not to say anything that might be quoted later to Shelley and be interpreted as criticism. She still had use for Shelley and didn't intend to jeopardize their friendship. In fact, she felt a little sorry for her, for all her advantages. Shelley might have an influential father, but everybody on the base was scared of Mrs. Pritchard, who was known to have so much influence with her husband.

Crystal intended to have the same kind of clout someday. Sort of "the power behind the throne" thing. It might be second-hand power, but she had no intention of turning herself inside out trying to make it as a career woman. No matter how high she rose on her own, she would never hit the top echelons of any field, not without a male mentor to back her. So why go to all that trouble? Why not simply latch on to a fast burner and ride his coattails to the top? In the end it all amounted to the same thing. Power was power, no matter how obtained.

Crystal's job—in the adjutant general's office at PACAF Headquarters—started the next Monday. She put a lot of thought into how to dress for her first day at work. This early in the game, she wanted to attract as little attention as possible, but she also wanted to impress her superiors. In the end, she chose a pleated skirt, a white silk blouse with a striped scarf at her neck, and a pair of white sandals that emphasized one of her best features, her long, slender legs. As she arranged her hair into a smooth, understated style, she was sure she would blend in with the other clerks during her training period.

Her immediate superior, it turned out, was a hard-bitten civil service veteran, who let Crystal know that she'd worked all over the world and had earned her GS 9 rating the hard way. She looked Crystal over, taking in her plain hairstyle and subdued makeup. When her manner thawed slightly, Crystal knew that her protective coloring had been successful.

Something her father had once told her slipped into her

mind. "Never let the bastards know what you really want—a job or a promotion or a man—because then they'll do their best to sink you. But if they think you don't really give a damn, they just might give you a hand up. But don't depend upon it, sweet cakes."

So why hadn't Maurice ended up at the top of the heap? Obviously he had ignored his own advice. . . .

"One of our most important duties here is to keep the data on the officers' record files up-to-date, Crystal," the woman was saying. She had introduced herself as "Ms. Forester," but she called Crystal by her first name immediately. "This is a very sensitive department—you'll get all kinds of weird calls."

"Weird calls?"

"Yes indeed. The little beasts are tricky, all right. You wouldn't believe the ploys they use. One called here yesterday, claiming to be General Knowlton's secretary. Said she was checking up on a Captain Browning as a possible candidate for an opening on the general's staff. First she asked about his background and the service schools he'd attended, and then she says, 'Oh, by the way, what is the captain's marital status?' Well, I knew right away what we had here, so I told her Captain Browning was married, had four kids. That cooled her fire."

Crystal was careful to look puzzled. "I don't understand," she said.

"She was a head hunter, checking up on the captain's eligibility," Ms. Forester explained impatiently.

"She must've been disappointed to find out he's married."

"He isn't married. Divorced, no kids. Serves her right, wasting my time. Believe you me, I've been around a long time and I've seen them all. I'm not easy to fool."

Crystal nodded agreement. She was glad that she'd been forewarned. What would Ms. Forester's attitude be if she suspected she was harboring a head hunter right in her own office? Crystal also felt a little chagrined. It hadn't occurred to her that other women might use the officers' records files to gather information on eligible men.

Later, Crystal invented a boyfriend who was off at college. She talked about him in such detail that her superior's eyes took on a bored glaze. Satisfied that she had allayed any suspicions, she concentrated on mastering the office equipment and learning the routine, in ingratiating herself with Ms. Forester and the officer in charge, Colonel Hightower, a middle-aged man with a trim, military body and a thinning hairline.

When her training period was over and she was sure that she was no longer under Ms. Forester's constant observation, Crystal initiated her search. It amused her that no one, watching her working so industriously at her desk or at the files, could possibly suspect what she was doing. For instance, what would Shelley's high-and-mighty mother think if she knew that it wasn't for job experience she'd solicited General Pritchard's help in getting work in officers' records?

Well, she'd accomplished her first goal, and the next step should be easy—choosing the right candidate. The records of every officer in the command were among these antiquated data files with their neatly keypunched information. Surely she would find the right candidate here.

The qualifications she was seeking were very specific. He must be single, of course. It was probably too much to ask that he'd never been married because he would, by necessity, be in the thirty-five-plus age category. But a widower would be quite acceptable—as long as there were no kids to clutter up the scene. Would she consider a divorced man? Well, that depended on the circumstances. Nothing messy in his background—no scandal and, again, no kids.

Also, she wasn't interested in anyone with less rank than a senior major—she preferred a lieutenant colonel—which narrowed things down. An academy grad, of course. No Officers Training School or ROTC types need apply. According to Maurice, a man who wasn't a graduate of one of the service academies usually retired as a colonel at the most—unless he was in a specialized field, such as science or accounting or law. And she wasn't willing to settle for that. She intended to be the wife of a general—the more stars the better.

For the same reasons, he must be rated, a pilot with tactical and command experience. His PME—professional military education—record was important, too, which meant he must have attended Squadron Officers School by his sixth year, Air Command and Staff College between his sixth and eleventh year, preferably in residence. If he was a colonel, it would be best if he had already attended Air War College—or better still, the National War College in Washington, D.C. Somewhere along the way, it was essential he pick up a graduate degree or two, preferably in management or logistics—or so Maurice believed.

Then there was the matter of appearance. It would be best if he were tall. Height gave a military man an advantage over shorter men—but he shouldn't be too good-looking. The handsome ones usually managed to scuttle themselves in the end, especially if they were womanizers. As an example, look at her own father and what his tomcatting had done to his career.

Most important of all, the man must have ambition. If he didn't have the right kind of drive, he was useless for her purposes. He should be popular with his men—but not too popular. Nothing chilled the brass faster than a liberal who fought for what he considered justice for his subordinates. Better that he be a conformist, a candidate for the "old-boy" club, someone who didn't make waves.

And he should have a mentor, someone higher up the ladder who was watching out for "his boy." Her father had pointed out that all the movers and shakers, no matter what their field, had a God complex and needed protégés to perpetuate themselves. Although he had failed miserably in his own career, still she trusted Maurice's shrewd hindsight on how the system really worked, and the word "mentor" was prominent on the list she'd made.

It was laughable how flattered Maurice had been when she'd steered the conversation to the subject of getting ahead in the air force after dinner one night. He hadn't suspected any ulterior motives, but her mother had caught on. Oh, yes, Janet knew what she was up to. But she hadn't said a word. She'd just listened with an expression on her face that said, "I'm on to your little tricks."

Eventually, Janet became bored and wandered off to the living room to watch television. She had been drinking—but when wasn't she drinking these days? For whatever reason, she had kept out of it, even though she'd turned the sound way up on the television set.

Maurice hadn't noticed. He was too busy expounding his theories on why some men made it in the military and why others failed. That's when he'd told Crystal. "If you show how hungry you are, they'll eat you up alive. So you put on this nice guy act—and then you show them that you've got the stuff, too. It's important to get the attention of the brass. None of it does you any good if you hide your assets under a barrel.

And you have to have the right attitude, sort of a fake modesty, that kind of crap. That was my mistake. I was too damned cocky, and I didn't brown-nose my superiors enough because I thought my record would speak for me."

He looked so pensive that Crystal wanted to reach out and pat his hand. A knot formed in her stomach as she remembered how close they had been until her mother had ruined everything and made them self-conscious about touching each other.

Ever since Crystal could remember, Janet had complained when Maurice was affectionate with her. She had called it unnatural, even though she knew it was his nature to touch and kiss and hug. Wasn't he always pawing at Janet? Just because he'd enjoyed teasing Crystal when she was a child, tickling her and pulling her down on his lap and nuzzling her neck— what was so wrong with that? After all, she was his only kid.

But the bitch had raised holy hell that time she'd come back early from bingo night at the club and found them taking a shower together. They were soaping each other, both of them laughing and having fun, and Crystal had felt so good, all tingly and warm—and then Janet was standing there in the bathroom door, her face so ugly that she looked like a witch, saying things that made Crystal cringe with shame.

After that, Janet saw that they were never alone together. The tickling sessions, the showering together—and the touch- ing—had stopped. Crystal had felt bewildered and betrayed, and she'd hated her mother, hated the power Janet wielded over her father. She had even resented Maurice for choosing Janet over her.

Oh, now that she was older, she knew all about his short- comings. He was a loser who might not have made it even with a different kind of wife. And all that fooling around he'd done with her when she was a kid—that hadn't been healthy. In fact, if Janet hadn't put a stop to it, it might have led to other things . . . but she hadn't understood that then. She'd loved it when he touched her, stroked her—and maybe there was something a little kinky about that, too.

Something—a stirring that was hot and furtive and secret— surfaced briefly, and Crystal looked away from her father, afraid that he might guess her thoughts. Sometimes she dreamed that she was a little girl again and that Maurice was undressing her, getting her ready for bed, stroking her hair, her arms, her body. The dream usually dissolved into a confusion of distorted images at that point, and when she awoke, she always felt guilty. Which was stupid. After all, she wasn't responsible for what she dreamed. Nobody could control their own dreams, could they?

And why was it that she'd never felt that same tingling warmth with any of the boys she'd experimented with? Her experience with Kimo in the backseat of his dune buggy had been the pits. When he'd climbed on top of her and started pumping away, she'd wanted to pick up the oily old wrench he kept under the front seat and hit him and hit him and hit him.

Well, she'd learned from that experience how easy it was to fool men. They had no way of knowing how a woman really felt or if she was faking—not if she were clever. And because she'd stayed in control and had put on an act, she'd had Kimo eating out of her hand as long as she'd wanted him. Now she intended to use her knowledge to snag herself a husband who was—what was that catchword everybody was using these days? Upwardly mobile?

Her father's voice intruded, and Crystal realized that he was still ruminating about the mistakes he'd made

"—a toss-up, even if you make all the right moves." Maurice rolled his brandy glass between his hands, warming the amber liquid, and she thought how small his hands were in contrast to his muscular build and above-average height. "There's only so much room at the top—it's like a pyramid. It narrows down drastically the higher you go. One slip, one black mark— and you're frozen in grade. Timing has a lot to do with it, too, being at the right place at the right time. The competition is murder—especially during peacetime. Sure I put in my stint in 'Nam, but so did everybody else because that flipping war lasted so long. The thing is, you need the breaks—and a wife who is willing to play the game doesn't hurt."

His eyes brooded over his brandy as he added, "I started out wrong. What chance did I have with an OTS commission? Only I didn't know that then. I thought I could beat the odds. I wised up too late—about that and a lot of other things. Hell, I was never even in the running. It's the old guard who runs things. The brass'll swear to high heaven there isn't any such thing, but the good ol' boys are there, all right, the movers and shakers, and they make all the decisions. Sure, I got my majority a little below the zone, but then I got into that trouble in France—"

He broke off and gave Crystal a quick look. "Not my fault," he said quickly. "Just one of those things. Some silly woman making waves. But it left a black mark on my record, and with the competition so tough . . . I should've resigned my commission, started another career. But no, I kept hanging on. I didn't realize how the system worked until it was too late. I just wish someone had laid it on the line for me. I wouldn't be clerking in a lousy liquor store now if they had."

As he went on talking, Crystal culled his words for truth, discarding his boasting, his self-justifications and self-serving explanations.

Later, when she went to her room, she sat for a long time, staring into space, digesting what she'd learned. In appearance, her father looked like a winner—and yet he'd been forced to retire as a major as soon as he had his twenty years in. So outward appearances could be deceptive, and that meant she should rule out good looks as a prerequisite for a husband.

Before she went to bed, she added a note to the diary she kept locked in her desk drawer.

"Don't be fooled by good looks. Could be handicap. Man with ordinary looks easier to handle, too. Less ego—and maybe more grateful for good sex."

Crystal found her candidate a month after she'd started to work at Hickam. His name was Grant Norton; although he was only thirty-six, he was already a lieutenant colonel, and he fit all her other requirements as if he had been custom made for her.

He had never been married, had attended the proper service schools—his latest one had been the Air War College—and he had the right mix of tactical and command experience on his records. Even more important, his superiors' evaluations of him were all superior, and he was a 1962 graduate of the Air Force Academy. He'd done two tours in 'Nam—one as a fighter pilot and the second as commander of a fighter squadron. At present, he held down an assistant staff slot in Manpower at PACAF Headquarters.

From the photo attached to his records, Grant Norton wasn't handsome, but he had something Crystal thought of as class—or maybe "presence" was a better word for that long, lean face and those cool, detached eyes. According to his personnel records, he was six feet one—and he weighed 165 pounds.

Satisfied that she'd found her man, she set about learning all she could about Grant Norton. With the same persistence she'd used to cultivate a select group at Punahou, she made friends with Gracie Cummins, who worked as a secretary in Manpower—and discovered that she'd struck pay dirt.

Gracie was what Crystal's mother would have called a plain Jane. She had the kind of fine hair that stayed perpetually limp in the humidity of Hawaii and a pitted skin that spoke of adolescent acne. Although she worked in the typists' pool, she sometimes filled in for Colonel Norton's secretary, and she was quick to admit that she had a grade-A crush on her occasional boss.

With Crystal's encouragement during the lunches they had together, she poured out everything she knew about Grant Norton, including the fact that he lived off base in a condo in one of the better sections of Pearl City. As far as the secretary knew, he lived alone. He was well liked by everybody in the office, but he also demanded—and got—his subordinates' best work. He dated around, never the same girl more than a few times— and he was known to be that old-fashioned thing, a gentleman. It was the secretary's private belief that he'd had a love affair that had gone sour.

The next weekend, Crystal haunted Grant Norton's neighborhood, eating lunch at a small restaurant a block away from the complex where he lived, prowling through the stores in a nearby shopping center. When it finally occurred to her that she was wasting her time, she sought out Gracie again, and this time the woman let it drop that Colonel Norton usually stopped at the Officers Club for a drink before he went home evenings, that sometimes he stayed on and had dinner there.

One of the young lieutenants in Crystal's office had taken a rather lukewarm interest in her and she set about warming him up. The next day, she wore a tight-fitting skirt with a side slit that showed half her thigh when she moved and earned a long stare from Ms. Forester. Not so surprisingly, the lieutenant lingered by Crystal's desk. With her encouragement, he ended up asking her out to dinner that night.

Crystal accepted—after a token hesitation. She let her eyes linger on his thighs as she told him that yes, she would love to have dinner with him—but since she had to be home early, why didn't they just make it the Officers Club?

When they reached the club, she looked around for Grant

Norton, but they had already ordered their dinner before he made an appearance. He paid no attention to them—or to anyone else—as he passed the door of the dining room on his way to the bar. Crystal waited a few minutes, then excused herself, saying she had to visit the powder room. As soon as she was out of her date's sight, she turned into the bar.

Grant Norton was sitting in a booth near the back, reading a newspaper, a drink at his elbow. Crystal paused briefly, sizing him up. Much better looking than his picture—that lean face, the dark hair and eyes, skin that stopped just short of being swarthy, reminded her of a young Basil Rathbone and added up to an attractive man. His features, although not conventionally handsome, were regular, well defined—he would age well. That lean kind usually did. Even if he lost his hair, he'd be a distinguished-looking man someday, a real asset in a high-ranking officer.

Crystal chose a barstool opposite the booth. When the bartender came up, she ordered a glass of mineral water with a twist of lemon. Since her plan was still nebulous, her mind worked feverishly, trying to come up with the right scenario.

In the end, deciding on a direct approach, she rose and crossed to the booth. She stood there, looking embarrassed and—she hoped—a little shy.

"Excuse me," she said. "Aren't you Colonel Norton?"

Grant Norton lowered his paper a shade too slowly, but his voice was courteous as he responded, "Yes, I am. Have we met?"

"Not exactly but—my name is Crystal Moore, and I'm a friend of Gracie Cummins. She pointed you out once. I wouldn't bother you, but I'm in something of a jam. My escort"—she paused to send a quick glance over her shoulder—"has had too much to drink, and I'm afraid he's going to create a scene. I wonder if you would call me a cab? I'd do it myself, but the phone booth is near our table and . . . well, I don't want any trouble. My father is a retired air force officer, and he'd kill me if he knew I got in a car with someone who'd had too much to drink."

She knew that she'd succeeded in arousing his sympathy when his eyebrows came together in a frown. "Who's your escort?" he said.

She hesitated, then shook her head. "I'd rather not say. If

I just leave quietly, that would solve the whole problem without embarrassing anyone."

When he nodded silently, she knew she'd hit the right note. Yes, this man would approve of someone who handled a tricky situation without causing waves. She looked away, as if fighting embarrassment, then hesitantly opened her purse and took out a dime. "If you'd make the call for me—"

He waved away the coin and stood, but she wasn't finished yet. "I guess I'll have to think up a good excuse for missing my carpool and coming home in a taxi. I forgot my mad money and . . . well, I hate to think what my dad's going to say when I ask him for money to pay the cab driver."

"That's easy to solve. Why don't I just lend you cab fare?"

She shook her head. "I'd rather not. If you'll make that phone call, I can manage."

Again, she read approval in his eyes. "I'm heading for home myself. I'd be glad to drop you off—provided you don't live on the other side of the island."

"I live a few blocks this side of Foster Village," she said. "If it isn't too far out of your way, I'd be very grateful. It would save me from a lecture."

"Okay, it's settled. Maybe it's best your escort doesn't see us together. Why don't you slip out the back door and I'll meet you in the parking lot in a few minutes? My car is a white Mustang."

Although she sensed that his offer stemmed from courtesy rather than from any personal interest in her, Crystal was satisfied that she had established a beachhead. During the short ride home, although he didn't say anything personal, Grant Norton asked her about her job, about her experiences as an air force brat. Crystal was careful to show an enthusiasm for the military way of life, to tell him how much she regretted her father's retirement because she really did miss moving around. She was so sure that she was making a good impression that she was disappointed when he still hadn't asked for a date by the time they were turning into her street.

She pointed out her parents' rented cottage. "My parents are still undecided about where they want to live permanently," she said. "Until they do, we're renting. They had to take what they could get because they aren't willing to sign a lease."

He nodded noncommittally and parked the Mustang at the curb. She bit her lower lip in frustration when he got out, but when he opened her door, she gave him her widest smile. "Thank you again, Colonel Norton," she said sweetly. "That's the last time I date anyone until I know more about them."

"That's a good idea." If he noticed the expanse of thigh she exposed as she slid out of the car door, he gave no sign of it. "Good luck—I hope you won't get in trouble with your father."

Seething with disappointment, she smiled again. She thought he was going to say more, but if so, he changed his mind because he got back in the Mustang and drove off.

"Shit!" she said explosively.

When she went into the house, she found her mother alone, curled up on the living room sofa with a women's magazine. For once, the television set wasn't on.

"Short date," Janet commented.

"The man was a dud," Crystal said. "I told him I had a headache."

"Good thinking. You're learning fast."

Crystal didn't answer. She went into her bedroom, shutting the door behind her. She picked up the phone beside her bed and punched out the Hickam Officers Club number with short, angry stabs of her finger.

"I'd like to speak to Lieutenant Rossiter," she said. "You'll find him in the dining room."

A few minutes later, a man's voice sounded in her ear. "Lieutenant Rossiter here."

"Bob? This is Crystal. You must be wondering what happened to me."

"To put it mildly. What the devil are you up to? Is this some kind of practical joke?"

"I'm sick. I began to feel nauseous when I got to the powder room and then . . . well, I got sick. You know, upchucked and all. I felt so rocky that I asked one of the waiters to call me a cab. I gave him a message for you. Didn't you get it?"

"No, I didn't." The lieutenant sounded more disgruntled than angry. "You okay now?"

"I'm in bed—I think I must've eaten some tainted food in the cafeteria at lunch. I'm really sorry to cut out on you like that, but I knew you wouldn't want me to . . . well, mess up your car or something."

There was a long silence. "Yeah. . . . Look, I'm sorry as hell that you're sick. Maybe we can do it again sometime—okay?"

Crystal assured him again that she was sorry, too, and hung

up. The evening had turned out to be a dud, but at least she hadn't made an enemy of someone she saw every day at the office. Her moves had all been correct, but it was obvious that she'd chosen the wrong man. Grant Norton had "rescued" her as she'd planned, but it was something that any reasonably decent man would do, given the same circumstances. Of course, that might be his weak point. People who always did the right thing laid themselves wide open to opportunists. So his manners just might be the thing to capture the king—if she ever got another chance.

Crystal went to bed early, having decided that she couldn't stand a whole evening of her mother's company. She was reading a book when the phone beside her bed rang. She picked it up and was stunned to hear Grant Norton's voice.

"This is Grant Norton," he said. "There's going to be a reception at the club tomorrow night. I wonder if you'd like to go with me?"

CHAPTER
↟ 8 ↟

THE LAST THING ON CRYSTAL'S MIND THE DAY AFTER GRANT Norton's dinner invitation was the tragic news about Sgt. MacGarrett's death, although she did call Tai to ask if there was anything she could do. Not to her surprise, Tai told her that she was fine, that everything was being taken care of, and Crystal hung up with a feeling of relief and the righteous feeling of having done her duty.

That afternoon after work, she went on a shopping trip. Although it nearly wrecked her small savings account, she bought a pale green shift that flattered her angular figure and brought out the highlights in her chestnut-brown hair.

Since she was twelve years old, Crystal had known that she would never be a beauty like her mother. She had inherited her paternal grandmother's small breasts, too narrow hips, and too long neck—or so Janet was always telling her. Since her facial features could only be described as average, she'd learned, through grim determination and careful experimentation, to use cosmetics to soften the sharp angles of her chin and nose and to extend the line of her too thin lips, to wear colors that flattered her sallow skin and emphasized the green in her eyes.

Tonight, as she went into the living room to wait for Grant, she was aware from her mother's sardonic stare that it was all illusion and artifice. Even when her father whistled and told her she was a knockout in that slinky new dress, she felt let down and wished she'd arranged to meet Grant away from home.

A few minutes later, her lips stretched into a welcoming smile, she opened the door to his ring. When she introduced Grant to her parents, she noted that her father's offer of a drink was a little too hearty, but she was gratified that Grant seemed unimpressed by her mother's catlike smile.

Even so, the reception at the Officers Club was a disappointment. Grant treated her with the utmost courtesy, getting her champagne cocktails, introducing her to a few people, making light, inconsequential conversation—and she found herself wanting to pinch him and remind him that she was a living, breathing human being, not some mannequin he happened to be escorting that evening. Was his aloofness part of a naturally reserved nature? Or was it more personal? Had he decided that he'd made a mistake and asked the wrong girl?

The only time Grant seemed to relax was when they were dancing. To her surprise, he was an excellent dancer. Since Crystal had wheedled dancing lessons out of her father while she was still in junior high, they made a good team. It was an older crowd, so there were few fast dances, which pleased Crystal. What she wanted was close contact, and the tangos and waltzes, even a few fast-paced fox trots, suited her purposes. Unfortunately, their closeness on the dance floor seemed to have little effect on Grant. It was only when the evening was over and he had taken her home that he told her he'd really enjoyed the evening, then leaned toward her to give her a goodnight kiss.

Crystal had been waiting for this moment all evening and was prepared to go all out to lure him into her net. To her disappointment, Grant's kiss was brief, perfunctory. After he drew away, he sat for a few moments before he asked, "Would you like to have dinner with me this weekend, Crystal? I hear the Willows is highly recommended by the local people."

Crystal nodded, concealing her surprise—and elation. "I've been there with my parents. It's a lovely place—and the food is very good. What time would you like to pick me up?"

"Is eight okay? Or we can eat earlier and take in a movie."

"Why don't we just have dinner? It will give us a chance to talk," she replied.

She expected another kiss, but he opened his door and came around the car to help her out, a courtesy that reminded her there was, after all, a seventeen-year gap in their ages. Although disappointed that he hadn't kissed her again, she discovered that she liked being treated with respect—and maybe her plan for a quick seduction was the wrong approach. After all, she wanted Grant to think of her as wife material. Proving it in bed might not be the best way.

A week later, she knew she'd made a mistake. Although the dinner had been pleasant and she'd taken pains to be charming and flattering, Grant hadn't asked for another date. In fact, since their dinner date, he hadn't even called.

She waited another week before she arranged to meet Gracie for lunch in the cafeteria. As they ate their sandwiches, Crystal plied the older girl with subtle compliments, then brought Grant into the conversation.

"How is Colonel Norton getting along?" she asked carelessly.

Gracie shrugged. "They say he's got a good chance of being on the next colonel selectee's list. General Krause really dotes on him." She paused a moment, the corners of her mouth drooping. "He took Maureen Goetz—she's that flashy blonde in civilian personnel—out last night. She was bragging about it in the restroom. She says they really got it on. God, I hate blondes!"

Crystal forced a smile. So she'd struck out—and to a blonde. Maybe she should dye her hair. And maybe her tactics had been wrong, and she should have gone along with her original plan to get Grant Norton into bed as quickly as possible.

She wasn't really listening to Gracie's prattle until the other woman asked her a question. "I'm sorry. What did you say?"

"I just invited you to an aloha party. Major Dunn is transferring back to the mainland—and it's also a promotion party for Lieutenant O'Hara. The Officers Club is all booked up, so one of the secretaries volunteered her parents' house on Mount Tantalus. I think she's bucking for a promotion."

Crystal started to refuse the invitation, then changed her mind because of the possibility that Grant might be there. If so, maybe she'd get an opportunity to maneuver him into another date. It was worth a try. If she got a second chance, she'd play her cards differently.

She chose her best holoku for the party, a fitted style that hugged her waist and fell in graceful folds to the floor. As she applied a light dusting of green eye shadow to her eyelids, she knew she was looking her best. A bitter thought marred her satisfaction. Yes, she could pass for attractive now—but for how long? Her kind of looks were only effective when a woman was still young and fresh. But youth was so damned short— already, when she was tired, there was a gauntness about her face that told her what she would look like as a middle-aged woman. . . .

Crystal discovered that she was breathing too fast, that a cold sweat had broken out on her forehead. She put her hand up to cover her left eye, even though there was no sign of the scintillating mist that usually heralded one of her headaches. What if her dreams never materialized? What if she ended up an old maid—or married to some loser, a liquor-store clerk like her father? What if she never got the chance to even try for the top of the heap?

Her lips thinned into a determined line. This kind of thinking was self-defeating. She was going to make it happen, just the way she planned. She was clever, resourceful—and she was prepared to do anything to bring it all about. Yes things *would* go her way—if not with Grant Norton, then with someone else. And it wouldn't be a one-way deal, loaded on her side. She would give her husband full value, be the perfect wife for an ambitious officer heading for the top—and at the moment, her only candidate was Lt. Colonel Grant Norton.

As far as Crystal was concerned, the party started out on a sour note. For one thing, she felt out of it because she knew so few of the people there. For another, the only person she wanted to see had yet to arrive. Although she was prudent enough to put on an act, talking vivaciously to anyone who spoke to her and dancing with the two men who asked, she kept a constant vigil for Grant, hoping that he would turn up.

The house where the party was being held was very old, one of the sprawling, turn-of-the-century Victorians that still existed in the hills above Honolulu. The lanai where Crystal sat was alight with electric Japanese lanterns, and the view of the valley below was spectacular, a treat for the eyes.

At the moment, Crystal was pretending an interest in the reminiscences of her hostess's father, a retired banker. In the background, his teenaged grandson was strumming a ukulele and singing an old Hawaiian standard. Several couples were dancing in the center of the lanai, and others were gathered around a trestle table that had been covered with tapa paper, sampling a conglomeration of island foods.

Crystal, whose appetite was always a barometer of her emotions, was picking listlessly at a piece of melon when she looked up to see Grant coming around the corner of the house. Her face muscles tightened when she saw the woman clinging to his arm. She was blond, very pretty in a clinging Hawaiian shift, and there was a predatory look in her eyes that told Crystal she would be a formidable rival.

Crystal waited until the blond woman had disappeared into the house before she rose and made her leisurely way toward Grant.

When she was a few feet away, she paused and gave him a surprised smile. "Oh, hello—I didn't know you would be here," she said sweetly.

Grant looked uncomfortable. "We just got here. It's a nice place, isn't it?"

"Lovely—one of my school friends lives in an old house like this. Her place always reminds me of home."

"Home? I don't think you ever told me where that is."

"My grandparents live in Omaha—in an old Victorian with turrets and bays and even a widow's walk. I always love visiting them," she lied. "Not that I'd want to live in Omaha all my life."

"No, it would be pretty dull after moving around the way you have." Crystal was sure there was relief in his voice as he added, "Here comes my date. Have you met Maureen Goetz?"

For the next few minutes, Crystal exchanged polite chatter with the blond girl, who was so obviously unconcerned about the competition that Crystal was steaming by the time she told them she'd promised someone a dance and retreated to her own table.

But her opportunity came later from a direction she hadn't expected. As the evening wore on, she noted that Maureen's color had heightened, that her voice grew increasingly loud, but it wasn't until she followed the blond woman to the powder room that she realized how drunk Maureen was.

As she pretended to be repairing her own makeup, she watched the woman in the mirror, and a sudden thought came to her. Suppose Grant's date passed out—wouldn't Grant be grateful to anyone who offered to help him get her home? The thing was—how to arrange that? Maureen had already told her, her laugh shrill, that she felt a little tight so maybe she'd better not drink any more.

Crystal's eyes moved toward the door that led to the adjoining bathroom. Hadn't she seen a medicine cabinet in there earlier? A few moments later she was standing in front of the cabinet, surveying its contents. The label on one bottle said it contained prescription sleeping pills; she took the bottle down, twisted off its cap and shook three tiny white pills into her hand, and then replaced it in the medicine cabinet before she returned to the powder room.

She held her breath when Maureen rose, her legs unsteady, then released it in a sigh of relief when the blond woman headed for the bathroom door. Quickly, she dropped the pills in Maureen's drink, stirred the punch with her finger until they were dissolved. By the time Maureen had returned, she was back at the mirror, combing her hair.

Before they left the powder room, she reminded Maureen that she'd brought a drink in with her. Although the woman giggled and said she'd already had too much, she picked up her glass and took it along. Since Crystal made it her business to be talking animatedly with Maureen as they approached the table where Grant was waiting, he had no choice but to invite her to join them. Crystal was sure he looked bored as he responded to his date's slurred comments about the other guests at the party.

But when Maureen picked up her glass and raised it to her lips, he took it away from her. "I believe that's my drink," he said smoothly. "You must've left your glass in the powder room."

Crystal, caught by surprise, could only watch as he drained the glass. Maureen looked rebellious, as if she meant to argue with him, but instead she yawned widely, not bothering to cover her mouth with her hand. Crystal bit her lip in frustration. This just wasn't her night—and what would those sleeping pills do to Grant? As far as she knew, he hadn't been drinking heavily, but there *had* been a warning on the bottle about not mixing the pills with alcohol. What if she was responsible for Grant having an accident?

She realized that Grant was on his feet, pulling out Maureen's chair, forcing her to stand. "It's getting a little late— why don't we say good-bye to our hostess and head for home?" he said.

Before Maureen could respond, Crystal spoke quickly. "I wonder if you'd do me a favor, Grant? I could use a ride home. I came with Gracie Cummins, but she's met someone and . . . well, I hate to ruin her evening."

"I'll be glad to drop you off." Grant rubbed the deep crease between his eyebrows. "I shouldn't have eaten that lomilomi. It seems to have disagreed with me—I have a busting headache."

"Maybe it's an allergy," Crystal said, hiding her dismay. "I think this is the time of the year when they burn the cane fields."

The blond woman looked from one to the other, her expression sullen. "I don't want to go home," she announced petulantly. "You're both a couple of parpy—party poopers. I want to have some fun—"

She sat back down, almost missing her chair. With a little sigh, she put her head down on the table, her eyes closed. Grant didn't try to hide his annoyance. "She's been drinking like a fish all evening. I'd better get her home. Dammit! She lives alone, too. I wonder if you would—"

"I'd be glad to put her to bed," Crystal said quickly.

Grant looked relieved. "That's great. Luckily, her apartment's not too far from where you live."

Crystal's emotions were mixed as she went to retrieve her wrap and purse from the house. She would be alone with Grant—but what good would it do if he didn't feel well? In the mood he was in, he wouldn't be interested in prolonging the evening. She'd be lucky if he even thanked her before he took her home.

Feeling aggrieved, she didn't bother to seek out Gracie to say she was leaving. She'd mend that fence tomorrow. For now, it was important to get out of here without Gracie seeing her—and offering to help, too.

"We don't want to attract any attention," she told Grant when she returned to the lanai. "I'll take Maureen around the side of the house while you bring your car to the front door."

Grant nodded and was gone. Crystal helped Maureen to her feet and steered her toward the edge of the lanai. If the other guests noticed their erratic progress, they kept their comments to themselves. When Crystal, half supporting an increasingly unsteady Maureen, reached the front of the house, Grant was already there waiting for them in his Mustang. He helped Crystal get Maureen into the backseat, where she sprawled out on her back and promptly went to sleep.

Although Crystal had hoped to make a few points once Maureen was out of the picture, she was disappointed. During the ride across town, Grant spoke to her only once, and then it was to ask if she would check to see if Maureen was okay.

When they got out of the car in front of a small stucco bungalow, she noticed that Grant rubbed the back of his head before he opened the back door to urge Maureen to her feet. Were the sleeping pills beginning to affect him—and if so, how could she warn him without giving herself away? God, it was one big mess. What she didn't want was to ride in a car with a man who was woozy from alcohol and barbiturates. What if a traffic cop stopped them? Wouldn't that look great in the morning papers? And what would a drunk-driving charge do to Grant's career? She didn't want to hurt him or even cause him embarrassment. Well, she'd just have to think of some way to keep him from driving again tonight. . . .

Half an hour later, having undressed Maureen without ceremony and dumped her into her bed, she joined Grant in the bungalow's small living room. She didn't have to pretend her concern as she looked at Grant's pale face.

"She's sleeping now—I'm sure she'll be okay. But you look terrible. Your allergy must really be acting up."

"I'm dizzy as hell," he admitted, resting his head against the back of the couch.

"Why don't you take a nap?" she suggested.

He seemed to be having a hard time focusing his eyes on her as he told her he was sorry to get her involved in his problems. Crystal felt a pang of guilt. It was obvious that the sleeping pills had reacted with the alcohol in his blood, just what she'd planned for Maureen, who hadn't needed any help after all. But at least the evening wasn't a total disaster because Grant seemed more approachable, less standoffish now.

Her voice solicitous, she told Grant that what he needed was a cup of coffee. When she went into the tiny efficiency kitchen, she looked with disgust at a sinkful of dirty dishes and greasy pans. Gingerly, she unearthed a coffeepot from under a pile of soiled dish towels, washed it quickly, then filled it with water. While the water heated, she searched for and finally found a jar of instant coffee and two clean coffee mugs, but when she finally returned to the living room, carrying mugs of coffee, she discovered that Grant was stretched out full length on the couch, sound asleep.

As she bent over to check his pulse, he stirred restlessly, mumbling something under his breath. She put her ear near his mouth, trying to make out what he was saying.

"—good sport." His voice was slurred, and she thought he was talking about Maureen until he added, "Should've taken you to the party 'stead that lush. . . ."

His voice trailed off, and Crystal fought back an impulse to slap him—hard. Was that how he saw her—as a goddamned good sport? Well, that was his mistake. Maybe a little demonstration was in order to remind him that she was very much a woman.

Crystal turned out all the lights except for one lamp across the room from the couch. She began to undress, tossing her clothes over the back of a chair. As she pulled off her chemise there was a ripping sound, and she cursed under her breath, knowing she had broken one of its narrow straps. Well, that was par for the night. Everything that could go wrong had gone wrong. But maybe she could salvage something from it, after all.

When she had stripped off all her clothes, she went back to the couch. Grant was lying on his back, his arms over his head. From his sonorous breathing, the sleeping pills and alcohol had finally taken their toll. It was harder to undress him than she'd expected. For one thing, she was unfamiliar with men's clothes; for another, his arms and legs were a dead weight that she had to manipulate without his help. When he was naked, she knelt beside the couch, trying to decide what to do next. He looked curiously helpless, his body exposed like that— and it was obvious that he was in no condition for sex. But then the idea was to make him *think* that something had happened, wasn't it?

She climbed over Grant's limp body and slid into the space behind him. It was a tight squeeze, and she had to raise herself to a sitting position before she could reach his right arm, which dangled over the side of the couch. She rubbed his hand against her breast, her teeth clenched tightly together. When he only snored louder, she slid it between her thighs, pushing his fingers deep into her flesh, but he still didn't respond, not even when she slid downward until she was lying with her head pressed against his stomach. She touched him intimately, then stroked

him, persisting until his body hardened under her nimble fingers. It just might work, she thought with satisfaction—if she
could control her disgust.

Wetting her lips, she pushed her hair back from her face
and bent over him. For the next few minutes, she used the
technique that had succeeded so well with Kimo. When it was
obvious that Grant was fully aroused, she slid on top of him,
straddling his hips. As she gingerly lowered herself upon him,
a shudder ran through his body and he moved convulsively.

"Give me your sweet ass, lover," he said distinctly.

Grimacing, Crystal rose and fell above him, each thrust
painful because her own body was dry and unaroused. It took
less time then she expected before Grant exploded inside her,
and she collapsed upon him, sighing with relief. Well, it was
done—and now for the really tricky part, convincing Grant
Norton that he'd seduced her tonight.

She crawled over him, went to the chair where she'd left
her clothes, and strewed them artfully over the floor. Satisfied
that she'd set the stage, she turned off the lamp and crawled
back onto the couch. Although she found Grant's sweaty body
and hot breath offensive, she stretched out facing him, arranged
his free arm around her nude waist and, sliding one leg between
his, half pulled him on top of her.

Her position was so uncomfortable that she was sure it would
be impossible to fall asleep. But then she didn't want to sleep.
She wanted to be awake when Grant came to and found himself
lying on top of a naked woman, the evidence of intercourse
all too apparent on both their naked thighs. Even when he
began to snore, his spasmodic breath fanning her face, she
didn't wriggle away.

Despite her miserable position, she must have dozed because
her next awareness was of Grant's voice saying, "What the
hell—"

She opened her eyes and stared directly into his red-rimmed
eyes. She was aware of a cold draft against her naked back,
of the early-morning light that turned Grant's face to granite.
Or maybe it was his awareness of what must have happened
that gave his skin a gray cast. In fact, he looked a little green—
as if he might vomit any minute.

She didn't have to fake her instinctive recoil. She gave a
little scream and pushed at him frantically, scrambling out from
under his flaccid body to cower at one corner of the couch.

"Oh, my God!" she said, putting both hands over her face. "Don't touch me, you—you bastard!"

"What the devil are you talking about? Surely you don't think—" Grant's voice broke off, and she knew that he had just discovered the evidence of intercourse on his body.

"God—Look, I don't know how this thing happened," he said, his voice hoarse. "I swear to you that I've never—someone must have put something in that punch I drank. It did taste funny—that's the only explanation that makes sense."

Crystal let her hands drop, let him see her teary eyes. "You didn't act drugged. I was sleeping in a chair and the next thing I knew, you were kissing me, and then we were undressed and—Oh, God, what if you got me pregnant? What will I do then? My father—he'll kill you if he finds out about this. He'll probably kill me, too." She added a sob for good measure.

Grant sank down on the edge of the couch. "Give me some time to think—my head's pounding like crazy. I'm sorry this happened—it's a nightmare. I swear to you that I'm not the kind of man who takes advantage of women . . . you have to believe that. And I'm sure you aren't pregnant—Look, when did you have your last period?"

"About two weeks ago." Crystal was silent for a moment. "That's not so good, is it?"

He groaned. "Maybe I didn't complete the act."

"But you did. I tried to get away, but you had me pinned down, and then it was too late—" She broke off with another sob.

"I'm sorry as hell. Look, Crystal, I'd give anything not to have had this happen. It's totally unlike me. I can only say again that there must've been something in Maureen's punch, the one I drank. It had to be someone's sick idea of a joke."

He massaged his temples, his face drawn and pale. He didn't look at her as he added, "I think we'd better put on our clothes. We wouldn't want Maureen to see us like this. I'll take you home—or maybe you'd better go to your friend Gracie's place. You can call your parents from there, tell them you stayed overnight with her. We'll talk on the way, but right now I think we'd better get the hell out of here before Maureen wakes up."

Crystal slid off the couch. She knew he was watching, knew that he must realize the significance of her torn chemise strap.

"I'll buy you some new clothes," he said suddenly. "That's the least I can do."

The least you can do is marry me, Colonel High-and-Mighty Norton, she thought. Only it's too soon to drop that on you.

"No, that isn't necessary," she said aloud, blinking her eyes rapidly. "I—I realize that you aren't totally to blame. I did enjoy you kissing me—until it got out of hand. All I want to do right now is put this whole night out of my mind and forget it ever happened."

He looked so relieved that again she wanted to slap him. "You're really pretty special," he said, his voice warmer than she had ever heard it before. "And I'm going to make this up to you—that's a promise."

You will, indeed, she thought as she gave him a tremulous smile. Oh, yes, you'll make it up to me but not for another couple of months. . . .

CHAPTER
✦ 9 ✦

THE MORNING AFTER THE PICNIC ON THE BEACH, SHELLEY
was up very early. Wearing a yellow bikini under a cotton shift,
she went to the kitchen to get herself an orange and a banana;
and to slap together a sandwich made from last night's roast.
In a few minutes Portagee would be there, and she wanted to
be gone before he arrived to put on coffee and squeeze oranges
for juice, to slice pineapple and fold the morning paper just
the way the general liked it.

And wasn't it strange that she always thought of her father
as "the general"? Was that because he was always so formal
with her—or because he was old enough to be her grandfather?
Of course grandfathers were supposed to be warm and loving
and indulgent, weren't they, which didn't describe her father
at all. True, he was formal with everybody, including his two
stepgranddaughters, who were scared to death of him. Only
with Tony, his son, did he thaw out enough to forget his dignity—
and why was she thinking about things she couldn't change on
a day like this—so fresh and new and promising?

An hour later, she parked her small sports car on the sandy
shoulder of the road near Mahuiha Beach. She didn't know if
she was disappointed or relieved that her car was the only one
there. She locked the car, mindful of the warnings she'd had
about local gangs that preyed on tourists, and then, taking her
time, she strolled along the path through the shoulder-high

growths of haoli-koa and Job's tears, sometimes detouring around a Christmas berry shrub.

When she came to the beach, she saw that it was empty. Again her reaction was mixed. Before she could pin down the source of her disappointment, she caught sight of a glass globe, tumbling in the surf, and she gave an exultant shout and ran forward to retrieve it.

The fishing net float, the size of a basketball, was covered with seaweed; a web of brine-soaked rope still clung to it. She cleaned the seaweed off with a pointed shell, then threw herself down on the sand beside it to gloat. A trophy for her room—and one she intended to keep. So many things she'd treasured through the years had ended up missing when she returned home from school, but this one she would take with her when she went away to Radcliffe. She would hang it up near her window, where it would capture the sun and tint the walls of her room green.

She was dozing on the towel she'd brought, her eyes shaded by dark glasses, when a voice hailed her. "Hi there. I see you've found yourself one of those Japanese glass balls."

Even before she opened her eyes and sat up, she knew it was the man who looked like Paul Newman. Something warm and pleasant happened to her as she met his smile. It wasn't because he was so attractive, she decided. She'd met other good-looking men and they hadn't affected her like this. Maybe it was because he so obviously took it for granted that she would not only remember him but be glad to see him as well. What would it be like to have such confidence in your ability to make people like you?

"I beg your pardon?" she said, and was chagrined to hear how husky her voice sounded. His smile widened, and she looked away, dazzled by the whiteness of his teeth. He looked ... well, like a young sea god. As to what he really was— Crystal had said something about an enlisted man's tag on his car. Was he a soldier from Fort Shafter or a navie from Pearl or maybe an airman from Hickam? Not that it mattered to her— but what if her father's rank mattered to *him*?

"How do you like the Islands?" the man asked.

"I like them very much."

"Is that your friend's car—the one parked on the road?"

Shelley considered the implication of his question. So he

thought she was a tourist. A sense of mischief prompted her answer. "Uh-huh. Her father is stationed here on Oahu."

"You're lucky to know someone who lives in the Islands. That's how I found out about this beach. I met this local guy, and we hit it off. He told me about this place, but he made me promise to keep it quiet."

"I can see why. It's so lovely and peaceful here."

He opened the knapsack he was carrying, took out a bottle of oil, and began rubbing it on his legs. Her eyes followed the movement of his hands. She wondered what it would feel like to have him oiling her back and arms, and a tingling sensation started up along her spine, a reaction that alarmed her. After all, what did she know about this man except that he was—what had Bobby Jo called him? A hunk? As for his easy, nonthreatening manner that made her feel they were old friends—that was probably his way with everyone he met.

"So when do you go back to—Where are you from, anyway?"

Shelley hesitated, not wanting to lie. She decided on a half-truth. "I was born in Dayton, Ohio," she said, and didn't add that her father had been stationed at Wright-Patterson at the time of her birth, that he'd been transferred to England two years later.

"Hey, we're neighbors. I'm from Pennsylvania. My old man's a mole."

"A mole?"

"A coal miner. My six brothers work the mines, too."

"Six brothers? How many sisters do you have?"

"None," he said grinning. "Mom gave up trying to have a girl after I was born. Eight males around the house was enough, she said."

Shelley looked away, afraid he might guess the effect his smile—white teeth flashing against tanned skin—had on her. "Are you Irish?" she ventured.

"Everybody asks me that—it's my coloring, I guess. I'm Polack. Hunkies, they call us at home. My name is Brotski. Theodore Adolph Brotski—but everybody calls me Tad." He smiled again, and another shiver ran along her spine. This time, he noticed it.

"You cold? Maybe you should put your dress back on."

"No, I'm not cold."

"Well, someone must be walking on your grave—and that's

a helluva thing to say, isn't it? What were we talking about?
. . . Oh, yeah. I was just getting ready to ask you if you were
Swedish."

"My grandparents on both sides came from England, but
there's Polish in my mother's family, I understand. A great-
grandmother," she said, and wondered what he'd say if she
told him her mother regarded it as an aberration that her ancestor
had married a Polish girl.

"So we have something else in common." Tad seemed
pleased. "I've got a confession to make. I came back here
today because I hoped you'd be here. I wanted to talk to you
yesterday, but you were with your friends."

Shelley looked away again. He spoke with such simplicity.
Maybe it was a line like the ones the preppies at the ski lodges
used, but she'd swear he was just what he seemed—an uncomplicated man who said what he thought and didn't hide what
he felt, either.

"Did I say something wrong? I didn't mean to—y'know,
come on too strong."

She met the worry in his eyes with a smile. "My name is
Shelley, and you didn't offend me. I guess the real reason I
came back today was because I hoped that you'd be here, too."

There was never any question of Shelley leaving the beach
alone that day. For the rest of the morning, she and Tad Brotski
played in the surf and explored the tide pools among the rocks
that bordered both sides of the beach, wading in occasionally
to examine an interesting shell. It pleased Shelley that Tad was
so careful not to step on the undulating water plants or to disturb
the tiny creatures who lived in the pools.

When they got hungry, they divided the sandwich and fruit
Shelley had brought and the candy bars that Tad had stuffed
in his knapsack. By midmorning they were holding hands, and
when they took a nap in the shade of a sand dune after lunch,
they lay side by side, their legs touching, their fingers entwined.

To Shelley, who had never felt this comfortable with a man
before, the day was pure magic—and yet so real that the world
around her took on a crystal-sharp edge as if the sand, the
curling, white-edged surf, the blue/green water, were etched
on metal. She marveled how at ease she felt, as if it were
perfectly normal to allow a strange man to brush back an errant
strand of hair from her forehead, to gaze at her fixedly and

without self-consciousness as if he wanted to drown in her eyes.

She loved the way Tad talked—naturally, openly, with no phony attempts to impress her. Surely it was safe to trust him, to believe that already she meant something special to him. A stab of doubt flared, but she told herself that she wasn't going to ruin the day by being suspicious. As she sat beside Tad, listening while he told her about his job, the past and the future seemed suspended, as unimportant as a dream. What matter if their backgrounds were so different? It had nothing to do with here and now, with the two of them holding hands at the beach.

Already, because Tad did most of the talking, she knew that he was a staff sergeant stationed at Hickam, that he loved working with his hands, and was proud of being a crew chief on a C-141, which he described as the best damned plane in the air force. Although she talked a little about her friends, saying that they had gone to school together, that their day at the beach had been something of a reunion, she didn't tell him that she lived at Hickam in Four Star House, that her father was General Pritchard.

Instead, she told him that she'd been so lonely the first time she'd gone away to boarding school that she'd been sure she would die; of how, gradually, she'd grown used to it, had even made a few friends. She talked about Tony, who was so much older than she, and about the special bond between them, even though they saw so little of each other. When Tad asked her what business her father was in, she hesitated then said he was in management. He didn't probe further; instead, he told her that he'd already guessed that she came from well-to-do folks.

Shelley asked him about his family, and for a while he bragged about his mom's great cooking, which he missed, then about his father's heavy hand when it came to discipline, which he didn't. Shelley, who had never been struck in her life, wondered how he could speak so casually about being whipped with a belt, especially when he grinned and added that he'd deserved it because he'd been a smart-ass kid who was always in some kind of trouble.

"Poppa couldn't understand why I was different from my brothers. They all went out for football or baseball in school, but I was into running. Which made me something of a freak in my old man's eyes. Football and baseball and other contact sports Poppa could understand. Those are things red-blooded American boys do, see. But running? That's for sissies. Even when I broke the state record for the cross country at a high school meet, he told me I was wasting my time. We just never did see eye to eye. That's one reason why I joined up instead of going to work in the mines—that and a little trouble I got into. The funny thing is that once I got away from home, I found out I wasn't weird at all. Nobody thinks there's anything strange about my running. Fact is, I still compete. I even won a couple meets last year in the interservice competitions."

"You ran for the air force in competition?"

"Yeah. How about that? Brotski the jock. It's a nice change in the routine, but I'm not really serious about it. No permanent jock assignments for me. They may look pretty cushy, but it plays hell with promotions when you're not working in your primary skill field. Besides, I'm a damned good mechanic. When I'm working on one of the big cargoes, it's like it's my own baby, and I wouldn't trade places with anyone, including the brass. Especially the brass, come to think of it."

"Have you ever thought about trying for a commission?" she asked.

"No way. Too much pressure. I like what I'm doing—why would I want to change?"

She couldn't think of an answer to that. Why indeed? He was obviously a happy man. She watched him as he rose and began brushing the sand off his arms and shoulders. The sun, halfway down the western sky, outlined his body and gave his head a bright halo. But she knew he wasn't a saint. He was down-to-earth and human, so human that she could hardly keep her hands off him. Even on this lonely beach, she felt safe with Tad Brotski. In fact, the thought of going home and leaving him was unbearable.

"It's getting late," he said. "Is your friend expecting you back at any special time?"

"No," she said quickly. "I'm free this evening."

"Then how about us going into town and grabbing something to eat?"

"I'd like that." She wondered if he guessed how hard it was to sound casual. "What should we do about my friend's car?"

"Why don't you follow me into town, park it in some safe place, and then pick it up later?"

She nodded agreement, and he gave her hand a squeeze as

he helped her to her feet. "I've got a feeling this is going to be one helluva evening, Shelley," he said.

Tad couldn't believe his good fortune. He'd never had any trouble attracting women, but never anyone like Shelley before. The girl sitting beside him in his old Chevy wasn't some waitress or beautician or divorcée on the prowl. She had class, real class. When she moved—to pick up a shell, to dash in and out of the surf, just plain walking—it was like poetry. Yeah, like poetry.

God, the way she was built! She was put together better than any woman he'd ever seen. Not one flaw, none that he could see—and in that yellow bikini she was wearing under her shift, there'd been little he hadn't seen. Even her knees looked as if some artist had sculpted them and then, at the last minute, had added a dimple behind each knee. There was something so damned sexy about those dimples that he'd had a hard time keeping his hands off them.

And that face. Those high cheekbones and the way the corners of her lips turned upward—it knocked him out. Right now, it was all he could do not to stop the car and kiss that sweetly curving mouth.

He didn't stop because instinct told him that she would be easy to spook. Sure, she'd admitted that she'd gone to the beach alone, hoping that he'd be here, and she'd let him hold hands an hour after they'd met. Still—something told him to take it easy, to make his moves carefully. Maybe some guy had given her a hard time, and she was a little leery of men— or maybe she was more inexperienced than she looked. Either way, he didn't intend to rush her, not when the payoff was so important.

"How'd you like to walk around the International Marketplace for a while?" he asked. "Some of the restaurants there sell local food. Or we can go to a steakhouse. There's one on Kalakaua Avenue that puts out a good sirloin."

"The marketplace sounds like more fun," she said. "I'd like to try something different."

Tad was pleased at her choice because it seemed to indicate an open mind and an adventuresome nature. Besides, he liked the International Marketplace with its exotic little shops, its tropical plantings, and the huge banyan tree that spread massive branches overhead, dominating the entrance. He often went there to sit on his favorite bench near the fish pond, watching the people pass by and listening to the staccato sound of Japanese or Tagalog or Taiwanese.

Tonight, there was something extra—a glow that had nothing to do with the luau torches hidden among clumps of bamboo and bird of paradise and red ginger. He wasn't sure just what it was, but he felt different, as if he'd been charged with electricity, as they strolled through the marketplace, pausing now and then so Shelley could examine a seabean bracelet or a kukui-nut necklace or a pink-tinged conch shell.

He searched for a word to describe his mood, but he couldn't pin down the right expression for the emotional high he was on. He couldn't help noticing the attention Shelley attracted as they wandered through the marketplace, and he was proud that he was the man who was walking beside her. Usually, that sort of thing didn't matter to him. He'd always been able to attract good-looking girls, but some of his best sex had been with girls other guys wouldn't look at twice. The instinct that was as natural to him as breathing told him the ones who were eager, accessible. Even without her looks, he would have noticed Shelley. Behind that cool exterior, there were hidden fires— and he wanted to warm himself in them, wanted her so badly that his loins ached.

During the next hour, they stuffed themselves with the wares of several small open-front restaurants in the marketplace— susui and lomilomi and broiled beef strips on slivers of bamboo—and then topped off their meal with Portuguese *malasadas*, hot from the oven and rich with cinnamon and sugar. When Shelley declared that she couldn't eat another bite, he led her to an iron bench, half-hidden among the giant leaves of an a'pe plant. As they sat there, watching the koa fish moving sluggishly in a small fish pond, Tad made his move.

"Look, it's too early to take you back to your friend's place. She's probably got her boyfriend there, right? This friend of mine has a cottage here in Waikiki where I sleep over sometimes. Right now, he's on TDY—y'know, temporary duty?— but he left me the key so I could water his plants. So how about it? We could make some coffee and talk—and later on, if we get hungry again, maybe we could scramble some eggs or something."

Shelley was silent; in the flickering light of a luau torch, her eyes were the color of smoke. The expression on her face, as if she were listening to some distant voice, puzzled him. Was it possible that he'd been wrong, that she didn't feel the same vibes he did? Or didn't she know what he was asking her? Had he been too careful?

"That would be nice," she said, so politely that his uneasiness increased. "I'm not much of a cook, but I *can* scramble eggs."

The cottage, on Liliuokalani Street, was part of an older resort that had fallen into neglect because it was a candidate for the wreckers' ball. Eventually the cottages, with their untrimmed hibiscus bushes and giant monkeypod trees and shaggy heart-palms, would be razed to make way for yet another high-rise hotel. For now, they still retained an aura of Waikiki as it had been fifty years earlier.

When Tad unlocked the door and switched on the lights, the odor of mildew, a constant in the Islands, filled his nostrils, and he went around the living room, opening windows to let in the trades.

"It looks so neat for a bachelor's place," Shelley commented.

"He's a neat guy—and he always keeps a six-pack in the fridge. You want a San Miguel's?"

"I'm not much on beer, but I would take a little wine if your friend has any."

"I'm sure he has something on hand." He gave her a sidelong look. "So you're a wino. I guessed that right off—from your red nose."

Shelley put a hand up to cover her sun-pinkened nose. "I should've brought a hat."

"No way. Golden girls and sun go together. By the time you leave here, you'll be brown as a nut."

"I doubt that. I never tan. On the other hand, I usually don't burn, either."

"Like I said—a real golden girl."

Tad got a dusty bottle of California mountain red from a cabinet, poured a couple of inches into a glass for Shelley, then got himself a beer from the tiny refrigerator in the kitchen.

"You seem at home here," Shelley said. She was sitting on a rickety rattan couch, her long, golden legs curled under her.

"I am," he said. He'd hedged on the truth a little. Although it was true that his friend was now on TDY, it was also true that Tad paid part of the rent so he could use the cottage whenever he wanted. In fact, some of the furnishings were his. He'd enjoyed cruising the local junk shops for the old brass wheel that had come from a defunct interisland ferry. It had been a real find, and now it was hanging in a place of honor on one of the koa-paneled walls. The tree fern tiki that stood near the door, which he touched for luck every time he went in or out, had come from the Big Island, and the unframed pictures of fighter planes and aerial views of Johnson Island were also his, as were the collection of shells, pinned on a weathered old fish net on the wall.

"I like the decorations," Shelley said, breaking the silence.

"Junk—but nice junk," he said, pleased.

They fell silent again. As Tad sat beside her on the battered couch and finished his beer, he was aware of the subtle odor of perfume that lingered on her skin. The light from a shell-encrusted lamp fell softly across her face, accentuating the high curve of her cheekbones and her full mouth. When he realized that she was just as aware of their closeness as he was, that she was breathing too fast, Tad knew it was time to make another move.

Carefully, he sat down his beer can and slid his arm around her waist. He kissed her gently, and the kiss was everything he'd hoped for—and more. There was a softness to her lips, a resiliency so pronounced that he was sure he could sink into her, drown in her. Her body, as he pulled her toward him, was supple, and he wanted to take her then and there. The only reason he didn't was because it was still too soon.

"My God—you're so sweet, Shelley. I want to gobble you up, make a meal out of you—and I'm almost afraid to kiss you again because I might not be responsible for what I do."

These were words he'd used before, words that had always been effective, but when she smiled at him, a tremulous, uncertain smile, he felt a flicker of shame. But not enough to stop. God, no, he couldn't stop. He touched the back of his hand to her cheek, then let it drop down to the pulse that throbbed so erratically in her throat. When the vein jumped convulsively and her eyes darkened, he laughed and ran his finger along her lips.

As he looked into her eyes, those chameleon eyes that changed color with her emotions, there was a swelling in his throat as if a lump had suddenly formed there. He wanted her urgently, wanted to possess her soft, sweet flesh, but he wanted something else from her, too, something he couldn't identify, but which he knew had nothing to do with sex.

His hand trembled a little as he stroked her hair, and the darkness in her eyes seemed to expand until it consumed her pupils. Was she afraid? If so, she didn't protest when he unbuttoned her dress, untied the yellow bikini, and slipped it off, his hands moving slowly, relentlessly. His mouth went dry as he felt her body heat, the smoothness of her skin, under his fingertips. Quickly, he stripped off his own clothes and then stood before her, his masculinity rampant. Her eyes widened, but she still hadn't uttered one word of protest.

Hungrily, he drank in her nudeness. Her breasts were the color of ivory, and her tight little nipples were dark pink, like rosebuds ready to bloom. But it was the golden pad, a soft triangular web between her thighs, that made him lose control.

Without finesse, he pushed her backward until she lay supine on the sofa cushions. With both hands, he separated her thighs and then knelt between them. As he caressed her warm abdomen, then probed her downy center, so spongy and moist beneath his fingers, he was sure that she was ready for sex, as he was.

With a muffled groan, he thrust himself against her, only to find that there was a barrier, a tightness that wouldn't permit the passage he craved. At the edge of his sexual excitement an awareness grew. She was a virgin—and he hadn't suspected, hadn't guessed.

But there was no turning back. The primal force that drove him was too strong; and once unleashed was all powerful. As his next frantic lunge broke the barrier, as he penetrated her and sank into her flesh, she made a keening sound, like a child crying out in the night. The world around him took on a red tinge, as if he were viewing it through a rainbow—or through a veil of blood. He rose and fell above her, unable to control the passion that consumed him.

It was later, after he was spent and his heart had stopped its wild pounding inside his chest, that reason returned. He held her close then, rocked her back and forth as she hid her hot face against his chest.

"It's all right," he crooned, filled with a tenderness he'd never felt for a woman before. "I promise it will be all right." He held her face between his hands, forcing her to look at him. As he kissed her lips that tasted of tears, he knew he would do anything to chase away the sadness on that still, white face.

"I should have told you," she said, her voice catching. "You're disappointed, aren't you?"

"Oh, my God—don't you know that right now I'm on top of the world? But I'm sorry that it wasn't good for you, Shelley. Next time, it will be better—I promise you it will be better."

He pulled her down until she was half lying across his lap so he could stare into her eyes. "Look, I don't want you to go back to Dayton, not in a few days, not ever. If I let you get away, it could all go sour. Sure, we'd write back and forth for a while, but then it would get complicated and other things would intrude, and the first thing you know, it would fizzle out. This thing we've got going for us is too special for that. That's why I want you to marry me as soon as we can get a license—"

"That's crazy. You know it's crazy," she said, shaking her head.

"It's the sanest thing I've ever said. You know you don't want to go back to Dayton. What do you have back there? You told me you don't want to go to that school your parents picked out for you. You and me—don't you feel it? We're right together, and I'm not just talking about sex. I'm not so hot with words, but—listen, Shelley, I can't stand the thought of you going away and never seeing you again. Stay with me—marry me. In a few more weeks, my tour at Hickam will be up, and I'll be rotating back to the Mainland. In the meantime, we can have our honeymoon in Hawaii. What better way to start off a marriage?"

"But people don't do things like that—"

"Sure they do. Or if they don't, they end up regretting it. I pay half the rent on this cabin, so we even have a place to stay. When my friend gets back, he can live in the barracks until my orders come through. We'd be together—I promise that it will all work out okay."

Desperation filled him when Shelley shook her head again. He knew his arguments weren't convincing—hell, he wasn't good at expressing himself. If he could just think of the right thing to say.

Shelley shivered convulsively, and he picked up the old afghan that covered the back of the couch and put it around her naked shoulders. She clutched at it as if she wanted to hide herself from his eyes, and his fear grew. She was right—it *was* crazy. Why would a girl like Shelley marry a mug like him, a mechanic with grease under his fingernails and nothing to offer her except his name?

Okay, she had let him make love to her the first time they were together, but maybe that was just because she was curious about sex. And why was she so quiet? Had he hurt her? Was she afraid of him? Didn't she realize that he'd never asked any other girl to marry him? Even though the first time hadn't been good for her, maybe if he made love to her again, she would change her mind. And God knew he was ready. He wanted her again, not with the same fierce urgency, but in another way. He'd been with so many women, but none had affected him like this, as if he would bust wide open if she didn't love him back.

"Say something, Shelley, before I explode," he said, his voice hoarse. "We can make it work—hell, I know I'm not good enough for you, but I'll always treat you right. I'm a hard worker—things won't be easy, but when I get more rank, it will be better. And the air force isn't a bad life. Sure, we'll have separations, but they can be good for a marriage. Some of the guys say it's like a honeymoon every time they come back from TDY."

Shelley gave a tiny sigh. When Tad started to go on, she put her hand over his mouth, stopping him. "There's something I have to tell you," she said. "It may change your mind about marrying me."

Tad stiffened. "Is there a guy back in Dayton?" he said jealously.

"There's no one else."

"Then it doesn't matter. Whatever it is, we can work it out."

"I'm not sure about that. I want to be honest with you. I didn't really lie. I just didn't tell you the whole truth."

"Okay—but I'm telling you up front. It isn't important."

"I hope that's true, Tad."

"Would I lie to you?" He ran his forefinger along the tense lines in her face and because he was afraid, he tried to make a joke out of it. "Relax, take a deep breath—and tell me this big secret. You have a criminal record, right? Or maybe you're really an exotic dancer taking an Hawaiian vacation."

She gave a shaky laugh. "I'm not on vacation. I live here."

His smile faded. "Why the devil didn't you say so?"

"Because—because I was afraid that if you found out who my father is, you wouldn't have anything to do with me."

"That's crazy. I don't care who your old man is."

"Not even if he's your commanding officer?"

"You're Major Barker's kid? Hell, I don't believe it. His kids are still little."

"I should've put that a different way. My father is General Pritchard."

Tad felt as if a fist had hit him in the solar plexus. "The hell you say," he said.

"Does it make a difference?"

"It bloody well does. Whatta you think?"

"I should've told you earlier," she said miserably. "You're really sore, aren't you?"

"No—yes. Hell, I don't know. Give me time to think. I have to figure out what this means."

She took him at his word. Huddled under the afghan, she watched him as he went into the bathroom to get his robe. He returned to the living room and paced up and down, deep in thought.

He turned to look at her finally. "I wouldn't want to be in your shoes when you tell your old man that you're marrying a grease monkey. Maybe we'd better elope and tell him later."

"You still want to marry me?"

"I have to make an honest woman out of you, don't I?"

"I thought you'd be furious—"

"Hell, I was all prepared to be—y'know, noble, if you told me something heavy, like your old man was a convict in Oahu Prison or a hood in the Hawaiian mafia. I guess I can't hold it against him for being a four-star general. The thing is—how are your folks going to take this? There's going to be hell to pay when they find out about me."

"If they don't understand, that's their problem." But the worry in her eyes didn't match her defiant words. "Once they get to know you, I'm sure that'll make a difference."

Tad was skeptical. "What you see and what they'll see is two different things. I'm an enlisted man, a miner's kid from Pennsylvania—and a Polack to boot. They aren't going to like any of that. Your old man's got a reputation for being—y'know, hard-nosed."

"Surely you're not afraid of my father."

"Of course I'm afraid. I'd have to be crazy not to be afraid. Staff sergeants don't take on four-star generals in this man's air force. In fact, this is probably the dumbest thing I've ever done in my life. Luckily, my tour's about up. I should have my orders in another two months. It'll be easier when we're off this rock. Once we're married and living at another base, all we have to do is keep our mouths shut and who's to know you're General Pritchard's kid? You'll be my DW—"

"DW?"

"Dependent wife."

A frown settled between Shelley's eyebrows. "I'm not sure I like that phrase."

"It doesn't mean anything. The air force has to use some kind of designation for wives, don't they?"

"You're probably right," she said, but she didn't sound convinced.

"So what do we do next? I think we should get married and then tell them."

She was silent for a long time. "I don't know—it might make things worse. Of course, if it's a fait accompli—"

"A what?"

"If it's already a fact, what can they do about it? I could call my mother and tell her I'll be staying with Tai for a few days. That way we can be already married when we tackle them. What do you think?"

"I think I've got one smart old lady." Tad untied the cord around his waist and let his robe drop. He pulled the afghan away from Shelley's shoulders and bent to kiss the deep valley between her breasts. "And right now, we've got more important business to take care of. What would you say if I told you that the world's greatest stud was going to make love to you again?"

"I'd say that I'd really lucked out."

"You don't know the half of it," he boasted. "In a few minutes you're going to find out something I already know about you—that you're one sexy lady."

Later, as they lay in each other's arms, Tad raised himself on one elbow and looked down at Shelley's drowsy face. "Well, was I lying to you? Am I or am I not the world's greatest lover? Let's hear one for the gipper," he said confidently.

Shelley was silent, staring up at him. In the dim light, her eyes seemed full of shadows. When she reached out and ran the back of her hand along his cheek, he felt the swelling in his throat again. "I love you," she said. "And that's one for the gipper."

CHAPTER

✦ 10 ✦

THE ONE THING TAD HADN'T EXPECTED WHEN HE'D AGREED to meet Shelley's parents was that he'd be so damned nervous.

Hell, he hadn't felt like this since he was twelve years old and his old man had caught him rooting through his oldest brother's sock drawer, looking for cigarettes. He'd known that he was in for two whippings, one from his father and the other from his brother, so he'd had good cause to be scared. But now—what could happen other than having General Pritchard chew him out for fooling around with his daughter?

He wasn't afraid that they could change Shelley's mind about marrying him. She might be quiet and easygoing, but there was a look in her eyes sometimes that told him she'd be like a rock once she'd made her mind up about something.

And why was he so sure he knew her so well when they'd only met two days ago? They hadn't done much talking—in fact, he hadn't been able to keep his hands off her long enough to carry on any long conversations. So he knew very little about her except that just looking at her blew his mind.

He glanced over at Shelley, who had been silent ever since they'd left Waikiki. Her face had a pinched look, as if she were cold, and she kept staring straight ahead, her hands twisting in her lap.

Was he wrong? Was she having second thoughts after all? Maybe she was one of those people who did everything on impulse—and then regretted it later. She had let him make out

with her so easily that he'd been sure she knew the score—
which was why it had been a shocker to be right in the middle
of it, going at it hot and heavy, and then find out she was a
virgin. Yeah, that had been some kind of shock.

But it had been too late by then, and when it was over, he'd
realized that this was it, the jackpot. The funny thing was that
he'd always known it would happen like this. Love at first
sight . . . well, at first sex. Not that it was all sex. He could get
sex any time he wanted it. So it was a lot more than that. It
was orange blossoms and forever more and a lot of other corn-
ball things. Maybe he hadn't really left home after all. Maybe
he was an old-fashioned, small-town guy at heart and not the
stud he—and everybody else—thought he was.

And just wait until his folks found out he was getting married. His brothers would really razz him. Of course, he'd have
to warn Shelley not to say anything about her old man being
a general. That would really complicate things, not only with
his family, but with his friends and his superiors at work, too.
He'd seen something like this happen once when that airman
in his old outfit at Pease AFB had married into money. Suddenly
everybody was acting tight-lipped around the guy, shutting him
out of the horseplay and the kidding. He didn't want that to
happen to him. One reason he was going for a career in the
air force was because he liked being accepted for what he was
instead of always being measured up against other people. He
liked knowing that if he did his job right, no one was going
to start pick, pick, picking away at him, finding fault because
he wasn't as big and tough as his fucking brothers.

That's why he didn't want anyone to know that Shelley's
old man was General Pritchard. He only had another few weeks
here, and why ask for trouble? Why the devil couldn't Shelley
be a tourist like he'd thought at first, the daughter of some
businessman back in Ohio? It would be so simple then.

As for this meeting with her folks, he'd be glad when it
was over. Real glad. What exactly had Shelley told them about
him? He'd gone in to take a shower, and when he'd come out
she'd been sitting on the edge of the bed, the phone still in her
hand, looking a little green around the gills.

"What's happening?" he said, and she looked at him with
her eyes sort of empty and said that she'd been thinking it over
and had decided that it was only fair to tell her parents the

truth, and now they wanted to see both of them as soon as they could get to the base.

He'd wanted to tell her that she should have talked it over with him first, that he needed time, but he didn't say anything. After all, they were her parents—and also, he hadn't been ready to admit that his stomach muscles cramped just at the thought of facing her old man. He'd seen General Pritchard once, and the guy's frozen fish eyes had really turned him off. Shelley's mom, too. Everybody knew what a hard case she was.

And these two were going to be his in-laws? It was enough to blow his mind.

Well, he wasn't going to let it get him down. He was as good as the next guy, maybe a little better than some. Okay, he wasn't rolling in dough, and he didn't have an officer's clout—hell, he didn't have clout at all!—but he would make Shelley happy. He wouldn't slap her around like some guys did their old ladies, and he'd bring home his paycheck to her every month. When they had kids, he'd be a good father, too. So he wasn't going to let Shelley's parents make him feel inferior or any of that shit. He was going to be himself, take it or leave it, and if you don't like it, kiss my ass. . . .

Shelley gave a long sigh as if she'd been holding her breath, and he reached out and took her hand. Her fingers were clammy, even though the wind blowing through the open window was warm and humid. He gave her hand a hard squeeze, knowing she was having an attack of nerves. And why not? These were *her* folks. She'd been dealing with them all her life, and now she'd be telling them something they didn't want to hear. Also, a heavy relationship with a man was new to her. Come to think of it, it was new to him, too. Not the sex, but the permanency of it. Getting married was for life—or it should be. Which was kind of scary.

So okay, he'd just have to tough it out today. After all, what could Pritchard do to stop them from getting married? Shelley was of age . . . or was she? On the beach that first day, he'd taken her to be twenty or maybe twenty-one. She looked older than her friends—except for the tall skinny one with the pointed chin. But if she'd just graduated from Punahou in June, then she could be as young as seventeen.

God, what if she *was* a minor? He never fooled around with jail bait, just as he'd never made it with a virgin before. That

"Hey, look at me! I got myself a cherry!" stuff was juvenile. Did Shelley have any regrets? She hadn't turned a hair when he started undressing her, just like it was something she did every day, but the evidence had been there—and since she'd agreed to marry him, it must have hit her the same way, the conviction that this thing between them was for life.

He liked it that she'd been honest about her old man. She could have waited, let him go on thinking she was a tourist. Actually, she hadn't really lied. She'd said that she'd been born in Ohio, which was true because her old man had been vice-commander of ATSC at Wright-Pat when she was born.

As for what happened when they got to Four Star House, he'd just play that by ear. Sure, he was a little nervous, but that was natural. He'd feel this way no matter who her folks were. Besides, what could her old man do? Throw him in the guardhouse? Of course if Shelley was seventeen, then things could get pretty hairy.

"How old are you, Shelley?" he said, breaking a long silence.

Shelley gave him a wan smile. "Don't worry. I'm eighteen. My birthday was last month."

"So you're legal—and your old man can't say shit about our getting married."

She looked away. "That's right."

"You aren't having second thoughts, are you?"

"I haven't changed my mind. How about you? It isn't too late."

He grinned at her, his good spirits restored. "You're my lady now. I'm not afraid of your old man."

"Maybe you should be. He's pretty formidable. And so is my mother. You don't have to go through with this, you know. I'd understand if you turned the car around and drove me back to the parking lot where we left my car. We can forget the whole thing right now"—she paused to give him a wobbly smile—"and if you do, I'll never forgive you—never!"

He laughed, and she bent toward him and ran her fingertips along his jawline. Her hand smelled of lilacs, one of the few flower odors he recognized. "Lilacs . . . my lady of the lilacs."

"It's your soap—how come you use lilac soap, Tad?"

"It must have been on sale—and I want you to promise that you'll wear lilac cologne from now on. Promise?"

"I promise."

"That easy, huh? Don't you want to bargain? Isn't there something you want me to promise?"

"That you'll never stop loving me, even if I get fat and old."

The thought of Shelley getting fat or old was so ludicrous that he had to laugh. "Okay, it's a promise. But if you grow a second head, all bets are off. I'm not into freaks."

"What are you into?" she teased.

"Foxy chicks with ash-blond hair and skin like one of those white flowers that smell so good——"

"Daisies?"

"No, not daisies. Daisies are weeds. I mean those flowers that—you know, they have thick petals that turn brown on the edges when they start to get old."

"I think you mean gardenias—and that's really romantic, comparing my skin to an old brown gardenia."

"Okay, I'm not romantic. But I'm good, lady. You have to admit that I'm good," he said confidently.

"And modest."

"Yeah—that, too." He reached out and squeezed her knee. "It's going to be great, Shelley. Wait and see. We're going to have a good life together. No matter what your folks say, we're going to get married, and the hell with them."

"The hell with them," she echoed.

A few minutes later, as he parked his Chevy in the driveway of her parents' quarters, Tad wasn't feeling so cocky. He told himself it was caffeine nerves because he'd had too much coffee that day, but as they walked up the driveway toward the large, sprawling house, he had to remind himself again that Shelley was crazy about him—and that he wasn't going to let her parents throw him. Okay, Pritchard was top dog at PACAF— but the guy put on his trousers one leg at a time, just like anyone else. So why this sinking feeling in the pit of his stomach, as if he were walking into a den of lions?

To Tad's surprise, Shelley rang the bell instead of just opening the door and going inside.

"If the door's locked, how come you don't use your key?" he asked.

"It isn't locked. I rang the bell because I wanted to—to make a statement that I'm serious about all this."

"I hope they aren't expecting Burt Reynolds," he said. "What did you tell them about me?"

"I said we were in love with each other and that we'd decided to get married but I didn't tell them that we just met two days ago. If I did, they'd really have a fit. Even so, it's going to be pretty bad—you know that, don't you? They're both used to having their own way."

Tad discovered just how intimidating General Pritchard could be when the door swung open and Shelley's father stood there, looking him over. He had expected one of the stewards to open the door, but the two of them must have been waiting because Mrs. Pritchard was right behind the general, her eyes frigid as she stared at her daughter, taking in the cut-off jeans and cotton T-shirt that Shelley was wearing.

Tad thought how much alike the Pritchards looked, both so pencil thin, the resemblance so striking that they could have been brother and sister. In fact it was hard to believe that they'd ever been intimate with each other—and yet, according to Shelley, she'd been born when her mother was past forty.

General Pritchard was wearing a sport jacket, which should have made him less impressive. But everything about him— his trim mustache, streaked with gray, his dissecting eyes, his sparse, lean body—spoke of authority, of a lifetime of giving orders, of having them obeyed without argument or discussion.

Even so, it was Shelley's mother Tad was most conscious of. He couldn't help comparing his own dumpy mother to this woman who looked so refined and who managed to keep everybody at Hickam in a turmoil.

"Mother and Dad—this is Tad Brotski. Tad, these are my parents." Shelley's voice was as polite as a well-mannered child's.

"What's this nonsense about getting married?" Mrs. Pritchard said, ignoring the introduction.

"It isn't nonsense. We plan to be married as soon as we can get the license."

Despite the firmness in her voice, Shelley's face was pale, and a thin beading of sweat glistened on her upper lip. Tad realized again what it was costing her to stand up to her folks, and he wondered if he deserved her sacrifice. The moment of doubt shamed him and revitalized his determination not to be intimidated. He returned Mrs. Pritchard's stare with one of his own.

"Good evening, ma'am." He moved his eyes to the general. "Good evening, sir."

"I want to know where you've been for the past two days, Shelley," Mrs. Pritchard said as if Tad hadn't spoken. "You left that message that you were going to stay overnight with your friend Tai, but of course we knew that was impossible."

"Impossible?"

Mrs. Pritchard's eyes sharpened. "Surely, you've heard about your friend's father. Sergeant MacGarrett was placed under house arrest two days ago. When I heard about it, I called the MacGarrett quarters immediately to tell you to come home, but your friend said you hadn't been there."

"How terrible—I'll call Tai right away—"

Mrs. Pritchard brushed aside her words. "I suppose you've been with this—this man? I'm really disappointed in you. To get involved with him at all is bad enough, but to even consider marriage—how can you be so irresponsible? How long have you known him—and I want the truth, Shelley."

"Long enough to know that I love Tad and intend to marry him."

Mrs. Pritchard's face tightened. "You're too young to know your own mind. Marriage with someone so—from such a different background couldn't possibly last. You've led a privileged life—what can he possibly give you that you don't already have?"

"Love. He can give me love."

"That's ridiculous. We've given you every advantage—what a cruel thing to say!"

"Is it, Mother? Do you realize that in the past eighteen years, I've lived with you a total of eight years? And six of them were before you sent me away to school for the first time."

"So that's what this is all about. You've been harboring some childish resentment toward your father and me. You know why we decided boarding school was best for you. Your father's assignments have always been very sensitive and not conducive to having a young child around. We sent you to the very best schools—is this our reward? This relationship with a common—with this man? Are you doing this to get back at us?"

Shelley rejected her mother's words with a shake of her head. "I love Tad—and he loves me. Except for Tony, no one's every really given a damn about me before. And I think you should apologize to Tad for insulting him."

Mrs. Pritchard's upper lip quivered; her nostrils flared as if she'd just caught a whiff of something rotten. "You're a fool,

Shelley. If you walk out the door with this man, you'll be leaving behind everything—your family, your clothes, your personal belongings. As far as we're concerned, we'd no longer have a daughter."

Involuntarily, Tad looked at General Pritchard, half expecting to see at least a shadow of resentment on that austere face. But the general's eyes reflected his wife's chill, and Tad realized that the two of them spoke with one voice. It was hard to believe that Shelley had been raised by these cold fish—how had she become the warm and loving person she was? Maybe they'd done her a favor, sending her away to school.

"That's what you've always wanted, isn't it, Mother?" Shelley said, echoing Tad's thoughts. "To be rid of me once and for all. I'm an embarrassment to you—a daughter young enough to be your grandchild. You must have hated it when your pregnancy began to show, proof that the general and his lady still got it on like ordinary people. Were you shocked when you found out that you weren't in menopause, and that it was too late to have an abortion? Oh, yes. I guessed that. Well, you're going to get your wish. You don't have to disown me, because I disown you—both of you. As far as I'm concerned, I'm an orphan from now on."

She caught up Tad's hand as if she needed something to hold on to. He looked into her bloodless face, her hurting eyes, and he wanted to take on that pain in her place. Most of all, he wanted to protect her from further hurt. Even his father, for all his heavy hand, would never treat him like this. Poppa had yelled at him, yes, given him a whipping now and then when he thought Tad needed it, but there was no way that he would ever cut his own son out of his life, no matter what he did.

Which made Adolph Brotski, for all the coal dust permanently embedded in his pores, a better man than General Curtis Pritchard, any day.

"Good night, ma'am," he said, speaking for the second time. "Good night, sir."

He put his hand on Shelley's shoulder and turned her around. As they started for the door, the back of his neck burned, and he half expected to hear the general bark, "Halt!" But there was only a dead silence behind them, and it seemed fitting somehow that he, a sergeant, hadn't been allowed to pass beyond the entrance hall of Shelley's home.

* * *

They were married three days later. The wedding ceremony was brief, in the registrar's office of the courthouse in downtown Honolulu. They were the only couple among the dozen or so waiting their turn to be married who weren't accompanied by at least one friend or relative.

The registrar, a middle-aged man of Hawaiian extraction, had such a heavy island accent that Tad said his "I do" in the wrong place and had to say it over again. He had bought Shelley gardenias. Their cloying scent dominated the small room where the ceremony took place, and he wished that he'd chosen violets or pansies, something delicate and fresh to match Shelley's radiant face.

Not that it really mattered. He'd never thought of himself as a romantic man. Just the opposite, in fact. But today, he felt like a winner, someone who had just hit the jackpot. He had won Shelley—and he still wasn't sure just how it had happened.

On the way back to the car, he asked her, "How did one guy get so lucky?", making a joke out of it but really wanting an answer.

"How did one gal get so lucky?" she replied smiling.

She was wearing white—a summer dress made of some thin, floaty material. It was sleeveless, and he'd never before seen such sexy arms on a woman—round and soft and not at all thin the way you'd expect in someone so slender. She was wearing a narrow wreathlike thing on her head, and it blended with her silver-blond hair, making her look so classy that he felt a little awed.

For one thing, he'd never seen her dressed up before. For the past few days, she'd been wearing his jeans, cut off at the knees, and one of his sweat shirts. Even in that, she looked great, but in this dress she'd bought at one of those boutiques on Kapiolani Avenue . . . well, he'd been shocked at the price, especially since he'd paid for it, but now he was glad that he hadn't complained. She looked so good that guys kept turning around to stare at her as they headed for the parking lot.

"Now that we're an old married couple," he teased, "I hope to get some good home-cooked meals."

Shelley gave him a stricken look. Too late he remembered that her first attempt at cooking breakfast for him had been a disaster. Not only had she burned the bacon, but she'd cooked the eggs so long they'd tasted like fried leather. He'd forced them down, but he hoped she was a quick study because he was particular about his food—his mom being the best cook in Tunsten.

"Too bad we don't live close to my folks," he said, speaking his thoughts aloud. "My mom is a great cook. You haven't lived until you've tasted her hot potato salad and her chicken and dumplings. All my brothers' wives use her recipes."

"I wonder if she—if your family will like me."

"Well, we'll find out in a few weeks. Even if my next assignment's on the West Coast, we can still take a delay enroute and go to Pennsylvania to see them. I want to show you off— man, I can't wait to see my brothers' faces when they get a look at you."

"But will they like me?"

"What's not to like? They'll be jealous as hell," he said, grinning. "My sisters-in-law, too, because they'll know what my brothers are thinking. Mom will be glad that I've finally married and settled down. I think she's been scared I'd turn out like my uncle, the one I look so much like, who never got married and ended up a bum."

"And your father? What about him?"

"Oh, he'll probably try to feel you up like he does all the girls," he said slyly.

She gave him a shocked look and he burst out laughing. "I couldn't help that one. You're always so serious—but I wasn't altogether kidding about the old man. He used to be a real chaser. My mom's had to put up with a lot from him."

"You mean he was—unfaithful?"

"Oh, sure, he was a real tiger with the women when he was younger." He took a closer look at her face. "Hey, don't worry. It won't be like that with us. You're my one and only lady. I won't promise not to look—but I won't touch. I'll come home every night to you and the kids."

"Do you want kids right away, or do you want to wait a while?"

Tad hesitated. Somehow it was hard to think of Shelley as a mother. Right now, all he wanted was the two of them— with no one else to worry about. Sure, they would have a social life. That was part of marriage. He liked to play pinochle with the guys, and she'd probably make friends with other wives and they'd have couples over for barbecue. But as for kids— it was too soon to think about that. At the moment, he had something else on his mind. He couldn't wait to get back to Waikiki, to take that pretty dress off Shelley and pull her down on the bed. . . .

He picked up Shelley's hand and pressed it against his thigh. "Let's not get into any heavy conversations today. I've got a hard-on you wouldn't believe. If we don't get home pretty quick, it's going to be too late."

She didn't pull away, but she didn't smile at him, and he knew that he'd disappointed her. He wanted to know what was bugging her—and yet he didn't, either. Well, it would take some getting used to on both their parts—but they'd just wing it and it would work out. Yeah, it would be okay. It had to be.

Two weeks later, Tad was called into his squadron commander's office. Usually, Major Barker was friendly and relaxed with the troops, but today he seemed to be having a hard time looking at Tad.

"Your orders just came in, Brotski. I'm sorry we can't give you any leave, but this is a hurry-up deal."

"They came in already? To where?" Tad said, frowning. His tour wouldn't be up for six more weeks, and besides, his career field was a common one, certainly not in short demand. So why was it a hurry-up deal?

"To the Philippines. Clark Air Base."

"You mean you're sending me on TDY? Hell, sir, I drew that TDY tour to Okinawa just five months ago."

"Not TDY. This is a PCS. You'll do a full tour at Clark."

A permanent change of station? But that was crazy! "There has to be some mistake—"

"No mistake. The orders have already been cut."

The truth hit Tad then. He felt as if someone had dropped a piano on his head. So this was what happened when you crossed a four-star general. A man with that kind of clout could break every regulation in the book, could do what he wanted with another man's life—and it wouldn't do a bit of good to file a complaint with the inspector general because PACAF Headquarters would only claim that his transfer was for the expediency of the government, and that would end it. In fact, if he made any waves, there'd probably be a coded entry on his service record—if you could believe the guardhouse lawyers—which would make him out to be a troublemaker, and he'd only be hurting himself.

He looked Major Barker in the eye. "I'd like a few days of leave, sir, to get things squared away with my wife. She'll need a new passport because her old one is—it got lost."

"You're scheduled to report in at Clark September first. She'll have to come along later. Look, Brotski, I'm sorry about this. You're a good man. Off the record . . . well, I don't know what's going on, but your orders came from Washington—way up the line. If you're smart, you'll let it ride and do like you're told."

"This whole deal stinks, sir. But I'll go along with it because I'm not about to give him—give anyone an excuse to put a bad mark on my record. I may be enlisted, but my career's just as important to me as yours is to you. So I'm not going to the IG even though I think this whole business is illegal as hell. And you can put that in your report, sir."

Major Barker studied him in silence. On the other side of the office partition, Tad heard men's voices, someone's laugh. He knew most of the orderly room personnel by sight, but at the moment, he felt as if he had wandered into the camp of the enemy.

"I think it stinks, too, sergeant," Major Barker said, lowering his voice. "If I had a choice, I'd see you stayed here until the end of your tour. I don't have that choice—and neither do you. But you're going to get one hell of an efficiency rating from me for your record just to even things out a little."

"Thank you, sir," Tad said. "Just be sure you cover your ass."

The major's face relaxed into a smile. "The first thing I learned at Officers Training School was to cover my ass at all times. I suggest you do the same. I don't know whose toes you stepped on, but it's obvious someone wants you off this base in a hurry. Since your orders are for the PI and not a remote like Thule, count your blessings. It could be a lot worse. Hell, Clark isn't a bad assignment. I was stationed there five years ago, and I extended six months so my oldest kid could finish first grade. The time'll go fast—you and that new bride of yours will probably enjoy it. And maybe your next assignment will be something choice in the good old U.S. of A."

CHAPTER
✦ 11 ✦

WHEN CRYSTAL HAD TURNED THIRTEEN, HER FATHER, IN an expansive mood, had asked what she wanted for her birthday. She'd told him she wanted a desk with a drawer she could lock. Although he'd made some quip about her being too young to have secrets, Maurice's eyes had met hers in a look of rare perception, and the morning of her birthday, a small desk with locks on every drawer had been delivered to their quarters.

Her parents had quarreled that night after Crystal was in bed. Janet said Maurice was spoiling Crystal rotten, that there was something unnatural about the way he doted on that girl.

Her father told Janet that she was a jealous bitch and he wished she'd get off his back. It had ended, as all their fights did, with them making up in bed, and Crystal had pulled her pillow over her head to shut out the grumble of their bed springs, Janet's moans, and her father's bellows of lust.

But the desk remained, and she felt reasonably secure about the things she kept there because she wore the tiny key around her neck. Even so, her diary was written in her own form of shorthand because her mother could wait for months, even years, like a spider building a trap for an elusive fly, for the right time to pounce. It was just conceivable that she would decide someday to jimmy open the locks.

The calendar she kept locked up with her diary was new. Crystal bought it shortly after her seduction of Grant Norton. Every morning she marked off the date with a cross. Two weeks later, when her monthly period was one day overdue, she wrote a triumphant word—JACKPOT!—on the calendar instead of the usual *X*—and then added a cautious *maybe*.

As it happened, she was wise to be cautious because three days later she awoke to find that she hadn't hit the jackpot after all. She was disappointed, of course. All that planning, not to mention that unpleasant episode with Grant, had been for nothing. It was especially galling because she suspected she'd never get another chance, not with Grant. Since that night, he hadn't phoned to find out if she was okay, much less to ask for another date. And two days ago, when they'd met by accident in the hall at work, he had looked past her as if she weren't there.

Not only was she furious because she'd wasted so much time, but she resented his high-handedness. Grant couldn't possibly know that she'd instigated that whole incident. He must believe that she had been a victim of his drunken seduction. So his lack of concern was intolerable, and her disappointment was exacerbated by a desire for revenge.

Not that she intended to stop trying to land him as a husband. No matter how indifferent he was to her as a woman, he was still perfect for her purposes. Her interest in him was strictly impersonal, but so much the better. Their marriage—if she managed to land him—would be a business deal, something undertaken for both their advantages. It didn't even matter if he wasn't attracted to her. At least he wouldn't be pawing at her all the time. Not that she intended to let him know how she felt. If he wanted sex, she'd give it to him. She knew a few tricks—she could satisfy him as long as necessary.

Crystal waited, more or less patiently, another six weeks. Timing was all-important—and her emotional reaction must seem genuine. If Grant suspected that she was lying about being pregnant, the whole thing would collapse like one of those blowfish the locals sold to gullible tourists. So she rehearsed in the privacy of her room—how she would approach him, what she would say, right down to the tears in her eyes and the quaver in her voice.

It was the middle of January when she called Grant's office, gave her name, and asked to speak to him. There was a long pause, during which she could hear the hum of a typewriter and muffled voices in the background, before Grant's secretary came back on the line to say, "Sorry. Colonel Norton is out of his office for the rest of the day. Can I take a message?"

"Tell him I'll call again tomorrow," Crystal said.

But the next day when she called she got the same answer. This time, she read embarrassment in the woman's voice and knew that Grant had given his secretary orders not to put through any calls from Crystal Moore. Her voice even, Crystal said that she'd call again, then hung up to plan her next move. Since he wanted to play games, she'd accommodate him. But they'd play by her rules, not his.

She was waiting for Grant that night when he got home from work. He was almost an hour late, and she was tired and hungry by the time he came up the walk, a briefcase under his arm. Since he seemed a little unsteady on his feet, she guessed that he'd stopped off at the club for a drink—and then had stayed for three or four.

She shook her head in disgust. Was the man self-destructive? Didn't he realize what a drunk-driving charge would do to his career? Well, she'd put a stop to that kind of thing once she was in charge. He would either stop drinking altogether, or she would do the driving. She never drank herself. Not only did she dislike the taste of liquor, but she hated to lose control, the feeling of not being on top of things.

Grant was fumbling with his key when she stepped out of the shadows behind a hibiscus bush. It pleased her that she'd managed to catch him by surprise. "What the hell are *you* doing here?" he blurted.

Secretly, she was glad for his rudeness because she always thought faster when she was angry. "I—I had to see you," she said, blinking hard.

"Can't it wait until some other time? I'm expecting company tonight."

"It can't wait. It will only take a few minutes."

"Okay, come on in. No use giving the neighbors something to gossip about."

Inside the apartment, Grant crossed the living room to open sliding doors that led out onto a lanai. A cool breeze, rich with the odor of pikake, ruffled Crystal's hair as she stood in the middle of the room. Grant didn't offer her a chair. He dropped his briefcase on a table and went to a small bar to pour himself a drink. Crystal glanced around the living room, noting its expensive furnishings, its almost painful neatness. Not a trace of anything personal. . . . Well, that figured. Grant was a cold, unemotional man. His quarters were bound to reflect that.

She realized Grant was waiting for her to speak. "There's something I have to tell you, but I don't know where to begin," she said.

"I hope you'll be brief. I'm really not up to any dramatics tonight. I told you I'm sorry—what else can I say?"

"Well, I'm sorry, too." She didn't bother to hide her anger now. "I'm in a jam—and it's your fault. My period is two months late—I guess you know what that means."

Consternation flooded his face. "Are you sure? Couldn't there be some kind of mistake?"

"I went to a doctor today—no, not at the base. It was a civilian doctor, Dr. Hong. He says I'm two months pregnant." She made a helpless gesture. "My father's going to be furious. He has a terrible temper, and where I'm concerned, he's very protective. When he finds out you—that it was your fault, he'll really stir up trouble. He's a very bitter man because he was passed over for Lt. Colonel and had to retire with only twenty years' service. He seems easygoing on the surface, but actually he's like a bulldog with a bone once he gets his teeth into something. I'm sure he'll take you to court over this."

She noted with satisfaction how Grant's face gradually changed color as she spoke. The glass in his hand began to shake, and he took a quick gulp of his brandy. "God, what a mess— Look, you'll have to get rid of it. I'll pay your expenses, of course—"

"I don't believe in abortion—no way am I going to murder my own baby!"

Grant sat down heavily in a leather easy chair. When he ran a hand over his hair, setting it on end, Crystal almost laughed out loud. He was really sweating—funny, he looked so boyish with his hair standing on end like that, not at all the arrogant man she knew him to be.

"Hell—I wasn't thinking," he said. "That was a terrible thing to say."

Crystal concealed her surprise with an effort. So he had a conscience—and it could be reached. So much the better. Blackmail wasn't the ideal climate for a marriage, even if it was a business arrangement. Other tactics seemed in order— at least they were worth a try. She could always fall back on blackmail.

"So what are you going to do?" he said.

"Do? The question is what are *you* going to do. You got

me into this. It's up to you to get me out of it. The only way to placate my father is to make it legal. He won't object to a baby that came too early if we're married."

"Married?" He said the word as if it were a snake.

"Why not? I'm a little young for you, but I'm also very mature for my age. And you don't have anyone else on the string. I've done some research, and I know that you date a woman a few times and then you drop her. You like to play the field and have your fun, but you stay away from serious involvements. But all that's going to change. Not only don't I believe in abortion, I also don't intend to be a single mother, raising a kid alone."

"You could put it up for adoption—"

"And what do I tell my friends? My family? My father's people are very old-fashioned. Everything is either black or white to them. All they understand is labels—and 'bitch' would be the least they'd call me. I could never go back to Omaha—and neither could my parents. As far as my grandparents are concerned, the sexual revolution never happened—and I feel the same way. I want a husband, respectability, support for my kid."

"Couldn't you go away? Make some excuse—I'd pay for the whole thing. Later, you can invent a husband—"

"I won't have to invent one if you marry me."

"Marriage to me would be a disaster. How could you possibly want to live with a man who—who isn't interested in you?"

"Not interested?" Again, she let him see her anger. In fact, she was so involved with her role that she'd forgotten he hadn't really seduced her. "What about the night it happened? You made a lot of promises—how could I know you didn't mean them? Maybe I could chalk it up to your being drunk if you'd acted halfway human afterward. But you never even called—and when I phoned you, you gave your secretary orders to tell me you were out. So all I want from you is marriage. I don't want any passionate love affair."

"You're out of your mind. I'd look like a fool—"

"Look, it can benefit both of us. I'd like being the wife of a colonel, and the right wife could help your career, too. I know how to play the game. After all, I *am* the daughter of an air force officer."

"I don't need a wife."

"But you do. The military still runs by the old rules. A wife and kid would help your career. And I'd be a damned good wife, too. I understand military protocol and how to behave around rank, when to be friendly and when to cool it. I'd be a good hostess and keep the senior wives happy. I've had a lot of time to think these past few weeks, and this is something I want to do, something I can do well."

Grant's eyes reflected a chill. "I'm not going to be black-mailed into marriage," he said evenly.

Crystal knew it was time to change tactics again. "This isn't blackmail. It's justice. After all, I didn't go to the police the way my friend advised, did I?"

"Friend? What friend?"

"My best friend from Punahou. She's the daughter of Gen-eral—well, that isn't important. I had to tell someone, and she's always been so sensible . . . she wanted me to go to the police and file charges against you, but I just couldn't. I was at fault, too, for being so gullible—and besides, I didn't want to hurt you. When you aren't drunk, you're rather—rather sweet. I'd forget the whole thing, but there's a baby growing inside me like a time bomb. He's your kid, too, you know. Your own son—or daughter. Fatherhood doesn't even have to change your life. Obviously, you get bored with women quickly, so I won't expect you to change your habits, only to be discreet. Is it a bargain, Grant?"

Grant stared at her for a long time. Her smile seemed to disconcert him. He got to his feet and went to splash more brandy into his glass. She watched him as he tossed it off in one gulp.

"That stuff'll kill you," she commented.

He didn't answer. He wandered over to the patio door and stood with his back to Crystal, staring out into the night. He turned so abruptly that it startled her.

"Look, I can't make a decision like this so quickly. Why don't I think it over tonight and call you in the morning? And don't worry. We'll work something out."

Crystal had to be content with that, although she was tempted to tell him that he had no choice, not if he wanted to save his career. As she picked up her purse and sweater, it occurred to her that he still hadn't asked her to sit down—or offered her a drink.

"Okay, tomorrow morning—and I'll leave you something to

think about. You're going to need a wife if you ever hope to wear stars. I can be that wife. I'll do everything in my power to help you advance your career, and I'm not going to insult your intelligence by pretending it will be for love. If you succeed, then so do I—and I've always wanted to be a general's lady."

She was gone before he could answer. As she got into her car, reaction hit her and she felt a little dizzy. Had she won— or would he suspect that she was lying and call her bluff? Her position was so weak that she was surprised he hadn't demanded proof that she was really pregnant. Either he was incredibly naive, which she didn't believe for a minute, or for some reason of his own he didn't really want to know for sure if he was about to become a father.

C H A P T E R
✦ 12 ✦

THE TROPIC CLUB, TUCKED IN AN ALLEY THAT BI-
sected the lower end of Honolulu's notorious Hotel Street, was
small, quiet, poorly lighted. It could also, on occasion, be
dangerous when a sudden fight erupted, which was something
the rare tourist who wandered in didn't know, or he would
never risk his wallet and his neck by going there.

It was also a place where everybody minded his own business. All kinds of exotic transactions took place there, including
the sale of contraband from all over the Pacific. Drugs and
diamonds and even warm bodies were sold or bartered in the
dark booths that lined the walls. It was a place where a business
girl could have a quiet drink without being bothered by a pesky
john, or where the heads of rival gangs could meet on neutral
territory.

The regulars recognized each other on sight. Although they
probably couldn't put a name to a face, they knew as much
about each other's business as it was safe to know. For them,
if not for outsiders, this was a safe house—which was why
Grant had taken pains to become a regular patron, eventually
fitting in so well that none of the bar's customers bothered to
look up now when he came through the door.

Through the years, he had frequented many such bars, always
choosing those that were off limits to the military. It was his
home away from home, the factor that allowed him to live a
double life.

Tonight, as usual, he settled himself in the shadows at the end of the bar, well away from the entrance. When the bartender, a burly man with bristly hair and a scant beard, brought him a Scotch-and-water without asking what he wanted, he nursed his drink carefully, not wanting to cloud his brain.

He felt safe and at ease here, even though there was always the danger that he would be picked up by the police during one of the brawls that occasionally erupted. Maybe it was the element of danger that added pleasure to these excursions. If so, he never worried about it. He just knew that the sordidness of his surroundings, so different from the world of order that was his natural habitat, satisfied some need he'd never tried to analyze.

But tonight, the magic wasn't working. Crystal's visit had robbed Grant of his peace of mind.

He had originally asked Crystal out for the same reason he dated other women at the base. Camouflage. And until now, it had always worked. After several dates, during which he was attentive, charming, mildly amorous, they began to preen themselves, chalking up his respectful attitude as proof that his intentions were serious or that they were different from the other women he dated.

Since he had a reputation for being something of a stud, what other reason could there be for his restraint? Then the slow retreat, the calls that came farther apart, the dates that ended a bit too soon. Sometimes they got bored and called it off themselves. Other times, he would confess that he had a commitment elsewhere, that he had to break their relationship off because he didn't think it was fair to them. The thing that amazed him was that no one ever blew the whistle on him. Maybe they didn't want to admit to their friends that they hadn't turned him on—or maybe they simply didn't think it was important.

But until now it had always kept the husband hunters off his back. It still seemed incredible that he'd been so aroused by Crystal that he'd actually made out with her. It was so foreign to everything he knew about himself—or thought he knew. She wasn't even that attractive. Oh, she dressed well, and probably some men went for that iceberg type, but the only kind of women he could tolerate for long were the pliant, nonaggressive ones.

And Crystal had too many sharp edges, including that clever

brain of hers. She'd end up looking like a harpy someday when she put on a few more years—could he tolerate living in the same house with her, eating breakfast across the table from her every morning, coming home to her at night?

On the other hand, this whole business had come on the heels of his conversation with General Krause this morning—which was why he was sitting here, sipping his Scotch, trying to make a decision.

He had known, when Krause took him aside after staff meeting, that it wasn't about anything official. But he'd expected it to be some task that the general, who often used Grant as his eyes and ears, wanted him to do. So when the old man offered him a drink and said he wanted to talk to him about a personal matter, his stomach muscles had tightened with apprehension. What the hell had he done? Was he in for one of the general's notorious ass chewings?

Krause's first words were innocuous enough. "Have you ever thought about settling down and starting yourself a family, Grant?"

"I'm having too much fun playing the field, sir."

"That's okay for a captain or even a major, but when a man reaches your rank and age—how old are you, anyway?"

"Thirty-six, sir."

"A thirty-six-year-old man who's wearing silver leaves has to think of priorities. You know how the military is—it only tolerates so much diversity, and then it comes down hard. A swinging colonel doesn't set well with the higher-ups. So maybe you'd better start looking around for a nice little woman who'll be a help to you. I don't know how many times I've given that advice to young officers, and it's still as true as it ever was, no matter how people tell you the military has changed. 'Find yourself a decent girl, someone who's supportive and who's willing to stay in the background,' I tell them. But no, they go for the sex kittens or the women's libbers, and then it's good-bye career. Now you—I think you've got the stuff it takes, Grant. There's no telling how high you could go if you play your cards right."

"Yes, sir. Thank you, sir," Grant had said, hiding his surprise.

General Krause might talk in clichés, he reflected now, and he might be a notorious ass pincher whom the younger wives all detested, but he also belonged to the select group who ran the air force, who could break a man and do it so smoothly that he could never be sure who had scuttled his career. Once designated a loser, the man just didn't advance. His assignments did nothing to help his career, and he didn't get appointed to the right service schools at the appropriate times. Instead, he got shuffled off to some jerkwater base or station, far from the center of power, and there was never anything tangible to point a finger at or file a complaint about.

So Krause's advice was valid—and something to be taken seriously. Very seriously. In his own devious way, the general was putting him on notice, telling Grant that if he watched his step, he would rise in direct proportion to the general's own advancement—and Major General Krause was known to be in line for his third star.

Which was why Grant had stopped off at the club after work to fortify himself and think over the ramifications of the general's advice. Then he'd run into Curly Browne, one of the few men on base he felt comfortable with, and they'd sat there hashing over old times at the academy, where they'd been classmates. He'd had too much to drink again—something that was happening too often these days—and then he'd gone home to be accosted by Crystal.

Well, Colonel Norton—full bull, eagle on the shoulder—did have a better ring than Lt. Colonel Norton. And General Norton sounded even better. It could happen. He could make it. And then maybe those two old men down in Florida, his father and his grandfather, with their pride and their expectations, would be satisfied. They'd been a millstone around his neck ever since he could remember. They hadn't been willing to settle for anything less than the best, so he'd never had the luxury of being able to fail at anything he'd ever done.

Despite the difference in their ages, his father (General Earl G. Norton, USAF Retired)) and grandfather (Major General Grant E. Norton, USA Retired) were as alike as twins, living side by side in that retirement community in Florida, both having outlived their wives by several decades.

"Too tough to die," his father was fond of saying.

"Too damned ornery," his grandfather always echoed.

Well, maybe when he got his star, they would be content. It wasn't that they bugged him about it. No, it never seemed to enter either of their minds that he wouldn't do as well as they had. They hadn't once, even when he was a kid, consid-

ered the possibility that he wouldn't end up a general, too.
Grant Norton, the third generation of generals, was to be their
crowning glory, the cherry on top of the ice-cream sundae. So
far, he had made his promotions below the zone, which kept
them off his back. The only thing they bugged him about was
his single state.

"Time you started producing the next generation of Nortons," his grandfather had said during Grant's last visit to Florida. "You're running out of time—you don't want to have kids
too late in life. Besides, older men make females. Takes a
young man to make boy babies."

Grant didn't point out the biological fallacy of his grandfather's old-fashioned beliefs. In fact, he never argued with
either of them because if he did, he knew he'd lose.

He also hadn't pointed out that being the son and grandson
of generals had been more a hindrance than an asset in his
career. No matter what he did, he couldn't win. Even at the
academy, there'd been those cadets who believed that the
instructors favored Grant because of his background. Later,
when his promotions had come along so quickly, he was aware
that other officers chalked it up to influence. And in that, they
were partially right. He had earned his silver oak leaf by hard
work, but the fact that he'd been assigned to jobs that gave
him a chance to show what he could do—that wasn't luck.

His mentor, Major General Krause, was fond of telling Grant
how he himself had been a snot-nosed shavetail, fresh out of
the Point, when he'd been assigned as junior aide to General
Earl Norton, that he'd learned everything he knew from the
old man.

So Grant didn't delude himself. He had inherited the chance
to make a run for the top. But that didn't mean that he couldn't
fall on his face. That conversation today had been a warning
as well as a promise. It would be stupid to take it lightly. A
paternity suit now—he didn't have to ask himself what that
kind of scandal would do to his career. He'd seen other men
scuttled by far less.

His eyes pensive, he stared at his reflection in the smoky
mirror behind the bar. It would be hard for anyone to recognize
Lt. Colonel Norton in this man who looked like a local with
his faded aloha shirt, his shapeless beachcomber's trousers, his
longish hair. The hair was a wig—very expensive and not
totally convincing. But he'd learned the hard way to camouflage

himself even in a bar that was off limits to military. Because there were always other military men who didn't give a rat's ass about off-limits signs.

The last time, it had been a sergeant from the motor pool, someone who had driven Grant, in the company of General Krause, to a couple of social functions in downtown Honolulu. The man had been sitting at the bar that day. He'd almost stared a hole in Grant when he'd walked in.

Luckily, he must have worried about the ramifications of his own presence there because he'd gulped down his drink and disappeared, and nothing had come of it. But Grant had bought the wig the next day, and he wore it every time he went cruising now.

The cruising was relatively new. At first, he'd been careful to stay away from other gays, either toughing it out when the urge came upon him or, when he got too horny, frequenting a bathhouse in whatever large city was nearest the base where he was currently assigned. But lately he'd relaxed his guard a little. With the wig as camouflage, he felt sure that his own mother wouldn't recognize him. People only saw what they expected to see—and no one would expect to see Lt. Colonel Norton in an off-limits bar near Hotel Street.

A hand touched Grant's arm, and he stiffened, only to relax when he realized who it was. The man standing there, smiling at him, was young, not much older than twenty. His tousled hair and heavy-lidded eyes gave him the appearance of a man who'd just crawled out of bed. Billy was Grant's latest paid lover—and sex with him was fantastic. Oh, he was businesslike about collecting his fee first, but after that he was surprisingly agreeable.

"You been waiting for me long, Hawkeye?" he murmured. The bartender brought a beer, dropped it in front of him, and moved away fast. He didn't seem to notice Billy's seductive smile. Billy was a flirt—he courted danger by coming on to every reasonably attractive male he came in contact with. He liked his partners rough and tough, and Grant liked playing the father, who could punish or reward in equal doses.

"I'm really hot tonight, lover," Billy said, squirming a little. It was one of his little tricks that was beginning to get on Grant's nerves. Billy leaned closer and, under cover of the darkness, slid his hand between Grant's thighs and squeezed hard. "Man, you're really hung—I don't think I can wait much longer. I feel horny as hell tonight."

"When aren't you horny?" Grant said. "You were born horny—and gay."

"Oh, no, you're wrong. I was perfectly normal until some older dude seduced me. Then I found out I was a flaming gay and probably had been for years. And what's your sad story, lover? Who brought you out of the closet?"

The question annoyed Grant. He didn't like talking about himself, and he especially didn't like remembering his first lover. It was a long time in the past, but it still hurt because the affair had been so casual on Jake's part.

Jake had been so blatantly a hedonist, someone who had no inhibitions as long as his sexual urges were gratified. Once he had admitted cheerfully to Grant that he would screw his eighty-year-old grandmother as long as she was a consenting adult. The only thing he drew the line at was kids and animals.

The first time hadn't been all that traumatic, even for Grant with his uptight moral code. It had been so spontaneous, something that could be excused because it had happened under unusual and favorable circumstances.

Jake and he had been thirdclassmen at the academy that year, and they had gone to Aspen over Labor Day, the three days when the doolies' parents took over the academy, leaving upperclassmen free. Although Grant wasn't interested in ski bunnies, he had gone along because he needed a vacation— and besides, he liked Jake with his breezy quips, his instant friendships with everybody he met.

The weekend had started out wrong. Not only did it rain instead of snow, a steady downpour that gave no signs of letting up, but the resort Jake had chosen was full of old people, not the singles they'd expected. Disgruntled and bored, they had gone to their room and ordered up a bottle of Scotch. They were both a little drunk, lounging on their beds in their khaki skivvies, swapping yarns and letting down their hair, a rare thing for Grant. He had been telling Jake about his own special bane, his father and grandfather, when he realized that Jake was staring at him, his eyes fixed, obviously not listening.

At first he thought Jake was bored by his reminiscences. Did Jake think he was bragging? Sure, everybody knew about his father and grandfather, but he'd never talked about them

before, and Jake *had* asked him the question that had started
the conversation.

"How come you never drag anyone to the hops?" Jake said
abruptly.

"I don't have time for females. You know the pressure on
me—I can't just squeak through. I have to shine, man."

"Yeah, but even grinds have fun sometimes. So how come
you've never let me fix you up with one of my sister's college
friends?"

"Hell, I'm not ready for it. First thing you know, you get
serious about some girl and then you end up trying to feed a
wife on lieutenant's pay. Not for me, chum," Grant said, wishing Jake would change the subject. Like most rationalizations,
it was only partially true. The truth was that he had no desire
to start dating. It took too much energy, and besides, he'd
always been a bust with women.

"How about a little refresher?" Jake said, picking up the
bottle.

Not waiting for an answer, he came over to fill Grant's
glass. But instead of moving away, he sat down on the edge
of the bed. His eyes, a shade of green that seemed almost
transparent in some lights, were very bright, and his face was
flushed, his lips very red. It came to Grant that his friend was
feeling his liquor. Hell, so was he. In fact, he found it too
much of an effort to shift his position when Jake's bare leg
pressed against his thigh. Even when Jake rested his hand on
his knee, Grant didn't move aside to give him more room.

He raised his glass to his lips, only to discover that it was
empty again. Without asking his permission, Jake filled it, then
reached forward to sit the bottle on the floor beside the bed.
The room got dark suddenly, and Grant realized that Jake had
turned off the lamp. He closed his eyes, too groggy to protest,
and also a little bemused by the sudden warmth between his
thighs. Was he sleeping? He usually only felt this horny when
he was dreaming, those strange, crazy dreams with faces and
images that disappeared when he awoke.

With a start, he realized what was happening, that it was
Jake's hand that was causing the warmth—and the pressure.
Jake was touching him—no, more than that. He was fondling
him, stroking him, and god, it felt good! He knew he should
sit up, should ask Jake what the hell he thought he was doing.
But the warmth had become a white-hot fire, and he didn't

move, not even when Jake bent and kissed him squarely on the lips.

The walls of the room seemed very close, as if he had suddenly expanded like Alice in Wonderland—or as if only one part of him had expanded, become a monster that was growing, engulfing him, negating all the things he always taken for granted. Nothing existed but the pleasure, the ache, the need. When Jake stopped stroking him, he groaned in frustration and frantically pushed Jake's hand down against his swollen member.

Jake laughed softly. "Don't worry—I'm not stopping. I just want to check the door and make sure it's locked."

Sanity crept back as soon as Jake left his side. Grant could have jumped up then, could have put on a righteous act and blasted Jake with his contempt. Instead he remained there, motionless, expectant, waiting.

When Jake came back and knelt beside the bed, pressing his mouth against Grant's belly, something inside Grant, some barrier, gave way, and he surrendered to the unthinkable. It was at that moment that he crossed over the line, moving from what he had always believed about himself, the excuses he'd given for his lack of interest in women—that he was fastidious, that he didn't have time for involvement—to the admission that what he wanted, what he needed for sexual satisfaction, was not a woman, but another man.

They didn't leave the room that night or the next day. They had food sent up, and they spent the time in bed. Jake was incredibly horny, a satyr, and he gave no excuses for his aberration. He loved sex—any way he could get it. He initiated Grant to all the ways possible between two men—and he did it so casually and unashamedly that there was no self-consciousness between them.

"I had this older cousin—he was a real stud," he told Grant as they were eating breakfast the next morning. "He liked it any way he could get it, and since he was about eight times bigger than the rest of us, he bullied us into doing what he wanted. We had this place in the woods, sort of a shack. The things that went on there you wouldn't believe. Then I found out that I liked girls even better than I did boys—but I don't think that's going to happen to you, friend, and that ain't good, not for a military man. You're going to have a hard row to hoe because the military won't tolerate gays."

He paused to pour himself more coffee. "Guys like me—we can get away with it if we're careful. I'm AC-DC, and I can use chicks as a cover. Soon as I get my bars, I'll look around, find myself a nice, wholesome girl, the kind that's willing to stay home and mind the kids—and I'll take care of her needs because I'm always ready. I wouldn't have approached you today except I was bored stiff—and besides I've had this hunch about you for a long time. Oh, it's nothing you do. Not a twitch or a simper—which is a lot of bullshit anyway. Most gays look as normal as hell. But we'll have to cool it when we get back to the academy. We can fool around now and then when we get the chance, but we'll have to do it away from the academy. It just takes one rumor and zap, that's the end. We have to think of our future in the air force—and take my advice. Don't stay a bachelor too long."

But of course Grant *had* stayed a bachelor. The thought of sleeping with a woman was abhorrent to him. Over the years, he learned to cover his tracks, to never patronize a bar where he was likely to meet men from his base. Usually, when he reported in at a new assignment, it didn't take him long to make a contact. He paid his lovers well for their favors, was careful to keep the relationships casual. No pretenses that it was love—it was sex, pure and simple, that he paid for.

Billy was his latest partner. He was good in bed, and he wasn't greedy. He liked to play games—but that came with the territory. Grant was pretty sure Billy had at least three other men on the string, that he got money from all of them. But that was okay. In fact, he preferred it that way. When the urge came on him, he called Billy and made arrangements to meet him at the Tropic Club. They had a couple of drinks, then left separately and met in a small, out-of-the-way hotel where Billy had registered earlier. Although he only signed one name to the register, Billy always paid for a double, saying that a friend might be staying with him overnight. That way there was no beef from the hotel management, who were only interested in collecting double room rate, not in the moral standards of their guests.

Sometimes they rented a projector and screen and watched a sex movie together while they had a few drinks, and sometimes they just got it on immediately. Either way, when he finally left the hotel, Grant was always at peace with himself, the raging need appeased for a while.

As for the women he dated, they were strictly cover. Better to have the reputation of being a swinger than to have it nosed around that he was queer. Even with the gay rights talk these days, a homosexual would never be tolerated by the military, which was a hundred years behind the rest of the country. Grant had no quarrel with that. Because one thing was constant. He might be gay, but he was also a genuine political conservative, which had helped him to maintain his secret. After all, it was liberals who were first to come under suspicion—

"What's the matter, lover?" Billy purred. "You got troubles? Tell your little ole chicken about it—maybe he can kiss it and make it right."

Grant looked at him with a jaundiced eye. The truth was that Billy was beginning to get on his nerves. All that coy talk—and he was also becoming a little nosy. Lately, he had asked Grant several times what line of work he was in and if he had a wife and kids at home. Well, it was time to cool things off. Maybe this should be the last time. Because he wasn't going to lay himself open to blackmail. He'd heard tales about how the chickens turned on the hawks. . . .

Grant winced, suddenly uncomfortable with his own thoughts. It was the labels that bothered him. Chicken and hawks . . . fairy . . . twitch . . . nance . . . gay. And yet, that's what he was. Before he'd known that he was homosexual, he'd always thought of gays in stereotype. High-pitched voices and lisps and swishy walk, all the clichés. He hadn't thought of them as being green-eyed hedonists with strong, muscular bodies, of being men like Jake.

Grant took a long drink of his Scotch. Even now, it hurt, remembering how Jake, flip to the end, had told him that since he was getting married he'd decided to stop the "kinky" stuff. Good luck and all that, chum. Don't get caught in any sticky wickets.

He hadn't realized until then that it was possible to feel jealousy for another man, to suffer from a sense of betrayal, just like a heterosexual. He had gone to Jake's wedding—to have stayed away would have caused talk—and he had hated Jake's bride in her white wedding gown, hated the way she'd clutched Jake's arm as they left the chapel. What had Jake really felt that day? Was it possible that he had given up men completely? Grant hadn't seen him since June week, hadn't tried to keep in touch. Now he wondered where Jake was, if he'd stayed in the air force, if he had any kids, how he was getting along. . . .

"Well, lover? Cat got your tongue tonight?" Billy said, his voice peevish. "I hope not. I got plans for all your parts—if you ever get it together."

"Why don't you go on over to the Clarkson? I'll be along after I've had another Scotch."

"Not too many," Billy warned. "You know what that does to your libido."

After Billy was gone, Grant motioned for the bartender to bring him another Scotch. He took his time over it, trying to sort out his thoughts. He was right about dumping Billy, but it did present problems—making a new contact and finding a new place to hang out. And every time he made a change, it got more dangerous because, in so many ways, Honolulu was still like a small town.

The whole island of Oahu was military oriented. Just going to and coming from the Tropic Club presented a problem, even in the getup he wore. Hell, you couldn't move a block in Honolulu without bumping into someone in uniform. If he was ever caught up in a raid at the hotel or in an off-limits bar, he'd be up the proverbial creek. Maybe he should create a false identity, keep a fake ID card on him when he went cruising— yeah, that might be wise.

He could ask the bartender, who knew where anything could be bought for the right price, about a fake ID card. But not tonight. Right now, he had to come to a decision about Crystal before he joined Billy for a little fun and games.

What a lousy break that he'd asked her out that first time! She had seemed perfect for his needs—good-looking enough to be an asset and yet not so good-looking that she wouldn't be grateful for the invitation. But something about her, some- thing calculating and watchful, had turned him off, and he'd dropped her after two dates.

Which made what had happened later so incredible. God, he hadn't realized it was even *possible* for him to get it on with a woman. He really must have been drunk—or more likely drugged. But the evidence that he'd had intercourse had been unmistakable. He could even vaguely remember pounding away—but he'd been so damned out of it that he'd thought it was a man he was banging.

So it was rotten luck that he'd gotten her pregnant—or *was* it? Was it possible that this was the solution to another pressing problem?

"Get yourself a wife," General Krause had said. He'd been talking about Grant's reputation for being a swinger, but it could apply just as well to his real problem. Crystal was no starry-eyed virgin, expecting fireworks on her wedding night. From what she'd said, she wasn't interested in having sex with him. Which wasn't so surprising, considering what a bust the first time must have been. What had she said—that he could go his own way once they were married? Did she suspect something—or was she telling him that she didn't want his services in bed?

If so, that would solve one problem. Not even to further his career could he make love to a woman. And she was right about one thing—she did have the qualifications for a good air force wife. She was shrewd, cool under fire, willing to do anything to get what she wanted—hell, it was possible that she had staged that whole business, which meant she was a very clever woman. Even though the age difference between them was bound to cause talk, still she would be his first wife, not a second wife who had replaced an older one he'd dumped. Also, Crystal was an air force brat, was familiar with the realities of service life and would have no illusions about it. She already had a good idea of how protocol worked.

Yes, he could do worse. In fact, she was just what he needed, so why was he still hesitating? Was it because, on a gut level, he simply didn't like her?

His sexual preferences didn't mean that he hated women. On the contrary. But he hadn't taken to Crystal from the first. Something about her, a feeling that she was weighing every word she said to him, had been a turn-off.

But maybe that part was all for the best. He wouldn't give out any signals that she might misunderstand. He would tell her he had an impotency problem. That way, there'd be no demands he couldn't satisfy—and no hurt feelings. So it just might work. He'd be killing two birds with one stone. A man headed up the military ladder needed the right woman behind him. Hadn't he heard that phrase a dozen times since his academy days when the commandant of cadets had laid it on the line, telling the graduating seniors the importance of choosing the right wife? And Crystal met all the requirements, including one the commandant *hadn't* mentioned. She was a cold fish sexually, which made her the perfect wife for a homosexual.

It might turn out to be a marriage made in hell, not heaven, but both of them would benefit from it—and there was the kid, too. No reason, just because he was gay, that he couldn't be a good father. He might even be a great father....

Late that night, after he returned to his condo, Grant dialed Crystal's phone number. She answered so quickly that he knew she must still be up.

"This is Grant," he said.

There was a brief pause, then, "Yes?"

"When do you want to tell your parents that we're getting married—and how soon should we set the date?"

CHAPTER
✦ 13 ✦

YEARS LATER, DURING A TIME OF GREAT CRISIS IN CRYSTAL'S life when she was reviewing the past, trying to come to terms with her mistakes, she looked back and realized that the morning she announced her engagement to her parents was that rare thing, a perfect day.

She had laid her trap adroitly, using her knowledge of her mother's nature, and when the trap was sprung, the part of herself that took pleasure in tormenting Janet savored every moment of her triumph. It almost made up for other, far less triumphant times in her life.

Her mother, to be sure, was suspicious as soon as Crystal wandered into the kitchen an hour later than usual, still wearing her robe, her hair uncombed and her face bare of makeup. Janet gave her a long look, then pointedly glanced up at the kitchen clock on the wall before she returned to her papaya.

So it was Maurice, sitting across from Janet at the breakfast table, who asked the obvious question.

"I thought you'd already left for work, hon. You sick or something?"

"Feeling *good*," Crystal said. She opened the refrigerator door, took out a plastic container of orange juice, and poured herself a glass. The juice had a metallic taste because it had been too long in the refrigerator, but she sipped it anyway, standing by the sink and staring out the window at a fat mynah bird who was scolding the neighbor's cat from the safety of a mango tree.

She was aware that her mother had put down her cup and was watching her openly now. Janet was wearing one of her cotton muumuus; it was so short that it showed her rounded thighs. Although she wore no makeup and her hair was screwed into a knot on top her head, her mouth had a too pink, swollen look as if she'd just climbed out of bed after a night of love.

Crystal discovered there was a sour taste in her mouth—and it wasn't from the orange juice. Although she was sure that this time she held all the cards, the old hurt/hatred/envy stirred within her. It was grossly unfair that her mother, who was more than twice her age, should still look like the first runner-up in the 1960 Miss America Beauty Pageant—which was what she'd been when Maurice, a young lieutenant with a brand-new OTS commission, had courted and married her.

It always galled Crystal when her mother casually dropped this tidbit of information into the conversation on meeting someone new. How many times had she heard that old refrain? "Oh, I see that paisley scarfs (or wedgie heels or cherry-red lipstick) is back in style. I remember how popular they were the year I was first runner-up in the Miss America Beauty Pageant."

And then the interested questions, the modest answers, dragged out of Janet so reluctantly, the compliments about how young she looked, and always, although it was never spoken aloud, the implied pity that Janet's daughter had not inherited her mother's stunning good looks.

Crystal, who had made a study of her mother, was on to all her tricks. What's more, she frequently borrowed them herself—but not, she was aware, with Janet's skill.

But give her time. Already, she was one up on Janet. By marrying Grant, a man with prospects that Maurice had let slide through his fingers, she had taken a step that Janet could never match. Her mother valued money, valued prestige, even though she was too indolent to go after them herself. In a few minutes, she would get a shock that would knock those scruffy Japanese zoris right off her slightly dusty feet. . . .

"You do know that you're already late for work, don't you?" Janet helped herself to a danish, buttering it with a lavish hand. "You could lose your job over this, you know. But then you can always go to your friend, General Pritchard, and ask him to use his influence to get you another one—that *is* why you were cultivating Shelley Pritchard before she dropped out of sight so mysteriously?"

It took every ounce of control Crystal possessed to look bored. So Janet knew how she'd gotten her job—and since she also knew about Shelley's disappearance, that meant the base gossip mills were really grinding away. Well, if Janet was trying to pump her, it wouldn't work. Personally, she thought Shelley had made an incredibly stupid move, eloping with that staff sergeant, but that didn't mean she meant to satisfy Janet's curiosity.

And just how long had her mother been sitting on the knowledge that General Pritchard had helped her get a job, waiting for the right time to plant one of her barbs? Right now, as Janet chewed on that danish like the pig she was, she looked very pleased with herself. But wait until she heard the real news.

"No problem," Crystal said, elaborately casual. "I called the office this morning and told them I wouldn't be coming back."

"You *what*?" Maurice set his coffee cup down with a clatter. "You mean you've quit your job?"

"You've got it, Maurice."

"You sure you want to do that?"

"I'm sure."

"I thought you liked working at the base."

"I loathed taking orders from that bunch of idiots."

"So what the hell do you intend to live on?" Janet demanded. Despite the anger in her voice, Crystal sensed the satisfaction underlying her mother's words and braced herself. "I hope you don't think *we're* going to support you. We've already committed our savings on a down payment on a condo in Huntington Beach. We're moving there the end of April."

Crystal took the news without blinking. When she gave her father a reflective look, his face reddened and he rustled his newspaper noisily. How long had they been planning this? And why the secrecy? Was it because he'd told her he couldn't help her with college tuition—or was it because they were so eager to be alone that they were moving three thousand miles away to get rid of her? Well, she had her own secrets—and this was the perfect time to drop her bombshell.

"How nice," she said. "I'm so happy for you. I know you've never been satisfied, living in this dump."

Janet frowned at her. "You do realize that there's no question of you sponging on us, don't you?"

"Sponge on *you*? I wouldn't dream of it."

"Then you'd better get yourself another job."

"Oh, that won't be necessary." She gave her mother a wide smile. "You see, I'm getting married."

The shock on Janet's face canceled out a lot of things. Crystal included her father's stunned face in her smile, noting in passing that the laugh lines at the corners of his eyes could only be called crow's-feet now. For some reason, the thought stung—and suddenly some of her satisfaction dissolved.

"I didn't know you were seeing anyone special lately," Maurice said.

"Oh, I've been dating someone very special. I just didn't feel like talking about it. Superstitious, you know. But last night, he proposed and I accepted. We're getting married the first of February. And don't worry about the expense of a wedding. Grant is taking care of that."

"Grant? Are you talking about that lieutenant colonel who took you out to dinner a couple of times?" Janet said sharply. "I thought he dropped you—"

"Wherever did you get that idea? I've been seeing him right along."

Briefly, some destructive emotion—anger, jealousy, rage—ravaged Janet's face. She must have realized how much she was giving away because she averted her eyes quickly, but when she picked up her cup, it rattled against the saucer. Her loss of control should have gratified Crystal, but instead the bitter taste was back in her mouth and a humiliating prickle stung her eyelids.

Why do you hate me so, Janet? she thought. Why couldn't you be glad for me? Is it because of that time you saw Daddy and me in the shower together? It wasn't my fault—I didn't know it was wrong for him to touch me there. After all, I was only ten years old. I wanted you to forgive me the way you forgave Daddy, but you never gave me another chance. . . .

"Well, this really is a surprise," Maurice said, and she was sure she read relief in his voice. "Why all the secrecy?"

"What secrecy? I'm a big girl now. I don't tell you everything I do. And anyway, you and Janet had your own little secret, didn't you?"

Maurice glanced at Janet, then away. "It wasn't that we

wanted—it wasn't really a secret. You knew things have been up in the air since I retired. Your mother is tired of Hawaii, and I'm ready for a change, too. But until we were sure . . . well, we thought it best to keep it to ourselves. You do understand, don't you?"

"Why, of course. Just like you understand why I didn't broadcast my relationship with Grant."

"Are you sure about this marriage? I wouldn't want you to rush into anything."

"I was sure of my own feelings for Grant right from the first, but I didn't know how he felt about me until last night."

"He's a lot older than you, isn't he?"

"Not that much older." Her eyes moved to Janet's stiff face. "Besides, I've always liked older men."

"You needn't think we're going to throw a fancy wedding for you," Janet said, her voice shrill. "I've got too much to do, getting ready for the move."

"I don't expect anything from you, Janet. Your only expense will be a new dress for yourself—that is, if you decide to come to the wedding. Grant is paying for everything. He's aware of your financial situation."

"We don't need his charity. I can pay for my own daughter's wedding," Maurice said quickly. "And your mother will take care of the preparations."

Although she didn't speak, Janet's eyes glittered with anger. Most of the time, she dominated Maurice, but that wasn't going to happen today, Crystal thought. This time, she would use some of Janet's own tricks on Maurice. Once it was a matter of pride, nothing or no one could change his mind.

"If you insist," she said blandly. "But Grant is perfectly willing to pay the bills. I told him that . . . well, that a wedding would be a real hardship for you and Janet."

"It's settled," Maurice snapped. "I don't want to hear any more about it."

Crystal blew him a kiss. "Thank you, Daddy," she said softly.

"Pretty proud of yourself, aren't you?" Janet said. "Well, don't expect it to all be peaches and cream. Being married to a military man isn't the easiest life in the world."

"Why, I'm looking forward to it! I consider it a real challenge, helping Grant with his career. Of course, he's already a lieutenant colonel, so we won't have to pinch pennies like

you and Daddy did when you were first married—not that
money is all that important to me."

"So you say. You mean to tell me that you'd marry the man
if he were an airman?"

"Of course I would. I love Grant—so don't you worry about
me. I'm going to be very happy. Of course, I hate to admit
that the possibility of being a general's wife someday isn't hard
to take."

"Don't hold your breath," Janet muttered.

"Oh, I won't. But it *is* a distinct possibility—did I tell you
that Grant comes from a very distinguished military family?
His father is General Earl Norton, and his grandfather—"

"Earl Norton is Grant's father?" Maurice interrupted. "Say,
he was commander of SAC when I was stationed in Nebraska.
You remember him, Janet. . . . Well, well, you're traveling in
high circles, little lady."

"I'm marrying Grant because I love him. And I intend to
do my best to see that he goes as far as his ability will take
him—if that's what he wants. I don't intend to hold him back
like some wives do."

"What do you mean by that?" Janet demanded. "If that crack
was aimed at me—"

"Crystal didn't mean anything—and don't be so damned
negative," Maurice said. "This fellow sounds like he'll make
Crystal a fine husband. Of course, I don't believe anyone is
good enough for my little girl, but she had to leave the nest
someday."

Or get shoved out, Crystal thought.

She laughed and went to sit in Maurice's lap, her arms
around his neck. "I'll always be your little girl, Daddy." She
kissed him squarely on the mouth. "I'm going to miss you. Of
course, Grant and I will always have room for you—and Janet,
of course—when you come to visit. We're getting quarters at
Hickam. One of those sets near the parade grounds that Janet
always drooled over."

Over Maurice's shoulder, she met the molten fury in her
mother's eyes. It was then that she was sure this was one of
the best days of her life.

It rained the morning of the wedding, which wasn't the
disaster it would have been anywhere but Hawaii. The rain was
gentle, warm, and it disappeared as quickly as it had appeared,

having washed away all traces of pollen and gasoline fumes, leaving the air so clear that it seemed to sparkle in the sun.

Crystal, wearing a wedding gown of white lace with a wreath of tiny white orchids in her hair, was in the front seat of her father's car while Janet, looking sulky and put-upon, occupied the cramped backseat. As they headed toward Hickam, Crystal saw a double rainbow, two half circles that began in a high valley in the Koolau Range and ended in a grove of kukui trees, always so much greener than other trees, at the base of the mountains. Although she usually had scorn for local superstitions, Crystal hoped the Hawaiians were right this time, that the double rainbow was a good omen, proof that she was doing the right thing—and that all the things she wanted were within her grasp.

There would be problems, of course. She would have to keep Grant happy, no matter what. His sexual preferences, for instance, were still a mystery, but she was prepared to cater to them. One thing she couldn't afford was a disgruntled husband who might go looking for sex somewhere else. Yes, she'd keep him happy in bed—that was one lesson she'd learned from her mother. Maurice, always so susceptible to female flattery, flirted with the little tootsies who came into the liquor stores where he worked, but it never went any further these days because he got all the sex he could handle at home.

And she'd do the same. She didn't want to devote the next fifteen years or so to furthering Grant's career only to have him take off with some sexy twit half his age when he reached male menopause.

Although they'd spent most of their evenings together since his proposal, he hadn't tried to make love to her. His goodnight kisses had been perfunctory at best. Part of her was relieved, but she was also a little piqued. She had prepared a speech about waiting to have sex until they were married, so it was galling that she hadn't been given a chance to use it. Well, it only proved that Grant had some sensitivity. Wasn't that one of the reasons she'd put him at the top of her eligibility list? Men with sensitivity could be easily manipulated—and she was just the one to do it. Yes, she had made the right choice, and she didn't owe anyone, especially Janet and Maurice, a thing. Not one bloody thing.

Of course there was a lot she had yet to learn about her groom. One thing that had surprised her was Grant's deference toward his father and grandfather, who had flown in two days ago to attend the wedding. She hadn't been flattered that they'd come all the way from Florida. She knew it was because they'd wanted to look her over and pass judgment on Grant's new bride.

Grant was a different man around them. If it wasn't ridiculous, she would have said he was afraid of those two old men. To see the three of them together was to look into the future and know how Grant would look someday. They all had those full heads of hair—although the older men's were salt-and-pepper gray—and the same lean, ramrod-straight bodies and cool, wary eyes.

Last night, Maurice and Janet had hosted a dinner party at the club for their future in-laws, one she knew they could ill afford. Maurice, although affable as usual, had seemed uneasy and had ended up drinking too much. Although he'd looked great in a well-tailored, tropical-weight sport coat, he'd been completely overshadowed by his distinguished guests—something Crystal had found herself resenting. It was one thing to be the object of their scrutiny herself. She had expected that. But it was infuriating, the way they'd dismissed Maurice, who was knocking himself out to impress them—and picking up the tab to boot.

As they'd put her through what could only be described as a grilling, subtle as it had been, she had felt like screaming, and when they'd finally left to return to their hotel, she'd been so relieved that when her mother, who'd been unusually quiet during dinner, said, "I've got a headache. Anyone want a drink?" Crystal had joined her in a rare glass of Scotch.

It was during the party that Crystal made the decision to wean Grant away from his relatives, just as she meant to loosen her ties to her own parents. With three thousand miles of ocean between them, that would be easy—but she wouldn't break off completely. If she did, how could she let Janet know about any triumphs that came her way in the future?

And why was Janet so quiet in the backseat now? She was staring out the window, her eyes veiled, her face expressionless. Was she still sulking over the expense of the dinner party at the club and the wedding reception—or was she counting the minutes until she would be rid of her daughter for good?

Crystal shrugged off her speculations. This was one day that Janet couldn't ruin for her. She was riding high—and it was only the beginning. The wedding, which would be held at Hickam's chapel, would be a success. Of that she was certain because she'd planned it herself. She just wished she could be as sure about the reception later, which Janet had arranged for. She had drawn up her own wedding invitation list with great care because she wanted a good show on her side of the aisle. She was satisfied with her choices—the most presentable of her parent's friends, a few Punahou classmates who were still on the island, three or four of the people she'd worked with, including Gracie Cummins and her former superior, Ms. Forester.

She had also invited Tai, knowing that if she didn't, it might cause comment since they had been good friends at Punahou; but she was relieved when Tai made the excuse that the boutique where she worked was short-handed and she couldn't get off for the wedding. She would have invited Shelley had she still been in Honolulu, but again, she was relieved that Shelley was in the Philippines with her new husband. Even though Shelley's father was General Pritchard, it might have been embarrassing if she'd turned up with her sergeant husband in tow.

Oddly, the one she really regretted not being there was Bobby Jo. How she would have liked to show off Grant to that nitwit with her soppy beliefs in romance. According to Bobby Jo's last letter, she was dating cadets now, but even if she married one, there was a wide, wide gap between a second lieutenant, fresh out of the academy, and a lieutenant colonel who might well be on the next colonel selectee list. Who knew? If Bobby Jo did marry a cadet, he might even end up serving under Grant—and, wouldn't *that* be delicious?

CHAPTER

✦ 14 ✦

IT WAS A LITTLE TOO WARM IN THE CHAPEL, EVEN THOUGH its thick cement walls and red tile roof were designed to keep out the heat of the Hawaiian sun. The spicy, slightly rank odor of white carnations from the lavish display of flowers that flanked each side of the altar, the too piercing perfume of one of the women guests, and a whiff of forbidden cigar smoke tickled Crystal's nostrils as she stood beside Grant at the altar, and she was afraid that she would disgrace herself and sneeze as she listened to the chaplain's droning voice.

"—join this man and this woman in holy matrimony—"

Holy matrimony—strange words for this particular bride and groom. As far as she knew, Grant was affiliated with no special denomination, although he'd entered his religion as Protestant on their marriage license application. She, on the other hand, hadn't been in a church since she was a kid, but from now on she would see that they both went to chapel reasonably often. It would look good to Grant's superiors.

The chaplain, a large man with a florid face, had reached the end of the ceremony, and Crystal made the proper response, feeling nothing, not even triumph now. Then it was over, and she lifted her veil for Grant's brief kiss.

The reception was held at the Hickam Officers Club. One of her mother's friends, the wife of a retired colonel, had decorated the tables with tropical flowers that she'd brought from her own yard—bird of paradise, torch ginger, heliconia, and anthuriums—which added a festive air to the barny ball-room. Unfortunately, the food was uninspired and obviously chosen for economy, even though Crystal had enlisted her father's aid in an effort to force Janet to abandon her parsimonious instincts. The champagne, too, was a bottom-of-the-list domestic brand, and the canapes and hors d'oeuvres were the cheapest available from the club's caterer.

Crystal was too elated to care. In her classically simple wedding gown, she was aware that for once her appearance eclipsed Janet's. Privately, she thought her mother's choice, an electric-blue dress suit, was much too flashy for a good mother-of-the-bride image. Was Janet trying to outshine her—or had it been an honest mistake?

Grant's manners were impeccable as he introduced Crystal to his colleagues and to General Krause, his mentor. Although she greeted the general with courtesy, Crystal resented the joking remark he made about their wedding night plans. She felt a little sorry for his wife, a tall, gaunt woman who talked with a hoarse, too breathy voice and was a nonstop smoker.

"Welcome to the club," said Mrs. Krause, who had already asked Crystal to call her Sophie. The diamonds on her fingers caught the overhead light as she waved away the smoke from her own cigarette. "I could say, 'You'll be sorry,' but since you're an air force brat, you already know the score. If you have any problem, give me a buzz. I've been through the officer's wife thing from the bottom up—and frankly, I don't think it's worth the bother."

"Oh, come now, Sophie." There was a forced joviality in her husband's voice. "You know you love the perks of being a general's wife. When we were stationed at SHAPE head-quarters, you got to know some of the most important men in the world."

"I got to *meet* them," Sophie corrected. Her words were slurred, and Crystal wondered how many glasses of champagne she'd already downed. "I could've been one of the maids for all the attention they paid me."

The general's fleshy face darkened, and Crystal quickly changed the subject.

It was later, when she was looking around for Grant, that Crystal saw General Krause dancing with her mother. It was obvious that he considered himself an expert at the tango. Janet gave Crystal a triumphant smile as the general lowered her in a deep dip, his face a little too flushed. Crystal watched with cynical eyes. Trust Janet to latch on to Grant's boss. And try to upstage her daughter at her own wedding.

When the music stopped, she approached the couple, her smile intact. "I see you've met my mother, General Krause," she said. "It took my wedding to get her out of the house. She's usually such a stay-at-home—except for bingo night at the club. She tells us that she hates crowds, but I think what she hates is having to put on shoes." She gave a tinkling laugh. "Some of my friends at Punahou got the idea we were locals because they never saw Janet in anything except a muumuu and go-aheads."

Janet gave her a furious look, which Crystal ignored. "Do you mind if I borrow General Krause for a while, Janet? I want to introduce him to some of my friends. They're all dying to meet him."

Laying her hand on General Krause's burly arm, she led him away. She didn't look back, but then she didn't need to. She knew that Janet was staring after them, her eyes murderous.

"You've got a great-looking mother, young lady," General Krause said.

"I'm very proud of her," Crystal said. "Did she tell you that she was a runner-up in the 1955 Miss America Beauty Pageant?"

"She did mention something about it, although she didn't give the year. I'm surprised she didn't win."

"So was she. It was the disappointment of her life. She wanted to be a dancer, but then she met my dad and they got married. She never lets him forget that she gave up a career for him, although . . . well, I happen to believe that being a wife and mother is better than any career. I guess that makes me sound pretty old-fashioned."

"Makes you sound very sensible. I have to admit I had my doubts when I heard how young you are, but as usual Grant knew what he was doing. I have high hopes for that boy. A chip off the old block—off both of them. Reminds me of myself at that age."

He looked so expectant that she said quickly, "Your age? There can't be that much difference between you and Grant, General Krause."

"Flattery will get you everywhere." As he reached out to take a glass from a passing waiter, his hand brushed her breast.

She knew it wasn't an accident, but she kept on smiling as if she hadn't noticed. God, he was really gross—that too red mouth and those piggy eyes and his round little paunch that looked as if he'd gone to the trough too often.

Crystal met the general's eyes, and she was nonplussed by the shrewdness there. It was impossible that he could guess what she was thinking, and yet—she'd better be careful. He might be a lech, like everybody said, but he hadn't earned his stars by being stupid.

"I was so delighted that you and your wife could come today," she said quickly.

"Wouldn't have missed it. Grant is something of a protégé of mine, just like I was a protégé of his father's. You two must come for dinner soon. I'll have Sophie call you."

Crystal hid her elation. "We'd love that, sir."

"We make a point of seeing my subordinates socially from time to time. Grant will tell you that I run a tight ship—but everybody is part of the same family, too. I'm sure you're going to fit right in. Yes, I'd bank on that."

"Thank you. I'll certainly try," she said, resisting the desire to pull away from the too warm, too moist hand he laid on her arm.

An hour later, when most of the guests were gone, Crystal slipped away to the women's lounge to renew her lipstick, glad for the chance to be alone for a while. Her face ached from keeping a perpetual smile on her lips, but she was satisfied that she'd made a good impression on the guests who mattered. She had made it plain, by innuendo and by seemingly artless comments, that although she was so much younger than Grant, she wasn't some chickie who had hooked him with sex. It helped that the senior wives at the reception were well aware she wasn't a second wife, the thing they resented the most. The quickest way to have them close ranks on her was to play the flirt, so she'd been very careful to act reserved around their husbands.

She was sure she'd succeeded when one of the senior colonels' wives, who was the current manager of the base thrift shop, asked if she would donate a few hours a week to the shop, and she'd also accepted an invitation to model at a charity fashion show. She had been polite but also a touch cool to the wife of one of the captains who worked under Grant. The woman, only a couple of years older than Crystal, was effusively friendly, but she'd kept her distance. After all, she *was* the wife of a senior officer now—and she intended to play that role to the hilt.

Grant was waiting for her when she returned to the reception room. He looked a little tired as he asked her, "Are you ready to go?"

As Crystal nodded, she tried to see her new husband objectively. He was attractive rather than handsome with his craggy face, his dark hair, and his brown, opaque eyes. Even so, she felt no physical attraction to him. Still, sleeping with him was part of the bargain. She could live with it—in fact, she'd have to be careful that he didn't guess how indifferent she was. A frigid wife would turn him off quicker than anything else—and she wanted this marriage to work.

She had moved her things to Grant's condo a day earlier, so there was no need to return to her parents' house. When they reached his place, Grant fixed them both a drink while she went into the bedroom to take off her wedding gown. After she had changed into a well-cut summer suit, she studied herself in the mirror, well pleased with her appearance, although the suit had played havoc with her checking account. She found herself wondering how Grant would like it, and when she went downstairs, she was gratified, from Grant's quick smile, to know that he approved of her taste.

Grant had arranged for a suite at the Halehana, a luxury hotel near Nawiliwili, Kauai, and had chartered a plane to take them there. Two hours after they left Honolulu, Crystal stood on the balcony outside their suite, which overlooked the hotel's famous lagoon.

She found herself humming along with a small group of musicians who were playing the Hawaiian wedding song in a clearing among the trees. As she watched a bare-chested Hawaiian youth running along the path, lighting luau torches that were strategically placed among the palms, she was aware of a nervousness she hadn't expected.

What would it be like to have Grant make love to her? Surely he wouldn't be as crude as that gorilla Kimo. He must have learned something from all those women he'd squired around, enough so it wouldn't be an ordeal. What a delicious joke if she'd hit the jackpot and had found herself a husband with excellent prospects, with a nice trust fund to augment his military pay, who also had enough skill to make sex interesting to her for the first time in her life.

She turned away and went to change into a dinner gown. It was backless and sheer; its deep emerald color did flattering things to her hair and eyes. When they went downstairs to the dining room, Grant seemed to be putting himself out to be pleasant, even though he'd been quiet on the brief plane ride to Kauai and during the trip up the coast in the hotel's jitney. He ordered a bottle of imported champagne, and as she sipped it during dinner, she couldn't help comparing the dry, aromatic burst of flavor in her mouth with the cheap domestic brand her mother had ordered for the reception.

After a dinner of broiled mahimahi and a salad of marinated artichoke hearts on a bed of taro leaves, she felt energized, far less exhausted than she'd expected. Grant talked easily about the reception, asking her questions about the guests she'd invited and listening to her answers as if he were really interested. Over brandy and Kona coffee, she told him, "I'm sorry your father and grandfather had to leave right after the wedding." At his nod, she added, "I liked both of them," although it would have been more accurate to say that she was impressed by their air of authority.

"They approved of you, too." Grant drained his glass before he added, "I'd rather they didn't know about the baby for another couple of months. They're pretty old-fashioned. When it's born, we'll tell them it was a premature birth. I want them to retain their good opinion of you."

The waiter, a husky Samoan, brought their dinner check for Grant to sign. Crystal waited until he was gone before she said, her voice tight, "It takes two to make a baby."

"I'm well aware of that. I didn't mean to insult you. I think this is the time to talk about ground rules. Being honest with each other is a good start, but sometimes it might involve hurt feelings. Honesty usually does. But it's the only way to make this marriage work."

She smiled into his eyes. "Oh, it will work. I guarantee that you'll be . . . pleased."

"You're sure of that, are you?"

"Of course. We have all the important things going for us. We both want the same thing—your success."

"And you're just the woman to help me succeed, aren't you? I'm a very lucky man."

There was an odd note in Grant's voice that made her frown. Then he smiled, and she relaxed because it was obvious he was trying to make this evening a success. She wouldn't ruin it by being suspicious and wary—not tonight.

"I'm a little tired," she said.

"Why don't you go on upstairs while I finish my drink? I'll be along shortly," he said.

Touched by his thoughtfulness, Crystal gathered up her purse. Of course, his tactful gesture wasn't really necessary. She wasn't a virgin, nervous about her wedding night. But she *was* a bride, no matter how the marriage had come about. He would expect her to act like one.

When he rose and came around the table to pull back her chair, she tilted her head and kissed his cheek.

"Don't be too long," she murmured.

Although Crystal took her time getting ready for bed, lingering over her bath, brushing her hair and applying lip gloss, Grant still hadn't come up by the time she slid between the cool sheets of the suite's king-size bed. She was dozing when the sound of his footsteps aroused her.

"Are you still awake, Crystal?" he said from the doorway.

She opened her eyes and sat up. As she stretched languidly, the sheet fell away from her shoulders, and she was well aware that her small, firm breasts were clearly visible through the sheer material of her gown.

"I've been waiting for you," she said.

She expected Grant to come to her then, but instead he turned his eyes away as if he were embarrassed. "Put on your robe and come into the sitting room. It's time we had a talk," he said.

He was gone before she could answer. When she came through the door a minute later, wearing her robe, he was sitting on a love seat, staring down at his clasped hands. His expression was so sober that her first thought was that he'd had bad news.

"What is it?" she said quickly.

He raised his eyes and stared at her fixedly. "I think I've made a mistake. We should have talked about this earlier. You must understand, Crystal—the intimacy of marriage is new to me, and it will take some getting used to. Also, I'm a very private man, and I find it hard to talk about personal things, so bear with me, will you?"

He looked so miserable that she almost went to him. She didn't because instinct, the instinct that so often warned her of impending rejection, was working full blast now. A feeling of pressure started up behind her left eye, and she massaged her temple absently.

"What are you trying to say?" she asked finally.

"That I have a very low sex drive. Which is the reason I've never married."

Pain, throbbing and deep, arched through Crystal's head. She pressed her fingers against her temple as if that could stave it off. "You got it up fast enough the night you got me pregnant."

Grant winced. "I can't explain what happened that night. God knows I've tried. All I can say is that I'm convinced someone spiked that drink I took away from Maureen. Some of those man-made hallucinogenics are unstable—they do weird things to people. Most of what happened is jumbled up in my mind, but I remember enough to know that we did have intercourse. But that doesn't change things. The doctors I've consulted about my problem tell me they can't find anything physically wrong with me."

He seemed unable to meet her eyes as he added, "I've been impotent since my late teens. I'm sorry if I misled you into thinking—I thought you understood that our marriage was strictly a matter of convenience."

A strangled laugh escaped Crystal's lips. She didn't believe a word of what he was saying. When would she ever learn? It was happening again. Once more, she had laid herself open to humiliation and rejection.

A lance of pain seemed to shatter the bone around her left eye. She pressed the palm of her hand tightly against her eye, held it there.

"Do you have a headache?" Grant asked, and the solicitude in his voice made her want to claw his face with her fingernails.

"I never have headaches," she snapped. "Why did you wait until now to tell me you were a—a eunuch?"

His face tightened. She watched him with savage, vengeful eyes, drawing pleasure from the knowledge that her words had stung. "I thought you understood that I had no interest in a real marriage. We never talked about it, but it was implied. . . . I was careful not to give you any reason to believe that I wanted sex with you."

The throbbing started up, deep inside her skull, a prelude

to the nausea and weakness that was the final manifestation of her migraines. Somehow she succeeded in producing a tight smile. "And what the hell makes you think I'm interested in having sex with you now?" she said.

He looked away. "I'm sorry. It seems I've made another mistake."

"You certainly did. The thought of you pawing me turns my stomach. I had a speech all prepared in case you tried anything."

"Then there's no problem, is there? As my wife, you'll have my support and respect, of course, but you're free to—to live your own life. I only ask that you be discreet. After all, we have the same goals. As I move up the promotion ladder, so will you. And we both want security for our child. There's no reason why this thing can't work out to both our benefit."

The nausea struck, twisting her insides. Careful not to jar her head, Crystal backed into a chair and sat down. She wondered dully why the room suddenly felt so cold—had Grant turned on the air conditioner?

How Janet, who believed all men were ruled by their penis, would love it if she ever found out the truth. She'd worry the subject like a terrier with a bone, stripping all the meat from it. Well, her mother was never going to have that satisfaction. Because this marriage was going to work, at least on the surface, no matter what sacrifices it took. As for Grant—at the moment, she wanted to hurt him, torture him on the rack, punish him. No matter how reasonable he sounded, she was sure that he was lying—lying through those perfect teeth.

Never mind that she had tricked him into this marriage. It was a lie that he was impotent—God knew he had responded with indecent haste the night she'd seduced him. As for his excuse that he'd been drugged and that was why he'd been able to perform—all she'd put in that drink was those lousy sleeping pills, certainly not some exotic aphrodisiac. He'd been groggy, of course, from the combination of drugs and alcohol, but it hadn't affected his libido. So what he was really saying, in his insufferably polite and superior way, was that he didn't find her desirable, not even to the extent of consummating their marriage.

And that she couldn't forgive him—that she wasn't good enough, attractive enough, sexy enough to warm the bed of the great womanizer, Grant Norton. Oh, she was acceptable as his wife. She could be trusted to be a good hostess, embrace the proper projects, make all the right moves—and she also wasn't so attractive that she'd make the senior wives jealous or resentful. In Crystal's opinion, it wasn't a coincidence that so many generals' wives were plain. It was almost an axiom in military circles that for a young officer to marry a real sexpot was to hurt his chances for advancement because the wives of senior officers didn't like having sexy young things around their husbands.

But Grant was wrong about one thing. She wasn't the sexual zero he obviously thought her to be. Kimo Kapiolani hadn't been all that interested in her at first, but after one session in his dune buggy, he'd been so crazy about her that he'd gone berserk when she'd broken it off. She could have done the same for Grant, satisfied his sexual needs, but not now. Not after he'd just delivered a body blow to her pride.

And maybe it was all for the best. Sex would just muddy the waters. Better to keep everything impersonal, a business deal. Love—if there was such a thing—involved jealousy and worry and the desire to put someone else's needs above one's own. She didn't need that.

Not that she wasn't going to enjoy telling Grant, in another month or so, how sorry she was that the doctor had made a mistake and she wasn't pregnant after all. She might even cry a little when she told him that the doctor was convinced her periods had stopped because she'd been in shock from her experience with him.

Maybe, in time, she would take a lover—maybe more than one. Grant had said they should be honest with each other? Oh, she would be honest all right. She would flaunt her affairs, tell him every bloody detail. Yes, she'd be discreet, but she'd do it because it suited her own best interests, not to save his face.

Crystal rose and smoothed the robe across her lap, knowing that there was little left to the imagination because of the sheerness of the material. It amused her that he looked—no, not apprehensive, but wary. Was it finally beginning to dawn upon him that she was in control, that despite the difference in their ages, he wasn't going to get his own way about everything?

"Okay, it's a deal," she said. "You may be a eunuch"—she rolled the word around her tongue— "but I'm not. I'm a perfectly normal woman, and I don't intend to live a celibate life. But I'll be careful. No one will suspect that you don't have the stuff to get it up. But if I have an affair with some good-looking stud, there'll be no recriminations, no jealousy. Is that understood?"

He was silent so long that she was surprised how agreeable he sounded when he finally spoke.

"It's a deal—although I don't like that word. I'd like to think that we're in this together for the sake of the baby you're carrying. I admit you're getting the short end of it. It's only fair that you have the freedom to—to look elsewhere for what I can't give you. I'm sorry about this, Crystal. It hasn't been easy for me to talk about something so personal. Like I say, I'm a very private man."

"And I'm a very determined woman. We should make a pretty good pair, shouldn't we? I'm also very tired. If you don't mind, I prefer that you sleep on the sofa tonight. Tomorrow we can talk about permanent sleeping arrangements. For now— good night. And pleasant dreams."

As she turned and walked unhurriedly toward the bedroom door, Crystal made a surprising discovery. For some reason obscure to her, the headache, which should have been raging by now, had totally disappeared.

CHAPTER
↟ 15 ↟

FOR THE PAST FIFTEEN MINUTES, BOBBY JO HAD BEEN HIDING out in the ladies' room—what her roommate, who was not only a self-styled intellectual but an Anglophile, called the "loo"—but she knew that eventually she would have to rejoin her date. She groaned under her breath, wishing she were back in her room in the freshman dorm. It wasn't that the cadet she'd been assigned was obnoxious or anything like that. It was just that he was so damned shy. No sparkle at all. And she did like men who were so sure of themselves that they carried most of the conversational load because being with someone shy made her tongue-tied, too.

So okay, she'd made a mistake, signing up for another blind date. It had seemed such a lark that first time, being interviewed by the academy's social hostess because they wanted to make sure she was presentable—and respectable. She'd gone along with it because it seemed the best way to look the cadet corps over. What she hadn't expected was to draw a Neanderthal the first time, and someone who looked about sixteen years old the second.

The hostess, a starchy type named Mrs. Gregory, had explained that just because a cadet signed up for a blind date, that didn't mean he was a social failure. "Our men are far from home, and their schedule"—Mrs. Gregory talked as if she had a mouthful of rocks, and she pronounced schedule as if it were spelled "shed-ule"—"is so full that they have no opportunity to meet suitable young women."

It had made good sense then, but that was before Bobby Jo met her dates. One who was incompatible she could shrug off and be philosophical about—but two? In fact, from what she'd seen of the cadet cadre so far, she was a little disappointed. Sure, a lot of them were prime physical specimens, but they looked so—so solemn, as if they were in training to be ministers or morticians, for God's sake.

No, they weren't at all what she'd expected. Next to the fun-loving, easy going boys at Punahou, they just didn't measure up. They might be "superior"—to use Mrs. Gregory's word—but most of them looked as if they had the weight of the world on their backs. Maybe it was because they were so brainy. They'd have to be smart to get into the academy.

Well, she couldn't wait till the hop was over so she could climb back on the chartered bus that had brought her here and end not only her date's misery but her own. Meanwhile, there were the next couple of hours to get through, and she wasn't looking forward to being pushed around the dance floor by someone with three left feet and sweaty hands. His name was Joseph Something—some unpronounceable name with lots of t's and z's—and he must have just squeaked by the academy's height requirements because he was only a couple of inches taller than her five-four-plus-heels.

He had average brown hair and average brown eyes and average everything else, and he was earnest. God, was he ever earnest! He hadn't smiled once, not even when she tried to lighten things up by asking him why freshmen were called doolies. He'd stammered something incoherent, and he'd looked as if he were in pain, which made her feel even more sorry for him. And he looked so young. Of course he had to be at least nineteen, a year older than she. He'd muttered something about putting in a year as an enlisted man before he bucked the quota—whatever that meant. It must be those short haircuts that made all of the doolies look like babies.

Well, there were no two ways about it; she was stuck. She had to go out there and face him again because no way was she going to hurt his feelings. But so help her, if he stepped on her feet or asked if she wanted another cup of punch one more time, she would scream—or faint dead away. At least that would take care of the dancing. The thing was, she still had to wait until that stupid bus left. So she might as well be a good sport about it. She really didn't want to make him feel bad.

"Did you come down from Denver?" The voice was female; Bobby Jo turned to meet the eyes of a plump girl in a floor-length shift that hugged her ample breasts and well-rounded hips.

"From Colorado College. I came on the chartered bus."

"Me too. I've never seen you around campus."

"I'm a freshman—I've only been at CC a few weeks."

"That explains it—how was your draw?"

"Draw?"

"Your date for the night."

"He's . . . very nice."

"A dud, huh? Well, sometimes you win and sometimes you lose. Mine keeps talking about the girl back home. I think he's afraid I'm expecting him to make a pass. The one I got for the fall hop was really neat. He hasn't called yet, but I keep hoping."

"Do you come to many of these dances?"

"As many as I can," the girl said cheerfully. "It beats sitting in my room. But this is my last year. I'm already a year older than most of the seniors. Luckily, I've been careful to keep on the good side of the Iron Lady." She laughed, but there was an edge in her voice that made Bobby Jo uncomfortable.

"Iron Lady?"

"Mrs. Gregory. You know, she's into corsets and all that."

Bobby Jo gave a dutiful laugh. "Why do you come if you don't have fun?"

"Oh, I have fun. At first, I used to think that . . . well, to tell the truth, I thought I'd catch myself a husband. But that never happened, and now the parade has passed me by—and that's *my* life story. I hope you have better luck."

"You've never—y'know, been serious about anyone?"

"Oh, lots of times. But no one's ever been serious about me. That's cadets for you. I think they indoctrinate them here at the academy about marrying the kind of girls that'll make good air force wives. Unfortunately, I don't fit the pattern. Wrong ethnic background and religion—and my mouth's too big. I pop off at the wrong times. I'm also a half-assed liberal, which doesn't set too well with military types."

Bobby Jo listened with fascination as the girl went on talking in a self-mocking way. Since she was saying some pretty derog-

atory things about the "military mind" and all that, Bobby Jo
wondered if she should let her know that her father was one
of those military types she was talking about. Of course, Daddy
was a chaplain—and besides, he'd voted for Jimmy Carter,
and he sent a check to the Democratic party every year.

It was strange this girl hadn't found a husband among all
those cadets. She was quite attractive, despite her plumpness.

"Are you having a good time?" the girl asked as if sensing
her wandering attention.

"My date's . . . well, he doesn't have much to say."

"He's probably overwhelmed," the girl said, her tone dry.
"Or maybe he's the silent type. The trouble is that the ones
with personality can have their pick of the females. They're
all spoiled—and very choosy." She looked Bobby Jo over with
frank curiosity. "You won't have any trouble scoring. Just look
around until you see one you like and then go after him."

"But I already have a date."

"Oh, come on. Where else are you going to meet a cadet?
They don't hang around the CC campus or the singles bar in
the Springs. My advice to you is to pick out one of the seniors
and then go for him. They're all so sex-starved that their glands
make them sitting ducks for a smart girl with your kind of
looks. Even with the pill, you wouldn't believe how many
babies are born soon after graduation every year."

She slid her hairbrush into her purse and rose. "I'll probably
see you around. I don't know why I bother coming to these
hops. Guess it's nostalgia—or maybe I've got a masochistic
personality. And good luck. Don't be afraid to drop your date
if something better comes along. It's a jungle out there, kid."

Bobby Jo stared after her, feeling depressed and vaguely
offended. After all, *she* wasn't looking for a husband. She was
only eighteen, and what she wanted at this stage of her life
was to have a good time without her parents breathing down
her neck and setting curfews and lecturing her about being a
"good girl."

After one last look at her freshly renewed makeup, she went
outside. She was looking around for her date when a hand
touched her arm and a familiar voice said, "Bobby Jo—that
is you, isn't it? I thought I saw you earlier, dancing with a
cadet, but I wasn't sure. You've done something new to your
hair, haven't you?"

Bobby Jo smiled up at Steven Henderson. She had always

liked Tai's fiancé—no, Tai's ex-fiancé. In the back of her mind, she had even hoped that she would see him here tonight like she had at the first hop. "I had it cut—and I'm really glad to see someone I know here," she said.

"This is your second hop, isn't it?"

"And maybe my last."

"Uh-oh. Another of the Iron Lady's prearranged dates?"

Bobby Jo giggled. Now that she thought about it, Mrs. Gregory did look as if she were wearing a steel girdle. "Guilty. I thought I'd give it another whirl."

"So where's your date?"

"He's probably getting me another cup of punch. He's already brought me three. Gurgle, gurgle."

Steven laughed. "Well, some of us were the grinds of our high school. We aren't all personality kids, but a lot of marriages develop from these hops. They're already calling Colorado Springs the mother-in-law of the air force."

Bobby Jo smiled and tried to think of something clever to say, but Steven was already going on.

"I was sorry to hear about the death of Tai's father, " he said.

Bobby Jo sobered immediately. "I always liked Sergeant MacGarrett. I can't believe he was guilty. Why, he wouldn't even put in a requisition for a new washer, and you know the base sergeant major could get anything he wanted from base supply. There must have been a mistake, or else someone—" She broke off, remembering that it had been Steven's father whom Sgt. MacGarrett had accused of lying.

"I liked him, too, even if he didn't want Tai to marry me." There was a tight line around Steven's mouth. "I was all torn up when Tai broke our engagement. That wasn't my doing. I wanted to work things out, but you know how loyal Tai is to her father. And she's got a stubborn streak as wide as her arm. Once she makes up her mind, nothing can change it."

"Don't I know! I remember when she decided that she wanted to take kung fu lessons. All those bruises and that sprained wrist, but she never gave up. I'm sure she did it to impress her dad, but all he said when he found out was that women shouldn't mess around in men's sports. It must've hurt, even though Tai made a big joke out of it. She never would admit Mac wasn't perfect. She's the best friend I have, Steven. I want to help her, but she's shut herself off from her friends. I think it's an Oriental thing—you know, about losing face."

"She wasn't raised as an Oriental. It's just her stiff-necked pride," Steven said shortly.

"Maybe they're the same thing," Bobby Jo said.

"Maybe. I've written her several times, but the letters come back. She didn't even leave a forwarding address when she moved off base." There was question in his voice, and Bobby Jo knew he was asking her for help. "I'd feel a lot better if I knew where the hell she is and how she's getting along. I don't suppose—"

He broke off, his jaw muscles tight, and it came to Bobby Jo that it wasn't only Tai who had too much pride. When Tai had written about her broken engagement, she'd only said that they'd both agreed to end their relationship because of the situation between their fathers, but it must have been a lot more than that—not that Tai would ever tell what had really happened. Well, her friend was close-mouthed—but that's what made her such a good friend. You could tell Tai anything, just *anything*, and it never went any farther.

And where exactly did her own loyalties lie? With Tai, obviously—but then Steven was asking for her help, and he looked as if he were suffering. Maybe it would be okay if she told him enough to relieve his worry about Tai. What harm could that do?

"Tai is getting along fine," she said. "You don't have to worry about her."

"Then you've heard from her lately?"

"Just a couple weeks ago. She's living in Honolulu, has a job, and is monitoring night classes at UH. I can't give you her address because I promised I wouldn't, but if you send a letter to her in care of the university, it should reach her."

"You're a jewel—you say Tai has a job? Is that necessary?"

"If she wants to eat, it is. The funeral and the lawyer's fees and the fine Mac owed the government took everything she had. She's clerking at a boutique in the Royal Hawaiian arcade. It's just temporary until next August when she reports in at the academy—" She broke off, her eyes widening with dismay. She'd really done it now. Tai would never forgive her for spilling the beans—and to Steven, of all people.

Steven's voice was controlled as he asked, "Tai is coming to the academy?"

"Listen, that just slipped out. She'd kill me if she knew I told you—"

"Why would she want to come here? She said she never wanted to see an air force uniform again as long as she lived. Or maybe she's going after a free education. That's it, isn't it? Once she gets her degree, she'll put in her five years of service and then the hell with the air force. But how did she get an appointment? Usually it's something you slant your last two years of high school toward, and I happen to know that she's a little weak on the sciences."

He frowned at Bobby Jo, his eyes narrowed. She knew the exact moment when he put two and two together because the crease deepened between his eyebrows and a muscle twitched in his jawline. She remembered, her heart sinking, that Tai had told her once how surprisingly intuitive Steven could be.

"Of course. Tai-*Ching* MacGarrett," he said. "She's related to Senator Ching, isn't she? And he got her the appointment."

"She doesn't want anyone to know," Bobby Jo said, thoroughly alarmed now. "She never talks about her mother's family—you won't say anything if you run into her next year, will you?"

"I won't say anything. She's really big on secrets. And she has a way of setting up standards for other people she doesn't bother with herself. She was pretty critical when I told her that an old West Point friend of my father's appointed me to the academy, but when it came to her own interests, she just went to her—whatever the senator is to her—"

"Uncle. He's her mother's brother."

"—uncle and got her appointment the easy way."

"It wasn't that simple and you know it. She had to meet all the requirements, and she still has to pass the final physical. However, Senator Ching told her she was his number-one candidate. He wouldn't go that far if he wasn't pretty sure she'd make it. After all, she had a three-point-nine cum—"

"At Punahou, a Hawaiian school. Hawaii schools lag way behind the national average in verbal skills—"

"Punahou is a highly rated school," she said, her loyalty stirring. "Besides, Tai's SAT scores were in the top two percentile. If it were anyone else, you'd be all for it. I don't understand why you're so bitter. It wasn't your father who got court-martialed and had a stroke."

"If I'm bitter, it's because I'm sure that Tai provoked our

quarrel on purpose. She knew I wasn't going to let her malign my father and not defend him. And when I did, she broke the engagement."

"If you believe it was deliberate, you don't really understand Tai or where she's coming from. She was hurting, and so she lashed out in all directions—you know what a temper she has. She keeps it under control most of the time, but after all that had happened, no wonder she blew up. But what was your excuse? That quarrel couldn't've been one-sided, Steven."

She knew her words had struck home when Steven's eyes darkened. "Okay, I blew it. At the time, I was so involved in some personal decisions I had to make that I wasn't thinking straight. You have to understand—the academy is a total environment. It isolates you from the rest of the world, and the smallest factor of academy life seems enormously important, especially your first two years. I was mentally all keyed up, like a wire getting ready to snap, trying to juggle half a dozen things at the same time. So when Tai accused Dad of letting Sergeant MacGarrett down, I said a couple of things I've regretted ever since. I want to apologize, but she's made that impossible—and maybe it's all for the best. Did you know that she sent back my ring without even enclosing a note?"

"You don't really mean that about it being for the best." Steven was silent so long that Bobby Jo added, "You aren't going to cause her any trouble when she reports in this fall, are you?"

"*If* she reports in. She still has to pass those tests, and they aren't easy. Even if she makes it, our paths aren't likely to cross. There's several thousand cadets enrolled here—and seniors don't associate with doolies."

His words stung Bobby Jo. "At the moment, you're surrounded by doolies," she pointed out.

"So? These dances aren't restricted to upperclassmen. And I'd better get back to my date. She'll be wondering what happened to me."

"It didn't take you long to get over Tai, did it?" Bobby Jo said, her loyalty surfacing again.

"What does that mean?"

"It's only been a few months since you broke up with Tai. Did you have a girl waiting in the wings?"

Bobby Jo was appalled as soon as the words cleared her

mouth. It wasn't any of her business what Steven did. He could have a hundred girls and it still wouldn't be any of her business.

"I'm sure Tai has found someone to console her by now." Steven's voice had a bite to it. "And there's a very skinny cadet over there glaring holes in me. A friend of yours?"

Feeling guilty, Bobby Jo gave her date an extra-warm smile. When she turned back Steven was already moving away, and she couldn't resist a parting shot. "I'll tell Tai I saw you. I'm sure she'll be relieved to know that you've already found a new girl."

"Do that. And while you're at it, tell her that if she comes to the academy next year with the wrong attitude, she won't even get through Beast. It takes more than an influential uncle to make the grade here."

Without waiting for her answer, he went striding off. A few seconds later, she saw him with a tall, auburn-haired girl. As he put his arm around the girl and led her out onto the dance floor, Bobby Jo felt frustrated because he'd had the last word, after all. She also felt guilty because she'd told him how to get in touch with Tai—if he still wanted to. When would she learn to keep her mouth shut and not blurt out whatever was on her mind?

Well, it was done. She'd have to write Tai and tell her she'd seen Steven and explain what had happened—or maybe she wouldn't. It could only add to her friend's worries. Even if Tai saw Steven in the fall, they probably wouldn't speak to each other. It was all over between them, Tai had said—and there was no reason not to believe her, knowing Tai's stubbornness.

And what had Steven's final remark meant? He had sounded so hostile. Surely, he wouldn't make trouble for Tai when she reported in at the academy this summer.

As Bobby Jo moved forward to join her date, who was looking more unhappy by the minute, she rubbed her upper arms, and she wondered why, since she was wearing sleeves and the auditorium was so well heated, she suddenly felt so cold.

It was two weeks after she'd met Steven at the hop before Bobby Jo finally wrote to Tai, although usually she answered her friend's letters quickly. Most of her letter was about Shelley's sudden move to the Philippines and Crystal's marriage—with a few lines about her own social life. Although she was careful to keep her letter gay, Bobby Jo felt depressed as she addressed the envelope to Tai. It was the things she hadn't told Tai, such as her encounter with Steven and her real feelings about Crystal's wedding, that were a downer. It wasn't that she was jealous of Crystal, but it did gall her that the one person who had seemed destined for a career, with her hard practicality and her drive, should be the first of their crowd to pull off what her mother would call a "suitable marriage."

And there was Shelley's marriage, too. From her letters, she was ecstatically happy with her sergeant husband. It made Bobby Jo feel so restless, as if she were just marking time while all her friends led exciting lives. Of course, she had all the dates she could handle considering the homework they piled on her here, but she still hadn't met anyone special, someone she was willing to give her all to.

Although she didn't like to admit it, she got homesick sometimes for her mom and dad and even for the gruesome four, her bratty brothers. Life had been so simple then. For some reason, she didn't feel as if she belonged here at Colorado College. She dated this one and that one, was socially active— to use another of her mom's phrases—but the chief subject of conversation seemed to be skiing, and she didn't know a schuss from a sitzmark. What's more, she didn't have any desire to learn, either.

She'd made a joke about it to Tai, but she was disappointed about her experiences with cadets. Either they were so gungho about the air force that every other word was some military term she didn't understand, or they were grinds—what they called "brainos" at the academy—or they were jocks, interested only in making it in sports. Maybe she expected too much— someone like Tai's Steven, who had a sense of humor and knew how to relate to a girl. Yes, she could go for another Steven— that cool way he had of talking, the way he looked at you, sort of challenging and sexy and all male. . . .

She sighed again and went to drop her letter in the hall mail slot. Next year would be better. Tai would be at the academy, and while her doolie year would be really tough, maybe they could get together once in a while for girl talk. And maybe Tai would fix her up with another Steven and she'd have that big sock-o romance after all, the one that had eluded her so far.

Tai had been trying to get around to answering Bobby Jo's letter all week. But first one thing and then the other had intervened. It was tourist season—when wasn't it tourist season in Hawaii?—and she'd been working long hours at the boutique, welcoming the chance to increase her earnings and yet resenting the time it took away from her studies. As busy as she was, she sometimes felt as if she were suspended in limbo while the world spun faster and faster, leaving her behind.

She knew that this was because, in her mind, she had moved on to the next stage of her life. Of course, her job served a good purpose besides supporting her. Before she reported in at the academy next summer, she intended to have a nest egg in reserve. Not that she had any doubts that she would make it as a cadet, but still—she never again intended to be so broke that she was down to her last dollar with rent due, no gas in her car, and only three packages of saimin noodles to last her until she drew her first week's wages. As a cadet, she would earn the same pay as a staff sergeant, and she intended to save as much as she could toward a car in her senior year—and a decent nest egg, just in case.

She had worries of another sort, too. How often would she see Steven at the academy? When they met, how would he act? Friendly? Hostile? Indifferent? That article she'd read in the *Honolulu Star-Bulletin* about the reaction of male cadets to the first females at the academy was sobering. Some of those interviewed had made it clear that they believed women didn't belong in the military. So she couldn't expect Steven to be friendly. In fact, she didn't want him to be. What she wanted was to be left alone so she could concentrate on her studies.

The breakup with Steven was still as raw and painful as an open sore, and she didn't want to be reminded of how it had once been between them, didn't even want to *think* of him. All their plans, their hopes and dreams—she had been a fool to lay herself open to so much heartache. When she thought of their final quarrel, she still seethed with resentment. And yet—and yet, it had been so fantastic when Steven made love to her.

Sometimes her body still played tricks on her and she dreamed about him. It was humiliating that physically she still wanted him. Well, she wasn't Shelley, willing to give up all for Love—with a capital "L." Once she'd graduated and her military obligation was behind her, she would be free to do anything, go anywhere. She didn't want any anchors holding her down. Not that she was against sex. But during her doolie year, she would tough it out. She already had enough strikes against her, just being a woman, without adding a man to her problems.

She started her letter to Bobby Jo that night when she got in from work, but after she'd written a few lines, she stopped, biting the end of her pen. How strange that she had so little to say to her best friend. They had lived out of each other's pockets at Punahou, swapping dreams and making plans and confiding in each other. Bobby Jo had known that Steven and she were lovers the day after it happened—and she knew something about Bobby Jo that no one else did, that all her arch remarks about sex were just so much window dressing because Bobby Jo was saving herself for the big love of her life.

But now she had so little in common with her old friend. In fact, she felt years older, a little impatient with Bobby Jo's preoccupation with finding the right man. Bobby Jo's letters seemed so—so juvenile, as if she were still going to Punahou.

There was an explanation for this distance between them, of course. So many traumatic things had happened in her own life that she'd matured overnight. Her values, her interests, her ambitions had changed. The eighteen-year-old Tai who had been in love with Steven Henderson and whose primary ambition had been to marry him and be the mother of his kids was gone, destroyed by reality. The new Tai was stronger, tougher— and determined to win out against the odds.

Someday she would be in a position where no one would have any power over her. When that day came, she would direct her own life. But for now, she would do whatever was necessary to survive at the academy, even if it meant playing the military game so well that no one would guess the contempt she felt inside.

And then, when the time was ripe, she would turn her back on the air force and never look back. . . .

CHAPTER
↑ 16 ↑

EVEN BEFORE SHELLEY BOARDED THE PLANE THAT WOULD take her to the Philippines, she felt totally disoriented. Although she was an experienced traveler, she had always flown first class or, on three occasions, on the plane assigned to her father as Commander-In-Chief of PACAF. Either way, there was always a solicitous steward hovering nearby to provide for her every need.

But this—this was bare-bones travel with little effort taken to make things comfortable for military passengers. For one thing, it was a "stretch" plane, with added seats to provide the maximum seating. For another, her flight had originated at Travis AFB in California and had already been airborne for five hours before it reached Hickam, which meant the aisles were strewn with candy and gum wrappers and Styrofoam cups, with children running up and down and people milling about, some just returning to their seats after the brief refueling stop at Hickam.

Shelley regarded the children uneasily. Not only wasn't she used to them, but she couldn't help thinking that their mothers should keep them under better control. There were other unpleasant things, too, besides the racket—the mingled odors of pine disinfectant, wet diapers, and stale coffee left too long in steel urns. Her stomach rolled suddenly, and she knew that the next hours would be a contest of wills—her determination to be a good sport warring with her weak stomach.

She tried to divorce herself from her surroundings by thinking of Tad and their reunion, only hours away now. After all, what was a little discomfort compared to that? Once they were together again, nothing else would matter, certainly not that humiliating encounter in the waiting room just before she'd boarded the plane.

She had been sitting alone, perched on the edge of a table because all the chairs and benches were taken, when a youngish woman, smartly dressed in a tailored pants suit, had joined her.

"Can you believe this? It's a madhouse," the woman commented. Although a No Smoking sign was tacked on the wall behind them, she lit a cigarette and held it below the edge of the table, turning her head away for an occasional puff as she talked. "Wouldn't you think they'd have a better system for getting us loaded on our plane?"

Feeling a little shy as she always did with aggressive strangers, Shelley nodded. "I guess there is a system—but being outsiders, it isn't apparent to us," she said.

"Well, I think it's the pits." The woman paused, looking Shelley over. "Are you traveling alone, too?"

"My husband had to go ahead because I didn't have the right shots or a passport."

"Well, I blew it. My own fault. I should've gone with Dean—that's my husband—but I figured it would be best if he went on ahead and rented a place for us. But this mess—it's going to be murder on that plane. All these kids, for God's sake!"

"It will be over soon—"

"Not for twelve hours—give or take a few centuries. I'm not looking forward to the next two years. When I think that Dean could be earning decent wages as a commercial pilot, I could scream." She took another puff of her cigarette. "I think I'll take a tranquilizer as soon as we board the plane. Maybe I can sleep all the way to the Philippines. Look, let's try to sit together. What I don't need is some woman with a couple of squalling brats climbing over me."

Shelley nodded, although she wasn't sure she wanted to spend the next few hours listening to the woman's complaints. Still, she was the only person who'd spoken to her since she'd arrived at the terminal, although she'd been aware of a few stares from other women, none of them particularly friendly. It couldn't be her appearance because she'd deliberately left off makeup this morning and was wearing her hair in a no-nonsense style, pinned back from her face. Like most of the younger women, she wore jeans and a knit blouse with a jacket around her shoulders to ward off the early-morning chill—nothing there to attract attention.

"I have the feeling I know you," the other woman said. "Maybe I've seen you at the club?"

Shelley chilled. It was more than possible—it was likely. "I doubt it—we seldom came to the base."

"Your husband *is* air force, isn't he?"

"Yes. He's a staff sergeant," Shelley said quickly.

The woman's eyelids flickered; she crushed her cigarette out on the side of the table and then let the butt slip to the floor. A young officer standing nearby gave her a sharp look but said nothing.

"Well, I've got to do something about my hair," the woman said. "See you around. . . ."

But Shelley had known that she'd seen the last of her. As she reviewed that brief encounter now, her cheeks grew hot. It wasn't that she'd wanted to be friends with the woman, but the knowledge rankled that if she'd replied, "Yes, it's possible you've seen me at the club. My father is General Pritchard," the woman would have fawned all over her.

Shelley rested her forehead against the cool window glass, feeling very tired and dispirited. It was stifling hot on the plane and would be until the air conditioning went on. They were already late taking off—something about the landing gear, one of the male flight attendants had said. Right now, he and two other stewards were rushing up and down the aisle, dodging kids and elbows and diaper bags, and although she was thirsty and would have given anything for a glass of water, she knew it would be useless to ask for service.

"Are you okay? You look a little pale."

Shelley turned her head to meet the eyes of the middle-aged woman sitting next to her. She had counted herself lucky that she'd been assigned a window seat on the narrow side of the aisle with only three seats across instead of six. As she smiled back, she decided that she'd had another stroke of luck, too. Obviously unruffled by either the noise or the heat or the strong odors, the woman, who had introduced herself as Dixie Beagle, was placidly knitting a pink baby sacque.

"It's awfully hot—I feel a little woozy," Shelley said.

"Why don't you take off your jacket and put it up above? If you need it later, you can get to it easily."

Shelley shed her jacket and put it away in a bin, then slid past the woman's plump knees to regain her seat.

"Wonder who has that one?" Dixie Beagle said, glancing at the empty aisle seat, which held a reserve sign, indicating that it had been occupied on the first lap from California. "You suppose they fell asleep in the terminal and didn't hear the boarding call?"

"Or maybe they got off the plane at Hickam."

"Well, I have to admit the extra space would be a blessing to these old legs of mine," the woman said comfortably. "I guess it's too much to ask, though. Someone with a middle seat in one of the wide rows is bound to move when they see an aisle seat's empty."

"Are you—is your husband in the air force?"

"Indeed he is. Chief Master Sergeant Clarence Beagle— the old fart."

Taken by surprise, Shelley laughed, and the woman looked pleased. "There—it's always better when you can laugh, isn't it? I call Clarence that when I'm mad at him, but he's really an okay guy. Since our youngest went off to school, there's just the two of us—and it's kind of peaceful. He'll have his thirty years in a couple of years from now, and then we'll be retiring to civilian life."

"Are you looking forward to it?"

"You'd better believe it. It's been a rough thirty years. Would you believe that I had all four of my kids while Clarence was off on TDY or on an unaccompanied tour? Every last one of them. Lucky thing I had good neighbors or I don't think I could've made it. When I say I've been through the mill, that's just what I mean."

But there was relish in her voice, and Shelley couldn't help wondering if she wouldn't find retirement too tame. "Won't you miss moving around when you retire?"

"Miss it? No, I won't miss it. I've had it with packing and unpacking, with scrubbing out ovens at the last minute so we can pass inspection and clear quarters while the kids are waiting in the car. I'm sick to death of living out of a suitcase in a rat-infested motel while we wait for housing, hemming up curtains because they're too long for the new place—then taking down the hem again because they're too short for the next set of quarters. And I've had it with making friends only to see them leave, knowing I probably won't see them again. But I guess I will miss some things—it wasn't all bad."

She looked Shelley over, her eyes puzzled. "I've been trying to figure something out. Is your husband an officer?"

"He's enlisted. A staff sergeant."

"Well, that's a surprise."

"Why do you say that?"

"It's the way you look, honey. Like you should be modeling in one of them fashion magazines. I haven't seen hair like that since the old Lizabeth Scott movies. You're going to have a time, keeping the color up in the PI. The base beauty shop is . . . well, adequate is the best I can say for it."

Shelley tried for a smile. Mrs. Beagle stopped knitting long enough to give her a sharp glance. "What is it? You look like you swallowed a gnat."

"This is my natural hair color—and I'm wearing jeans and a knit shirt like half the women on the plane."

"Well, I suspect you're one of those women who could wear a towel and still look great. I never did have style, even when I was young. And if you want my advice"—she paused and waited for Shelley's nod—"you should try to loosen up a little. I can tell you're a very nice girl, but you look so—so aloof, I guess you could call it. Like you're saying, 'Don't bother me.'"

"But I don't feel that way at all," Shelley protested.

"There now—I didn't mean to hurt your feelings. I only meant it for your own good. Clark Air Force Base is . . . well, it'll take some getting used to. You have to be real security conscious all the time, what with the terrorists and the stealing and all. And Clark is like a small town. You know—everybody gets to know everybody else's business. After a while, you see the same people so much that it's a real relief when a plane comes in with some new faces to stare at."

She shifted her position and gave a deep sigh. "The whole air force is different these days. Some things are better, of course, but these days, you don't have the old traditions that used to make you feel as if you really belonged to something bigger'n yourself—you know what I mean? I can remember back when the neighbors would come over with a cake and maybe a casserole when you moved into new quarters. Now you can live next door to someone for a year and never exchange two words. That's one reason why I'm ready for retirement."

She paused to catch her breath, and Shelley asked quickly, "Where do your children live now?"

"Three in the Washington, D.C. area, one in Honolulu. I've been staying with my oldest daughter while she had her baby—our fifth grandchild, the second girl. This assignment to Clark is our last one overseas—unless there's another war before Clarence puts in his papers."

Her eyes got a little misty suddenly. "And here you are, just starting out. Well, it can be a lot of heartache, being a service wife. I wish civilians understood how fast the money goes when you're always moving around, especially if you have kids, and then they wouldn't scream about every pay increase we get. On the other hand, you do get to meet people different from yourself and see something of the world."

"I'm looking forward to it," Shelley said, smiling at her.

"Just don't let the climate and the isolation get to you. The trick is to make friends with other women who'll be here as long as you. After a woman's been at Clark a while, she starts counting the days till her husband rotates, and she loses interest in making new friends."

"I'll remember that," Shelley said. "I met one woman, an officer's wife, at the terminal, but when she found out I was enlisted, she lost interest."

"She was right. It's best to stick to your own kind. There's a good reason why enlisted and officers shouldn't mix. A young officer, just starting out, has enough trouble getting any respect without having to worry about maybe having to give orders to someone he sees socially."

Shelley digested this for a moment. "I never thought of it that way, Mrs. Beagle."

"Call me Dixie—I don't think I caught your name?"

"Shelley Prit—Brotski."

"Shelley's a real pretty name." She gave Shelley a weighing look. "How long have you been married?"

"Just a few weeks. Tad got his orders for Clark just after we were married."

"Bad timing, that. You got on in Hawaii, so I guess your husband was stationed there?"

"At Hickam."

"And when he popped the question, he told you how great

it was, traveling all over the world, I'll bet. That's a man for you. Well, you'll get used to military life because if you don't, you're in big trouble. Lucky for me the worst of it happened when I was still young. Later on, we got longer assignments. Those first years when Clarence was in SAC, I used to wake up in the morning and have to think a minute before I could remember where I was. Once I went to a movie in the afternoon, and when I came out I started looking for the bus back to Barksdale—only we were stationed in Ohio at the time. So it's a real adjustment. But you'll make it to retirement—provided you have a good solid marriage."

"We do," Shelley said, so fervently that Dixie laughed and patted her hand.

"Well, hang in there. Come and see me after you get squared away. We were lucky enough to draw one of the barns—that's what they call the older quarters with a screened-in verandah all around. Clarence likes to eat his lunch out on the verandah. He comes home every day for a home-cooked meal and sometimes for a—well, never mind that."

Shelley smiled to herself. She liked this earthy, talkative woman—and she hoped they would be friends. Dixie's advice and reminiscences were like coming upon a familiar house from another direction. As the daughter of a general, she had seen military life from one narrow angle. Now, as an enlisted wife, she would see it from another point of view.

One thing already was coming clear—to the enlisted ranks and their wives, the officers and their affairs were important only when it affected their own private lives. The enlisted people lived in their own world, which had its own set of rules and priorities—and if she wanted to make a success of her marriage, she must learn those ways.

Luckily, for the next few hours, she had a good teacher sitting right next to her—and one who was obviously willing to let her in on the nuances of being the wife of an air force sergeant.

Shelley had fallen into a fitful nap when a voice on the cabin loudspeaker brought her back to consciousness. A little confused, she sat up and looked around. The aisles were clear now, but from the noise, chaos still reigned. There were new odors, none of them pleasant, and her stomach rolled persistently, making her swallow hard.

Next to her, Dixie had already put away her knitting needles and her yarn. She had also fluffed out her short gray hair and was putting on lipstick. Her eyes were very bright, and Shelley had a clear picture of what she must have looked like when she, too, was a bride. Was it possible to keep love alive so many years—or was she just looking for hopeful signs?

As if she knew what Shelley was thinking, Dixie confided, "This is the good part of being married to a military man. Separations are hell, but when you're back together again, you forget the bad times."

Shelley made a mental vow that it would be like that with Tad and her. No matter what lay ahead, he would never have any reason to be sorry he'd married her. They would have their differences—already there were times when she noticed things about Tad that grated on her nerves, such as his cursing—but she would overlook them and hope he would overlook the things about her that irritated him—such as her inability to cook an egg without burning it and her total lack of housekeeping skills.

Because she mustn't—*couldn't*—fail. What else did she have? A small talent for painting—and not the slightest chance of earning a living from it without a teaching degree. She could never go back to her parents, not after the way they'd treated Tad. Besides, they wouldn't take her back—and she had too much pride to ever let them know that she was anything except deliriously happy.

So she had to make a success of her marriage. That would be the ultimate revenge against the parents who'd never really wanted her.

And wasn't she lucky that Tad did? It was some kind of miracle that he loved her. She must learn not to hold back, to open her heart to Tad, to be honest with him—except for one thing. She would be the kind of wife he wanted, but she'd never let him know that she wasn't the sexpot he thought her to be because that would be a terrible blow to his male ego.

So she would continue to fake her response in bed. After all, she did love it when he cuddled her, when he held her in his arms before and after they made love. So not really enjoying the sex act itself didn't matter that much when it came to sharing the rest of her life with Tad.

It was midafternoon when the plane finally landed. The problem with the landing gear hadn't been corrected after all, and they were forced to circle the airfield for almost an hour while it was being lowered manually. Although some of the children slept—Shelley suspected from pure exhaustion—there was still a constant hubbub of noise, and she wanted to put her hands over her ears and shut it out. Even Dixie had finally lost her tolerance and was making acid comments about the inefficiency of leased airplanes. Only the realization that if she was exhausted, the children's mothers must feel even worse kept Shelley from complaining, too. She wondered at their patience. Across the aisle, a young woman, a two-year-old on her lap, had fallen asleep. As Shelley studied the woman's pale face and the dark shadows under her eyes, she felt a surge of sympathy. When the toddler awoke and began to scream, she leaned forward impulsively and offered, "Would you like me to hold your son for a while?"

The woman gave her a wary look. "He won't let you. He's not used to being around strangers. Thank you anyway."

Although her words were polite, she busied herself with her son, so obviously dismissive that Shelley felt rebuffed.

"Don't let it worry you," Dixie said in a low voice. "It's not personal. She's scared stiff. Lots of the young wives are that way—and some of the older ones, too. It's going off to a foreign place so different from what they're used to. When she gets to Clark, she'll just mark time, never going anywhere except to the commissary and the BX, counting the days until orders come for them to go back to the States. Some of the wives can't hack it. They cut and run back home. If they can't talk their husbands into getting out, they let them go overseas alone the next time—those who stay married. It's a shame there isn't some kind of pill the medics could give wives to make them accept things the way they are."

She gave Shelley's troubled face a long look. "You going to be okay? Sometimes I talk too much."

"I'll be fine. Don't worry. I won't be one of the ones who cut and run. I can put up with anything to be with Tad."

"Well, you've got the right attitude. Just relax and give a little when you have to. Things are going to go wrong—that's part of life. Make some friends and laugh it up every chance you get—and leave the military stuff to your husband. Nothing more boring than one of those wives who're always talking about their husband's job. If I was you, I'd find something to do to take up the slack time once you've hired a housegirl to do your cleaning. Take up ceramics at the service club or join a sewing club or maybe do some volunteer work, and then when your Tad is off on TDY, you can stay busy. Of course, once you start your family, you'll have your hands full. That was my hobby, raising kids."

"I took painting courses when I was in school," Shelley said.

"That's a nice little hobby," Dixie said, her voice indulgent.

Shelley didn't tell her that it had been more than a hobby, that it had been the thing she planned to do with her life. She nodded instead. I'm already learning, she thought.

"Just don't let your outside interest take you over," Dixie went on, tucking a stray strand of hair behind her ear. "When your man comes home, he'll want all your attention. The military is a rough life, and they take a lot of . . . well, I won't say the word, but you know what I mean. It isn't like civilian life, where you can always walk away and get another job if you don't like your boss. If some NCO or officer's on your man's back, he's stuck until one of them transfers out. You can't buck the officers, not openly. Of course, any NCO'll tell you that there are ways of holding your own with them once you know the ropes. You take my Clarence. He always knows where the bodies are buried. Covering your ass, they call it in the air force—and there I go, talking too much. Guess I'm nervous— all this circling around. What I'm trying to say is to be there when your man gets home nights because he'll need you."

He'll need you. . . . Yes, she would always be there when Tad needed her. No one else had ever needed her. Not even Tony, who had been away so much that she hardly knew him. But now someone did—and she would repay him by being what he wanted in a wife.

Shelley's first impression of the Philippines when she disembarked from the plane was the heat—a breathless, stifling heat that struck her in the face like a slap. Then warm hands were gripping her shoulders and Tad's arms were lifting her for a kiss. Around them, the wives who had traveled unaccompanied were being greeted, too, but she was blind to everything except Tad's eager face, Tad's kiss.

"God, I've missed you, Shelley," he said hoarsely.

"I've missed you, too. I thought the past weeks would never end."

"Did you get things squared away with your folks? In your last letter, you said they sent your clothes, but you didn't go into detail."

"One of the house stewards delivered them—but there wasn't any message. I'm surprised my mother didn't send them to the Salvation Army."

Tad gave her a hug. "The hell with them. You've got another family now. You're going to love my folks—you won't need anyone else."

"I don't need anyone but you, Tad."

"Let's get into the shade—it's hotter'n hell on this ramp. I want to get you alone—as soon as I get your customs clearance and collect your luggage, we'll go on home." He hesitated, his face sober. "I couldn't get those quarters I told you about. So we'll have to make do with temp quarters for now."

"I don't care where we live. Not as long as I'm with you," she said confidently.

"You say that now, but wait until you see the trailer we drew. It's pretty miserable," Tad said as he steered her toward the terminal.

An hour later, he was packing her luggage into a ramshackle jeep that looked as if it were a survival of World War II. "I really lucked out on the jeep," he bragged. "It wiped out the money I had saved, but you just about have to have wheels if you live off base."

He helped her into the jeep, then ran around to slide under the wheel. "It's really hot in our quarters," he warned. "There's a power shortage right now because of the drought, so the Philippine government is regulating the electric power. The base gets the short end of the stick because it's considered industrial. The air conditioning will be back on in a couple of hours—until then we just have to sweat it out."

Ten minutes later, they pulled up in front of a long, rusty-looking trailer, one of a long row of trailers, set up on cement blocks. Shelley's heart sank as she took in the metal roof and siding, the painted-over windows.

"It'll be a lot better when the power comes back on," Tad said. "This is the hot season—it's a lot different from Hawaii, isn't it?"

"I prefer it here—with you," she said, determined not to show her dismay.

Tad gave her a hug. His uniform was stained with sweat,

and she repressed a desire to pull away. She wanted to be close to him, but surely he wouldn't try to make love to her until the air conditioning came on.

"You must be tired," he said, a question in his voice, and she knew that he wanted sex.

"Oh, no. I slept on the plane," she said thinly.

"Then let's get inside," he said. "And I hope to hell nobody knocks on the door for the next couple of hours."

Later, as they lay in bed, a large metal fan humming above their heads and sending a flow of hot air over their sweating bodies, Shelley was ashamed how relieved she was that it was over. She had tried to respond, but, as always, just when she felt the first stirrings of excitement, the whole thing was finished. Well, no big t'ing—as the kinds at Punahou were always saying. It had been good for Tad—and that's what mattered. So she wasn't all that crazy about sex. No big t'ing. She was only thankful that Tad was satisfied so quickly. What if she had to endure a prolonged siege of lovemaking every night? What if he drew it out and drew it out until she felt like screaming? No, she was lucky. He'd never commented on the fact that she didn't initiate sex—was he disappointed? Maybe he would like it if she did once in a while. Well, she'd think about it—but not now, not when she was so tired that she felt just like crying. . . .

CHAPTER
↟ 17 ↟

DURING THE WEEKS FOLLOWING SHELLEY'S ARRIVAL IN THE
Philippines, she often felt as if she were Alice in Wonderland,
who had wandered into a strange land with strange new rules.

It didn't help that, after the first few days, Tad seemed
morose and withdrawn, not the exuberant lover she'd known
in Hawaii. When he came home at night, she had so many
things stored up to talk to him about, and yet, when she asked
him anything about his job, he brushed off her questions and
retreated into silence.

And when she tried to ignore his silence and went on talking,
he turned the radio on and listened to canned football games
on Armed Forces Radio. Only when they were making love
did he seem to be the man she'd married. She knew that something was worrying him, but until he decided to confide in her,
she also knew that there was nothing she could do to help him.

It had never occurred to her before that Tad might be secretive. On Hawaii, he had seemed so open. There were other
things, too, about her new husband that she was discovering,
just as he was finding out things about her—some of which,
she had to admit, must be quite a shock.

He had teased her about her lack of cooking skills in Hawaii,
but now, with food so expensive and limited in scope, her
failures couldn't be overlooked so easily. After the third time
she'd ruined dinner by overcooking the rice or burning the
hamburgers, he had finally exploded.

"This has gotta stop, Shelley! We can't afford these fucking food bills. What's so hard about frying a little meat or boiling some potatoes? Are you doing it on purpose so I'll get a house-girl? You know that's stupid until we move off base—you don't have enough to keep you busy as it is. And even if we get one, I'll tell you right now, I'm not about to eat any of that gook food. You'll still have to cook—and you'd better learn fast before you put us into bankruptcy."

In the end, she had gone to Dixie, who had obligingly come over a few times to teach her some of the basic cooking skills, and their meals did improve after that. But there were so many mysteries that she never seemed to grasp, things that other women picked up by watching their mothers in the kitchen. It didn't help that the foods Tad liked, such as stuffed cabbage and chicken and dumplings, were so unfamiliar to her that she had no idea what they looked or tasted like when properly prepared.

In the heat of the cramped trailer, the smell of sausage frying or cabbage cooking made her stomach roll, and she often couldn't eat the food she'd just prepared. She longed for a decent beef roast, but when she bought one and fixed it as a treat, Tad hit the roof at the price.

She sometimes wondered if she didn't have a mental block against learning how to cook. Was it some inner rebellion against the way Tad had changed? If so, it hurt her more than it did him because so often she threw out her failures and he never knew about them.

But he was well aware of the food bills. When she had to ask him for more money two weeks after she arrived, he demanded, "What the hell's going on, Shelley? How could you possibly spend the food money I gave you already? Do you have any idea what I make a month?"

"No," she said honestly, trying to hold on to her temper. "You told me not to—I think your exact words were that I wasn't to bother my pretty little head about such things."

He shook his head as if to ward off a pesky fly. "I'm putting you on a food budget. And you'd better follow it or we'll starve to death."

She was silent for a moment. "About your beer—does that come under the heading of food, or is that a personal expense?"

"What the fuck does that mean?"

Shelley was already sorry she'd let her temper get out of

hand, but she was determined not to retreat. "Your beer takes quite a hunk out of our food budget," she pointed out.

Tad slammed his hand down on the table. "Look, I work hard every day in that stinking heat. When I get home, I want to forget the mess your father got me into and have a couple beers. So get off my back, Shelley."

"Is *that* what's been bugging you? You resent me because of what my father did? Well, think about this. You only had a taste of what my parents are like. I had to live with them all my life. You went into this with your eyes open. I was honest with you. You were the one who was so sure that we could work things out. I was the one who had doubts and had to be persuaded."

"Yeah, and you're never going to let me forget it, are you?"

The unfairness of his remark took her breath away for a moment. "I've never brought it up before today. So how can you say such a thing, Tad?" she said finally.

In answer, Tad, picked up his shirt, which he'd tossed across the back of a chair, and put it back on. "Shit. I'm going over to the Top Hat to drink my beer in peace. I hope your head's on straight by the time I get back."

Shelley was in bed, the sheet pulled up around her shoulders, when Tad tiptoed into the trailer several hours later. She lay motionlessly, her body rigid, resenting the smell of beer on his breath, resenting his elaborate attempts to be quiet. But when he undressed and got in beside her, when he touched her, his hand seeking out the softness of her breast, when he whispered that he was sorry, she let him make love to her. Afterward, when his heavy breathing told her he was asleep, she lay staring up at a patch of mold on the ceiling, wondering if things would ever be right between them again.

The next morning Tad made promises, and she pretended to believe that their quarrel had been unimportant, one of the norms of any marriage. But she tried even harder after that, and for a few days things went smoothly.

It was the standing rib roast that instigated the next quarrel. She wanted something special to celebrate Tad's twenty-fourth birthday. The price on the roast made her wince, but she shook off her doubts and put it in her grocery cart anyway. After all, this was a special occasion. She'd make up the difference somewhere else—serve Tad beans for the rest of the week if she had to.

Dixie had given her explicit directions on how to cook the roast, and although the oven in the rusty old stove was temperamental, she was satisfied it would turn out okay, especially since she'd baked a cake in the oven that morning that had turned out only a little lopsided.

The odor of roasting beef wasn't as appetizing as she'd expected, and she was glad the air conditioner was going full blast to keep down the heat. As she added french dressing to a concoction made from slightly wilted iceberg lettuce and a can of three-bean salad, she hummed to herself. This would be a special evening, and maybe, just maybe, they could talk afterward and Tad wouldn't retreat into his shell—or take out one of those aircraft manuals he was always studying.

Tad's step made her turn, smiling. She flew into his arms and hid her face in his chest, so it was a minute before she realized that he wasn't alone.

"I want you to meet my wife, Sergeant Harnessey." There was something, a reserve, in Tad's voice that made her look at the man closely. "The sergeant wants to see that portable tape deck I put up for sale on the bulletin board."

She stared at him in bewilderment. "I didn't know you were selling—" She broke off, realizing that he was shaking his head slightly. "It's in the bedroom," she said weakly.

Sgt. Harnessy's eyes were busy, cataloging her long dress, the table with its bowl of gardenias she'd cut from a bush in Dixie's yard, the two wineglasses she'd bought at the BX. They lingered longest on the wine she was cooling in a bucket of ice cubes.

"Something smells awfully good," he commented.

"It's prime ribs," Shelley told him.

"Yeah? You sure live high on the hog, Brotski. Wish I knew your secret. Last time my old lady gave me prime ribs was when I made E-eight."

Shelley started to tell him that this was a special treat because it was Tad's birthday, but the two men were already moving toward the bedroom in the rear of the trailer. The back of Tad's neck was rigid, and she felt an ominous sinking in the pit of her stomach. She had done the wrong thing again—when was she going to start getting things right?

Tad waited until Sgt. Harnessey was gone before he exploded. "What the hell's wrong with you? This fancy spread you put on will be all over the outfit by tomorrow. By the time Harnessey tells his old lady and she tells the wives' network, everybody will be wondering how we can afford it—and you know what they'll be thinking. Black market—or worse. Besides, you know we can't afford prime ribs. How much did that roast cost you?"

She told him, trying to keep her lips from trembling. Although she added that it was his birthday, that she'd wanted a special treat, he didn't seem to be listening.

"You're going to have to shape up, Shelley." Tad went to get himself a beer, ignoring the wine. "We had this all out before—what are you trying to do to me?"

Shelley didn't answer. Why should she make excuses for everything she did? Who the hell did he think he was—her master? Silently, she turned and went into the bedroom, closing the door behind her. She lay on the bed, and it seemed to her that her whole life was crashing down around her head.

A few minutes later, the bedroom door opened. Tad sat down beside her and laid his hand on her shoulder. "Come on, Shelley. I didn't mean it. I know you knocked yourself out, fixing that meal. It was just that—that the timing was so rotten."

She sat up, pulling away from his hand. "Happy birthday," she said bitterly.

"Yeah. I blew your surprise, didn't I? Look, it isn't too late. The roast smelled great—how about it? Shall we eat now? I'm hungry as a bear."

Shelley knew he wanted to smooth things over. But why didn't he tell her he was sorry? And why was he selling his tape deck, which he was so proud of? More important, why hadn't he said anything about it to her?

They made up, of course, but some of the shine had gone off their marriage. Her love hadn't changed, but she viewed Tad differently now, as someone who was fallible and sometimes impossible to deal with. She found herself being careful what she said to him, placating him instead of speaking up and voicing her opinions. Where was the easygoing man she'd married? Had he never existed except in her own mind? Only occasionally did she see that man these days. Were all marriages this way after the honeymoon was over?

As the days passed, Shelley had other things to think about. She learned the hours the commissary and BX were open, discovered the best time to shop to avoid the daily power-outs that turned the sprawling buildings into infernos. She became familiar with the schedule of the rattling old buses that circled the huge base, but one thing she couldn't seem to get used to was being alone most of the day.

Although Tad came home every day for lunch, he gulped down his sandwich and iced tea, then pulled her into the bedroom for what he called a "nooner." She grew to dread these fast, sweaty couplings. Since he was always so rushed, she didn't even have the comfort of being held afterward, the thing that made sex endurable to her, and she sometimes found excuses to leave a sandwich in the refrigerator for him and be away at lunchtime.

When he complained, she told him that it was too hot to do her shopping during the afternoons, especially since she had to buy groceries three times a week because she could only carry so much on the base bus. She hoped he'd offer to leave her the jeep, but he changed the subject, and because she was trying so hard not to say anything that might start another quarrel, she didn't press him about it.

A month after she arrived at Clark AFB, they moved into off-base housing in a compound just outside Peace Gate. The rooms were large and airy—and almost totally bare because there was a shortage of government-issue furniture at Clark.

Even so, it was a relief from the stuffy trailer. Again, Tad vetoed hiring a housegirl, saying that until they got their furniture, there wasn't enough work to keep one busy, a decision Shelley thought absurd since there were vast amounts of floor to keep waxed—and she still hadn't adjusted to the change in climate.

Despite this, Shelley would have been content if she had felt better. At first, she blamed her spells of nausea on the heat, on the change in her diet, on everything except the obvious reason. When she finally counted back and realized she'd skipped two periods, she wondered how she could have been so blind. She made an appointment at the base hospital, and when her suspicions were confirmed, she knew she had to tell Tad what she was sure would be bad news.

He was lounging at the enamel-topped table where they ate their meals, ruffling through a *Sports Afield* magazine after what could only be described as one of Shelley's worst attempts at fixing him the kind of food he was used to. After trying to get down a few bites of stewed chicken that not only had a strange taste but was stringy and tough, and dumplings that were undercooked and soggy, he pushed away his plate and said it was too hot to eat.

Silently, Shelley began gathering up the dishes, and because her sight was a little misty, she knocked his plate off the table. The sight of the stringy chicken and the leathery dumplings splattered all over the kitchen floor was too much and she burst into tears. When Tad began to laugh, she cried even harder and flew toward the bedroom, always her refuge when things went wrong between them. Still laughing, he tried to catch her, but she evaded him, slammed the door in his face, and threw herself down on the bed for a good cry.

It was a while before Tad followed her. She was still snuffling into a pillow when his hand turned her over. His face, inverted above her, was very somber.

"Okay, I shouldn't've laughed. But it was funny as hell—the expression on your face, I mean. Look, you knew what I was when you married me. I warned you that I might not measure up to the kind of guys you were used to. But I've been trying real hard. Haven't I eaten everything you've put before me for the past month—even that crazy curry dish that about burned off my tongue? So why don't we strike some kind of bargain? You overlook my uncouth ways and I'll eat your cooking, even if"—the laugh lines beside his mouth deepened—"you poison me someday."

She started to answer when a rolling wave of nausea caught her by surprise. It had always been morning sickness before, which was easy to keep from Tad, but there was no hiding this. She twisted frantically, breaking his hold, and flew into the bathroom. A few minutes later, feeling wretched and weak, she returned to the kitchen. Tad was sitting at the table. He had cleaned up the mess on the floor, washed and dried the dishes, and put them away. Since this was the first time he'd raised a hand to help with housework, she stared at him in surprise.

"You okay, Shelley?" he said, setting down his coffee cup.

"I guess so. I don't know what caused that—"

"Probably that chicken," he said, his tone deadpan.

"Oh—oh, shut up!" she wailed. "If you mention that chicken one more time, I'll throw something at you. You think you're so smart—why don't you do the cooking?"

"Hey, that's woman's work," he said, and although he was

smiling, she knew he meant it. "Me Tarzan, go out and earn the bread, and you Jane, stay home and cook and clean house."

"You should have been born in the eighteenth century," she said crossly. "That's where you belong."

"Uh-huh. And you belong with me—preferably in my bed."

The anger bubbled up in Shelley, exploded into words. "Is that all you ever think of? Getting me into bed? Well, I'm more than a bed partner. I'm a person. I'm not your slave who's only good for sex and keeping house for you."

The expression on Tad's face was almost laughable—if she'd felt like laughing. Although she was sorry she'd lost her temper, something stubborn and resentful and sick to death of the heat and the nausea and Tad's moods kept her silent.

A wave of color rose in his face, and his eyes took on a hard shine. But even when he rose and came toward her, she wasn't afraid of him. Only when he grabbed her arm and jerked her to her feet did she understand how angry he was. She stared into his eyes, and a feeling of helplessness paralyzed her. He shook her, and another fear came to her—for the baby she was carrying.

She began to struggle, frantic to get away, and his hands tightened around her arms. She moaned with pain and went limp, and only then did he let her go. She clutched at the edge of a chair, staring at Tad. He was breathing hard and the wild look in his eyes, as if he had just seen a ghost, startled her into silence.

"God," he said. "Oh, God, Shelley!"

He turned and, walking unevenly, started for the door. Part of her was still afraid and thankful that he was leaving, but the part of her that loved him had a sudden revelation.

"He did that to your mother, didn't he?" she said to his retreating back.

At first she thought he hadn't heard her. Then he turned, and the misery on his face told her she was right. Her only thought to comfort him, she flew toward him, her arms outstretched. When he put his head on her shoulder, she began to cry again, but this time she cried for both of them.

She'd been so busy feeling sorry for herself that she hadn't thought of what he was going through. If the past month had been hard on her, what had it been for him? She already knew that he was dissatisfied with his job, that he didn't like the senior master sergeant who was his immediate superior and who, according to Tad, was always on his back. Now she finally understood tht he was ashamed because he couldn't give her the things he thought she deserved. And why hadn't he said something, talked about it, brought it out into the open? Was there some lack in her that kept him at arm's length except when they were making love?

She pulled away and looked into Tad's face. "We should talk more," she said. "I know you aren't happy with your job— why don't you tell me about it?"

A closed look came into his eyes. "I don't believe in bringing my work home nights," he said.

"Where else would you bring them? I'm your wife—it would help if you talked your problems over with me."

"No! I want to forget them when I leave work."

She was tempted to let it drop, but she knew that if she did, if she didn't persist, the pattern of their life together would be set. There would always be two camps—her problems and his problems.

Had she made a mistake, not telling him about the things that bothered her instead of putting on the happy little bride act all the time? Could that be the reason both of them flared up so easily, the reason why Tad had been driven to the edge of violence? Did they hold too much in? Or maybe he had noticed her lack of response when he made love to her. He never complained, always told her how great it was, but what if he suspected something was wrong?

She'd been told so often how fragile men's egos were when it came to sex—but then it wasn't Tad who had the problem. He was always ready for sex. It was this—this frigidity she'd discovered in herself. She loved it when he kissed her, when he took her in his arms and petted her, loved the preliminaries of lovemaking, but then, right in the middle of their love-making, something always happened, a wall rose between them, and suddenly she only wanted it to be over and finished with.

She wasn't ignorant of sex, only inexperienced, so she knew very well what was supposed to happen. But it never did— never. Only so far and then no farther. Would it always be this way? If so, he must never know. Because what an irony if he'd given up his precious freedom and taken on so many new problems only to have a frigid wife on his hands.

But other avenues were open for a better understanding and closeness between them. Yes, she had to persist, had to make him confide in her, as she must learn to be open with him about her true feelings. And if he didn't listen at first? Then she would keep trying until he did. For their marriage to succeed, they simply had to communicate, had to be friends as well as lovers.

She pulled away from Tad, forcing him to look at her. "If you don't want to talk about your job, that's okay. But I'm not going to fall into that same trap. I've been trying to be a good sport, and I guess I overdid it. You think that everything is great, but I need help, Tad. I need to talk things out with you. This life is so new to me, more than you realize, I think. I lived in Europe so long that lots of things you take for granted are strange to me. And except for you and Dixie, there isn't anyone I can turn to for help."

"So talk," he said, but there was an edge in his voice.

"I'll start by explaining what must have happened to the chicken. It smelled a little strange when I put it on to boil, but I thought maybe stewed chicken always smelled that way. Besides, I've been a little—my stomach's been a little upset lately. The chicken was already partially thawed when I bought it. I stood in line at the commissary for almost an hour and then waited in the heat another hour for the shuttle bus, so the chicken was out of refrigeration for almost two and a half hours."

"So next time you'll have to make sure the meat you buy is still frozen solid."

"That isn't always possible. But you could take the shuttle bus to work one day a week so I can use the jeep."

He shrugged, not looking at her. "You don't want to drive that old jeep. It's got a bulky clutch—and it's not automatic, either."

"You can show me how."

"If you had the jeep, I couldn't come home for lunch."

"Oh, you can manage with something from the snack bar one day a week."

"But they don't serve nooners at the snack bar," he said, grinning. When she didn't smile, he added, "What else is bugging you? Spit it out."

"That business of shaking me. You can't do that again, Tad. Ever. If you do, if you ever try anything like that again, I'll walk out on you. I know something's wrong at work, but you can't take it out on me."

"I don't know what the hell you're talking about."

"When you come home nights, you're wound up like a clock. You don't unwind until you've had a few beers—or sex. But that isn't healthy. You should be able to talk to me. I'm your wife. I'm on your side. You can tell me anything and I'll still be on your side—"

"Hey, you're making like a nagging wife. How about cooling it?"

She almost gave up then. Only the gut feeling that if she did, they would eventually lose what they had together prompted her next words. "We have to have this out—and right now. If we don't, if we go on pretending nothing's wrong, then we're heading for real trouble. But first, I want your word that what just happened won't happen again. I'm not about to be battered wife. Not even once. That anger you carry around inside you— what's going to trigger it off the next time?"

"Shelley, I swear to you that I'll never lose my cool again like that—"

"How often did your father hit your mother? Often? Just once in a while when he'd had too much to drink? You hated it, didn't you? And yet something deep inside you believes that this is the way to express anger to your wife. When you saw yourself as an image of your father, it scared you. Well, it scared me, too. I'm not your mother. I have too much pride to let you mistreat me. If you ever raise your hand to me again, I'll walk right out of your life and I won't come back—and if I walk away, you'll lose more than a wife. You'll lose your child, too."

"Are you saying that you're—"

"I'm pregnant. Almost three months. I just found out today."

"Haven't you been keeping track of your periods?"

"They've always been irregular. I thought it was—you know, the stress of getting married." Her face flushed as he grinned at her. "How do you feel about it, Tad? You aren't mad, are you?"

"Mad? You've gotta be kidding! Hey, your old man is some kind of stud, isn't he? It must've happened the first time—or damned near it. And what you want to bet it won't be a boy? The Brotski men always make boys."

Shelley watched him, smiling, but she was aware of disappointment, too. He had reacted so casually—but what did she expect? In his family, babies were a normal occurrence.

His brothers had a dozen kids between them. But still—hadn't he seized upon the subject too quickly? Was he using it as an excuse to end any serious discussions with her?

For now, maybe it was best to leave it alone. Later, she would approach him again. And he hadn't agreed to let her use the jeep once a week, either. In fact, he hadn't committed himself to anything—was that part of the Brotski life-style? This separation of the sexes, of roles? Was this how it would be in their marriage, always that division except when they came together for sex?

As for having a baby, how strange that she felt so—so empty, so unloving of the child she was carrying inside her womb. As a lonely girl, spending Christmas holidays with boarding-school matrons because her parents were going to be away for the holidays or because her parents' "obligations" didn't leave any time for their daughter, she had dreamed of having a big family of her own someday.

But now that she was pregnant, she realized how little she knew about children of any age, much less how to take care of an infant. Was motherhood so natural that when the time came, she would know what to do by instinct? Or were her mixed feelings about the baby unnatural? Would her child be a replica of her, unwanted and unloved by its own mother?

"Hey, you're awful quiet over there. Come sit on my lap. You'll soon be so big I won't be able to get my arms around you. Better make up for lost time now."

Although he was smiling, there was something unnatural about his teasing, and she suspected that he was ashamed of his violence earlier. But why didn't he talk about it? Why did he lock it away inside?

"I was wondering how you'll react if the baby is a girl," she said.

"Oh, I think we should keep her," he said. "In fact, I like the idea of a little girl. If she looks like you, I'll have to beat the boys off with a bat someday."

"Maybe she'll take after your side of the family. All muscles and no brains."

She had meant it as a joke, but he didn't laugh. Instead, a flush spread over his face.

"Is that how you think of my folks?" he said. "As ignorant hicks?"

"No, of course not. I was kidding—you're always saying that I have no sense of humor. So I made a joke. A *joke*, Tad."

"Well, it wasn't all that funny," he muttered.

Shelley felt a wave of weariness that made her bones ache. She slipped off his lap and stood up. "I think I'll go to bed early tonight. I'm still a little woozy—I guess my morning sickness has shifted to the evenings."

She bent and brushed her lips against his cheek, then moved away so quickly that his outstretched hand fell short of the mark. By the time he came into the bedroom, she was in bed, pretending to be asleep. He touched her shoulder, said her name softly, but she didn't answer or open her eyes, and after a moment, he slid into bed beside her.

Only when his breathing deepened and she knew he was asleep did she relax and shift her body to a more comfortable position. Her thoughts were painful—and edged with guilt. It was the first night they'd gone to sleep without making love, and although sex wasn't anything like she'd expected it to be, still she wanted to be close to him, the closeness that they only seemed to obtain in bed. Was this to be the pattern of their marriage? Both of them pretending that everything was fine between them except when one of them exploded into angry words? Because if it was, wouldn't she be better off without him, even though it meant raising a child alone!

The next day, she went to tell Dixie about the baby. Dixie's assumption that it was good news seemed to put things back into perspective. Over glasses of iced tea, they talked about babies, about pregnancy, and Dixie's advice, as always, was practical and down to earth.

When Dixie went to replenish the tea in their glasses, Shelley looked around her friend's neat quarters with envious eyes. It was strange how quickly her standards had changed. If she had moved directly into these quarters, she would have been disappointed by their shortcomings—the ancient wood floors that must be murder to keep polished, the sagging cushions on the rattan sofa and chairs, the utilitarian furniture. But after a month in temporary quarters and then living in a near empty house, these quarters looked like a mansion, especially because Dixie had made her living room cheerful by putting out trinkets, the kind sold in the BX, camouflaging the sofa with bright cushions, hanging framed temple tracings from Thailand and embroidered pictures from Hong Kong on the wall.

"I can't wait until we get some furniture," she told Dixie when her friend came back into the room.

"I know what you mean. But you do have decent housing, which is a plus. Not up to stateside standards, but still livable. Some people never move on base at all, you know."

"Why not? Base housing is so convenient—"

"It's the security problem. The guards in those civilian compounds where you live are off-duty Philippine National Guardsmen. Not only do they have permission to carry guns, but they'll use them if they have to, which the local hoods know."

"But the base has plenty of guards, too."

"Who aren't allowed to carry guns. So the rip-off artists hit the base quarters regularly. We've been burglarized twice—the last time, they got all our small appliances and some pesos I had hidden away in an old purse. Serves me right. I knew better, but I was going into Angeles City to have some dresses made, and I had just bought a good supply of pesos."

"How do they get on base? There's a high fence around the perimeter."

"Fences—" Dixie stopped to shake her head and laugh. "Why, sometimes they steal the fences, too. Any kind of metal, even wire, is valuable here. Just yesterday, Clarence went over to the Nigrito village to do some bartering, was driving along the perimeter road when all of a sudden something didn't look right. It took him a while to realize that a whole section of fence was gone—cut out as neat as you please."

"So it's more secure in the off-base compounds?"

"Some people think so, yes." She gave Shelley a long look. "Don't you start worrying about it. Just keep your eyes open—and be careful. You're bound to be approached to sell your cigarette ration on a regular basis as soon as it's known that you don't smoke. You can get enough for them to pay your housegirl and your yardboy, but it's tricky. Sometimes they make an example of someone, and—it could be you."

"Oh, I wouldn't do anything illegal! Tad would kill me."

Dixie started to say something but obviously changed her mind because she got to her feet and went into the kitchen. When she returned with a plate of cookies, the conversation took another direction.

That evening, Shelley repeated some of the things Dixie had told her. To her surprise, Tad was upset.

"You be careful what you say to Dixie. It sounds like she's part of the wife network. All that bunch does is cause trouble."

"Dixie isn't like that at all," Shelley protested. "Besides, she's my only friend here. I'm alone so much during the day——"

"There's plenty of things to keep you busy," he said impatiently. "You've got your housework and laundry and cooking."

"But I get lonesome, Tad. And what if you go on TDY? What do I do then?"

"What all the other wives do——wait until I get back," he said shortly. "Hell, take up a hobby or something. Or get acquainted with some of the other women here in the compound. What about that buck sergeant's wife next door? She's about your age."

"I spoke to her yesterday, but she just nodded and went right on walking."

"Yeah, well, you'll have your own kid to keep you busy in a few months. You won't have time to gossip with the other wives. Most of what you hear is all blown out of proportion, anyway."

Shelley stared at him, trying to make sense from his words. His face was wet with perspiration, and lines of fatigue cut into his face. She had a mental picture of her father, who always looked so impeccably dressed, even during his infrequent hours of leisure. What would the general say if he saw Tad now in his sweat-stained T-shirt, with rubber go-aheads on his bare feet and a can of beer in his hand? Would he tell her that it was just what he'd expected when he'd learned she was marrying an enlisted man?

Shelley gave herself a mental shake. She, of all people, knew that there were no stereotypes among enlisted personnel. They weren't the dog faces of yesterday——most of them were trained technicians, many with college degrees. And enlisted men didn't have a priority on casual dress during their off-duty hours. Most of the high-ranking officers she'd met were woefully careless about their civilian clothes. Hadn't she heard her mother's caustic remarks about her husband's subordinates and their Hong Kong knit suits?

And what her father might or not think of Tad shouldn't matter. And yet——it did. It irritated her because it forced her to make comparisons. She didn't want to notice anything about Tad that wasn't favorable——such as the four-letter words he used so often and his failure sometimes to take a shower before he made love to her.

Some of it, she was aware, was her own fault. She'd been so reluctant at first to say anything that might seem critical. Now it was too late. If she asked him to take a shower at noon before he took her to bed, he would think of the other times they'd made love and know that it had bothered her. And why did it bother her, come to think of it? He showered regularly, both morning and night. Was her aversion to a little honest sweat a manifestation of something deeper, a resentment that she didn't dare put a name to?

Of course, she had faults that annoyed him, too. How often had Tad mentioned, if only by a joking remark, that she'd left a dirty pan soaking in the sink overnight or that she'd missed a spot when she dusted the furniture? Was his mother a fanatic housekeeper? Or was it more of the same, that when she didn't conform to some ideal he had in his head, he felt cheated?

Well, she felt cheated, too. She had expected sex to be—how had Bobby Jo once described it? Bells to ring and chimes to chime? She had been assuming that it was her fault—but what if Tad was simply a rotten lover?

If only they would talk more. But he had shut the door on that—or had he? Maybe it would be different after their furniture was delivered and she had a housegirl to help with the work. Maybe then she wouldn't feel so tired and depressed all the time.

The next week their furniture arrived. Tad, as an E-5, rated items that were long past their prime. Although the felt-filled cushions of the rattan sofa and chairs had the strong musty odor she had come to associate with the Philippines, Shelley didn't complain. She was too grateful to have reasonably comfortable chairs to sit on and a real bed instead of an air mattress on the floor—and a roomy buffet for their dishes, even though so far she had nothing to store except the thick gray-white plates and cups they'd drawn from the base's "lending closet."

But the mattress on the bed was another matter. It sagged so much in the middle that it gave her a backache and kept her squirming at night, trying to find a comfortable spot. But when she asked Tad if they could buy one of the secondhand foam-rubber mattresses she saw advertised on the bulletin board at the commissary, he shook his head.

"You'll just have to put up with some inconveniences. Your

husband is a sergeant, not a general. You said you could handle it. Why don't you try being a good sport? You don't hear other wives complaining."

"I don't hear other wives—period. So far, not one soul has been over here to say hello, welcome to the compound, how are you. I don't think it's my place to make the first move—"

"It'll take time. Maybe it's your attitude."

"My attitude? What does that mean?"

"It's that look you get when you meet someone new. Like you're afraid they're gonna bite you. You might trying smiling more and acting more human."

"I'm very human, Tad."

"Oh, hell—I didn't mean to hurt your feelings. Look, I know what a great person you are. You're warm-hearted and . . . well, fantastic, but the women in this compound, they don't know you. They judge you by—other things."

"What other things?"

He ran his fingers through his short hair, looking irritated. "The way you take advantage of the yardboy, for instance. He does twice as much work for you as he does for the neighbors. They resent that—after all, we all chip in the same amount for his services."

Shelley looked at him in bewilderment. "Why, I just point out what needs to be done and he does it."

"But that's the point. It's so easy for you. You take household help for granted. You've had people waiting on you all your life. Ordinary people don't feel comfortable ordering paid help around. So okay, some of the housegirls and yardboys take advantage of that. So what? It's expected. But the other women notice how much the yardboy does for you and they don't like it. Which could be one reason they're so standoffish."

"It seems I can't do anything right," she said bitterly. "Maybe you married the wrong woman."

"I married the right woman—but you did say we should talk more and be honest with each other, didn't you? This isn't easy for me, either, honey. All day long, I put up with a lot of shit, and when I come home nights, I want peace and quiet. I don't want a wife nagging at me—so let's both drop the subject, okay?"

She started to do just that, but suddenly angry words were

spewing out of her, surprising her as much, she suspected, as they did Tad.

"I'm not going to drop it. Being open isn't supposed to be one-sided. You seem to think it's okay for you to say what's wrong with me, but I'm not allowed to say anything about you. Okay, you've had your say. So now it's my turn. You aren't perfect, you know—"

"I know that. I never pretended to be perfect."

"You haven't? Funny. I've had the idea lately that you think you're God's gift to women. All you've talked about for the past week is that new female airman in your shop."

"Oh, God! Look, Susie is . . . well, she's one of the guys. Sure, I like her. That's because I can talk to her about things at work you wouldn't be interested in."

"I haven't had a chance to be interested in your work. You refuse to discuss it with me."

"You know how I feel about bringing—"

"Your job home at nights. Yes, I know. You've made it very clear. But I want to be part of your whole life. It's obvious you've been getting a lot of sympathy from this—this Susie Whatsit. You could get it from me if you'd just open up and tell me what the hell's bothering you."

"Don't curse. You know I don't like to hear a woman curse."

"I thought you loved four-letter words. They come out of your mouth often enough. I don't like to hear *you* curse, either. Does that matter to you? Or is this more of the old double standard? Men curse but women don't? You may have left home, but you brought it right along with you, Tad. You have all these rules about what women can and can't do, and you expect me to accept them. I don't even know what they are! You drop them on me out of the blue like you expect me to assimilate them by some kind of osmosis or something."

"Okay, so you know some big words. So what? This conversation is getting too heavy for me—why don't we drop it?"

"I'm not finished. You said that sure, we should be honest with each other, but what you really meant is that you can criticize me all you want, but I can't do the same to you. I'm supposed to live by your rules. Well, that isn't going to happen, Tad. I'm sick of it. Sometimes—"

She stopped, warned by the flush that swept over his face. Instinct told her to back away, but she knew that if she did, she would lose the battle—and the war, too. So she faced him down, stared into his furious eyes, not giving an inch, and after a moment, it was Tad who backed down.

"Okay, spit the rest of it out," he said.

"I don't want our marriage to fail. I love you, Tad, and I know you love me. We got married so we could be together for the rest of our lives. It's too good between us most of the time to let it slip away. I'm trying very hard to be the kind of wife you need. But you have to give a little, too. For one thing, I asked you to leave me the jeep once a week. I know that some of the men in your outfit carpool with each other. You could arrange something so I could have the jeep once a week. I hate shopping in the afternoons—it's so damned hot in the commissary with the air conditioning off, and I have to go so often because I can't carry much on the bus. If I could take a turn at providing transportation, maybe I could carpool with the other wives in the compound. And you already know all this. What's the real reason you don't want to leave me the jeep? Don't you trust my driving? If so, you're wrong. I'm a very good driver."

For a moment, she thought he wasn't going to answer. When he did, his voice was tight.

"The jeep doesn't belong to me anymore. I sold it to one of the guys on the line who wants transportaton back and forth to work so his wife can have their car all the time. The deal is I pick him up mornings, bring him home at lunch and after work, and I get to use the jeep the rest of the day and on weekends unless he needs two cars for some reason. So far, it's worked out pretty good, although I'll have to turn the jeep over to him when he gets the price he wants for his other car. When he gets his orders to go stateside, I have first dibs on buying the jeep back. I'm hoping I can swing it by then."

She waited for more. When it didn't come, she asked the obvious question. "But why did you sell him the jeep in the first place?"

"Because I needed the bread."

"You've never said anything about needing money. In fact, you told me that we were getting along fine."

"You really have to pull it all out of me, don't you? Okay, we're down to rock bottom, stone broke. I had to borrow from Air Force Aid—and it's a loan, not a grant. No interest, but I have to pay it back."

"But why are we so broke?"

"Because it's so damned expensive, living here I had to put down a big deposit on this place, and then I bought the jeep, and . . . well, I thought we could swing it, but I underestimated the expenses and first thing I knew, I was busted."

"Why didn't you say something? No wonder you were so upset about the grocery bills. Why didn't you tell me the truth?"

"Hell, Shelley, how do you think I feel, not being able to support my own wife? I thought I could make it up, but then—"

"You should have been honest with me."

"I didn't want to worry you. You've never had to think about what things cost. You don't know the first thing about handling a budget."

"And it's the money that's been worrying you?"

"That and my job. The old man called me in last week and laid down the law. I have to straighten out my finances or it goes on my records. That spread Harnessey saw didn't help. He told everybody in the outfit how high on the hog we live. I came here under a cloud, you know. Everybody figures I must've really fouled up at Hickam for them to assign me to Clark six weeks before I was supposed to rotate back to the States, especially since there's no slot for me here right now. Hell, I hate the job they've got me on. I'm filling an E-four slot, for God's sake, working as a supply clerk. I'm a damned good mechanic, and that's what I want to do. It drives me crazy, handing out stinking screws and tools all day long instead of working on the line."

"Oh, Tad, I'm sorry. But you can't expect me to know this unless you tell me."

"It's just that . . . hell, a guy is supposed to take care of his wife."

"He's supposed to talk to her, too—except maybe in Pennsylvania."

He grinned at her. "My old man never told Mom any of his business. He said you couldn't trust a woman to keep her mouth shut. I guess I picked that up from him. So from now on, you tell me your sad stories and I'll tell you mine."

Shelley felt like crying. He was trying to make a joke out of it, but she had won a small victory today, one that she hoped would make things easier. And this Tad, showing his vulnerability, his concern for her, was the man she'd married.

She put her arms around him. "We'll make it, Tad. It just takes time."

It was a week later that Tad told her he was taking her to Camp John Hay, the military rest camp in the mountains near Baguio. He came in from work, stripping off his olive-green fatigues at the door. Dressed only in shorts and T-shirt, he caught her up and whirled her around. "Hey, hey, little mother, you got a kiss for your old man?"

Shelley, who loved him when he was playful, laughed out loud. "I do, I do," she said, and kissed him.

"In that case, I've got a surprise for you. How'd you like a little vacation? Cool mountain air, no cooking, no housework, nothing to do but stuff yourself at the mess hall, maybe go to a movie and do some sight-seeing, make love, and just laze around?"

"I'd love it," she said. "And now I suppose you're going to try to sell me the Brooklyn Bridge?"

"I'm not kidding. We're going to Baguio—I made a reservation at Camp John Hay for next week. Cabin in the pines, fireplace—and cool, cool, cool nights. Five whole days—how about that? So what do you think of your old man now, huh?"

"I think he's great," she said slowly.

"Well, let's show some enthusiasm, girl!"

"I love it, I love it. Only . . ." She hesitated. Although she had hoped that they would talk more, so far there had been no confidences, only a few bits of information about the job he hated so much—and he hadn't mentioned the female airman again.

"Only what?"

"Can we afford it, Tad?"

"Would I go for it if we couldn't?"

"I hope not. This isn't—you don't have to prove anything to me, Tad. I only—"

"I'm not trying to prove anything. I knocked myself out getting time off. What does it take to please you, Shelley?"

"Okay, I'm pleased. I'm delirious. I really mean it. And if you found a way to clear up those debts, then that's it. But we did say we were going to talk things over from now on, didn't we?"

"Get off my back, Shelley. I'm doing the best I can, but I

keep getting the message that my best isn't good enough for you."

"You're being unreasonable." Tad's face blurred suddenly, and Shelley had to sit down quickly because the room was rocking around her.

"Hey, what's wrong? You're white as a sheet." Tad's voice was full of concern as he took her hand.

"It's just a little dizzy spell. It's perfectly normal for pregnant women."

"So you say."

"I went to the doctor for my checkup today—remember? Everything's fine. In fact, he's happy because I've only gained a few pounds."

"If you ask me, you could stand a little more weight. You're a lot thinner than you were in Hawaii."

"It's the heat—and getting adjusted to the change in climate."

"And then I come home and pick fights with you. I don't know what the hell I do that for. Maybe this lousy heat is getting to me, too."

"Or maybe—" She broke off. How could she say that maybe he felt guilty? How could she convince him that she was speaking the truth when she told him that the trappings of her former life had never mattered to her, that all she wanted was him—the way he'd been on their honeymoon?

CHAPTER
↟ 18 ↟

TAD LAY ON HIS BACK, HIS ARMS FOLDED UNDER HIS HEAD, staring up at the wooden beams above the bed. The odor of woodsmoke, from the fire they lit the night before, lingered in the cabin, and the blanket that covered his loins covered Shelley, too, and he was aware, as he always was when they were close, of the warmth radiating from her body.

He had thought he would mind when she began to show her pregnancy, but instead he felt proud—proud that he was the one who had planted his seed inside her womb, proud that she belonged to him, that he'd put his mark on her. Although he was ashamed of it, there was another reason why he welcomed the thickening of her waist. He hated the way other men stared at her. But soon her pregnancy would protect her from their stares, and she would be completely his.

He rolled to his side and rested his hand against the curve of her abdomen, fancying he could feel the movement of their baby, although Shelley had told him it was too soon. He wished now that he had paid more attention to the "women talk" of his sisters-in-law when they got together with his mother. Was Shelley telling him the truth when she said that her occasional dizzy spells were normal? Well, there was something he meant to do before he left for Korea, and that was to go have a talk with her doctor.

Before he left for Korea . . .

He still hadn't told Shelley about his TDY assignment, and

yet they'd been here at Camp John Hay for almost three days. But things had gone so smoothly, as if they were back in Hawaii during those first weeks. He hadn't wanted to ruin it by telling her that the reason he'd been given leave was because he'd be going to Korea for four months. He would have to tell her soon, of course, but not the rest of it, that he had volunteered for TDY to prove he wasn't a goof-up and also because it meant returning to his old job as a line mechanic.

It hadn't been an impulse. He'd been thinking about it ever since he'd overheard Sgt. Myles telling one of his cronies that he wished he could get someone to take the TDY assignment he'd drawn because his old lady was raising hell and threatening to go back to the States. It had been too good a chance to pass up, so Tad had volunteered for the four-month tour. The guys had all looked at him like he was crazy. They probably figured he was having domestic troubles. If Shelley was farther along in her pregnancy, he wouldn't dream of leaving her for four months, but—hell, she'd said herself that she was in perfect health. And separations were part of being an air force wife, weren't they? She knew the score—after all, she'd been an air force brat.

So why hadn't he told her? He'd had a dozen opportunities. In fact, why hadn't he told her a lot of things? Like how he'd sold their cigarette rations for the next year to one of the guys for the money to pay for this little vacation. She'd suspected something, but . . . well, some things were best kept quiet. Besides, it wasn't any of her business. The fact that she'd tried so hard to get him to open up had only made him more determined to hold his tongue. He wasn't about to become a pussy-whipped husband, asking his wife's permission for everything he did. Hell, he was a man—and he meant to make his own decisions.

Sometimes he thought he'd go crazy, trying to figure out what Shelley wanted from him. Nobody he knew—at least, nobody back home—worried about communication. If a man took good care of his family, he was a considered a good provider, which was just about the best compliment you could pay a guy.

And if he had a few beers and played some poker with the guys on Friday nights—it was his own business. Women were expected to keep house, raise the kids, take care of a man in bed—and if they did these things, a man was counted lucky.

So why was it so complicated with Shelley? Was it all those foreign schools she'd attended, that fancy education her folks had given her? Those two cold fish didn't look as if they had to communicate with each other. If ever he saw a couple of clones, it was General and Mrs. Curtis Pritchard.

The thought of Shelley's parents chilled him. Come to think of it, he was a lucky man. What if they'd approved of the marriage and he had to see them all the time? Yes, he was lucky—and he was going to stop this kind of stewing before it drove him crazy. This vacation had been a good idea because it gave Shelley and him time to enjoy each other again. They had made love last night, and it had been good—sex with Shelley was always good.

But not perfect. Not like it had been at first. Lately, he'd been aware that something was wrong in that department. Oh, Shelley never refused him, not even when he woke her up at night for a second round, but she was always so quiet while they were making love. Some of the chicks he'd made out with in the past had clawed and scratched and moaned how good it was—which made him feel pretty much of a man. Not that any of those women could compare to Shelley. No, she was something special, a class act.

He raised up on one elbow to look down at Shelley. She was lying on her face now, her head buried in the curve of her arm, and from the way she was breathing, deep and slow, he knew she was still asleep. He reached out to touch her shoulder, and the twin mounds of her buttocks caught his attention. Carefully, he folded back the covers, exposing her smooth back and the dimples above her buttocks that he thought were so sexy, and he thought how fantastic she was, a woman with dimples behind her knees and above her buttocks.

Unable to resist, he cupped the soft warm mounds in his hands. Almost immediately, his arousal was pushing against his leg, pulsating and throbbing, and he nudged her thighs apart with his knee, kneeling between them. When he rubbed himself against her, she didn't move, but he knew she was awake because she stiffened under the stroking. He had intended it as a joke, a bit of love play before he coaxed her into sex again, but suddenly he was caught up in an urge so strong that he fell upon her, grunting under his breath as he entered her. A few lunges later it was all over, and he collapsed on top of her, panting.

She still hadn't moved. It occurred to him that she hadn't moved or said a word, not even when he'd taken her. Gently, he rolled her over. The tears on her cheeks glistened in a ray of morning sun that slid through the window louvers, and when he tried kiss her, she shook her head violently and pulled away.

"Hey—what's wrong? Did I scare you or something? You looked so damned sexy that I couldn't resist—look, I'll make it up to you. Next time, it'll be good for you, too. Okay?"

She still wouldn't look at him, and he tried to make a joke out of it. "I shouldn't have done that, right?"

"I wasn't ready for you, Tad. It's painful when I'm not ready. And you didn't even kiss me before you climbed on top of me."

Tad rolled away to sit on the edge of the bed, feeling a little aggrieved. "I got carried away. I was fooling around and then it got out of hand. You looked so damned tempting—you've got the best-looking tush I've ever seen. You mad at me?"

She sat up, too. "I'm not mad. But sometimes I have the suspicion that my feelings don't really count."

"Of course they count. You're one fantastic lady. The guys you dated before we were married must've told you that a hundred times."

"I didn't do much dating, Tad. I went to all-girl schools—and the matrons watched us like hawks. Even during the vacation tours my mother arranged for me, I was always well chaperoned. I know Europe like the back of my hand—the resort areas and the parts you can see from a tour bus. But I never got a chance to know the people—including boys. Sometimes we found ways to meet them, but they all seemed so young, except—" She broke off.

"Except who?"

"Karl Breuner. He was a ski instructor at a resort near Grenoble. My ski team went there for a month, and he gave us advanced lessons. I sneaked out at night a couple of times to meet him."

"So what happened?"

"I found out he was meeting one of the other girls, too. I thought my heart was broken—but of course it wasn't."

"And that's the only serious relationship you had before you met me?"

"The only one."

Tad was silent, aware of mixed feelings. He should be glad

that she'd only had one boyfriend before she met him, but instead he felt jealous as hell. She'd been a virgin the first time they made it together, but some kinds of heavy petting were almost the same as going all the way. Maybe the other guy had known some tricks he didn't know—and she was measuring him up against a real lover-boy type. Because something was wrong with their sex life. Was it possible that she was still hung up on this Karl Breuner?

"This ski instructor—did you keep in touch with him?"

"After we left Grenoble. I never saw him again."

"Are you saying that that one experience turned you off men until you met me?"

"Why are you asking all these questions, Tad?" A tiny smile curved the corners of her mouth. "Don't tell me you're jealous."

"Hell, yes, I'm jealous. I don't like anyone to even look at you," he said truthfully. He knew other guys at work, even some of the happily married ones, envied him his good-looking wife. But he didn't like the way they stared at Shelley, as if they wanted to undress her. Some of it wasn't their fault. It didn't matter what Shelley wore, she still looked sexy. No wonder she had a hard time making friends with other wives. It was those incredibly long legs, that blond hair—and her mouth. No red-blooded man could look at that mouth and not want to kiss her. Sometimes he wished that she looked like— well, more like other wives. Some of them were pretty as hell, but they didn't have that extra something that made Shelley stand out no matter where she was.

Tad studied Shelley's averted face, and it occurred to him how hard it had been for her to tell him about the ski instructor. At the time, it must have—what had she said? Broken her heart? Girls that age got these violent crushes, and when it fizzled, yeah, it could hurt like hell.

And why should her silly little romance suddenly make him feel so sad? What had happened to his jealousy? Sometimes he didn't understand himself—and he certainly didn't understand Shelley. It made his head ache, just trying to figure out what made her tick. Life had been so simple before he'd met her. For one thing, not once since he'd rolled in the hay with Marcy Leske when he was twelve had he ever doubted that he was a superstud. Every girl he'd ever slept with had told him how great he was—so why was he having doubts? And if

Shelley wasn't all that sold on the way he made love, why had she married him?

Hell, it didn't make sense. Sex *was* love, wasn't it?

He opened his mouth to ask her the question, but the words wouldn't come. For one thing, it was embarrassing to talk about. Sure, he had no inhibitions about sex. He'd even done kinky things when the girl was willing and it seemed right. But to talk about sex seriously, not in a kidding way—no, that just wasn't his thing.

And for all her talk about communication, he was sure Shelley felt the same way. Sometimes, when he made a crude remark or told her a raunchy joke, her face got stiff and she changed the subject. If dirty jokes turned her off, why didn't she just come out and say so? Was it because she didn't want to make him mad? Was she scared of him, for God's sake?

"How come you never said anything about this sex thing before?" he said finally.

She didn't answer. She reached for her robe, put it on.

"Come on—open up. If you don't like some of the things we do, why don't you say so? I can't read minds, you know."

"I didn't want to hurt your feelings," she said.

The answer was so surprising that it was a while before he asked. "You aren't afraid of me, are you?"

"Of course not. Why would I be afraid of you?" She sounded genuinely puzzled.

"Sometimes . . . well, I blow off a lot when I get irritated—like when I shook you that time. I thought maybe that scared you."

A smile tugged at her mouth. "I know why you did it, and it's okay. Really it is."

Tad was relieved that the conversation had lightened. Even so, one question still nagged at him. "Some of the things we do when—you know, we're in the sack together don't feel right to you, do they?" he said suddenly.

He thought she would laugh off the question, but she didn't. "No, I don't like all of it. Women—women are different from men. We aren't ready for sex so fast."

"I never had any complaints before," he said, and despite himself, his voice sounded stiff.

"I know. Maybe that's the trouble."

"What the hell does that mean?"

"It means—I don't think we should talk about this right

now. You're only going to get mad—and besides, I don't know whether I'm right or not."

"Say it," he growled. "You know you're just dying to get it out in the open."

"Not when you take that attitude. I think we'd better talk about this some other time."

She rose and started for the bathroom. He grabbed her hand, holding her there. "Tell me what's bothering you, Shelley—and start with why you got so uptight when I said I'd never had any complaints before."

"You won't like it."

"Say it, dammit!"

"Okay—but remember you insisted. I suspect that the girls you've slept with . . . well, they know you can get just about any woman you want, so they're afraid to be honest with you. You've never had the chance to find out what really turns women on because the women you were with always told you how great you are in bed."

Tad released her hand and stood up. "So what you're saying is that I'm a lousy lover?"

"You're not a lousy lover, Tad. But sometimes I want you to hold me and talk to me before we make love. And I want you to—I'm not always ready for sex so quickly. I get the feeling sometimes that you're trying to prove what a man you are, but you don't have to prove anything, not to me. I love you. Just having you hold me is enough sometimes."

Tad felt the hurt deep in his guts. It stirred up an earlier hurt, opened an old wound that he'd thought was healed. He had been ten, maybe eleven, when he'd come in from school one afternoon and heard his father talking to his mom in the kitchen, heard his own name. He hadn't understood, not at that age, what his father meant when he said that Tad acted like a goddamned fairy sometimes. But he'd noted the word and later he'd asked one of his brothers about it. That's when he'd found out that there were men who preferred to have sex with other men—and that his father was afraid his youngest son would turn out to be one.

It had taken a long time to get over the anger—and the fear that his father just might be right. His first experience with girls had ended that worry—or so he'd thought. But now, with Shelley's words ringing in his ears—"sometimes I think you're trying to prove what a man you are"—the anger, black and raging, came rolling up from deep inside him, catching him unaware. He felt depleted, less than a man—and boiling mad.

He wanted to strike out at Shelley, hurt her as she'd hurt him. The muscles in his arms tensed involuntarily, and his hands formed into fists. Realizing that he didn't dare stay in the same room with her, he turned and headed for the door, ignoring Shelley's cry of protest.

For a long time he ran along one of the paths that led from the cabin area through the woods and up to a hilltop lodge. He met no one, for which he was grateful later because he was sure he must have looked like a madman, loping along with his face tight with anger. It was when exhaustion finally stopped him that he knew their vacation was over. And it served Shelley right. She had started the fight—or had she? Hadn't he insisted on the truth? But what the hell kind of truth was that? That she didn't like the way he made love? No, the real problem here was that Shelley was frigid, a cold fish of a woman. . . .

It was past noon when he returned to the cabin. Shelley was still in bed, but now she was lying on her back, the blanket pulled over her shoulders, one bare arm covering her face. "Get packed," he said abruptly. "I'll be back here in an hour, and you'd better be ready to leave on the two o'clock bus or I'll go back to Clark without you."

Her arm dropped away from her face. Her eyes were swollen, her nose red, and she'd chewed her lower lip until it was raw. She wasn't pretty now. In fact, she looked like hell, and the sight of her shattered his anger, filled him with shame.

"What's happening to us, Shelley?" he asked, his voice hoarse with fear. "What are we doing to each other?"

She began to cry—silent tears that ran down her cheeks. He'd never seen anyone cry like that before, without trying to wipe away the tears. He went to her and pulled her into his arms. He rocked her back and forth, and he knew that nothing mattered except staying together. The hurt, the blow to his masculine pride—that wasn't important. Shelley loved him, and he loved her—why had he never said those words to her? She said them to him all the time. But no, he'd been too busy polishing his image as the big macho man from Pennsylvania. Instead, he'd told her he was crazy about her, told her how she turned him on, that she had the best-looking eyes or tush or tits in the world. And still she loved him so much that she hadn't told him the truth, that he had a lot to learn about making love to a woman.

Well, she was right about him being spoiled. Why hadn't he figured this out for himself? All those women, those easy conquests—they had served only one purpose. Every time he'd taken one to bed he'd really been thumbing his nose at his old man and yelling, "Yah, yah, yah—look what a stud I am, you old bastard!"

Well, who needed it? Like Shelley said, he didn't have to prove anything. It was time he did some fence mending, time he learned to—to communicate with his old lady. And the way to start was to admit that he had a lot to learn.

"I guess this means the honeymoon is over," he said, making a joke of it because old habits died hard.

She stopped crying and wiped her eyes. "You bastard," she said. She giggled then, and suddenly he was grinning, too. "Where have you been for the past few hours? Why didn't you stay here and fight?"

"I've been running, trying to get my head straightened out."

"And is it on straight now?"

"You'd better believe it." He had to do it, dammit, had to say the words, but it wasn't easy. "I'm sorry, Shelley. I'm the world's biggest fool. I love you. I love the hell out of you."

She started crying again, and he thought she was the most beautiful thing he'd ever seen with her red eyes and her swollen mouth and her runny nose. He said some things, made some promises, and she did the same. Afterward, he couldn't remember what either of them said. When she had stopped crying, he pulled her onto his lap on the edge of the bed.

"You have to promise that you won't let me get off course again. When we make love, tell me what you like—I want you to be happy, Shelley. That's the most important thing in the world to me."

"I'm not sure what I like," she confessed. "Maybe we'll just have to play it by ear."

"Right. Just think of all the fun we'll have, experimenting. For instance—how about this?" He touched her breast with the tips of his fingers. "You like?"

She sighed deeply. "I like," she said.

"And this?" He explored the softness of her breasts with his lips and tongue, then stroked her hips, her inner thighs, taking his time, prolonging the love play. Somewhere along the way,

he made a discovery. Pleasing Shelley, making her moan with
pleasure, was an aphrodisiac—why hadn't anyone ever told
him this before? When he finally stopped, she made an incoherent sound deep in her throat, and he told her, "I'm all
sweaty—I have to take a shower."

"You do and I'll turn off the hot water," she threatened. Her
face was flushed, and there was a fever in her eyes that made
him feel very humble. She was giving him her trust, not holding
back, putting it all on the line—but what if he didn't come
through and satisfy her this time? For a moment, fear paralyzed
him, but he pushed it out of his mind. If it didn't happen this
time, it would happen the next—or the next. Because now he
was putting her pleasure on the same plane as his, and that
made all the difference.

As he nuzzled the spot behind her ear that had her own
natural scent, he discovered that he was willing to wait for his
own pleasure. Always before, the sex act had been a high—
intense and sweet and quickly over with. But now, as he stroked
the incredible softness between her thighs, as he watched her
eyes take on a blind, feverish look, he wondered how he'd
missed the boat so long.

How many of the girls he'd laid had been faking as they
thrashed around under him, moaning and groaning? Shelley,
so obviously in the first stages of orgasm, seemed to be lost
in her own world, blind to everything but sensation, and he
felt proud that he was initiating her to what sex could be. Since
he was getting incredibly excited and she still hadn't touched
him, that proved something he'd always heard, that the brain
was the real erotic zone.

Shelley gave a moan; she exploded with a suddenness that
caught him by surprise. Her eyes frantic, she pulled him down
on top of her, and as he sank into her, she cried out his name
and he felt a rush of excitement that brought him to a thunderous
climax only a few seconds behind her.

"I love you, Shelley," he said, and wondered why it had
taken him so long when the words were so easy to say.

"I love you, too—but don't you ever go off like that again
and scare me to death, you hear?"

He buried his face between her breasts to hide his expression. His little mouse was growing teeth—and while he approved
on one level, he felt uneasy, too. They hadn't thrashed everything out yet. Maybe they never would, both of them being

who they were. But for now—God, he felt good! How could he have been sexually active so many years and never realized that a woman had her own needs, her own desires? Would Shelley be repelled if he tried other things—if he got really kinky?

Later, he discovered that she didn't mind at all. In fact, she had a few ideas of her own.

CHAPTER
✦ 19 ✦

It often seemed to Shelley, those first weeks after Tad left for Korea, that her life had become an endurance race. First, there was the loneliness. It accompanied her wherever she went, gibing at her, whispering an insidious stream of fears into her inner ear.

"Nothing's really changed . . . you're still alone, just as you've always been . . . you expected too much. . . ."

And then there was fear—fear of the unknown, fear of being pregnant in a foreign land, fear of the rumors that were epidemic at Clark, rumors that even she, so isolated from other people, heard as she sat in the waiting room of the GYN clinic, or drank a Coke at the BX snack bar, or waited in line at the commissary.

At night, when the wind hummed through the louvers of her bedroom windows, she huddled in bed, listening to the sound of the domesticity in the other compound quarters, wishing she were part of the life going on around her. As it was, she talked to no one except the yardboy or the jeepney drivers who took her to the base to shop or sometimes to one of the Filipino clerks at the BX. She was included in none of the coffee klatches in the compound, as ignored as if she didn't exist. Worst of all, she was plagued by something else, the suspicion that Tad had volunteered for TDY, that another man had been slated to go instead.

There was physical fear, too. Although reason told her that

the compound was well protected by off-duty National Guardsmen, instinct told her differently. If someone broke in while
she was asleep, how long would it take the guard to get there?
Would her neighbors even bother to come to her aid if she
screamed!

As week followed week, she found herself sinking into
lethargy, sometimes not leaving the house for days on end. She
began barricading herself in the bedroom, a chair pushed under
the doorknob, as soon as it got dark. Lying there on the bed,
she read or listened to Armed Forces Radio or simply stared
up at the ceiling. She kept a light burning all night, too, more
afraid of the dark than of their already high electricity bill.
Although Tad hadn't mentioned their finances again, she knew
that they were barely holding their own, that he must be having
problems stretching his meager personal allowance in Korea.

It would have been different if she still had Dixie, but Sgt.
Beagle had rotated back to the mainland, taking Shelley's only
friend at Clark with him. Once, as she was returning from the
base, she made a gesture of friendship toward one of her neighbors, the wife of a technical sergeant who lived across the
compound, but the woman only nodded when Shelley called
out, "Nice morning, isn't it?" and began picking up the toys
strewn around her strip of lawn.

Twice a week, Shelley took a jeepney to the base to do her
commissary shopping, go to the library, and prowl through the
thrift shop and the BX. It used up time, and although she was
increasingly reluctant to leave the house, she knew that it was
good for her to get out and see other people even if she never
spoke to them.

Since they hadn't hired a housegirl, housework took up a
few hours a week. Even though Tad wasn't there, she kept the
rooms spotless, trying to master the secrets of handling the
balky cooking range and how to steam rice so it didn't stick.
By practicing on a couple of uniforms that Ted had left behind,
she even learned such esoteric things as how to iron a shirt—
and how to wax a floor until it gleamed.

Her appetite had vanished the morning Tad left for Korea,
and she lost so much weight that it wasn't until she was five
months pregnant that her clothes began to feel tight around the
waist. Since she couldn't afford to buy anything new or have
maternity clothes made by the local sew girls, she shopped at
the base thrift shop and found three maternity blouses and a

skirt that fit. Even when they'd been new, the clothes could never have been stylish, but there was no denying that they were dirt cheap—and very comfortable.

Until now, her neighbors had ignored her, and after her attempts to make friends had been rebuffed, she had retreated into her shell, too proud to court rejection again. But a week after she began to wear maternity clothes, one of the younger women spoke to her when she went outside to toss a dish towel over the clothesline.

"Hi. Another sizzler, huh? I don't think the rainy season is ever going to get here."

"Well, at least it would cool things off," Shelley said, feeling a little rusty at small talk.

"Everything okay with you?"

"Why . . . yes, things are fine."

"Your guy on TDY? I haven't seen him around."

"He's in Korea. He'll be there another couple of months."

"Tough. Last time Kevin was on TDY, I was climbing the walls by the time he got back."

"You have a little boy, don't you?"

"Yeah—Johnny. A real handful." Her eyes rested on Shelley's maternity smock. "If you ever need anything—just holler. I'm Judy Beaumont—we live over there." She pointed across the compound.

"I'm Shelley Brotski. Would you—I was wondering if you'd like some iced tea?" Shelley asked hesitantly.

"Well, I'm kind of in a hurry. Commissary day. Say, why don't you come along? Even if you don't need anything, it helps to kill time."

"I'd like that," Shelley said. Unexpectedly, her eyelids prickled, and she turned quickly and went into the house to get her fish-net shopping bag.

During the short trip to the base, as they drove past the clusters of tiny shops where rattan and wood carvings and other souvenirs were sold, past the bars that catered to GIs, the eating places, and the sew shops that lined Perimeter Road, Shelley listened gratefully to Judy's repertoire of what she secretly thought of as "rumors and rumors of rumors." Cheerfully, her neighbor related some of her own experiences as a military wife, reciting a stream of disasters with such aplomb that Shelley envied her.

"Your old man's really good-looking," Judy said. "I love that black Irish type. How'd you two meet?"

"He—Tad was stationed at Hickam, and I was visiting a friend," Shelley said cautiously.

"Yeah? It must have been a short courtship."

"We were married a week after we met."

"Wow! He's really a fast worker. How long you been married?"

"Seven months."

"What about your folks? Have they met him yet?"

Shelley hesitated, then told a half-truth. "They met him just before our wedding. Tad was transferred a month later, so I haven't met his family yet. I guess we'll take a delay enroute and go to Pennsylvania to see them when we rotate back to the States."

"Well, I wouldn't want to be in your shoes, meeting your in-laws for the first time. I've known Kevin all my life, just about. We got engaged when he got drafted and married when he came home from boot camp. Boy, what a letdown his first assignment was. It was at a new radar site in Utah, way out in the boonies, the nearest town forty-five miles away. Would you believe that we lived in this converted henhouse? The old farmer we rented from had tossed in some electric wiring, laid down a few pine planks for a floor, installed some beat-up old plumbing that must have come from Noah's ark—and that was our cozy little home. Charged us two hundred and fifty a month for it, and then had the nerve to tell us that he'd fixed up the place because he wanted to do something for the "boys." It's enough to make you throw up, isn't it?"

At Shelley's laugh and nod, she added, "Say, I'm sorry I haven't been over to see you until now. We heard—the other gals and I—that you two were newlyweds, so we figured you'd rather be alone." But the evasiveness in her eyes said different. Shelley wondered what the real reason for her isolation was, but she knew it was a question she didn't dare ask.

"Well, I'm very glad we did meet," she said aloud.

"Me too. Are you from the east, Shelley? That *is* a Boston accent, isn't it?"

Shelley hesitated. "Actually, I'm from the midwest," she said finally. "I guess I picked up the accent from—my parents."

"English, are they?"

"My mother is," she said, relieved that she could tell the truth.

"Well, my folks are pure east Tennessee hillbilly. Scotch-Irish, I guess, way back there somewhere."

Judy went on talking about her hometown and her family, and as Shelley listened, she wished it weren't necessary to lie about herself. Still, if she told the truth, that her father was General Pritchard, instinct told her that her new friendship would die a quick death.

After that, although she didn't see her neighbor every day, she felt as if she had a friend. There were areas in their conversations that she stayed away from, but luckily Judy was a nonstop talker and didn't seem to notice how little Shelley had to say about herself.

The week after she met Judy, Shelley went to the hospital for her fourth checkup, only to find that she had a different doctor again. A brusque man, he asked her the standard questions, renewed her prescriptions, and then told her to return in two weeks.

"Two weeks?" she said, puzzled.

"Yes. Make an appointment with the nurse at the desk." He picked up a folder from the pile on his desk, obviously dismissing her.

"But I'm only five months pregnant," she protested. "Why do you want to see me again so soon?"

"I want to keep an eye on you."

"Is something wrong with me?"

"Wrong? Having a baby is a perfectly normal procedure," he said, and she knew he was hedging.

"I want to know why you want to see me in two weeks," she insisted.

"You seem a little run-down. Are you dieting?"

"No. I've never had a weight problem."

He grunted. "How much milk do you drink a day?"

"Not much. I hate reconstituted milk. It tastes like rubber."

"Well, the air force can't have fresh milk shipped in here just to suit your tastes, young woman."

His remark was so unfair that she could only stare at him as he went on, "I can prescribe calcium supplement for you, but it's better if you get it from your food. Stay away from sweets and other empty calories. And eat plenty of fresh fruit and green vegetables."

She didn't bother to tell him that she didn't eat "sweets" because she couldn't afford them—or to point out that fresh fruit and green vegetables were seldom seen in the commissary. She rose to go and was halfway to the door when he added, "And lay off the cocktails. Just because booze is cheap here is no reason to overdo it."

She turned and gave him a long, level look. "I don't drink at all, doctor," she said.

He shrugged. "If you say so." He returned to his paperwork.

She told Judy about it later, her resentment still simmering.

"Too many military doctors are like that," Judy said. "I guess they think it's a waste of time to cultivate a bedside manner when they're the only game in town. The ones that were drafted are the worse—most of the career doctors are really dedicated or they wouldn't stay in. Of course, if you were an officer's wife, he probably would have treated you better."

"I doubt that. I've heard—" Shelley stopped just in time, appalled that she'd been about to say that she'd heard some of her mother's friends complaining about indifferent military doctors.

"Heard what?"

"Oh, just rumors."

"Well, the good medics outnumber the bad ones. Just your luck that you got one with some kind of attitude problem. At least it's free. Imagine what having a baby costs in civilian life."

"We do pay—or at least Congress claims that the reason military wages are low is because we get free medical care—and early retirement," Shelley reminded her friend.

"Right—and I've got some oil stock I'd like to sell you."

The two women were sitting in the ice-cream parlor near the BX, eating the ersatz concoction that was sold as ice cream. Judy took a final bite and pushed her dish away. "I hear the base commander vetoed an offer by Baskin-Robbins to put in a franchise ice-cream parlor here. He claims that we already have an adequate supply."

"You could've fooled me," Shelley said. "And all the time I thought we were eating frozen clay."

Judy giggled. "Right. Say, you haven't told me yet what you're going to name your kid," she said, her grasshopper mind moving to another subject.

"Tad and I haven't really talked about it yet."

"We named Johnny after Kevin's grandfather. What's the name of Tad's old man?"

"Adolph," Shelley said.

"I see what you mean. How about your dad's name?"

Shelley hesitated. "Curtis."

"Well, that isn't so bad. You could call him Curt, I guess."

Shelley nodded and changed the subject. As they were walking toward Judy's car, she stretched her back, trying to relieve the ache under her shoulder blades.

"Baby kicking?" Judy asked.

"Just beginning to. Sometimes I feel like I'm carrying it right under my ribs."

"Carry it high and that means a girl," Judy said wisely. "Carry it low and it's bound to be a boy."

"So where did you carry Johnny?"

"Up under my chin," Judy said, grinning.

"You're something else—what am I going to do when you go back to the Mainland?"

"Oh, you'll make other friends."

Shelley shook her head. "I don't make friends easily. Besides, the other women in the compound don't seem to like me."

"That's just your imagination."

"No, it isn't. What's the matter, Judy? Why are they so standoffish?"

"It's because—okay, it's because they think you're stuck-up. Oh, *I* know you aren't, but you do give that impression."

"So why did you decide to be friendly?"

Judy gave her a sidelong look. "You really want to know?"

"I do."

"Well, it was that maternity smock you wear sometimes—the striped one? That used to be mine. I knew you bought it in the thrift shop, and I figured that if you shopped there like the rest of us, then you couldn't really be stuck-up."

Shelley met her eyes, and they both burst out laughing. "Thank God we have the same taste in maternity smocks," she said when she could speak again.

Two months later, when she was seven months pregnant, Tad came home. His homecoming was everything Shelley had dreamed about, so much so that she remembered an old saying that being married to a military man was like having a series of honeymoons. Tad was an ardent lover, so ardent that she had a few fears for the baby, even though it was too early to curtail intercourse. To her surprise, since Tad had always been so proud of her slender figure, he insisted that he loved the sight of her nude body as much as ever, rounded abdomen and all.

When she confessed she was afraid of getting stretch marks, he volunteered to rub her skin with coconut oil, which led to far more exciting things.

"You don't think I'm fat and ugly?" she asked later as they lay in each other's arms.

"You're beautiful, Shelley. I love seeing you like this. You're carrying my baby—what could be more of a turn-on? Of course I expect you to get back in shape after junior arrives. If you stay fat, I may have to trade you in for a new wife."

"Is that so? And if you start losing your hair, does that give me the right to trade you in?"

"Oh, the Brotski men never lose their hair," he bragged.

"So what's all that hair tonic and stuff doing in the medicine cabinet?"

"Just insurance, baby, just insurance." He put his arms around her and rested his head on her abdomen. "I can hear him in there, splashing around. What a life—it can only go downhill for him once he's born."

"But there's compensations for growing up," she said slyly, and ran her hand along his thigh.

"Yeah—how long can we fool around?"

"Until the final six weeks. I asked the doctor on my last visit."

"What's your doctor like?"

"Which one? So far I've had four. Just as I get used to one, he leaves and I get another."

"That's the military for you. Nothing ever stays the same."

"Except us. We'll stay the same—you promise?"

"I promise," he said, and kissed her.

Judy came for coffee the next morning. "How was the homecoming?" she asked.

"Fabulous."

"Well, enjoy, enjoy," Judy sighed. "The honeymoon ends eventually, and then everything goes back to normal."

Privately Shelley was sure her friend was wrong, but that

night Tad complained that the rice was sticky and she knew the honeymoon was over, just as Judy had warned.

The next day was commissary day. Since Judy was in Baguio on vacation, Shelley took one of the old base buses that serviced the compounds and was cheaper than the jeepneys. There was no air conditioning, and the hot, humid wind that blew in through the open windows provided little relief from the stifling heat. As she rested her aching head against the back of the seat, she wondered if the weather would ever break. Even the rainy season, which Judy had compared to living under water, would be better than this.

When she got to the commissary it was so crowded that she wished she'd chosen another day. The power was off again, and even though the doors had been propped open, the barny building was like a steam bath inside. She chose only a few essentials, then headed for the cashier. Not for the first time since she'd become pregnant, she was grateful for the special checkout line that was reserved for pregnant women and men in uniform.

But today even the prego line was long, and as she took her place behind a middle-aged sergeant, she felt so dizzy that she had to lean upon her cart. The skin that covered her ankles felt tight, as if they were swollen to twice their size, and her smock stuck to her back, an added irritant. She was tempted to just leave her cart there and go home, but that would mean she'd have to come back tomorrow—and besides, she was low on milk and bread.

The man in front of her inched forward, and she moved, too, pushing her cart. The woman behind her, who must have been in her last month of pregnancy, looked so exhausted that Shelley felt a pang of pity for her.

"I shoulda stayed in bed this morning," the woman said with a sigh, and Shelley nodded agreement.

The line was moving faster now, and Shelley was almost to the cash register. She was thinking positive thoughts, promising herself a glass of iced tea and a cool shower when she got home, when a movement at the corner of her eye caught her attention. She turned just in time to see a familiar figure go sailing past.

Everybody at Clark knew Mrs. Blackwell on sight. The wife of General Blackwell, who commanded the Thirteenth Air

Force, she was never seen without an open-crowned tennis cap on her head.

Bestowing gracious smiles in all directions, the tall, thin woman moved to the head of the line, pushing a cart before her. "Do you mind if I go ahead?" she asked the sergeant, her tone perfunctory. "I'm in a dreadful hurry." Without waiting for an answer, she turned her basket into the space in front of him.

"Look at her—the old bat," the woman behind Shelley whispered. "If she wasn't General Blackwell's wife, so help me I'd tell her off. She wears that tennis hat all the time so everybody will recognize her—or so I've heard. And look at what she's got in her cart. She's got a standing order for any filet-mignon steaks that are shipped in. Her excuse is that because her husband's head of the Thirteenth Air Force, they have to do so much official entertaining, but I've got my suspicions. I'll bet the two of them have steak for dinner every night."

Shelley didn't answer. She was staring into Mrs. Blackwell's cart. It held several packages, wrapped in brown butcher's paper. Each package bore two words—"filet mignon"—and a price, written in black crayon. Shelley felt a little dizzy. Tad and she hadn't been able to afford even hamburger the last few days. . . .

There was no warning. Everything—the heat, her aching legs and swollen ankles, the frustration of the past few months— came boiling up, sweeping away caution and prudence. Without a moment's thought, she reached around the sergeant and tapped Mrs. Blackwell on the shoulder.

The older woman turned, looking surprised. "Yes?" she said.

"Are you pregnant?"

"Why—why, of course not!"

"Well, since you aren't pregnant and you obviously aren't in uniform, get the hell out of the prego line," Shelley said.

There was a dead silence about them; even the cashier, a slightly built Filipino girl, stopped ringing up sales, looking scared.

Mrs. Blackwell drew herself up, her face flushed. "Do you know who I am, young woman?" she demanded.

"Everybody knows who you are, Mrs. Blackwell. Do you know who I am?"

"No, I don't but—"

"My name is Shelley Brotski, and I'm seven months pregnant with the baby of an air force sergeant, and if you don't get out of this line, so help me I'm going to throw you out."

The woman started to say something. She met Shelley's eyes and then she was walking away, her heels tapping angrily on the cement floor, leaving her cart standing there.

From somewhere behind Shelley, there was a ragged cheer, a smattering of applause. Shelley knew she had the audience with her, but reaction was already setting in and she felt like crying.

Why had she done such a stupid thing? And why had she given Mrs. Blackwell her name? As she pushed the cart forward, her hands were shaking so that she had a hard time getting out her wallet and CEX card. The cashier hurried to ring up her order, and after her purchase had been recorded by the merchandise control monitor, Shelley hurried away, carefully avoiding the eyes of the other patrons.

All the way home on the grumbling old bus, questions haunted her. What would Tad say when he found out? She knew his temper so well. Even though he seldom lost control, it was still there—and they had been getting along so well lately, too. What would this mean to his career? Would this put a black mark on his record, keep him from getting promoted to tech sergeant? If so, he would never forgive her—never! She had already caused him so much trouble, just being who she was. . . .

It was almost five when the wooden stairs outside the kitchen door creaked under Tad's weight. When he came into the kitchen, Shelley pretended to be busy peeling a potato, but when he didn't speak, she was finally forced to look up. She knew immediately that he had heard the news, and she put the knife down slowly, staring at him.

"You've heard, haven't you?" she said.

"Yeah—about half an hour after it happened. Mrs. Blackwell called her old man, who called the base locater to find out where I was assigned, and then the general called Major Snyder. It took the old man about five minutes to have me on the carpet."

"Was it bad?"

"Depends on what you call bad. The major told me that my wife had stirred up a hornet's nest, that I'd better keep her under control or else."

Shelley digested this for a moment. "I guess you're pretty mad at me, aren't you?"

"Hell, no. You did the right thing."

Shelley sat down o the kitchen stool, staring at him. "But this may keep you from being promoted, Tad."

"No way. What are they going to do? Put it in my records that my wife had a run-in with the commander's wife because the old bitch bucked the prego line?" He looked at her closely. "Hey, cheer up. You didn't think I was going to yell at you, did you?"

"I didn't know what you'd do."

"Okay, so you blew up. That dame's been asking for it for a long time. You only did what everybody on the base has been wanting to do. It's about time someone put her down."

"But it could mean trouble for you—"

"It won't. After the major chewed me out, he winked, said he hoped I wouldn't be too hard on you—and then he reminded me that his old lady was seven months pregnant, too."

"They could ship you back to the States."

"I should be so lucky. That'd be some kind of punishment, wouldn't it?"

Shelley took in the small tic in his cheek and knew that there was more to it than he'd told her. She also knew she'd get no more out of him.

"I love you, Theodore Adolph Brotski," she said softly.

"Yeah? I'll remind you of that statement when the going gets tough—like when I have to go TDY again."

"I'll remember. And I'll make this up to you someday."

Tad looked a little sheepish. "How about a cold beer?" he said.

CHAPTER

✦ 20 ✦

THERE WAS SOMETHING UNREAL ABOUT THE HUGE AUDITO-rium, packed with so many young people, both male and female, all so sober and silent, something unreal about the whole day, in fact. Tai wondered if it was because she'd visualized this day, the day she reported in at the Air Force Academy, so often during the past year that every nuance of difference struck her as ominous. She had read everything she could get her hands on about the academy to give herself an edge, but it hadn't helped because her mental image was so far off reality.

Some things, of course, were as she'd expected . . . the impressive buildings that for all their size seemed dwarfed by the mountains that served as a backdrop . . . the incredibly lush parade ground, surrounded by hills . . . the chapel that sat aloofly above it all with its roof flaring against the sky like a falcon in flight. These were scenes whose photographs she'd studied in the brochures she'd sent for. But the sense of purpose, of measured and intimidating order—this was so different from her expectations that she felt as if she'd taken the wrong turn somewhere and had stepped into an alien world.

She had reported in that morning, along with what seemed to be an army of new cadets—and she hadn't stopped since except for a lunch she couldn't eat and now for this orientation. She had expected a certain air of camaraderie, of bravado, to offset the confusion, the endless barking of instructions from upperclassmen who were supervising their orientation, the being loaded down with so much equipment and clothing that she'd staggered under their weight as she trotted to her assigned room in Vandenberg Hall.

But her fellow doolies seemed interested only in getting through the arduous day without doing anything that might draw undue attention to themselves. Later, she couldn't remember what the commandant of cadets and other officers said during the hour's assembly, although she knew that their words were meant to be inspiring. She did recall an edict against fraternizing, about upholding the tradition of the academy, about the complexities and responsibilities of being an officer—and of course, about the honor code, which she had already memorized.

We will not lie, steal, or cheat, nor tolerate among us anyone who does. . . .

After orientation, when she returned to her room in Vandenberg Hall, she was relieved to find that it was empty. She hadn't yet met her roommate, although her gear and clothing were all neatly stowed away. Although ashamed to admit it, Tai felt the need for a few minutes alone to recoup her courage. There had been several other females sitting near her in the auditorium, but they had seemed unapproachable. Were they as confident, as sure of themselves, as they'd looked? Or were they just as uncertain and scared as she was? She had certainly tried to *look* self-assured. Perhaps they, too, were fighting butterflies in the stomach—and wasn't that a comforting thought?

She was sitting on the edge of one of the bunks, trying to remember the instructions she'd been given, when she heard a sound at the door. She looked up—and up and up. The girl standing there was tall, a Brunhilde of a woman. She was also extraordinarily pretty, with thick black hair and lustrous eyes—and there wasn't an ounce of superfluous flesh on her long, well-knit body. In fact, Tai thought, fighting a wave of hysteria, she would have looked perfectly at home at the head of a Roman legion.

"Hi. I'm Cassie," the goddess said, smiling.

Tai discovered that she'd lost her voice. In fact, she had lost all the ground she'd gained during the past few minutes. This—*this* was the kind of woman she was expected to compete against? This perfect specimen of womanhood?

"Hey, don't let it get you down. Look, we're going to be roommates. We have to talk to each other."

Tai finally found her voice. "My name is Tai—and I guess I was a little overwhelmed. You're pretty impressive, you know."

"Yeah. I scare a lot of people. But I'm a pussycat at heart. To know me is to love me. I can get downright kittenish—with the right guy." She put her hand over her heart and rolled her eyes. "And did you ever see so many right guys? I can't wait to do a little fratting, can you?"

"Fratting?"

"Fraternizing—you know, like with those heavenly cadets."

"I thought that was forbidden."

"Rules are made to be broken," Cassie said, winking.

Tai laughed—for the first time that day. Cassie was kidding, of course—or was she? "I was too scared to do much looking," she confessed.

"Gotcha. Scared. I'll bet the guys did some looking at you, though. I caught a few glances myself, and I can't wait to get acquainted."

"How would you manage without getting caught? I got the impression we'll be watched every minute here."

"That's the fun of it. Nothing like a few obstacles to get the old ingenuity going. Of course you understand I'm just talking about the chase—I'm a good Catholic girl, as a lot of guys have found out. A little fooling around is okay, but that's my limit."

"How do you know so much about . . . well, how things work here?"

Cassie held up two fingers. "I had two teachers—count 'em. Two of my older brothers graduated from the academy. They told me what to expect."

"And I think I just lucked out, drawing you as a roomie."

"And vice versa. The thing is—I'm not so sure it's good to know what to expect. Maybe it's better to come in cold and just let it all happen. That way you don't worry in advance about obstacle courses and drills and inspections."

"Or maybe you worry more—the fear of the unknown."

"Maybe. One thing for sure, it's going to be rough competing against all these overachievers. I made straight A's in high school, but I had to study like the devil to do it. How about you? Are you a braino? Can I pick your brain when the going gets tough?"

"Afraid I can't help you. I got good grades, but I had to work for them."

"So we'll do it the hard way, I guess. Oh, well. Midnight oil and all that stuff. But we'll make it. We roomies have to stick together, right?"

"Right." Tai had just made a discovery. She was no longer afraid. She held out her hand. "I think we should shake on that."

They shook hands solemnly.

"What nationality are you, Tai?" Cassie said curiously. "As you can see, I'm Italian as spaghetti."

"I'm one-fourth Scots, one-fourth French, and one-half Chinese."

"Wow! That's pretty exotic." Cassie studied Tai with frank interest. "If you don't mind me saying so, you look pretty frail. You sure you can hack the physical stuff during Beast? It's really grueling."

"Oh, I'm tougher than I look," Tai said dryly.

"Yeah—yeah, I can see that now. The wiry kind that can run rings around the muscle men. I have a hunch you're going to blow a few minds. It's sort of a no-win situation, you know, being a female cadet. If you excel at anything physical, it's one big surprise. You know—'Hey, look what the monkey did!' But if you have any trouble keeping up with the male cadets, it's a self-fulfilling prophecy of failure. You have to be better than they are to stay even."

"So what else is new?"

"Well, we've got a chance here to strike a blow for womanhood—not that I'm into the ERA. Every gal for herself, I say. I just want to get a good education, learn to fly a plane for the hell of it, and then see what happens. How about you?"

Tai hesitated. "I want pretty much the same thing," she said, although the truth was she had already decided not to take flight training. Flying might be a challenge, but it wasn't necessary for the career in engineering she wanted. And anyway, it was too far off in the future to worry about. Except for a few hours of instruction in a Cessna during her senior year, formal flight training wouldn't begin until after graduation. She had more immediate problems now, such as getting through basic cadet training—what the academy called BCT and the cadets called Beast.

Cassie grinned at her. "Well, now it's all the horrors of Jacks Valley, such as obstacle courses and bashing each other with cudgels. We dun signed away our souls to the air force, and for the next four years we're just a couple of cogs in the system. You ready?"

"Ready," Tai said, and wasn't ashamed that her voice sounded a little hollow.

It was the day following BCT, and Cassie and Tai were comparing notes, able to laugh at the mishaps that had seemed so tragic at the time but which now could be put in perspective because they hadn't washed out. Cassie was telling Tai that she'd gone into the air force because her father, a colonel, had been so close to retirement that he'd told her, the youngest of a family of eight, that she'd either have to get an appointment to the academy, find a way to finance her own college education, or go to work.

The knock on the door that interrupted her was sharp, intrusive. They exchanged consternated glances before they sprang to their feet, their backs stiffened into a brace even before the door opened and an upperclassman, a female, came in.

"Basic Cadet Tai-Ching MacGarrett?" she asked brusquely.

"I'm MacGarrett, ma'am," Tai said.

The upperclassman looked her over with expressionless eyes. "Report to the vice-commander of cadets immediately. Follow me," she said, and swung on her heel.

Cassie groaned and whispered, "God—what did you do?"

Tai's mouth was too dry to answer, so she only shook her head. As she followed the silent messenger through a warren of halls, she searched her memory but could think of nothing that could have provoked this summons. She had done very well during Beast, which she suspected had surprised her cadet instructors, and she felt satisfied that she could hold her own even against the male jocks in her class. Had she broken some rule inadvertently? She was tempted to ask the upperclassman, but she checked herself in time. For the first six weeks, according to the credo, doolies were permitted to say only five things to upperclassmen: *Yes, sir. No, sir. I don't know, sir. Permission to speak, sir. I have no excuse, sir.* Even though BCT was over, to initiate a conversation would be more than a faux pas. It could very well be a disaster.

The upperclassman left her when they reached an unmarked door at the end of a long hall, but not before she issued a warning to Tai to remember that she would be speaking to a senior—and that she was that lowest of the low, a doolie.

After the cadet was gone, Tai hesitated, staring at the door. Should she knock—or go right in? In the end, she gave the door a sharp rap, then waited for an answer. When a voice told her to come in, she felt as if she'd just been hit behind the ear because the voice was all too familiar. Why hadn't she remembered that Bobby Jo had told her that Steven was vice-commander of cadets this year? Had she unconsciously blocked it out of her mind?

Before she opened the door, she squared her shoulders and wet her dry lips. There was nothing she could do about her flushed face or the slight buzzing in her ears, but she was determined not to give Steven any reason to suspect how off balance she felt. She went in fast, looking straight ahead, and stopped in front of the desk where Steven sat. Putting everything in it, she snapped the salute she had been practicing for the past few weeks.

"At ease, Fourthclassman MacGarrett." Steven looked her over so long that she knew he wasn't going to make it easy for her. After all, he had her where he wanted her—and there was nothing she could do except grit her teeth and take it.

"According to your element sergeant, you were late for the acceptance parade," he said. "What have you got to say for yourself, MacGarrett?"

"No excuse, sir," Tai snapped, even though his accusation wasn't true. She and Cassie had been in place before half their unit had assembled.

"You're right. There's no excuse for tardiness or for anything else you do wrong here at the academy. A doolie doesn't even have an excuse when he's right. Remember that—and if you go around showing your resentment when you're corrected, it's going to go hard for you. You understand?"

"Yes, *sir*."

He winced. "Don't break my eardrums, MacGarrett!"

"Yes, sir," she said, just as smartly but not as loud.

"That's better. I'm going to overlook your infraction—but just this one time. Any comments?"

"No, sir." For being tardy for an assembly, she had gotten off easy, even though her element sergeant had made a mistake in reporting her. Or had she really been reported? Somehow she doubted it.

"Permission to speak, sir."

"You have it."

"Why is my punishment so mild, sir?"

"I can arrange for you to walk a tour if you like. Would that please you?"

For the first time, she looked directly at Steven instead of at a point above his head. He wasn't smiling, but there was something in his eyes—was he laughing at her? The suspicion infuriated her, and her voice had a strangled sound as she said, "I would not, sir, unless demerits for this offense are the norm."

"Are you asking if I'm favoring you? I am not. It was your first offense. It's normal to be a little lenient the first time. Next time, it'll be different, I assure you."

His tone was so short that she expected to be dismissed, but instead he kept her standing there while he examined her short hair, her lack of makeup, her short nails. His mouth twitched suddenly, and she wanted desperately to reach out and claw his smug face.

"I'm going to talk to you off the record, Tai," he said. "In view of our past—friendship, I have a few tips that might help."

"Yes, sir?"

"It's a highly competitive business, being a doolie at the academy, but you don't have to prove yourself superior in every aspect, you know. You've been really knocking yourself out, I understand—how much weight did you drop in Beast?"

She forgot herself long enough to frown at him. "Eleven pounds—sir."

"Which you couldn't afford to lose. I suggest that you pay attention to your diet and try to gain those pounds back."

"Yes, sir. Is that an order, sir?"

His face stiffened. "It is."

"I'll drink an extra milk shake every night—sir. Is that all, sir?"

"No, dammit, it isn't all! Hear me out."

"Yes, sir."

"Listen to what I have to say because it's for your own good. During the next year, you're going to be competing against a lot of gung-ho jocks, male and female—and knowing you, you're going to try to prove that you're better than all of them. Okay, you're strong for a girl—deceptively so. You're a master at kung fu, and you're a champion swimmer, and you surf like a dream. Great. You'll need that stamina. But what you don't need is to show up your competitors. So cool it. Do a good job, but don't try to be the best in everything. Compete—but don't try to be a champion, not as a doolie. I know how competitive you are, but there's such a thing as the whole-man concept—"

"Whole person, sir," she said.

To her surprise, Steven's face relaxed into a smile. "Whole-person concept," he acknowledged.

"I don't understand—are you saying that I shouldn't do my best?"

"I'm saying that there's a thin line between achievement and fanaticism. You won't be diminished if you don't have the highest grades and the best athletic record. In fact, it's impossible for you to have either. There are cadets here who can scan a page in a textbook and repeat it word for word ten years later—and some of them are top physical specimens, too. These are the ones who major in the tough subjects like biology and physics, and make the top ten of their class. Be content to get good grades, with competing on your own level. And learn to conserve your energy or you'll wash out before you have time to learn the floor plan of Fairchild Hall."

"Would you give the same advice to a male cadet, sir?"

"It's different with a male cadet. He doesn't have the handicap of being a woman in a man's world."

"If ever I heard a sexist remark, that's it—sir. In other words, it's okay to be competitive if you're a man, but if you're a female, for God's sake, let's not outdo a male cadet or he might get into a snit."

"I didn't mean that."

"You didn't? Sorry, sir, I misunderstood. Tell me, what did you mean, sir?"

A flush rose to Steven's cheeks, a sure sign that he was losing his temper. "Okay, forget it. I only want to help you survive—"

"Or have you been trying to put me down, sir? If you really mean what you say, there's something you don't understand. I don't need your help. I don't want your advice, either, not on a personal basis. If it's official and you're giving me the same advice you'd give a man, okay. But I don't need or want protection. I wouldn't be here if I did. I'll make a lot of mistakes—I'm prepared for that. I might even wash out, but *I'll* be the one who makes those mistakes and who pays for them.

And if I make it through and graduate, then *I'll* be the one who earned that gold bar on my shoulder."

Her voice had risen. She broke off, her face hot and stiff. She stood at attention again, and he made a helpless gesture and then said, "Dismissed, Cadet."

She saluted him so smartly that her hand slapped against her forehead. As she turned on her heel and left the room, she should have felt triumphant because she'd bested Steven during their first encounter. Instead, she felt like crying.

Some of her depression must have shown when she returned to her room because Cassie gave her a sympathetic look. "What was that all about?"

"I was reported for being late to the acceptance parade."

Cassie whistled. "Someone needs glasses—or something weird's going on around here. What happened? How many demerits did the vice-commander give you?"

"He just gave me a warning."

"Wow! How did you manage that?"

"Influence in high places."

"Right. High places. Next thing you know, you'll be meeting someone from high places behind the chapel."

"No way. I'd rather meet King Kong on top of the Empire State Building than meet Cadet Steven Henderson behind the chapel."

"God, you're sick, sick, sick. I got a look at him during muster—I'd frat with him anytime!"

"Uh-huh. I thought you had something going with that third-degree type who was ragging you so during Beast."

"He dun me wrong. He's been making eyes at our glamour girl—and I figure that if his taste is that bad, he ain't for me no way, no how."

Tai laughed at Cassie's wry words. One of their classmates had earned the nickname of glamour girl during Beast because of her exotic appearance—and also because she'd been singled out for the special attention of the upperclassmen instructors.

"Did you hear the latest?" Cassie said.

"Which latest?"

"About *her*. According to her tentmates, the little twit got up ten minutes early every morning to put on a full makeup job."

"God, I wouldn't lose ten minutes' sleep to meet the president, much less to put on makeup. The sweat would wash it off anyway."

"Well, you don't need it. What wouldn't I give for that poreless skin and those black eyelashes. You even have naturally pink lips."

"You're great looking—as you know very well."

"Oh, I'll pass. Just a homespun beauty, that's me."

"Homespun—like Sophia Loren is homespun. I wonder how our glamour girl managed to smuggle in makeup?"

"Maybe she's got friends in high places, too."

"Wash your mouth out with soap," Tai said lightly.

They exchanged smiles. Cassie sobered first. "This part makes it worthwhile, doesn't it? Even if we end up covered with old battle scars, we have each other for backbone. That counts for something—and besides, next year just has to be better."

"At least this doolie crap will be over. Believe me, I'm going to be kind to the poor beasts that take our place next year."

"Wanna bet? Oh, you won't treat them like some of those jerks treated us during BCT, but once you're third degree, you'll be bracing some poor doolie for running in the halls and almost knocking you down."

"Maybe," Tai said, unconvinced.

"Well, we'd better get some sleep. Tomorrow the real fun starts—academics. The question is—when will it ever end?"

"Four years from now—if we make it that far," Tai said heartlessly.

Later that month, when Tai got her first test scores, she discovered that while she hadn't made the top ten percentage of her class, she was very close.

And that for *you*, Cadet Vice-Commander Henderson, she thought.

Cassie had also passed—by the skin of her teeth. Not that it bothered her. "Better to blend with the crowd," she sang out as she danced around the room, looking like a manic Brunhilde. "Miss Average Cadet of 1977—that's me!"

Tai, watching her, felt a pang of sadness. Next year, she would be assigned another roommate, and no matter how they clicked, it wouldn't be the same. There was something special about the roomie who'd shared the trials of being a doolie with you.

One consolation—she had made a lifelong friend. And that wasn't something to sneeze at.

C H A P T E R
↟ 21 ↟

ALTHOUGH BOBBY JO WAS AWARE OF THE INTERESTED STARES
of male cadets as she waited for Tai in one of the visitors'
lounges in Arnold Hall, her mind was on other things. She had
so much to tell Tai—and she was anxious to find out how her
friend was getting along. Although they'd spent part of Christmas Day together, eating roast goose and getting tipsy on wine,
they hadn't seen each other since because of Tai's busy work
schedule and because Bobby Jo had been studying extra hard,
too, trying to bolster up her sagging grades.

Tai had called her twice, which was a treat, but the last
time she'd sounded so exhausted that Bobby Jo was determined
to find out what was going on—provided she could get her
close-mouthed friend to talk. She'd expected to see her at the
winter hop, which she'd attended, but Tai had given the excuse
that she couldn't be there because she was walking off demerits
that evening.

Bobby Jo looked up now and saw Tai moving toward her,
her step light and quick.

"You look marvelous, Tai-Ching-a-ling," she lied as Tai
came up. Tai did look trim in her smart blue uniform, but she
didn't look marvelous. She was so pale, in fact, that Bobby
Jo wondered if the harassment of some of the upperclassmen
was getting her down. She'd heard some of the derogatory
remarks the seniors and juniors made about women cadets. In
fact, the juniors, the final class without female cadets, were

calling themselves the "Last Class with Balls," and there was even a rumor that they were having the initials "LCWB" engraved on their class rings.

"And you look like a sexpot, as usual." Tai collapsed into a chair. "What chance do the rest of us poor females have with you around?"

"Uh-huh. Well, you don't see any engagement ring on my finger, do you? Shelley and Crystal are old married women, and here I am, still a spinster."

"Oh, come now! You must have a dozen boys on the string."

"But I still haven't met anyone who—you know, really rings my chimes. And how is *your* love life?"

"Love life? What's that? Doolies don't have love lives. They don't have lives, period. Our bodies and souls belong to the cadre. Everybody is on our backs—from our element sergeant right up the line to the cadet commander. Oh, not physically. They're too civilized for that—and besides, it's against regulations. But they chip away at our egos until we could crawl under a snake's belly. I know the reasoning behind it, but that doesn't help much. They hassle you because it—supposedly—hardens you and desensitizes you. I guess they're right. If you snub your big toe at the same time someone socks you in the solar plexus, you tend to ignore your aching toe. And of course they've all been through it themselves and survived, so that proves something, I guess. So I just grit my teeth and hang in there. But sometimes, when some muscle-bound jock is barking at me because I don't move fast enough to suit him, I could just belly up and die. The only thing that keeps me going is the other doolies, and the fact that it would give someone-who-shall-be-nameless too much satisfaction if I washed out."

"Tell me the truth—don't some of those muscle-bound jocks come on to you?"

"Oh, sure. But they're just flexing their sexual muscles. As soon as their little Barbie dolls from back home come for a visit, they treat us as if we had the plague. You'd have to be a fool to take that kind of thing seriously. Besides, fraternization is forbidden. No hanky-panky behind the chapel allowed."

"Meeting behind a chapel would inhibit *this* ol' minister's daughter like crazy."

"Some of the girls take a chance, but it's risky as hell. Fratting can get you into more trouble than socking an upperclassman. But still they do it, and I don't know why. My sex drive is so low these days that I couldn't make love to Burt Reynolds if he crawled into my bed. My roommate has a special guy, but she won't meet him anywhere except in the library. Holding hands among the stacks is her limit. Even that much is dangerous if you get caught. I don't know where she gets all her energy. She's into intramural basketball, and she's the mainstay of her team. Well, at least it keeps the jocks off her back. Automatic respect for a fellow jock."

"What kind of sports are you in?"

"Swimming and fencing at present. Did you ever get the impression while we were at Punahou that I was hot stuff in the sports department?"

"Oh, sure. Well, you never bragged about it, but everybody knew you were a champion swimmer and a whiz at kung fu and other sports. Why do you ask?"

"Well, I got my comeuppance. Some of those big bruisers make me look like a one-year-old kid learning how to walk. Women cadets don't compete directly with men in most of the contact sports, but the comparison is there all the time."

"What about the martial arts?"

"Unarmed defense is what the females do. It's coming up next term for me."

"So earn your automatic respect there."

"I'm not sure if I should try. It might be better for me if I just slid through. Or so I've been told by the great expert at playing it cool."

"Who are you talking about—no, don't tell me! It's Steven, isn't it? Are things warming up between you two?"

"No way. The ice is still a mile thick. In fact, he's been playing tootsie with the daughter of the commandant of cadets. An overendowed redhead who is always hanging around him, oozing sex—or so I heard. And if he gives me just one more demerit for a spot on my uniform that nobody else can see, so help me I'm going to spit on that bacon-and-tomato sandwich he has every morning for breakfast. Wouldn't you just know that I'd be assigned to his squadron?"

"But he seemed so concerned about you when I saw him at the winter hop. When he came over to talk to me and my date, he asked how often I saw you and said you needed a friend right now."

"Well, he was playing the good guy for your benefit. He never speaks to me that he doesn't bark. I hate his guts."

"Uh-huh. I don't think you know how you really feel about him, Tai."

"I'll tell you how I feel. I want him to leave me alone. He watches me like a—a bloody falcon. If he picks on me one more time, I'll—"

"You'll what, Cadet MacGarrett?" a male voice said.

Bobby Jo swallowed hard when she realized Steven was standing beside their lounge chairs, staring down at Tai. To her eyes, Tai seemed to be moving in slow motion as she rose and stood in a brace.

"Relax, Cadet MacGarrett. I'll be joining you and Bobby Jo. You have my permission to sit down."

Tai's face was devoid of expression as she dropped back into her chair. It was obvious to Bobby Jo, who knew her so well, that Tai was fighting mad. She gave Steven a covert look as he pulled out a chair and sat down. God, but he was good-looking! It wasn't fair that one man could have all those assets. No wonder Tai had ambiguous feelings about him. . . .

"So how's school, Bobby Jo?" Steven said.

Despite her loyalty to Tai, Bobby Jo couldn't help smiling at him. "Great—I just might squeak through this term."

"Too much social life?"

"Too few brains," she said ruefully.

"Anyone special in your life?"

"Not really. I'm still available."

"We'll have to do something about that, won't we? How about letting me fix you up with my roommate? He's a good Joe—and I happen to know he hasn't asked anyone to the dance next month."

The temptation was strong. Bobby Jo risked a glance at Tai, saw that her friend's eyes had a glazed look as if she were about to explode. "Thank you just the same. I can get my own dates," she said with dignity.

"Suit yourself," Steven said amicably. His eyes wandered to Tai's stiff face. "Now Cadet MacGarrett here—she could use a little help with men. I haven't seen her at any social affair since she reported in. Too bad—but some of us have to be wallflowers, I guess. Isn't that right, Cadet MacGarrett?"

"If you say so, sir."

"I do. And why is it that you don't turn out for any of the dances?"

"Too busy studying, sir," she said.

"Or maybe it's because no one's asked you?"

"I've been asked—sir. I said no."

"Indeed. Well, well. What do we have here? An antisocial doolie? Describe a doolie to your friend."

"A doolie is garbage, lower than a worm, a zero, sir."

"Very good. You have a good memory."

"Yes, sir."

"Is that all you have to say for yourself? You sure you don't have something to say along the lines of what I overheard as I came up?"

"Are you giving me permission to speak freely, sir—without repercussions?"

"No repercussions. Speak freely, cadet."

"You, sir, are a class-A asshole, sir," Tai said, her tone even.

"Temper, temper." Bobby Jo, who had stopped breathing, saw that Steven was smiling. "And I'll let you off this time. Next time, it's up before your peers for you. Can't let a doolie get by with talking nasty to her superiors, can we?"

"No, sir. Thank you, sir."

Steven gave Bobby Jo another smile and rose. After he strolled off, Tai collapsed against her armrest with a long sigh.

"Does he do that often?" Bobby Jo asked.

"Not as often as he did at first. These days, it's only when he thinks he can catch me off guard. One thing that helps— the other cadets in my unit think the way Steven picks on me is rotten. So I don't let him get to me." But there was a shine in her eye that belied her words.

"Is there much harassing—you know, in general?"

"Varying degrees of it—and most of it subtle. Almost exclusively from seniors and juniors. The instructors, no matter what their private opinion of women cadets, are professionals. They treat us all alike. And the male cadets in our own class are super. Very supportive—with an exception here and there. As soon as there are women first degrees and more women instructors at the academy, things will improve, I'm sure. One of my element sergeants is female and she's all business. If she chews me out, I know it's because I really goofed up. The ringleaders among the seniors, who organized the harassment, will be gone next year. That will help. But there will always be strict discipline—which is as it should be because it molds us into a ... well, a fighting force. What might seem pretty Mickey

Mouse stuff to outsiders does toughen you. I know it has me. Next to these four years, the rest of my life has got to be a breeze."

"Well, it's still so unfair. All those guys coming down hard on you."

"You should hear some of the upperclassmen when the officers aren't around. They're really pigs. But their little verbal games don't really bother me. I just say 'Yes, sir' or 'No, sir' and let it roll off my back. One day I'll walk out of here with an engineering degree, do my military obligation, and then it's 'kiss my ass, air force.'"

Bobby Jo giggled. "How many years do you have to serve?"

"If I don't take pilots' training, it's five years. Six if I do, which is why I'm not signing up for PT."

"Didn't you tell me that you were pilot eligible?"

"That's automatic when you pass the admittance physical— and there's other considerations, too."

"Well, I don't blame you for opting out. The thought of piloting a plane scares me to death."

Tai looked at her, her eyes very serious. "I'd give my back teeth to take pilot training," she said. "But I'm not going to give those bastards that extra year."

"You still feel the same way about the military?"

"Right down the line."

"You're careful who you talk to like this, aren't you?"

"Even Cassie doesn't know how I feel—but I'm sure Steven suspects. I play the old rah-rah game, right along with the rest of the doolies."

"And you think Steven suspects?"

"I'm sure he does. That's one reason he comes down hard on me. He's a real gung-ho military type."

"Well, at least he hasn't turned you in."

"What could he say? That he suspects I'm in for the free education? That could describe half the cadet cadre. Besides, I think he'd rather I stayed at the academy so he can bug me."

"I don't understand him at all. After all, it was his father who was in the wrong."

"*I* know that and *you* know that, but Steven thinks his precious father is a saint. Well, so be it. Even if it kills me, I'll stick it out."

"And that's what worries me. You look like death warmed over. Why don't you just give it up? You told me once that you don't have a military commitment until the end of your sophomore year—"

"Never. I'm in it to the bitter end."

Tai's face was so grim that Bobby Jo cast around for something to lighten the conversation. "How are you and your roommate getting along?"

"Cassie? She's my bud, my backbone. I don't think I could have made it this far if she hadn't been there to psych me up. That's one thing that makes it endurable—the friends I've made. By now, our unit is like a family—everybody supportive of everybody else. I love them all . . . well, almost all of them. There's always a few bootlickers and finks. But they don't count. Friends like Cassie do."

"Well, I'm sure you'd make it without her," Bobby Jo said jealously. She had met Cassie during Christmas vacation, and she'd felt inadequate in the presence of Tai's friend. "I don't think she likes me."

"Oh, most female cadets are cool toward the women who date the male cadets. It's a defense mechanism. For one thing, you can wear your hair down to your ankles if you like while we go around looking like cropped poodles."

Looking pensive, she patted her cap of shining black hair, which Bobby Jo secretly thought made her look like an Oriental Joan of Arc. "On weekends, the guys, even the doolies, strut around with their little tootsies, showing them off, so what do you expect? And the dances—Steven knows very well that hardly any of the female cadets go to the dances. Most of us wouldn't be caught dead wearing our mess outfits when the drags are all gussied up in formals and spike-heeled shoes."

She gave Bobby Jo a dreamy smile. "I have this fantasy. I'm walking into the ball room with this prime specimen, a civilian in evening clothes. He's about eight feet tall and has four-foot shoulders, and all the male cadets are glowering, and their drags with their Farrah Fawcett hairdos are positively green—" She broke off and gave Bobby Jo an apologetic look. "Sorry—you don't come under that category, of course."

"No offense taken," Bobby Jo said; she gave the saucy flip of hair that fell over her forehead a furtive pat.

"Tell me what's happening in your life, Bobby Jo," Tai said tactfully, and for the rest of their visit they talked about Bobby Jo's struggles with math, about old friends and old

times at Punahou, both careful to keep the conversation light
and cheerful.

When Tai finally left, Bobby Jo returned to her car, an
ancient VW that rattled like a castanet when she started the
motor. She was feeling a little let down. Tai seemed so different, so abrupt and quick talking and—and different. She
wasn't sure she approved. Well, Tai had been through so much
even before she came to the academy. Surely she would revert
back to the old Tai eventually—and not too soon to suit
Bobby Jo.

As she drove along one of the academy's winding, woods-
edged roads, she was careful to watch out for the mule deer
that sometimes wandered down from the higher valleys. The
whole area looked like a well-kept park, and she thought
it was a shame that the cadets had so little spare time for enjoying it.

A few yards past South Gate, she slowed down her car. It
was customary for visitors to offer a ride to any cadet who was
waiting in the small shelters beyond the academy gates. Although
forbidden to solicit rides, it was well known that if asked, they
could accept. Today, the shelter held two cadets, one dark-
haired and studious looking, the other taller, with crisp brown
hair and a husky athlete's body.

Shelley rolled down her window. "I'm going into Colorado
Springs," she said. "Do you want a lift?"

She met the taller cadet's eyes and inhaled a long breath.
God, what a fox. He put Steven in the shade. Not that he was
all that handsome, not really, but that cleft in his chin and those
white, white teeth when he smiled really turned her on.

When the two men loped toward her car, she opened the
passenger's door, her heart pumping too fast. Of course, he
was probably taken. That kind always was. No doubt he had
a dozen groupies hanging around and someone special waiting
back home—the lucky girl.

"Hi," the tall one said. "We really appreciate this. My wheels
are in for repairs in the Springs—I'm suppose to pick my van
up today, but we missed the bus." He climbed into the car next
to Bobby Jo, folding his long legs under the dashboard, leaving
the second cadet to squeeze into the backseat. "I'm Josh—
short for Joshua—Springer. And you're Ms. Farrah Fawcett-
Majors, right?"

Bobby Jo wasn't sure whether to be insulted—or flattered. "I'm Bobby Jo Clark," she said.

"Bobby Jo Clark. A name made in heaven, just like its owner. And this is my friend, Cadet Owens. Unfortunately, Cadet Owens is under strict quarantine, so I have to do his talking for him. Some kind of social disease, I understand."

The stocky cadet grinned good-naturedly. "Stow it, blubber lips. You don't get rid of the competition that easily."

Bobby Jo felt excited and expectant. It was probably a line, one this Josh used with all the girls, but God, he was attractive.

She started up the car, feeling a little self-conscious when her shoulder brushed against Josh Springer's arm. When she gave him a covert glance, she saw that he was sitting sideways in his seat, staring directly at her.

"What is it?" she said, startled.

"You're a knockout, Bobby Jo. I think I'm having a heart attack."

"Well, don't do it in my VW," she told him. "Wait until you get back to the academy."

"I may never go back. I may follow Bobby Jo Clark to the ends of the earth, provided I can do it before curfew. I don't suppose—no, I won't ask. It would be too much."

"What's too much?"

"That you're free between now and the witching hour of midnight plus thirty minutes when we cadets have to be back at the academy?"

Bobby Jo felt a thrill of excitement, but she kept her voice cool as she said, "Well, I do have some studying to do."

"Let me guess. I'm very intuitive. You go to Colorado College, right?"

"That doesn't take intuition."

"Ah, but I have another brainstorm coming through." He pressed his finger against his temple as if screwing it into a socket. "I have it! You come from a place far across the sea, and your father—hmmm, I see him in some kind of uniform. Is he a mailman? A bus driver? No, I've got it! He's in the air force, right? And I see these flowers all over the place. Now how does that compute? Is it a floral shop? No, damned if they aren't growing in someone's yard. And the house has a red tile roof and lots of grass and—could it possibly be on an air force base? And what's this? A dog? Scrunchy little thing with ragged ears. Looks like a mouse that stuck its tail in an electric socket—"

"She does not!" Bobby Jo said. "And the only way you could know all this is if you were at Hickam and saw me there."

"Or pumped your date after he spotted you at a hop," the other cadet grumbled—not quite under his breath.

"Saw you at Hickam, fell in love with you on the spot," Josh said, ignoring his friend. "Unfortunately, there wasn't any time to get acquainted because I was heading back to the academy after my summer orientation stint at Hickam. And now you turn up here, the answer to a dream. There's something I've been wanting to tell you for a long time. I love you, Bobby Jo Clark."

Bobby Jo laughed—and then couldn't stop laughing. She felt light-headed, as if she'd just caught a whiff of ether—or drunk a glass of champagne. Did it happen like this? she thought. Could it possibly be this easy, this fast?

CHAPTER

✦ 22 ✦

EVEN BEFORE BOBBY JO WENT DOWNSTAIRS TO MEET JOSH Springer in the dorm lounge, she knew it was going to be a special evening. Everything pointed to it—the pleasurable fluttering in her stomach, her inability to concentrate on anything, not even the important business of blow-drying her hair so that it looked as if she'd simply flipped a brush through it.

Although she applied her makeup as carefully as ever—a touch of contouring blush beneath her cheekbones, a brushing of powder, followed by a spray of mineral water to give her skin a matte look, deep pink lip gloss applied with a camel's-hair brush—her thoughts kept drifting to the evening ahead. As she conjured up images of Josh's infectious grin and the outrageous things he said to her, she wondered uneasily if she could keep him interested for a whole evening.

She was well aware that clever repartee was not her strong point. Usually, she simply sat back and let her dates do the talking, smiling at their jokes and their compliments. If the conversation got too heavy, she steered it back to lighter things, getting them talking about movies or TV shows or their favorite recording artists. But would this work with Josh? He seemed so—so clever, even if he did like to kid around a lot. What if he turned out to be one of those people who made her feel inferior—like her roommate?

He might even think she was dull, once he'd spent several hours with her. She'd been accused of that by a boy she'd once dated for a while. He'd told her she was like a mirror, reflecting what was around her but giving nothing of herself back. Of course, that had been the evening she'd told him she didn't think they were right for each other. He'd been furious—which was why she'd discounted the things he'd said, such as calling her a . . . well, it wasn't a nice word, but it meant she was a tease.

But what if he'd been right about her being dull? She wasn't kidding herself. She felt out of her depth when the conversations got too serious—like those rap sessions her roommate's cronies were so fond of. A half hour of that and she was yawning and wishing they would shut up and go away. What she really enjoyed was . . . well, laughing and joking and flirting a little. Was that so wrong? Tai didn't think she was awful for wanting to have a good time before she settled down. God knew she deserved a little gaiety in her life after all those hours of sitting on a hard bench in church, trying not to fidget while her father droned on and on and on. . . .

"—must be someone special, the way you're primping." Her roommate's caustic voice intruded upon her thoughts. At Bobby Jo's blank stare, Lois added, "Don't tell me Little Bo-Peep has finally found her sheep."

Bobby Jo felt exasperated as she so often did when her roommate's oblique remarks stopped just short of insult. Although she resented it, she usually pretended not to understand Lois's sarcasm. She hadn't even made a fuss about the nickname—Bo-Peep—that Lois had saddled her with, nor had she let on how her roommate's ridiculous attempts to imitate her southern accent bugged her. It wasn't as if Lois even came close. Nobody at home talked like that. They certainly didn't address just one person as "you all," for God's sake!

But in the interest of peace, she ignored Lois most of the time. Lately, it was true, her roommate was getting worse, dropping snide remarks that didn't even make sense. Well, she could put up with it for a few more months, but next year she'd be a junior and she meant to get a place off campus—provided she could talk her parents into raising her allowance—even though she'd still need a roommate to share expenses.

And the roommate wouldn't be Lois. She'd had it with that one. What's more, she wasn't going to miss dorm life. She'd thought it would be so much fun, living with a bunch of girls, but the ones in her dorm seemed to resent her. Why, she couldn't figure out. She was always friendly, always willing to help fix their hair or to lend them a stamp or even clothes sometimes. And yet they were so cool that she wondered sometimes if they had a grudge against southerners or if they were simply born snobs, period.

Well, her conscience was clear. She was always careful not to flirt with their boyfriends. Could she help it if sometimes one of them asked her out? She'd never accepted a date from a boy who was going with a girl she knew. She was polite to them, of course—it wasn't her nature to be rude to anyone.

"Who's the lucky man tonight?" Lois asked.

Bobby Jo hesitated, reluctant to answer. Not that she was secretive. It was just that Josh was so special she felt a superstitious fear about saying his name out loud, especially to Lois. "A cadet I met when I went to visit Tai, my friend at the academy," she said.

"Oh . . . the female jock."

Bobby Jo gave her a hard look. Lois, who was tall and angular and who looked as if she'd stepped off the pages of a body-building magazine, should talk about female jocks.

"As a matter of fact, Tai is very petite and feminine." Bobby Jo's eyes lingered on her roommate's too full hips. "She just managed to squeak by the academy's height and weight standards. She's smart, too—a whiz at math."

"And you two are friends?"

"Very good friends," Bobby Jo said firmly.

"I understand the cadets don't want females at the academy. Of course it's pretty convenient, having women close at hand when they get the mating urge."

Bobby Jo laid her brush down; she turned to face her roommate. "Tai is one of the most decent girls I know. And if you make one more crack like that, I'm going to march downstairs to Ms. Campbell's office and demand another roommate. I've put up with your nasty remarks about me, but when you insult someone you don't even know just because she's my friend— that's too much. Now you apologize or so help me I'll repeat this conversation to Ms. Campbell and ask for another roommate."

The skin on Lois's cheeks took on a splotchy look, but to Bobby Jo's surprise, she said, "Sorry—just having a little fun. How come you're so touchy today?"

"I'm not the one who's touchy. You've been jumping on

everything I've said for the past month. If something's bugging you, say so. Otherwise, knock it off."

"You don't know—you really don't know, do you?"

"Know what?"

"About Ronnie James."

Bobby Jo searched her memory. Ronnie James? A vague image stirred. Wasn't he that lanky guy who used to sit across the aisle from her in English II, the one who'd been so upset when she refused to go out with him?

"Is he sort of blondish—with a thin beard?"

"You didn't even remember his name. Well, that figures. The guys in your life come and go so fast it's no wonder you lose track."

"That isn't true. And if he's the one I think he is, I never went out with him."

"Oh, he asked you out all right. Only he wasn't good enough for you, was he? And of course you didn't know the two of us had a thing going, did you, when you started giving him the eye?"

"Giving him the eye? I don't remember ever speaking to him before he asked me out. Are you saying you two were going steady?"

"Going steady? God, I can't believe you! That's one thing that really gets to me. You talk like you stepped out of a 1950 movie, and the guys think it's cool, that you're putting it on, when actually you're just a hick from some small town in— where the hell is it? Oklahoma? You must really be hot stuff in the backseat of a car—that's the only explanation. Sure, you've got looks, but you don't have anything else going for you."

Bobby Jo scooped her makeup into her handbag and snatched up her wrap. "Tomorrow I'm going to ask matron to move me to another room," she said with as much dignity as she could manage. "But right now, I have someone waiting for me downstairs. I don't have time to continue this conversation."

She sailed out of the room, her head high. She'd never been so insulted in her life. She just hoped the other girls hadn't heard Lois yelling at her. Or maybe they felt the same way, that she was some kind of dimwit. Okay, she'd just managed to pass this semester, even though all her electives were "snap" courses, but that was because she wasn't really interested in school. As for that Ronnie James person—she hadn't encouraged him. Lois was just trying to find someone else to blame for a bad relationship. . . .

She passed one of the freshmen, who gave her a sidelong glance but didn't speak, and it occurred to Bobby Jo how few friends she'd made at Colorado College. Which didn't make sense. She'd been so popular at Punahou—and not just with the boys. Was it possible that was because she'd been Tai's friend? Everybody looked up to Tai so—maybe the other girls had accepted her because of that.

The suspicion that she couldn't quite make it on her own hurt. She'd been so excited when she'd come to Colorado, but the truth was it hadn't turned out the way she'd expected, not at all. Sure, she went out a lot, but when was the last time the girls in the dorm had included her in one of their hen sessions? Sometimes, when she came in from a date, she heard them talking and laughing in one of the other rooms—did they all share Lois's opinion of her?

She rounded the curve in the stairs. When she spotted Josh, standing by the reception desk, talking to the freshman monitor, some of her depression vanished. He laughed at something the girl said, and involuntarily Bobby Jo stopped on the stairs. Josh turned and saw her. His lips widened into an admiring grin that made her heart beat faster, and suddenly she didn't give a hang what Lois thought about her. The admiration in Josh's eyes was balm to her ruffled feathers, and she gave him a smile that made him whistle softly as she came up to him.

"You are one high-powered lady," he said. "I don't know if an old country boy like me can handle it."

Bobby Jo couldn't think of a flip answer, so she just smiled again. He executed a sharp right turn, presenting his arm for her to take, making her—and the monitor—laugh.

"That's better," he murmured as he escorted her toward the door. "You looked so solemn when you came down those stairs. I thought maybe you'd just remembered that you'd forgotten to turn off the faucets in the bathtub."

"Our dorm has showers," she said.

"A very literal lady, I see. So tell me—what *was* bugging you a few minutes ago?"

"I just had a run-in with my roommate."

"What's her problem?"

"She . . . well, she accused me of flirting with her boyfriend, but it isn't true. He did ask me to go to a rock concert, but I turned him down. Why, I hardly knew him. In fact, I had no idea she was dating him. She acted as if they had a heavy relationship, but—I can't help it if someone asks me for a date, can I?"

"I suspect every guy you meet does. I can't understand why when you're so ugly."

She giggled at his deadpan delivery. This kind of talk she understood and felt comfortable with. It was almost as if she were back at Punahou with all the boys hanging around, trying to make her laugh.

The melodrama they attended was held in a converted barn in Manitou Springs, a small community that huddled between Colorado Springs and Ute Pass, one of the natural entries into the Rockies. Bobby Jo was delighted with the rustic setting, which reminded her of Arkansas, and while she was pretty sure that Josh was a little bored, she enjoyed the slapstick comedy, too.

Afterward, they stopped at a small tavern for a drink. Josh chose a back booth, well out of sight of the door, explaining that he didn't want to attract any attention. As they waited for their drinks, he kept up a constant string of jokes. When she laughed, he told her she was a perfect audience since she thought everything he said was funny.

His compliments warmed her, especially since her ego had taken such a beating earlier, and she felt very proud when she noticed the interested glances of other women. Not that Josh was the best-looking man in the taproom, but the cute way he had of complimenting her at the same time he seemed to be insulting her, his admiring glances, and his crazy jokes made up for it. Without thinking, she had a second planter's punch, although her limit was usually one, and when he ordered a third round of drinks without asking her, she shrugged mentally. Tomorrow was Sunday—she could sleep late.

By the time they returned to Josh's car, one of the new personalized vans that were becoming so popular, she felt a little tipsy. In fact, although Josh had his arm around her waist and was holding her so tightly that the side of her breast was pressed against his chest, she felt as if she were floating a couple of inches above the ground.

"Are we going back to the dorm now?" she asked, hoping he'd suggest a ride first.

"Later. First I want to show you my favorite Colorado view," he said. "I'll bet you've never seen Helen Hunt Falls by moon-light, have you?"

"I've never even heard of it," she confessed.

"You know the legend of Ramona, don't you?"

"I don't think so."

"She was a character in an old novel. Her lover was an Indian—the falls were one of the settings in the book."

"Sounds lovely."

As they headed south, Josh was quiet, concentrating on his driving, and Bobby Jo rested her head against the seat, her eyelids heavy. She must have dozed because it seemed no time at all before Josh was shaking her arm. "We're here. I could use a little pick-me-up before we take a walk down to the falls. How about you?"

She started to tell him she'd had more than enough to drink, but he was already handing her a small flask. Rather than appear to be a poor sport, she tipped it up and took a long swallow. The liquid burned her throat, and she almost choked before she got it down.

"What *was* that?" she said when she found her breath again.

"Jim Beam. The military man's champagne," he said. "It'll put hair on your chest."

The idea of hair growing on her chest was so ridiculous that she began to giggle. Josh put his arm around her and pushed her face against his chest. "Shhh. You'll disturb our neigh-bors—you might even give them heart failure."

She stopped laughing and peered out into the darkness. Against a faint glow in the sky, she saw the outline of several cars.

"You mean we aren't alone?" Her voice sounded a little queer, and she said the words over again, this time enunciating them carefully. "You mean we aren't alone?"

"They won't bother us. They're much too busy."

"Doing what?"

"Oh, lady, lady—you are something else," he said. "Uncomplicated and to the point—and so am I. Which point is really giving me fits right now. I just hope you're the kind to take pity on a poor Joe from New Jersey who's a long way from home."

His words didn't make sense, but when she told him that, he laughed and pulled her closer. "Relax and go with the flow, Bobby Jo—God, that name kills me. It could only belong to you. You really turn me on, you know? The way you walk—it's enough to drive a man crazy."

His breath against her face was very warm. She snuggled closer, feeling relaxed and excited at the same time. He kissed her, and the warmth in her stomach spread—up to her breasts and down to her thighs. The pressure of his body increased, and his tongue slid between her lips, but she didn't pull away, not even when he slipped his hand inside her coat and rubbed his thumb over the swell of her breast.

Ordinarily, she didn't go in for heavy petting, as the boys she dated found out pretty quickly. Sometimes, if she really liked a boy, she let him fondle her breast, even kiss it through her dress, but never anything more. But Josh was so eager—he was talking again, his voice going on and on in the dark—and she felt very confused. Everything was all jumbled and out of whack—she and Josh kept shifting position, moving around on the seat, and he was telling her, his voice urgent, that he was crazy about her, that he was in pain, that if he didn't at least touch her, he would go out of his mind. Besides, it was so dark and comfortable here in the back of the van—and when had they moved out of the front seat, anyway? She couldn't remember climbing back here.

And Josh's hand—should his fingers be touching her *there*? Didn't he realize that she wasn't that kind of girl, that she was saving herself for the right man? But oh, it felt so good when he did that to her, when he stroked that special spot....

Sometimes she tried to imagine her wedding night, the first time she did it with her husband, but she never got farther than how exciting it would be to undress while her bridegroom watched her with worshiping eyes. Why hadn't she known that having a man touch her in that very special place would feel so good? Josh's fingers kept stroking her, and she wanted—she didn't want him to stop, even though it was so moist down there that she was a little embarrassed—and what had happened to her panties? When had he taken them off? He'd unbuttoned her blouse, too—was he actually suckling her nipples as if he were a baby? And that pressure against her leg—it was so hard and hot and somehow very threatening. When had he taken off his trousers—was that his *thing* he was rubbing against the inside of her thigh?

An alarm rang under her confusion. She tried to sit up, but Josh's hands were like vises, holding her down. He murmured reassurances in her ear, told her how wild he was about her, that he'd fallen crazy in love with her the first time he'd seen her, that he'd never felt this way about another girl. His voice was like a bell, setting her vibrating, and suddenly it seemed so silly to make a fuss when all he was doing was fondling her.

And it felt so delicious when his hair tickled the flesh between her thighs like that, when he did that with his tongue. Only—wasn't that sort of nasty? Something nice girls didn't allow? What must he think of her for not stopping him before this? But oh, it felt so good. It sent hot little thrills up and down her body, made her stomach muscles quiver. And after all, it wasn't as if he were trying to go all the way. He was just kissing her, touching her—and how did he know about her secret place, the tiny hidden spot she rubbed sometimes because it felt so good? This—what he was doing with his tongue—felt even better. This was heaven. Pure heaven. And there was no harm in it. Surely, he wouldn't try anything else. He knew that she was a nice girl, the daughter of a chaplain. It couldn't hurt anything if she just let him go on doing that. It wasn't as if she were actually encouraging him. After all, she was just lying there, letting him touch her. . . .

And why was he stopping? She didn't want him to stop, not even to kiss her breasts again. His mouth was so wet—and that pressure between her thighs—what was he doing now? My God, that was his thing he was trying to push inside her!

She started to tell him to stop, but his mouth was covering hers now and he was holding her down—and then it was too late. He was inside her, moving frantically up and down, and she—she didn't want him to stop now, didn't want him to stop, didn't want him to—oh, God, she was soaring, and now her whole body was exploding and she was in heaven . . . heaven. . . .

She realized Josh was lying on top of her, his breath rasping in her ear. "God, that was good, baby—it was good for you, too, wasn't it?"

Bobby Jo didn't know what to say. Would he think she was easy if she told him that she'd loved it? Did women—decent women—feel that way? She knew the girls in the dorm talked about sex all the time, but she'd never been sure if they really liked it. After all, until tonight, the only thing she'd ever felt when a boy kissed her was a little pleasant flutter. Most of the

time she'd been worried about her lipstick smearing or whether
the boy was messing up her hair.

But this—what had just happened—was catastrophic. And
scary. Because what if it didn't mean anything special to Josh?

"I guess you think I'm easy now," she said finally.

"Easy? You've got to be kidding—no, you aren't kidding.
Don't tell me—" He broke off.

A sob escaped from her tight throat, and then Josh was
holding her, nuzzling her ear. "Baby, baby—don't you know
I'm crazy about you? Did you think this was just a casual thing
with me? Next time, it will be even better. We'll go to this
motel I—that I've heard some of the guys talk about. I'll show
you how great it can be when we don't have to hurry. It'll be
out of this world, just the two of us in a big, soft bed. You'd
like that, wouldn't you?"

She let him reassure her, coax her, and later she let him
make love to her again because after all, it was silly to make
a fuss when he'd already taken her cherry. But this time, there
was a cold, watchful core inside her that held back, that wondered if Josh's compliments, his vows of love, weren't just a
bit too glib—and practiced.

CHAPTER

✦ 23 ✦

TAI SO SELDOM GOT MAIL THAT WHEN SHE DID, SHE ALWAYS
felt compelled to stop everything else to read it on the spot.
She had kept up an erratic correspondence with a few of her
old Punahou classmates, and three times Crystal had dropped
her a note, usually when she had some personal triumph to
crow about. From her accounts, she was leading a whirlwind
social life at Hickam, playing the colonel's wife to the hilt.
Although Tai wished her well, she hadn't yet answered Crystal's last letter, mainly because there seemed so little to say.

Shelley's first letter, the summer after Mac's death, had
come as a surprise. Written in what Tai thought of as boarding-
school script, Shelley wrote about Tad and her pregnancy, about
life in the Philippines, about the adjustments that becoming a
military wife demanded. Although the letter was cheerful
enough, Tai sensed a deep unrest. Which was why, despite her
grueling schedule, she had answered promptly, minimizing her
own trials and, following Shelley's lead, trying to make them
sound funny.

But it was Bobby Jo's breezy notes, as inconsequential as
the wind, that always gave her a lift, so when she saw the
characteristic blue envelope in her mailbox, she shifted her
books to one arm and tore it open, standing in the hall.

But this time, even though the letter exuded enthusiasm and
was dotted with exclamation marks, she didn't smile. This Josh
Springer Bobby Jo had met—she'd heard that name somewhere

before, and she had the feeling that it hadn't been in any favorable way.

She realized that time was ticking away, and she tucked the letter inside a notebook and hurried toward Fairchild Hall for her first class of the morning; but all during military history she was preoccupied and found it hard to concentrate on the lively debate raging in the small room.

Usually, she was quick to state her opinions, to parry opposing arguments with the instructor, a young captain who was secure enough to permit his students to challenge him. Today, her mind was on her friend's letter, on trying to figure out why it disturbed her so.

Cassie, who took the same class, commented on her lack of attention as they were walking down the hall after class.

"What's up? You were a million miles away today. Captain Roderick asked you what you thought the roots of the war in 'Nam were and you told him that you had no opinion. Which about floored me—and him, I suspect. What I mean is—Tai-Ching MacGarrett without an opinion? It blows the mind."

"I guess I wasn't paying any attention," Tai confessed. "Cassie, what do you know about a cadet named Josh Springer?"

The smile slipped off Cassie's face. "You aren't interested in *him*, are you?"

"Answer the question, ma'am."

"Okay, okay. He's a senior, high achiever, very cool, popular with other cadets. He's also into women—and I do mean *into* them. You know, a real joystick man. I hope you aren't hung up on him because he's got a line that won't stop—not that I wouldn't mind fratting with him if he liked my style, which he obviously does not. But it would strictly be for laughs. He's not your steady type."

"Nothing more?"

"So what were you expecting?"

"I don't know. My friend Bobby Jo met him, and it sounds like she really fell for him."

"Well, that wouldn't be hard to do. He's a charmer. Only he's the kind who strikes hard and then moves on fast. I wouldn't advise your friend to take Josh Springer too seriously."

"Maybe I'd better—no, it isn't any of my business," Tai said. "Bobby Jo's had three dozen boyfriends to my one. She can take care of herself."

"Right attitude, roomie. And you've got your own troubles.

Hell, all God's children's got troubles. Today we start the heavy stuff—unarmed defense and all that. The guys are really looking forward to this day, you can bet."

"Guys? But it's an all-woman class."

"That's the way it's supposed to work, but I've heard this rumor—from one of the female elements, who should know—that we're really in for it. The first class is coed because it's mainly a lecture and a demonstration of martial arts as a whole, which gives the macho types a chance to prove their manhood." She put the back of her hand against her forehead in a poor imitation of a swooning Victorian heroine. "Will it never end, will it never end?"

"Will you never stop, will you never stop? And what's this rumor you heard?"

"Karen Dill took me aside this morning as we were coming out of the dining hall. Seems the seniors are cooking up a little surprise. They plan to match up some poor female with their top jock during the demonstration. She thinks sisters should stick together, even if she's third degree and I'm a lowly doolie, and she also thinks I'm the prime target, because of my height. So she told me to stay in the background, preferably behind some big male. Of course, they might get a surprise. I didn't survive five older brothers, all of them jocks, by being a shrinking violet. I don't know shit about martial arts, but I can arm wrestle with the best of them."

She sounded so cocky that Tai was still smiling when they split at the end of the hall to go to their respective classes. As she ducked down a branch corridor, she wondered what to do if she were picked as the butt of the joke the seniors were cooking up. Steven's advice, however personally demeaning, did make good sense. There was no percentage in making waves or in trying to best an upperclassman when they held all the cards. And to get the reputation of being a smart-ass with the juniors, who would be seniors next year, would be suicide.

Besides, she wasn't sure how well her kung fu skills would stack up with their martial arts expert—whoever he might be. With the whole cadre probably in on it, all prepared for their yuck of the week at the expense of the women doolies, it might not be wise to deprive them of their fun. Better to be a good sport—and land on the mat as lightly as she could manage.

Having made this decision, she put it out of her mind,

knowing she would need all her wits during her aerodynamics class. It was her most interesting subject—and also the most satisfying when she managed to master some tricky theorem. As always, she tried to lose herself in the lecture, in the interplay of questions and answers later.

In the past few months, she had sat in on many informal rap sessions where the doolies, looking ahead to the future because it was better than dwelling on the present, talked knowingly about how to beat the promotion system. They weighed the pros and cons of one field over another, of making the right moves and attending the right service schools all the way up the ladder, quoting as gospel the opinions of senior cadets and/or officers, older brothers, military fathers, and, Tai often thought, the man who policed the parking lot.

Since Tai had no intention of making a career of the military, she didn't feel involved and seldom joined in the sessions. Her own goal was simple—an engineering degree and anything else that might make her future more secure. Against the advice of her counselor, who wanted her to major in the humanities, she knew what she would choose as her major at the end of her sophomore year. Her dream was to be an aeronautical engineer—maybe she would someday help design the planes her fellow doolies would fly, a dream she was careful to keep to herself.

Despite her interest in the subject, the aerodynamics class seemed to drag today. Her mind kept drifting to Bobby Jo's letter. What was her responsibility to her friend? A subtle hint about Josh Springer's reputation as a womanizer? A carefully couched warning? But surely Bobby Jo didn't need her advice. She had dated dozens of boys and had obviously handled them all—wouldn't she resent a warning from someone who had only seriously dated one man? It would be like an old maid giving a mother of five advice on raising children.

On the other hand, Bobby Jo could be surprisingly naive at times. She still believed in romance and all the old-fashioned fairy tales. What if, in this Josh Springer, she'd encountered someone outside her experience? Still—how much of a Don Juan could a twenty-three-year-old cadet be?

When the bell rang, Tai was the first one out of the classroom. As she hurried down the hall, she was careful to stay just under a full-fledged run, which was forbidden inside Fairchild Hall. She had almost reached the exit when she saw

Steven up ahead, moving leisurely toward the same door. He was the last person in the world whose attention she wanted to attract, but she didn't dare slow down. She had only a scant ten minutes to get from the farthest reaches of Fairchild Hall, where classes were held, across the broad expanse of the parade grounds to her room in Vandenberg Hall to change clothes, then hurry back to her squadron's position at the far left of the formation, all the while making sure the room she shared with Cassie was left in perfect order for inspection.

So she didn't dare slow down, even though she knew she was tempting fate by passing Steven on a near run. She had almost reached the door when his voice snapped out her name.

"Cadet MacGarrett!"

Tai had no choice. She had to stop. Even so, she went on another two steps before she slowed and turned.

"Yes, sir?"

"Your shirttail is hanging out."

It wasn't. She had tucked it in securely before she'd left the classroom.

"Sorry, sir."

She made a show of tucking it in. The hall was clearing out rapidly now, but she was aware of curious stares—and a few covert smiles. The little clock that seemed a perpetual part of her these days ticked faster, warning her that time was slipping away.

"Is that all, sir?" she said—imprudently.

"It is not. And that was a little foolish, wasn't it? Showing impatience to an upperclassman, I mean."

"No, sir—I mean yes, sir."

"In fact, it's a big no-no, isn't it?"

"Yes, sir."

"And you know what's going to happen now, don't you?"

"Yes, sir."

"I have to put you on report for untidiness, for running in the halls, and also for rudeness. How many demerits do you think that would add up to?"

"I don't know, sir."

A trickle of sweat ran down Tai's neck. This was hazing, the kind that was officially forbidden. From Steven's half smile, she knew that he was baiting her, hoping to force her to lose her temper—the temper he was so familiar with. And she was equally determined that he wouldn't succeed. She stared him straight in the eye and had the satisfaction of seeing him frown. He glanced down at his watch.

"And now it looks to me like you're going to add tardiness to your sins, Cadet MacGarrett. You're dismissed."

As Tai saluted him smartly, she felt a little dizzy. There was a distressing moisture under her eyelids. I will not cry, she told herself fiercely. This was one humiliation he hadn't managed to inflict upon her since he'd started his harassment.

Although she dashed toward Vandenberg Hall at breakneck speed, she was still three minutes behind schedule when she reached the room she shared with Cassie. To her relief, her clothes were laid out on her bed. Cassie must have guessed what had happened and had taken some of her own precious time to give her a hand. Even so, she was the last one in position by the time she reached her place in formation. Cadet Dill, her element sergeant, gave her a hard look as she slid into place.

"You're on report, Cadet MacGarrett," she snapped.

"Yes, ma'am," Tai said woodenly.

The sidelong glances of the other cadets held sympathy. Which wasn't going to help her walk off those demerits if Steven chose to enforce them. And she desperately needed every minute she could get for her studies. As it was, she was only averaging five or six hours of sleep a night. No wonder she was down to ninety-five pounds.

Well, it was the milk shake routine for her again. If her weight was still off by her next physical, she was in trouble. And trouble was one thing she had an abundance of—thanks to Steven.

The bitterness welled up inside her, and this time she didn't quite succeed in keeping her eyes dry. As she stared straight ahead, afraid to blink for fear the tears would run down her cheeks, she cursed the day she'd ever met Steven. How could she have misjudged him so? It seemed impossible to reconcile the man who had been her lover, the man she'd planned to marry, with the man who was making her life miserable.

Later, when they dispersed, Cassie fell into step beside her.

"You okay?"

"Okay. Thanks for laying out my clothes."

"You're my bud, aren't you? You'd do it for me—in fact, you have a couple of times."

Tai started to make a joking reply when a man's voice

intruded. "Tough going, MacGarrett. That jerk Henderson really is an asshole."

Tai looked around, but there were several cadets walking behind them and she couldn't be sure who had spoken. Cassie shook her head. "The guys think it's very uncool the way Henderson picks on you. They figure you must've turned down an invitation to take a late-night spin in his car with him."

Tai was tempted to tell her the truth, but instead she said, "He'll be gone next year. I can tough it out until then."

"Yeah, and then those turkeys in the junior class will be seniors. The sophomore class has just about accepted female cadets, so maybe we'll get a break when they're seniors and we're juniors. Oh, happy day! If you ask me, most of the seniors would ignore the whole female cadet thing if it wasn't for a few ringleaders who keep them stirred up. It's peer pressure—there's only a few who've been causing all the trouble. Imagine when those same jerks are in charge of the big red button. It makes me shudder."

Tai found she could still smile. "Meanwhile, it's more demerits for me—and I thought I'd finally walked them all off."

"Tough. Maybe he'll lay off you now. I hear the seniors get downright mellow the closer it gets to June week."

"That'll be the day." Tai sighed.

It seemed to Tai, in her heightened state of consciousness, that there were too many spectators in the boxing room—in fact, why were there *any* spectators?—for the preliminary session of an unimportant class. It was obvious that at least half of them were upperclassmen. In the rear of the gym she recognized several seniors, one of them the cadet Cassie called "the leader of the rat pack."

Cadet Armstrong was, which always seemed so strange to Tai, extremely attractive, a high achiever with all the attributes of a natural leader. It puzzled her that this particular cadet should be the ringleader of the group who made life rough for the female cadets. Surely it couldn't be hatred of women. From his reputation, he was a real killer with the girls who attended the hops and other social events at the academy.

From the corner of her eye, she watched as he talked quietly to another senior. At first, the instructor, a young captain who had been on the 1974 Olympic boxing team, explained the philosophy of unarmed defense and martial arts in general, which were concerned with defensive, not aggressive, conflict, emphasizing the fact that a practitioner used the strength and aggression of his opponent to put the odds in his own favor.

The captain's tone was so earnest that Tai decided Cassie's rumor must have been just that—an idle rumor. But Cassie nudged her when the captain paused, then added, "And then there's the old saying you'll hear so often that knowledge of martial arts makes the weak equal to the strong. This is only true, I assure you, if the weak has a gun—and it's always possible that the strong has also been trained in the martial arts."

He beckoned to the senior cadets standing in the back of the room. "Cadet Commander Armstrong is going to demonstrate some of the technique with which you'll become familiar before you finish this course. He'll need a partner—I won't ask for volunteers, although I know each and every one of you is just panting to put up your hand." He waited, smiling, for the obligatory laughs. "Since this is Cadet Armstrong's show, I'll let him pick his partner and I'll assume that you're all volunteers."

Cadet Armstrong took his time threading his way through the audience toward the mat in the center of the room, his insolent stare roaming over the doolies. To Tai's prejudiced eyes, it seemed that even the largest of the male cadets shifted uneasily, careful not to meet Armstrong's stare. Her pride prevented her from looking away when he paused to examine her expressionless face. Beside her, Cassie's breath sucked in audibly as he turned a ferocious look in her direction. He raised his hand and pointed his finger—but at Tai, not Cassie.

"That one'll do," he growled.

Tai didn't move for a moment. There was a wave of murmurs, quickly subdued, from the other doolies, and she knew that her classmates resented his choice. She was, after all, the smallest cadet in the room—and a woman. They, too, must have heard the rumors and knew that she was being singled out to take the fall for all of them.

The instructor hesitated, frowning. He gave Armstrong a hard look, then asked Tai, "What's your name, Cadet?"

"Fourthclassman MacGarrett, sir,"

"You don't have to volunteer, you know—"

"But I do volunteer, sir," she said.

"Okay then. Front and center, Cadet MacGarrett."

Tai moved through the crowd; she had the feeling that their eyes were burning holes in the back of her head. Cadet Armstrong looked her over silently, then turned out his hands in a shrugging gesture as if to disclaim what was about to happen.

"We'll start with a basic over-the-arm toss," the instructor said. "You'll all be familiar with this move before you finish the course."

Armstrong circled Tai leisurely, his eyes roaming over her. When his back was to the instructor, he mouthed, "Say your prayers, cunt," and then moved in quickly. Tai didn't resist; when he flipped her over his arm, she landed lithely on the mat, still on her feet. There was a ripple of applause that made Armstrong frown.

"Into gymnastics, are you, Tai-*chink*?" he said sotto voce in her ear. "Well, let's see how you handle this one."

Not waiting for the instructor to describe the next move, he reached out confidently for a hold. Instead of resisting, she used his own muscle strength and flew over his shoulder in a graceful arch, landing lightly on her feet again.

The instructor, who looked as if he wanted to laugh, broke in quickly, "The next move is a real bone cruncher, so you'll be learning how to take a fall as well as the countermoves to protect yourself."

He nodded to Cadet Armstrong, who was already circling Tai. She flinched a little when he bent toward her and hissed, "You won't get up from this one, slant eyes. Time I'm through with you, the only thing you'll be good for is a gang bang."

A flash of heat rose to Tai's head, followed by a sudden chilling of her skin. She recognized the chill for what it was, knew the danger of letting anger direct her, but at the moment, all she wanted was to wipe that mocking leer off Armstrong's face. Balls, was it? She'd show him balls. . . .

Cadet Armstrong's eyelids narrowed slightly, and she knew he was about to make his move. Quick as a cat, he reached for her—but she wasn't there. She was behind him, her foot buckling his knees, and for a second he was too surprised to resist. Using his own weight and bulk, she flipped him—over her shoulder and onto the canvas mat. She didn't pull the move to blunt his fall. He crashed upon the mat and then lay there, the breath knocked out of his lungs. For a few seconds there was a dead silence in the room, and then a male voice yelled, "Way to go, MacGarrett."

Armstrong sat up, shaking his head to clear it. He rolled to his feet and came at her again, his eyes murderous. But his timing was off, and she sidestepped easily, then darted forward to grab his arm and pull him toward her. He was flying through the air again before he had time to realize what was happening.

This time he didn't get up. The room erupted into applause, and although she knew she'd just made a mistake, humiliating the ringleader of the female baiters, her blood was up and she didn't give a damn. She circled the fallen man, her knees loose and slightly bent, her hands poised for the next move. But the fight had gone out of Armstrong—even if his rage hadn't.

"You almost broke my fucking ankle," he snarled.

There was wave of disapproving catcalls, and a feminine voice said, "Shame, shame." The instructor, looking as if he didn't know whether to laugh or explode, bent over Armstrong and examined him quickly.

"You just got the wind knocked out of you—but maybe we'd better get you over to the medics for a look-see." He beckoned to two of the cadets, who helped Armstrong to his feet and out the door. When they were gone, he told the silent class, "Tomorrow we'll start with exercises to limber up the muscles you'll need for your training. And now, everybody clear out—except Cadet MacGarrett."

When the room was empty, he turned to Tai. "Okay, explain yourself, MacGarrett."

"I'm sorry, sir. I don't understand the question."

"You've had martial training—kung fu, I'd guess. How much?"

She hesitated, then said reluctantly, "Three years."

"It isn't in your records."

"I'm sure it's in my original application and resumé."

He grunted. "Okay, I'll buy that. You do know you did a stupid thing today, don't you?"

"Sir?"

"Okay, play dumb. But stay out of dark corners for the rest of the year and watch out for low-flying balls—and if you repeat this conversation to anyone—*anyone*—I'll deny it and put you on report for lying." He paused, then added, "For what it's worth, Cadet Armstrong was supposed to pick the biggest jock in the class. That's the whole point—to prove how effec-

tive martial arts can be. To choose the weakest cadet in class—
hell, I'd better modify that. To choose the one who *seemed* to
be the weakest cadet negates the message we try to impress
upon students."

"Yes, sir. I didn't think you were in on it, sir."

"You can go now—but think about this. It would have been
better for you if you'd faked a couple falls and taken your licks.
You've got the kind of pride that can get you in a lot of trouble
in this man's air force."

Suddenly it seemed important to Tai to have this man's good
opinion. "May I speak off record, sir?" Tai said.

"Can I stop you?"

"Yes, sir. Just tell me to shut up."

"Speak your piece."

"Cadet Armstrong called me a cunt and told me I was only
good for a gang bang. I couldn't let that pass."

He stared at her for a long moment. To her surprise, a wave
of red washed over his face, and she realized that her words
had embarrassed him. "You want to file a complaint?"

"No, sir!" she said, surprised that he'd even ask.

"Then I suggest you forget it. And I have a hunch that you
just might make an adequate officer someday. Dismissed, Cadet
MacGarrett."

She thought over his words as she headed for her billet. Did
being a good officer mean taking any insult, no matter how
unfair or humiliating, without complaining? It seemed a dumb
way, a man's way, to run an army.

Steven didn't hear about the incident until late that evening.
He was at his desk, putting the final touches on a book report
that he hoped would bring up his sagging English grades.
Although he was a good student, he found it hard to keep his
interest in mundane subjects like English from flagging. Since
he'd discovered the fascinations of computer science, it had
become his passion—to the detriment of other subjects.

His current roommate—and best friend—was lounging on
his bunk. John Potter—better known as John-John to his inti-
mates—was plunking away at the battered old guitar he had
managed to smuggle into his room when he was a lowly doolie,
a feat that had earned him a reputation for ingenuity among
his classmates.

Steven took in John-John's dreamy expression and knew his

roommate was thinking about his girl. They had been pinned since his junior year and would be married in June. John-John, who freely admitted to being oversexed, was straining at the reins like a stallion who had just caught the scent of a mare in season. If he had already bedded his fiancée, he was keeping it to himself, a reticence Steven heartily approved of.

His mind wandered away from the sentence he was polishing, back to the hazing incident in Fairchild Hall. Tai had been furious—it had taken all her willpower to snap out those "yes, sirs" without exploding. Which was the whole point of his hazing. Tai needed self-discipline, hardening. The next three years wouldn't be any picnic—and he wouldn't be here to look out for her. No one except John-John realized why he kept bugging her—and his harassment had earned Tai the sympathy, respect, and the loyalty of her fellow doolies. Next year, she would be third degree, still subject to a lot of hard knocks, but she would have good friends among the male cadets, too—and a female at the academy needed that.

In his own way, he had also insulated her from the hassling of his own classmates. Because they believed she was his special project, they left her alone—not that Tai had any idea what he was up to. The hatred in her eyes when she looked at him hurt like hell—but then, what else was new? The chasm between them would never be crossed. He owed his father, the man he admired most in all the world, his loyalty—and Tai felt the same way about her own father. And never the twain shall meet. . . .

"You brooding over that girl again?" John-John asked, and Steven realized his roommate had stopped strumming his guitar and was watching him.

"What girl?"

"I'm not talking about that redhead you've been rushing for the past year. I mean your little Chinese friend."

"We had another—encounter."

"So I heard."

"News does get around."

"When it happens in the middle of Fairchild Hall, yeah, it does get around. Which is your intention. Don't you think you were a little too rough on her this time? She just finished walking off that last tour you instigated."

"She can take it. She's tough as they come. She'll be a lot tougher when this year is over."

"Yeah. Something your friend Armstrong found out this afternoon. The whole corps is buzzing about that little incident."

Steven swung around to face him. "What does that mean?"

"You haven't heard? Everybody was talking about it in the dining hall—come to think of it, where were you at dinner?"

"The Flowerses invited me to their quarters for steak."

"Ah so—making time with the commandant of cadets' daughter, eh? Are you going to marry the girl? It wouldn't be a bad deal—as long as she's the one you really want."

"Never mind that. What's all this about Armstrong?"

"Well, you know that old gag the seniors pull on the doolie martial arts classes? You know, they pick some big bruiser to be the demonstrator's partner and he comes swaggering up, full of confidence because no way is this guy, about half his size, going to throw him, martial arts expert or not. Then slam bang, thank you, ma'am, and he's on the mat, looking up instead of down. So he gets up again—this just has to be a mistake, see?—and this time he really concentrates on flexing his muscles. Then slam bang again. It gives everybody a big laugh, and it's an incentive for the nonjocks in the class to try a little harder."

"I know all that. So what has this to do with Tai?"

"Captain Goetz was conned into using Armstrong as his demonstrator. Armstrong was supposed to pick Cadet Glover—he was all-state back in Nebraska, where they grow 'em rough, tough, and ugly. He's also something of a braggart. Just the guy everybody'd love to see stretched out on the mat. But Armstrong picked Tai instead. More of his pussy baiting. I'm sure Goetz wasn't in on it. I heard he almost countermanded Armstrong's choice, but he must've decided it was a bad policy to jump Armstrong in front of a bunch of doolies. The other doolies didn't like it, but you don't go around making enemies when you're a chicken-shit fourth degree, not with someone like Armstrong, who has a reputation for being vindictive. He's got too big a following—which shows how stupid some people can be. Anyway, he picked your favorite doolie, and—"

Steven groaned, and John-John grinned at him. "You already know the end, right? Seems she's some kind of martial arts expert. She floored him twice, and the second time he stayed down with the wind knocked out of him. During the fracas, he made a foul remark that some of the guys overheard. If

MacGarrett had wanted to bring him up before the board for harassment, I think she would've had backing. But I heard she told Goetz to forget it, which is smart—"

"The little fool—I told her not to call attention to herself."

"You may be the reason she lost her cool today, big man. I figure she was still pissed off at you when Armstrong started hassling her. He called her a cunt and said something really gross to her about a gang bang just before she slammed him to the mat."

Steven got to his feet slowly, his jaws clenched. John-John gave him a worried look. "Hey, you aren't going to do anything stupid, are you, like calling Armstrong out? Me and my flipping mouth—"

Steven didn't wait to hear any more. His head seemed to be on fire—and yet his thoughts were ice cold. Despite his anger, there was a purpose to what he intended to do. He knew what a bastard Armstrong was, had watched him in action for three and a half years. If he didn't call him out, Tai's life wouldn't be worth living for the rest of the year. And since he knew John-John's assessment was right, that it was probably his fault that Tai had lost control of her temper, it was up to him to straighten things out.

He didn't bother to knock before he went into Armstrong's room. Armstrong's roommate was working at his desk, and Armstrong was sprawled out on his bunk asleep, a *Playboy* lying open across his face. When Steven said his name, he snorted and sat up.

"So what's up, Henderson?" he said, rubbing his eyes.

"A grudge match—between you and me."

"What's your beef, hotshot?"

"How about tomorrow afternoon?" Steven said, ignoring the question.

"Hell, you're crazy. I'll wipe up the floor with you."

"Or we can make it tomorrow evening—provided one of the rings is free."

"You're calling *me* out? You really are crazy."

"Let's say tomorrow, any time I can arrange it. I'll talk to Coach Abernathy and let you know."

Steven turned and headed out the door. Just before it swung shut behind him, he heard Armstrong's roommate say, "What the fuck's eating *him*?"

"Who knows? I've been wanting to tangle with that smart-ass for four years. I'm going to enjoy every minute of this."

Steven wasn't surprised that the wooden benches surrounding the ring were almost full when he arrived for the match the next evening. John-John, who was acting as his second, whistled softly and muttered something about Roman spectacles and gore. Steven ignored him. He was too busy fighting the hollow feeling in his stomach.

He'd had no problem getting permission for the match. It was an accepted method, although not official, for handling trouble between cadets. As long as it wasn't touted as a grudge match, it served a good purpose. Usually, the combatants exorcised their anger and became, if not friends, at least not open enemies.

That there was a special interest in this particular match because of the status of the cadets involved, both of whom were class officers, was inevitable. Ever since Steven had been selected vice wing commander and Armstrong wing commander, an uneasy truce had existed between them, but it was well known that they seldom saw eye to eye about things. So speculations were rampant about the cause of the match, speculations Steven was careful not to satisfy.

A large block of seats were occupied by Armstrong's cronies and hangers-on, but Steven was gratified to see that his own friends were well represented. Not for the first time, as he met Armstrong's smirk, he questioned the cadet system. Why was it that men who possessed the worst qualities—lack of empathy, an overabundance of personal ambition, overweening vanity—so often were chosen as leaders?

Not that he himself wasn't competitive. But it was a secondary thing with him, not a gut reaction. Sometimes, when he thought of the years ahead before retirement, he had to remind himself of his goals and priorities. As for Armstrong—he was all the things Steven disliked in a man. He played by the rules in public, but in private he was a bastard with a knack for making the right contacts. It was well known that he was dating the only daughter of General John Larsen, present Commander-In-Chief of Air Defence Command. Steven pitied the girl if she married Armstrong.

As he looked around, nodding to his friends, he was well aware that he might not end up the winner of this match.

Armstrong overweighed him by some twenty pounds—and it was all solid muscle. On the other hand, he *had* been on the boxing team during his first three years at the academy and had done well for himself in intramural contests. So it was a toss-up who would win. . . .

Coach Abernathy, who supervised the boxing team, beckoned to both men. Steven loped forward, eager to get it over with. Knowing the importance of appearing confident, he clenched his hands over his head and gave a cocky grin after he threw off his terry-cloth robe. As the coach intoned the rules and he touched gloves with Armstrong, he noted the thin beading of sweat on his opponent's forehead. Was that heat—or was it possible that Armstrong was nervous about this match?

Almost before the thought could form in his mind, his opponent attacked him—a split second before the coach signaled for the fight to begin. When Steven's counterblow, squarely on his opponent's jaw, sent Armstrong reeling into the ropes and then to the floor, Steven was totally nonplussed. The last thing he'd expected was for Armstrong to have a glass jaw.

Since his own adrenaline was still pumping away, it was all he could do not to jerk Armstrong to his feet and deliver another punch. As he bent over his opponent, ostentatiously checking to see if he was okay, he was aware of the cheers and shouts in the background. Knowing his voice would be covered by the noise, he told Armstrong, "If you've got plans to get even with Tai MacGarrett, forget it. The next time I'll knock your fucking head off—and it will look like an accident, you scudball."

He didn't wait to see the effects of his words. He turned a grin, a good-ol'-sport grin, upon the audience. "I'm quitting while I still have my teeth. My opponent is a real tiger—all bets are off now!" and earned a hand that included Armstrong's cronies.

"Okay, you heard the guy. That's it for tonight," Coach Abernathy said. He clapped Steven on the back. "Too bad you didn't keep on with your boxing, Henderson. Could've used you this year."

"Thank you, sir. Academics are taking up too much of my time," Steven said.

Just before he left the auditorium, he glanced back.

Armstrong was standing with his cronies, and the expression on his face was anything but happy. Slowly, Steven raised one hand as if to give him a friendly wave—but his middle finger was pointing straight up. As he walked down the hall, he found himself swaggering a little. So much for good sportsmanship, he thought.

It was two days later that he found a note, written on a scrap of yellow tablet paper, inside his mailbox.

"North corner of chapel tonight at nine," it read—and it was signed "Moongirl."

He reread the words, trying to figure out what they meant. Except for the signature, he would have chalked it up to a gag—or some kind of trap that Armstrong was cooking up for him. But no one, no one in the world except Tai, would use that name. It was something he had called her only while they were making love, usually in the back of his father's car or on some lonely beach.

So the question was not who had sent the note, but *why* Tai had sent it. Was it possible she wanted to mend fences? If so, why hadn't she requested a meeting through channels, starting with her element sergeant?

After all, he *was* vice-commandant this term, in the direct chain of command. So why had Tai taken such a risk just to meet him alone? She could have cited the confidentiality of the meeting she was requesting to her element. It might not be official, but everybody looked the other way, knowing that sometimes a cadet had a personal problem so delicate that he/she wanted to discuss it only with someone at the top of the chain.

As for whether he was going to the chapel tonight—wild horses couldn't keep him away. But first he intended to take out a little insurance on the off chance that it could be a trap, after all.

He showed John-John the note. "How about taking a walk with me tonight?" he said.

"Right. Could be the little lady is planning on having you up for rape or something."

"Not Tai. She may be a walking headache, but she has a strict sense of—call it honor."

"Well, you know her best. So what do you want me to do? Stand guard?"

"Just stay in the shadows. If everything looks okay, I'll give a signal and you can melt away into the night."

"Anything you say. But you'd better take along some rattlesnake antidote. She just might take a bite out of you."

It was a few minutes before nine when Steven rounded the sharp angle of the chapel. Although there was a moon, the building cast a darkness over the area. He couldn't make out Tai's figure, but he sensed she was already there—and alone—even before she stepped out of the deep shadows. He made a surreptitious gesture and knew John-John would draw back, out of earshot.

"What's this all about, Tai?" he asked.

"You bastard—you had to do it, didn't you?" she hissed.

Whatever he'd expected—an offer of reconciliation, even a simple "thank you" for risking his neck—it wasn't this. "Do what, Cadet MacGarrett?"

"Don't give me that Cadet MacGarrett crap. There's no one else here. I'll call you 'sir' when there are witnesses. Right now, the only word that fits you is 'bastard.'"

"Okay, spit it out. What's your problem?"

"My problem is you. You had to get involved, didn't you? Why did you do it? Were you trying to be the big hero—or was it because someone else was picking on your own private whipping boy?"

"Is that what you really think?"

"I think you're a sadist, that you get your kicks out of hassling me. So why the big hero act? It couldn't be your conscience because you don't have one—any more than your lying father does."

"Knock it off. Don't bring my father into this."

"I feel sorry for you—you know that? Someday you're going to find out the truth about him, and when you do, I hope you have the guts to come to me and apologize. Not that I really give a damn. It can't bring Mac back. But for the good of your soul, I hope you can do it."

"And this is why you asked me here?"

"What did you think—that I wanted to make out with you? I'd rather kiss a snake."

"You didn't use to feel that way, Tai," he said softly.

"I was a fool. I'm a lot smarter now. I've changed since—"

"Oh, you've changed all right. You used to be a lot different—and what the hell happened to your sense of humor?"

"Listen to me, Steven—and take notes. In the past two years, I lost everything that mattered to me—starting with my father. The medics said it was a stroke, but Mac died of a broken heart because your father didn't have the guts to tell the truth and take responsibility for his own mistakes. Or maybe he simply saw a chance to break up your engagement to me. But those years gave me backbone. I worked hard and studied hard—and when I'd finally made it into the academy, there you were, making life miserable for me. And now you tell me that you don't like the change in me? Well, you can go to hell, Cadet Vice-Commander Henderson!"

She was gone before he could formulate an answer. He stood there for a long time, the arctic-cold wind that whistled around the corner of the chapel chilling him to the bone. If he could have gone back, altered the way he'd handled things, he would have done so willingly. But it was too late. He'd made too many mistakes, and he'd lost Tai for good.

A month later he pinned Carol Flowers, the daughter of the academy's commandant of cadets. Two days after graduation, he married her in the same chapel where he'd finally given up on Tai MacGarrett.

CHAPTER
✦ 24 ✦

EVER SINCE HER FATHER HAD BEEN ASSIGNED TO HICKAM AFB, Crystal had wanted to live in one of the spacious old senior officer's quarters near the parade ground. She was well aware that strings had been pulled by General Krause to get Grant a unit that usually was occupied by a full colonel, which was why she was so careful never to make a big thing about it to other wives. In fact, she complained occasionally about the shortcomings of the fifty-year-old house, just as if she didn't know that no amount of inadequacies could negate the prestige of having full colonels as neighbors.

She had taken a particular delight in showing off their quarters to her mother before her parents had moved back to the mainland. Not that Janet had given her the satisfaction of showing envy. Her voice bored, she had pointed out the lack of closet space, the dearth of work surface in the kitchen. She'd called their set of quarters an old barn—which of course it was. But that had just been spite. Crystal knew very well that before Maurice's retirement, her mother would have given half his pay to have been assigned these quarters.

Today, as Crystal stood in the dining room, adding a few last-minute touches to a table setting, she thought of Janet's parting remark—"Take my advice and don't get too confident. You aren't living on general's row yet, Crystal—and chances are you never will be."

Well, of course she wasn't there yet! Grant had a long way

to go before he made general, but she was satisfied to wait—and to work hard toward that day.

Grant seldom complimented her, but she knew he was pleased with her efforts so far. She had been careful to move slowly, knowing that to be pushy, to stand out too much from the other lieutenant colonels' wives, was to ask for trouble. The committees she'd served on, the volunteer work she'd done, were grub jobs, the dirty little chores that no one else wanted, which was fitting to her position in the officers' wives' pecking order.

But she always managed to see that her good works were noted by the right people, too. Hiding one's light under a barrel was all very well, but it didn't make points where they counted.

As for her appearance, no one could fault her there. Her clothes were chosen for their appropriateness, not for current fashion. Although Grant's private income, if not his air force pay, was generous enough to permit her to shop in Honolulu's most exclusive stores, she patronized the various base exchanges on the island and some of the less expensive dress shops. Her clothes, although of good quality, were as understated as Grant's three-year-old Mustang. Even the few pieces of furniture she'd bought to supplement their government-issue furnishings had been carefully chosen to add a personal touch, not to be ostentatious.

In the same vein, she wore her hair in a classic style, coiled around her head, and although she was always perfectly groomed, her nail polish was a rosy pink, never a flashy scarlet. They could have afforded a full-time live-in housekeeper, but she'd settled for a twice-a-week cleaning woman, knowing that to have better domestic help than officers who were Grant's seniors would only cause resentment. Day help was acceptable on a lieutenant colonel's pay; a live-in housekeeper would have aroused jealousy and the suspicion that the Grant Nortons were living above their rank.

The restrictions of military protocol didn't bother Crystal. The rewards were too great. She was willing to pay her dues and to wait a reasonable time to collect the payoff. Even as she cozened up, with the proper degree of deference, to senior wives, letting them hog the spotlight and take the credit for work she'd done, it didn't really touch her inner core.

Let them have their day, she told herself. She would have hers—and when she was the wife of a general, she'd know what to do with the power. Oh, she would make them, the women junior to her, jump through her hoop! She wouldn't stagnate in her quarters like that lush Sophie Krause did! Everybody would know who General Grant Norton's wife was, and if that came under the heading of wearing her husband's rank, so be it. Mrs. Pritchard, Shelley's mother, was her role model, not Sophie. No one ever took *that* lady for anything but what she was—the wife of PACAF's Commander-In-Chief.

To Crystal's satisfaction, Mrs. Pritchard still maintained a casual relationship with her. Once, she had called to offer Crystal a minor committee chairmanship on one of her lesser charities, and again, she'd asked Crystal to step in during an emergency to help arrange flowers for a last-minute dinner party General Pritchard was giving in honor of a group of visiting congressmen. Crystal and Grant hadn't been invited to the dinner party, of course, but that was all right with Crystal. It wouldn't have been appropriate—and besides, she was supremely confident that her own day would come.

Wisely, Crystal never mentioned her tentative friendship— if that's what it was—with Mrs. Pritchard to anyone. She let the older woman direct the pace of their relationship, but she got a secret satisfaction when Mrs. Pritchard unbent enough to tell her that she wished Shelley, her own daughter, had Crystal's good common sense.

And tonight—tonight was special, her first really important dinner party, because they would be entertaining General Krause and his wife. She had considered the guest list carefully, not wanting it to be apparent that she was courting Grant's mentor. At earlier dinners and barbecues she'd given, she had practiced on officers who were the same rank as Grant and, on one occasion, two of his academy classmates and their wives. She'd been friendly, seemingly absorbed in woman talk, and no one watching her would have guessed how bored she was and how she longed to join the men, who were talking shop in another room.

This evening, as she finished setting the table, she congratulated herself on what she was sure would be a successful evening. She hadn't made the mistake that so many young military wives did of planning an elaborate meal. That would come later, when Grant was a colonel. In the interest of camouflaging the real object of the dinner party, she had invited the most presentable of the couples she and Grant had entertained before, as well as a lowly major and his wife. They were an attractive, well-bred couple, who would fit in very well—but that wasn't why she had included them. It was to make sure that she didn't appear to be an opportunist. Better if it was thought that she was still too inexperienced with protocol to realize that mixing such diverse ranks as a major and a lieutenant general was a little ... well, gauche.

After long thought, she had decided to use a presentation silver serving dish, engraved with the name of Grant's grand-father, that had been a wedding gift. Reminding their guests that Grant's roots were firmly planted in a solid military family was a plus—as long as it was subtly done. The food, too, was the kind military men preferred—roast beef and baked potatoes and a crisp green salad with a piquant dressing and apple pie for dessert. Nothing so fancy that it would excite the envy of the women or make them suspect that she had gone all out for this dinner. On the way home tonight, the women would tell their husbands that Mrs. Norton was a good cook, but their praise would be indulgent rather than envious.

It was rather like walking a tightrope, Crystal thought, trying to keep the correct balance, staying in the background but maintaining visibility, too. Too bad Janet wasn't here to see how well she was doing. And oh, how she did enjoy manip-ulating the senior wives, besting them at their own game! It was better than a tonic, certainly better than sex—

"You're purring, Crystal," Grant's deep voice said from the doorway. "I can hear you all the way over here."

The smile she turned on him was approving. He looked so distinguished in his dark sport jacket, with just that hint of silver at his temples. Maybe he looked a few years older than his thirty-eight years, but that was an asset at this stage of his career.

The past two years had held more than a few surprises. Because Crystal had tricked Grant into marriage, she had taken it for granted that they would live together in some kind of armed truce, tolerating each other only because of their mutual goal. But it hadn't been that way at all. She found Grant surprisingly easy to get along with. In fact, she enjoyed his company and looked forward to their lively conversations at dinner. The thought had come to her more than once that their relationship could be described as friendship, the kind she'd never really had with anyone else, male or female. Grant took such a keen interest in her activities, even going so far as to offer to shop with her—an offer she'd accepted because his taste was surprisingly good. Also, he never quibbled about money and, in fact, had turned over a sizable checking account to her soon after their wedding.

Sometimes, it was true, he seemed to withdraw within himself, shutting her out, and then there were those evenings when he disappeared without explanation. After she'd found a match cover from a rather notorious Hotel Street *go* parlor in the pocket of one of his old jackets, she'd surmised that he was a secret gambler, but she never questioned him about his nights out.

Even when she'd finally told him that the doctor had been mistaken and she wasn't pregnant, he had taken it well. That he'd been disappointed was obvious, but if he had any suspicion that she'd been lying about her pregnancy, he kept it to himself. In company, his treatment of her was affectionate, and she knew other women envied her and took it for granted that theirs was a love match. Well, they didn't have to know, no one ever had to know, that her marriage was so impersonal that Grant had never once undressed in front of her or that they slept in separate bedrooms.

Crystal realized that Grant was patiently waiting for her answer. "If I'm purring, it's because I'm sure everything will go smoothly tonight," she told him. "If the guests get here before the roast is overcooked, this should be a successful dinner."

"But not so successful that the older wives will resent you," he said, his tone dry. "Where did you learn so much about power plays?"

"From an expert—my mother. Janet has the instincts of a barracuda. If she wasn't so lazy, she would've pushed Maurice right up the promotion ladder."

"Well, if he'd really wanted success, he would have made it anyway."

"What does that mean?"

"That the right kind of wife is an asset, yes, but if a man is ambitious enough, he'll make it up the ladder in spite of an inadequate wife."

"This isn't your subtle way of telling me you intend to throw me back, is it?"

"Never. And if I don't tell you often enough how I appreciate your hard work, forgive me. I guess I picked up my habits from my illustrious parent. I can't remember my father—or grandfather—ever complimenting me. They just assumed that I'd never make a mistake, never let them down."

"They *are* rather hard to get acquainted with," she said, and didn't add how delighted she was that Grant's relatives hadn't returned for another visit. "Maybe we'll see more of them after you report in at Wright-Patterson next year."

"About that assignment to Wright-Pat—I'm afraid it isn't all that certain yet. General Krause called me into his office this afternoon and told me he's had second thoughts about getting me assigned to his staff at Wright-Pat. He thinks it might be best for me to get some more tactical experience— maybe as a wing commander. According to him, it also might not be wise if I become too closely associated with him. If he gets shot down, I could, too—or so he says."

Crystal worried her lower lip with her teeth, trying to absorb this information. "But you don't believe him?"

"I don't know what to believe. He got his rank by riding my father's coattails. It's an accepted way for a man to get ahead in the military."

"You didn't do anything to—you know, offend him, did you?"

"Not that I know of. He's satisfied with my work—I'm sure of that. I don't know what's going on. I did have that stint as a squadron commander in 'Nam, so I already have combat commander experience on my record. Being a wing commander is a whole different ball of wax, of course, but—" He shrugged.

"Maybe—maybe he's playing some kind of game to keep you off balance and make you sweat," she said, trying to hide her disappointment. A position on Arnold's staff when the general took over command of Logistics Management Center and DCS/Logistics Management Systems at Wright-Pat would almost have guaranteed Grant a "below the zone" promotion to colonel, which meant he would have made it years before his classmates at the academy did.

"He's a devious bastard. We'll see how it goes tonight. But I sure as hell would like that assignment at Wright-Pat. There's a lot of visibility there—it's a good spot for a logistics man."

"So when he leaves for Wright-Pat, the general won't be taking you—is that what it boils down to?"

"As of now. On the other hand, he's just about promised that he'll look out for my best interests. I have to accept that part in good faith. One thing—he's very impressed with you. He told me today that marrying you was one of the smartest moves I'd ever made."

There was a hint of irony in his voice that made her wish, not for the first time, that she could read what was going on behind that bland smile and those impeccable manners. Was he thinking of their bargain—or did he still feel uncomfortable about his impotency? Surely he must realize she'd been relieved that she wouldn't have to service him in bed—or was that still true? There were times lately when she found it hard to sleep at night, when erotic images kept her awake. She might even have approached him again except that the last time she'd made a tentative play for him, he'd been as elusive as smoke escaping from a room.

It had been about six months ago, and she'd been feeling restless all evening. After she'd taken her bath and changed into a gown and negligee, she'd gone to the small room off the kitchen, originally intended for a maid's room, which Grant had turned into a den. She'd brought both of them drinks and then had sat on the arm of his chair, sipping her gimlet and letting him see that she was willing—if he wanted to try again.

He'd been courteous, pleasant, but when he'd finished his drink he'd excused himself, saying he'd had a hard day, leaving her alone to nurse her disappointment.

She'd never made that mistake again. Their relationship remained impersonal, like two roommates of the same sex sharing an apartment. But they also shared a few laughs because she found his dry sense of humor to her liking—or maybe it was a sense of the ridiculous that they shared. Sometimes she even found herself laughing at herself these days—and that was a completely new phenomenon in her life.

When the doorbell rang, she left Grant to greet their guests and went to check out things in the kitchen. Her part-time housekeeper was the wife of a navy enlisted man, stationed at Pearl Harbor, and sometimes Crystal had the fancy that it was Shelley she was ordering around. The woman gave her a tentative smile as she came through the door.

"Everything in order here?" Crystal asked crisply.

"All ready to go—I only need to toss the salad."

"You know what to do when I ring the bell, don't you?" Crystal said.

"First I serve the canapes—Colonel Norton will take care of drinks. Then, when you give the signal to go into supper—"

"Dinner, Nancy."

"—into dinner, I serve the lady sitting next to the colonel first, then go around the table in the order of how they're seated."

"And do keep the water goblets filled. Colonel Norton will handle the wine."

"Okay—I've got that. How about dessert? Do I clear the dirty plates off before I serve the dessert?"

"Of course. And do it as unobtrusively as possible. Later, when we go into the living room, you can finish clearing the table—you did tell your husband that you'd be home late, didn't you?"

"Oh, sure. He didn't much like it, but I told him what you promised, that I could stack the dishes and do them tomorrow. After all, you don't ask me to work evenings often, and you pay me extra."

Crystal nodded. Nancy's husband was a problem. He didn't like his wife working as a housekeeper, and yet the poor slob didn't make enough money to support his wife and kids. Well, that was their problem. She paid good wages—not as much as some, but a lot better than others. . . .

All of their guests, including the Krauses, had arrived by the time she rejoined Grant. She gave Sophie's gown a quick appraisal as she came through the door. Very expensive—but it still looked tacky on Sophie's shapeless figure. It wasn't that she was fat—but she had let herself go, and now she had a dumpy look. Too much alcohol and too many years of sitting on her can. Personally, Crystal thought, she didn't intend to make that mistake. She might not have the sexiest figure in the world, but she was trim, and that's the way she intended to stay—by watching her calories and doing her exercises every day without fail, no matter how boring they were.

Talking amicably, she steered the older woman toward the sofa and sat down beside her. As Sophie speculated about the latest base scandal, a key club that was reputed to be operating among some of the younger officers and their wives, she listened with seeming interest, but her attention was on Grant and General Krause, who were talking together across the room.

General Krause was obviously in an expansive mood. He had looked her over, his gaze lingering just a shade too long on her breasts, when she'd come into the room. When she'd bent over him to add an ice cube to his drink, his eyes had taken on what could only be described as a gleam.

Just how far should she let this interest of his go? To stop it, she knew, she only had to make the proper remark, something casual and joking, to warn him that she wasn't interested in one of his little flirtations, his "feelie-feelies," as one of the younger wives had indiscreetly called his wandering hands.

If it were anyone but Krause—but his pudgy hands and sweaty palms and those porcine eyes were just too much. Well, she would handle it without involving Grant. Something told her that he wouldn't approve of those sly little pinches and the accidental touchings Arnold was so adept at. All very commendable to be protective of his wife, but also unrealistic.

During the next few minutes, as Nancy served the canapes and Grant kept the drinks flowing, Crystal put herself out to be charming to everyone, to not single out Sophie for her attention as a hostess. As she took pains to make sure the major's young wife was included in the general conversation, she discovered that she was enjoying herself immensely. It would be so different if she weren't playing a game, if she were frightened and uncertain and over her head, as so many of the younger officers' wives were. What a ghastly evening this would be then! As it was—yes, it was a real high. She should have been an actress because who would guess, watching her, that she was bored out of her skull with the small talk, the inconsequential conversation of these very ordinary women?

It was after dinner, when Nancy had cleared the table, packed most of the dishes into the dishwasher, and left, that Crystal went into the kitchen to get more ice. She was closing the refrigerator door with her hip, an ice tray in each hand, when she sensed someone behind her. She started to turn, but she wasn't quick enough. The hands that cupped her derriere were hot; she fancied she could feel their moistness through her gown. Her first instinct was to jerk away, to tell Arnold Krause to keep his filthy hands to himself. Her next thought, a split second later, was not to do anything stupid.

Arnold crowded closer, holding her there with his rotund paunch, the evidence of his arousal pressing against the back of her thigh. She felt like gagging, but instead she managed to slip to one side, breaking his hold, and when she turned, she was smiling, her eyebrows raised.

"Naughty, naughty, General. What if my housekeeper should walk in?" she said archly.

"She's already gone home, and I've been wanting to do that for a long time." His eyes were very bright, and his mouth had a too moist look. "You're a very attractive woman. Grant is a lucky man, bedding you every night."

"Well, I'm lucky, too," she countered, dumping the ice into an insulated container. "And we'd better get back to the party before someone gets the wrong idea—"

"Be quiet and listen to me, Crystal. We don't have much time, and I want to make sure you understand how this thing is going to work. I'm hot for you, really hot. You scratch my itch and I'll scratch yours. Grant must've told you about our conversation this afternoon. What happens next to his career depends on you—and how you play your cards. You understand?"

Crystal stood there, frozen by shock. She understood—only too well. If Grant was assigned to a second-rate job at this stage of his career, he could forget about promotion. Other men, farther down the ladder in seniority, would pass him by, and that would be the end of his chances of ever making general. Arnold Krause was laying it on the line. He wanted her. In payment, he would see that Grant got what he wanted. So it came down to this—could she stomach this man with his hot eyes and his wet hands in order to get Grant that coveted staff position at Wright-Pat?

And why—why the hell was the man so hot for her, anyway? She didn't come off as sexy or provocative. In fact, she was anything but. She'd heard rumors about Arnold's current affair with one of the typists in his office, a local girl with a lush figure and dark, come-hither eyes. So he obviously got all the sex he wanted. Was it the *chase* that turned Arnold on, having power over the wife of a protégé, of cuckolding a man who, in so many ways, was his physical and mental superior? And if this was it, then surely it wouldn't be long before he got bored with her and started chasing someone else. What it all boiled down to was how strong her stomach was. The thought of having him climb on top of her was repulsive. On the other hand, she'd done a lot of things that had taken guts and hard work already. It would all be wasted if she didn't come across now.

From some inner reserve of cunning, Crystal produced a

provocative smile. "I thought you'd never ask, Arnold," she said softly.

Arnold Krause's eyes narrowed briefly, and then he was smiling, too. He took her hand and pressed it against the bulge in his trousers. "You're a very smart girl," he said, his voice thick. "You're going to end up a general's lady someday."

"I'm counting on it," she said, and as he slid his thick fingers over her breasts, she thought, I hope it's worth it. If you don't come through for me, Grant, so help me I'll kill you. . . .

CHAPTER

↟ 25 ↟

July 1, 1978,
Belmont Resort Hotel, Bermuda

Dear Mrs. Joshua Springer,

Your new name sounds so grand, Bobby Jo! And your wedding was fabulous. White lace and orchids from Hawaii and crossed swords—I have to admit that there were tears in these old ex-doolie eyes of mine when you walked down the aisle on your father's arm.

And now, in a few months, you'll be giving your mom and dad their first grandson—or granddaughter. I'm glad they've accepted the situation without playing the heavy parents. And no, I'm sure no one at the wedding guessed. If you hadn't told me, I wouldn't have known you were four months pregnant, not in a million years. In fact, you looked radiant, just like brides are supposed to look, with nary a bulge to give away your secret.

As for me, I'm taking my "free time," a three-week breather before I plunge into my second year at the academy. As you can see by the address, Cassie and I treated ourselves to a vacation in Bermuda, a place as different from Colorado as we could think of!

In a couple more weeks, I'll be off for a three-week stint in the Philippines with a group of cadets to get a behind-scenes look at how things operate on an overseas

*air base. I'll be seeing Shelley and her new son there,
but I won't get to meet the fabulous Tad because he's
on some kind of training exercise right now. I can't wait
to see Shelley with her baby. She sounds so happy in her
letters—*

Tai paused to stare down at the words she'd just written.
Happy—weren't Shelley's letters a little *too* cheerful? It couldn't
be all that much fun, living on sergeant's pay. Well, if Shelley
slanted the truth a little, who could fault her? Didn't they all
do that? Her own letters to her old schoolmates were invariably
optimistic. But what if she told Bobby Jo how depressed she
felt this very minute, even with the Atlantic sea breezes blowing
through her hair, rustling her pad of writing paper, and the
dazzling blue pool she was sitting beside tempting her to take
another swim?

Maybe if she hadn't made that stupid mistake about the time
of Bobby Jo's wedding, hadn't arrived just in time to see Steven
and his bride leaving the chapel—but she had, and their image
still haunted her. Steven's bride was tall, red-haired, pretty;
she'd been clinging to his arm as they passed under the arch
of swords. And Steven had looked like a fatuous fool, grinning
sheepishly at his friends.

One consolation—he hadn't seen her. She could be thankful
for that. Would it have mattered to him if he had, if he'd guessed
how torn up she'd felt inside?

Tai returned to her letter, impatient now to be done with it.
As she hurried through an abbreviated description of the resort
hotel where she and Cassie were staying, one thought cheered
her. Three weeks of precious freedom lay ahead, and she meant
to enjoy every minute of it. She might even have a torrid affair
with one of those bronzed muscle men sunning themselves
beside the pool. After all, she'd been through the mill these
past couple of years. Time she had a little fun and games.

Shelley's first thought when she saw Tai coming down the
ramp at the air terminal was that her friend was just the same—
except for her short hair and her trim uniform. An hour later,
as they sat drinking coffee in her sparsely furnished living room,
she realized that her first impression had been wrong.

The Tai she'd known in Hawaii had been reserved, but she'd
also possessed a natural warmth that never questioned the good-

will of others. This Tai was self-contained, cautious, and there was a wariness in her eyes that reflected the discovery that life could kick you in the teeth when you least expected it, that it wasn't wise to believe in such things as love and forever-afters.

I'm sorry, Tai, Shelley wanted to say, even as they exchanged personal news and then talked about Hawaii, marveling at how much had happened to all of them since that last beach picnic two years ago.

"You look fabulous in your uniform. That hat has real flare," Shelley told Tai.

"Unfortunately, they didn't take womanly curves into account when they designed these uniforms," Tai said ruefully. "For once, a runt like me had the advantage. Most of the female cadets have to watch their diets."

Shelley sighed. "Don't we all—I gained twenty pounds at the very end of my pregnancy. I still haven't taken them all off."

Tai shook her head. "My heart bleeds—don't you ever look in the mirror? You are . . . well, I guess the word is "blooming." Marriage is obviously good for you. I have to admit—"

She broke off, looking uncomfortable.

"You have to admit you thought I'd dived into marriage too fast? You're right, you know. It could have been a disaster, and in some ways . . . well, Tad and I have our problems. We're two different kinds of people, which takes getting used to. But I don't regret marrying him. I love Tad—and I feel loved back. Which makes it worth all the trouble our elopement caused."

"Do you ever hear from your parents?"

"They haven't contacted me since we got married. I asked my brother to tell them about the baby, but—nothing. No messages. Well, it's their loss. Larry is the image of my brother's old baby pictures—and it's possible that he'll be the only natural grandchild my parents ever have."

"I'm sorry." Tai hesitated, then said, "I've been wanting to thank you for showing up at Mac's funeral. About all I can remember about that day is sitting on that hard bench in the chapel and holding on to your hand for dear life."

"I didn't know how to comfort you, Tai," Shelley confessed. "Later, I thought of so many things that I could have said—"

"Just being there was enough. I really needed—what you gave me that day. Not only had I lost Mac, but I'd lost everything else that mattered to me, too."

"You're talking about Steven, aren't you?"

"He was part of it. Of course, I realize now that I never really knew him."

"You told me in one of your letters that he gave you a pretty hard time at the academy. That really surprised me."

"And me. I didn't expect it, you see. But I survived—did you know that he's married now? He and his bride had a chapel wedding—the same day that Bobby Jo married Josh. I got to the chapel too early, and who should be coming out the door but Steven and his bride. Ironic, isn't it? It could have been me, passing under that arch of raised swords."

"Did it—bother you?"

"Not really." Tai's voice was even, but the look in her eyes told a different story. It had hurt all right, hurt badly—and that meant Tai still wasn't totally over Steven Henderson. . . .

Later, looking back, Shelley wasn't sure how it happened. She had always found it so difficult to confide in anyone, even Tad, but suddenly the barriers were down and she was telling Tai about her marriage, about the money problems that kept them insolvent despite Tad's recent promotion to technical sergeant, about the day-to-day irritants that were so small in themselves but added up to so much trouble.

She realized suddenly that she was talking too much, and she stopped in dismay. But when she stammered an apology, Tai stopped her.

"Don't apologize, Shelley. If you can't talk to an old friend—and I *am* your friend, Shelley—who can you talk to? We're a lot alike, you know. Both of us find it hard to—to open up to other people. Luckily, I have a friend at the academy that I can say anything to—and believe me, I've pounded her ear a lot this past year."

"I don't mean to give the impression that I'm unhappy with Tad," Shelley said. "Most of the time everything is great—except when he's TDY. Being alone, having to cope with the baby and everything else on my own, is pretty grim. In fact, just being married to a military man can be grim at times." Shelley gave a shaky laugh, then added, "I've always admired you because you're so all together, Tai, so sure of where you're going. Talking to you today . . . well, I guess I was suddenly conscious of the goals I turned my back on when I married Tad. I wanted to study design at Parsons, to find out just how much natural talent I have, and sometimes I feel . . . well, as if I stopped growing at eighteen. You'll never have that problem. You don't need other people in order to be happy—"

"Happy? What's that? I think what you have with your husband and baby is closer to real happiness."

"But you still wouldn't trade places with me," Shelley said with certainty.

Tai was silent, as if reviewing her own feelings. "No," she said finally. "I'm not ready for marriage—or any other serious commitment. There are too many things I want to do with my life. I wouldn't be surprised if I never got married."

In the bedroom, Larry awakened from his afternoon nap with his usual roar of outraged hunger. As she went to get him, it occurred to Shelley that while she had opened up to Tai, confiding the things bottled up inside her, Tai had said very little about her own problems—if any.

Shelley was sitting at the small rattan table she used as a desk, trying to balance her checkbook, so absorbed in the irksome task that she didn't realize Tad was calling her until he came to the living room door and said, "Hey, honey, you got cotton in your ears? I asked you if everything's ready for tonight."

Shelley put down her pen and looked around at Tad. He was wearing the light blue shirt made of piña cloth that had been her welcome-home present to him, and she thought he looked very sexy with his hair still glistening wet from his shower.

Tonight was their turn to entertain their pinochle group, and it wasn't something she was looking forward to.

The men, including Tad, seemed to think that they had to drink as much beer and bourbon as they could get down—and then there was the strain of carrying on a conversation with their wives, all of whom were several years older than Shelley. She was well aware that they had their reservations about her. Always, it seemed, there was that barrier—and she wasn't sure whose fault it was. God knows she tried to be friendly, but it was as though they spoke a different language and lived in a world she couldn't enter.

Even playing pinochle was tricky. She had played bridge for as long as she could remember and was very good at it, so pinochle, a relatively simple game, was easy for her. But after she'd caught a few pointed remarks about her "luck" with cards, she'd stopped counting tricks. Sometimes, she even made deliberate mistakes so she wouldn't win so often.

"Everything's ready," she told Tad. Thankfully, she put away the checkbook to finish later and got to her feet. She was wearing a three-year-old cotton shift, sleeveless and simply cut, but a designer's label was sewed inside the neckband, and she hoped no one would guess that it had cost more than all the clothes Tad had bought her in their two years of marriage.

"There's plenty of Cokes and beer, and I made ham-and-cheese sandwiches ahead—they're in the fridge, along with the dip, covered with plastic wrap. Everything else is ready to go into those teakwood bowls you bought me for Christmas. No use putting anything out until the last minute. You know what the humidity does to chips and pretzels."

"I hope you didn't fix any more of that green stuff. I won't tell you what it looked like."

Shelley's face tightened. "No, I didn't. You let me know several times what guacamole reminds you of. Since I don't have your mother's recipe for dip, which I'm sure must be fabulous, I fixed the usual Lipton's onion soup mix and Philadelphia cream cheese. I'm sure everybody will like it because that's what they all serve. You know—innovative cooking."

"No need to be sarcastic," he said.

She shrugged. "Just getting my own back."

"Yeah . . . well, do me a favor. No literary discussions tonight with Turner's wife, huh? Talk about people getting glazed eyes—and be careful what you say to Lara Morgan. She didn't appreciate it when you told her that picture she's got hanging in her living room was an interesting attempt at a primitive."

"How was I to know she'd painted it herself and that it was supposed to be modern art? It looked like a very bad primitive, and actually I was being kind. It was a natural mistake."

"You make too many mistakes. Sometimes, I wish—" He broke off.

"Why stop now? Sometimes you wish I were different—was that what you started to say? Maybe you should have married some waitress from the BX snack bar. At least she'd fit in with your crowd."

"Don't start anything, Shelley. I know your nerves are all on edge with the baby teething, but other women manage. I never heard any of my sisters-in-law complaining—"

"Not to the Brotski men. They'd probably get their teeth knocked out."

Tad looked at her for a long time. She braced herself for an angry remark, but unexpectedly, he said, "What is it, Shelley? Something's wrong. Ever since I got back from TDY, you've been acting weird. It isn't like you to put people down. Tell me what's bugging you, and maybe I can help."

Shelley wasn't sure how she felt. Guilty, for one thing—and if she were honest with herself, also a little provoked because Tad's understanding had disarmed her and made her feel in the wrong. Why was it that every time she thought she had him figured out, he managed to surprise her? Was it because, despite what she thought of as her tolerance, she still saw Tad as a stereotype: blue collar, small town, coal miner's son. . . .

"I'm sorry," she said—and meant it. "I'm bitchy because . . . well, your son's the world's greatest kid, but he's also a handful. I guess motherhood is getting me down."

"Hell, honey, if that's all it is, why don't you sign up for one of those all-day tours the Silver Wing Rec Center sponsors? Make it on a Sunday and I can baby-sit Larry."

Shelley put her arms around Tad's waist and buried her face in his chest. "Why are you so good to me when I'm such a grouch sometimes, Tad?" she said. "Dammit, I was just itching for a good fight, and now I feel ashamed of myself."

"That's the idea. Keep 'em off balance." His voice was smug. "And I meant that about you taking off for a day. You haven't seen anything of the PI except Angeles City and that trip we made to Baguio. And the only times we go out is to the movies or to the Sunday barbecue at the Top Hat. You think about it, okay?"

"I just might take you up on your offer," she said, knowing that she wouldn't. With a transfer coming up in just six months, they were trying to save every cent they could. Technically, the air force paid for a PCS—a permanent change of station—but it was never enough to cover even half the expenses. Most couples put money aside between tours or took an advance on their pay so they could afford to go home, see their folks, and to pay for restaurant meals and motel rooms while they waited for quarters at their new base. There were other expenses, too—cleaning bills and deposits for utilities and car repairs and all the emergencies that seemed to come up during a transfer. . . .

"Is the storm over?" Tad teased, and she kissed him, knowing that he was right. The storm *was* over—for now.

—thought I'd catch you up on the news, Bobby Jo. Grant just got orders for Wright-Pat—a great assignment, as he's going to be Lieutenant General Krause's assistant deputy and senior administrative aide. I think I wrote you when Grant made full colonel, didn't I? Well, that means we're sure to get the senior officers' quarters they call the "brick houses." They're the oldest on base, but they're incredibly roomy and just made for entertaining. Besides, they're very close to the club, which is really convenient—

Bobby Jo was trying to read Crystal's letter while, at the same time, placate the baby, who was fussing in her playpen. But after the first couple of paragraphs, Vicky started to wail, and she laid the letter down without finishing it. After she'd put a bottle on to warm, she picked up Vicky, jostling her up and down on one hip until the bottle was finally ready. As she settled down at the kitchen table to feed her daughter, a line from Crystal's letter slipped into her mind.

You wouldn't believe how hectic our social life is these days!

Social life—what was that? She hadn't had any social life since her "honeymoon"—that dreadful trip to New Jersey to see Josh's mother. She had been four months pregnant with Vicky, and Mrs. Springer had been horrid, so cold and touchy. And since they'd reported in at Williams AFB in Arizona and Josh had started flight training, his idea of a night on the town was to drive to a MacDonald's for a Big Mac and fries.

Bobby Jo looked around the tiny kitchen, which was filled with baby clutter, and she wanted to scream. I didn't bargain for this, she thought.

From the living room, she heard Josh turning another page of the textbook he was studying. He was muttering some data he was trying to memorize, and it could've been Greek for all the sense it made to Bobby Jo. When he was studying, he demanded absolute silence, which meant she had to keep the baby quiet and couldn't even turn on the radio. For the past three evenings, he'd been cramming for something he called a systems exam, and he might as well have been on Mars for all the company he'd been.

As she carried the sleepy baby into the bedroom and got her ready for the night, she remembered the orientation program she'd attended soon after Josh had reported in at Williams AFB.

"You wives are as much a part of the air force team as your husbands, and you have almost as many responsibilities," the wing commander had told them. He was a stern-looking man with a trim mustache and a pompous manner, who made Bobby Jo feel like a schoolgirl being lectured by her teacher. "Your husband's success may well depend upon your support these next eleven months, so it's very important that you handle day-to-day domestic problems on your own. UPT—pilot training—is very demanding, and he'll need freedom from domestic worries so he can concentrate on his studies—"

Bobby Jo shrugged mentally as she returned to the kitchen to start dinner. It was all so different from what she'd expected. For one thing, she'd thought there would be more camaraderie among the wives. The reality was that they were spread out so far geographically, being forced to live all over the area in tiny apartments or mobile homes or run-down farmhouses, that they seldom got together. So many of them worked, too, at whatever jobs they could find—or, like her, already had babies to tie them down.

Well, Josh couldn't say she hadn't tried. She'd been so gung-ho that day, so determined to be the perfect air force wife. But it got old after a while—very old. Okay, she'd known the excitement of June week couldn't last—the parties and teas and being the center of attention. But the change had been too sudden, too extreme—like diving into ice-cold water on a hot summer's day. Surely married life didn't have to be like this. There was no reason, for instance, why they couldn't go out to dinner at the club once in a while, was there?

"Why don't you do something about Vicky? She's been yelling her lungs out for the past five minutes," Josh said from the door.

He was wearing the old cotton flannel shirt and cords he studied in, and he looked irritated and tired with dark circles under his eyes.

"She's your daughter, too," Bobby Jo said, rebellion stirring.

"Taking care of the kid is your job, Bobby Jo. Is it too much to ask that I have a little peace and quiet? Either I put in my evenings studying or I wash out of academics. And if I wash out, that's the end of it. I won't get a second chance. It isn't as if you didn't know the score. I warned you what flight school would be like."

"I know, I know. You don't have to go through it all again. I'm doing my best, but being trapped in this grubby place day after day gets me down. I'd like to have a little fun once in a while—"

"Doing what? You know I can't drink while I'm flying. And I'm too tired to push you around a dance floor even if we could afford a baby-sitter. Besides, there simply isn't enough time. I'm only getting a few hours of sleep a night as it is, trying to stay on top of things." He frowned at her. "And don't start sulking. God, I hate it when you sulk!"

"I'm not sulking," she said, infuriated because his accusation was true. "I'll be glad when this year is over. Maybe then we can start living again. We don't even have a sex life these days."

"Whose fault is that? Every time I touch you, you develop a headache or something. I know you're worried about getting pregnant again, but there *is* such a thing as the pill."

"You know my religion forbids me to take the pill. It'd be a sin."

"Well, I don't belong to that fundamentalist religion of yours and I'm not about to get a vasectomy and I don't like rubbers, so you'd better do something—quick. If you think taking care of one baby is hard, try two or three."

"My mother managed with five."

"Bully for her. If you don't want to take the pill, okay. But don't cut me off, Bobby Jo. I'm a normal man and I need sex. I'm going to get it one way or another."

Although he hadn't raised his voice, Bobby Jo felt a chill. Was that a threat?

"I'll think about it," she said.

"You do that. If you'd thought about it earlier, we'd have it made right now. It never entered my mind that you were dumb enough not to be on the pill."

Bobby Jo felt a quivering in her stomach. "Would you have married me if I hadn't gotten pregnant?" she asked.

"What kind of a stupid question is that?"

"I haven't forgotten how deliriously happy you were when I told you about the baby. 'Jesus Christ, how did you let that happen, you dumb broad?' Really loving words."

"What did you expect when you sprang it on me in the middle of the dance floor? Your little bombshell knocked the props out from under me. 'Josh, I have some news to tell you—we're going to have a baby.' Right in the middle of the flipping dance floor, for Christ's sake!"

"I wish you wouldn't use the Lord's name in vain," she said.

"Okay, preacher's daughter. You weren't so holy in the back of my van that first night we made out. I don't remember you struggling or trying to get away. In fact, I had nail marks on my back for the next three weeks."

"I'd been drinking," she said with dignity. "I'd never had more than one planter's punch before in my life, much less three—plus a shot of straight bourbon."

"Well, baby, things sure have changed. You lap up more than your share these days."

"That's not true—okay, I have a pick-me-up now and then, but so what? When we were dating, you were always trying to get me to drink. To loosen me up, you said. I just can't please you, can I? You act like you hate me sometimes, Josh."

Josh's face lengthened. "I don't hate you, Bobby Jo. But I want you to get off my back. You have to grow up and start acting like an adult. I'm hanging on by my fingernails at school. To graduate and then get into fighters, I have to jack up my academic grades, and it's really rough going. The guys who batch it here have an edge. No problems at home to distract them. I wanted you to stay with your folks this year, but no, you had to come along and you made all those promises—"

"Is *that* what this conversation is all about? You want me to go home so you can move into the Bachelor Officers Quarters? And what happens when you want sex? Are you planning to get it from those groupies who hang around the bars in town and service the flight students? Well, I don't want to go home to my folks. They have enough problems—"

"You could stay with my mom in New Jersey. You know she wants to see the baby, and there's plenty of room in that big old house. It would only be for six months. When I switch over to the T-38's next week, things are going to be even tighter than they are now. Besides, Mom could take care of the baby once in a while and give you a break."

"I hate Trenton," Bobby Jo said, her voice rising. "And I

don't want to stay with your mother. I want to be with you. Have you stopped loving me?"

"No—hell no, I'm crazy about you, Bobby Jo, but you drive me up the wall sometimes! I don't know whether I'm coming or going these days. Maybe I *should* move into the BOQ. If things don't calm down, I'm going to wash out. The flying part is okay because I've made all excellents on my check flights—but the academics are a different matter. And one doesn't balance out the other—"

"I know all that. And I'm trying to do my best. I didn't bargain for this, you know. I thought . . . well, that it would be different. Going to the club for dinner and dancing on Saturday nights, that sort of thing. And this awful apartment—it's even worse than the dorm. At least there weren't any roaches there, and we had all the hot water we wanted."

"I know it isn't easy for you. But it's going to get better. Maybe we can look for another place to live—but not until exams are over."

He returned to his books, and she went to change Vicky and get her back to sleep. As she sat holding the baby, she felt so—so old and unattractive and unwanted. How long had it been since she'd had her hair done at a beauty parlor? And she hadn't bought a new dress since . . . well, since her mom had sent her that money for a trousseau. She wished now she'd spent it on more practical things. Jeans and shorts and tops to wear around the house and to the commissary instead of those fancy cocktail dresses, but then—how could she have known that she would be stuck in this awful place night after night while Josh pored over his damned books?

As she wandered out into the kitchen to check on her dinner casserole, she saw Crystal's letter, still lying on the table. She picked it up and finished reading it. It didn't escape her notice that every other sentence was about some social function Crystal had attended. Was it deliberate? It would be just like Crystal to brag, in her offhand way, about how exciting her life was. Deliberate or not, the letter left a bad taste in Bobby Jo's mouth and she decided that her answer—she'd wait a month or so, of course—would be all about her sexy—and *young*—husband and her beautiful baby.

The thing that dismayed her was the suspicion that being married to a junior officer was going to be more of the same, even after Josh finished his training—not enough money and being put down by the wives of senior officers and all that. If so, she dreaded to think of the years ahead. Of course, Josh wouldn't ask her to play the game the way Crystal did. All he really wanted to do was fly. If he had ambitions to be a senior officer, he never mentioned it. All he ever talked about was getting into fighter school and then, when he'd logged enough flying hours, to go to test pilot school.

What was it one of the older wives, who'd been to the punch bowl too often, had said to her at a luncheon she and the other student trainees' wives had attended?

"Just hope your husband doesn't go into fighters—or worse yet, become a test pilot. If he does, you'll have to learn to live one day at a time. I know because I went through it and almost had a nervous breakdown. When my husband got grounded because of a heart murmur, I felt like celebrating—not that I ever told him how I felt."

Well, *she* didn't want to spend her life waiting for the chaplain to knock on the door and tell her she was a widow. It didn't happen all that often now that the war in 'Nam was over, but she could still remember how her father used to come home all gray and wrung out emotionally from having to tell some strange woman that her husband had been killed.

So was it wrong to hope that Josh wasn't as good as he thought he was, that he didn't really rate as a "stick"—a hot pilot—even though the other guys called him Josh the Stick? Was it wrong to hope that he couldn't qualify for fighter training?

CHAPTER
✦ 26 ✦

BOBBY JO'S LETTER CAME WHILE SHELLEY WAS PACKING. It must had gotten lost somewhere in transit because the postmark was a month old. Even though she was surrounded by packing crates and crumbled newspaper, Shelley opened it and read it immediately, smiling at Bobby Jo's breezy style. The letter was mostly about Josh, who had finished UPT, had his wings, and now was being sent to fighter school. "Just what he wanted," Bobby Jo commented. The rest of the letter was about the baby, who looked like Josh and who was a real handful.

Shelley felt a pang of sympathy at this last observation, although her own son had been an unusually "good" baby. Her friend seemed to be growing up finally, she thought absently—and then wondered who she was to talk.

Despite her determination to be a good sport, she was having a hard time coping with the coming move, which was filled with all kinds of potential problems. In addition to having to travel so far with a toddler who was at the getting-into-everything stage, there were other, far more important problems, such as finding a place to stay in northern California while they waited for quarters at Travis AFB, sweating out the delivery of their hold luggage and household goods—and hoping everything would arrive in good condition.

And then there was the problem of furniture. What if they had to live off base? They didn't have money to buy furniture, especially expensive appliances. Could they borrow the essentials they'd need from base housing at Travis? She should have checked on that long before this. On top of this was the trauma of moving to a new place, of having to make new friends, of finding a trustworthy baby-sitter, all the problems of starting a new life—and all the time stewing over the possibility that Tad would be tapped for another overseas tour, possibly an unaccompanied tour, in two years.

It was hard now for Shelley to remember how miserable she'd been at Clark those first few months. She had made friends, felt at home here, was coping so well these days. She had even picked up quite a bit of Tagalog, the most common language of Pampanza Province, by taking lessons at the recreation center. And it was very rewarding, talking to Filipino nationals in their own language even though one of her neighbors had told her that she was a fool, wasting time learning a language that was useful only in the Philippines.

Shelley had shrugged it off, but she'd been careful not to use her new skill again in front of the woman, even when she suspected that the neighbor's new housegirl, fresh out of a barrio, had misunderstood instructions to clean the fingerprints off the toaster. Sure enough, the girl immersed the toaster, cord and all, into a pan of soapy water, and while Shelley had managed not to laugh, she also hadn't felt guilty about keeping her mouth shut.

As for Tad, he seldom objected to anything she did as long as she was there when he got home—preferably with dinner waiting for him on the table. Other than that, he was pretty indulgent—except for his occasional attacks of jealousy, which pleased her more than it annoyed her because it proved he cared, didn't it?

"What's that you're reading?" Tad asked her. He was perched on a packing crate, sorting through his sports magazines. As far as she could tell, he was saving more of them than he was throwing away.

"It's a letter from Bobby Jo. I can't imagine her with a baby. In so many ways, she still seems like a kid herself."

"I'll bet she says the same thing about you." Tad dodged the wad of newspaper she tossed at him, grinning. "And there's no question that you're all grown up. Fact is, I think you've gained a little weight lately."

Shelley was silent. Was this the right time to tell him? He'd given her the perfect opening. On the other hand, they had so many things to worry about right now. . . .

"A woman usually does gain weight her first few months of pregnancy," she said, making up her mind.

"Say *what*?"

"I'm two months pregnant—according to the doctor who examined me this morning at the GYN clinic. So we should be settled in at Travis before I start getting clumsy. Good timing, wouldn't you say?"

"How did it happen when you're on the pill?"

"'No birth control method is a hundred percent certain except abstinence,'" she said, quoting her doctor.

"Hell, this really is a surprise. I hope you don't have any morning sickness this time. That could be rough during that fifteen-hour flight to California—and while we're driving across country to see my folks."

"So far, it hasn't been a problem. Maybe I'll get lucky this time." She hesitated, then said, "Tad, I've been thinking about going to see your parents. Why don't we postpone it until next year? It would be a lot easier on us—"

"Honey, the folks are expecting us. You know how Ma is looking forward to meeting you and seeing her grandson. She'd be all bent out of shape if we don't go to see them."

"But if she knew I was pregnant—"

"She wouldn't understand. Hell, she was doing the wash the day I was born. She got up the next morning and finished the job."

A mental image of a peasant woman, all muscles and brawn, slipped into Shelley's mind, and she had to stifle a laugh. Well, nothing for it but to go through with the visit. Maybe it wouldn't be so bad, even though it was going to knock a hole in their budget. As soon as they reached California, they'd have to buy a car, and since it was late fall, that meant the baby would need warm clothes. Then there were car expenses and motels and meals on the road, not to mention rent and utility deposits if they had to live off base. Well, she wouldn't say any more about it. Tad was looking forward to seeing his family again— and eating his mother's cooking, no doubt. . . .

After a quick lunch, she returned to the job of sorting their possessions for the move. As she added half of their skimpy supply of pots and pans to the hold luggage, which would arrive at their new station first, she wondered what Tad's parents would think of her—and if they would accept her into the family.

Larry was asleep on the back of the five-year-old station wagon Tad had bought in California when they pulled up in front of a large frame house, set among a scattering of maple and evergreen trees. Shelley resisted a shudder as she stared at the house; it looked as if it hadn't had a fresh coat of paint in twenty years. She had expected—what? Certainly not this run-down place with its neglected lawn and overgrown shrubs.

"The house always looks its worst this time of year," Tad said, and she knew he was seeing it through her eyes. "The old man . . . well, he's a hard worker on the job, but he doesn't do much at home. Taking care of the house and yard is women's business, he always says."

"It looks very comfort—"

"Hey there, you old son-of-a-bitch!"

A few seconds later, it seemed to Shelley that the station wagon was surrounded by big, burly men, so alike that she was sure she would never be able to tell them apart. None of them looked like Tad—although the one pounding him on the back and shouting insults in his ear had Tad's blue eyes. Tad responded good-naturedly, but when one of the men stared at Shelley and gave a long wolf whistle, Tad turned a hard look upon him.

"Shelley, these are my brothers," he said. "That one's Earl, and the one with the egg on his face is Roscoe, and the ugly one over there is Morris—"

Although Shelley had been sure she'd never be able to tell Tad's brothers apart, a few hours later, as they sat down to dinner at a long yellow oak table, she had already noted that Roscoe was the one with the foulest mouth. Which was saying something, since all of Tad's brothers cursed a blue streak and her father-in-law was the worst of the lot. When he first met Shelley, he gave her a bear hug that almost broke her ribs, and then he told Tad that he wasn't surprised that he'd found himself a looker since he'd always had an eye for women.

As for Tad's mother—Shelley was sure Mrs. Brotski didn't approve of her. She had so little to say, for one thing. A short, plump woman, her black hair was streaked with gray and her eyes were the same light blue as Tad's. In fact, he was the only one of her children who resembled his mother. His brothers were the image of their father—barrel-chested men with big voices and loud, intrusive laughs.

Although Mrs. Brotski hadn't made a fuss over Larry, their two-year-old had capitulated without a murmur and was already calling her "Gran-gran." He found his new cousins, who came in all ages from a toddler his own age to a teenager in high school, a little intimidating at first, but he finally decided to accept them, too. Right now he was outside, watching the kickball game in the front yard. Shelley wouldn't allow herself to worry about him since it was obvious that no one else did.

Although the kitchen was filled with women, Shelley's mother-in-law was doing most of the cooking. Like a small, plump whirlwind, she stirred the contents of the pots on the huge wood-burning range, slipped pans, blackened with use, in and out of a cavernous oven, tasting everything frequently with a wooden spoon.

When the food was finally dished up, Shelley had trouble hiding her surprise. She had expected, if not gourmet food, at least something special in country cooking, but the cornbread was soggy in the center and too brown on the outside, and the thick slice of ham on her plate dripped with grease, as did the fried potatoes. A dish of sweet potatoes swam in butter, and the stewed chicken, which Tad had raved about for the past three years, was overcooked, the dumplings so soggy that they resembled the ones that had precipitated their first quarrel.

She glanced at Tad, half expecting his sheepish smile, but he was helping himself to more dumplings, telling his mother that he'd missed her cooking, that he wanted her to give Shelley some of her recipes.

As she watched him wolfing down his food, a glimmer of understanding came to Shelley. By Tad's mores, it would be unmanly to say how much he missed his mother, just as it had taken him so long to tell his wife that he loved her. But it was different with his mother's cooking. He could go on in great detail about how much he missed her dumplings and her apple-custard pie. And wasn't it about time she accepted the fact that Tad, while straightforward in most things, was not the uncomplicated man she was always expecting him to be?

As Shelley sawed away at the thick crust of a wedge of apple-custard pie, she set herself a new goal. She would make a special effort to fit in with Tad's family, to make them like her—and she would start by helping with the dishes, even though his mother had rejected her earlier offer of help.

But after dinner, Mrs. Brotski again refused her offer. "Now you sit over there and get acquainted with your sisters-in-law. I'm used to doing the redding up after Sunday dinner. Besides, I know where everything goes."

She bustled off, leaving Shelley with the other women. Was it possible that Tad's mother was jealous of her role of food preparer for her brood and their families? Or was it the same old problem—was there something about her, Shelley thought, that turned off other people?

Although she hadn't changed out of the jeans and ribbed cotton sweater she'd worn in the car, it was possible that Mrs. Brotski had labeled her as useless, as someone unable to cope with such mundane things as doing dishes. Of course, the other women hadn't even bothered to offer their help. Maybe they had learned that their mother-in-law meant it when she said she preferred to do it alone.

Shelley took a chair with the other women, a forced smile on her face. She listened to family jokes she didn't understand, gossip about people she didn't know, allusions to events that meant nothing to her. The women ignored her except when one, a dark-haired woman with sharp features, commented that she thought Larry had the Brotski nose, so it was a while before Shelley realized how curious they were about her.

It was Sara, the wife of Tad's oldest brother, who finally directed a personal remark to Shelley. "So you're a Buckeye," she commented.

It took Shelley a few moments to realize what she meant. "I was born in Ohio, but my parents moved from there when I was just a baby."

"Didn't Tad say your pa was in the military?"

"Yes—in the air force," Shelley said cautiously.

"Well, it's a good thing you're used to moving around now that Tad's decided to make the military his career," said another woman—Shelley had yet to learn her name.

Sara ignored the interruption. "What do you use on your hair?" she asked abruptly.

From the sudden silence, Shelley knew that this was something they had all wanted to ask. "I'm a natural blonde," she said. "My mother is very fair, and my brother and I inherited her coloring."

"You don't say! That must cause him a peck of trouble."

"Why would it cause Tony any trouble at all?" Shelley asked, puzzled.

"You know—people thinking he was some kind of sissy, having that blond hair."

Shelley couldn't help a smile. It had just occurred to her that she and Larry were the only ones in the house who didn't have dark hair—and why on earth would anyone associate blond hair with weakness in a man?

"No one would dare accuse Tony of being 'some kind of sissy,'" she said firmly. "My brother is six feet three and was a weight lifter in school. He was also All-American his last year at the academy."

"Does that mean he's an officer?"

"He's a colonel."

"Is your pa an officer, too?"

Shelley hesitated. Hadn't Tad told them anything about her? "Yes—he's an officer," she said reluctantly, hoping they wouldn't ask his rank.

"You gettin' hitched to Tad musta given your folks a turn. What'd they say when they heard you was marrying a sergeant?"

"I didn't ask their permission," Shelley said, suddenly tired of the conversation. Why didn't Tad rescue her or at least check to see how she was getting along? But no, he was having a great time, laughing and talking with the men outside on the porch. . . .

The afternoon dragged on. She was glad when Larry became whiny because then she had an excuse to ask her mother-in-law where she could put him down for a nap. Tad's mother led the way to a downstairs bedroom that was so immaculate, despite its shabby furnishings, that she suspected it was seldom used.

"I keep a crib set up in here," Mrs. Brotski said, pointing to one corner. "The daughters-in-law are always dropping off their kids for me to watch when they want to go somewheres. Me and Adolph sleep upstairs, but I thought you folks would be more comfortable down here. I'll fetch you an extra quilt before you turn in. It gets right cold at night this time of year."

It was the longest speech she'd yet made, and it took Shelley a while to realize that her mother-in-law was letting her know, in her matter-of-fact way, that she and Tad would have privacy at night while they were staying there. It seemed odd that this woman, so worn out and old, was sensitive enough to realize that she and Tad were still ardent lovers. And yet—why did that surprise her? Tad had picked up his sensitivity somewhere. He certainly hadn't inherited it from his father.

By now, she was aware that she wasn't going to like—or understand—her father-in-law. It wasn't anything he'd said to her or even because every other word he spoke was an obscenity. No, it was the way he looked at her, his eyes flat and measuring, that made her skin crawl. . . .

"You mustn't mind my boys—and Tad's pa," Mrs. Brotski said abruptly. "They're hardworking men, and they're all good providers. It's the life that makes them talk so rough. Tad was never like the others—I was glad when he joined the air force. He's got himself a good trade now even if he leaves the service. I never wanted him working in the mines. My other boys don't mind, being underground like that, but it wouldn't be right for Tad. I'm just so glad he found himself a decent girl like you to marry, too. You two—you're real happy together, aren't you?"

The question was diffident, and Shelley felt a sudden shame. Where did she—who had never managed to come up to her own parents' standards—come off making judgments about Tad's people? What did she know about sacrifices and hard times, about labor strikes and poverty and grueling physical work?

"I love your son very much," she said. "We're very happy—and Tad is so silly about his son that it's almost comical."

For the first time, Mrs. Brotski smiled at her, and Shelley realized that she must have been a very pretty woman at one time. Why had she married a man like Adolph? Surely she could have done better—and why had she stuck to him all these years?

"A good marriage . . . well, it's the only thing a woman really needs," her mother-in-law said. "Hard times, they come to us all. They come to a miner's family more than to most, but if you've got a good marriage, it don't matter. Adolph—he's got his faults. Sometimes when he's drinking he does things he don't really mean, but the rest of the time, he's real good to me. I reckon he'd just curl up and die if anything happened to me. That's why I'm hoping he'll go first."

At first, Shelley thought Mrs. Brotski's last remark was an

attempt at black humor. She met her mother-in-law's eyes and knew that she was speaking the literal truth. Adolph would be lost without his wife—and she knew it, knew her own worth. She had found her place in the scheme of things.

Which is more than I have. . . .

"May I ask you a favor?" Shelley said impulsively. "Do you mind if I call you something besides Mrs. Brotski?"

"Why, you can call me anything you like—my first name's Bernice."

"I wasn't thinking of your first name," Shelley said.

"Why don't you call me Ma, like everybody else does? Or maybe that's what you call your own mother?"

"I call her *Mother*," Shelley said. "Sometimes I used to think I should call her Mrs. Pritchard."

Her mother-in-law digested her words—or maybe the tone of her voice. "You don't get along with your folks?"

"My parents haven't spoken to me since I married Tad."

"Well, I wouldn't fret about that. I don't have a daughter, but I suspect I'd feel the same way if the good Lord had seen fit to give me one—that no one was good enough for her, I mean. Your folks will come around in time."

She laid Larry down on the bed. Together, the two women undressed the sleepy child and put on his pajamas. "He's a good-looking boy, Shelley," Mrs. Brotski said, stroking Larry's hair. "He don't look much like you except for his coloring—nor like Tad, either. Does he take after your folks?"

"He looks like my father's side of the family. I just hope he has a lot of you in him."

Mrs. Brotski looked pleased. "That's a right nice thing for you to say. And I guess I'd better get back to the kitchen and put on some coffee for the men when they come inside. You can set out some cups if you've a mind to," she added, and Shelley knew that she had been accepted, that she no longer came under the category of company.

Shelley tucked the blanket under Larry's chin, knowing it would stay there only long enough for him to squirm into another position.

"You hoping the next one will be a girl?" Mrs. Brotski said abruptly. At Shelley's look of surprise, she smiled briefly. "You can't fool someone who's had seven kids of her own and twelve grandkids," she said. "If you're keeping it a secret, we won't say anything to the others."

Shelley made a quick decision. "It's no secret. I have a hunch Tad is just itching to let his brothers know that he's doing his best to populate the world with little Brotskis."

CHAPTER

✦ 27 ✦

THE ONLY WAY CRYSTAL COULD ENDURE THE BOREDOM OF an Officers' Wives Club board meeting was to play a little mental game in which *she* was the president instead of the long-winded wife of the base commander. Because she had been offered the job of chairman for the refreshment committee, a thankless job but one she couldn't very well refuse, she was forced to attend these deadly dull meetings during which a controversy as insignificant as the size of the lettering used on name tags could take up an hour.

When Grant's assignment to Wright-Patterson in Dayton, Ohio, had come through, it had seemed such a step up the air force ladder, but she'd forgotten how much brass was assigned here. A colonel with a recent date of rank was at a disadvantage, even if he was the senior aide and assistant deputy to a lieutenant general. Which was one reason the quarters she'd wanted hadn't materialized. Oh, they were on the list for the "brick houses," as they were called, and Arnold Krause had made some vague promises about seeing what he could do, but meanwhile they were living in one of the newer, smaller, and, in Crystal's opinion, much inferior quarters.

Another thing diluted her satisfaction in Grant's promotion. For the past few months he'd been remote and indifferent, as if her conversation, her opinions, didn't really register. When she asked if something was bothering him, he denied it so vehemently that she'd been even more convinced something

was wrong. Not that he acted worried or unhappy. It was just
that he seemed to be wrapped up in his private thoughts all the
time, shutting her out and destroying the rapport that had made
them a team with a single goal.

On the other hand, Sophie Krause's increasing dependency
upon Crystal did bolster her spirits—and her ego. By now, she
knew that what Sophie referred to as "my rotten liver" was
cirrhosis, necessitating a strict diet, which Sophie followed
religiously, and complete abstinence from alcohol, which she
didn't. Sophie loved to gossip—when she wasn't talking about
Arnold. Sometimes Crystal was sure that if she heard one more
complaint about Arnold's stinginess or Arnold's women or
Arnold's personal hygiene, she would spit.

After all, *she* was the one servicing him these days during
those afternoons when he summoned her to meet him at some
out-of-the-way motel. Thankfully, he spent half his time in
Washington, but even twice a month was too often for her. In
fact, she felt downright nauseated when she let herself think
about the things he expected from her during those afternoons.
It wasn't that he jumped her right off and started banging away.
She would have preferred that. Oddly, he really tried to satisfy
her, too. Since she wanted to get the whole business over with
as quickly as possible, his clumsy attempts to arouse her added
to her irritation. Only by mentally divorcing herself from what
was going on did she manage to continue with the charade,
and during their sessions together, she often prayed that he
would lose interest, develop impotency like Grant, or even
drop dead, anything to extract her from an increasingly tiresome
situation.

Early in their affair, she had decided that if she wanted to
have any real influence over Arnold, he must believe that his
threats to have Grant transferred to a dead-end job had had no
part in her decision to have an affair with him, that she wanted
him as much as he wanted her. Otherwise, she reasoned, he
would distrust everything she said or did.

At their first rendezvous, in a back street Waikiki hotel that
catered to tourists, she had pretended an ardor she didn't feel,
and Arnold had been fast to accept the fact that it was love—
or lust—that motivated her. She had only contempt for an ego
so swollen that he could actually believe she'd prefer a paunchy,
balding man with broken veins in his nose to a distinguished-
looking man like Grant, but she played his delusions for all

they were worth, never showing for a moment how distasteful she found him.

She'd even hinted several times at her dissatisfaction with Grant as a lover, a fact he seemed to accept almost too complacently. Was he jealous of his protégé? She had her suspicions, even though he'd been Grant's mentor ever since her husband had graduated from the academy.

If it wasn't for the payoff she expected someday, she would have found a way to break off the relationship long before this. And it did have its pleasant moments—none of them sexual. Arnold, for all his personal conceits and swollen ego, was shrewd, a walking encyclopedia of air force power structure. The three stars on his shoulder proved that he knew how to play the game for all it was worth.

Crystal found this aspect of his personality fascinating, and after they'd gone through the rituals of sex, she listened with genuine interest while he talked about behind-scenes power struggles in the military community. Relaxed and expansive once his sexual urges were satisfied, Arnold told her things she knew must be indiscreet on his part. She never repeated anything he told her, not even to Grant. Instead, she filed the information away for future reference.

From the beginning, Crystal had sensed a perversity in Arnold's nature that drew pleasure from thwarting other people's expectations. She suspected this quirk had worked in Grant's favor for the simple reason that her husband never asked his mentor for anything, never curried his favor or showed in any way that he expected anything from Arnold except the friendship of an old family friend.

When Arnold dropped an occasional plum in Grant's lap, he was always properly grateful, of course, but never obsequious. Taking this as her guide, Crystal pretended not to realize the obvious, that Grant's star rose in direct proportion to the success of her affair with Arnold.

There were other rewards, too, these material. Although Arnold never offered her money, sometimes he dropped a gift into her lap with the casual remark that here was a little something he'd seen and thought she might like. Sometimes it was perfume—Joy or some other expensive brand—or satin underwear, exquisitely hand-sewn in France, that she knew must have cost him a small fortune. Having heard so often about Arnold's stinginess from Sophie, Crystal couldn't help thinking that Arnold would do well to lavish a little of his generosity on his wife.

But she always thanked him sweetly and wore the garments when she was going to meet him—which of course was what he intended. Only twice did he give her anything that caused a problem. Once it was a solid-gold Swiss watch, which she hid away in the bottom of her jewel box, wearing it only occasionally and never when Grant was with her. The other gift was an exquisite string of pearls with a diamond clasp.

Arnold had been to Japan for a conference when he brought her back the pearls. "Take good care of them," he said. "They aren't cultured."

She would have loved to brag about them in a discreet way, but since a colonel's wife would be hard put to afford a perfectly matched set of natural pearls, she was forced to tell anyone who complimented her on them that they were cultivated. Even then, she was the recipient of a snide remark from Sophie, who had a jealous streak. When Grant, always so observant about what she wore, commented on the superior color of her new pearls and asked her where she'd bought them, she told him one of the wives at the club needed money quickly and had sold them to her at a bargain price.

Her main bone of contention, other than her affair with Arnold, was the quarters she coveted. So far, Arnold's promise to take care of it hadn't materialized. Aware that she'd already brought the subject up too often, she didn't dare press him again, at least not openly. If only she hadn't jumped the gun and written her mother and her old Punahou schoolmates that she would soon be living in Wright-Pat's prestigious brick houses. Already Janet had made a remark in one of her infrequent letters, asking when Crystal was moving out of those tacky old Capehart units and into the brick houses—only she'd called them "those barny old white elephants near the club."

It was this remark that renewed Crystal's determination to approach Arnold again. Since she was meeting him that afternoon, she meant to prod him a little by complaining about the condition of their unit and see if that didn't stir up some action.

The method they followed for their clandestine meetings was always the same. Arnold, wearing civilian clothes and carrying a salesman's case, would register at some second-rate motel under the name of Mr. and Mrs. Thomas Eden—for some reason, that name amused him—always choosing one with covered parking so his car, with its military tag, wouldn't draw attention. As soon as he'd registered, he would phone Crystal and give her his room number so she wouldn't have to stop at the desk. Later, she would park at a downtown garage as if she were going shopping and take a taxi to the motel.

That afternoon, as she got out of her cab, she looked with distaste at the run-down motel he'd chosen. Although it didn't really matter—she would have hated the assignation even if he'd booked the honeymoon suite at the Dayton Hilton—she felt degraded as she hurried along the row of shabby cabins, looking for the number he'd given her.

When she rapped lightly on the last door in the row, Arnold opened it immediately. He was already nude, and when she saw his fatuous smile, she groaned inwardly, knowing that he was in one of his playful moods with some fantasy he wanted to act out.

When she lifted her face for a kiss, pretending eagerness, he thrust his tongue into her mouth, his lips hot and wet. He ran his hands down her back, then locked them behind her hips, pulling her up against his body. His paunch pressed against her abdomen, and she wished she had the luxury of slapping his fat face which always reminded her of a Chinese pug.

"I'm horny as hell," he breathed in her ear.

"Me too, lover," she murmured, and slid her hand between their bodies to touch his swollen member. He was already fully aroused—maybe he would get it off fast today so she could go home early and take a long, hot shower. . . .

"Arnie's been a bad boy since the last time he saw you," he said, nuzzling her throat. "He deserves to be punished. Wait until he tells you all the naughty things he's done—"

As he enumerated his "sins," everything from masturbating while he looked at a *Playboy* centerfold to a quick copulation with his middle-aged secretary in the office supply closet, she concentrated on keeping her cool. Although she had long suspected that most of his "sins" were pure fantasy, she wasn't really sure, and she wondered why, if he had access to so many compliant women, he bothered with her.

She felt rebellious as she contemplated the scenario expected of her. First she would undress, and then she would "punish" him by turning him over her lap and spanking his flabby, dead-white buttocks while he howled with lust. Then, while she pretended anger—she never had to pretend this—he would grovel at her feet, kissing them fervently with his moist lips and begging her forgiveness, which she would withhold for a while until she finally pushed him down on the rug with a foot on his chest, then climbed on top of him to ride him to a climax. Not only was it messy, a total turnoff, but it was all so damned boring. Even so, it was better than the times when he tried to give her a good time by prolonged foreplay.

Sometimes, she tried to imagine what boyhood experience had spawned this punishment fixation of Arnold's. Had he harbored a forbidden lust for some young nun at that Bronx parochial grade school he'd attended? Whatever its origin, this was one time she wasn't going to prolong it, not with her nerves jangling like electric wires after that interminable board meeting.

Smiling coolly, she pulled away from his clutching hands and began to undress, removing her garments one by one and revealing her body with tantalizing slowness, aware that Arnold's excitement was growing in direct proportion to the amount of bare skin she exposed. When she had stripped down to her garter belt and hose, she sat cross-legged on the bed, facing him, and slowly removed her hose, one by one. By now, Arnold's face was the color of a cooked beet. When she lay back on the bed, her arms and legs widespread, his assault was violent and mercifully fast.

When he was spent, she snuggled up against him, running her hands over his body as if she were so entranced by his performance that she wanted more, secure in the knowledge that he seldom managed to get it up more than once an afternoon.

"I was a little late today because I went to see the housing officer again," she said, her tone casual. "Can you believe it? We've dropped back two slots on the housing list for the brick houses. Two colonels reported in—and they both outrank Grant. The way it's going, we'll be transferred before we get to the freeze zone."

Arnold rolled away from her and sat up. "Give it time," he said. "You've only been on the list for . . . how long now?"

"Ten months."

"Well, those quarters are in great demand. I don't understand why you're so hot for them, anyway. The place you have is much more modern."

"It's so hard to entertain in such small quarters. Sophie is always asking me to take over a committee meeting when she has one of her spells. If I could hold them in our quarters, the way she does, it would save me the trouble of trying to arrange for a conference room at the club at the last minute."

Arnold looked at her so long that she felt an impulse to squirm. "It means that much to you?" he said.

She hesitated, not sure what to say. The shrewdness in his eyes told her that he was one step ahead of her. Her reasons were valid—as far as they went. Sophie *had* asked her several times to take over a meeting, and it *had* been inconvenient, arranging for a conference room at the last minute—but that wasn't why she wanted the brick quarters.

"It's for Grant, too," she said. "He'd like to entertain more."

"Maybe I can oil things for you. In Grant's double capacity as my aide and assistant deputy . . . yes, that's reason enough to bend the rules a little. I'll give the housing officer a ring, tell him you act as my hostess when Sophie's under the weather. That should do it."

Crystal squealed and threw her arms around him. "You're a love," she told him. "You're always so good to me!"

"So why don't you show your appreciation?" he said, and she saw that he was aroused again. Since there was no help for it, she set about satisfying him the fastest way she knew, wanting to be gone from the shabby room with its soiled bedspread and cracked wall plaster and the odor of disinfectant so strong that it overwhelmed her expensive perfume.

After Arnold left, she took a long, hot shower because she fancied that his body odor still clung to her skin. It was almost six o'clock before she finally pulled into her own carport. Feeling mentally exhausted, she sat there for a while, staring at the no-style building that she despised because it had no class.

Or did she hate it so much because it was identical to the unit where she had lived with her parents when Maurice had been stationed at Wright-Pat? Another thing that galled her was the rank of her neighbors—a lieutenant colonel on one side and a major on the other—quite a letdown from their first set of quarters at Hickam.

Luckily, that would change shortly. Too bad she couldn't tell Grant the news. But if she did, he would wonder how she knew that they would soon be assigned the quarters she wanted. Maybe she could hint at it, tell him the housing officer had been encouraging today. She did want to start making a few purchases for their new quarters. . . .

As she let herself into the house, she called Grant's name, but there was no answer. Which was strange because his Mustang was parked in the carport. Well, maybe he was in the spare bedroom he used as a den and hadn't heard her.

She headed down the central hall and went into the kitchen. To her surprise, she found Grant there, sitting at the kitchen table, a mug of coffee in his hand. His face was so gray that her first thought was that he was ill. Her second was the fear that he'd found out where she'd spent the afternoon. If so, what could he do about it? Did this come under the heading of "going her own way"? God knew she had fulfilled the other part of their bargain. She had certainly been discreet. . . .

"Grant?" she said tentatively.

He turned a brooding stare on her, but she had the impression he didn't really see her.

"Is something wrong?" she said. "Is it your father—or your grandfather?"

"This is going to kill them," he said in the leaden voice of someone who had just taken a hard punch.

"What are you talking about?"

This time her words seemed to register. Unexpectedly, a dark flush spread over his face. When he gestured toward a chair, the motion was slow, as if his hand weighed a ton. "Sit down, Crystal," he said. "This concerns you, too. You may as well be in on it."

Her knees weak, Crystal sat down opposite him. "What is it?" she asked, thoroughly alarmed now.

"I'm in trouble—big trouble," he said heavily.

"What kind of trouble?"

"I'm being blackmailed."

"Blackmailed? Is this some kind of sick joke?"

"It's not a joke."

"Why would anyone blackmail *you*?"

"Because I'm gay," he said, and there was relief in his voice now, as if by sharing it with her, he had somehow taken a step back from his trouble.

CHAPTER
↟ 28 ↟

GRANT HAD BEEN AT WRIGHT-PAT SEVERAL MONTHS WHEN
he first noticed Paul Jenners. He'd been so busy at first, taking
over his new duties and helping Crystal get settled, that there
hadn't been time for personal concerns. As a result, he hadn't
had a chance to cruise the Dayton gay bars and bathhouses, so
he'd been forced to abstain from sex—which, as he was later
to realize, made him a sitting duck for a smart operator.

He had gone to the Officers Club after work that day to
have a drink, a habit he still followed because it gave himself
a chance to unwind before he went home. As long as he bypassed
the bar and chose a booth out of the way of traffic, he was
seldom bothered by unwanted invitations to join some acquaintance for a drink.

A newspaper at his elbow as additional insurance, he sat
sipping his Scotch on the rocks, slowly shedding his tensions.
It had been a difficult day. Someone had messed up—a mis-
placed report that delayed the general's weekly staff meeting
by thirty-five minutes and put Krause in a foul, snappish mood.
The general, who didn't suffer fools easily, had pounced on
every premise, questioning every opinion, however well considered, even chewing out that poor stick Lt. Reynolds for
transposing two numbers in the dateline of an unimportant
memo.

Well, that was the military for you. Rank not only hath its
privileges, it also tolerated eccentricities in its general officers.

Grant sometimes thought the brass stored it up during the early years when they were forced to conform, then let it all hang out once they'd attained their stars.

But there would never be any tolerance for *his* particular eccentricity. A gay general was unthinkable—although Grant had his suspicions about a couple he'd encountered, including one particularly macho general who delighted in chewing out his younger subordinates.

Of course, as the old saying went, it took one to know one—did the two he wondered about have their own suspicions about *him*? Somehow, he doubted it. The mantle of normalcy he wore was too good. Having Crystal for his wife helped. One look at her, so obviously an affectionate, supportive wife, and who could doubt that they had a satisfactory sex life? Yes, Crystal was good. Fact was, he owed her one hell of a lot.

Which was why he went along with her demands most of the time. Sometimes he thought the whole situation between them was a comedy of errors, a joke on nature because their roles should be reversed. Crystal should be the aspiring career officer while he was the supportive wife who played footsie with the wives of senior officers.

Why was she so eager to be a general's wife, anyway? Funny that he'd never asked her that question. He suspected it had something to do with her blowsy ex-beauty queen of a mother, an "I'll show the bitch" sort of thing. And it didn't really matter. They scratched each other's backs, were two different sides of the same coin. Without Crystal, it would be difficult to maintain the façade. . . .

Grant took a long drink of his Scotch, then set down his empty glass. When he was still a teenager, his grandfather had once told him that a good Scotch was God's gift to men with balls. Grant had made a note of this, and when he came of age and was going through an agonizing identity crisis, he'd adopted Scotch as his drink. Now he liked it for its own merits, liked the burst of dry flavor, like aromatic ashes, in his mouth. He was contemplating whether to have a second drink or to go home to the excellent meal he knew would be waiting for him, when a shadow fell across his newspaper.

He looked up into the quizzical eyes of one of the bartenders. According to the badge on his uniform, his name was Paul.

"Can I get you another drink before I go off duty, sir?" He was young and well built, with a lean, hawklike face. In contrast, his eyes were luminous, fringed with dark eyelashes, and his mouth, full-lipped and dark pink, would have looked more at home on a feminine face. His smile, Grant noted with quickening interest, had a feline look—and there was definitely an invitation in his eyes.

"No, I've had enough. I'm about to head for home myself," Grant said; he discovered a dryness in his mouth.

"Look, sir, I know this is presumptuous, but my car is on the fritz. If you're heading home, could you drop me off near the gate so I can catch a bus into town?"

Grant felt a warning flash of caution. But since he couldn't think of any good reason to refuse, he nodded silently and gathered up his newspaper. He hadn't realized until he stood up how slightly built the bartender was, and he felt self-conscious as the two of them headed for the door, Paul in the lead. Which was stupid. The man was simply looking for a ride. To read anything more into this incident was dangerous.

Later, he would realize that Paul had played him like a master fisherman snagging a fat trout. As they drove toward the gate, he talked so casually that Grant's suspicions were lulled. But when he let the bartender off at the covered bus stop, Paul bent to look in at him through the open window. "If you're ever out on the town for the night, why don't you drop in at the Locust Grove Bar? I hang out there—I'll be glad to introduce you around."

His tone was still casual, but there was no mistaking what the invitation implied. Grant grunted, a noncommittal sound, and drove away, but the image of Paul's face, those full lips and those moist eyes, remained with him as he headed for home.

During the next week, he avoided the Officers Club and went home right after work. A week later, restless and bored with Crystal's harping on the shortcomings of their quarters, he stopped at the club for a drink and discovered that Paul was off duty. He started for home and then, on impulse, decided to drop by the Locust Grove for a second drink. No harm in it, he thought. He'd just have one Scotch, see what the action was, then go home—but first, he'd change into the civilian clothes he kept at his office.

The Locust Grove Bar was easy to find. A soft-porn movie theater nudged it from one side while a nightclub, featuring topless dancers, flanked it from the other. As Grant came through the door, the first person he saw was Paul, sitting alone at a long, curved bar.

When Paul saw Grant, he smiled and patted the seat of the barstool next to his. Grant hesitated, then joined him. Now that his eyes had adjusted to the murky light, he saw that the place was full of men, some of them dancing together. Later, he would reflect that he should have turned on his heel and left at that point. Always before he'd been so careful to assume a false identity when cruising, but it was already too late for that—and besides, his predatory instincts were going full blast.

For the next two hours, they talked—and drank. Paul was a little too ingratiating for Grant's taste, but he had a sense of humor, edged with a touch of malice, that Grant found amusing. He had suffered through so many evenings of dry, meaningless exchanges that passed for conversation in military social circles that it was a relief to let down his hair, to talk freely—much too freely, as it turned out.

Around midnight they ended up in what Paul called "his pad." Grant expected something bohemian, but it was a well-furnished apartment in a modern building in a good neighborhood. They had a few more drinks, and then they went to bed, and Grant discovered that Paul was that rare thing, a lover who put his partner's needs first.

It was only when Grant was dressing to return home that it came to him why Paul had seemed so familiar the first time he'd seen him at the club. Except for his mouth, with its feminine fullness, he was the spitting image of Jake, Grant's first lover.

He saw Paul again the next night and the next, excusing his absence from home by inventing an urgent report he had to get out for Arnold. At that stage of their affair, he could no sooner have stayed away than he could have flown.

Paul was an excellent cook, and the second night he fixed bouillabaisse for dinner. Wearing matching velour robes that Paul produced with a charming smile, they ate on the sofa in front of the apartment's white marble fireplace, and it didn't occur to Grant in his besotted condition to wonder how Paul, a bartender at the Officers' Club, where the tips were known to be parsimonious, could afford the rent on a luxury apartment in one of Dayton's newer apartment buildings.

A month later, Paul asked him for a "loan."

"That bucket of rust I've been driving is about to fall apart," he said easily, flashing a grin. "I need wheels, man, something reliable."

It was then that Grant, usually conservative about money, made another mistake. "Why don't I get you a good secondhand car for your birthday next week?" he said impulsively.

Paul's eyes gleamed. "You're one generous dude," he said. "I insist on making it a loan."

But after he had picked out a car, a far more expensive model than Grant had anticipated, the matter of paying back the loan never came up again. By now, Grant was obsessed with Paul, who had a frank sexuality that was both giving and taking, and a generosity during the sex act that fed something in Grant that had been untapped until now. Never having known his mother, who had died when he was an infant, he had little experience with love of any kind, so he chalked up his desire to see Paul every evening to their common taste in music and books, and even in the kind of food they both liked, and he begrudged every evening he was forced to spend with Crystal at some social event. In his desire to repay Paul for what he thought of as a generosity of soul, he bought him gifts—replacing a tape deck that had burned out, then a television set that was beyond repair.

Occasionally, it occurred to him that Paul was inordinately unlucky with mechanical things, this after his lover told him a little shamefacedly that he'd just wrecked his microwave by running it empty. But he enjoyed the role of provider, especially since Paul's gratitude was so touching, so it was a shock to find out that Paul had another lover who paid the rent on his apartment.

Grant's disillusionment transcended anger. At first Paul denied it, claiming the man was simply an old friend, and then, when Grant produced a love letter Paul had carelessly left lying on the bedroom dresser, he changed his story and claimed that Calvin was the man who had initiated him to sex.

His eyes moist, he swore that he detested the man, who was a brute, but that he was afraid to break off with him— and besides, he couldn't afford to drop him because Calvin paid all the expenses on the apartment.

And then Paul made his second mistake. "My wages are so lousy that I really need the bread he gives me," he whined. "I'd break off with him in a minute if I had another steady source of income."

Grant almost hit Paul then. Although he'd been wearing blinders, he wasn't stupid, and he knew that he'd been had. A strong sense of self-preservation warned him to extract himself from the relationship without delay.

He took off the velour robe—had Paul's other lover worn it on the nights Grant wasn't there?—and put on his clothes, ignoring Paul's increasingly threatening tirade. Without a word, he left the apartment, Paul's shrill voice following him down the hall.

He was sure that would end it—until the next evening when the phone rang in the middle of a dinner party. It was Paul— and his threat to have a talk with "the little wife" sickened Grant. He hung up, but Paul called him right back. This time, Grant left the receiver off the hook, only to have Paul call his office the following morning. Grant refused the call; he left word with his secretary that in the future, he was "out" to Paul Jenners, an insurance salesman who'd been making a nuisance of himself.

Whatever she thought of this thin excuse, his secretary must have gotten the message across because Paul changed his tactics. The first letter arrived at Grant's quarters two days later. Crystal was curious about the letters that began arriving every day, each minus a return address but with a Dayton postmark. Grant shrugged them off as a sales campaign by a pesky insurance salesman, but the next time Paul called him at home, he agreed to meet him downtown "to settle things."

Settlement, he discovered, was to be in cold cash—ten thousand dollars. In return, Paul would turn over the snapshots that his friend, who was a professional photographer, had taken of their romantic interludes through a two-way mirror in the bedroom. He produced the snapshots, and as Grant stared down at the proof of his homosexuality, he saw himself through the eyes of his superiors. He almost threw up in that dark, smelly little bar.

He could have paid Paul the ten thousand dollars and never missed the money. As Paul pointed out, it was a reasonable exchange for a career. But he knew that this wouldn't be the end. There would be another payment, more photographs, and then in a few months, it would start all over again. Because blackmailers were insatiable—and that kind of torture he didn't intend to endure. So he told Paul to do his worst—and left the bar quickly before he put his fist in the mouth that he'd once thought so sexy.

Reaction set in when he reached home. Crystal was out, and as he stood by the living room windows, looking at the orderly street with its well-trimmed hedges and its green lawns, he considered the probable result of his actions. Paul was vindictive—if he didn't come up with the money, Paul would certainly send the snapshots to Grant's superiors, and that would be the end of his air force career. He would be asked to resign, and he would do it, rather than have his father and grandfather learn that he was a homosexual.

Or maybe Paul would send copies to them, too. When Grant was still in the first throes of infatuation, he had told Paul about the two old men, about their political conservatism and their roots in the past. Never in a million years would they tolerate a sexual deviate in the family. And Crystal—he would have to tell her the truth. It was only fair that she be given a chance to bail out of their marriage before this whole mess became common knowledge.

He was sitting in the kitchen, holding a cup of coffee that had grown cold, when Crystal came home. Dimly, he realized she was asking him a question, but her voice seemed to come to him through a thick wall. Only when she said his father's name did her words finally penetrate.

"Is something wrong?" she said. "Is it your father—or your grandfather?"

"This is going to kill them," he said.

"What are you talking about?"

Grant met the worry in her eyes. His face felt very hot, and he realized he was blushing, a phenomenon so foreign to his nature that it snapped him out of his stupor. He knew he had to tell her the truth, but it was hard to get the words out. In her own way, he knew, she was fond of him—or maybe it was more accurate to say that she was tolerant of him by now. Either way, he owed her something.

"Sit down, Crystal," he said. "This concerns you. You may as well be in on it."

Crystal dropped into a chair. "What is it?" she said.

Somehow he said the words, the damning words that would explain so many things to her. He expected shock, revulsion, disbelief, but not the fury that twisted her face. She jumped to her feet, flew at him, and hit him with the open palm of her hand. The blow stung, but he didn't retaliate or try to defend himself. She hit him again, this one across the bridge of his nose—and then, unexpectedly, she burst into tears. He had never seen Crystal cry. Impotently, he stared at her distorted face, unable to do anything, say anything.

At her best, she wasn't a pretty woman, although she had style, a trim body, and an intensity that he knew attracted some men. Now, he discovered that when she cried she was downright ugly, with her skin splotched with red and her eyes swollen. But at that moment he came closer to loving Crystal than he ever had. Motivated by regret, he reached out and laid a consoling hand on her shoulder. She looked up at him, and although she stopped crying, she didn't pull away.

"That bastard's not going to get away with it," she said fiercely. "You can't pay him off—he'd only come back for more money."

It took him a minute to recover from his surprise. "I'm not going to pay him off. But he's very vindictive—he'll expose me out of pure spite."

"He's also greedy—greed makes a person careless. If you call him and tell him you've changed your mind, he'll come running, won't he?"

"He'll come all right, but—"

"It'll be up to you to stall him. Get to the meeting place late and pretend you want to make things up with him. I'll need time to break into his apartment."

He saw her plan then. It just might work if Paul was confident—or stupid—enough to keep the snapshots at his apartment.

"He gave me a key," he said reluctantly. "But I can't let you take that kind of risk—"

"You don't have any choice. I've put too much into this marriage to let that pervert wreck your career."

Grant let her persuade him to go through with it. He convinced himself that Crystal would be in no real danger because he wanted to believe it and because he had invested seventeen years in the air force.

While Crystal listened, he made the phone call to Paul. "I've been thinking it over," he said into the mouthpiece, "and maybe we can make a deal—as long as I have your guarantee that this will be a one-time thing."

"Oh, you can be sure of that," Paul said quickly. "Hell,

man, I wouldn't even ask except that I'm in a bind. Once I get my act together, I'm leaving town and that's the last you'll see of me."

"Then I think we should talk—in some public place. That way there'll be no surprises on either side—understand?"

"Sure, sure, man," Paul said.

They agreed on the Salamander Bar, a quiet place that catered to neighborhood trade. Grant hung up, satisfied that Paul had no suspicion that the meeting was anything but setting-up time.

"It's all set," he told Crystal. "Eight o'clock at the Salamander Bar—which is across town from Paul's apartment. I'll call the bar at eight and leave a message that I'll be fifteen minutes late. Any more than that and he might smell a rat. And when I get there, I'll stall him as long as I can. Maybe I can get him talking about old times."

"Let him think you want to resume your—what do you people call them? Affairs?"

You people. . . . Of course she would think of it that way. Why not? All her life she had heard stories about queers, perverts. How could she know that finding out Paul was a blackmailer had hurt him as much as the betrayal of a lover would hurt her? At the moment, she was looking at him as if he were some kind of strange animal. Would it be that way from now on? There had never been any love between them, but there had been respect, which had made their forced intimacy endurable. Would that change? Would she stick it out, knowing what she knew now?

"Do you want a divorce?" he said abruptly.

"You'd like that, I suppose."

"No," he said honestly. "I'm satisfied with our life. But if you're going to look at me as if I'm some kind of child molester, all bets are off. I've never corrupted anyone, Crystal. I was born with my sexual preferences, but I didn't realize that I was a homosexual until I was at the academy. Before that, I always had some rationalization for why I wasn't interested in girls. And after I found out the truth, I was careful not to approach anyone I wasn't sure of. For the most part, my lovers have been professionals, although I thought Paul really cared for me. I was sure we were both in the same boat, misfits who had learned to live with our aberration and go on from there. It seems my judgment was in error, but I swear I'll never embarrass you again. If I get out of this jam, I'll keep away from that kind of temptation."

"I'm sure you will, because if it happens again, I'll throw you to the wolves myself," she said grimly.

He read the determination, the fury, in her eyes, and an errant thought came to him—that it might be better in the long run if he simply resigned from the air force and walked away from the whole rotten mess.

Crystal had never been so furious in her life. Everything she'd worked for, all the sacrifices she'd made, rose up to taunt her, that long litany of humiliations and compromises, not the least of which was the boredom she'd endured. Well, she wasn't going to let it all go down the drain. She would do what she had to do—and if those lousy photographs weren't in Paul's apartment, she'd think up another plan.

The apartment building Grant had directed her to was surprisingly elegant. When she looked in through the lobby door and saw a middle-aged man in a guard's uniform, sitting behind a bleached wood desk, eating a sandwich, she cursed Grant for not warning her about him. A group of chatting men and women, wearing evening clothes, converged on the lobby doors, and in the confusion she dropped in behind them, a smile plastered on her face, hoping the guard wouldn't notice that she was wearing slacks and her London Fog raincoat.

Luckily, the contrast in her clothes didn't seem to register. The guard was too busy trying to cover up the snack that they had interrupted. He waited, more or less patiently, while they argued noisily whether or not to drop in on "old Corny" or hit another nightclub, and Crystal, still smiling, slipped onto the elevator and punched the button for the sixth floor.

The elevator seemed to rise with agonizing slowness. Any minute she expected a red alarm light to flash on, and she was glad she'd taken the precaution of punching the button for the floor above the one Grant had given her.

A few minutes later, when she opened the fire door to the fifth floor, the corridor was empty. As she hurried along, looking at door numbers, it occurred to her that she should have an excuse ready in case she were caught prowling the halls. The wrong building? Yes, that might do it—after all, who could disprove it?

The key Grant had given her was already in her hand when

she stopped in front of apartment 5-D. It turned easily in the lock, and a second later, she was inside with the door shut behind her.

The apartment was dark. She stood there a moment, trying to decide whether or not to turn on a light. Since she hadn't thought to bring along a flashlight, she was finally forced to take the risk. When she pressed the button beside the door, soft light flooded a small foyer, and she shrank back instinctively, her heart beating very fast.

An awareness of time passing and the fear that Grant might not be effective at fooling his ex-lover sent her hurrying toward the living room. Quickly she searched a small desk, then an antique cabinet used for storing tapes, restoring order as she went along because she didn't dare leave any evidence that she'd been there in case she was unsuccessful and had to come back another time.

A bow-fronted chest of drawers in the hall was next, but all it yielded was a collection of hard-core porn magazines. Had Grant and his lover looked at them together? Although so many things were clear now, she still found it hard to envision Grant, so austere and fastidious, poring over pictures of naked men. What did she really know about the man she'd married? For all his denials, he could even be a child molester, but he was all she had—and she'd already invested so much time and effort in him.

Crystal had finished searching the kitchen, bathroom, and bedroom with no success when impulse sent her back to the kitchen for another try. She opened the refrigerator door, examined the stock of white wine, all expensive imported brands, the gourmet cheeses and fancy condiments, and wondered if Grant had paid for them.

The cupboard was next. A quick search behind boxes of sugar and flour and spices and a large box of oats revealed only a slight feathering of dust. As she was turning away, a faint memory stirred. Hadn't she read a story once about a woman who hid her silver in a box of cereal? And come to think of it, wasn't that outsized box of oats out of place in the apartment of a man who obviously had a taste for more exotic foods?

She found the photographs and two metal containers that held negatives buried in the box of Mother's Quick Oats. As she stuffed them in her purse, she felt so triumphant that she wanted to throw the oats around the room as a way of thumbing her nose at the blackmailer. But she resisted the impulse and replaced the box exactly as she'd found it, back side facing outward, before she closed the cupboard door.

She turned off the kitchen light and started for the foyer. In a few minutes she would be back in her car, and Grant would be safe—provided the blackmailer didn't have a duplicate set of negatives hidden away somewhere. She had saved Grant's ass for him—would he remember this the next time she wanted something he considered unreasonable? If not, she would remind him. Oh, yes, in the coming years, she would remind him many times who had gotten him out of this jam. . . .

She was reaching for the doorknob when the door flew open. She was so startled that she could only stand there, staring at the powerfully built man in the doorway. He looked as startled as she felt.

"Who the hell are you?" he demanded.

Crystal's mind went blank. After all, what excuse could she give for breaking in—but no, she *hadn't* broken in. That was the point. She had let herself in with a key. . . .

"You bastard," she said, pumping anger into her voice. "You don't have to put on an act. You know who I am—and let me tell you, I don't intend to share my husband with a creep like you. Your affair is over, as of now, or I'm going to his superior and blow the whistle on him and tell them that my husband is a lousy gay. What do you say to that, you—you pervert?"

The man moved fast. He grabbed her by the shoulders, shoved her back into the foyer, slamming the door shut behind him with his foot. "I say you're a lousy burglar. I'm calling the police and charging you with housebreaking."

"What burglary?" she said quickly, her mind moving very fast. "I didn't take anything from your love nest. I came here looking for my husband—and I used a key I found in his jacket pocket. So go ahead and call the police. I'll have a few things to tell them myself. Like where did Grant get the money to buy those expensive presents for you? He dipped into the petty cash account at work, that's what he did. That's a crime—and you're an accessory."

"I think you're bluffing, lady. Something smells here. . . . How come you came looking for your old man tonight? I told that lamebrain something was up, but no, he was so sure it was all coming together."

Crystal stared at him, trying to make sense from his words. "If you aren't Paul—then who are you?" she said finally.

"Paul and me date back a long way, from when he was just a chicken, soliciting johns on street corners. And I think you'd better hand over your purse. I want to take a look in it."

Crystal knew she was trapped. She was also afraid. Something about this man, about the coldness in his eyes, told her she was in danger.

Self-preservation took over. She let her eyes fill with tears, but the man only told her, "You're wasting your time. That kind of shit doesn't work with me. Why don't you save both of us a lot of trouble and hand over that purse before I have to take it away from you—which could make me very mad. I'm going to have to punish you as a lesson to your old man, but if you cooperate, I won't mark you up too much with my little friend here."

A knife appeared in his hand. It was small, narrow, and it looked as deadly as a rattler. He tossed it from one hand to the other, his eyes gleaming, and she knew he was enjoying himself, enjoying her fear—and that he wasn't going to stop with a few token strokes.

Her next move was instinctive. She gave way before him, retreating down the hall. When her back was pressed against the side of the bow-fronted chest, she reached behind her, her eyes never leaving the man's face as he advanced toward her, taking his time. With a quick movement, she grasped a small music box she'd searched earlier. Using the aim that had won her a pitcher's slot on her junior high baseball team, she threw the box into the man's face.

There was dull thud as it struck the side of his head, spinning him around. Not waiting to see how much damage she had inflicted, she flew past his prone body and out the door. When she saw a couple getting into the elevator at the end of the hall, she called out frantically for them to hold it for her.

A few minutes later, she was back in her car, but her hands were shaking so that she couldn't turn the key in the ignition. She folded her arms on the steering wheel and buried her face in them. So this was what panic felt like—she was glad she wasn't a man and would never be called upon to fight in a war. On the other hand, she had kept her head and saved herself from being carved up. In fact, she had just discovered that she had physical courage, something she hadn't known before.

When she got home, Grant was there, waiting for her. His face was so pale that a small patch of pigment discoloration on his forehead, usually unnoticeable, stood out like a brown strawberry. Instead of feeling relief, his hangdog expression aroused her fury, and she forgot that the whole scheme had been her idea. While he'd been drinking with his ex-lover, she had been taking all the risk, laying herself open not only to a burglary charge but to personal danger.

She stalked toward Grant and flung the packet of photographs in his face. He didn't put up his hands to protect himself, and the end of the manila envelope left a red mark on his cheekbone.

"There's your snapshots. I'm keeping the negatives as insurance in case you forget that I risked my life for you tonight. Your lover's friend caught me in the act, and if I hadn't moved fast, he would've cut up my face as a lesson to you. I saved your career for you tonight, and you're going to pay me back by promising that this is the end of your lousy perversions."

His silence increased her rage, and she added, "And the payoff has changed. I'm not going to settle for being a brigadier general's wife now. Oh, no, I want more. I intend to be the wife of a four-star general someday—and you'd better come across because you owe me, Grant. You really owe me."

"I know I do," he said heavily. "I promise that I'll do my best to get you what you want."

CHAPTER
✦ 29 ✦

SHELLEY HEARD THE RADIO BLARING OUT COUNTRY MUSIC as she was coming up the walk of the apartment building that housed the families of four middle-grade enlisted men. Since her arms were full of groceries, she pressed the doorbell with her elbow instead of digging her keys out of her purse. It was so long before the door swung open that she was beginning to think Tad wasn't home, after all.

"Oh, hi, honey. Forget your key again?" Tad said, taking the sack of groceries from her arms.

"It's in my purse—but I knew you were home because I heard the radio all the way down the street. And where do you get off with that 'again'? I got locked out once—"

"Twice."

"Okay, twice—Mr. Elephant Child," she said, irritated by the Indian summer heat and her aching arms, by the persistent wind that never seemed to stop blowing at Travis AFB, and, if the truth be known, by Tad's pragmatic mind and selective memory.

She turned to go back to the station wagon for another bag of groceries, but he stopped her. "I'll bring in the rest—did you get plenty of chow for the party tonight?"

"The usual stuff. Chips and Fritos and gourmet cold cuts."

"Uh-oh. In one of those moods, are you?"

She studied his grin suspiciously. "What's up? You look like you just won the Irish sweepstakes."

330

"Oh, nothing like that." His tone, if not his smile, was elaborately casual. "But how'd you like to kiss a master sergeant hello?"

It took a moment for his words to penetrate. She squealed then and grabbed him, knocking the bag of groceries he was holding to the floor. As cans of beans and coffee and boxes of cereal flew in all directions, he kissed her enthusiastically, then lifted her off her feet to swing her around in a big circle. "How about that? I got the news today. Man, I couldn't believe it! A line promotion—how about that?"

"We're rich! We can afford steak now—"

"Whoa! Hold it! Not yet. We have to finish paying off the credit union before we start buying T-bones."

"Not even one?"

"Well, maybe a couple." He looked so pleased with himself that she hugged him again. "And where are the kids? I went next door to Meg's apartment to pick them up, but nobody's home."

"Oh, I changed off with Beth since Meg's coming to the party. She's going to keep them overnight, and then I'll watch her three boys next week sometime," she said absently, her mind still on the news. She tried to figure out how much his pay raise would be. Now they could pay off that loan at the credit union—and if they didn't transfer for another year, they might even save a little money for emergencies—or for a newer car.

"So how about helping me clean up the mess?" Tad said, and she realized he was picking up spilled groceries from the floor.

"Right. Can we tell the gang tonight, or did someone slip you the news on the q.t.?"

"It's official—but maybe we'd better downplay it, hon. Let them find out some other way. I did jump ahead of several senior guys in my outfit."

"And you worked for it. No one can say you didn't. I think I'll tell Beth, though. Her husband's already got six stripes, so it won't matter to her. God knows we were happy when Ron got his promotion."

"Yeah—remember that jerk who asked him how come he got promoted when he didn't play golf with the officers?"

"I remember, I remember."

"Well, that's how it goes. God, it was some kind of jolt

when the old man called me in and gave me the news! A line promotion—no sweating out the selectee list and all that jazz. It knocked me for a loop."

"I was sure you'd make it," she said—not altogether truthfully.

"Well, I do know aircraft engines," he acknowledged.

"It isn't just that. You get along well with people. You get them working together."

"Now where'd you get that idea?"

"Major Lunigan. At the squadron picnic last spring. He had a few too many beers, and he was telling me how you'd pulled the shop together since we came here."

"Well, that was the beer talking. I do my job and and keep my nose clean—and take orders."

She wanted to argue with him, but he looked uncomfortable, as he always did when he was praised, so she turned away and began putting away groceries.

The party was a success—or at least everybody seemed to be having a good time. At Tad's suggestion, she had invited their neighbors so they wouldn't have to worry when the noise level shifted into high. The cold cuts and potato salad, the coleslaw and pickles and chips, disappeared at a record rate, and so did the beer and mountain red. As usual, the men gravitated to the kitchen like lemmings to the sea while the women remained in the living room, everybody, it seemed to Shelley, talking at the same time.

Since they had transferred to Travis, she had been to many of these get-togethers, and while she felt much more relaxed these days, it was still an ordeal of sorts. It was obvious Tad felt no such restraint. As usual, he was in the center of it all, laughing and joking, having a wonderful time. She envied him his ease with people. It was a gift she wished she possessed, but she was realistic enough to know it would never happen, not to her.

But she kept circulating, keeping the food supplies coming, and as she passed around another bowl of mixed nuts, she couldn't help comparing this party with one of her mother's sedate entertainments. How horrified she'd be if her guests had the gall to turn up dressed so casually—the men in short-sleeved shirts and the women in long muumuus or cotton shifts. In fact, she would turn up her nose at every aspect of her daughter's life. So wasn't it lucky that she and the general had yet to acknowledge the existence of their grandsons?

"Why the long face?" Marcy Downing lived in the end unit of their apartment building. She had followed Shelley into the service room off the kitchen, where an extra supply of chips and pretzels was stored.

"Didn't know I had one."

"You did. You should be dancing on the tables, gal. The pay jump to master is really a big one."

"How on earth did you know about Tad's promotion?"

Marcy looked smug. "David is in wing personnel—remember? But my lips are sealed. I understand why Tad and you don't want to make a big thing of it tonight. Noses out of joint and all that."

"That isn't the reason. Tad just isn't one to blow his own horn."

"Uh-huh. He's an okay guy—and you aren't so bad, either. At first, I thought—" She broke off, looking embarrassed.

"At first you thought *what*?"

"Well, it was those shorts you used to sunbathe in. I looked out the window at this long-legged blonde, stretched out on the grass in the backyard, and I asked myself, 'Who needs a sexpot like that living next door?' But then I met you in the laundry room, and—"

"—and took me under your wing, got me into the baby-sitting network, and became my all-round good friend," Shelley said, smiling at her.

"Yeah. We were lucky enough to be assigned a good sponsor when we were transferred here from Reese, so I try to pass the favor along when I get the chance. Those first few months, I was a candidate for the loony bin. Three kids and two of them still in diapers. But I muddled through. What else? You adjust or you don't—and adjust is better than don't. Oh, I still have times when I'm tempted to talk David into getting out and moving back to San Diego so we can be close to our folks. He could get a decent job in the shipyards and . . . well, it always passes. Because David would be miserable away from the air force."

"Tad, too. He calls it his home away from home. He says it as if he's kidding, but actually he means it. And it isn't so bad. How else would ordinary people like us see the world?"

"Yeah. The world as seen through the eyes of a DW. Every time some jackass calls me that, I get the urge to kill—"

"Hey, Shelley, we're running low on vino," Tad called from the kitchen, ending the conversation.

The next morning, Shelley went to pick up her two boys at her friend's house. Larry, at five, had his father's outgoing personality and sometimes startling candor, while Mark, who was just past three, was quieter and took his time making up his mind about strangers. When she came into her neighbor's living room, Larry lookd up from a game he was playing with Beth's children, gave her a welcoming smile, and then returned to the game. Mark, in contrast, flew across the room his arms outstretched, and buried his face in the hollow of her throat.

She kissed the top of her son's head, knowing that in another year or so he would be as independent as his brother, who already had decided that mushy stuff such as kissing one's mom in public was not for him.

When they reached home, Larry was out of the car and already heading toward the door, eager to share his adventures with Tad. He's already growing away from me and identifying with his father, Shelley thought, and unconsciously her arms tightened around Mark.

She had put them both down for their "quiet time," over Larry's indignant objections, when the phone rang. "Will you get that, Tad?" she called. "I've got my hands full."

She heard Tad's voice, then a long silence; when he appeared in the door, she started to ask him who it was, but the look on his face stopped her. She dropped a kiss on each of the boys' heads and left their bedroom, closing the door behind her.

"What is it?" she said, not really wanting to know because instinct told her it was bad news. Possibilities flickered through her mind. Not the children, thank God. Was it his mother, his father—or one of her parents?

When he still couldn't seem to get the words out, another possibility came to her, and she felt a great rush of apprehension, the prelude to grief.

"Oh, my God . . . something's happened to Tony," she whispered.

"I'm sorry—that was your sister-in-law's cousin. He—your brother went down over Puget Sound. It was some kind of freak accident. A private plane drifted into his flight pattern a few minutes after he took off, and—"

He went on talking, but his voice seemed to come from a long way off. She heard words ... midair collision ... funeral services ... but they had no meaning. She was seeing a small girl, sitting in the entrance hall of some shadowy house, the details of which were long lost to her memory, waiting patiently for her big brother, who was due home on leave.

And another image—the same little girl, older now, going into the headmistress's office at one of the schools she'd attended, sure she had been summoned for some infraction of the rules, only to be caught up in the arms of a tall smiling man in an air force blue uniform....

"But it can't be true," she said aloud. "Tony went all through the war in 'Nam without getting hurt. He can't be dead—there has to be some mistake!"

Tad's arms closed around her. For a moment, she had the illusion that they were Tony's arms, and now the tears started—tears she knew would never stop falling in her heart whenever she thought of her brother.

It was later that Tad brought up the subject of the funeral again. "The woman who called—I never did catch her name—told me the memorial service would be at the Air Force Academy day after tomorrow. Your folks wanted it that way, I guess. I know you'll want to go—and don't worry about the expense. I'll go to the credit union and get the money for your plane ticket."

"But the kids—"

"That's what emergency leaves are for. I'll take care of them—and we've got friends to help out. You won't be gone that long, but your folks need you right now."

She started to tell him that her parents had never needed her, that they never would, but the words didn't come. To Tad, such an idea would be unthinkable. No matter how his family might feud among themselves, a funeral brought them together. There were rules, customs, mores that were ironbound in his life—and this was one of the strongest. That the news had come to her from her sister-in-law's family told her she still hadn't been forgiven—but how could she say that to Tad?

In the end, she went to Colorado, but not for the reason Tad assumed, to be a comfort to her parents. She went to honor her brother, to pay homage to him for all those years that he'd found a small place in his busy life for his kid sister.

* * *

The memorial service was held in the Protestant wing of the students' chapel. Outside, the temperature was just above zero, and while the chaplain, a rotund man with a pink pate, was intoning words that seemed to have nothing to do with the brother she remembered, Shelley could hear the popping of the steam radiators along the wall. She was wearing a five-year-old coat, but because she'd had no use for winter clothing in Hawaii or the Philippines or northern California, it still looked respectable, if a bit out of style. She was glad of that. At least she wouldn't disgrace her parents by turning up in shabby clothes at Tony's funeral.

Even so, she knew her presence was unwelcome. Her parents hadn't snubbed her; they had greeted her politely enough, but they hadn't asked about Tad—or their grandsons. True, Tony's wife had clung to her briefly when Shelley arrived in the car she'd rented at Denver's Stapleton Airport, but now, as they sat in the front row of the chapel, divided by several members of her sister-in-law's family, she was aware that Gretchen and she were as far apart as ever, that they would never have the chance to become friends now.

Tony's teenaged stepdaughters were awkward with her, too, as if they didn't know quite what to say to this strange aunt who was so near to their own age. She had tried telling them how close she had always felt to Tony despite the difference in their ages, of how she had adored him as a child, but they'd looked embarrassed, as if they didn't believe her, and she wondered what they'd heard about her from their mother—or their stepgrandparents.

At the altar, the chaplain was finishing his litany of praise for the dead. Good husband, father, and soldier—was that the sum of what Tony had been? The Tony she'd known had been a laughing, joking man who always made her feel important. He had helped shape her character for the very reason that he had accepted her, loved her without reservations. Knowing that this man, who loomed so large in her life, thought she was worthwhile, had given her a sense of self-respect that had nurtured her through those lonely years when she'd felt abandoned by her parents.

It occurred to her now how strange it was that she had never been jealous of her brother. All her parents' hopes and dreams had been wrapped up in him. Their only disappointment had been the fact that Tony hadn't produced sons to carry on the family name—and traditions.

And now—what were they feeling behind their impenetrable calm? Grief? Anger because they had just discovered that even the high can suffer loss? Had it occurred to them yet that there never would be another Pritchard male to carry on the family name, attend the academy, become an air force officer? Would her father, who had fought so hard to keep women out of the academy, do an about-face now and try to talk one of his stepgranddaughters into trying for a military career? Somehow she doubted that. With the single exception of his wife, women held so little value to her father. And wasn't it strange that he did have grandsons, even though they bore another man's name, and that both of his grandsons looked so much like Tony as to be uncanny?

The service ended, and she went over to Tony's widow to murmur something comforting, to kiss her cheek and tell her that if there was anything she could do, just ask. She added that she had a plane to catch, and then, having done her duty, edged away, knowing that nothing she said really mattered to Gretchen—or to her parents.

It was impulse that made her turn back and seek out the oldest of her nieces in the milling crowd. She pressed the snapshot of her sons that she kept in her wallet into her niece's limp hand.

"See that your grandparents get this," she said, and was gone before the girl could answer.

It was with a sense of relief that she joined Tai, who had gotten permission to cut classes to attend the service, and who was looking very solemn and pale. As they walked along the base of a high cement wall, heading for the visitors' parking lot, Shelley wondered if the ceremony had stirred up memories of Mac's funeral for Tai.

Feeling the need to break the silence, she gestured toward the building that loomed above the wall. "The whole place is so much larger than what I expected," she said.

"I know," Tai said. "When I first reported in, I thought I'd wear my feet down to the ankle, trotting back and forth to class in those hallowed halls."

Shelley smiled at her friend. Tai looked much the same as she had during her visit to Clark AB three summers earlier, but to Shelley's eyes, there was a new authority in her step, even in the way she held her head. "It's better for you now, isn't it?"

"Seniors are the cocks of the walk," Tai said. "Little tin gods—but wait until we report in on our first assignment. Then we go to the bottom of the pecking order again."

"Have you heard any news about Steven?" Shelley asked.

"Sometimes I hear a rumor or two via the grapevine, but not from the great man himself, of course."

Her tart tone made Shelley smile. "Do you still feel bitter toward him?"

"Not bitter. That finally wore off. But I have no desire to see him again—ever. As far as I'm concerned, he's past history." But having said that, she added, "It's sort of ironic that his marriage broke up. She was just what his parents ordered— WASP, daughter of a career officer, all the proper ingredients for an ambitious officer's wife."

"Steven is divorced?"

"So I hear. I wonder what his parents think about that."

"They probably blame you," Shelley said.

"I wouldn't be surprised. Would you believe that I actually felt sorry for him when I heard the news? A broken marriage . . . well, it leaves scars."

And so does death, Shelley thought. She rushed into speech, trying to keep her voice steady. "When was the last time you heard from Bobby Jo?" she asked.

"She writes pretty regularly since they were transferred to George AFB. She says she has a lot of spare time with Josh gone so much. She sounds . . . well, she isn't the same happy-go-lucky Bobby Jo we knew. Motherhood and the realities of being a service wife seem to have changed her."

"Don't I know," Shelley said, more fervently than she intended. Tai laughed, and the conversation moved to other things during the remainder of their walk.

Shelley flew back to northern California that evening to grieve alone, to try to accept a world that didn't, somewhere in its vastness, hold a man called Tony. She had seen him so seldom, only once since her marriage to Tad, but she had known that he was there, that if she needed him, he would be at her side in hours. Now she had a sudden sense of her own mortality, the strong feeling that despite Tad, despite her boys and the friends she'd made, she was out there naked and alone in the world, with nothing solid to cling to.

It was a week later that the letter came from her mother. For a long time, she stood by the mailbox, staring at the return address—*Mrs. Curtis Pritchard, 1243 Garden of the Gods Road, Colorado Springs, Colorado*—before she went back into the house. With her nerves still so raw from grief, she was tempted not to open it, to drop it in the desk drawer until more time had passed. But what if one of them—her father, perhaps—had contracted a fatal illness? What if he wanted to see her?

She knew she had to open it, but she made herself a bargain. If the letter held recriminations, she would know by the first line, and then she would stop reading, tear up the letter, and throw it in the garbage.

She opened the letter and scanned it swiftly. Her eyes widened with surprise as its meaning sank in.

> *I want to apologize for the behavior of your father and myself at Tony's memorial service. I can only say that we were both in shock and felt that we just couldn't face any more emotional upheavals. We also weren't sure how you felt about us. Now I realize that you might have wanted to resume family relations. If so, I would be very happy to correspond with you and possibly arrange a visit. Do let me know as soon as possible.*
>
> *Mother*

They came two weeks later. Her answering letter to her parents had been guarded, every word carefully considered. Not too eager—because what if this were some kind of mistake?—but not cold, either, even though she wasn't eager to see them. Tony's death had cut her up emotionally, and she wasn't sure how much more she could take. And anyway, her mother's letter hadn't made much sense. They must have known at Tony's memorial service that she was waiting for some sign from them. So why the sudden change of heart?

"It's the boys," Tad said when she voiced the question aloud. "They took a look at that snapshot you left for them, and it turned them around. Didn't you tell me that the boys look like your brother? With him gone, it's natural they'd want to mend fences."

"They could have done that when Larry was born," she pointed out.

"Maybe they hoped your brother and his wife would still come up with a boy," he said.

She knew he was right. It was the only thing that made sense. Her parents were inflexible people who seldom changed their minds once they'd made a decision—and yet they had asked permission to visit her. What would they say if she told them to come ahead—but that unfortunately both her boys were visiting friends and wouldn't be there?

But she had answered the letter civilly, even with a cautious warmth. As Tad, always so pragmatic, said, "They're your folks, hon. You don't have much choice."

At Shelley's request, her parents arrived in a rental car instead of having a staff car and a driver sent out from Travis AFB to pick them up at the airport, a courtesy her father's rank entitled him to. True, her father, even in a dark business suit, looked just like what he was—a man of authority. At least he wasn't wearing his uniform, Shelley noted thankfully as she watched her parents' arrival from the living room window.

Her mother, too, looked out of place in her expensive silk chambray suit and matching coat as the two of them stood in front of the four-plex. Afraid that they might catch her watching them, Shelley drew back from the window and gave her immaculate living room one last appraising look.

"They're here," she told Tad.

Tad snapped off the sports program he'd been watching. "Calm down, Shelley," he said. "After all, they aren't going to eat you."

"Some parents do eat their young—guppies and tigers and even pigs," she said.

"But we're talking about people. Under all that starch, they're human enough to want to see—"

"—their grandsons. They couldn't care less about me. I don't expect anything good to come of this."

"Just don't expect it to be all bad, either," he said, and went to answer the doorbell.

Tad was right, as he so often was. Her mother was surprisingly cordial, even unthawing enough to tell Shelley that she looked very well. She knew this was true because she'd been fussing with her hair and makeup all morning. Tad had thought she was making too big a thing about how she looked, but then he could wear rags and still be acceptable to *his* mother.

The conversation was impersonal—the unseasonably early winter in Colorado, the election in November. Her mother even talked at length about an art exhibit she had attended at Kennedy Center on their last trip to Washington.

"Are you doing any painting these days, Shelley?" she asked.

"The boys keep me too busy. When they start school, I might sign up for an art class at the service club."

"I see—and where *are* your boys?"

Beneath the casual question, Shelley sensed her mother's tension. So Tad was right on all counts. They had come to see their grandsons, to weigh Larry's and Mark's worth, and evaluate their potential.

"They're playing next door. I sent them over there to get them out from underfoot while I . . . uh, did some housework," she said. "I'll get them now."

Tad stood up immediately. "No, I'll get them. You stay here and visit with your folks."

The general waited until the door closed behind Tad. "I see your husband is wearing master sergeant stripes. That seems to indicate a certain ambition."

"Tad's career is very important to him," Shelley said, her anger stirring.

"I'm sure you're right," her mother said with a warning look at her husband. "As your father is always saying—it's the noncoms who really run the air force."

The lie was so blatant that Shelley could only stare at her mother. Her mother's voice was crisp as she asked, "How much longer do you expect to be here at Travis?"

"We hope it will at least be another two years. Tad shouldn't be tapped for overseas duty for a while since he did that tour in the Philippines—as I'm sure you remember."

"I'm sorry about that," her father said immediately. "That was a very bad move on my part. I'm afraid that I was thinking of the embarrassment of having my daughter married to an enlisted man stationed at the same base. But surely the tour wasn't too bad, was it? I understand that most air force families consider Clark AB a very choice assignment."

Shelley thought of the termites that swarmed once a year, their discarded wings turning the streets and walks and even the floors of the quarters slippery and dangerous, of the tiny lizards that were tolerated as house pets because they kept down the insects, of the heat and the humidity, of the dry season that shriveled the skin and the rainy season that seemed never-ending, of the loneliness and the fear of being eighteen and having a baby so far from everything that was familiar to her. And yet she had come through it okay. Wasn't she a stronger person because she had learned to cope with whatever life tossed at her?

"Our tour at Clark was quite pleasant," she said, her tone neutral.

The boys arrived with their usual gusto—until they saw the strangers. Mark's fingers went into his mouth as he studied his grandparents with wide eyes, while Larry looked them over with his usual brash curiosity.

"Are you friends of my mommy and daddy?" Larry demanded.

"Come here, young man," his grandfather said, and to Shelley's surprise his voice was husky. "Did your mother ever tell you that you look just like your uncle Tony did when he was your age?"

Larry edged toward him. "She said I have my Grandmother Pritchard's hair, only I've never seen her. She and my grandfather live so far away that they can't come to see us."

"Well, I'm your Grandfather Pritchard, and this is your Grandmother Pritchard."

"Are you really?"

"Really. You want to shake hands with me?"

"You're supposed to kiss grandmothers and grandfathers," Larry said doubtfully.

"Then you can kiss my cheek—and your grandmother's, too."

Larry studied him, then his grandmother. "Okay," he said agreeably, and moved forward to kiss first his grandmother, then his grandfather.

Shelley saw it happening, but she couldn't reconcile what she knew—or thought she knew—about her parents when they produced a bagful of toys, perfectly matched to the ages of their grandsons, and then got down on the floor to help the boys play with them.

Tad watched for a while and then disappeared into the kitchen for a beer. Shelley murmured something about making coffee and followed him.

"I saw it, but I don't believe it," she said.

"Believe it. Everybody's soft on their own grandkids," Tad

said, popping open a beer can. "What about supper? It looks to be a long visit. Why don't we take them to the club instead of you trying to fix something here?"

"Can we afford it?"

"Let me worry about that."

Later, when they went out to dinner, Shelley felt a certain pride in the knowledge that the NCO Club at Travis, which was partially supported by the constant flow of transients going to and from military bases in the Pacific, was as attractive and well run as the Officers Club. If her parents found it strange, being surrounded by the families of enlisted men as they ate, they said nothing. Once, a passing sergeant did a double take when his eyes rested on General Pritchard, and Tad, who obviously knew the man, looked uncomfortable. Shelley shook her head slightly, letting him know that he wasn't to worry. No one would believe the man anyway if he said he'd seen one of the line chiefs having dinner with General Pritchard, NORAD's Commander-In-Chief, in the NCO Club dining room.

Shelley's parents left for the airport after dinner. Before they left, her mother asked permission to write—and to come by for another visit "the next time we're out this way." Shelley told her of course, that would be great, just as if she hadn't been ignored for the past six years.

As Tad said after they were gone, "Family is family. You can't help who your relatives are"—a remark Shelley would have given both her eyeteeth for her parents to have heard.

CHAPTER

✦ 30 ✦

SOMETIMES FOR DAYS ON END, BOBBY JO DIDN'T BOTHER to open the living room drapes. It wasn't because the sun shone on that side of the house in the afternoons, but because there was nothing interesting to see from the windows. On both sides of the street a row of "ranch houses," all as small and squat as her own, marched along, interspersed with poorly kept lawns and an occasional palm tree. It didn't help that someone was always saying that she and Josh were lucky to have found decent off-base housing.

The view from the kitchen window, that cramped, narrow room with its antiquated appliances, was just as dreary—a weedy backyard that Josh was always promising to "do something about," one scrawny palm tree, and the gray boards of a rickety redwood fence that made each house its own island, unlike the split-log fences with friendly gates that she remembered from her own Arkansas childhood.

Most mornings since Josh had left on his most recent TDY, she stayed in bed until past ten and would have stayed in bed until noon except for Vicky's whining. Vicky was almost six now, and while she was smart and intimidatingly precocious, she gave no sign that she was going to be a beauty. In fact, she was the image of Josh, but what in him—his well-shaped nose, his thick eyebrows that met above his eyes, his jutting chin—was so attractive was much too strong for Vicky's small face. Even her teeth, large and square like her father's, crowded the narrow jaw that she had inherited from Bobby Jo and had already cost them more than they could afford in orthodontist bills.

By nature, she was a secretive, watchful child, always economical in how she dispersed her rare hugs. Bobby Jo often wondered how Vicky could possibly be her daughter. She would have loved an affectionate, responsive child who laughed easily and gave her spontaneous kisses and confided in her. Sometimes she had the feeling that there'd been a mix-up at the hospital and she was harboring a changeling.

Which, of course, was absurd. Still, it was disconcerting to be talking to her neighbor, Iris Contanti, who was the wife of one of the pilots in Josh's squadron, and to look up into Vicky's unwavering and undeniably hostile stare. At such times, Bobby Jo always felt like slapping her—but of course she never did. Instead, she sent Vicky to her room or next door to play with a friend.

Bobby Jo wasn't sure what she would do without Iris, who was a native Californian from Los Angeles, and who had a whole repertoire of witty sayings and expressions that made Bobby Jo laugh. And she did need to laugh. Even when Josh was home, he wasn't good company, certainly not the fun he'd been while they were dating. Of course, as she reminded herself so often, it wasn't Josh's fault that he had a deadline on that correspondence course he'd been taking for the past year. It was important that he get his master's degree in management, what he called his "degree in military." From his sour tone, she knew it wasn't meant as a compliment. Still—it was either that or sign up for graduate school, which would mean he'd be away from his precious flying for several months.

Bobby Jo hated it when Josh was studying and she had to stay quiet, not even turning on the TV. She loved to watch old movies, which always seemed so much better than the newer ones. Deanna Durbin and Audrey Hepburn and Humphrey Bogart—those were real stars. And having to tiptoe around so as not to disturb Josh—it reminded her too much of Arizona, that first miserable year when she'd been pregnant with Vicky and Josh had been in flight training.

Even when Josh put his studies aside for an evening, he wanted to watch football on TV or invite someone from his squadron over, which meant fixing a big meal and listening to a lot of boring shop talk about F-15s and the newest X-planes at Edwards AFB.

At first, after he'd left on this current exercise, she'd tried to keep busy. She'd gone to wives' club meetings at the base with Iris, mainly because Josh had told her it was expected of her, and she'd even volunteered to be a Gray Lady at the base hospital, which was quite a sacrifice since she felt so uncomfortable around sick people. Also, she put in four hours a week at the thrift shop, where she rang up sales and helped unpack contributions. Sometimes she set aside a good buy for herself instead of putting it out on the shelves, which was officially frowned on but was something everybody did. Sort of a perk for working so hard and ruining her fingernails sorting through boxes of junk.

So her afternoons weren't too bad. It was the evenings that were such a drag, even when Josh was home. Oh, he still made love to her when he was in the mood, but even that wasn't the same, and she often felt as if she were a convenience instead of a living, breathing person. Not that he wasn't quick to notice her appearance, especially if she put on a pound or two. Well, what did he expect? She needed to get out of the house and do exciting things—go dancing, for instance. But no, he didn't have time for that, and when they did go to the club, it was more of the same, he and his buddies talk, talk, talking shop while she sat at a table with their wives, trying to find something they had in common to talk about.

More and more, she was sympathetic to Iris's way of dealing with boredom. When Iris's husband was home, she was the perfect wife, cooking up a storm and being a good hostess and playing the game. But when Jimbo was on a training exercise or on TDY for a few months, she didn't let it slow her down. She went out and had a good time.

A lot of the women did. They went to bingo night at the club, then stayed on to dance with young unattached officers, mostly transient pilots from other bases. No harm in it, Iris said. She had tried several times to get Bobby Jo to go along, but of course Josh would never put up with that.

Once she had said something about going to the club with Iris while he was gone, and he'd ordered her, loud and clear, to stay away from the club because it was a good way to get a bad reputation. He didn't like Iris, never wanted to invite the Contantis over when he was home, even though he and Jimbo

Contanti were good friends on the job, both being in the same squadron. Sometimes she just didn't understand him. After all, Iris was good company—and she was always so careful what she said around Josh.

The next morning she had repeated the conversation to Iris. They were having coffee and danish together as they often did, and Iris hadn't even bothered to change out of her robe before she'd slipped across the street to ring Bobby Jo's doorbell.

"You don't believe that crap about getting a bad name, do you?" Iris said, tossing her long dark hair. Iris took very good care of herself and spent a lot of money at the base beauty shop on perms and facials and manicures. "You can bet the guys have *their* fun when they're away from the base. There's groupies everywhere, just itching to keep the flyboys happy— and there's all those unattached nurses and female officers who live in the BOQs, too. Most of them are promiscuous as hell."

Bobby Jo didn't like disagreeing with Iris, but she knew she couldn't let that one pass. "I don't believe that. My best friend is a senior at the academy, and she wouldn't even look at a married man."

"You're so naive sometimes, Bobby Jo. Even if they don't chase married men, how do they know who's married or who's single? The guys can tell them anything when they're away from home—and they do."

"Josh isn't like that. He doesn't run around on me," Bobby Jo said.

Iris gave her a long, measuring look. To Bobby Jo's relief, she returned to the subject that had started it all. "There's no harm in going to the club without Josh. After all, the air force is one big extended family, right? Isn't that what the CO's wife is always saying?"

Bobby Jo giggled. "She *is* pretty gung-ho at times. But counseling junior wives is part of being a commander's wife, isn't it? And she's really pretty nice."

"Well, she makes me sick. Who does she think she is? She came out of some small town in Texas, I hear—and so did that stick she's married to."

Bobby Jo, aware of her own small-town background, was silent. One thing about Iris that she didn't like was the way she put people in categories. Her father was "in the market," which Bobby Jo had learned meant he was a stockbroker. The home she'd been raised in, as Iris often pointed out, would make twenty of the crackerboxes the air force provided junior officers—when they provided them at all.

"It's the preacher's kid in you that keeps you from having a good time," Iris went on. "We don't have to go to the club, you know. There's a couple of places in town where unescorted women can go to dance, and no one's the worse for it." She laughed suddenly. "Last week, Millie and I went to that place where the men do a strip. One of the strippers was a real hunk. He really came on to me. I played along with him, but of course I didn't meet him later like he wanted."

Bobby Jo shivered. "Josh would kill me if I went to a place like that."

"Well, if our guys keep going off on those lousy exercises, you may change your mind. It would serve Josh right. He doesn't worry about you, does he? As long as you're neatly tucked away while he's gone, what does he care? He won't even let you go to work—not that a job appeals to me. Let the men earn the bread, I say."

"Josh is old-fashioned about some things. He says it doesn't look good for an officer's wife to work."

"Garbage. That's not true anymore. Everybody knows you can't hardly make it on a junior officer's salary even if your husband draws flight pay. Maybe when he has enough rank to land a command slot, he'll need a full-time wife, but who cares if a junior officer's wife works as long as she doesn't do something grubby, like being a cocktail waitress?"

Bobby Jo decided it was time to divert her friend or she would go on for hours, talking about what was wrong with the air force. She asked what Iris was going to wear to the Officers' Wives Club luncheon the next day, which launched Iris on a long tale about the bargain she'd found at this little dress shop in Victorville, of all places. Later, when Iris took herself off, Bobby Jo cleaned up the breakfast dishes, then turned on the TV and settled down to watch her favorite soap. But today's episode didn't hold her attention, and finally she turned it off.

Feeling restless and bored, she wandered into Vicky's room. Her daughter was sitting in her pint-sized rocker, rocking her favorite stuffed toy, a koala bear that Josh had brought back from a trip to Australia. When she saw her mother, she stopped rocking and gave her a wary look.

"What you doing, sweetie?" Bobby Jo said, determinedly cheerful.

"Don't call me that, Mommy. It sounds so silly."

"Sweetie? Why, everybody says that."

"No, they don't. You talk so funny—Bonnie's mother told her you were a—an Ozark hillbilly, she called you."

Although her words seemed guileless, her expression gave her away. She's been planning this, Bobby Jo thought, hurt and also very angry. She wanted to grab Vicky and give her a hard shake. Why was her own daughter so hateful to her? Was it some lack in her own nature? God knew she wanted the same kind of relationship with Vicky that she'd had with her own mother—warm and confiding and mutually admiring, even when they'd disagreed. But the only person Vicky really cared for was her father. She was always quoting him, acting as if it were Bobby Jo's fault that he wasn't home more.

Luckily, Vicky would be starting school in the fall. Surely, things would get better then. Maybe it was time to have another baby, and this time, maybe it would be a boy. She understood boys so much better than she did little girls. Boys were . . . well, affectionate and loving, not always looking at you with critical eyes.

After she left Vicky, Bobby Jo threw herself into the task of relining the kitchen cabinets with paper, and somehow she got through the day. She went to bed early, was already asleep when the phone rang. She was tempted not to answer it, but of course she had no choice. Pilots' wives answered the phone even when they knew it might ruin their sleep for the rest of the night—or for the rest of their lives.

It was Josh's voice that answered her sleepy "Hello?"

"Hi, wife. I just called to say that I won't be home for another month. Someone messed up, and the old man is really pissed off. So now we have to go through the exercise again. Sorry about our anniversary dinner—but that's how it goes."

"Okay," Bobby Jo said.

There was a long silence. "What did you say?"

"I said okay."

"You sound funny. If you're sore about—look, it isn't my fault. My squadron got an excellent on that fucking exercise."

"I'm not sore. I *said* okay, didn't I? I'll see you in a month."

She hung up. A few minutes later the phone rang again, but this time she didn't answer it.

In the morning, after she'd had breakfast, she called Iris. "This is Bobby Jo," she said. "I've changed my mind—when did you say you were going to that dance place again?"

The Club—that was its only name—had once been a road-house, a truckers' hangout, Iris told Bobby Jo. But then the town had spread outward, surrounding it, and now, refurbished and enlarged, it catered to a younger, livelier crowd.

"Nobody cares if you don't have an escort," Iris assured her. "In fact, the management encourages single women because it brings in the men customers. You can have a few drinks, dance with the guys, and then go home alone. Nobody's going to hassle you. Of course, some of the women go there to pick up men, but that's their business."

Despite her friend's assurances, Bobby Jo hung back as they went inside, letting Iris precede her. The building was long and rectangular with a low ceiling. A country rock group was playing on a rustic-looking bandstand, and there were far more men than women, certainly at the dark, smoky bar they passed as they headed for an empty table at the edge of the dance floor.

As she looked around, Bobby Jo wondered if she was dressed appropriately. Some of the women wore jeans and tank tops, but others were dressed to the hilt in fancy cocktail dresses. Iris looked . . . well, she certainly didn't look as if she were going to the Officers Club for dinner. Her dress was tight and glittery and showed too much of her too skinny legs. In fact, Bobby Jo thought her friend looked a little like Ida Lupino in that old movie where she played a roadhouse owner.

The two of them were a strange combination because she had worn a conservative shirtwaist. In fact, she felt a little dowdy and wished she chosen something with more . . . well, pizzazz. What if no one asked her to dance? After all, she wasn't eighteen any longer. Maybe she was too fat, like Josh was always saying, since she'd picked up those extra ten pounds.

A few minutes later, the fear that she would be a wallflower was laid to rest. Her first partner was a rangy man who was dressed like a cowboy but who talked like one of the boys she'd dated at Colorado College. He said she was the best-looking chick in the place, that she really turned him on, compliments that she parried with a smile. She was having such a good time that she was sorry now she'd made the decision not to dance more than one set with the same man. Even so, when the music stopped, she refused another dance and returned to her table.

Her next partner was short, stocky, and dark-haired. He told her she had a great bod and how come he hadn't seen her there before? She wasn't sure she liked him, but his compliments were balm to her bruised ego. After all, when was the last time Josh had paid her a compliment?

Somewhere during the next three hours, she lost track of Iris, who had been dancing with a bearded man with bold, coal-black eyes. Several times, when Bobby Jo returned to the table between sets, she looked around for her friend, but since she was so busy dancing, she didn't have time to worry about it too much.

It was after midnight when she became seriously concerned about Iris's absence. For one thing, it was becoming increasingly hard to fend off the passes of her dance partners, most of whom hinted that they wanted her company for the whole night even though she made it plain that she wasn't that kind of person. Just when she was wondering how she would get home, Iris reappeared.

"Hi. Having a good time?" There was a feverish glitter in Iris's rather prominent eyes, and although she was wearing a fresh coat of lip gloss, her mouth had a blurred, undefined look, and her clothes looked a little wrinkled.

"Yes—but it's getting late. I told the baby-sitter I'd be home by twelve o'clock," Bobby Jo said.

"No sweat. We'll be home by one—who did you dance with?" Iris said easily. "Anyone special?"

"Not really—where were you? I looked all over for you."

"In the bar, talking to this friend of mine. I don't know how you missed us—we were sitting in one of the booths."

Bobby Jo started to tell her that she'd looked in the booths, but Iris was already heading for the door. On the way home, since Iris obviously didn't want to talk, Bobby Jo closed her eyes and rested her head against the back of her seat. When they reached home and she got out of the car, she still felt a little woozy from the drinks she'd had—and from the stuffy air in the roadhouse. Luckily, her baby-sitter, the teenaged daughter of a neighbor, didn't complain about her lateness, probably because Bobby Jo paid her double for the extra hour.

Bobby Jo slept late the next morning, awaking only when

she heard the blare of the TV in the living room, turned to cartoons. She sat up, her pounding head telling her that she was going to suffer for those extra drinks she'd had. She added them up and was shocked to realize that she'd downed at least six over the course of the evening.

Well, that settled it. No more nights out on the town for her. Not only because she'd drank too much, but because there'd been too many uncomfortable moments—like when that bushy-haired man had gotten so mad because she'd refused to go out to his car with him. Only the intervention of one of the bartenders had saved her from a nasty incident, and the whole episode had left a bad taste in her mouth. She loved to dance— but why did men have to be so stupid?

She told Iris her decision over coffee that afternoon. "It isn't that I didn't enjoy myself," she said. "It's just that going out without Josh makes me uncomfortable. If it was only dancing, I'd love it—but the men at that place come on too strong for me."

"If you say so—it was just that I thought you could handle it. So how about going to the club on bingo night? A bunch of us usually go. Surely Josh couldn't object to that. Safety in numbers, right?"

"If a whole bunch of you are going, maybe it would be okay," Bobby Jo said. She thought bingo was a bore, but at least it would get her out of the house. The way it was, sometimes she thought she'd go stir crazy.

"After bingo, we usually stay on for a round of drinks, and if someone asks us to dance and they don't have two heads, we go ahead and dance. Why not? Who could object?"

Josh could, Bobby Jo thought. "Okay, I'll go with you next time," she said.

Iris's mouth curved into a smile, and Bobby Jo was suddenly reminded of something her mother had once said to her. "Be careful of anyone whose face isn't improved by their smile."

"Now you're talking. You need to get out more—and it's all perfectly harmless. Besides, I need an alibi. Jimbo is really into the jealous-husband thing these days. Seems he called a couple of nights, checking up on me, and both times I happened to be out. If he knew I was with you . . . say, playing bingo, it would cool things down. It's okay for him and Josh to fool around when they're on TDY, but we're expected to sit home and vegetate."

A sickness rose in Bobby Jo's throat. It was a while before she said, "What do you mean about Josh fooling around?"

"Did I say that? I'm sorry—just a slip of the tongue."

"It wasn't a slip of the tongue, Iris. What are you trying to say?"

"I think we'd better drop this before it gets too heavy."

"It's already too late. What did you mean?"

Iris made a production of stirring sugar into her already oversugared coffee. "Okay—I might as well tell you," she said finally. "Josh has the reputation for being . . . well, when the guys in the outfit call him Josh the Stick, they aren't talking about how he pilots an F-15."

"I don't believe you," Bobby Jo said, her voice flat.

"Look, kid, that's the way things are with flyers. Fighter pilots attract women, and there's nothing we wives can do about it. I'm sure old Jimbo takes a roll in the hay with some chick every time he gets the chance. Which is why I don't feel guilty about having a little fun of my own. Of course," she added quickly, "I don't sleep around. I just like to get out of the house, have a few drinks and some laughs—you know?"

Bobby Jo felt as if she'd been blind and now had gained her sight. She wondered what she had ever seen in Iris, who had deliberately made that slip about Josh just as Vicky had deliberately let her know what her friend Bonnie's mother thought of her Arkansas accent.

But why? What was there about her that brought out the cat in Iris—and even in her own daughter? She herself was seldom catty. In fact, she usually changed the subject when the back-biting started. Was *that* her sin? Did she give the impression that she thought she was better than other women because she didn't gossip and tear other people apart?

"Hey, Bobby Jo, I didn't mean to upset you," Iris said, and the concern in her voice seemed genuine. "Look, don't pay any attention to me. I'm sure it's Josh's old academy nickname that gives the guys the wrong impression. The girls make a fuss over him because he's good-looking, so the guys assume he's sleeping around. I've never heard anything specific, you understand—and I should learn to keep my damned mouth shut."

She went on talking, and because Bobby Jo wanted so desperately to believe her, she finally let herself be persuaded that it was because of Josh's nickname and his bedroom eyes—and maybe a big dose of male jealousy—that the guys in his outfit thought he was running around on her.

CHAPTER
✦ 31 ✦

Two evenings later, Bobby Jo went to bingo night at the Officers Club at George AFB with Iris and two other wives. Afterward, they stayed on to have a nightcap. As she looked around the crowded room, Bobby Jo was relieved to see only a few couples that she knew by sight. She reflected that this was probably because Josh's whole wing had gone to Alaska for the exercise.

When a dark-haired man with a smile that reminded her of Josh stopped by their table to talk to Iris, her friend introduced him as Deke Picon.

"This is my friend, Bobby Jo," Iris said. "Her husband's in Jimbo's outfit. They're on that exercise in Alaska, and since she was climbing the walls, I talked her into coming along tonight."

As the man smiled at her, Bobby Jo decided he was very attractive. She'd always liked men whose eyes crinkled up when they smiled. When he asked her to dance, she accepted, and while they danced, he told her he was new to the base, just having come back from a tour in Saudi Arabia. "Where the wild Arabs roam," he said.

Bobby Jo laughed and found that she was really enjoying herself, but even so, after they'd danced once more, she told him she had to leave, that her baby-sitter was expecting her back by twelve o'clock. When he asked for her phone number, she reminded him that she was married, and he took the rebuff good-naturedly, saying it just wasn't his lucky day. Because he'd acted like a gentleman, her voice was warm as she told him she'd enjoyed dancing with him—and maybe they'd run into each other again sometime.

When she returned to her table, Iris and the other two women weren't ready to leave. Rather than sit alone at the table, she danced with a captain she knew slightly and even let him buy her another drink. After that, the evening seemed to blur pleasantly. The after-dinner crowd was thinning out when Iris, who had been dancing with a young major, came back to the table, the major at her elbow.

"How'd you like to go nightclubbing, Bobby Jo?" she said. "Johnny's with a friend who's dying to meet you. There's this great floor show at the Victory Club. The last show starts at midnight, so we'd be home by two."

"I can't—I promised my baby-sitter I wouldn't be later than midnight," Bobby Jo said quickly.

"Little Miss Cinderella," Iris said to the man, who laughed and whispered something in her ear. "Sorry, Johnny—maybe next time. I did promise to get her home by twelve."

The man shrugged, gave both of them a mock salute, and sauntered off. Iris looked a little disgruntled as she gathered up her purse and jacket, but her voice was pleasant when she asked Bobby Jo if she'd had a good time.

"Yes, I really did," Bobby Jo said.

"How did you and Deke get along?"

"He's nice. We danced twice."

"Only twice?"

"I told him two dances with the same man was enough for an old married woman."

"And of course you had other guys standing in line, just dying to dance with you."

"I don't know what you mean."

"Oh, come on. Did you ever, in your whole life, have to sit out even one dance?"

Bobby Jo gave her an uncertain look. Was Iris being catty? She was glad that they had arrived at Iris's car so she didn't have to answer.

The next week she went to the club again, this time with Iris and the wife of a pilot who said she was about to go crazy shut up with two squalling kids twenty-four hours a day. Bobby Jo looked around during bingo and recognized several other wives from Josh's outfit. Obviously it was accepted that wives use the club facilities when their husbands were TDY. When Josh came home, she would have it out with him. She'd be diplomatic, of course, because she hated his long, cold silences even more than she hated his bursts of temper.

But when Josh came home two weeks later, he was in such a foul mood that she knew it was the wrong time to approach him. Since he hadn't had a chance to work on his management course and the deadline was fast approaching, he came home after work, ate dinner, then went to his desk to study until late. When he finally came to bed, he immediately fell asleep, leaving Bobby Jo disappointed and frustrated. When she found herself wishing that he would go TDY again, she felt guilty and put forth an extra effort to have his favorite meals waiting on the table for him when he came home.

In the end, she decided not to rock the boat by telling him that she'd been going to the Officers Club while he was away. Since he never brought the subject up, she was sure no one had mentioned seeing her there. She was especially glad when he finally finished the study project he'd been working on and announced that he was taking her out to dinner.

On the way home that evening, he reached over and gave her knee a squeeze. "You've been a good sport, Bobby Jo. Sorry I haven't been much company for you lately."

Bobby Jo's eyes filled with tears. When Josh was like this, all was right with her world. They made love that night and the old magic was back, and she was sure that everything would be the same again. She had missed sex, missed the closeness, the physical contact, the feeling of being wanted and needed by Josh. Not that he was one for talking after sex, but he always told her she was fantastic in bed before he fell asleep, didn't he? Which was why she wasn't going to even *think* about what Iris had said about his being unfaithful. After all, Iris had admitted that she'd let her tongue get away from her.

During the next few weeks, things were so normal that sometimes Bobby Jo wanted to pinch herself. With his current crop of lessons behind him, Josh had more time for her. She didn't even mind how Vicky ignored her while vying for Josh's attention. In a way, she understood how Vicky felt. It was only when Vicky started sassing her that she finally lost her temper and restricted her to her room for the rest of the day.

"You're a bad mommy," Vicky yelled. "You're nothing but a tramp."

Bobby Jo reached her in three short steps and gave her a hard shake. "You're never, never, to say that to me again, do you hear?" she said fiercely.

Vicky looked frightened. "You're hurting me, Mommy," she whimpered.

"Where did you hear that word?"

"From Bonnie. She says it all the time about her mother. Is it a bad word?"

"You know it is or you wouldn't have used it," Bobby Jo said, her tone short. "From now on, I don't want you playing with her, you hear?"

"But she's my best friend—"

"She isn't really your friend. She's too old for you—and besides, she's always making fun of you and putting you down. You'll make some real friends when you start to school."

That night she talked to Josh about sending Vicky to nursery school for the rest of the summer. "She needs to play with other kids her own age," she said.

"What about that little girl—what's her name? The one she plays with all the time?"

"I don't like Bonnie's influence on Vicky."

"Well, do what you think is best."

Bobby Jo bit her lip, irritated by the indifference in his voice. It didn't seem fair that while Vicky adored her father and put him on a pedestal, he so often ignored her.

Two months later, Josh was ordered to report in at Maxwell AFB to attend Squadron Officers School. Although she knew that SOS was a necessary part of his training, Bobby Jo found herself resenting his cheerfulness as Josh handed her a list of clothes and toiletries he wanted her to pack.

After he had gone off to have the car serviced, she choked back her resentment and resolved that she wouldn't raise a fuss because Josh had decided it would be too expensive for Vicky and her to accompany him to Alabama, even though it was permitted. Well, she'd keep busy while he was gone, and one of the first things she intended to do was clean out Josh's closet because he'd been complaining that he couldn't stuff any more clothes into it.

It was true that his closet was packed full of clothes, but then it was twice the size of the one in the guestroom that she used. He needed more space because he had two separate wardrobes, one military and the other civilian, but it would help if he would throw something away once in a while.

Also, he just plain bought more clothes than she did—so why was he always griping about the bills? She hadn't bought a new dress in over six months—and yet he'd returned from that trip to Hong Kong in January with three new suits, bragging about all the money he'd saved.

It was the same with sports equipment. He had golf clubs, tennis rackets, a bowling ball, fishing and skiing gear, the best the BX offered, all of which he seldom used. And yet, when she'd asked him to go through his clothes and sports equipment for donations to the officers' wives' white elephant sale, he'd told her that there wasn't anything he wanted to get rid of.

Josh the Pack Rat—that's what the guys should call him instead of Josh the Stick. Some of his clothes dated from his high school days, including that old corduroy jacket he had on his list to take to Maxwell with him. Well, she could understand that. It was warm and comfortable, and even in Alabama it would probably be cool at night, but why would he also need three sport jackets and half a dozen shirts just to hang around the Maxwell Officers Club or attend keg parties on the BOQ lawn?

She started down the list he'd given her, packing away the items in his luggage. The corduroy jacket was in the back of his closet, crushed between two tweed sport jackets. After she'd extracted it, she gave it a hard shaking to get out the wrinkles. There was a spot on one lapel that looked like a coffee stain, but since there wasn't time to send it to the cleaners, she decided to use a spot remover. If she had her druthers, she would pitch the jacket out—but then Josh would have a fit.

She went through the pockets, looking for handkerchiefs. It never seemed to occur to Josh to unload them into the clothes hamper when he took off his clothes. She was removing one from a side pocket when his car keys fell onto the floor. So that's where they'd been all this time—he'd looked all over for them, and then he'd accused her of borrowing them and losing them. Well, she was going to enjoy producing them when Josh got home and telling him where she'd found them. Maybe then he wouldn't assume that it was her fault every time something got lost around the house.

She thrust her hand into the other front pocket, and her

fingers touched paper. She drew out a piece of blue stationery, scented with a floral perfume. A letter from Josh's mom, she thought. He seldom shared them with her—not that she minded. The way Mrs. Springer referred to her as "your wife," never by her name, was enough to make her blood boil. Of course Josh was Mrs. Springer's only son, and it was natural that she'd think of his wife as a rival. Well, she'd made it her business never to say a word against her mother-in-law and to write her regularly, even though Mrs. Springer never wrote back. No, Josh couldn't fault her for the way she treated his mother.

Idly, she unfolded the letter. She read the first line, and the blood drained from her head. She had to sit down hard on the edge of the bed because her legs had given out on her. When the dizziness passed, she picked up the letter, which had fallen to the floor, and read it through from beginning to end.

Hi, lover! Surprise, surprise! I tucked this in your pocket because I wanted to tell you again how great you were last night. Wow! You're some kind of stickman, just like the guys say. My toes are still curled into knots! Here's my phone number in case you've lost it. Give me a ring the next time you're out this way. Better call after six because that's when I get home from work. Love ya! Maxine.

Bobby Jo crushed the letter in her hand as if it were a snake that she was squeezing to death. She was so sure she was going to vomit that she made a dash for the bathroom, only to discover that the sickness was in her mind. As she sat on the edge of the bathtub, she tried to bring order to her chaotic thoughts. This Maxine—was she one of those groupies Iris had told her about? God, Iris had been right, so right. Josh had been cheating on her all along.

Josh the Stick. . . .

An obscene image, of a man and woman writhing on a strange bed, flashed through her mind. Although she was alone, her face felt hot suddenly and she buried it in her hands. How many women had Josh slept with since their marriage? His reputation for being a stud was obviously true because the woman who'd written the letter had wanted more. Since she seemed to know very little about him, it must have been a one-night stand. Did that make it worse—or better? Did it matter at all?

Bobby Jo rose and stood in front of the bathroom mirror, trying to see herself with objective eyes. This was how a woman looked when she'd just discovered that her husband had been cheating on her. Her eyes had a wounded look, but aside from that, she was much the same as she'd been the day she'd first met Josh. So why wasn't she enough for him? Where had she failed him? No matter how tired she was, she always opened her legs to him and never made excuses about having a head-ache, not even when she really did. Was it too much to ask that he be faithful to her? After all, she did without sex when he was away, too—and it was hard on her sometimes, really hard. So why did he do it? Was it the novelty, the chase? Did everybody in Josh's outfit, including the wives, know that he cheated on his wife?

God—what a bloody fool she'd been! And what did she do now? At the moment, she wanted to crawl into bed with a bottle of vodka and drink herself to oblivion. She wanted to go home—only there wasn't any room for her at home. Her father was stationed in Germany now, and her mother was always complaining that their quarters were too small, even though two of the boys were away at school. What's more, she wouldn't be welcome, not if they knew she had left Josh for good. Her parents believed that marriage was for life, that you stuck to your spouse through thick and thin. Besides, she couldn't run home with her tail between her legs. She'd be too ashamed.

If she left Josh and tried to make it on her own, how could she support herself—and Vicky? She had no job skills, no work experience. And yet—how could she stay with him, knowing what she did? How could she pretend that everything was normal? Josh would be home in a little while. As soon as he saw her face, he would know something was wrong. She couldn't face him—what kind of a woman was she that she couldn't even keep her own husband from straying?

Moving stiffly, as if she'd suddenly aged a dozen years, she washed her face in cold water, then rubbed it briskly with a towel to restore its usual high color. But she couldn't erase the pain, the soul sickness she felt, and she was sure that it would be with her always, that her world would never be right again.

* * *

Bobby Jo was waiting for Josh when he came home from having the car serviced. She had sent Vicky across the street after asking Iris if she'd take care of her because she had something to talk over privately with Josh. Although Iris must have been dying with curiosity, she only said, "Why not? But you've got that wrong. That little gal is five going on forty-five. She should be baby-sitting *me*."

When Josh came in, he looked around the kitchen with a frown. "I hope you aren't planning on eating out tonight," he grumbled. "I have to be at the terminal early tomorrow morning—remember?"

"Sit down, Josh," Bobby Jo said.

"If you've got some beef, this is a helluva a time to start anything."

Bobby Jo laid the letter on the table. "I found this in your corduroy jacket."

Josh picked up the piece of blue stationery. He read the first line and his face darkened. Not to her surprise, he attacked first.

"What the hell were you doing snooping through my things?" he demanded.

"I was looking for dirty handkerchiefs," she told him. "And it won't work, trying to make me feel guilty when you're the one who's done something wrong."

"What the hell is this? An inquisition?"

"Who is she?" She gave the letter a contemptuous look. "How long have you been screwing her?"

"Now that really sounds cool. Be sure to say it loud enough so Vicky can hear it."

"Vicky isn't here—and what would *you* call it? Making love?"

"Look, I don't need this. Even you aren't dumb enough to think I'm going to stay celibate when I'm out there for weeks at a time, working my butt off. It doesn't mean a damned thing, hasn't anything to do with you. Hell, I'm human—I need the release. So okay, I take advantage of what's being offered, but I come back home to you, don't I?"

Bobby Jo wanted to hurt him, wanted to pick up something and hit him, wanted to scratch and scream and call him every name in the book. Instead, to her shame, she burst into tears for the simple reason that she knew he was sincere, that he really believed he was justified in breaking their marriage vows.

He wasn't even going to apologize or promise not to do it again. In fact, he sounded aggrieved, as if she were the one who was being unfair.

Holding her hands over her face, she turned and ran from the kitchen and down the hall to their bedroom. Before she threw herself on the bed, she locked the door behind her.

Through the door, Josh pleaded with her to come out, promised that he would sit down and talk to her without yelling. When she didn't answer him, his tone changed and he told her to grow up, for Christ's sake, and start acting like an adult. But she only lay there, too sunk in misery to cry now, and in the end, he shouted that there was no reasoning with her, that he was taking his flight bag with him and would spend the night in the transient BOQ, that maybe when he returned from Maxwell, she would be ready to listen.

Bobby Jo was off the bed by the time the outside door slammed. By the time she had reached it, Josh's car was already moving down the street, going very fast. She stood in the doorway, not caring if the neighbors saw her tearstained face.

Was this the end of their marriage? Could she ever forgive him? If she was still here when he got back, she knew that he wouldn't change. Their marriage would continue on his terms, just as everything in their relationship had always been on Josh's terms. He would expect her to stay home, be the dutiful wife, while he was free to do anything he wanted. He could also expect her to keep her mouth shut and ask no questions, complain about nothing.

On the other hand, if she left him—how would she live? She had no idea how to look for a job, much less hold one down. And then there was Vicky—she didn't doubt for a minute that Vicky would want to stay with her father. She would never understand why her mother had left him.

And what about the rage trapped inside her that made her feel as if she would explode any minute? How could she get rid of the rage now that Josh was gone?

CHAPTER
✦ 32 ✦

ALTHOUGH THE DAYS FOLLOWING JOSH'S DEPARTURE FOR Squadron Officers School were stifling hot with summer heat, Bobby Jo often felt cold, as if her body had been invaded by a permanent frost. She told herself she was catching the flu that was currently making the rounds, but she knew in her heart that it was a malady of another kind, a sickness caused by Josh's betrayal of their marriage vows.

She had expected Josh to call before he took off the morning after their quarrel, but the hour of his ETD passed and there was no message. On top of everything else, she had to placate Vicky, who blamed her mother because her father had left without saying good-bye. Since she knew that this time Vicky's accusations were true, Bobby Jo was patient as she explained that since Josh had left so early in the morning, he'd decided to sleep on the flight line that night.

Vicky didn't believe her, which wasn't surprising since Bobby Jo was a poor liar at best. Vacillating, as she did, between longing for Josh and anger, she got through the next few days without falling apart at the seams. But the tension inside her, having no outlet, built until she was sure her blood pressure must be sky high.

For one of the few times in her life, she lost her appetite, and her clothes were soon so loose that she had to use a safety pin to keep her jeans and skirts from slipping down on her hips. Her hair needed a perm and her nails were a disaster and her skin had a waxy, too white look because her tan had faded and she was too apathetic to renew it. Her eyes, without the makeup she usually applied as soon as she got out of bed in the morning, had a bald, unfinished look that made her avoid her mirror.

It was Iris who finally coaxed her out of the house. When she insisted that Bobby Jo and Vicky go with her to the base theater to see a movie matinee, Bobby Jo agreed, but only after her neighbor promised not to ask her any questions. The movie was a comedy, and it made Bobby Jo laugh, which surprised her, and on the way home she discovered that some of her depression had lifted—until Iris told her bluntly how terrible she looked.

"You need some action," her friend said. "Why don't you come along with me and Martha tonight? We're going to that male strip place I told you about. It's all perfectly harmless, so do say *yes*. You know you're just dying to go."

Bobby Jo wasn't dying to go. The whole idea of men stripping in front of women turned her off. But the thought of spending another evening watching television and listening to Vicky's whining about her father was suddenly unbearable. Before she really had time to think it through, she found herself asking what she should wear.

There were four of them, all wives of junior officers. One of the women, a few years older than the others, who was married to a Special Services captain, freely admitted that she'd stretched the truth and let her husband think she was going to a Tupperware party.

"What he doesn't know won't hurt him," she said blithely. "And I'm dying to see if those jackasses look as ridiculous as the women strippers in Las Vegas do."

Privately, an hour later, Bobby Jo thought it was the women in the audience who looked ridiculous. As they screamed their approval of the men strippers, egging them on to show more skin, she cringed in her seat. It surprised her that so many of the audience were middle-aged and even older. Or maybe it wasn't such a surprise at that. To quote Iris, who was always so quick to analyze other people's motives, most of them were here for revenge on their own men for ogling centerfolds and patronizing strip joints.

When one particularly boisterous woman rushed up to the stage, the tip of a dollar bill showing in her cleavage, and invited the current stripper to retrieve it, Bobby Jo looked away, embarrassed for the woman. Iris poked her in the ribs. "Relax—it's all in fun."

Feeling gauche, Bobby Jo forced herself to watch, and as a new stripper, very virile in a swarthy-skinned, dark-eyed way, strutted around the stage, flexing his muscles and rolling his hips, she felt a familiar warmth invading her loins. Afraid that the others would guess her reaction, she murmured something about going to the john and slipped away, determined to wait out the rest of the program in the ladies' room.

Iris followed her there a few minutes later. "Hey, this just isn't your thing, is it? What say we split? Since we came in two cars, it won't inconvenience Sharon and Martha. We can stop at the club for a good-night drink—when was the last time we had a real heart-to-heart?"

"Too long," Bobby Jo said, smiling. It was true that she'd been avoiding Iris—but right now, her reasons didn't seem valid. After all, Iris had enough sensitivity to see how the whole scene outside embarrassed her—and why should she feel apologetic, anyway?

Half an hour later, they were sitting at the bar in the Officers Club, sipping Gibsons. Around them, voices rose and fell, and the music from the dance floor was soothing and unobtrusive. Iris was putting herself out to be funny, and Bobby Jo felt a wave of gratitude for her friend and was ashamed that she'd made the decision to drop Iris.

"Well, well—the two prettiest ladies at George. This has to be my lucky day."

Bobby Jo looked up into a familiar face. She groped for a name, came up with Deke—Deke Something-or-other, the man Iris had introduced her to a few months earlier. When Iris asked him to join them, she moved over automatically, and he slid onto the barstool next to hers. His smile was as warm as she remembered—it transformed a rather ordinary face into a very attractive one.

For the next hour, she listened as Iris and the man exchanged banter. Iris was good at it—she and Josh would make a good pair, Bobby Jo thought. Why was it they didn't like each other when they were so much alike?

She was puzzling over the question when Deke turned to her. "Haven't seen you around. You been away?"

"No—just under the weather a little with the flu," she said.

"Sorry. You don't look as if you've been sick. In fact, you look great." His gaze was so admiring that Bobby Jo flushed with pleasure. It had been so long since she'd felt pretty— funny what one compliment from an attractive man could do for a woman's ego.

"Bobby Jo always looks great," Iris said, shaking her head. "When she gets out of bed in the morning with her hair standing on end, she still looks great. If she wasn't such a good friend, I'd be jealous as hell!"

Bobby Jo expected Deke to tell Iris that she had no reason to be jealous of anyone, but instead he said, half under his breath, "Yeah, I can see why you're jealous."

The compliment aroused an echo in her mind. Josh used to compliment her like that—but that was years ago, and so much had changed since then. Sometimes she got the feeling that he didn't see her at all these days—and yet he was her mirror, her image of herself was what she saw reflected in his eyes.

Unexpectedly her eyes filled with tears, and she looked away from Deke, afraid he might guess how seldom anyone told her she was pretty these days. When the waiter brought her another Gibson, she drank it thirstily, the tartness easing her dry throat. Feeling more at ease, she listened as Iris told Deke a comical story about her PCS move from Castle AFB to Victorville. When Deke drew Bobby Jo into the conversation by asking what her worst moving experience had been, she told them how the packers in Arizona had wrapped their breakfast garbage and sent it to George AFB along with their dishes and silverware, and how, two weeks later, she finally discovered what was causing the foul odor in their shipment of household goods.

"That's a real horror story, Bobby Jo," Deke said, laughing at the face she made.

A phone call came for Iris as Deke had ordered them another round of drinks. She came back looking annoyed. "That was Jimbo. Would you believe that he sprained his wrist and has been grounded for the next month? He'll be landing in fifteen minutes—he got a hop on the shuttle. He wants me to pick him up at the air terminal."

Bobby Jo started to get up, but Iris stopped her with a gesture. "No need for you to go with me. I'm sure Deke will drive you home."

"I'd be honored—as long as you don't mind riding in a jalopy. I picked it up because I needed wheels to get around the base. I ordered a new Renault in France on the way home from Saudi Arabia, but the red tape has got it tied up somewhere."

Bobby Jo couldn't think of any good excuse to refuse his offer, although she felt uneasy about having the neighbors see a man bringing her home. Still—it wasn't all that late. And it was perfectly innocent, wasn't it?

During the ride to her neighborhood, Deke talked easily, as if they were old friends. They were deep in a discussion of a movie they'd both seen and liked when they pulled up in front of her house. Bobby Jo hesitated, then on impulse asked if he'd like to come in for a cup of coffee. Deke accepted so quickly that she thought it prudent to add that she hoped her daughter hadn't talked the baby-sitter into letting her watch anything scary on television because it gave Vicky nightmares, thus letting him know that they wouldn't be alone in the house.

She paid her yawning baby-sitter, then stood at the doorway watching until the teenager had crossed the street and disappeared into her own house. When she returned to the living room, Deke had already made himself comfortable on the sofa.

"How old is your daughter?" he asked.

"Five. Iris says she's five going on forty-five, and I'm afraid she's right. Vicky has her father's brains."

"And your good looks?"

Bobby Jo hesitated, not sure how to answer. "She has beautiful brown hair and eyes—like her father," she said finally.

She went into the kitchen and plugged in the coffee maker, then set out cream and sugar and, after a moment's thought, a plateful of cookies. A little domesticity was in order, just in case Deke got the wrong idea, she thought, pleased with herself because she was handling the situation well.

But the precaution wasn't needed because Deke's conduct was impeccable. They talked about movies for a while, then he asked Bobby Jo where in the South she was from. She liked it that he didn't crack a joke when she admitted she was the daughter of a minister.

"I lost my father when I was three, and I didn't get along with my stepfather," he told her.

She listened as he talked about his academy days. Although the years he'd been there overlapped Josh's by two years, he knew her husband only by reputation, he told Bobby Jo. Before she could question him further, he changed the subject and asked where she'd gone to college. She told him Colorado College and didn't add that she hadn't graduated.

The conversation was so impersonal that when he moved closer, put his hands on her shoulders, and gave her a quick kiss, it took her totally by surprise and she was too stunned to pull away.

"Sorry—I just couldn't resist. I've been wanting to do that all evening. And I'd better leave before I disgrace myself and do it again."

He was gone so quickly that it wasn't until he was out the door that she realized she hadn't said one word to him after the kiss, not even "good-bye." What a strange man he was. But nice. Even though he had kissed her, a married woman, he'd apologized. It was obvious he knew she wasn't the kind to go in for any extramarital affairs.

Bobby Jo turned off the lights and went to bed, only to find that she couldn't sleep. She felt restless and keyed up—and despite herself, she kept reliving the moment when Deke's lips had touched hers so briefly. When she found herself wondering what making love to him would be like, she gave her pillow an angry thump, then got up and took a sleeping pill and went back to bed.

Josh's letter came three days later. He said he was sorry that he'd left in a huff and then added that he hoped she'd had time to think and would be more reasonable in the future and not expect him to be an angel. Although he must have written the letter to placate her because he went on to say that when he got back they'd take off for a few days in Carmel, a sort of second honeymoon, something cold and hurting inside Bobby Jo refused to be appeased.

She waited a week to answer the letter, and she didn't mention his apology or his offer of a second honeymoon. But she also didn't point out that they had yet to have a first honeymoon—unless he was talking about that hurried trip to see his mother before he'd reported in at Williams AFB for flight training. Instead, she wrote that Vicky had the sniffles and mentioned the unseasonable rain, which had cooled everything off and had also flooded out two sets of quarters on base. She told him about the trip the Officers' Wives Club was organizing for Disneyland and the San Diego Zoo that she was going to take Vicky on if she was over her cold by then. When she was finished, she read the letter over and knew it sounded stiff and unforgiving, but she folded it up and sealed it in an envelope anyway.

The phone rang as she was putting the letter out for the mailman. She recognized Deke's voice, and a strange sensation, an inner quivering, started up inside her chest.

"I thought you might like to take in a movie tomorrow evening," he said. "That new musical we were talking about is showing in Victorville this week."

Bobby Jo opened her mouth to tell him that she wasn't interested, so it was a shock when she heard her own voice asking what time the movie started.

"Seven o'clock—why don't we have a late dinner in town afterward?"

After she'd hung up Bobby Jo had second thoughts. What if someone saw her with Deke and told Josh? Of course, everybody she knew went to the base theater, which showed first-run movies for a fraction of off-base prices. It was very unlikely she would run into anyone she knew at a movie house in Victorville—and anyway, what could be more innocuous than taking in a movie with a casual acquaintance, even if he happened to be a man?

She had Deke pick her up in the parking lot of the branch library in her neighborhood, reasoning that if anyone who knew her saw her car parked there, they would think that she was at the library. When Deke opened his car door for her, she slid in quickly, feeling self-conscious, but within a few minutes she was laughing and talking and enjoying herself.

The movie was just as good as she'd hoped it would be. They rehashed it as they walked to the car, and while Deke told her he usually wasn't that interested in musicals, he had to admit that this one was pretty good.

The restaurant he took her to was surprisingly nice. She hadn't expected it to be so fancy, and she wished now that she'd worn a dress instead of a blouse and slacks. But Deke evidently didn't agree because he told her how great she looked with that blue blouse setting off her eyes and auburn hair. Bobby Jo basked in his praise. It might be a line, but it was nice to have someone sweet-talk her instead of complaining because she'd forgotten to make an entry in the checkbook again.

Deke ordered champagne. They finished off the bottle somewhere between the entree and dessert, and he ordered another and told her to drink up, that a little wine was what she needed to make her relax.

Everything got a little out of sync after that, but Bobby Jo she knew she was having a wonderful time because she couldn't seem to stop smiling. Which was why she agreed to go to a place Deke knew where they had a Dixieland band, despite the lateness of the hour. She liked dancing with him, although something seemed to be wrong with her feet tonight. Later, as he helped her into the front seat of his car, he drew her toward him. She expected a kiss, and when he only touched her cheek with his lips, she felt both reassured and disappointed.

As they drove along the highway, heading for home, she knew Deke was talking to her, asking her a question, but she was too sleepy to answer. She must have fallen asleep because the next thing she knew, he was helping her out of the car, guiding her through the dark. She thought she saw neon lights, but when she tried to focus her eyes, all she could make out were multicolored blurs. Deke stumbled, almost fell, and she giggled, then giggled again. She wanted to sing, only she knew she mustn't wake up the neighborhood. She put her finger to her lips and told Deke that they had to be quiet or they would wake up Vicky and then she would snitch and tell Josh that her mommy was out with a man.

"We don't have to worry about Vicky here," Deke said in her ear. "This place is very private—no one will bother us."

Bobby Jo clung to his arm, swaying a little, fascinated by the golden haze that filtered through her eyelashes. She decided that she liked the haze—and she liked Deke, too. Had she told him yet how much she liked him because he knew how to treat a woman?

She was aware that he was lifting her, carrying her, and she clung to his neck, humming one of the songs from the movie. When he put her on her feet and turned on a lamp, she stared around, surprised to discover that she wasn't in her own living room. In fact, it wasn't a living room at all. Through a shimmering mist, she saw a chest of drawers, an easy chair with wooden arms—and a very large bed with a gold-colored spread that looked as if it had been to the laundry too many times.

She realized Deke was lifting her again, and she started to tell him she could walk, for gosh sakes, only the words got away from her. She sank into softness, and now she was looking up at him, feeling very dizzy. His hands were fumbling at the front of her blouse, and she knew he was taking her clothes off, which seemed such a joke because wouldn't Josh be mad if he knew? Oh, it was all right for him to undress his floozies, but he wouldn't like it if he knew another man, even a nice one like Deke, was slipping her blouse over her head, unsnapping her bra, sliding her slacks down to her knees and over her feet.

The sheet beneath her felt very cold, and she was glad when Deke joined her on the bed and pulled her up against his warm body. He kissed her—a kiss so long and deep that she was afraid she would strangle. His lips moved to her throat, then to her breasts, and she felt so tingly all over that she put her arms around his neck so he wouldn't stop.

She knew that Deke was talking, asking her to do something, but his voice seemed so far away—and besides, she didn't want to move. Because if she did, maybe that wonderful feeling between her thighs would stop. She heard someone moaning, and she knew the sound must be coming from her own throat because Deke was talking again, his lips close to her ear.

"Don't pass out on me now, baby," he said, and she giggled, thinking how silly he was. Why would she pass out when all she'd had to drink was a little champagne and a couple of Gibsons? And besides, if she did, she would miss the best part of it, wouldn't she?

She didn't miss it because she didn't pass out. Although everything seemed to be happening in a thick fog now, she knew when Deke rolled her over on her back, when he crouched over her, touching her, fondling her, when his hoarse voice told her she had the most fantastic body he'd ever seen and he'd wanted to fuck her since the first time he'd seen her. She started to tell him that she didn't like that kind of dirty talk, but now he was doing something to her that sent little darts of hotness up and down her body. She felt him pressing against her, then moving inside her, faster and faster, and suddenly a pulsation, a throbbing encompassed her, wiping out everything else.

She heard Deke's voice, saying she was great, that he was so hot for her that in a few minutes he wanted an encore, but the mist was moving in fast now, and she sank into the spiraling darkness with a sigh of utter contentment.

* * *

It was when she awoke that regret came pouring in and she began to cry. Deke tried to console her. He told her that if he'd known she couldn't hold her liquor, he never would have ordered that second bottle of champagne. When she kept on crying, he put his arms around her, kissed the tears off on her cheek, and suddenly the excitement was back, full force. Deke's breathing took on a strident sound as he rained butterfly kisses on her breasts, her stomach, the sensitive flesh of her inner thighs. She was ashamed when she realized how quickly she'd become aroused, but it was too late to stop. This time, she understood the things he wanted her to do, and when she shook her head Deke took it with a shrug.

"Just feeling you out. Some will and some won't," he said philosophically.

He slipped under the sheet, his hands and mouth busy, and it was very exciting, lying there quietly on her back while he did things to her with his lips and tongue, things that Josh had stopped doing years ago. She was soon writhing under the rush of pleasure, begging him not to stop. Later, when he asked her to take him in her mouth, she didn't refuse. How could she when he'd satisfied her so completely and yet was still unsatisfied himself? When he groaned and told her again that she was fantastic, she felt a sense of power that she could bring him such pleasure just by doing something so easy.

Afterward, as she lay in Deke's arms, listening to his breathing, she wondered what was wrong with her. Why didn't she feel guilty and ashamed for allowing a man she'd only seen three times to have sex with her? Was she easy—a tramp like Vicky had called her? Of course, she'd let Josh make love to her on their very first date, but that had been love. Was this love, too? It had to be something more than casual sex, or she would never have given in so easily. If it wasn't love, would she feel so good right now?

The following week, she saw Deke almost every night. For the first time in her life, she was indifferent to what the neighbors thought, although she did invent a night-school course at the local junior college to explain her absence to her babysitter. Since she and Deke could only spend a few hours together, they didn't bother to go out to dinner first. She drove directly to the motel where Deke had taken her that first time, then drove herself home later. As eager for sex as Deke, Bobby Jo couldn't get enough. Once, she told him about Josh's unfaithfulness, and he laughed and said he'd wondered if Josh the Stick was still living up to his academy reputation.

"I don't know why he's making out with other women when he's got a hot little number like you at home," he added.

His words struck a wrong note. Deke must have felt her stiffen because he laughed and pulled her close. "Sorry, baby. I forgot that you like things said nice. What I should have said was that I think he's a fool to even look at another woman when he's got a sweet little gal like you waiting for him at home."

Bobby Jo laughed, but his words had jarred her. It was after that that she began to notice other things—such as how careful Deke was with his money. Once, he asked her if she could help out with the motel bill as he was a little short. Another time, he suggested that she bring the wine the next time because it was a real drag taking a side trip to the liquor store on base after work.

Bobby Jo noticed these things, but only in passing. A fever seemed to burn perpetually in her veins, a thirst that could be quenched only by Deke's lovemaking. She didn't let herself think of tomorrow. It was enough to live for each day. After all, there was plenty of time to talk about where they were heading. Josh had only been gone three months—and for now, it was enough to be with Deke almost every night, to have him make love to her.

Deke seldom called her at home because so often Vicky reached the phone first and then Deke had to pretend it was a wrong number. So she was surprised, three months after their first date, when she picked up the phone to hear Deke's voice.

"Look, baby, I've got to talk to you. I know this is Sunday and we aren't supposed to see each other until tomorrow, but something's come up. How about meeting me at the motel at the usual time?"

After Bobby Jo had hung up, she sat for a while, wondering what was wrong—and why he couldn't tell her over the phone. She also found herself reluctant, for the first time, to meet him. For one thing, she was so tired that she'd planned to get to bed early. Maybe she was belatedly coming down with the flu— or maybe this dragged-out feeling was simple lack of sleep. Also, she hadn't been eating right. Vicky was a fussy eater, and she had fallen into the habit of eating the things her daughter liked—peanut-butter sandwiches and milk, canned spaghetti and hot dogs—none of which seemed to agree with her lately.

Well, tomorrow she'd go to the base clinic and see if they wouldn't prescribe a tonic, but for now—she had to meet Deke. He had sounded so strange on the phone. Was it possible that he was coming to the same conclusion she had, that it was time to admit that what they had together was more than sex? How long did it take to get a divorce, anyway? This was California, so even if Josh fought it, she could be free in a few months. Vicky would be a problem—but then, when wasn't she? Somehow they would work out that part. Vicky was bound to love Deke once she'd met him. In so many ways, he was like Josh—how could Vicky help liking him?

Bobby Jo felt her spirits sag as soon as Deke opened the door to her knock. His face was pale, and although he kissed her, he quickly pulled away.

"What is it you want to talk to me about?" she asked.

"Sit down, Bobby Jo." Deke poured her a glass of wine and put it in her hand. From his breath, she knew that he'd been working on the bottle while he waited for her.

"Look, I have something to tell you—and it's something you aren't going to like," he began. "I thought we had more time, or I would've gone about this a different way and prepared you ahead of time. And I guess I might as well come right out with it. My wife's decided to give up her job in Albany and move out here with the kids."

"Your *wife*?"

"Look, you must have known I'm married. Iris and Jim were our next-door neighbors at Pease."

"She never told me anything about you—and why haven't you ever talked about your wife? How would I know you're married?"

"I never mentioned her because . . . well, it didn't seem diplomatic. And besides, what does it matter? After all, you're married, too. So don't put on that righteous act with me."

"I never lied to you," Bobby Jo said, her voice low.

"Okay—you've been square with me. And I'm going to be square with you. You don't know my old lady—she's jealous as hell. Now that she's given up that cushy job of hers, she's going to want her pound of flesh, and there's no way I can get away nights. So this has to be our good-bye meeting, Bobby Jo. One more night together and then it's all over. I'm going to miss you like hell, but I have to think of the kids. What other choice do I have?"

Bobby Jo stared at him, but she was seeing another image—her own. And it wasn't a pretty sight. Once again, she had let a man make a fool of her. When was she going to stop being a patsy?

Silently, she rose and picked up her purse. Deke started to speak, but something in her eyes must have warned him because he sat back down, his shoulders slumped. The last thing she saw before she went out the door was Deke taking another long swallow of wine directly from the bottle.

In a state of calm that she knew was unnatural, Bobby Jo went home, paid the baby-sitter, watched a late movie on TV until she finally fell asleep on the couch with the television screen still flickering.

The next day, when she awoke and was immediately so sick that she barely made it to the bathroom in time, she knew that fate had handed her a double whammy—like those two-handed gestures the kids in her hometown made when they wanted to show special contempt.

She was pregnant—and there was no way in the world that she was ever going to make Josh believe she was carrying his child.

CHAPTER

↑ 33 ↑

As Tai told her old roommate, Cassie, making a joke of something too complicated to talk about seriously, a funny thing had happened to her on the way to graduation.

"I think it's all that talk about honor and duty and loyalty, all of it somehow mixed up with flying, that finally got to me," she said ruefully. "And then there's Old Glory, running up and down the flagpole every morning and evening, and the bull sessions and the propaganda from the instructors. It's enough to turn anyone around, for God's sake. I stand there, day after day, with my chest stuck out and my gut sucked in, just itching to make our element the best in the group, our group the best in the squadron, our squadron the best damned one in the cadre. When that tinny old bugle plays taps at night, the notes echoing off Fairchild Hall, the shivers run up and down my spine and I'm ready to do my all for the grand old air force."

"I know what you mean—but what has that got to do with flying a plane? They also serve who man the desks, mine friend."

Tai gave Cassie a sheepish smile. "Some of it's those planes sitting over there on the academy landing field. They really get to me—like they're some kind of challenge, right? Dammit, they're only Cessnas, and something the sticks crack jokes about, but they did get to me. Right now, I'm practically frothing at the mouth, wanting to get my hands on the controls of

a T-37, wanting to see if I have the stuff to be a hot pilot—
and the only way I can find out is to take flight training."

"Even though it means you'll have to commit yourself to
an extra year of duty?" Cassie asked.

"So what's a year? Only that I'll be that much closer to
thirty before I finish my military obligation. I'll probably end
up kicking myself, but what the hell. Maybe pilot training will
come in handy later on when I turn civilian. Who knows? I
might want to pilot the corporate plane when I own my own
engineering firm."

"Uh-huh. Excuses, excuses." Cassie was lounging in Tai's
bleached-oak desk chair, her feet propped up. As far as Tai
could see, her irreverent sense of humor hadn't changed one
bit in the past four years—which was some kind of miracle in
the humorless halls of the academy.

"So go for it, Tai. Just don't forget one thing—the battle
of the sexes isn't over yet for you, not if you go into flight
training. If you perform as well as the men, it's still 'Hey, look
at the clever monkey!' and if you don't, then it's because you're
a woman, and didn't they always say that only the half of the
human race that has balls belongs in the cockpit of a plane?
Hell, even the word—*cockpit*—gives it away. You'll notice
they don't call them boobpits."

Tai grinned at her friend. "You're b-a-d, Cassie. Real bad.
What would your mother say if she heard that kind of language?"

"She'd flip. But don't worry. At home, I'm still little Miss
Goody Two Shoes."

"And everywhere else, too."

"Right. I go to church every Sunday—and I don't fool
around. Well, not much and then nothing heavy. Besides, now
that we're first degree, the choices for frat partners have really
narrowed down."

"You have the same friends you made four years ago," Tai
pointed out. "Our class is still a team."

"But who do our male teammates ask to the Hunter's Ball,
huh? The Barbie dolls from back home with their Princess Di
hairdos and their long white gloves."

"I don't envy those girls," Tai said, thinking of the gradual
change in Bobby Jo's letters. "I'd much rather be an officer
than be married to one."

"You'd better believe it. But it's still galling to see those jerks strutting around during June week, showing off their home-grown dollies."

Tai didn't really care whom the senior men cadets asked to June week activities, but she didn't say so because it might have sounded like sour grapes. "What's going to happen to us in the next few years, Cassie? Will we stay in touch after we get our commissions?"

"You and I will always be friends," Cassie said with certainty. "Even if we only see each other once every ten years, you'll always be my number-one bud."

Tai caught the wistfulness in her friend's voice. Yes, they were still best friends, but hadn't there been a small rift in their relationship since her decision to become a pilot? Cassie was content with her own career choice—management and personnel. Even so, Tai suspected that her friend felt out of it when bull-session talk turned to flying, the pros and cons of fighters over tankers or cargo carriers as a longtime career choice, the merits of the new long-range bomber currently being tested at Edwards, the endless wrangling and in-depth discussions and hot opinions about every aspect of flying.

Until Tai's conversion, she had felt the same way, that she could take or leave planes and/or flying. It had been an added bond between Cassie and her. Her own change of attitude had come on so gradually, so insidiously, that it had caught her completely by surprise. During her first couple of years at the academy, she'd never doubted that she could keep a proper distance between herself and flying, that she would continue to concentrate on things that would help her in her civilian career as an engineer. And yet—starting in her junior year, she had found herself thinking flying, talking flying, until she'd finally accepted the whole mystique.

Maybe, she thought now, it has something to do with Mac, who had been a frustrated pilot. If her father's education and his eyesight had permitted it, he would have been a pilot. Instead, he had been an aviation buff who could recite the specifications of every plane in the air force and who could identify any plane flying overhead by the sound of its engine. So maybe some of it had rubbed off on her. All she knew for sure was that when the time came to make the decision, she had to choose flight training.

As if Cassie was following her thoughts, her friend said, "I really hate it that we'll be splitting up after graduation. I'd sign

up for FT, too, but when the chips were down, I found I just
didn't have any desire to be a sky jockey. I'm perfectly content
to work behind a desk. So call me a shoe clerk."

Tai hadn't argued with her, although she'd hoped that Cassie
would share her year at flight school. This wish was renewed
a dozenfold a month later when she reported in at Williams
AFB and discovered that she would be one of only four women
in her flight.

There was Marta Tailor, a doe-eyed girl who hailed from
California and had a perpetual tan to prove it; Twyla Williams,
a black girl from Atlanta who had been in the same squadron
as Tai at the academy; and Janice Popadaris, who looked like
a female boxer and was a flaming women's libber.

Tai, who was half her size, hadn't been intimidated by
Janice's belligerence at the academy, although most of the other
women cadets—and even some of the men cadets—had been.
When they reported in at Williams, Tai arrived first and took
the bunk nearest the window because she was a fresh-air addict.
When Janice, swaggering and aggressive, arrived, she decided
she wanted the same bunk. Tai told her to back off, and because
of Tai's reputation as a martial arts expert, Janice had let it
drop.

Later, to Tai's relief, Janice contrived to get her room
changed, and Marta Tailor became Tai's roommate. Since then,
she and Janice had maintained an uneasy truce.

Janice wasn't Tai's only problem. At the academy, most of
Tai's male classmates had eventually accepted women cadets
because of class loyalty. She soon discovered that it would be
different at Williams. Again, she—and the other females—
would have to prove themselves, and she wondered wearily if
the day would ever come when women in the military would
be treated as people, not as women in a man's world.

Not to her surprise, Janice started off on the wrong foot.
Determined to prove that she was as macho as any man, she
swaggered around the halls and the rec room with a chip on
her shoulder, and when one of the men made the mistake of
opening a door for her, she let loose her whole repertoire of
four-letter words.

Tai caught the looks the men exchanged, and she knew that
she and the other females would be tarred with the same brush.
She also knew it wouldn't do any good to take Janice aside
and advise her to keep her mouth shut and let her achievements

prove that women could perform as well as men in the cockpit of a plane. So they were all on their own. With luck, she would make it through the next eleven months without any trouble. But if she had to, she was prepared to defend herself as best she could. When hadn't she had to fight for what she wanted?

When she reported in at the orientation briefing, she discovered a familiar face among the instructors—Steven Henderson's. He didn't see her at first because she'd taken a seat at the back of the room and the lieutenant sitting in front of her was tall and broad-shouldered. But it was obvious that Steven knew she was there somewhere. He examined the rows of seats leisurely, and even though she stared straight ahead, her eyes fixed on Colonel Hastings, the wing commander, who was giving the orientation speech, the back of her neck prickled and she knew when he'd spotted her.

She concentrated on the briefing, even though Colonel Hastings's words were typical of all orientation speeches.

"—will be no student-instructor pilot relationships. No IP will date a female student. No first-name basis, even between men students and IPs—"

Tai's attention wandered as he launched into the usual jack-'em-up speech. Of all the rotten luck—why had she ended up at the same flight school as Steven? She had heard he was at Pease AFB, which was obviously the wrong information. Was the next year going to be more of the same? Would he continue his harassment? One thing in her favor—she was no longer a doolie. She was an air force officer, albeit on the lowest rung of the ladder. And if he bugged her, she would remind him of that, loud and clear. . . .

The briefing ended, and she was leaving the room with the other students when a hand seized her elbow and pulled her to one side. "I want to talk to you, Lt. MacGarrett," Steven said brusquely.

Aware of curious stares, Tai was forced to stop. The expression on Steven's face was all business and unsmiling, but on the other hand, he wasn't frowning, either. So what the hell did he want?

His first words when they were alone cleared up the mystery. "I think we'd better set up some ground rules for the next eleven months, Tai. You'll need all your energy for your studies, so I suggest we declare a truce. We'll pretend we're complete strangers and start from scratch. Otherwise it might affect your performance—I'm sure you don't want that."

Tai had some hard thoughts about how he'd hazed her that first year at the academy. It was an effort to keep her voice even as she told him, "That's agreeable with me. I'll treat you just as I would any other instructor."

It was a compromise, of course. She'd vowed at their last meeting that she would never speak to Steven again, but of course she had no other choice.

Later, in her room, she tried to sort out her feelings and was surprised to find that at some point during the past three years, her hostility toward Steven had lost its sharp edge. Either she had a very poor memory or her values had changed, because she knew that she would honor her promise to treat him without hostility—as long as he didn't try to reopen old wounds.

During the next few days, she discovered that Cassie's warning about her status at flight school had been prophetic. From being seniors, cocks of the walk, she and the others who had just graduated from the academy were novices again, as scared of making a mistake as any of the ROTC or ATS graduates in the class.

They all knew the statistics. Twenty percent of their class would wash out—for one reason or another. And because all of them—man or woman, products of ROTC or ATS or the elite academy—were in the same boat, they formed an uneasy alliance. Even Janice, who had already managed to insult almost everybody in her class, was tolerated because she was one of them, too.

There were all kinds of rumors floating around, some about the first female students to take flight training. One concerned an ATC graduate who'd been popular with the other students because of her gung-ho attitude and yet had been the first of her class to wash out.

It seemed particularly poignant to Tai because the reason for this earlier female trainee's failure had been physical. Although only five feet four, an inch shorter than Tai, she had been given a waiver because her sitting height, the distance from the end of her spine to the top of her head, met the standards, but when she got into the cockpit of a T-37 for the first time, it was soon clear that she didn't have the physical strength in her arms to control the brakes, even though she'd passed all the physical tests.

When Tai heard this tale, one of many that the men students seemed to delight in telling the females, she increased her daily physical workout, concentrating on increasing the muscle tone of her biceps and pectorals.

The first three weeks were devoted to academics, including physiological training and T-37 systems. Tai studied long into the night, making sure that she understood every aspect of the mass of information in her textbooks and manuals before she went on to the next phase. Even when she got her first grades, which were all in the very good to excellent range, she didn't allow herself to relax. Up ahead loomed her first flight lesson— and she had no idea how she would do. The sixteen hours she'd spent in a Cessna in her senior year had been promising, but that was child's play next to the reality of flying a T-37 or, later in her training, the more advanced T-38.

Even after she and the others went "on line," it was another two weeks before they saw the inside of a cockpit. First there were the simulators and academic ground training to master before they were finally allowed to put on flight helmets and climb inside the cockpit of a T-37 for flight training.

To Tai's dismay, when she reported in for her first flight, she discovered that Steven would be her IP. She would have assumed it was an accident except that she'd originally been assigned an instructor pilot named Lt. Cross. In line with their truce, she had been polite to Steven the rare times their paths had crossed, and he had been just as polite—and impersonal— to her. Now she knew that her patience would be tried to the limit, and it was hard to contain her anger as she fastened her helmet under her chin and climbed into the cockpit of the trainer.

During the next hour, she tried to shut Steven out of her mind, to regard his voice, coming through her helmet ear-phones, as part of the plane. She concentrated on his instructions, his comments, and since he was totally professional, she allowed herself to hope that his assignment as her IP had really been a coincidence. Even so, she found it impossible to relax.

Steven must have sensed her tenseness because his voice took on a deeper tone. "Relax, Tai—just flow with the program. Don't tighten up—there's no need. This plane can practically fly itself. All you have to do is nudge it a little and it'll do anything you want, just like the thoroughbred it is. All the kinks have been worked out—it's a sweetheart of a flying machine—"

His voice was hypnotic. Tai found herself believing him, trusting him. After he'd allowed her a few more minutes at the controls, he took them over again and they returned to the base. When she slid out of the plane, Tai found herself wanting to pat the trim airplane as if it really were the thoroughbred Steven had compared it to.

"You'll be okay," Steven said, and she felt so good that his next words were like a dash of cold water. "But you're going to have to work a little harder than some of the others. I advise you to put in extra time in the stimulators."

With a nod, he strolled off. As Tai stared after him, the wind, straight off the Arizona desert, whipped her hair to a frenzy, chilling her—or maybe it was the knowledge that he was right that chilled her, the realization that she wasn't, as she'd hoped, a natural-born, seat-of-the-pants flyer.

During the next few weeks, she would think of Steven's words many times. What appeared to be so easy for others to master so often seemed nearly impossible to her. Almost, she thought in despair, as if she had a mental block against succeeding. She gave the problem different names—nerves, fatigue, even fear—but she knew this was just rationalization. The truth was that the thing she wanted to do most in the world was something for which nature, perverse as always, was denying her because of some physical or mental or judgmental lack. For yet another time in her life, she had to face the fact that she might fail, and the knowledge kept her awake nights when she desperately needed her sleep.

The schedule, where maximum utilization of daylight was adopted, didn't help. One week she was on "early week" and the next "late week." Which meant that every other week she set her alarm for an hour before sunrise so she could make the briefing and be in the T-37 fifteen minutes before sunrise. The next week it was just the opposite, and she was on the line later in the day and had to get used to a different sleep pattern again. That others were having the same problem adjusting wasn't reassuring, even though it meant that she wasn't the only one having trouble.

The first two washouts in her class had been men who couldn't hack the academics, but the third was Twyla Williams, who was so violently airsick every time she went up that she was finally declared unfit for pilot training. Then the fourth, one of her flight's most promising students, took himself off the program, and the rumor was that he was afraid of flying. Six of the students were already on probation, having failed two academic tests, and three had failed their midphase check ride and were slated for the dreaded eighty-eight, one of the recheck rides that could wash them out.

Tai renewed her attack on academics and continued to draw excellents, which engendered a remark from Jack Ripson, one of the men students in her class, about female grinds. Despite this, most of the other male students had begun to accept her when Janice, eternally finding grievances where none existed, decided that an instructor's casual remark was sexual harassment and filed charges against him.

Overnight, the climate changed. Now the women were regarded with suspicion—and wariness. When Tai came into the rec room, the joking and horseplay stopped, and she no longer felt welcome at the bull sessions. She was chagrined at how much it hurt. In her own mind, she had accepted these men as friends. To have them consider her as the enemy, to lump her with Janice, made her feel like an outsider again.

All of this took second place when she passed her first check flight. She had been afraid that she would tighten up, but her extra hours in the simulator paid off, and when she felt the power between her hands, suddenly she was back in Hawaii, riding the pipeline off Ala Moana, the surfboard beneath her bucking and yawing like a skittish mare, sensitive to her every movement and shift of weight, and she was in control again, responsible for her own safety, for the safety of this million-dollar piece of technology.

She felt exultant and humble at the same time, and when the flight was over, she found a distressing moistness in her eyes. The check rides were never given by the student's IP, but by an instructor from another flight, and when she slid out of the plane and saw the smile of the check pilot, a captain named Chase, she knew that he understood and shared her feelings.

"A real high, isn't it, MacGarrett?" He was a lean, dark-haired man with the aloof eyes so common to pilots, and rumor had it he had been accepted for Fighter Training School in the fall. "There's nothing quite like it—except sex with someone who really matters. You aren't the greatest I've ever flown with, but you've got the stuff for it. Just hang in there, keep going—and don't look back."

Although she only nodded before she left for weather class at the student squadron, she felt exultant—and very proud of herself. It was only much later, when she started T-38 training, that she realized that along with his praise, Captain Chase had also issued her a warning.

The next student to wash out was her roommate, Marta Tailor. Tai had become fond, if not intimate, with the dark-eyed girl, but she'd been too busy to notice her roommate's gradual withdrawal until it was too late to help her. It was Janice, always eager to spread bad news, who yelled to Tai across the dining hall. "I hear your roomie took an SIE, MacGarrett. No guts, huh?"

Tai was too stunned to answer. SIE stood for self-initiated elimination—and that meant it had been Marta's own choice. But why hadn't her roommate given some hint of her doubts? Was it possible that Marta had—and that she'd been too wrapped up in her own problems to notice?

Steven came to her room that evening. She was sitting at her desk, studying for a test—and trying not to notice the empty bunk next to hers—when his knock came. In no mood for company, she was tempted to ignore it, but when it came again, more insistent this time, she went to open the door to Steven's grave face.

"I want to talk to you," he said.

"You're the IP. So talk."

"Not here. Come to the visitors' lounge. Nobody's there right now."

She started to tell him she had to study for a flight planning exam, but she changed her mind and nodded. Steven was, after all, her instructor. It wouldn't be prudent to refuse him.

"It's still hard for you to give even a little, isn't it?" Steven said. "Well, maybe that kind of rigidity is needed to get through UPT—but don't let it get out of hand."

His words rankled, and when, a few minutes later, she joined him on a brown leather sofa in one corner of the empty lounge, she didn't try to hide her resentment.

"You've heard the news about Marta?" he said.

"Janice couldn't wait to let me know."

"Marta didn't tell you herself?"

Tai shook her head. "I didn't even know she was having a problem."

"And that bothers you. Haven't you learned by now that you can't be your sister's keeper, Tai? You have to accept the fact that some people go their own way without confiding in you. And some are going to fail—you can't let it get to you."

She gave him a hostile look. "That's easy for you to accept. You don't have a heart. Sometimes I wonder if you're even human, Steven."

"I'm human enough to care what happens to you, Tai."

"And I'd like to end this conversation—unless it's official."

"Oh, it's official all right. It's my job to help you take your lumps. But in your case, it's more than duty, Tai. I want you to make it. You have a real passion for flying. In a way, I envy you that part. To me, it's just a job. But I do understand how you feel about planes. With me, it's computers. Give me a program with bugs to be worked out, the tougher the better, and I'm lost to everything else. Which is why I took computer science as my major."

He went on talking about a software program he was working on in his spare time, and she realized that he was trying to relax her. Part of her resented his tact. After all, she wasn't a nervous mare who needed gentling. But another part of her was grateful, and this scared her because it meant Steven's opinion of her still mattered—and it mustn't. If she ever let down her guard and forgot he was the enemy, she could be hurt again. She might even find out that the reason she'd never had another serious relationship with a man was because her old feelings for Steven were still there, hidden under the scars.

"I'm really bushed," she said, interrupting him. "Do you have anything else to say? If not, I'd like to go back to my room."

He studied her, his face tight. "No, that's it. But before you get back to your books—remember this. I'm not your enemy. I never have been."

"You could have fooled me. What was all that special attention I got during my doolie year at the academy?"

"Don't you realize that by hassling you the way I did, I created a hundred champions for you? I knew I wouldn't be around the next year to look after you, so—"

"You condescending bastard!" she said, jumping to her feet.

"What made you think that I needed your help? I *earned* the respect I got—and don't you forget it!"

"Of course you did. But you had a few strikes against you the other females didn't have. Your background, for one—"

"You can call it by the right name. My race, you mean. Well, most people aren't bigots like your father. They don't give a hang if I'm Chinese or—or Martian. And if they do, that's their hang-up, not mine. So get off it, Steven. Don't try to tell me that you hassled me for my own good because I don't buy it. You were sore because I broke off with you. That's why you gave me such a bad time."

"That isn't true—but maybe you want to believe it because you don't want to admit that what we had is still there—for both of us."

"How can you say that? You were already having second thoughts, even before Mac's trouble."

"Where the hell did you get that idea?"

"Don't bother to lie. I know you had reservations about us even before you called me the day before Mac's funeral."

Steven winced. "Okay, I did make a few mistakes. For one thing, I didn't know how to handle a relationship that heavy. Your letters were so—so intense that they scared me a little. Because what if I didn't measure up? Also I was third degree, and I had a lot of important decisions to make by the end of my sophomore year. I was having serious doubts about my career choice, and—surely you went through the same kind of thing? I'm not trying to excuse myself. I should have provided you with more moral support after Mac was arrested. If it's any comfort to you, I've paid for my mistakes, including a marriage that never had a chance because I still love you, Tai."

Tai stared at him. Why was he telling her this? "And that's why you came down so hard on me when I was a doolie?" she said, skepticism sharpening her voice. "You got married the day after graduation because you loved me? Come off it, Steven. I don't know why your marriage failed, but it wasn't because of me."

"I'm not saying I didn't believe it would work at the time. Otherwise I would never have married Carol. We were good together in bed—and I'm human, no matter what you think, and I'd given up all hope that you and I would ever get together. Hell, our marriage should have worked, but even as early as our honeymoon, we both realized the truth, that something very vital was missing in our relationship. We went through the motions for a while, and then Carol went home on a visit, met someone else she liked better, and never came back. Which was a relief to me because it meant I didn't have to carry around another load of guilt for the rest of my life."

"I don't know what you're trying to prove by telling me all this," Tai said wearily. "Your idea about us treating each other as strangers was right."

"Okay, I'll have to live with your distrust. But believe me when I tell you that I want to help you. You can make it through flight training, but not if you continue the way you are. You're too determined to be perfect. Allow yourself a little slack. When you're flying, loosen up a little, trust your instincts. That's your worst hang-up. You're afraid of your gut instincts. Don Chase agrees with me that you're too tight. You think out every move before you do it—and that inhibits you, throws off your timing. Sure, you need every bit of training you can get—the drills and the simulator time and the academics. But in the air, it's just you and that plane. Allow your instincts a little freedom. And use me. I'm here to be used. If you have any questions, if you need any advice or just want to talk—come to me. I promise that from now on, I'll be completely objective with you."

He paused, as if waiting for an answer. When she was silent, he gave her a twisted smile, then rose and strolled off.

Later, when she was back in her room, Tai thought over the things he'd said and discovered that one thing had changed. She was convinced now that Steven had meant what he'd said about wanting to help her. The question that kept her awake that night was—did she really want to let Steven back in her life, even as a completely objective adviser?

When Steven returned to his room in the BOQ, Tai's image lingered in his mind. She looked the same as she had three years ago, and yet she was so different. Cooler, more sure of herself, tougher perhaps, more considering—and also more guarded—in stating her opinions. He missed the softer, more flexible and spontaneous Tai he'd known in Hawaii, even though, during the years of their estrangement, she had grown as a person into someone he respected—and still loved. But of course he had no right to feel that way—or to interfere in her life. He had forfeited his chance to take care of her.

He turned into his room and found Charlie Fogle waiting for him. Charlie had a blunt nose, protrusive eyes, and a wide mouth that always reminded Steven of an amiable frog. With his barrel chest, stocky build, and voracious appetite, he would probably have a serious weight problem someday. He was also Steven's best friend at Williams, which was why Steven didn't freeze up when Charlie said, "I saw you getting cozy with the Chinese chick in the lounge. You got something going there?"

"She's upset because her roommate went out on an SIE."

"Well, that's to her credit. Proves she cares. Chase was talking about her today at lunch. Says he gave her a check ride and he's sure she's got the stuff to go the route. Too bad she's a female."

"Why do you say that?"

"Because of the numbers. A few years of duty and then out she goes—into industry or marriage or both."

"So do a lot of men."

"Sure—but the numbers say she'll only stay around long enough to do her six years and then get out."

"And whose fault is that? If the brass would utilize female pilots better, maybe the numbers would change."

"So write your congressman. They're the ones who put the restrictions on women taking any duty connected with combat—including fighters. And it probably doesn't matter in the long run. You know what happens when a female flyer gets pregnant—nine months off flight duty, and then she has to requalify to get back on flying status. You can't change physiology. It's the females who have the kids, not the men. A man can father a whole squad of house apes and it doesn't affect his status, but a woman who gets pregnant has different priorities—of necessity."

"Not very fair, is it? Some women are just as serious about their careers as men."

"That's life for you. What's with you and MacGarrett, anyway? You've got a thing for her, haven't you?"

"Is it that obvious?"

"Not to anyone but me, your old buddy and psychology minor. One thing about this yen you have for MacGarrett—it means you've stopped carrying the torch for your ex."

"I was over Carol long before we got our divorce. If I

seemed to take it hard, it's only because no one likes to fail. Can you imagine eating at the same table, day after day, sleeping in the same bed every night—and not one damned thing to talk about except the latest Ann Landers column or the weather? It was so different with Tai. We never stopped talking when we were together. We agreed or disagreed about everything under the sun, but we always had a thousand things to say to each other—" He broke off and gave his friend's smug face a chagrined look. "Me and my flipping tongue. I let the cat out of the bag, didn't I? I hope you have a poor memory."

"It's forgotten, although you sure bent the rules, taking on a student you once had a personal relationship with. Just remember this—complete objectivity is the way to go. You sure you can handle it?"

"I'm sure."

Charlie shook his head. "If you didn't have first dibs on her, I'd make a play for her myself, even though it's pretty dangerous business, romancing a female officer."

"Why dangerous?"

"Oh, come on. You know the pattern. Officers who marry officers are asking for a lot of misery. Suppose you get assigned to separate bases?"

"There's always the Joint Spouse Assignments route."

"Which doesn't always work. Look at that guy Peterson—he's been separated from his wife for almost a year now with no relief in sight. He's pulled every string he can find, but there simply isn't any slot for her here at Williams, nor for him at Los Angeles Air Station where she's assigned. Doesn't that make you think?"

"It's not something I stay awake nights worrying about," Steven said dryly.

"Maybe you should—provided you're thinking about warming up your romance with your little friend, Mai-Tai."

Steven frowned at him. One of the men students had started calling Tai by that nickname when he'd found out she'd been born in Hawaii. Because it was a natural, it had soon been picked up by others. Tai didn't seem to mind, but Steven didn't like it one bit.

"Sorry." Charlie grinned at him, looking like a slightly over-weight leprechaun. "Why don't you make it easy on yourself and ask to have Tai switched to another instructor?"

"Because it would look as if she'd done something to deserve being dumped on another instructor."

"And besides, you don't want to let go, do you?"

"Did anyone ever tell you that you're a smart-ass?"

"Only about a thousand times. On the other hand, I don't get involved in personal relationships with my students, either," was Charlie's parting shot as he unwound his legs and ambled out of the room.

It was the next day that Steven got an unexpected visitor—his father. He was on his way to a conference at Travis, Colonel Henderson told Steven, and had decided to take a detour to see his son. They went through the father-son thing, slapping each other's shoulders and exchanging insults.

"So how are things going for you, son?" Colonel Henderson said finally.

"Everything's great. How's Mom—"

"I've put in my retirement papers, Steven."

His father's words were such a surprise that it was a moment before Steven said, "I always figured you were in for the long haul, Dad."

"I got an offer from industry I couldn't refuse. Top pay, expense account, the works." But his father's voice was a little too glib, and Steven knew that it wasn't the whole story.

"What's up? This isn't the first offer you've had, all of which you've turned down before."

"I'm getting a bit long in the tooth—or haven't you noticed?"

"Okay, if you don't want to talk about it—"

"Hell, I *am* talking about it. I need a change—anything wrong with that?"

"Not for ninety-nine percent of the air force. But for you—yeah. It doesn't compute—as we computer freaks say."

"Computers are a waste of time. You should've taken my advice and chosen aeronautical engineering as your major."

"Computers run the world—including the air force. And don't change the subject. What's the real reason you're retiring?" A sudden fear sharpened Steven's voice. "Is something wrong with your health—or with Mom's?"

"We're both fine. And don't make a big thing out of this. I decided it was time to quit, and so I put in my papers."

Steven wasn't satisfied. It was unthinkable for his father, whose whole life was the air force, to retire with only twenty-five years of service under his belt.

"Okay, but it'll come out eventually. Might as well tell me now."

"Dammit, Steven, are you calling me a liar? You've changed—I don't know if it's your divorce or that blasted MacGarrett girl. I knew there'd be problems when I heard she was in flight training at Williams. What's she been telling you? That I didn't back MacGarrett's lies because I was covering up my own poor judgment? Let me tell you something—that man lied. He couldn't produce my signature on that purchase order, could he? Hell, I've always been too careful about covering my ass to sign any fucking requisition that might backfire on—" He stopped in midsentence.

Even before dark color stained his father's cheeks, Steven knew the truth. He was guilty as hell, and everything Sgt. MacGarrett had claimed was true. His father had made a mistake in judgment, which wasn't so bad, but then he had allowed an innocent man to take the rap for him. . . .

"My God, Dad—you crucified that man! And you let Tai go through all that misery just to cover up your own mistake? How can you live with yourself?"

"Watch what you're saying, boy. And open your eyes. You told me once you couldn't figure out why some men make it in the military and others, just as competent, don't. Well, it's because the smart ones learn to cover their asses right down the line. The ones who don't, get passed over and retire young."

"Like you, Dad? Is that why you're getting out? You've been shoved into another dead-end job, haven't you? All that crap about an offer you can't refuse is just that—crap. Even though you knew I'd find out eventually, you still had to put up a front. Why the hell is that, Dad? Why is it so hard for you to admit that you aren't perfect? And when did your superiors find you out? Before or after you railroaded an innocent man into his grave? Because they did. I don't know how I missed it when all the signs were there. For the past few years, you've been shuffled from one second-rate job to another, filling in temporarily until you were replaced by someone permanent. All that talk about being a troubleshooter was garbage, wasn't it?"

"Now listen here—"

"Funny that I never added it up. Maybe I didn't want to. Did some new evidence turn up that pointed the finger at you? Naturally, the brass wouldn't set the record straight. It would look bad, a colonel throwing a sergeant to the wolves to save his own hide. But they don't want you around, do they? So you got shoved aside, and now you're going to save face and get out. What a farce the whole fucking business is."

Even then his father tried to bluff it out. He blustered and roared for a few minutes before he finally subsided into silence. Steven wondered how he could have been so blind. The signs that his father's values were flawed had always been there. Those lectures about knowing where the bodies were buried, the advice to play the game not by the rules but by the odds— all signs of a weak man who saw the world through his own narrow self-interest.

"You never liked her, did you?" Steven said, breaking the silence.

"Liked Tai? Is that who you're talking about? I didn't like or dislike her. She was wrong for you. She would've held you back. How would it have looked, a senior officer with a chink wife standing beside him in the reception line?"

"Tai was right about that, too," Steven said, sickened. "You're a bloody bigot as well as a liar and a perjurer."

"Aren't you forgetting something?" Colonel Henderson's voice was sharp. "What about that missing liquor? Someone took it—and MacGarrett couldn't account for his key."

"But there were two keys, What did you do, Dad? Lose your key somewhere and when you realized it was missing, steal Mac's key?"

Again, he'd made the right guess. There was a telltale flicker in his father's eyes that told him the truth.

"Here now, this is your father you're talking to, Steven!"

"Yes, you're my father. I can't change that. But think about this: That man you framed is dead. He might still be alive if you'd told the truth from the beginning. In the long run, it wouldn't have made any difference on your promotion. Somewhere along the line, they caught on to you or they wouldn't have put you out to pasture so soon. I've always looked up to you and taken your word as gospel, but no longer. I'm wise to you now. And I've taken the last advice from you I ever want to hear."

He left his father standing there—a well-preserved man with gray streaks in his hair, a trim military bearing, and silver eagles on his shoulders.

Steven took a long walk out along the flight line, needing

to be alone to sort out his thoughts. At some point during that walk it came to him that he couldn't blame all his mistakes on his father. What a self-righteous, pompous ass he'd been five years ago! So full of his own problems, his own importance. Well, it was too late to change that, but it wasn't too late to tell Tai the truth. Maybe she would forgive him and forgive his father, but even if she didn't, it was still something that he had to do—for the sake of his own self-respect.

CHAPTER
✦ 34 ✦

Tai had expected her difficulties to increase when she moved from T-37s to the more complex T-38s. Instead, it was as if she'd reached a truce with her own recalcitrant body. Suddenly she was doing everything right, without undue effort, and she wondered if her problems had been psychological after all. Despite her new assurance, she still felt as if she were treading on raw eggs, afraid the tension—or whatever it had been—would return, afraid that the next time it would be so bad that it would wash her out, especially since her class had already diminished by eighteen percent.

When nothing happened, she put it out of her mind and devoted all her attention to learning the intricacies of the T-38. And all the time, behind her concentration, another hunger was growing, one she knew would be impossible to satisfy.

Whenever the men students got together, they talked fighters. Almost universally, they wanted to get into fighter training, and while she suspected that it was less an itch with some of them than with others, she felt left out. After all, it was the fighters that stirred her imagination. To have that kind of power under control, to be alone in that slender piece of metal and glass with only her skill, knowledge, instinct between her and the ultimate adventure—it would be like riding a thousand surfboards at the same time.

Every class, Tai had been told, had an unofficial student leader, and her class was no exception. His name was Jack

Ripson, an ROTC graduate from UCLA, and he made no secret of his aversion to women pilots, especially if they were academy graduates. He must have sensed Tai's fascination with fighters because she became the target of his derogatory remarks. When their flight started formation flying, the training that proves a flyer's mettle, Jack Ripson took it upon himself to call his fellow students together for a pep talk in the briefing room.

"Okay, you guys, pipe down," he said, raising his voice above the din. He was a whip-slim man with a cocky smile, always superbly confident of himself, and, it was rumored, the scourge of the groupies who hung around the local watering holes that catered to student pilots at Williams. When the room was quiet, he went on, "This is the best class to go through Williams in years, so let's show them our balls. We're all going out for fighters, right?"

After the roar of agreement had subsided, he said, "That's the stuff. Since we're all going for fighters, we gotta have fighter call signs. From now on, you can call me Ripper." He grinned at the catcalls and shower of insults. "Chuck—you're an old Iowa farm boy, so you're Hogcaller, and Kennedy over there is Whizzo—"

Tai listened, her face frozen, as he went around the room, giving out names like Macho and Tender and Starchaser. He paused when he came to Tai. "Now what we've got here is a female pilot—she don't need a fighter call sign 'cause she can't do fighters. So we'll just leave her slot blank. Tough shit, Mai Tai."

He went on to the next man, leaving Tai fighting mad—and hurt. Which was stupid. After all, she knew the rules. Female pilots could fly a WC-130 right into the eye of a hurricane, could be the aircraft commander of a C-5, the largest transport plane in the world, but no woman could pilot a fighter or any other plane used in combat. Nor could they go through Fighter Training School—although it was true that a few female engineers had.

The next morning, when she reported in for preflight briefing, the first thing she saw was the fighter call signs, chalked up on the blackboard opposite each student's name. All the others in her flight had call names—except her. The space beside her name was blank. From the sudden cessation of voices and the covert glances in her direction, she knew her fellow students were waiting to see what she would do.

She didn't hesitate. Walking swiftly, she went to the board, picked up a piece of chalk, and wrote the word "Tiger" in the space next to her name.

When she turned, she saw that most of the men were smiling—all except Jack Ripson, whose face looked like he'd just swallowed a frog. He jumped to his feet and started forward, but Tai blocked his way. "If you touch that board, I'm going to wipe the floor up with you," she said quietly. "And if you don't think I can do it, just try me."

Although not particularly tall for a man, Jack Ripson towered above Tai—and he outweighed her by forty pounds. Even so, her challenge stopped him—but only briefly. When he took another step forward, one of his cronies told him in a low voice, "Let it go, Jack. Either way, you can't win." Another student, who had graduated with Tai, drawled, "Maybe I should warn you—Tai's a kung fu expert."

Jack gave him a furious look. "I don't need your advice, asshole," he said, but he moved back to his chair. The door opened and the briefing officer came in. He gave Tai a curious look, but when she took a seat in the front row, he started the briefing without comment.

Tai listened attentively to the instructor as he outlined what they would be learning the next few weeks. She knew that she would need every bit of information she could absorb when she started formation training. She had already heard, via the school grapevine, that Jack Ripson didn't want to fly formation with her because, to quote him, "everybody knows women have rotten coordination."

A few of the male students, the ones called "sticks" because they were naturally hot flyers, had already taken their formation check ride, and while all of them had passed, none had received a grade higher than very good. Tai was determined to be the first to draw an excellent rating. It wasn't an unrealistic goal since she'd already discovered that she had an instinct for judging distances and better-than-average hand-eye coordination.

On the day she was to go for her check ride, Captain Nelson, the instructor who had replaced Steven when she'd moved to T-38s, took her aside. "Captain Marko is going to give you your check ride. He was top IP last year, so you drew a good one. Also, since he's got no hang-ups about women pilots, he'll evaluate you on your merits. Just keep your mind on what you're doing and you'll be okay."

Tai nodded, too tense to speak. She'd been relieved to learn during briefing that her partner for the formation check ride was Bob Jenkins, one of the class's four black students and a natural pilot—until she'd overheard Jack Ripson's comment— "What is this, equal rights day at Williams?"

During the first few minutes of flight, she was much too wound up, but her instructor's voice was so relaxed that she found herself calming down. Although it wasn't an instruction flight, it was permissible for the evaluator to give advice, and as the calm voice in her ear gave her a few tips on technique, then let her practice them, suddenly everything came together for her and she was back in control. By the time the check ride was finished, she knew she'd never done better, but even so she was surprised to learn that she had earned an excellent.

She had no intention of telling the others. That wasn't her way. But as she came into the briefing room after her check flight, Jack Ripson accosted her.

"So how'd you do with your check ride, Tiger Lily?"

The arrogance in his voice, the use of yet another nickname that pointed out her race, infuriated her, especially when one of Jack's cronies sniggered. But she shrugged and tried to pass him, only to have him block her way.

"So? Did you pass?" he persisted.

"I did."

"Fancy that. So what was your grade?"

"Excellent," she snapped.

"Right on, Tai!" one of the men called.

Jack's eyes narrowed. "What'd you do?" he drawled. "Sleep with the instructor?"

There was dead silence in the briefing room. Everybody seemed to be holding their breath. Anger flooded through Tai, and her hands began to shake. Afraid of what she might say— or do—if she didn't leave immediately, she turned on her heel and marched out of the room. It was one of her lowest moments since her father's death.

Captain Nelson, her IP, caught up with her at the end of the hall. "What's wrong, Tai?" he said.

She gave him an incredulous look. "I can't believe you just said that," she said. "You were there in the briefing room. You must've heard what Ripson said. How dare you ask me what's wrong? You guys—the whole damned bunch of you piss me off. Male loyalty sucks. I'm leaving the program—no, I'm not! I'm going to stay and make that idiot eat his words. Just tell him to stay out of my way or so help me, I'll floor him. And I can do it. That muscle-bound creep's a sitting duck for a body slam."

"Are you going to file charges? You've got witnesses—you can take him out of the program, you know."

It hadn't occurred to Tai that Jack's remark had given her a weapon for revenge. What he'd said was enough to wash him out—but did she really want that? For a female student to make waves, to use equal rights to fight back at the jerks who bugged her, was asking for ostracism from the other male students. That part didn't bother her—she'd been alone before—but did she really want to see Jack, who for all his machismo and bigotry, was a damned good pilot, out of the program? The answer was *no*. . . .

"I'm not going to file charges," she told Nelson, who looked relieved. "I'm going to take it in and suck it up. But you tell Jack the Ripper to keep out of my way—no, I think I'll give him that message myself."

She turned and went back to the briefing room. Despite the size of the crowd, it was very quiet. Jack gave her a wary look as she marched up to the blackboard. She picked up the chalk from the holder, wiped out the word "Ripper" next to his name, and wrote in a new word—ASSHOLE—in capital letters. Still looking neither right nor left, she left, and it was only when she was back in her room, safe from watching eyes, that she had a good cry.

But it didn't last long. She had a systems class to attend in five minutes, and she wasn't going to give Jack the satisfaction of making her miss it.

The next morning when she reported in, she glanced at the board, expecting to find that Jack had restored his old call name. Instead, the one she'd chosen for him was still there. Involuntarily, she turned her head to meet Jack's eyes. Looking sheepish, he made an okay sign, and she knew that she'd just had the only apology she'd ever get from him. She and Jack would never become friends, but the feud was over—and maybe they both had learned something.

When she checked her box in the mailroom late that afternoon, the letter waiting for her made her smile. A letter from Bobby Jo was always an upper. But as she read it, her smile faded because the letter held only a ghost of Bobby Jo's usual optimism. Not that Bobby Jo complained about anything. It was just that she was trying too hard to sound cheerful—and then there was the postscript she'd tacked on at the end.

"Funny how life can kick you in the teeth when you're already down, isn't it?"

Tai was tempted to go to a phone and call her friend, but it was almost dinnertime, and she had some tall studying to do before she went to bed that night, so she decided to postpone the call until morning. But the following day, she was so caught up in the next phase of her training that the letter faded from her memory. Only much later would she realize that the postscript had been a cry for help—and that she hadn't offered it.

Then it was April, and Tai was packing for the cross-country trip that was customary near the end of flight training. The official purpose was to give students experience in dealing with other flight patterns and new conditions while they acquired valuable experience on approaches at bases other than Williams. The students considered it a holiday, especially since they were allowed to choose their own flight plan—within reason. Since Captain Nelson would accompany Tai, she took his advice and put Travis AFB on her agenda because it was possible that at some point in her career she would fly C-151s and C-5s.

"We can refuel at Edwards," her instructor told her. "Not much use to spend any extra time there. You won't get close to the X-planes."

"Any chance of talking to some of the test pilots?"

"I doubt it. That's a pretty exclusive crowd. Some are okay, and some are jerks—but when they *are* jerks, they take it to the limit. Of course, I'm hoping to be one myself someday, provided I make it through fighter school, get in my thousand hours of air time, and finish my master's in engineering. A lot of ifs, right?"

"You'll make it."

"Or buy it trying."

"No way—and I really envy you. I'd give my left arm for a crack at fighters."

"It could happen. You could even end up the first female test pilot—provided you're also the first female fighter pilot."

"Don't hold your breath. It's really a farce. Women can go into space, but they can't fly fighters," she said, and then, because it was a sore point with her, she changed the subject and asked him a question about their cross-country trek.

"When we reach Travis," he told her, "we can rent a car and go into Frisco if you like. It's only an hour's drive from the base."

"What would your wife say to that?" she teased.

"She's all for those little jaunts. It gets me out of her hair for a couple of days—or so she tells me."

Tai shook her head in mock despair. "I don't envy her. Being married to a pilot must be rough."

"Yeah. A woman has to be crazy to marry a pilot."

"Or be in love," she said, remembering how close she'd come herself.

When she reported in the next morning, wearing flight gear and carrying a canvas bag that held the outfit she planned to wear on their night out in San Francisco, it was Steven, not Captain Nelson, who greeted her.

"Nelson had an emergency. One of his kids fell and broke his arm," he said. "I'm subbing for him."

Tai didn't try to hide her dismay. What could have been a real holiday now looked to be an ordeal. Being in Steven's company for three or more days—no, she couldn't hack that.

"I'll get someone else," she said, matching his businesslike tone. "I don't want to inconvenience you."

"Let it go, Tai," Steven said softly. "Flow with the program. If it were anyone else but me, you wouldn't suggest getting another instructor. I'm the logical one—I had you for T-37s."

She knew he was right—but she still didn't like it. "Okay—but let's go over those ground rules again before we start. This is strictly official, right? We're just a student and her IP, doing a cross-country. Nothing heavy, okay?"

"Nothing heavy," he said, and she had to be satisfied with that.

Two evenings later, they were ordering dinner at the Top of the Mark, high above San Francisco on the top floor of the Mark Hopkins Hotel. They'd been lucky enough to get a table by the window, and as Tai sipped a wine cooler and looked down at the lights below, she thought how deceptive they must look to other diners. She was wearing heels and a coral-colored dress, and at the moment she was very much aware that she was a woman. Part of it was the novelty of wearing heels and having a skirt swishing around her knees when she walked, but part of it was the release from having to constantly prove that she was as good as a man. At least for this short time, she could be herself, even though she still wasn't reconciled to her escort. Still, it was flattering to have the complete attention of an attractive man, to be the object of interested glances from other male diners.

Over steaming cups of clam chowder, Steven told her that he had decided against Fighter Training School. "This is my final year as an IP. I'm sweating out my next assignment now. I suspect it'll be an overseas assignment—I'm due for one."

"It's your choice, of course—but if I had the chance at fighters, I'd grab it in a minute."

"I know. Maybe things will change for women someday."

"It had better happen soon. I've got six more years after I get my wings, and then I've had it with the military."

"If you hadn't signed for flight school, it would have been five years."

"We all make mistakes."

"Your academics are top drawer, and you're a damned good pilot. It's a shame to waste all that training."

She shrugged. "So when I'm a civilian again I'll take up flying as a hobby." She hesitated, then added, "I never thanked you for your advice."

"No thanks needed. I'd do the same for any—"

"Student. Yes, I know."

"But I have to admit that I sweated you out a little more than I did the others," he said, grinning at her.

She looked away, disturbed by how much his grin affected her. What the hell, she wasn't a teenager with her head full of dreams anymore. She was as tough as most men and tougher than most women. She'd proven herself—so why the fireworks when she let down her guard with Steven, even a little? Was it sexual abstinence? Since she and Steven had broken up, she'd only had two affairs, both of them brief, and maybe that was a mistake because it left her vulnerable to any reasonably attractive man. The trick was not to mistake biology for something else.

"What are you thinking, Tai? You look a million miles away."

"I was thinking about—about Hawaii. It's been five years since I left there. I was wondering if there's any chance I'll get assigned to Hickam."

"Well, it's good duty, but I suspect that your first assignment will be at Williams or one of the other flight training bases as an IP. Your academics and flying marks are tops—and it's a good way to pick up the maximum flight hours."

It wasn't a new idea to Tai. The limited assignments open to a woman pilot had been discussed ad nauseam at student bull sessions. "It's a possibility," she acknowledged.

Steven waited until the waiter had replaced their soup cups with plates of salad before he said, "There's something I have to tell you. This might be the only chance we have to talk without interruption, so hear me out."

"What is it?"

"You'll let me have my say?"

"Okay."

His voice unemotional, his eyes steady, Steven repeated a recent conversation he'd had with his father. Even before he was finished, Tai's eyes were filled with tears.

Her loyalty to Mac had never wavered, but in the deepest recesses of her heart there must have been some small doubt that he hadn't told her the whole story because she was conscious of an overwhelming relief. By repeating Colonel Henderson's confession, Steven had laid that particular ghost to rest.

He had also told her the truth at great cost to his own pride, when most men would have let things alone. But of course Steven wasn't like most men. He was himself, Steven, who never compromised, not when he was sure he was right, and who owned up to his mistakes, no matter what it cost.

"Thank you for telling me this," she said.

"Are we friends again?"

"We were once lovers, Steven, but I didn't think we ever were friends."

"I've always been your friend—and I want you to say the words. Will you accept my apology for assuming that Mac was guilty?"

"Apology accepted, but not really necessary. You had to believe your father, just as I had to believe mine."

"I think this calls for a celebration. How about some champagne?"

"Why not?"

Even with the champagne and their truce, Tai expected the evening to be awkward, but she was soon laughing at Steven's quips. Strange that she'd forgotten this about Steven, that he could always make her laugh. For the time being, it was easy to pretend that they were back in Hawaii, eating mahimahi at their favorite restaurant. The only thing missing was the tropical plantings and a Hawaiian combo in the background.

Steven seemed to be thinking along the same lines because he touched his glass to hers and said softly, "Here's to Hawaii."

"It all seems a long time ago," she said.

"It was. You've matured since those days."

"Is that a compliment?"

"It is. You used to look like a little girl. Sometimes I felt like a dirty old man when we were making—when we were together. The academy—and flight school—have changed you."

"I would have changed anyway, even if we'd followed our original plans."

"I wonder. So many military wives stay in the same old groove. Have you ever noticed how some of them still wear the same hairstyle they had when they graduated from high school—or college? It's like they've been trapped in amber."

"That's crazy. Why are you picking on military wives? With all the moving around and having to cope with all kinds of problems and changes, a military wife either grows up fast or she doesn't stay married."

"I disagree. Too many of them don't grow as people. They do all their shopping at the BX and commissary, associate only with other military wives, never make the least attempt to become a part of the civilian communities where their husbands are stationed. Sometimes they don't even bother to leave base, not even to go sight-seeing. In other words, they just mark time to retirement and have no life outside the air force."

"Well, you may be right, but that wouldn't have been my style," she said.

"No, your style is to make waves and fight windmills. Good thing you're not staying in. You'd probably be court-martialed the first time you took on a senior officer."

Tai grinned at him. "Or a general's wife? Did I tell you what happened to my friend Shelley?"

When she told him about Shelley's adventure with Mrs. Blackwell, Steven laughed so hard that he attracted curious glances from other tables. "And there were no repercussions?" he asked.

"None at all."

"She was lucky. It could have been different. Your friend must have lots of guts."

"The funny thing is that she seems so gentle, not like a fighter at all. I'm having lunch with her tomorrow. They're stationed at Travis now."

"Is her husband a pilot?"

"Crew chief on a C-five. He just got assigned to Korea for a year."

"Did I ever meet her?"

"She came to Punahou late in our senior year, but I may have mentioned her in my letters."

He snapped his fingers. "Shelley—of course. She's General Pritchard's kid. And you say she married an enlisted man? That must have shook up the old man."

"It was pretty bad. They disowned Shelley for a long time, but after her brother was killed, they wanted to make up. Seems they're crazy about their two grandsons. Shelley says they want her and the boys to stay with them in Colorado while Tad is in Korea. She's thinking about it."

"How come she didn't accompany him to Korea?"

"No quarters for dependents at his base. It's really been rough for Shelley. She had to move off base when he left since it's an unaccompanied tour, not TDY. She rented an apartment in Vacaville, and of course everything that can happen has happened—their old station wagon broke down, the refrigerator konked out, the kids have been sick. She tries to make it sound comical in her letters, but of course it can't be—"

She went on talking about Shelley, and although Steven's interest seemed genuine, Tai felt increasingly restive. Once, he touched her hand to draw her attention to a passing couple who were wearing Hawaiian leis. Which was a natural gesture—except that he didn't take his hand away again after the couple were gone. On one level, she was ashamed of her own awareness of him. After all, she wasn't on her first date, in an agony about what to say, how to act. On a more visceral level, she didn't want him to move his hand. Which was one hell of admission to have to make.

Later, she would wonder if Steven had planned the whole evening with one object in mind—to seduce her. She would even try to make herself believe that it was the wine that befuddled her mind and lowered her defenses. She would make other excuses, too, but the truth was that she never once raised an objection, not when he took her to the door of her hotel room, opened it with her key, and then, instead of saying good night and going off to his own room, followed her inside. Nor did she protest when he ordered drinks to be sent to their room, or when he settled himself on the edge of the bed and pulled her down beside him.

By the time their drinks were delivered, she was already partially undressed and had to retreat to the bathroom. There was plenty of time for second thoughts as she stood there in her bra and panties, waiting for the waiter to leave. But instead, she came straight back to Steven's arms, and when he had trouble with the fastening of her bra, she was the one who took it off, then slid out of her panties and stood in front of him naked and without defenses.

They never did finish their drinks. Steven lifted her in his arms so he could bury his face between her breasts, and he told her how many times he'd fantasized about making love to her on a soft mattress instead of in the back of a car or on a moon-drenched beach. It had been so long since they had made love, so why did it seem so familiar, as if they'd been sleeping together all those years between?

True, Steven's lovemaking was more skillful. He had learned new techniques, new ways to arouse a woman. And yet, it seemed as if time had stopped and this was their first time together, that tentative, gritty session of lovemaking on the beach. Her body hadn't forgotten Steven. Already her arms and thighs were accommodating to his shape, his touch, his arousal. Why was it that *this* man, no different from any other attractive and well-conditioned male, was so exciting that she felt as if she were dying when he touched her, fondled her, tasted her? It was a mystery, but there it was. She wanted to ask him to explain why he, not someone else, was what she wanted in a man, but at the moment she was much too busy. All that mattered was the need, the hunger, that only he could relieve.

Steven, too, was so caught up in the frenzy of their love-making that he had no desire to talk, so Tai had no way of knowing that her lover was also remembering that first time at the beach. Nor did she suspect that he was trying to find answers to his own questions.

Tai's appearance had changed, yes, but she felt the same in his arms. That supple body, those finely honed muscles, the texture of her skin, which looked so firm and yet was so incredibly soft, the musky odor when she was in passion that aroused him so quickly—why had he ever thought that voluptuous curves were sexy when this woman, so lean and close to the bone, had only to look at him to turn him on? What was the source of her appeal—and why, six years ago, had he given her up when he could have been sharing her life and her bed all this time?

The questions faded because he'd reached the moment of no return. As a keening cry came from Tai's lips, as her hands beat out a tattoo of climax on his shoulders, he knew that he couldn't take another chance, that he had to bind her to him for good before something else happened.

He proposed that night as they lay in each other's arms, and it was an indication of the strength of their renewed love that Tai didn't hesitate, didn't say a word about the difficulties of such a marriage.

"Yes, I'll marry you, Steven," she said.

CHAPTER

↑ 35 ↑

SHELLEY HAD ARRIVED AT THE BASE A LITTLE EARLY AND
was still sitting in the two-year-old Ford sedan that had replaced
their old station wagon, not wanting to get to the Officers Club
too soon, so she saw Tai drive up and park a few feet away.
To her surprise, Tai wasn't alone. She and the dark-haired man
who was driving talked for a minute, and then he kissed her
thoroughly before Tai got out of the car. She was smiling as
she watched him drive away.

Belatedly, Shelley opened her door and called to Tai. Her
friend waved and came toward her.

After they'd exchanged hugs, Shelley asked, "Well? Who
is he?"

"Steven Henderson," Tai said.

"Steven Henderson? Correct me if I'm wrong—this is the
same Steven Henderson who gave you such a bad time at the
academy? The one you used to be engaged to?"

"The very same. But things have changed. We're going to
get married as soon as I get my wings. He's got some business
at MAC Headquarters and then he'll be joining us. You'll like
him, Shelley."

"I'm sure I will," Shelley said, feeling a little dazed.

"I love him, Shelley—and he loves me. I know there's a
lot of problems ahead, but we're not going to borrow trouble.
Whatever comes up, we'll work it out."

Impulsively, Shelley put her arms around Tai and gave her

a hug. "I know you will. After all, look at the odds against Tad and me, and yet we're still together."

"How are things going? Did you straighten out that problem with your checking account you wrote me about?"

"It was my mistake, after all. The account was really overdrawn, just like the bank said."

"Sorry—look, if I can help you out—"

"No, it's all taken care of. And let's not talk about anything grim. Tell me about your wedding plans—"

For the next hour, over a luncheon salad and iced tea in a quiet corner of the Officers Club dining room, they rehashed old times and talked about old friends. They exchanged wry smiles when they compared notes and discovered that the only time either of them heard from Crystal was when she had some personal triumph to relate.

"You wonder why she bothers to keep in touch at all," Tai said. "Well, I wish her well. Her mother gave her a really rough time. I was over there once and Mrs. Moore kept making nasty cracks about Crystal. I felt so sorry for her."

Shelley found it difficult to feel sorry for someone so single-minded about feathering her own nest, an observation she kept to herself. "I keep thinking I'll take the boys down to Southern California to see Bobby Jo," she said instead. "It's just that it's such a long drive, and with Larry in school now—maybe I'll wait until spring, just before Tad gets back from Korea."

"You must be counting the days until his tour is over." Tai sighed. "I wonder how many times Steven and I will be separated in the next few years?"

"Maybe you'll get lucky. It's—it isn't easy. I miss Tad—and there's something so scary about being the sole person responsible for yourself and your kids."

"Have you decided what to do about your parents' invitation?"

"I'm going to stay here. Tad doesn't want me to go—and I don't want to stay with his parents in Pennsylvania, so it's a stand off."

Tai started to say something, but just then Steven Henderson joined them, and Shelley discovered that she did indeed like him. He was personable, attractive—and when he looked at Tai, his eyes seemed to devour her. No wonder they hadn't been able to forget each other. What had Crystal once said about them? That they sizzled like two firecrackers when they were together?

When Tai and Steven finally left to return their rental car to the terminal, Shelley walked to the parking lot with them, then stood watching as they drove off. For some reason, she felt very lonely and—she had to admit it—a little jealous. It wasn't that she begrudged Tai her happy ending. No, she was happy for her friend. But it was a little ironic that Tai, who had started out with so little, wouldn't have to face the same financial problem that she did—what would it be like to have two salaries coming in every month?

That night, after the boys were in bed, Shelley wrote her twice weekly letter to Tad. She mailed it the next day, even though, in reading it over, she was dissatisfied with it. Although she'd tried to sound cheerful, it seemed to her that some of her depression had crept in.

She was also fighting a strong case of guilt, which had made it doubly hard to hit the right note. True, the overdrawn check fiasco had been settled, but not the way she'd let Tai believe. It had almost killed her to borrow money from her father, but even that was preferable to having Tad find out that she simply couldn't manage on the allotment she got from him. He had his own worries—and the allowance he kept for himself was pared to the bone. She just couldn't ask him to get along on less when she'd been so stubborn about not staying with his parents while he was gone.

"The boys and I will be just fine," she'd said. "I think it would be taking advantage of your mother to accept her invitation."

"My mother doesn't make invitations she doesn't mean." Tad's voice had an edge. "Financially, we're just keeping our head above water now. You can't live in base housing while I'm gone, and off-base rent in this area is sky high—I don't think we can swing it. If you stay with my folks, that'll cut expenses way down. Hell, we might even be able to save a little for a change."

"I know what condition our finances are in," she said. "I write the checks—remember? If I stayed with anyone, it would be with my parents in Colorado Springs."

"Where you'd have stewards to run after the kids, cook your meals, and do your laundry, right? Yeah, I can see why you'd prefer that to living with my folks."

"If that sort of thing mattered to me, I wouldn't have married you, Tad," she said tightly.

Unexpectedly, Tad's face softened. "Hell—I know that. But how do you think I feel? I want to give you all those things, but it's never going to happen. You must have your doubts at times."

"Never! And I really don't want to stay with my parents. That was just—bitchiness. Mother and I would be at each other's throats five minutes after I got there. She'd interfere with the way we're raising the kids, and she and Dad would load them down with expensive toys and . . . well, it just wouldn't work. It's bad enough when they make those whirlwind visits."

"Yeah. It's funny how you suddenly notice the spots on the rug when they drop in," Tad said dryly.

"And how cramped the living room is—and how many cracks there are in the plastic cushions of that old recliner I bought for you at the thrift shop."

"Well, at least the general hasn't made another offer to see that I got an educational waiver so I could get into OTC," Tad said. "If I wanted to be an officer, I'd try for a scholarship under the Airman's Education Program—and I wouldn't need his help, either."

"I think, in his own way, he was trying to be helpful. He didn't realize you'd be insulted by his offer."

"Let's face it, Shelley. Your old man only wants to help me get a commission because it means his grandsons would have a more acceptable background—in his eyes. He doesn't give a damn about me."

"I didn't realize you felt that strongly about it, Tad. Why haven't you said anything about this before?"

He shrugged. "Why stir things up? Your folks don't come that often. Besides, the boys love them—and why not, when they come loaded down with expensive gadgets? My folks can't match that, but I wouldn't worry about you and the kids if you were staying with them. I know they don't measure up to your standards—"

"Is that your way of saying you think I'm a snob?"

"No—but you don't really like my family, do you? You think they're pretty low class."

"I think no such thing! I love your mother."

"But not enough to stay with her for a year?"

Shelley wasn't sure what to say. How could she tell Tad

that it was his father she couldn't stand? True, Tad had left home the first chance he got to get away from his father's heavy hand, but still—they were *his* people, his own flesh and blood.

"It isn't anything personal," she said diplomatically. "I do feel I should stay here. For one thing, the winters are so cold in Pennsylvania—"

"You loved Switzerland. It's even colder there."

"I was young then and didn't have to worry about the boys catching colds—"

It had ended in a quarrel, one that had festered even after they'd made up and rented the apartment in Vacaville, where she would be close to base facilities—and the base hospital.

But it also put the burden of proving she was capable of managing alone upon Shelley's shoulders. She was in the position where she couldn't complain, couldn't tell Tad how tired she got at the end of the day, so tired that she went to bed soon after the boys did most evenings. She couldn't complain about money, either. Every emergency, such as when the station wagon's transmission gave out and she had to buy another car, cut into their small reserve, until one day it was gone.

Since then, she'd watched every penny, shopping for food bargains, never spent money on a magazine or a lipstick. The meat and fruit she bought went to the boys, while she subsisted mainly on starchy—and filling—foods. Her sons were blooming, of course, while she had gained ten unneeded and unhealthy pounds.

Even so, she had managed okay until she'd made a mistake in her bookkeeping and had written a check for money that wasn't there. That's when she had gone to her father for a loan. He had not only sent her what she'd asked for but double that amount—along with another invitation to come to Colorado for the remaining months of Tad's tour. Desperately tired of living at rock bottom, she had kept the extra money, even though she'd refused the invitation.

So now she lived with the fear that Tad would find out. He had so much pride—God knew how he would react. How many times had she heard him say that the Brotskis would rather starve than accept charity, which was what he would consider the loan?

Fighting depression, she tried to put the whole business out of her mind for the next week. When that didn't work, she decided that she needed some time to herself, and she asked a neighbor to watch the boys while she went to the base exchange alone, a luxury in which she seldom indulged. She didn't tell her friend that there wasn't even an extra dollar in her wallet for shopping. Instead, she put on her best skirt and blouse, dropped off the boys, and drove to Travis. She treated herself to a Coke at the snack bar, then took her time, looking over the display cases full of cosmetics and perfumes and jewelry that she couldn't afford to buy.

Aware suddenly that she was feeling sorry for herself, she gave herself a mental scolding. How dare she think like that when she had so much! Tad was still the lover she'd married—that never changed, even when other things got rough. In fact, he was at his most tender when they were in financial hot water. Yes, Tad had a temper and he didn't confide in her as much as she would have liked, but he loved her. That she never doubted, not for one minute.

And the boys—they were so sturdy and independent. Didn't her parents realize that the grandsons they doted on were so much like the son-in-law they disliked? Not that they said anything against Tad. Oh, no, it was those little remarks her mother dropped, bits of news about her friends' children, about someone's son graduating from Yale or West Point, or a friend's daughter getting some honor at Stanford, a slow chipping away at Shelley's contentment. Tad had been right about that. She would be miserable, living with her parents—but oh, it would be such a relief to have someone share the responsibility of the children and not have to watch every lousy penny, to have a little time to herself. . . .

"Is that you, Shelley?"

The voice was female—and very familiar. Shelley looked around—into Crystal's eyes. Her first thought was that Crystal looked marvelous, almost pretty—and the second one was to thank God that she'd put on a skirt today instead of her usual jeans.

They touched cheeks and exchanged hugs. "This is really a surprise, Crystal. I thought you were still at Wright-Pat," Shelley said.

"Oh, we are. Grant is General Krause's vice-deputy now—I think I wrote you about it, didn't I? I came here with Sophie Krause—she's visiting a friend in Fairfield, but since she hasn't been too well, the general asked if I'd come along, too." She made a face. "What could I do? When a general asks a favor, you say *yes*."

Despite her bright tone, it was obvious that her first warmth was fading fast. "I intended to call you and see if we couldn't spend some time together, but . . . well, it's been so hectic. We're leaving late this afternoon, or we could still arrange something—"

"There you are, Crystal. I've been looking all over for you." The woman standing next to Crystal was bone thin. Although her features were sharp and her face had a fleshless look, Shelley thought she must once have been a very attractive woman.

Crystal introduced them hurriedly. "This is Shelley—we went to the same private school in Honolulu. I was just telling Shelley that we'll be leaving this afternoon."

Sophie Krause smiled at Shelley. "You're General Pritchard's daughter, aren't you? I met you at one of your mother's bashes. You still have that gorgeous hair, I see. Since you're wearing a wedding ring and you're shopping at the BX, I presume you married an air force man?"

"Yes, I did. My husband's in South Korea right now, teaching maintenance techniques to Korean aircraft mechanics. It's an unaccompanied tour, so my sons and I took an apartment in Vacaville."

"I see—well, I've been through it. I remember how lonely those UTs can be." She hesitated, then added, "I am so sorry about your brother, my dear. His death was a loss not only to his family, but to the air force. I understand he was an outstanding officer."

Shelley sensed that her words were sincere. There was no condescension here, although Mrs. Krause must know, from her description of Tad's assignment in Korea, that she was married to an enlisted man. How sad that Crystal was fidgeting, anxious to get away. Didn't she realize how obvious she was? Or maybe Crystal was only obvious to someone who had known her before she had perfected her act—and she did look smashing in that turquoise suit, which made her own clothes look like they had come off the racks at K-mart.

"Why don't you have lunch with us, Shelley?" Sophie Krause was saying. "As my guest, of course."

Shelley hesitated, tempted by the invitation—until she caught the flash of annoyance in Crystal's eyes. She declined, inventing a doctor's appointment.

When Crystal, with Mrs. Krause in tow, took herself off, after another round of cheek brushings and promises to write soon, Shelley went to the ladies' room to bathe her hot cheeks in cold water. She felt diminished, as if Crystal's subtle snub had somehow reduced her worth as a human being. Although she knew it was absurd to feel this way, suddenly she couldn't wait to be back with her boys. There, at least, she was certain of her importance—and welcome.

The thing about the encounter with Crystal, she reflected as she drove home, was not that she envied Crystal her husband's rank or her social life, because she didn't, not one iota. What bothered her was the certainty that Crystal *believed* she did—and that was humiliating, an irritant that had ruined her rare outing.

Tad didn't open Shelley's letter immediately. He waited until he was alone, stretched out on his bunk in the cubicle he shared with another instructor, before he slit it open with his thumbnail. It had the peculiar briny odor that he associated with the hold of a ship—or the belly of a cargo plane—and he wished that Shelley would perfume her letters like some of the other wives did. Or maybe that was another thing she considered too low class.

The thought startled him. Where had *that* come from? He, of all people, knew Shelley wasn't a snob. She was reserved, yes, but she never looked down her nose at anyone because of her own background. But what tightened his jaw right now was not Shelley, but her old man. Although he hadn't told this to Shelley, General Pritchard was still at it. He'd called from Colorado just a week ago with another offer to pull wires to get Tad a commission, this time through some kind of direct commission deal that sounded as illegal as hell to Tad.

Well, he'd set the general straight—and he hadn't minced words. Hell, he didn't want to be an officer, didn't want the responsibility, the game playing, and the backbiting. Just about every officer he met was running scared, scrambling for promotions. In his opinion, they never formed real friendships with each other because they were all competing too hard for the same promotion slots. Only officers who'd been in the same class at the academy or ROTC or ATS seemed to really groove together—and how often did a man get stationed with an old classmate, the air force being so big?

No, he preferred being a sergeant—not that he didn't intend to be an E-9 someday, which was pretty exclusive company. Someone had told him once that there were more damned colonels in the air force than there were chief master sergeants! And everybody knew who really kept the planes flying. Where would the pilots be without the mechanics? As far as he was concerned, pilots were just glorified bus drivers.

Out of curiosity, he'd taken one of those pilot potential tests once and had made a higher score than the squadron commander, who was supposed to be such a hot pilot. The old man got all fired up and tried to talk him into signing up for flight school. Fat chance. He didn't want to be a pilot, depending on other men's mechanical skill to stay alive. No, he was doing just what he wanted to do, keeping the planes in the air.

Which was why he'd flipped when Shelley's old man had offered to arrange some kind of waiver so he could get a direct commission. Of course it wasn't Shelley's fault that her old man was a jerk. Still, he couldn't help thinking sometimes how simple life would be if Shelley came from ordinary folks.

The old man had been pissed off at his refusal, even though he'd tried to hide it behind that cool way he had. Tad might even think this latest tour in Korea had been instigated by the old bastard if his orders hadn't already been cut before the general's last offer. Come to think of it, Major Hastings *had* been surprised as hell when the orders came in out of the blue, just like the time Tad had been sent to the Philippines. But he had to be wrong about that because this job was genuine. It was a rough slot to fill, too, because teaching these Koreans proper aircraft maintenance was like trying to read through molasses. For one thing, there was the language barrier. All of them were supposed to speak English, but it was the strangest English he'd ever heard.

The familiar noises of the barracks—voices, coughs, someone singing a country-western song off key—filtered through the thin walls of his room as he reread Shelley's letter. When he was finished, he stared into space for a while, trying to sort out his impressions.

Usually she wrote such long letters, which he enjoyed, even though he had to agonize over the short notes he sent her in return. But today's letter was short—very short. When she asked him to write more about the Koreans he met, was she hinting that his own letters were too brief? God knew he didn't have the knack of putting words down on paper. Before Shelley had taken over the job of writing to his mom, he'd seldom written home more than a couple of times a year. As for making a big thing about the local customs here—what did he know about that? Did she think he associated with the locals off duty? If so, she really had her signals crossed.

The truth was he had this . . . well, uneasy feeling around Orientals. Didn't know just how to handle them because they seemed so damned alien. After all, he'd been in his late teens before he'd seen his first one—except in the movies or on TV.

And this business about Shelley taking art lessons. Somehow that didn't set right with him. Sure, he had told her once to take up a hobby, but didn't she have enough to do with him gone? And didn't they use . . . well, nude male models and stuff like that in those classes?

Maybe it was time they had another kid. Even on his pay and allowances, they could manage one more. After all, the medical part was free, and they already had a lot of baby clothes and equipment. This time, he'd like a girl, especially if it took after Shelley. Of course she changed the subject every time he brought it up, but when he got home, he intended to talk her into it. A new baby would keep her busy.

Funny that he always felt so good when Shelley was pregnant. Why the hell was that? It wasn't as if she had easy pregnancies and was all smiles like some pregnant women were. Her morning sickness was more like all-day sickness— and this for four or five months instead of the usual three. Hormones, the doctor called it, but personally, Tad suspected at least part of it was mental. When one of his brothers' wives complained about morning sickness, his father's favorite remark was, "It's all in your head, girl."

Unconsciously, Tad grimaced. Why, when he couldn't get along with the old man, did he quote him so often, as if his opinions were gospel? And why, when he'd been so eager to leave home, what with Poppa always on his back, had he tried to talk Shelley into staying with his folks while he was in Korea?

It wasn't the money, no matter what he'd said. It was— hell, it was because he wanted to know that she and the boys were tucked away in some safe place until he was able to look after them himself. And maybe some of it was because he didn't like the idea of her being around the base with the men looking her over. Oh, he saw them—not that Shelley ever seemed to notice. She didn't have any idea what she did to guys. Even when she was pregnant, he'd seen them ogling her. But what if some guy who had a lot more to offer than he did came along—and she started thinking about all she'd missed?

He was rereading the letter when Chuck Malley, the tech sergeant who shared Tad's room, came barreling through the door.

"Hey, hey—more mail from your old lady? She must really like to write letters," Malley said, his voice too loud in the small room.

Tad looked at him with jaded eyes. In his opinion, Malley represented the worst type of noncom. Subservient to officers, overbearing with men of lesser rank, a goof-off from the word go, he also had a filthy mind.

Before I leave here, Tad thought coldly, I'm going to have to deck that guy. . . .

He put the letter away without answering. Malley didn't seem to notice. "How about mixing it up with the local talent tonight? There's this gal who's related to my moose who'll give you a good time. She does everything—and I mean everything. A real four plus, if you dig me."

"No, thanks," Tad said. "I'm going to take in the movie tonight."

"Hell, man, that won't loosen your bolts. If you're worried about taking something back to the wife, this little gal is clean. She just takes on one guy at a time, stays with him until he rotates. She lives with her old lady, who rents out a spare room with bed privileges—you know what I mean? How about it? You want me to fix you up?"

"I want you to keep your nose out of my business," Tad said, his voice tight. "I don't run around on my wife."

"Oh, shit. Nothing worse than a holy Joe," his roommate said in disgust. "I hope you don't think that wife of yours is sitting home, minding the kids. A looker like that—half the guys at Travis must be ringing her doorbell. Wise up, Brotski. That's how it is. I'm smart enough to know that someone is probably banging my old lady right now."

Tad wanted to smash in Malley's face. Instead, he looked him in the eye and told him, "That's your problem. Like I said,

I want you to keep out of my business. One more word about my wife and I'm going to kick your fucking face in."

He was sure that Malley would take him on, and he discovered that he was itching for the fight. But his roommate just shrugged and muttered, "Try to do someone a favor and you get kicked in the teeth. If you want to tough it out, that's your business."

He changed his clothes and was gone, leaving behind the odor of cigarette smoke and the musk after-shave that he used instead of taking a shower. Tad opened the window to clear the air. The winter wind came whistling in, ice cold and filled with a dozen odors, including those from the open sewers of the workers' settlement close by.

Despite Tad's contempt of Malley, the man's poisonous words rankled. True, there was no resemblance between Shelley and the slut Malley was married to, but still—it was true that the guys must be looking Shelley over, ready to move in if they got half a chance. In lots of ways, she was so damned dumb. Look how fast she'd fallen for *his* line. And it had been a line—until he'd discovered that he wanted something more than sex. Hell, she'd needed a keeper then, and he sometimes wondered if she still didn't.

And that letter—there was something about it he didn't like. The thing was, he wasn't good at figuring out people. He just went by instinct. "By gosh and by golly," they called it back home.

For the third time, he read Shelley's letter, and his frown deepened. She'd made a big thing about her friend Tai visiting her. Was that what was bugging him? Tai and Shelley had kept up with each other pretty regularly, which was strange because Shelley had told him once that they hadn't been all that friendly at school. They were so different, you wouldn't think they'd have much in common. Still, Shelley really admired Tai. She'd written, "Sometimes I feel—you know, embarrassed because I haven't done much except get married and have two kids. I'm really proud of Tai. It takes guts to make it in a man's world."

It sounded almost as if she regretted marrying him. Wasn't being a wife and a mother enough? Why would she envy Tai, who was neither? Was it because her friend was marrying that pilot, an officer?

That night, he answered Shelley's letter. He told her that

while he understood that she needed a hobby, he thought she should wait until he got back before she signed up for that art course.

"I don't think you should leave the boys with other people," he wrote. "After all, they're your responsibility, not the neighbors. When I get back, we'll talk about this. Until then, why don't you just forget it?"

Shelley got the letter a week later. Tad hadn't written anything about the Koreans he worked with, nor did he comment on Tai's visit. When she got to the last paragraph, saying he wanted her to postpone signing up for the art class, Shelley crushed the sheet of tablet paper between her hands. Damn him, anyway—who did he think he was, giving her orders? She was an individual, not a puppet. She didn't need Tad to point out her responsibilities. Who did he think took care of his kids twenty-four hours a day while he was in Korea? Didn't he realize that she needed a break once in a while? Or maybe he didn't. Maybe he thought she was some kind of superwoman—like his mother or his sisters-in-law.

That evening, as Shelley was heating tomato soup and grilling cheese sandwiches for dinner, the phone rang.

Bobby Jo's voice cut through her "Hello?" "Shelley, I need help. I'm in trouble, and there isn't anyone else I can turn to."

"What kind of trouble?"

"It's . . . oh, I don't want to tell you over the phone. I'm sick, really sick, and I need someone to take care of me for a few days. I can't ask any of my neighbors or friends here because it would be all over Josh's squadron and then he would find out. And my parents—if they knew about it, they'd just die—"

She broke off with a sob.

"Calm down, Bobby Jo," Shelley said soothingly. "You'll have to tell me more or how can I help you?"

"Okay—only I feel so rotten and ashamed. You—you're going to think I'm terrible. You probably won't have anything more to do with me."

"Tell me, Bobby Jo," Shelley said firmly.

"I—I had an abortion two days ago. I went to this doctor in town because how could I go to the base hospital? It would be in my medical records and then Josh would find out—"

"I don't understand. I thought you and Josh wanted another child," Shelley said, thoroughly bewildered.

"But it wasn't his baby. I had to get rid of it because . . . oh, Shelley, I didn't mean for it to happen. It was because I was so upset about Josh and that letter I found in his jacket pocket. It was from this girl he'd had sex with. When I jumped him about it, he said all the guys did it and it wasn't any big thing. We had a big fight and then he went off to Squadron Officers School and I was so mad that I went out with this guy I met. He was really sweet, and the next thing I knew we— we were having an affair. Then his wife moved here and he broke it off. I found out I was two months pregnant, and with Josh gone for four months, how could the baby be his? I was so desperate that I—I got rid of it, only now I have this fever and I feel so weak. I can't go to the base hospital and have it put on my medical records, and two of the wives from Josh's outfit do volunteer work for the abortion clinic in town, so I can't go there. I tried to call the doctor, but all I got was his answering service, saying he was on vacation, would be back in two weeks—and he didn't give a referral to another doctor. So now I don't know what to do—"

"Calm down, Bobby Jo," Shelley said, alarmed by the panic in her friend's voice. "Everything's going to be all right. You'll have to find another civilian doctor."

"But who's going to take care of Vicky? She's already asking questions. When I went to that doctor, I arranged for her to stay with a friend of mine, only I didn't realize that I'd be so sick afterward. If Josh finds out, he'll divorce me—I know he will. It's all right for him to sleep around, but not me. Oh, no, I'm supposed to not say a word about it—"

"Go back to bed, Bobby Jo," Shelley said. "Tell Vicky that you have the flu. And try to get some sleep. It will take me a couple of hours to get things squared away here, but if I drive all night, I can be there by morning. And don't worry. Everything's going to be all right."

She hung up on Bobby Jo's fervent thanks and went to feed the boys and then to pack.

CHAPTER
↑ 36 ↑

WHEN SHELLEY ARRIVED AT THE DEVELOPMENT OF TRACT
homes in the outskirts of Victorville, where Bobby Jo lived,
she noted it looked much the same as her own shabby neighborhood in Vacaville. So much for being married to an officer,
she thought as she drove past the rows of small ranch houses,
differing only in the varied colors of their doors.

A few minutes later, when a small, dark-haired girl opened
the royal-blue door of Bobby Jo's house, she had a hard time
concealing her surprise. It was hard to reconcile this sulky,
rather plain child with the one her friend had described in such
glowing terms. Vicky looked Shelley over, then turned the same
appraising stare on the boys, who eyed her back warily.

"You're Shelley, aren't you?" she said before Shelley could
speak. "I didn't know you were bringing *them*, too. They can't
play with my things—and they can't go in my room, either."

Shelley ignored her rudeness and introduced Larry and Mark.
"Would you see that the boys get something to eat?" she said,
only later realizing that she was treating Vicky as if she were
an adult. "We didn't stop for breakfast because I was anxious
to get here. Peanut-butter sandwiches will be fine."

To her relief, Vicky nodded. She marched off toward the
back of the house, followed by the silent boys.

Shelley brought in the luggage she'd packed so hurriedly,
then went looking for Bobby Jo. As she passed through a small,
sparsely furnished living room, its disorder dismayed her. She

423

would have chalked it up to Bobby Jo's illness except that the scattering of magazines and newspapers, the discarded clothing draped over the backs of chairs, and the dust on the furniture was obviously nothing new. Through an open closet door in the hall, she saw a cardboard box full of empty vodka bottles, and her worry changed to exasperation.

The odor of illness, sharp and immediate, assaulted her nostrils as she opened the next door she came to. Bobby Jo was lying crossways across the bed as if she'd been too weak or tired to turn around the proper way. She was wearing a soiled cotton wrapper, and when she heard Shelley's "Are you awake, Bobby Jo?" she opened her eyes and struggled to a sitting position. She met Shelley's appalled stare, and tears gathered in her eyes.

Shelley was speechless. She had never seen Bobby Jo look anything but immaculate, with her face made up and her hair carefully arranged. It was hard to reconcile this woman, with her drawn face, lusterless hair, and haunted eyes, with her vivacious friend who was always so quick to laugh.

"How do you feel?" she asked as she bent over to kiss Bobby Jo's cheek.

"Terrible. I'm so sorry to be such a bother, but I just didn't know who else to turn to."

"You'd do the same for me, so let's not hear any more of that kind of talk. I'm going to give you a sponge bath, then I'm taking you to a doctor. Do you think you can walk to the car? If not, I can drag you on a chair. Learned that in summer camp—one of my few useful talents."

Bobby Jo giggled. "Oh, Shelley, it's so good to see you," she said, wiping her eyes.

"Never fear, Shelley's here." Shelley went on talking, determinedly cheerful, as she gave Bobby Jo a quick sponge bath, then got her into a clean gown and robe. Bobby Jo submitted docilely, as if she had abdicated all responsibility to her friend, but when Shelley suggested that she call the base hospital to send out an ambulance, she shook her head frantically.

"No—not the base hospital. They'd know that I'd had an abortion."

"Then I'll call a civilian doctor. Maybe we can get one to come here and examine you. If not, I'll take you there in my car."

Half an hour later, having called several local doctors, none of whom would make a house call, she found a doctor who was willing to come. Perhaps he read desperation behind her careful explanations and guessed why she wouldn't consider taking Bobby Jo to a hospital emergency room because he broke in and told her brusquely, "I'll be there in half an hour."

He got there in less than that, and when she opened the door, some of her anxiety subsided. He was a short, stocky man, younger than she'd expected, but something in his manner gave her confidence as he examined Bobby Jo thoroughly, then turned to Shelley and motioned for her to follow him to the living room.

"Infection—but it isn't out of control. Antibiotics should do it. I don't think she needs hospitalization."

Shelley said, "Thank God for that."

"Are you a relative?"

"A friend. She—you understand why she doesn't want to be hospitalized?"

His eyes moved around the cluttered living room, then stopped at a picture of Josh in his uniform. "Yeah. Well, she'll be okay. Next time, I hope she's more careful."

He wrote out a prescription, got a sample bottle of pills from his bag, and handed them to her. "For pain—every three hours." He snapped his bag shut with an air of finality. "Get that prescription filled, and keep a close watch on Mrs. Springer's temperature. If it goes any higher, give me a ring. And see that she takes all her antibiotics. No stopping them just because she feels better and her temperature drops to normal."

"About the bill—"

"My wife sends them out the first of the month. The complaint will be listed as the flu. There's a charge for the house call—but not too much. I'm just getting started. Later on, it'll cost your friend an arm and a leg to get me to make a house call."

His words startled Shelley into a laugh, and his face relaxed into a brief smile before he added, "Keep an eye on her. She's too apathetic. Some of it's the fever, but some of it's mental, too. This—what she's been through can cause all kinds of traumas in a woman. If she doesn't come out of her depression after a few days, think about getting her some professional help."

After he was gone, Shelley rejoined Bobby Jo, a determined smile on her face.

"Am I going to be okay?" Bobby Jo asked.

"It's just a mild infection. The doctor left you some pain pills and a prescription. I'll get it filled right away. Meanwhile, you try to get some rest."

Bobby Jo sank back on her pillows with a sigh. "You're a real friend, Shelley." And then she added, "I'm sorry we weren't closer when we were at Punahou together."

The next few days were hectic, but Shelley, who had never thought of herself as being a takeover person, found the role of nurse strangely satisfying.

Bobby Jo slept a lot, maybe from the medicine or simply as a retreat from reality, and Shelley used the time to put the house in order. The boys, much to her surprise, got along well with Vicky. As meek as lambs, her two rough-and-tumble sons took Vicky's orders, and when she got her own way, which was most of the time, she shared her games and toys with them, fussed over them, even mothered them. As Shelley was preparing dinner, she listened to their conversation in the living room, and despite herself, she had to smile.

Vicky was "reading" to them from a book, and although it was obvious she was simply repeating an often heard story, the boys listened with awed attention.

It was only with Bobby Jo that Vicky seemed hostile. She seldom went into her mother's bedroom, and when she did, she didn't stay long. Since Bobby Jo seemed unable to cope with her, Shelley finally took Vicky aside for a little talk.

"You're very mature for your age, Vicky," she started out.

"I'm almost six," Vicky said.

"Larry's seven—and yet you seem years older. Which makes me wonder why you and your mother don't have a better relationship. You and my boys get along so well—"

"They don't bug me," Vicky said.

"But your mother loves you—"

"No, she doesn't. She thinks I'm ugly."

"Oh, I can't believe that! Why, you have such lovely hair and your eyes are spectacular—"

"What does that mean—spectacular?" Vicky asked suspiciously.

"It means you have very pretty eyes."

"*She* doesn't think so. She wanted a boy. I heard her telling Poppa that she could—could cope better with boys, that she didn't know how to treat a girl. And he said—"

"I don't think you should repeat your parents' private conversations," Shelley interrupted quickly. "And I'm sure Bobby Jo didn't mean she wanted *you* to be a boy. It's just that she was used to boys, having all those younger brothers. I felt the same way when Larry was born because I was the youngest child and I'd never had any experience with babies."

"So how did you learn what to do with him?"

"From books," Shelley said ruefully. "Which isn't the best way. Also, my husband came from a large family. He helped a lot—and I learned as I went along. Your mother is doing the same. You'll understand this better when you have kids of your own someday. Remember—she didn't have her mother to help her when you were a baby. She had to do it all by herself because your father was taking flight training then, and later he was gone so much of the time. She's still so afraid of doing something wrong that when you're . . . uh, rude to her, she doesn't know how to handle it. After we're gone, she's going to be weak for a while. She'll need your help. She also needs a lot of love and understanding, and I think you're mature enough to give it to her. Your mother . . . well, she doesn't have a lot of confidence in herself right now."

"It's Poppa," Vicky said. "He doesn't listen, no matter what she says. He doesn't listen to me, either, but then I'm just a little kid. Adults never listen to kids, do they?"

"Not enough. Sometimes I'm so busy telling the boys what to do that I don't really hear what they're saying," Shelley said. "We get so wrapped up in our own lives that we let you kids down. It's just that we have so many responsibilities—"

"I don't ever want to grow up," Vicky said fiercely. "But I don't like being a kid, either."

"You're a great kid, and you'll be a wonderful woman someday. I have a feeling you'll be able to cope with just about everything."

Vicky's dark eyes considered her. "I like you—and I don't like most of Mommy's friends. They all talk so silly."

"Well, thank you. You know, Vicky, you have to get through the years until you grow up. Might as well do it the easiest way. You could start by making friends with your mother. She needs a good friend. And she's really a very nice person."

"She's okay, I guess. It's just that she doesn't much like me. How can you like someone who doesn't like you?"

"She loves you. You should read the things she says about

you in her letters. She brags about how well you can cook and how you take care of your own room and how helpful you are when you two go shopping at the commissary."

"She said *that*?"

"Of course. Surely she's told you all this."

"Yeah—only she says nice things to everybody, so I didn't believe her. She tells Poppa he's so great, and yet he treats her ... well, he never listens to her. He comes home from a trip and they go into the bedroom right away and fool around, but he never talks to her. He thinks she's dumb. Of course, he never talks to me, either, and I'm real smart."

Shelley sighed. She already knew more than she wanted to know about Bobby Jo's marriage, having been the recipient of her friend's confidences, too. Suddenly she couldn't wait to get back home. Tad might work with his hands and bring home half the pay Josh did, but she was sure that she'd never find any love letters from another woman in his jacket pocket. And why she should be so sure of this when women couldn't keep their hands, much less their eyes, off Tad, she didn't know. But she did. Was all life a trade-off? You gave up one thing, but you gained something else?

Well, this week had given her something to think about. Seeing what complete dependence on a man had done to Bobby Jo had been a revelation. Bobby Jo had turned into some kind of doormat, an extension of Josh's ego, and when he wasn't around, she'd been a sitting duck for the kind of man who exploits vulnerable women. That couldn't happen to her, she was sure of that, because she had too much pride to let anyone walk over her, and yet—sometimes she did give in when she and Tad had a real difference of opinion, just to keep the peace. Maybe it would be a mistake to give up that art course she really wanted. What harm could it do to steal a few hours for herself? Compromise meant that both sides gave a little, didn't it? And except for one thing, refusing to stay with Tad's parents while he was in Korea, she had gone Tad's way during most of their marriage.

When she got home, she would make a decision or two. Right now, three hungry kids were waiting for their dinner—and she hadn't even started peeling the potatoes.

Shelley and her boys left a week later. As Bobby Jo stood at the doorway beside Vicky, watching Shelley's Ford sedan slowly move down the street, she already missed them. She had grown very fond of Larry and Mark in the past two weeks, and she knew the house would seem too quiet with them gone. Vicky would miss them, too. She'd actually cried when Shelley's car pulled away from the curb. Was she that lonely for brothers and sisters? What would she think if she knew how her mother had wronged her by getting an abortion?

An intolerable ache filled Bobby Jo's empty body. How strange that before the abortion, the baby hadn't seemed real. And now, when it was too late, she mourned for the human being who had never had a chance to be born. Well, it was too late for regrets, but not for learning from her mistakes. She had made a choice, and now she had to live with it. From now on, no matter how painful it was, she had to take responsibility for her own life and not just drift into things. And the place to start was with Vicky.

Seeing Shelley, so loving and yet so firm with her boys, made her realize how much she'd shorted Vicky. If it wasn't too late, she had to find a way to reach her. Right now, Vicky's hostility was so deeply entrenched that it seemed impossible to change it, but somehow she must learn how to act—and feel?—like a real mother.

As she turned to go back in the house, it came to her that maybe she'd made too much of doing the right thing. Since she seldom knew what the right thing was, she usually ended up doing nothing. Maybe if she treated Vicky as another person instead of as her daughter, it would help. And what would she do right now if Vicky were a friend? Why, she'd try to comfort her.

After a moment's hesitation, she put her arm around Vicky's thin shoulders. When Vicky leaned against her, the strength of her own reaction—of affection, of relief—surprised her.

"I wish they lived closer," she said aloud.

"Can we go see them, Mommy?" Vicky said eagerly. "Shelley invited us, you know. Or maybe the boys could come here for a visit sometime—I really like them."

"So do I."

"You like boys better than you do girls, don't you?"

"Not really," Bobby Jo said, feeling her way. "Boys are so . . . well, they're so wrapped up in sports and that sort of thing. Girls are better company because they're more concerned about people things. There's an old saying about a son being a son until he takes a wife, but a daughter is a daughter all her life."

Vicky fixed her with a disconcerting stare. "What does that mean?"

"Oh, that mothers and daughters are friends all their lives."

"Are *we* friends?" Vicky said doubtfully.

"Of course. Even if you weren't my daughter, we'd like each other, wouldn't we? That's being friends," Bobby Jo said, resisting the impulse to cross her fingers.

"Like you and Shelley?"

"Right."

"She's really neat—and so pretty. Are you jealous because she's prettier than you?"

Out of the mouths of babes, Bobby Jo thought, but she was more amused than piqued by Vickey's question. How many of the hurtful things that Vicky said weren't insolence at all, but simple honesty?

"I'm not jealous of her. She's my friend—and besides, what people look like aren't nearly as important as what they do," Bobby Jo said, hoping she didn't sound too preachy.

"But you're always primping—that's what Poppa says," Vicky pointed out.

"Maybe that's because I want to look my best for your father. It's so important to him that I look nice."

Vicky was silent for a moment. "I look like Poppa, don't I?"

"Indeed you do. A miniature Josh, that's you. You're going to be a beautiful woman someday, but I don't think you'll ever waste much time worrying about how you look."

"But I want to look like you. I think you're pretty."

Bobby Jo discovered that she was deeply touched. One thing about a person who was devastatingly honest. When they did compliment you, you knew they meant it.

"If *you* say so, I know it must be true," she said, her tone light.

Vicky gave her a wary look. "Are you laughing at me? I don't like people to laugh at me."

Bobby Jo hugged her. "Oh, Vicky, I'd never do that—and we should talk together more. I think having Shelley here was good for us. Maybe I can get my act together now and be a better mother."

"Are you going to stop drinking that stuff that makes you act so silly?"

Bobby Jo's heart skipped a beat. "I'll try," she said carefully.

"I wish Poppa would stop, too. His face gets so red and he talks so loud when he's drinking."

"I can't promise for your father, but I can promise for myself." A sudden weakness in her knees warned Bobby Jo that it was time to get off her feet again. "I think I'd better go lie down for a while. Why don't you watch TV until lunch?"

"I can fix lunch—as long as you don't want something fancy," Vicky said importantly. "Shelley said I should take care of you until you get over the flu."

"Bless Shelley," Bobby Jo murmured. "She's a good friend— and your old mommy needs friends right now."

"I'll be your friend," Vicky said.

During the next few weeks, Bobby Jo often thought of the promise she'd given Vicky so easily and that was so hard to keep. Most of the time she succeeded, although sometimes she slipped back into her old apathy and then only a drink would make her mental pain endurable. But most of the time, she kept her promise. She spent more time with Vicky, playing games or taking walks or going to the city park. To keep herself so busy she wouldn't have time to brood, she decided to fix up the house a little. She bought supplies at the hardware store in the shopping center and painted the drab walls of the living room a soft, sunny yellow, then framed two travel posters and hung them behind the sofa.

When she asked Vicky if she'd like to choose a color for her own bedroom, Vicky offered to help with the painting. It was a little daunting to realize that Vicky, at six, was neater at trimming the edges of windows and baseboards than her mother was. Bobby Jo regretted all the skills she hadn't learned, but since she wasn't an expert at painting—or anything else— at least she couldn't tell Vicky what she did wrong, which made for a certain harmony.

Despite the improvement in her relationship with Vicky, Bobby Jo had to fight constant depression. She seldom allowed herself to think about Josh because it only added to her misery. As the days, then the weeks, passed, she found herself dreading his return more and more. Not just because of her guilt but because it was so peaceful, just she and Vicky.

Sometimes, her marriage, her whole life, seemed unreal, as if she were a shadow instead of a real person. She had always done what was expected of her—by her parents, her friends, her husband. No wonder Josh found her boring, her opinions unimportant. She was just a convenience to him, someone who kept his house and shared his bed. And when he was away from home, she was interchangeable with other women. She couldn't blame it all on Josh. His opinion of her had obviously been shared by Deke, her lover, whom she'd thought really cared for her—and who had dropped her so quickly when his wife appeared on the scene.

Well, she didn't like the person she was. She didn't want to be a shadow person. The thing was—she didn't know exactly what she did want to be. She had no special talent, no special interest—except in old movies. Josh had made so much fun of her taste in books that she'd even stopped reading the historical romances she loved. She had loafed through school, just getting by—and she had taken the easy electives because everybody had advised her to.

"Choose some easy courses," her own father had advised. "You probably won't use what you learn, anyway, but it can't hurt to get a diploma."

And her advisers had steered her toward a liberal arts degree. Josh had laughed at that, too, saying she'd wasted her time. When she'd looked hurt, he'd kissed her and added that he was glad she wasn't an intellectual because nothing was more boring than a woman with brains. Still, she hadn't done too badly when she put her mind to it. That poetry class she'd taken her sophomore year at Colorado College—she had made all A's. Not that this would help if she decided to get a job. She could type a little—but she didn't want to be stuck in an office typists' pool.

What she'd really like was a job where she could deal with people. Maybe she could get a job clerking in a store. No, Josh would never stand for that. Not classy enough for an officer's wife. Still—there must be something she could do to keep her from climbing the walls. . . .

The day after Vicky started first grade, Bobby Jo went job hunting, hoping to find part-time work. If Josh made her quit when he got back home, so be it. Meanwhile it would be good experience—and keep her busy.

By the end of the week, her efforts had been so fruitless

that she almost gave it up. At first, she thought her failure was because she had no work experience or work skills, but after she'd been turned away several times without even being allowed to fill out an application form, another pattern began to emerge. When she first spoke to the employment clerks, they were cordial enough—until she told them that her husband was stationed at George AFB, and then the climate changed and they told her they were sorry, but there were no openings.

Two of the jobs—receptionist for a doctor and word processor trainee for an insurance company—she was sure she could have filled. The pay was minimal, so the requirements were less exacting, but even so, when they heard the words "My husband's with the air force," their interest died, and she soon was being ushered out.

She'd heard other military wives talk about the prejudices against them, but only now did she realize the feelings of rejection that they'd covered up with jokes. It was humiliating to be turned away, not for lack of talent or training or experience, but simply because you were married to a service man who was likely to be transferred somewhere else someday.

"Military wives are second-class citizens," one of the wives in Josh's outfit had once complained, and Bobby Jo knew now it was true—and that it hurt to be considered second class.

Only the knowledge that she wasn't alone, that she was experiencing something thousands of other women had, kept her going. Most of her life, she had drifted into things, including both of her pregnancies. For the sake of her own pride, she had to win this battle—or return to the bottle.

Even so, she was deeply discouraged after a particularly traumatic experience. One interviewer had been so rude—and this for a job that paid slave wages—that she decided to stop at a small, side-street cafeteria for a cup of tea to restore her courage.

She was sitting in a rear booth, sipping her tea and munching on a sandwich she didn't really want, when she heard the two men in the next booth talking. She didn't mean to eavesdrop, but the booths were so close together that it was impossible not to hear their conversation.

"Have you found anyone to replace Josie?" one said.

"Not yet. The employment agency is sending out some applicants tomorrow. Actually, the main requirement is someone who can make the clients comfortable."

"I know what you mean. Buying a house is a big step to most people. They do get uptight easily."

"What I need is someone who'll make them feel welcome, and get them a cup of coffee without acting as if she's doing them a favor. Sort of an office hostess. Josie was perfect for the job—easygoing and reliable."

"When is her baby due?"

"In a few weeks. She was going to work until the end of the month, but her husband's raising hell, doesn't want her on her feet so much. She's only staying on until I find a replacement."

"Well, don't get one of those libber types because they get insulted if you ask them to serve coffee to the clients."

"Women have a right to be touchy. It's time they got a little respect in the business world, but in this case—acting as a hostess is part of the job requirement."

"I hear you talking."

The other man laughed, and the conversation moved to a discussion about business. Bobby Jo, who had been sitting very still, not wanting to miss anything, returned to her sandwich. An idea had come to her, one that excited her. The job the man had described was tailor-made for her. She liked people, liked making them comfortable and putting them at ease. Even Josh never faulted her for that. Everybody said she was a good hostess, and that's what this job was—being a hostess. The man had even used that word.

If she needed typing skills, she had enough to get by on. She could answer the phone—people said she had a good phone voice. And she certainly didn't think it was humiliating to be nice to people and to serve them coffee. What difference was there between that and waiting tables in a restaurant or clerking in a store?

She paid the waitress so she'd be ready to leave by the time the two men were finished with their lunch. When they rose, she rose, too, and followed them to the door, only to realize that they were going in opposite directions, that she had no idea which man was looking for a receptionist.

The rather stocky, older man, she decided finally. Surely that rumbly sort of voice suited him better than it did the younger man with the sharp features.

Half a block from the cafe, the man she was following turned into a small white brick building. The sign painted across the front read SAMUEL SHOULDERS, REAL ESTATE, and when she went in through the bronze-trimmed glass door, the murmuring of voices, the ringing of a telephone, and the clicking of a word processor greeted her.

The woman at the front desk was very pregnant. She gave Bobby Jo a friendly smile and asked, "May I help you, miss?"

"I'd like to see Mr. Shoulders," Bobby Jo said, taking a chance on the name.

"Do you have an appointment?"

"No—do I need one?"

"Not if Mr. Shoulders isn't busy," the woman said cheerfully. "Could you tell me what your business is?"

"It's—I'd like to see him about a job," Bobby Jo said.

The woman punched a button, spoke briefly into the phone, then smiled at Bobby Jo. "Mr. Shoulders is in his office." She pointed toward an open door. "Right through there. He has an appointment later, but he has fifteen minutes free now."

Aware that the woman was watching her, Bobby Jo hurried toward the door. And what if Mr. Shoulders wasn't the man she had overheard talking? Should she apologize and turn around and leave?

But when she went into the office, the stocky man was sitting behind a large mahogany desk. He rose, held out his hand, smiling. Like his voice, his smile was pleasant, and she saw now that his face was unlined, that it was the streaks of gray at his temples that had made her think of him as an older man. And how appropriate his name was. He definitely did have shoulders.

"I'm Sam Shoulders," he said. "Have we met before?"

"No—my name is Bobby Jo Springer."

"So you're here about a job—the employment agency sort of jumped the gun. I wasn't expecting anyone until—"

"The agency didn't send me. I—I overheard you talking to your friend at the coffee shop, and since I'm job hunting—I'm sure it's something I would be good at."

"I see . . . well, you have one qualification. You have initiative," he said. "Yes, I do need a receptionist. The one I have is taking maternity leave—and in fact, it's doubtful if she'll return. Why don't we talk about your background, and you can tell me why you're so sure you would be good at the job."

For the next few minutes, Bobby Jo answered his questions. When she explained that she was a service wife, his expression didn't change, which was encouraging. In fact, she felt so at ease that she found herself telling him about the problems she'd had job hunting.

"I know there's a certain prejudice against military wives," he said. "What most employers don't consider is that there's no guarantee that *any* employee will be permanent. Josie— she's the woman who spoke to you—is a local woman, born and raised here in Victorville, but she's only been working for me seven months. This is a rather ingrown town—but it's also a good one. Low crime rate, stable population, good schools."

He grinned suddenly, and she decided again that he must be younger than she'd first thought. "Which is really important to me, a widower with two sons."

"You have two sons? I've always wanted a son—not that I'm not happy with my girl," she told him.

"One of these days I'll have to introduce you to my boys," he said. "We have an office dinner coming up next month— it'll be a good chance for you to get acquainted with the husbands and wives of the other employees."

Bobby Jo gaped at him. "Are you saying—"

"You have the job—and everybody calls me Sam." He stood and held out a large, squarish hand. "Welcome to Shoulders Realty Company, Bobby Jo. When can you start?"

CHAPTER

✦ 37 ✦

BOBBY JO WAS HAVING TROUBLE WRITING A LONG OVER-due letter to Shelley. It wasn't that she didn't have anything to write about. She'd already filled two pages with descriptions of her new job and her new boss, but the one thing she knew she should say—that she was eternally grateful to Shelley for coming to her aid—those words she found difficult to put down on paper.

For one thing, writing to Shelley made her think about that terrible abortion, which was still a black shadow that haunted her dreams. Since she'd gone to work, she'd been able to push it to the back of her mind most of the time—except when she thought of Shelley. Not that Shelley had mentioned it in her own letter. No, she'd written about the art course she was taking that was so fulfilling. She told an anecdote about her boys' encounter with the neighborhood bully and then had described a surprise visit from her parents as being very traumatic. But still the incident was there between the lines, reminding Bobby Jo of the thing she wanted to forget. Also, the knowledge that Shelley alone knew her secret didn't help. Which was why she had postponed writing the letter for so long.

Bobby Joe gave it up finally. She'd finish it later—when she got home. She leaned back in the desk chair, yawning and rubbing her temples. The singing of wheels on the street outside and the soft hum of the office air conditioner were the only sounds. It was late Monday afternoon, and business had been so slow that Mr. Shoulders had asked her to stay until six to take any calls so he could let the others go home a little early.

Bobby Jo didn't mind. Vicky was going to a birthday party right after school, and there was no reason to hurry home. In fact, she'd felt flattered that he'd given her the responsibility of closing the office. Of course all she was expected to do was record phone calls and the names of any customers who came in so they could be contacted later. Still—it meant he trusted her not to foul things up and leave the lights on or the door unlocked when she left.

When no customers had come in, she'd decided to write to Shelley. And wasn't it funny how many things she didn't dare put down on paper? How could she tell Shelley that she still woke in the middle of the night, sure she heard a baby crying? Or that she hadn't been to church since she'd started that affair with Deke? How could she describe, to someone who was such a straight arrow, that she still dreamed she was in bed with Deke at the motel, that she was wild for him to make love to her . . . until he touched her, and then, abruptly, he changed— into the doctor who'd done the abortion, and then everything got nightmarish and horrible and all mixed up with the operation and the pain she'd felt afterward.

And she couldn't tell another woman, not someone like Shelley, about her self-doubts, the suspicion that she was easy, a pushover. She'd let two men make love to her practically the first time she'd met them, and both of them had ended up treating her like dirt. How could she possibly say these things to Shelley, who was so sure of her own husband's love?

Well, she *could* talk about her job, couldn't she? In fact, it was pleasant to be able to let Shelley know that she was doing something right for a change. . . .

Bobby Jo returned to her letter with the comment that it felt great to be earning money of her own. What she didn't say was that she loved being treated as if she were good for something else besides putting a meal on the table or being a bed partner.

She had just finished the letter when she heard a noise at the door. When she looked up, Mr. Shoulders was standing there, watching her. "You bucking for overtime? It's past six," he said.

Bobby Jo smiled at him, knowing he was teasing. "I'm

writing a letter to a friend. Vicky went to a birthday dinner, so I don't have to hurry home tonight."

"Your daughter's six, isn't she?"

"Going on forty-five—as a friend once said."

"One of those old-soul types, is she?"

"Sometimes she scares me. She inherited her brains from her father, so she's always one jump ahead of me."

Mr. Shoulders gave her a quizzical look. "Why from your husband? You aren't exactly a moron."

"You should have seen my grades in school. Most of the time I just squeaked by."

"There are different kinds of intelligence. Getting along with other people is as important as book knowledge."

"Well, I do like people. I used to think—" Bobby Jo broke off because it seemed vain to say that she'd always thought she'd be good in some kind of public relations job.

Sam Shoulders didn't seem to notice that she hadn't finished the sentence. "When is your husband due back?" he asked.

"In two weeks."

"I hope this doesn't mean you'll be leaving us."

"Oh, no—at least, I don't think so."

"Have you been thinking about that real estate course I told you about? It might be a fine career choice for you. You could sell real estate no matter where you're transferred. Of course you'd have to be relicensed in a new state."

"It sounds great. The thing is—isn't there a lot of complicated legal stuff to learn?"

"In a narrow sense, yes. But there are plenty of guidelines and study plans to help you, and you have the whole office crew here, including me, to advise—and supervise—you at first. Even after you get your license, you wouldn't be starting out with the complicated stuff. At first, you'd just be showing property with one of the other salespeople, learning the ropes."

"I'd love that part—you know, finding the right house for people, a place where they could put down roots," Bobby Jo said.

"You aren't all that keen about moving around, are you? It seems strange that you'd marry an air force pilot."

"I didn't plan to. It just happened that way. You see, my best friend in high school was going to Colorado College, and she talked my parents into letting me go there, too. I'm not all that good at striking out on my own, so it seemed the right thing to do. As it happened, my friend had some personal problems and she ended up going to the academy, so I was on my own, after all. Then I met Josh, and we got married right after he graduated—" She broke off, a little embarrassed that she was talking so much about herself.

"How do you like Victorville?"

"It's nice here, Mr. Shoulders. I'm used to the climate now, and the people are very friendly."

"Why don't you call me Sam?"

"Okay—Sam," she said, and discovered it wasn't difficult, after all, because he seemed more like her friend than her employer.

(Excerpt from a letter to Tai written by Crystal, dated November 1982.)

Well, Tai, you are full of surprises! I never dreamed you'd make it up with Steven. I do hope things work out the way you plan. Grant tells me the Joint Spouse Assignment process is a shambles, but then I'm sure you must know all this, right?

At least you shouldn't have too many financial problems, which is more than poor Shelley can say, I guess. Honestly, I feel downright guilty sometimes. Here I ended up with a senior officer, who also has a substantial income from a trust fund, so I've never had to pull in my belt. Like I say, I do feel guilty sometimes.

Grant just returned from a trip to Washington to see his friend, General Krause. (Did you see in the Air Force Times where Arnold had made his fourth star and is being assigned to Hickam to take over as Commander-In-Chief of PACAF, the same position Shelley's father had?) Grant came back with some exciting personal news, too. I can't discuss it yet, but don't be surprised at a change of address for us soon—

Crystal laid down her pen and considered the words she'd just written. Indiscreet, perhaps, but she couldn't resist dropping a hint. It wasn't official yet and in fact wasn't all that sure, but it looked very much like Grant would be taking over as Deputy of Manpower at PACAF Headquarters when Arnold became Commander-In-Chief—and that was a brigadier general's slot. Officially it would be a temporary assignment, but if Grant did a good job, it could become permanent. So once again, because she'd played her cards right, Arnold Krause had come through for Grant.

In fact, life was very good these days—with a couple of gray spots here and there. She enjoyed the perks of being a colonel's wife, even though she still found it irksome to cater to the wives of men senior to Grant. With Arnold at the Pentagon now, one odious chore had almost vanished from her life. It was a relief not to have to service that old fool every time he got the urge. She didn't even have to cater to Sophie these days. In fact, poor Sophie was in Walter Reed Hospital. The official word was that her liver trouble had flared up again, but Crystal suspected she was in there to dry out.

Crystal glanced at the small clock on her desk and saw it would soon be time for Grant to get home from the office. She finished the letter quickly, wishing she could say what she really thought about Tai's marriage. Wait until that little fool found out what she'd bitten off. Officers married to officers had a couple of strikes against them. Everybody knew that it was enough to stop a man—or woman—dead in their promotion tracks. . . .

Grant came in as she was addressing the envelope.

"Pretty pleased with yourself about something," he commented. "What did you do—stab someone in the back today?"

She frowned at him, noting that his face was flushed, his eyes a little glazed. How had he managed to down a few drinks already? Did he keep a bottle in his desk at work—or had he left early to go to the club?

"I do hope you aren't in one of your moods tonight," she said.

"I'm always in a mood of one kind or another—or haven't you noticed? No, you wouldn't. Well, no matter. All's well in the household of Fast-Burner Colonel Norton and his charming wife." When Crystal was silent, he added, "You look festive. Whom are we entertaining tonight?"

"The Andres—I told you this morning that I'd invited them for dinner and bridge."

"I don't remember. And don't blast me for not consulting that terribly efficient social calendar you made out for me. I may be a logistics type, but that's my professional mode. Off hours, I avoid schedules like the plague."

"The Andres will be here at eight," she said, ignoring his remark. "I suggest you change into civilian clothes—and don't choose something too casual."

"You mean you haven't already laid out the clothes you want me to wear?" he said in mock surprise.

"You *are* in a mood. Do be polite to our guests—and watch the liquor. You know what happens when you drink too much. I'm still smoothing over your remark to General Collins about cost overruns. I know you have a thing about waste in government, but after all, he *is* in procurement."

"Yes, dear."

She frowned at him. How much had he had to drink? Lately, he'd been hitting the bottle more than she liked. A little social drinking was expected, but Grant drank as if he had to psych himself up to get through the evening. Surely, after the debacle with that blackmailer, he'd learned his lesson. For the sake of his career, he simply had to exercise control.

"No, I haven't taken another lover—if that's what you're thinking," Grant said, his smile twisted. "I hope you appreciate the sacrifice, but I suspect you don't."

"What does that mean?"

"It means that to a cold fish like you, sex must seem pretty easy to give up."

Involuntarily, Crystal glanced toward the door. "Please lower your voice if you don't want this conversation to be repeated all over the base. Betsy is in the kitchen."

He shrugged. "I'm sure she gets her share of sex—with five kids, she's done it at least five times."

"You're so vulgar at times—you certainly didn't learn that at home. You come from people of culture and taste—"

"Are you talking about those two old farts in Florida? They know every four-letter word in the book—and some that aren't. They use them frequently, too."

"But not in mixed company," she said sharply. "I don't know what's gotten into you lately—"

"Maybe I'm finally coming out of the closet," he said, grinning.

Crystal ignored the inneundo and glanced down at the small gold watch on her wrist. It was the one Arnold had given her, and she got a secret satisfaction from wearing it to social events, her way of thumbing her nose at the bores she had to put up with.

"Why don't you change, Grant? I still have to check the dinner table."

"Yes, you do that. We wouldn't want General Andre and his fat wife to be insulted because a knife was turned the wrong way. Not that they would know the difference. Did it ever occur to you that all that perfection could work against you—and your ever-loving husband? Flo Andre serves the world's worst food at her table. She might take it as an insult that you put one of your gourmet dinners in front of the general everytime we return their hospitality."

A sharp retort rose to Crystal's lips, but Grant was already moving toward the bathroom. She stared after him, fighting the desire to scream. What was wrong with the man lately? His career was going so well—all his promotions had been well below the zone, and his job titles got progressively better. She wasn't really worried, of course, that he would step out of line again. He never asked her about those snapshots, but he knew she'd use them against him if he ever decided he didn't need her any longer.

On the other hand, *something* was bugging him. He seemed . . . well, as if he were coming apart at the seams. Several times in the past few months she'd had to remind him to shave and even to take a shower before some social event—and this to a man who had always been so fastidious about his personal hygiene. And his jokes were coarser, his language less refined—was he going through some kind of midlife crisis?

Well, just so he behaved in company, she could put up with it. After all, she'd expected him to resent her because she'd found him out—and because she now had the upper hand. His snide remarks she could overlook. She'd been the recipient of that kind of thing all her life from her mother. But if he ever got the idea he could cheat her out of her just rewards, she still had those photographs tucked away in a safety deposit box. He was just as ambitious as she was, which gave her a hold on him—and besides, there were those two old men in Florida. Grant would die before he'd let his father and grandfather know that he was queer. . . .

"Oh, I forgot to tell you," Grant called from the bathroom. "General Krause sends his regards. He called today to tell me he's coming to Wright-Pat for that gymnasium dedication ceremony next week and will be staying over an extra couple of days. I invited him for dinner—I knew you'd want to make some points with him."

Crystal counted five before she asked, "Is Sophie coming with him?"

"No, she's still in the hospital. I would've offered to put him up, but I wasn't sure you'd want him underfoot for two days."

"He'll be more comfortable in the VIP quarters," she said absently. God, two whole days of Arnold—just what she needed. He was sure to want to get together with her—how come he still hadn't cooled off? Maybe she'd been a little too creative in bed. It was obvious he got something from her he didn't get from his one-night stands. Unfortunately, she still needed him, but once Grant had his first star, she was dumping the bastard.

She dropped the letter she'd written to Tai in her purse to mail the next day, but something had happened to the satisfaction she usually got from writing to her old Punahou classmates. Suddenly, she was remembering Tai and Steven together—the sexual tension had fairly sizzled between them. They would probably spend most of their married life in bed. Well, she didn't envy Tai that. Sex was highly overrated—not that it wouldn't be a change to make out with someone with muscles instead of flab....

The phone rang as she was heading for the dining room, but she didn't turn back since Grant was closer to the extension phone than she. She was refolding a napkin at the dining room table when she heard his step in the hall.

"Bad news," he said from the doorway, his face so grave that she paused to stare at him. "That was Krause. He won't be coming after all. Sophie had a heart attack last night. She died this morning. We'd better plan on going to the funeral."

Crystal's first thought was conventional: Poor Sophie—she was only forty-five. Her second thought was totally selfish: Thank God, I won't have to put up with Arnold pawing me next week.

(Excerpt from a letter to Bobby Jo from Tai dated February 1983.)

So how's it going, Bobby Jo? Not much news here, but I thought I'd answer your last letter anyway. Your job sounds terrific. I was a little surprised that Josh is so against you working, though. You'd think he'd be glad

*that you had something to do, since he's gone so much
of the time.*

*The situation with Steven and me is the same. I'm
still at Williams, and he's still in Germany. Everybody
keeps promising to do something about getting us assigned
together, but I'm afraid it will have to wait for a while.
The problem is that Steven has already put in three years
as an instructor (that's about the limit before burnout),
and it's unlikely I'll be tapped for transport planes until
I get more flying hours in.*

*I went to see Colonel Sharon at wing headquarters
again. He's a real old fog-bottom. The only advice he
had for me was to get pregnant and then try to get out
on a medical! I wanted to spit in his eye—the sexist pig.
(Sorry—I've met some pigs I rather like!)*

*I was looking through an old photograph album yes-
terday, and I came across a snapshot you took that day
we all went to the beach together. Can you believe that
it's been seven years now? The snap just shows the three
of us—Crystal and Shelley and me—but your shadow's
there on the sand in front of us. We look so young. Funny
to remember that the roof fell in on me that day. Things
changed for all of us after that, didn't it? Shelley met
Tad the next day, and you went off to college and Crystal
started her job at Hickam, where she met Grant Norton.*

*Do you remember the pact we made to have a reunion
in Hawaii in ten years? Somehow I doubt that will ever
come off, although it would be fun, of course. . . .*

Two days after she mailed the letter, Tai got a phone call
from Germany. Although she and Steven had made the decision, in the interest of keeping their phone bills in line, to write
more often and phone less, one of them was always making
an exception. Consequently, their phone bill was astronomical,
especially since Steven charged his calls to the home phone.

"Hi, love—you miss me?"

Tai smiled to herself. Steven always started his calls out
that way. What would he say if she told him that no, she'd
been too busy to miss him? He wouldn't believe her, of course,
and no wonder. He knew very well that she had a hard time
getting to sleep nights in that king-size bed they'd bought. . . .

"I do, I do. Is this a social call—or is something up?"

"Both. First things first. Did I tell you lately that I love you?"

"You did. But say it again, Sam."

"I miss you like crazy."

"I miss you, too. Abstinence is hell."

"Hang in there. Something's got to break." Steven paused briefly, and when he went on, his voice had changed slightly. "No soap on the swap deal between you and that C-151 copilot who wants to go to Williams. For one thing, you need to be checked out on C-151s and to have logged quite a few hours. Dammit! I almost ran amok when I got the word—can you imagine the stink if an academy grad ran amok?"

"I've heard of an academy grad bursting into tears," Tai said soberly. "So when do you think you can get some leave? You know how it is here—I can't cut out on my students in the middle of training."

"I'll get away next month if I have to go AWOL. This separation thing is getting old. We're going to have to have a serious talk about it, Tai."

"You aren't starting in on that family thing again?" Despite herself, Tai's voice was cool. "I'm not ready for it, Steven. I want your kids someday, but not now. I have to put in five more years, and I want to do a lot during those years, get more experience, explore the envelope."

There was a long silence on the other end of the line. "Let's talk about it when we get together again. Meanwhile, I want you to do some serious thinking about—about possible solutions. Promise me that you'll keep an open mind?"

After Steven hung up, Tai felt dissatisfied and uneasy. Maybe she should seriously think about getting pregnant. Only—only it just wasn't fair. Being pregnant meant being grounded for nine months and then having to requalify before she could go back on flying status. She had worked hard to get her wings, and she wasn't ready for the responsibility of raising a kid. And wasn't it strange that *she* was the one who had gone to the academy to get a free engineering degree while Steven had been so gung-ho about his military career? When had she changed? When had flying become much more attractive to her than being an engineer? She still wanted that, of course, but—not yet. No, not quite yet. . . .

* * *

It was humid, stifling hot, in Victorville. Bobby Jo lifted the hair away from the back of her neck, thinking dully that she really should get it cut—maybe in one of those new layered hairdos. Josh had made a remark about her hair just a couple of months ago. He'd come in from work in a rotten mood, something he did so often since he'd returned from school. When he'd grunted instead of answering Vicky's "Hi, Pop!" their daughter had prudently gone next door to play with her best chum, while Bobby Jo had wondered if Josh was getting bored with being home for such a long stretch.

That's when, out of the blue, he'd made that remark about her hair.

"Do you realize that you haven't changed your hairdo in years? For God's sake—do something with it. I'm tired of seeing it flopping down over your forehead."

That was just the latest of his complaints. He fussed about the meals she fixed, saying she should do more baking, and when she'd said the obvious, that baking took more time than she had to spare, he had really blown up.

"It's that flipping job! Why the hell don't you quit? I don't like what's happening to you, Bobby Jo. All you talk about is work. 'Mr. Shoulders sold that colonial in Rolling Hills to so-and-so today,' Who cares? I'm working my butt off since they dumped that maintenance squadron CO job on me, and I don't need any problems at home. Besides, you should be here when Vicky gets out of school afternoons."

"She's never alone, Josh," Bobby Jo protested. "She goes over to Mrs. Willis's house after school, and it's only for an hour. Besides, Vicky doesn't mind me working. She enjoys helping around the house—"

"I don't approve of you paying her for chores she should be doing anyway. You two are a real pair—I don't know which one is the dumbest."

"Vicky's grades are the best in her class," Bobby Jo said, stung into anger. "And I'm smart enough to hold down a job."

Josh slammed his fist down on the arm of his chair. "That's what I'm talking about! Ever since you got that two-bit job, you're always mouthing off. I think that guy you work for is doing a job on you—and you'd better watch it. You're a real pushover when it comes to men."

If he'd struck Bobby Jo, it couldn't have hurt more. Josh had said some cruel things to her during their marriage, but this remark hit her in her most vulnerable place. Not trusting herself to speak, she went into the kitchen to start dinner. A few minutes later, Josh called for a beer. Silently, she took it to him and set it his elbow. When she started to turn away, he caught her hand and held her there.

"Ah, come on, honey. I was just kidding you. Sometimes I get a little upset. You have to admit you aren't the same girl I married."

"No, I'm not. For one thing, I'm not pregnant," she said, her voice tight.

"Hey, don't lay that guilt trip on me. I didn't rape you—remember how it was?" His voice deepened as he added, "We couldn't get enough of each other—you're still the sexiest lady I know. And didn't I marry you without kicking up a fuss? I would've married you anyway. It was just that I wanted to wait a year until I'd finished flight training. That was the advice we got from the commandant. 'Get flight training under your belt before you marry your girls, men.'"

"Why is it always 'men' and 'girls' with the military? Why not 'men' and 'women'?" she asked.

"Hell, that's an expression everybody uses. And I've got no complaints about our marriage." He pulled her down into his lap and nuzzled her throat. "Hmmm. . . . You smell good—and I'm nuts about you. That's why I get uptight when you start acting like a nagging wife."

Bobby Jo felt his body stirring under her buttocks and knew he wanted sex. An errant thought slid into her mind. I could be any female body and it wouldn't make any difference to Josh.

As Josh fondled her breasts, she felt cold, detached. Although she submitted to his lovemaking, she was glad when it was over. Later, as he was lying beside her, his arms folded under his head, Josh told her he'd applied for test pilot training and was sure he'd be accepted.

"I've logged more than the thousand flying hours I need, and with my engineering degree under my belt, it should be a shoo-in." When Bobby Jo was silent, he added, his voice defensive. "You knew this was what I've been aiming for all along."

"No, I didn't," she said.

"Why else do you think I've been busting my butt to get in all the flying time I can and qualifying on those other planes? I thought you understood how it was."

"How could I? You never bother to discuss your plans with me."

"Look, it's for you and the kid, too. If I make it through the flight school and am lucky enough to get assigned to Edwards as a research pilot, it means we can stay put in one place for years. I won't be going on exercises all the time, and I'll be home every night."

"It's a year's course, isn't it?"

"Yeah . . . well, almost."

"What happens to Vicky and me? Do we come along, too?"

Josh rolled to the side of the bed and sat up. "Actually, it's permitted, but most wives stay behind. You remember how it was at Williams? This'd just be more of the same. You'll be a lot better off if you stayed here that year. I'd get some leave time, of course—"

He went on talking, but Bobby Jo had stopped listening. She was busy trying to figure out why, when Josh was telling her that they would be separated again, this time for almost a year, she didn't feel worse. In fact, she felt relieved, as if a crisis in their marriage had been diverted—or maybe just postponed.

Josh took Bobby Jo out to dinner at the Officers Club the night before he left. He was in a good mood, reminding her of how it had been during their courtship days. Tonight, as they joined three other couples, it was possible to forget the past months—and her own guilt. Dancing with Josh, with his off-key humming in her ear, she felt nineteen again, especially when he told her she was the prettiest girl in the room, bar none, and kept his arm draped around her shoulders at the table, even though it made him the target of some good-natured teasing.

During the day, the Officers Club was a shabby place with its drab wallpaper, faded carpets, and commonplace furnishings, but at night, with candles reflecting off the women's jewelry, with music playing in the background, it could have passed for a high-class restaurant.

Bobby Jo was content to relax, not participating in the conversation. The men were all fighter pilots, and there was a lot of shop talk along with the jokes and the kidding. It occurred to Bobby Jo, as she listened to the men's exchange of in-jokes and professional jargon, that their wives, including her, looked much alike. As if there were a government regulation about the kind of women pilots were expected to marry, she thought. Or maybe that was one of the courses they taught at flight school. Did the commandant have a set speech, like the ones they used at the wives' orientation briefing?

"Men, be sure the girl you marry is supportive, submissive, and knows her place. She can be pretty, too, but that isn't required, only that she be proper air force wife material. She should smile a lot but always keep her mouth shut and never, never state an opinion of her own. . . ."

"You're a thousand miles away, Bobby Jo," Josh said in her ear. "You thinking about what's going to happen when we get home?"

"No," she said honestly. "I was thinking about the orientation speech the commandant of cadets' wife gave us during June week."

"'Give your man lots of loving and treat him right because a good man sure is hard to find,'" Josh half sang, wiggling his eyebrows at her.

Bobby Jo thought how young he looked tonight. For so long, she had thought of him as being the mature one of their marriage, and yet—lately, she sometimes felt as if he'd been caught in a time warp and now she was the older one.

"The gospel according to the air force is to keep your man happy and don't make waves. And smile a lot," she said aloud, and despite herself, there was an edge in her voice.

Josh's smile dissolved into a frown. "What's got into you tonight, Bobby Jo? You aren't going to turn into a nag, are you? My mom . . . well, she's a great old gal, but she does have a tongue like the edge of a razor. I think that's why the old man cut out on us when he did. Couldn't take it."

And so you looked for someone dumb and easygoing to marry, did you, Josh? she thought, but didn't say aloud.

The music started up again, and Josh pulled her out onto the dance floor, ending the conversation. Later that night, he made love to her as fervently as he had on their honeymoon. But as he sweated and groaned above her, she felt unmoved, and again she was glad when it was over.

The next morning, Josh left for school. A week later, after a lot of soul-searching and not a little apprehension, Bobby Jo signed up for the real estate course at the local college.

In June, she passed the course with respectable if not spectacular grades. During the next summer, Sam Shoulders tutored her, directing her studies into the areas she would need, and in September she took the California real estate exam. She passed—by a very narrow margin—and got her real estate broker's license.

CHAPTER
↑ 38 ↑

BOBBY JO SAT IN THE SHADE OF A PLANE TREE, WATCHING Vicky and her best friend, Georgette, as they jumped up and down on a trampoline, shrieking joyfully. It was peaceful and not too cold under the tree, even though the winter wind was nippy. The tension she'd felt all day slowly seeped from her body, leaving her relaxed and somnolent. She must have dozed because a familiar voice, saying her name, made her start violently.

"Whoa—didn't mean to startle you, Bobby Jo," Sam Shoulders said, sounding amused.

Bobby Jo returned his smile automatically. Meeting her boss here in the park was quite a coincidence—or was it? She'd told him once that she often brought Vicky and her friend to this particular park on weekends. Had he thought her remark was some kind of invitation?

She saw that Vicky and Georgette had been joined by two boys. From their size, they looked to be nine or ten—and they were as alike as two peas in a pod.

"Are those your boys?" she asked.

"Dennis and David—a real handful, both of them."

"They look a lot like you."

"So I've been told. Actually, except for their coloring, they resemble their mother."

"She's been gone for quite a while, hasn't she?"

"Nine years. She died in childbirth. She was a tough lady—

452

the doctors told her not to have kids, but she was determined to give me a son. She lived long enough to know that she'd given me two." He paused a moment, his eyes reflective. "She was a very special person. Very reserved—with a backbone of steel. I still miss her."

His quiet words touched Bobby Jo, but she felt another emotion, too—envy. "She would be proud of you—it can't be easy, raising your kids alone."

"But of course that's just what you've been doing, isn't it?"

"I don't understand. My husband is still—I'm not alone."

"I only meant to say that your husband is gone more than he's home."

"He'll be back from test pilot school in another month," Bobby Jo said quickly, and then wondered why she sounded so defensive when there'd been no hint of criticism in Sam's remark.

"If he's assigned to another base, you'll be leaving us, I suspect. I'll—we'll miss you at the office. I hope you continue in real estate wherever your husband's next assignment takes you."

"If Josh gets Edwards AFB, my California real estate license will still be valid. Even if we get base quarters, maybe I can commute to a nearby town."

"Well, I hope it all works out for you."

Vicky came bustling up, her eyes fixed on the strange man talking to her mother. Bobby Jo introduced them, and, quixotic as always, Vicky decided Sam Shoulders was worth charming. She smiled at him demurely, then ruined it all by declaring, "Those awful boys are bothering us. I told them I was going to tell my mother, but they just stuck out their tongues and told me to get lost. I think twins suck."

Bobby Jo gave Sam a quick look and was relieved to find that he was smiling. "They just want to be friends," Sam said. "Boys don't know how to behave around girls until they get a little age on them. Girls mature faster than boys—don't you agree, young lady?"

Vicky preened herself. "I can handle those big lummoxes." She flounced away, fire in her eyes.

"Lummoxes?" Sam said.

"One of my expressions. She picks up my worse ones," Bobby Jo said ruefully. "I've been trying to stop talking like an Arkansas hillbilly for years."

"Now that's a mistake. I love your Arkansas accent. What if we all were alike? Wouldn't this be a boring world?"

"But Josh—" She didn't finish the sentence, afraid he would think she was criticizing her husband. "Anyway, no one would dare laugh at Vicky, no matter what she says, or they'd have a fight on their hands."

"A handful, too, is she?"

Bobby Jo started to nod, then changed her mind. Was Vicky really a handful—or was she simply her own person? And how had she, of all people, produced a child like Vicky?

"She's independent, but she's also pretty special," she said.

"And so are you, Bobby Jo." Sam's voice so low she wasn't sure if she'd heard him right. At her uncertain look, he stood up, smiling down at her. In the sunlight, his hair had a silvery sheen, and suddenly she was very curious about his age.

"May I ask you a personal question?" she blurted.

"Of course."

"How old are you?"

"Thirty-five—and if the hair throws you, it does that to a lot of people. It runs in my father's family. His hair was snow white by the time he was forty. I suspect mine will be, too."

"It's—actually, it's very attractive," she said.

"Thank you. What say we take the kids somewhere for a treat before they slaughter each other?"

Bobby Jo followed his gaze to the four children. Hands on hips, Vicky was haranguing the boys while her friend giggled in the background. From the way they watched her, as if she were something totally new to their experience, she knew that Vicky had the upper hand.

"Vicky strikes again." She sighed. "Sometimes I feel as if she's bringing me up instead of the other way around."

"Just think what a woman she's going to be someday. No holds barred. And she'll need it. That's the kind of world we live in these days."

"One I'm not very well equipped for."

"Why do you say that? You function very well in this world. I don't know of anyone in the office who is more diplomatic. You even have our razor-tongued Mrs. Green eating out of your hand."

She eyed her employer doubtfully. Was he making fun of her? No, he was smiling, as if he approved. Well, she did get along well with her coworkers, even though, technically speaking, she was in competition with them for sales.

Sam Shoulders called to the children, and at the mention of a treat, they came running. For the next hour, in an old-fashioned ice-cream parlor near the park where the prices, Bobby Jo secretly thought, were outrageous, they slurped sodas and dug into sundaes as if they hadn't eaten for a week. Since they were too busy eating to quarrel, it gave Bobby Jo and Sam a chance to talk quietly to each other, pleasant adult conversation that put her at ease.

It was getting dark when she and Vicky returned home. When she saw that the lights were on in the living room, she paused, her heart beating very fast. Had someone broken in? She was trying to decide whether to go to a neighbor's house for help when the front door flew open. Josh stood there, glowering at her.

"Where the hell have you been?"

"We went to the park—what are you doing here? Are you sick or—"

"Do I look sick?" he snapped. He turned and went back into the house.

Bobby Jo reflected that what Josh looked was drunk—and in a foul mood. Feeling a little sick herself, she told Vicky to go to her friend's house next door for a while.

"I don't want to leave you alone with Poppa, Mom," Vicky said, tossing her head. "He looks mad."

"He's just tired. You stay with Georgette until I call you to come home."

"Well . . . okay. But if you want me, I'll be right next door."

When Bobby Jo went into the house, Josh was sitting in the living room, staring at the blaring television set. When she saw the half-empty bourbon bottle on the coffee table in front of him, she knew she'd been right.

"Can I get you something to eat?" she said quickly.

"Hell, I fixed myself a sandwich an hour ago. I could've starved to death, waiting for you to fix dinner."

"I had no way of knowing you'd be home today," she pointed out. "You told me that you couldn't get leave until after graduation."

"There's not going to be any graduation. I got washed out. My IP had it in for me right from the start—he was always hassling me about something. He said my reflexes were off—which is lot of crap—"

"Maybe it's your drinking," Bobby Jo said without thinking.

She had no warning because Josh's expression didn't change. One minute she was standing near his chair and the next she felt a blinding pain in one side of her head, and then she was lying on the floor, her face stinging, in shock from the suddenness of his attack.

"Goddamn it, I expect a little loyalty from my own wife!" Josh roared. He hauled her up by one arm, his eyes red-rimmed with rage. "It's time you found out who's the boss around here, you whining little bitch."

Even when he picked her up, staggering in his effort to keep his balance with her dead weight in his arms, and started for the bedroom, she didn't understand what he intended to do. Only when he tossed her on the bed and jerked her skirt up over her thighs did she realize that he meant to have sex with her. She didn't fight. She was too afraid to resist, but the tears poured down her cheeks as he pulled her panty hose down over her knees, then stood over her, fumbling with his zipper, not even bothering to take off his trousers.

It was over quickly. There was no pain because he was too drunk to complete the act. Afterward, when he was snoring on his pillow, Bobby Jo slid off the bed and went into the bathroom. She stripped to her skin, then bundled up her discarded clothes, stuffed them in a paper sack, and put them in the trash can under the sink. For a long time, she stood in the shower stall under a stream of hot water, scrubbing herself until her skin stung. It was only later, when she looked at herself in the mirror, that she realized that a large bruise, already turning blue, stood out plainly on her cheek.

She spent the night in Vicky's room, sleeping on a canvas cot. When the alarm went off, she got Vicky ready for school, grateful that her daughter didn't ask any questions. Vicky, unusually quiet, stared at her bruised face for a long time, but all she said was, "I think Poppa sucks," before she ran off to catch her school bus.

Josh was still asleep when she looked in at him. As she stared at his bloated face and his slack mouth, she felt nothing—not even fear. But she wasn't yet ready to face him, so she dressed quietly, then left the house. Since she couldn't think of any other place to go, she went to work as usual.

To her relief, everybody seemed to accept her explanation that she'd fallen over one of her daughter's toys and had hit her face against the edge of the coffee table. She was glad when the first customer came in because then everybody returned to work and stopped commiserating with her.

She busied herself with two referrals, making the necessary phone calls to set up appointments to show the listings the clients were interested in. It was almost lunchtime when she got an inquiry about the Marriot mansion, one of their prime leasing properties. She was feeling so rocky by now from stress and loss of sleep that she was tempted to refer it to someone else, but the commission was a respectable one—and she knew that whatever happened next in her life, she would need money.

She made an appointment to meet the customer at the mansion at one o'clock, but when she arrived, no was was there. For a while, she wandered around, inspecting the richly appointed house, which was to be rented furnished. When two o'clock came and the customer still hadn't shown up, she shrugged philosophically and prepared to leave.

She was combing her hair in the master bedroom bathroom when she heard footsteps outside the door. She hurried into the hall, a polite smile on her face, expecting to see her client, but it was Sam Shoulders who greeted her.

"I tried to call you, but the phone service here's been cut off," he said. When his eyes narrowed, she resisted the impulse to turn her head away so he couldn't see her bruised cheek. "Your customer called and postponed the appointment until tomorrow, but you'd already left."

"I was just getting ready to leave."

"Maybe you should take a break for the rest of the day. You look as if you need it."

"I'm fine—"

"I can see that you're in tip-top condition," he said dryly. "Who did it, Bobby Jo?"

"I fell and hit my face against the coffee table."

"Was it your husband? Is he home on leave?"

"He's home, but that has nothing to do with—" To her distress, her voice thickened and she had to stop. Sam moved across the space that separated them, so quickly that she didn't have time to retreat before his arms were around her shoulders. Momentarily, she relaxed against him, but when she realized what she was doing, she pulled away.

"I'm sorry," she said, "but I'd rather that you just—that you didn't mention it again."

"Okay. It's your business. But you don't have to put up with abuse, Bobby Jo. Violence feeds upon itself, you know. Once you accept the image of yourself as a victim, it will happen again and again."

"You've got it all wrong," she said. "It was an accident."

"Okay. But remember—I'm your friend. You can call on me for help any time of the night and day."

She started to answer, to reiterate that he had it all wrong and she didn't need his help. Instead, she began to cry. As the tears streamed from her eyes, she was so ashamed that she put her hands up to hide her contorted face. This time, when he put his arms around her, she didn't move away. She hid her hot face against his jacket, as much from vanity as from a need for comfort because she was well aware that she wasn't one of those women who look appealing when they cry.

Sam's touch was gentle as he stroked her hair, murmuring meaningless words. His lips brushed her forehead, and his breathing suddenly quickened. When he kissed her closed eyelids, her only reaction was pleasure—not that it was wrong or dangerous to let him touch her like this.

Then he kissed her fully on the mouth, and she knew it was time to pull away. But she didn't. It wasn't that she felt a great rush of sexual desire. It was just that she liked having him kiss her like that—gently, tenderly.

His kiss deepened, and something that had been slumbering in Bobby Jo for the past few months suddenly stirred. It blossomed into full-fledged need, and she pressed herself against him and opened her mouth under the pressure of his lips. His arms tightened around her, and the kiss that had been meant to comfort was suddenly demanding and urgent.

A word, one that Josh had once used to describe her, clawed itself up from her subconscious, but it had no meaning. All that mattered was the elementary force that, for this moment in time, ruled her body. Later, she would realize how vulnerable she'd been. She would think that the circumstances of this meeting—the empty house, the knowledge that they wouldn't be disturbed, her deep anger at Josh, and her long abstinence—had worked against her. For whatever reason, when Sam began to stroke her hair, when he nuzzled the cleavage between her breasts with his lips, she didn't stop him, not even when he led her to the huge bed that dominated the master bedroom and sank down with her upon a pile of cushions.

As he kissed her breasts through her blouse, he was breathing so hard that she felt a moment's pity, followed by a rush of tenderness, and when he began to undress her, she helped him with zippers and buttons and fasteners. While he undressed, she watched him with mesmerized eyes, realizing that what she'd thought was a stocky build was really a well-muscled body.

He bent over her, touching her in ways that told her he would be a good lover. How was it that she had already known, in some deep recess of her mind, that this man's sensitivity to other people's feelings would extend to lovemaking? When she was ready, he took her with tenderness, and the things that had been frozen for a long time unthawed and she responded fully, crying out his name at the moment of release.

When she came back to earth, she was too ashamed to look at him. *Easy*—that was the word Josh had used to describe her. Back in Arkansas, they said women like her had round heels. It seemed some things never changed—once a pushover, always a pushover. She rolled away from Sam and buried her face in a cushion, wishing he would go away without saying anything, wishing she could wipe the past hour out of her mind, wishing she were dead. . . .

Sam brushed back the hair that their frenzied lovemaking had dislodged. "I love you, Bobby Jo," and she knew he meant it—at least at the moment. "I know I took advantage of your— your generous heart just now, but I'm not sorry. How can I be when it was so good for both of us? If you don't want to go on with this, I'll understand. I realize that the next time it would be something we'd planned ahead of time—and that would make a difference. But I'll never forget this hour—and I mean it when I say that if you ever need a friend, I'm here for you."

She didn't answer him. Avoiding his eyes, she gathered up her clothes and went into the bathroom to clean herself up and to dress. When she returned to the bedroom, Sam was gone. For a long time, she stared at the bed where they'd made love before she smoothed the spread and arranged the cushions.

When she returned to her car, she sat there for a while, thinking. Words Sam had said to her echoed through her mind. "You don't have to put up with abuse, not from anyone, Bobby

Jo . . . it feeds upon itself . . . once you accept the image of yourself as a victim, it will happen again and again—"

It came to her then that she had been blaming the wrong person for her marital problems. By allowing Josh to misuse her, she was not only debasing herself, but she was perverting him. It was time to admit that their marriage, always so fragile, was a lost cause. Maybe it had always been because they'd married each other for all the wrong reasons. Her only choice now was to leave Josh and put their marriage behind her. The thing was—could she possibly make it on her own?

When Bobby Jo got home, Josh was sitting on the sofa. When she saw the shame in his eyes, some of her resolve began to fade. But she took a deep breath and said the words she'd rehearsed.

"I've taken all I intend to from you, Josh. You've never treated me like a human being with rights of my own. To you, I'm just a convenience. Any woman would keep you satisfied in bed."

"Oh, God, Bobby Jo—that isn't true. I'm crazy about you, always will be. I know I'm a selfish bastard and I'm sorry about the other women and the way I treated you last night. I was sick when I woke up this morning and remembered what happened. It's the system that did it. They keep telling you how special you are, that you're a state-of-the-art, a hotshot pilot, and after a while, you begin to believe it. Then I washed out and it did something to my head, made me crazy. But it didn't really have anything to do with the way I feel about you—"

"It's too late—"

"Don't say that, honey! I can't make it without you. Don't knock me down. I promise I'll stop drinking, but don't give up on me. I—I need you."

The chill inside Bobby Jo began to thaw, and because she hated it that his words could still reach her after what he'd done, she looked at him with resentment and near hate. Why was he doing this to her—what did he really want from her? A doormat to walk on, to take out his frustrations on? She met Josh's eyes, and knew that his need, no matter what it was, was genuine, that he was really sorry for hitting her—and maybe for other things.

A part of her still fought back. It reminded her how hard she'd worked for her small victories, warned her that if she submerged herself in Josh and their marriage again, her tentative groping for independence would wither and die on the vine.

You can have it the way you want it, the voice whispered. There's even a man, the one you should have waited for, who will give you the kind of life you've always wanted, stable and prosperous and comfortable, and he'd be a real father to Vicky, too. All you have to do is turn your back on Josh and walk away. . . .

But the voice was self-defeating because it aroused another question, one she could only answer with honesty.

Sam can give you what you need, yes, but what can you give him, Bobby Jo?

And of course there was her guilt, the guilt she still hadn't resolved. Not once but twice, she had betrayed Josh with other men. Never mind that he'd had other women. That didn't change the fact that she had committed a sin. Then there was the baby she'd aborted. Someone had to pay for that—and the crime had been hers, not Josh's.

Even so, she didn't give in right away. She demanded concessions, concessions that Josh agreed to. He promised that he would stop drinking, that he would never lift his hand to her in anger again. She could keep on working—if that's what she really wanted. And if she did quit, now that he was home full time, it would be her own decision.

In the end, Bobby Jo promised to stay with Josh and make a fresh start, to try again to make the marriage that had started for all the wrong reasons work. And to give it every chance, the next day, she resigned from her job at Shoulders Realty.

CHAPTER
↟ 39 ↟

THE LUNCHEON/FASHION SHOW AT WRIGHT-PAT'S IM-
pressive Officers Club had been very successful, which didn't
surprise Crystal since she'd supervised every detail. Well advertised in advance not only in the Officers Club bulletin and the
base newspaper but in the major Dayton papers, enough tickets
had been sold to assure a nice profit for the cause it represented—to buy new furniture for the base hostel that housed
air force families in crisis. The luncheon menu had been well
chosen, and the fashion show, sponsored by a local dress shop,
had gone off like clockwork, with the models, all of them
officers' wives, performing like professionals.

So Crystal was satisfied—and also very tired. She had been
there early to rehearse the models one last time to make sure
there would be no slipups. Since they were all wives of junior
officers, there had been no complaints.

As she drove home that afternoon, she reflected that she
had done her duty well—as she always did. This time she
could tell Grant about it in detail. Other things, not the least
being her long affair with Arnold Krause, she kept to herself,
as she did most of her machinations. Her latest intrigue had
been a campaign to put her own candidate in as president of
the Officers' Wives Club. She had been too canny to run herself—everything that went wrong was always laid on the president. Besides, it was very possible that she wouldn't have

been elected, not by secret ballot, and a personal failure like that would have reflected badly on her.

But with the election of her surrogate, the popular wife of a lieutenant colonel on Grant's staff, she was now in the position to see to her own interests—getting appointed to run the fashion show being the most recent example. Its success would be noted in the right quarters, and it was results that mattered in the military, not motives or what happened behind the scenes. Success and keeping your nose clean and playing the game were what really counted.

Crystal thought about the letter she planned to write her mother as soon as she got time. Although she still maintained the pretense that Janet was interested in what she did, her mother's indifference had deepened during the years. Not that it mattered. Crystal didn't expect any accolades from that quarter. In fact, Janet's too elaborate lack of interest added to her own pleasure when she wrote about some new triumph. This was one of the perks of success, probably the most enjoyable one of all.

At the moment, she would have been totally content, despite her fatigue, except that one of her migraines had been plaguing her all day. By now it had reached the pulsating stage, and a long soak in the tub, followed by a nap before she had to start thinking about dinner, was in order.

When she reached her quarters, the "brick house" she'd schemed so to acquire, she sat in the car for a moment, savoring the sight of it. Constructed of red brick, it was undeniably old-fashioned, with the deficiencies inherent to a house built at a time when each senior colonel had his own live-in household help. But it was also a symbol—and she loved the prestige of living there.

As she went up the walk, she noted a flower bed that needed replanting. She paused when she heard the hum of a lawn mower in the backyard, then decided to let it go until the next time. Their gardener, a high school boy who was the son of a master sergeant, was reliable and hardworking. He could be trusted to do what was necessary. Besides, she needed a couple of pain capsules—fast.

She swallowed the capsules and had a long bath, then put on her robe, not bothering with a gown because she loved to nap in the nude. There was something sensuous about her bare skin against the sheets that always made her feel deliciously wicked. Feeling the need for a cup of tea, she went into the kitchen and put on the teapot, then slumped down at the kitchen table to wait, resting her head on her folded arms.

The kettle was singing when a scraping noise alerted her that she wasn't alone. When she looked around, the gardener— she couldn't remember his name—was standing there, looking awkward and embarrassed. He was a tall, well-built boy, about sixteen; his hair was shorter than that of the boys she remembered from her own high school days in Hawaii, giving him a clean-cut look.

"Sorry, Mrs. Norton. I knocked twice, but no one answered. Then I heard the teakettle whistling, and I figured someone must be home. I wanted to ask you about that flower bed in the front. You said something about putting in some annuals—"

"Oh, yes," she said, rubbing her neck muscles. "I did pick up some petunia starts at the garden shop. They're in that patch of shade under the catalpa tree."

The boy nodded, his eyes on her face. "You got a migraine, Mrs. Norton? My mom has them all the time."

She started to tell him that she didn't get headaches, but he looked so concerned that she found herself saying, "I thought I'd have some tea and then take a nap. Sometimes that helps."

"You want I should massage your neck? I do that for my mom, and she says it helps."

Crystal stared into his earnest face. She gave a mental shrug. Why not? The capsules certainly weren't doing the trick today.

"Okay. But I doubt it'll do much good. Usually, they just have to wear off."

She liked it that the boy—what *was* his name?—washed his hands carefully before he approached her. She studied his back as he stood at the sink, really seeing him for the first time. He was wearing a dark green sweat shirt and jeans; his hips were very slim, but the rest of his body was so muscular that she wondered if he was into football or weight lifting. His hands were large, with square fingernails and blunt tips, so she was surprised how gentle his touch was when he began massaging the back of her neck, pressing his thumbs into the nerves on either side of her spine. She closed her head and relaxed, yielding herself to the pressure, the circular movement of his hands.

It was a while before she realized what was happening to her. The sensation was such a novelty that at first she didn't recognize it for what it was. It began as a hollowness, not altogether pleasant, in the pit of her stomach, then spread across to her chest. A tingling started up along her inner thighs, followed by a flush that brought the blood rushing to her face and throat.

Her first, instinctive reaction was indignation, which quickly gave way to curiosity. Since it was obvious that the boy wasn't doing anything offensive, she sat there, totally bemused, as the warmth spread, finally becoming both aggressive and urgent. When she stood and turned, it was so abruptly that the boy had no warning. His hands fell away, brushing her breasts, and a wave of red spread over his face.

He stammered an apology, but she didn't answer him. She stared into his eyes, and before he could move away, she put her arms around him, and kissed him fully on the lips. For a moment, she thought he would resist, but then he was kissing her back—a little clumsily, but with enthusiasm. His breath whistled in his throat when she thrust her tongue deep into his mouth. They were standing so close that she felt his body heat, and she knew that he was already aroused. Freeing one hand, she pulled at her belt, untying it. Her robe fell open, exposing her nude body to his startled gaze. When she pressed against him and ground her hips against his, he groaned and clutched at her with both hands, filling her with a hot excitement she hadn't felt since she was a small girl, aroused and confused by the caresses of her beloved father.

The boy was awkward, uncertain, but he wasn't totally inexperienced. He knew what to do when she bent backward over the table and pulled him down on top of her. His eyes feverish, his hands trembling, he dropped his jeans down around his ankles, and there was no doubt that sexually he was fully mature as he slid between her spread thighs. When he thrust against her, penetrating her, Crystal had the first orgasm of her adult life. It came so quickly, so unexpectedly, that she was totally helpless under the force that convulsed her.

Secretly, she had believed that she was frigid, but as she lay there, the cold edge of the table biting into her back, the aftermath of the orgasm slowly ebbing, she felt as if she'd just awakened from a long sleep. So this was what Grant had robbed her of all these years—why hadn't she taken a lover long before this?

Her mind worked feverishly. She didn't want this experience

to be a one-time thing, a romp in the hay that was over quickly, never to be repeated. So even though the boy hadn't reached his own climax yet, she pushed him away, murmuring that there was a better place to make love than a kitchen table. Taking his hand, she led him upstairs to the bed where she'd slept alone so long. Tenderly, she finished undressing him, rubbing her hands over his hard, muscular body, savoring the sight, the touch, and later the taste of him, wooing him with the skills she'd used to keep Arnold Krause interested so long, initiating him to other possibilities of gratification, giving him what she knew he'd never had from any girl his own age.

Later, she would teach him what pleased her. For now, she concentrated on bringing him, sweating and trembling, to the verge of climax time after time, proving to him that sex could be more than a few quick thrusts and groans.

And when he was finally satisfied and had rested a while, she showed him other things, this time for her own gratification. He was an eager and uninhibited student. He learned fast, and he loved his lessons. With him, she was the leader, the teacher, in control as she always had to be. She whispered promises in his ear, telling him what they would do the next time. Her words—the raw, coarse words that she'd learned from Arnold—inflamed him and excited him again, and she realized that he was a natural lover, insatiable in the way that only a sixteen-year-old boy can be insatiable. They made love again and would have done it a third time, only it was getting late and she knew Grant would be home soon.

"Come back tomorrow after school," she told him. "The door will be unlocked. I'll be waiting for you here—oh, what's your name, anyway?"

"Jason, Mrs. Norton," he said.

Despite the lethargy left over from lovemaking, Crystal had a hard time falling asleep that night. She was torn between the demands of her body, which had been awakened for such a short time, and what she knew was a very dangerous situation. To take a lover, one her own age, was one thing. Other wives did it all the time, and if they were discreet, no harm came from it. In fact, she personally knew several wives of senior officers who were visited regularly by junior officers when their husbands were at work or on TDY. But to become involved with a boy of sixteen—if such a thing became common knowledge, it would cause a scandal that would permanently ruin Grant's chances for promotion.

On the other hand—god, she didn't want to give up Jason, not yet! Maybe just one more time—and then she would give him some money and break it off. Because she'd just made the discovery that she wasn't, as Grant often said, a cold fish. She wanted to explore this new thing—with Jason as her sex partner. So she'd take the chance and later—later, there was no good reason why she couldn't look around, find a lover closer to her own age.

The next afternoon, when Jason came to her bedroom, looking both hesitant and eager, Crystal was lying naked on her bed, waiting for him. She opened her arms to him, and they kissed for a long time before she helped him to undress. After they made love, she held him in her arms, stroking his hair, so relaxed that she felt like purring.

"Do you have a girlfriend?" she asked him idly.

"Sorta. I've been dating this girl—nothing heavy, just going places together."

"Don't tell me you struck out with her, lover," she teased.

He flushed dark red, and she remembered that boys his age had little sense of humor. "Well, she's real . . . you know, uptight. I haven't even got past second base yet."

Crystal sat up and bent over him, tickling his ear with her tongue. "Why don't I teach you a few tricks? I'll be your girl and you be yourself, and before I get through with you, you'll be able to go all the way home with any girl."

It was an exciting fantasy, one with endless ramifications. During following afternoons, they played it over and over— she the shy virgin and he the seducer—with variations. For the first time, she understood why Arnold was so fascinated by his sexual fantasies because she found herself totally entranced by the things they did during those long afternoons.

The one meeting she had planned became several, and then they were meeting every afternoon. When she realized that Jason's visits after school were curtailing his gardener's income, she discreetly tucked a couple of bills in his jeans pocket. At their next meeting, he didn't mention it, and after that, it became a habit to slip money into Jason's jeans before he dressed, something they never discussed.

On weekends when Grant was home or on days when she had appointments she couldn't break, she missed her love sessions with Jason, missed his ardent young body, the fantasies they acted out. She became so absentminded during dinner parties and other social events that she finally had to take herself in hand and make a special effort to keep her mind from wandering to Jason when she was with other people.

She knew that what she was doing was very risky, but she didn't realize how important Jason had become to her until Grant came home one evening to tell her that Arnold Krause had called to say that Grant's PCS orders to Hickam Air Force Base, where he'd be Arnold's assistant vice-deputy at PACAF headquarters, were being cut, that they would be reporting in at Hickam in September.

It was her dismay at news that would have delighted her just a couple of months earlier that made Crystal realize an unpalatable truth. She didn't want to move to Hawaii for the simple reason that she was hung up on a sixteen-year-old high school boy.

CHAPTER

✦ 40 ✦

CRYSTAL SUFFERED ALL THE PANGS OF WITHDRAWAL HER first month in Hawaii. It wasn't purely physical. There was something endearing about Jason that she missed almost as much. For one thing, they had become friends. During their afternoons together, he had confided in her, telling her about the troubles he was having at home and at school, and she'd felt a tenderness she'd only experienced once before, for her father—and even that had changed after her mother had taught her shame.

She had also been Jason's teacher and mentor as well as his lover, a role that satisfied another facet of her nature. The fact that he came from an unhappy home with an alcoholic mother had created a bond between them so strong that she had allowed herself to think of him as her child as well as her lover. The very perversity of their relationship had been an aphrodisiac that had heightened her enjoyment of their lovemaking.

Even so, there was never any question of not giving Jason up. The prize she had been working for, which she had sacrificed so much for, was too close at hand. Not only would Grant be working in a position usually filled by a general, but Arnold had promised to pull every string possible to see that it became a permanent assignment, thereby insuring that Grant would get his star.

Although Crystal had known that she would be expected to perform sexually on cue, to be at Arnold's beck and call, even this she had been resigned to. The thought of doing with Arnold what she'd done so willingly with Jason had sickened her, but it was part of the price she was willing to pay. She'd consoled herself with the knowledge that once Grant had his star, she could ease out of her odious relationship with Arnold once and for all.

Later, she'd discovered that there were other compensations for giving up Jason. Without her urging, Arnold obtained a set of quarters for them on the parade grounds, claiming that since he was now widowed, his subordinate would often be expected to entertain in his stead. Since these quarters were reserved for generals, Crystal knew there'd been speculation and gossip, especially since two brigadiers, both from tenant organizations not part of PACAF, were living in colonels' quarters at present. It was very satisfying to have generals as neighbors; it almost made up for her own thwarted sexual drive.

As soon as they arrived at Hickam, she began working herself into the fabric of the base. She became so busy making new contacts, renewing old ones, and ingratiating herself with the right people, that gradually the memory of Jason faded. In fact, she became impatient with his letters, which she found surprisingly juvenile. They had agreed that it was too dangerous to carry on a correspondence, something Jason seemed to have forgotten. He wrote Crystal impassioned letters that alarmed her with their recklessness. When the letters continued, even though she was too prudent to answer them, she finally called him at home, gambling that he would answer the phone.

But it was a woman's slurred voice that said, "Hello?" in her ear.

Crystal hesitated, then decided to risk it. "May I speak to Jason, please?" she said.

"Who is this?"

"I'm a friend of Jason's—from school."

"Well, I don't like girls calling my son—if you *are* a girl. And if you're who I think you are, you better watch out. I don't want no older woman teaching my boy bad habits—"

Crystal hung up, appalled at her own carelessness. What had she been thinking of, taking a boy that young for a lover? And if his mother was suspicious, it was even more imperative that she convince Jason it was all over. But how to reach him? She didn't dare write or call him at home again. Maybe she could call him at school—yes, it was worth a try.

Posing as his mother with an urgent message, she called Jason's high school the next day. It took a while, but he finally came on the line. For some reason, he sounded more immature over the phone than he did in person, and again, she wondered what on earth had possessed her to get involved with a youngster, no matter how attractive.

"Jason, this is Crystal. I know you can't talk now because you aren't alone, so just listen to me."

"Okay, but—"

"You have to stop sending me letters. We talked it over—remember? And you agreed that it had to end."

"But I miss you, Crystal. I—I want to at least write—"

"No!" she said, so sharply that she heard his breath suck in on the other end of the line. "It's over. You're a wonderful person, but it has to end. Besides, you should be interested in girls your own age."

"You didn't use to think like that," he said sulkily.

"I know. My head wasn't on straight then. It was wonderful while it lasted, but you have to get on with your own life now and finish your education. I'm a married woman—and eleven years older than you. Do you understand? No more letters. I do love you, but there's no future for us."

"But I get to thinking about—things. You know what I mean. And then I can't sleep—"

"There are plenty of girls your own age to date, Jason. The girls at school must be coming on to you all the time."

"Yeah, sure. Only I'm not interested."

"Well, give them a chance." Her voice softened. "Remember the games we used to play? You could play them with someone else—"

She kept on talking, and when she finally hung up, the sweat was streaming down her face, but she knew the crisis was over. Never again, she vowed as she went to take a shower.

At least, never again with a boy quite *that* young.

Grant was sitting at the bar at the Tropic Club, nursing a beer instead of his usual Scotch and water, sipping it slowly because of the ache, deep in his gut. He had gone to see the medics the week before and had taken an upper G.I., which had revealed a thickening in his stomach lining that had tentatively been diagnosed as a small lesion. Nothing to worry about—yet, the doctor had told him. Just watch your diet, cut out spicy foods, and keep away from alcohol and stress.

Keep away from stress—with Arnold Krause for a superior? Stress was synonymous with Krause. It could be his middle name. He fed on it, thrived on it, and if things were going too smoothly, he deliberately stirred up trouble among his subordinates. The man reveled in pitting them against each other, playing out an endless game of who's on top—today.

Grant knew why he did it—and it wasn't because Krause was a power freak. There was a practical reason for keeping his staff off balance. It cut down on laxness, a resting-on-laurels attitude, too much complacency. And the credit for their efficiency, as always, went to Krause.

Gloomily, Grant took another sip of his beer. He was sick to death of being Krause's whipping boy. Yes, a lot of men envied him, knowing he was marked for promotion, but sometimes he wondered—hell, all the time lately he wondered!—if it was worth it.

It hadn't helped that Crystal was in some kind of strange mood these days. Since they'd moved to Hickam, she'd been irritable, hard to please, overly critical. With Crystal on his back at home and Krause bugging him at work, he got it from two sides these days—and it was getting to him.

Which was why he'd changed into an aloha shirt and had gone downtown after work for a drink at his old hangout. Although he had no intention of trying to make a sexual contact, there was something satisfying about being here again, just another face in the crowd. No one to bug him with questions about the old man's thinking. No veiled speculations about his own status. No hostile or curious or envious looks. No one at the Tropic Club gave a damn who he was or what he did for a living—as long as he minded his own business.

As for carrying it any further—he'd learned his lesson. In fact, he had avoided eye contact with a couple of men who'd looked him over with interest when he'd first arrived. It was a little gratifying that the bartender had recognized him; he'd asked if Grant wanted a Scotch and water as soon as he sat down on a barstool.

"Good to see you again," he'd added, and Grant had nodded, then said he wanted a beer this evening.

Grant jumped nervously now as a hand touched his shoulder. Turning, he saw it was Billy, his former lover.

"Hey, hey—long time no see, brudda. You dropped outta sight so fast, I figure maybe you died on one of those sales trips to the Mainland," Billy said with fake joviality.

Grant eyed him without interest. Billy, it was obvious, had fallen into hard times. His face was thin, verging on gaunt, and his reddened eyelids twitched as he slid onto the next stool.

"Buy you a drink, Billy?" he asked reluctantly.

"Sure t'ing. A beer's fine."

Billy waited until the beer was sitting in front of him before he asked, "Where you been, man?"

"Oh, here and there," Grant hedged. "I'm working another territory now."

"You ain't been in stir, have you?"

"Why would you think that?"

"Oh, you know. You was always so cagey, never talked about what you do, like that. I figured maybe you was in the rackets." Billy fiddled with his beer can, his eyes flickering toward Grant, then away. "Look, brudda, I'm a little short and I'm really hurting—y'know what I mean? How about a loan? You'll get it back when this deal I'm working on falls into line."

Grant felt like kicking himself for laying himself open for a touch. Reluctantly, he gave his former lover enough for a fix, then watched as Billy hurried away, leaving his untouched beer on the bar. As Grant paid the bartender and said, "Be seeing you," he knew it was a lie, that he'd paid his last visit to the Tropic Club.

The next day was the weekly staff meeting, something he had come to dread. Krause had been touchy, impossible to please for the past few weeks, and today was no exception. Without provocation, he jumped Grant about a late report even though he himself had okayed the delay until current information could be assimilated.

"You better get it together, Norton," he growled. "You can be replaced, you know."

Grant didn't bother to answer. He caught the speculative glances of the other staff members, and he wondered why he'd never realized what a total bastard Krause was. Sure, he'd seen how the general rode men who were out of favor, but he'd always seemed immune to the same kind of treatment before. To be this man's subordinate for another two or three years— could he hack it? What kind of game was the old man playing, anyway? One minute he was all benevolence, and the next Krause was treating him like shit. So the question was—how long could he take it without losing his cool and blowing the whole thing?

When the meeting broke up, Krause told him gruffly to stay behind. Hiding his apprehension, Grant nodded and began gathering up papers, tucking them away in his attaché case, not looking at the others as they left the conference room.

But when they were alone, Krause's face broke into a smile. "Well, my boy, I told you I'd take care of you. The word got to the right places, and you're on the next BG selectee list."

Grant was silent. Why, when he'd just been handed the prize he'd been working toward most of his adult life, didn't he feel more elated? Intellectually, he knew that he had it made now, that those two old men in Florida would finally get off his back, that Crystal would be the general's lady she'd always wanted to be—so why did he feel so let down? Dammit, he'd eaten dirt for this promotion—so where was the triumph, the high?

"Thank you, sir. I'm overwhelmed," he said, realizing Krause was waiting for his reaction.

"I thought you'd be. And let me caution you—this is unofficial, just between the two of us. Don't even tell that little wife of yours. Other good men have their own friends in high places who want to see them make it. Could be they have more clout than I have."

"I understand, sir—and thank you."

"You'd better get used to calling me Arnold—at least in private. I hope you weren't offended by that chewing out I gave you today. Best way I know to scuttle any rumors. It wouldn't do to have the staff know I had a hand in all this."

"Yes, sir—Arnold."

But didn't my hard work have a little to do with the promotion, sir? Grant thought.

"You scratch my back and I scratch yours," Arnold said expansively. "Speaking of the wife—how's Crystal? You two getting along okay?"

"She's fine. We get along great, always have."

"Well, you're a very tolerant man—that's one thing I like about you, Grant, that you can overlook things that would send another man into a tailspin."

"I don't understand what you're talking about, sir."

"You don't?" Although Krause sounded surprised, there was a hint of mockery in his voice.

"What is it, sir?"

"This is a little awkward, but maybe the best way to handle things is to come right out with it. I got a letter from the wife of a master sergeant at Wright-Pat recently that . . . well, take a look at this." Krause opened a desk drawer, took out a piece of flowered stationery, and handed it to Grant. Silently, Grant read the letter, then handed it back.

"This is a lot of garbage," he said with certainty.

"You're sure of that?"

"It would be totally out of character for Crystal to take a sixteen-year-old boy as her lover. The only reason she'd have an affair with anyone would be because—" He stopped, realizing in time that he'd been about to say that the only reason she'd have an affair would be for material gain.

"Because of what?"

"Because something had gone wrong with our marriage. Which isn't true. Also, I have a habit of dropping by the house unexpectedly at all hours of the day to take a shower and change into a clean uniform. I would have known if something was going on," Grant improvised. "And if I had any worries at all along those lines, I'd look for someone older, more mature— and certainly with more clout than a boy still in high school."

His words, spoken as a diversion, seemed to echo in the room. Krause's eyes shifted to the letter, then back to Grant's face, and when a line of pink showed at the edge of the general's collar, a dark suspicion blossomed in Grant's mind.

God—God, what a blind fool he'd been! He'd been cuckolded by his own mentor—and he'd been too stupid to read the signs, to put two and two together. . . .

"I didn't think there was any truth in the letter," Krause said. "Crystal's too smart to do anything so stupid."

He clapped Grant on the shoulder, looking so relieved that Grant wondered if jealousy had prompted Arnold to show him that letter. "Well, boy, count your blessings. You've got a real helpmate there—good hostess, great organizer—the kind of wife a general should have."

Grant managed a noncommittal nod. He was glad when Arnold dismissed him, because now he could escape from the room. He made it to his car, but he didn't start the motor for a while. The depression he'd been fighting for weeks was upon him, a crushing force squeezing his chest and paralyzing him, and the nagging ache in his stomach was suddenly full-fledged pain, cutting him in half.

He leaned his head against the wheel, trying not to retch. How long had Crystal and Arnold been having an affair? When had she first let that lech get to her? Was it possible that it had started back when they were first married? And where did they meet? In a hotel—or in Arnold's office after hours? Surely not at Four Star House.

They had been so clever—never a word or a gesture to give themselves away, and yet all the time that Arnold had been calling him "My boy" and patronizing him, doling out little tidbits to keep him happy, he had been screwing his wife behind his back. Had Sophie known? Maybe the drinking had been her way of escaping the knowledge that her husband was having an affair with the wife of his protégé, a woman half her age.

What did they do together? Did Crystal enjoy it? Somehow, he found that impossible to believe. But it was obvious she knew how to keep Krause happy. Oh, yes, Crystal was full of tricks. She'd even succeeded in getting him to perform with a woman for the one and only time in his life. But she must have had her hands full with Krause. According to his reputation, he was the kind who climbed on and off like a rabbit nibbling at a lettuce leaf, half the time unable to get it up at all.

Sometimes lately he caught strange looks from other men. He had thought it was envy because of his rapid advancement, but what if everybody in the whole damned air force—including his old classmates at the academy, including his father and grandfather—knew that he'd gotten his promotion below the zone because Arnold Krause had been sleeping with his wife? Did they think that he condoned it, that he was in on it?

The bile rose in Grant's throat. He barely got the car door open in time to vomit upon the cement beside his car. When the spasms finally stopped, he slammed the door shut and started up the car. On his way home, he was careful to drive below the base's speed limit because this wasn't the time to be stopped for speeding.

When he reached his own driveway, he killed the motor and sat there, staring straight ahead. He felt hollow inside, all burned out and used up. One thing was certain—he couldn't go on working for Arnold. He would have to ask for a transfer, no matter how it looked on his record, because how could he face Arnold every day, knowing what was going on? While they were in bed together, did Crystal talk about him? Maybe she'd told Arnold that he was gay, that he couldn't perform with a woman. It would be natural for her to confide in her lover—didn't they call it pillow talk?

Moving like an old man, Grant got out of his car and went into the house. As he looked ahead, he saw only darkness, with no hope or joy or anticipation to fill the emptiness of his life. After he'd given up his secret life, he'd subjugated his sex drive—and everything else—to his career. To find out at this late date, just when he was on the verge of finally making general, that the promotions he'd thought he'd earned with hard work had come through Crystal's prowess in bed—no, he couldn't stomach that, couldn't live with it.

He went into the enclosed sun porch off the living room that he used as a den, opened his desk drawer, and took out the antique gun that his father had given him for his eighteenth birthday.

"'Bout time you had a gun, now that you're a man," he'd said. "Take good care of it—your granddaddy gave it to me when I graduated from the Point."

Grant had been very proud of the gun. Through the years, he'd kept it well oiled and in perfect condition. He unwrapped its chamois cloth protector now and loaded the gun, then sat at his desk, looking down at it. Its metal barrel glistened in the late-afternoon light, and when he picked it up and laid the barrel against his cheek, it felt very cold.

So lethal—and yet so beautiful with its carved ivory handle, its brass barrel. And now it was loaded, ready to fire. One twitch of his finger on the trigger and it would all be over— the emptiness, the futility, the darkness, the gut feeling that he'd been a fool to give up so much for so little return.

He put the gun against his temple.

Crystal was under the dryer at the base beauty shop when one of the operators touched her shoulder. "Phone call for you, Mrs. Norton."

Crystal thanked her and raised the hood of the hair dryer. Who would be calling her *here*? Whatever it was, surely it could have waited until she got home.

She picked up the phone and put it to her ear, and because

she was irritated by the interruption, her voice was tart as she said, "This is Crystal Norton."

"Temper, temper," Arnold's voice said. "You need some loving to mellow you out."

Crystal swallowed her annoyance. "That might be fun. Want to try it?" she said, her voice honeyed.

"How about coming over to my office before you go home? I want to tell you something."

When she hesitated, he added, "Everybody's gone. You can come in through my private entrance and bypass the guard desk. Use the key I gave you."

"I have dinner guests tonight. I can't stay long."

"Long enough for one of your fast blow jobs?"

It was all Crystal could do not to slam the receiver down. She gave a husky laugh. "How about a slow one?" she said.

"It's a deal. You won't be sorry. I promise you'll get your reward."

After Arnold hung up, she stood there for a moment, the phone still at her ear. More and more, Arnold was treating her like a call girl, summoning her whenever he felt like it, using language that made her stomach roll. Well, her day was coming—and wasn't she going to enjoy telling off that bastard when it did?

She realized the receptionist was eyeing her with interest, and she said quickly, "I'll see you at home, dear," and hung up.

Half an hour later, she was rounding the corner of the big, sprawling PACAF Headquarters building. As she glanced up at the wide expanse of windows that faced the control tower on the flight line, she wondered what Arnold had meant by saying she'd get her reward. Did he have another gift for her?

It was surprising how generous he had been through the years. Sophie had complained so much about his stinginess that Crystal hadn't expected him to be so lavish with his gifts. Besides her gold watch and her matched pearls, she had several drawersful of expensive lingerie at home, and then there was the jewelry she kept locked away in a metal box in her bedroom desk—a collection of heavy gold chains and charms, a pair of one-carat diamond earrings, a beautifully carved antique cameo from Italy, and Arnold's latest gift, a sapphire necklace with a diamond clasp. Sometimes, back in Ohio, she had paraded around in front of Jason, decked out only in her jewelry because he had loved seeing her like that, glittering and sparkling in the sunlight that crept between the closed drapes of the bedroom windows. . . .

Momentarily, Crystal felt an ache, a yearning, but she shrugged it away. That part of her life was over—and she would never be that foolish again. Yes, she still missed Jason, but no longer because of the great sex they'd had together. He had been . . . well, to say he'd been like a son sounded kinky, and yet it was true. Maybe that was how some women felt toward their sons, tender and loving and sure that nothing was too good for their man-child.

Of course her affair with Jason couldn't have lasted much longer. The age difference between them had been too wide. There toward the end, she had sometimes found his mixture of naiveté and brashness irritating, and eventually he would have started looking around at girls his own age. Right now, he probably had a dozen on the string, using the skills she'd taught him. . . .

It was past six when she used the key to Arnold's private entrance to let herself into the building. Krause was waiting for her in his spacious office on the second floor; he had a drink, rye whiskey and spring water from his bar, ready for her.

He kissed her after he'd locked the door. "Hmm. You look delicious in that mint-green dress—like a dish of lime sherbert," he said. "I've been sitting here, getting hornier by the minute, waiting for you."

She returned his kiss, then pulled away. "What's my surprise, Arnold."

"Surprise? I don't know what you're talking about."

"Oh, aren't you the tease. No surprise, no fun," she said lightly.

"No fun, no surprise," he countered. He cupped her hips with his hands, pressed himself against her. "Mmm . . . you really get to me, Crystal, and I've never figured out why."

"Well, thanks a bunch!"

"What I mean is—you're a good-looking woman, but you don't show off what you have, which is what makes you a good officer's wife. You act like a lady, but you're really all bitch. Maybe that's what it is—the contrast between what you look like and what you are. All I know is you really turn me on."

He unzipped his trousers and dropped them to his ankles. "See what I mean? I'm really in pain."

Wanting to get it over with fast, Crystal set about satisfying him. Even though it didn't take long, her nerves felt like tiny wires, jabbing into her skin, by the time it was over. After she'd repaired her lipstick, she asked, "What's your big surprise?"

"How would you like to be a general's lady?"

Ever since her affair with Arnold had begun, Crystal had been waiting for this moment. She had pictured it in her mind a dozen different ways. Grant coming home with the news or calling her from the office, or sometimes she'd even fantasized that she heard it from one of the senior officers' wives who had a line into the Washington rumor mills. She had rehearsed how she would feel, what she would say, so it was all that more surprising now it had finally happened, her initial reaction was disbelief.

"What is this? Some sick joke, Arnold?" she said coldly.

"No joke. Grant is on the BG selection list—he should be wearing stars by the first of next year. It has to be officially confirmed on the hill, but that's just a formality."

Reaction hit Crystal then, a slow trembling in her knees. "You did come through, didn't you?"

"I helped. But there's something I want you to understand—which is why I'm telling you this in advance. Grant deserves that star. He's a top-grade officer, and his record as a commander is impeccable. He's also one of the best administrators and logistics men I've ever known. We need more men like him in the air force. So don't get the idea that you put that star on his shoulders. He would've made it anyway—but maybe it would have taken him a few more years."

Crystal stared at him, trying to interpret his words. He sounded—angry.

"I know he deserves it," she said stiffly. "I've never underrated Grant. But there are thousands of men in the air force who are just as good and deserving who don't have a chance in hell of rising above the rank of colonel before they retire."

"There's a grain of truth in that," Arnold admitted. "Well, enjoy it. I hope neither of you ever has reason to regret Grant's promotion. Looking back, I realize I was happiest when I was a snot-nosed lieutenant, fresh out of the Point and still full of illusions. You're going to make a good general's wife—just don't try to wear Grant's star for him. Sophie never made that mistake—but then she also hated the responsibility of being a general's wife and eventually retreated into a Scotch bottle."

The leather couch creaked as he got up and pulled up his trousers. There was a strange smile on his face as he looked Crystal over.

"Nary a hair out of place after all that exertion. In your own way, you're a natural. After Grant makes general, I suppose you'll want to end our relationship, but for old times' sake, I hope you give me a blow job once in a while. You're the best, you know. With your talent, you would've made one helluva call girl."

He pushed down a button on his intercom to alert his driver, who was waiting down the hall, that he'd be leaving for the day. He gave her an ironic salute, but no kiss, before he left the room.

A minute later, she heard the distant sound of the elevator descending and knew it was safe to leave, but she stood there for a while longer, staring at the door. Why had he waited to tell her about Grant's promotion until after she'd serviced him? What facet of that clever, twisted, conniving mind prompted him to tell her at all? Well, he was right. As soon as it was official and too late for a slipup, she would drop Arnold. And wouldn't that be a relief? With hard work and a little luck, there was no reason why Grant should stop with one star. Why not two or three or even four?

On the way home, she decided that when she wrote her mother about Grant's promotion, she would treat it casually as if it weren't all that big a deal. God, what wouldn't she give to be there when Janet opened that letter! Of course Janet would play it cool. She'd either ignore it or point out the negative side—as if there were any—but underneath, she would be livid with envy. Yes, it was going to be delicious, letting her—and a few others—know that Grant had done the thing Maurice had never been able to do.

Crystal was still in a holiday mood when she reached home. She hummed under her breath as she let herself in with her key. Grant's car was parked in the driveway, so she knew he had beaten her home, but when she passed the living room, it was dark and so was the kitchen. She thought she heard a sound in his den, and she went through the living room, opened the

door to the sun porch. She saw his shoulders and head silhou-
etted against the darkening window behind his desk.

She switched on the overhead light. "Why are you sitting
in the dark?" she asked. Grant didn't answer; his face was so
gray and stiff that she felt a stirring of fear. "Are you okay?"

"I'm fine. Better than I've been in years."

"So you already know," she said, smiling at him.

"Know what?"

"Come on, Grant. Don't play games with me. Arnold must
have told you at work."

"I haven't the foggiest idea what you're talking about."

"Well, if you want to be coy, I'll give you a clue. What
have you been working for ever since you left the academy?"

"Retirement?"

She made a face at him. He was so seldom playful—but
then how often did a man become a general? "I'll give you
one more clue. What comes after colonel in the chain of command?"

"So you know about that. Who told you?"

His question took her by surprise. Who indeed? She couldn't
very well admit that Arnold had told her—or could she?

"I ran into General Krause as I was leaving the beauty shop.
We got to talking, and something he said gave it away. When
I called him on it, he admitted that you were on the BG selectee
list. He told me he was jumping the gun, telling me, but he
also said it was a sure thing."

Grant's eyes moved over her. "You're good. I give you that.
You're really good. I'm curious about something. Did Arnold
tell you before or after he fucked you?"

For one of the few times in her life, Crystal was speechless—but not for long. "What a lousy thing to say!" she said,
pumping indignation into her voice. "Even if that's your idea
of a joke, I resent it."

"It isn't a joke. I know you've been sleeping with him—
to put it delicately. You see, I finally figured it out. How do
you like that? Your thick-headed husband finally caught on that
his wife was fooling around with his boss. You two must've
really yukked it up, laughing at me. Was it good? Is he as good
at sex as he is at stabbing people in the back?"

"You're insane. There's nothing between Arnold and me.
There never has been."

"You really must think I'm a fool—and you're right about

that. But even a fool can put two and two together sometimes and come up with four. Do you know what I've been doing for the past hour?"

"I have no idea."

"I've been sitting here, staring at this gun." He lifted his hand and she saw the gun, gleaming in the overhead light. "It's an antique, you know. Brass barrel, carved ivory handle— worth a mint. But it isn't a toy. It's a lethal weapon that fires real bullets. If I put it to my head, I could blow my brains all over the desk. Instant nirvana. The easy way out. I got that far, you know. I thought of all the things I'd given up—the rotten things I'd done to get where I am—and I put the gun to my temple, ready to pull the trigger.

"Then I thought of Arnold, of that twisted mind of his. He wanted me to know about you two—and right after he'd given me the news about my promotion. But he outsmarted himself. Because there's something he obviously doesn't know about our marriage. I couldn't care less that you have a lover. You could have a dozen and it wouldn't matter. What did matter was my pride, that he'd made a fool out of me.

"When I put that gun to my head something clicked, and it all came together. That's when I realized how stupid it would be to blow my brains out when I had another out. All I have to do is walk away. I don't have to live this shitty life. And that's just what I'm going to do. Walk away. I've given the air force twenty years of my life, and tomorrow I'm going to put in my retirement papers. And then I'm going to accept that job offer at the Hoover Institute I told you about. It's some kind of irony, isn't it? That the institute should be at Stanford, so close to San Francisco, right smack dab in the middle of the gay scene?"

"You're crazy—"

"Crazy? Oh, no. I'm finally sane—after a lifetime of trying to do what other people expect of me. But that's all over. I think I should warn you that I'm coming out of the closet. Whatever happens, I'm going to live life on my own terms. And about time, too. As for you—you have plenty of grounds for divorce. I'll sign over half my pension to you. You can squeak by on it if you're careful—or you can go to work. I don't care what you do as long as I never have to see you again as long as we both live. As far as I'm concerned, you're dead."

Crystal discovered she was breathing too fast, that her head was spinning, and she realized that she was hyperventilating. All her hard work, the times that she had toadied to fools, the currying of favor and the frustrations and the setbacks and the humiliations and those odious sessions with Arnold Krause— it had all been for nothing. For *nothing*! Grant would waltz away from it all, scot-free to do what he wanted, while she was left behind, out in the cold again. No, it couldn't be endured. If anyone walked away, it was going to be Crystal. . . .

She reached forward and grabbed the gun off his desk. She pointed it directly at his head. "You're wrong, Grant," she said. "You're the one who's dead."

She pulled the trigger.

CHAPTER
↑ 41 ↑

TAI WAS DREAMING. IT WAS A BITTERSWEET DREAM, HALF pleasure and half pain. Just when it reached a climax, a hand touched her shoulder and shook her awake.

"Wake up, Tai," Steven said. "You're having a nightmare."

She opened her eyes and discovered it was morning, that she was safe in bed, safe with Steven. Filled with relief, she put her arms around Steven, and he laughed and kissed her.

"Sorry to wake you, but the way you were thrashing around, I was afraid you were having the granddaddy of all nightmares."

"It wasn't really a nightmare. I dreamed I was flying one of the X-planes at Edwards."

Steven was silent for a moment. "You haven't given it up, have you? That you'll be the first female fighter pilot."

"And the first female test pilot, too," she said.

"Well, go for it, Tai—if that's really what you want." But his voice held strain now. "How about I fix us some breakfast? Waffles and sausage okay?"

"Wow. I'm really getting spoiled." Tai stretched languidly, then rolled to her stomach and buried her face in her pillow. "When we both hit home base at the same time, I live it up."

"It'll cost you, woman," Steven said, swatting her rear. "I expect my pound of flesh in the sack. Lots of good, home-grown loving."

Tai sighed and sat up. "God, I wish we could get this schedule thing worked out. When we both got assigned to

McChord, I was sure our troubles were over, but we still don't see much of each other. Tomorrow you're heading out for twenty-two days on the Pacific circuit, and I'm doing my special services bit, squiring Tacoma school kids around the base. Then, when you get back, I'll be five days into the European run. We won't see each other for almost a month—sometimes I think those creeps in scheduling do it on purpose."

"Hey, cut out that kind of talk. I don't like it any more than you do, but you have to admit that when we *are* together, it's prime time."

Tai bit her lip and didn't say, as she could have, that honeymoons were great, but when did you get down to putting together a real marriage? So many important things they should discuss never came up because they had so little time together they didn't want to waste it with serious talk—or anything that might start a quarrel.

And she didn't say that there was something unreal about their snatched hours together, however sweet. Even the condo they'd bought near the base reflected it, she thought as she looked around the bedroom. Everything was so—so bland and standardized. There were few personal touches because she didn't have the time and the leisure it took to put her mark—and Steven's—on their townhouse.

Sure, there were the usual souvenirs, brought back from their trips—cherrywood carvings and cloisonné vases from Hong Kong, ceramic figurines from Germany, a lace tablecloth from Belgium, the silk wall screen from Japan, and the black lacquer floor screen with its tiny inlaid bits of ivory and gemstones that Steven had picked up in Taiwan. All very interesting, but like the showrooms in a furniture store window, there was nothing that she'd made herself or that Steven had put together in a workshop or that they'd bought together at some antique store. . . .

"I'm giving you to the count of three to get up before I pull off that sheet and expose your beautiful hide to my lewd gaze. Breakfast is waiting—and we have one whole day together. Let's not waste a minute of it, woman."

But that's the trouble, Steven, Tai thought as she slid out of bed and began dressing. Don't you see? We need to have time to waste. Either we're separated by half a world or we're trying desperately to cram every bit of excitement into the days we do have together. I'm so damned tired of it, and yet I can't say anything because the minute I complain, you get that look.

Oh, you don't say it out loud, that if I'd get out when my six years are up, most of our problems would be solved. Or that if I got pregnant, I'd be grounded for nine months, and if I didn't requalify, then I'd be here when you came home from your flights. And then, in two years, I could get out, settle in as an air force wife, and we could lead a normal life.

But don't you understand? I'd have to give up flying—and flying is in my blood, in my bones, inside my head. With you, it's a job, something that doesn't touch your emotions. You're much more stimulated by your computer, with tinkering around with that new software program you work on when I'm gone and you're here alone. With me, the excitement comes from flying, not from having the label of pilot or the prestige of being the aircraft commander of a C-5, in charge of a seven-man crew. It's the *act* of flying that excites me—and I'd be lost without it.

And yet—the two of us are important, too. I need you in my life—and the situation is tearing me apart. Not being able to talk about it to you is tearing me apart. Because there's no solution that would satisfy both of us. . . .

They had dinner with old friends at the club that night, then made love with the desperation that came from knowing that it would be weeks before they saw each other again. It was the following day, after Steven had left on his Pacific flight, that Tai had a surprise visit from Cassie, her old academy roommate.

Although she and Cassie kept up a lively correspondence, it had been almost a year since their paths had crossed. So when Tai came in from her special services jaunt, a little out of sorts because she always felt as if she were on exhibit during these tours as the little girl who flew the C-5, the biggest plane in the world, Cassie was waiting for her in the office Tai shared with three other rated officers.

"Hey, roomie—you got time for an old friend?" Cassie said, smiling at Tai from her desk chair. Tai flew toward her friend, and after they'd hugged and kissed cheeks, they stood grinning at each other.

"So what're you doing here?" Tai demanded. "I thought you had another year at that cushy desk job in Japan?"

"I'm on my way to Detroit to get married, Tai-Ching-a-Ling," Cassie told her. "Can you believe it? Mr. Right was living next door to my grandparents all the time. He came to Japan on business—he's an automotive engineer—looked me up, and bingo! It all happened fast. We're giving our folks what they want—an old-fashioned white-gown-and-lace wedding. Even a ring bearer—my little beast of a cousin, may he not throw up in the middle of the ceremony."

"I must be dreaming—no, I'm awake because it hurts when I pinch myself!"

"Look, Tai, I know this is awfully sudden, but can you possibly get away for the wedding? You're my bud and I'd like you to be there. For one thing, I want to show off my guy. He's . . . well, he used to be long and skinny and the bane of my life when I visited my grandparents during summer vacations. Now he's long and not so skinny and wonderful. Five inches taller than me, too. Which means I can wear high heels for the rest of my life if I want."

"I wish I could make it, but I traded off with another pilot so Steven and I could have a few days together this month." Tai hesitated, then added, "You're sure this is the right thing to do? What about your career?"

"My career so far has consisted of doing flunky duty for an assortment of senior officers, most of them over the hill. I'm getting out, Tai, when my time is up next year. I have my degree, and I can get a job at one of the auto plants—once I brush up on design and a few other pertinent things. I'm going into automotive designing—and believe you me, I'm ready to give up the hot pursuit and the cold nights. Who needs it?"

Her voice was earnest as she went on, "I want the husband-and-kids bit. I've never made any secret of being an old-fashioned girl. Once the babies start coming, I may even stay home and raise little engineers instead of holding down a job. Whatever I do, I'll be a better person for having gone through the academy and doing my stint in the air force. Not to sound maudlin, but it made a stronger person out of me. For one thing, I'm in no danger of sinking into domesticity—and maybe I'll raise better kids."

Tai was aware of envy, which surprised her. It would be nice to know exactly what you wanted out of life. Cassie would be a wonderful mother. Once she started a family, she would never look back in regret at paths she hadn't taken. She would revel in the security of a husband, a home, kids. But maybe security, real security, was a myth these days. The world was constantly changing, evolving. Maybe the only true security was in being strong and flexible.

That evening, she and Cassie had dinner at a small French restaurant near Tai's townhouse. Later, they sat over coffee and cognac for an hour, reminiscing and catching up on personal news, before Tai drove Cassie into Tacoma so she could catch her flight to Detroit.

After she'd seen her friend off, Tai felt so restless that she went for a long drive. Although she was sure that Cassie's solution was not for her, she couldn't help thinking how easy it would be to throw in the towel. After all, she hadn't come up with anything better. She was exactly where she'd been when she'd married Steven four years ago, with no solution in sight—none that would satisfy both of them.

In three weeks Steven would be home, and if they were lucky, she would be back from Europe before he was scheduled for his next flight. For the first time since their wedding, she wasn't looking forward to their time together. The last thing he'd said before he left this morning was to be thinking about their future and to come to some decisions. She still hadn't done that because there were no solutions that she could live with.

The thing was—how much longer would Steven wait?

CHAPTER
✦ 42 ✦

TAD AND SHELLEY HAD QUARRELED THE NIGHT BEFORE, and, as always happened after a quarrel, depression had dogged Shelley's footsteps ever since she'd awakened that morning. Even as she went about preparing breakfast, frying Tad's eggs in bacon fat the way he preferred—and which she abhorred—she kept rehashing the argument in her mind.

She was aware that she had provoked the quarrel by telling Tad about her mother's phone call, choosing the wrong time, when he was tired from a particularly rough day at his job as line chief at Barksdale AFB, where they'd been stationed ever since his return from Korea two years earlier. But she'd suddenly become sick of pretending that everything was right between them, that they had no problems or decisions to make. It wasn't just Tad's new assignment, his sixth PCS in the ten years of their marriage, although she did love it here in Louisiana. She had weathered so many of these transfers that she'd learned to take them in stride, to even enjoy the change.

But this one was different. Why was it that Tad, of all the men in his outfit who had the same AFSC, he'd been the one tapped for another unaccompanied tour? He would be gone a year, and then, if they were lucky, they might have two years together before they had to sweat out another overseas tour. And she was sick, sick, sick of it.

It wasn't that she blamed Tad. He had to go where the air force sent him. Intellectually, she knew that it was just as hard on him as on her. He loved her, loved their boys, loved family life. When he was away, he missed them. But *she* was the one who was left behind to cope with all the day-to-day problems of raising two lively boys.

Besides, the one left behind always had it the hardest. Tad would have his work to keep him busy. He'd be living in new surroundings, absorbed in his new job, with a new place to explore during his time off, while she faced the same old dreary routine and the responsibility of taking care of the children twenty-four hours a day, seven days a week—alone.

In Greenland, where Tad was going, everything would be provided for his comfort. Now that he was a senior master sergeant, he would be assigned a comfortable room in the NCO barracks. On his days off, he could go sight-seeing, see something of Greenland, go to the NCO Club for a few drinks and long bull sessions with the other sergeants, all the time knowing that back home, the little woman and the kids were waiting for him.

It would be a minivacation from domesticity for Tad. But not for her. Her responsibilities doubled when he was gone, and the loneliness was like a black cloud that hung over her, day and night. Especially at night.

Then there was the business of having to move off base, away from neighbors who would have been a comfort if Tad were going off on TDY those months. Oh, she would meet her friends for lunch now and then, but as a single, she wouldn't fit into their evenings. They would throw barbecues and have parties to which she wouldn't be invited, not because they didn't enjoy her company, but because she would be a fifth wheel among couples. And then there were the inevitable crises and alarms she would face alone—why was it that the car always broke down or the boys had fights with the neighbors kids or got sick when Tad was gone? It was almost a rule, it seemed.

Which was why it was so unreasonable of Tad to forbid her to accept her mother's invitation to stay with them the year he was gone. She had explained why this time was different, repeated her mother's concessions and promises, the proof that her parents had changed. And, as her mother had pointed out, they did have all that extra room in that big house the government had leased for them in Manitou Springs when her father had become Commander-In-Chief of NORAD.

She and the boys wouldn't even have to stay under the same roof with them. The guest house on the estate was more than adequate as living quarters for the three of them. They would still have their privacy, but with a difference. She would have someone she could trust to watch the boys while she did other things—like going back to school.

It was her mother who had suggested that Shelley enroll at Colorado College while Tad was gone.

"We're just rattling around in this big house—and we do have more than adequate household help. It makes sense that you come here. After all, you did say something during our last visit about going back to school when you got the chance."

Shelley's mother hadn't added the obvious, that it would be a help with Shelley's finances not having to pay rent, but it had been implied. And it would be great to go back to school and start getting credits toward an art degree. Later on, when the boys were older, a degree would be necessary if she wanted to work as an art teacher, perhaps in some private school. Of course Tad was touchy about her going back to school while the boys were still so young, but they could work that out later. Right now, she would be content if he just gave in and agreed to let her and the boys go to Colorado while he was gone. It wasn't even as if his reasons made sense. In fact, he hadn't given a reason, only that he didn't think it was a good idea.

"You still sulking?" Tad said.

He had finished his eggs and bacon and was having a second cup of coffee. Shelley pretended not to hear him because she knew that if she answered him, the quarrel would start again. She cleared the table and put the dishes in the dishwasher, then paused to look around the roomy kitchen. When she and the boys moved off base, they couldn't possibly afford anything like this. She really loved these lovely old quarters at Barksdale, had loved fixing them up with plants and macramé wall hangings and bright throw rugs. . . .

"One good thing about this tour," Tad went on, ignoring her silence, "it takes me off the hook for a few years. We should have at least four years stateside duty before I get another overseas assignment, and next time, you and the kids can go along—"

"That's what you said when we were transferred to Louisiana," she reminded him. "That we'd be here at Barksdale for at least three years."

"So I was wrong. But this time the law of averages is working in our favor. I should make E-9 in another three or four years, and that means one giant pay step. That'll ease the pain."

Shelley looked at him with cool eyes, resenting the reasonableness in his voice. At the moment, she even resented it that he'd changed so little in the past ten years. He still had that lean, well-knit body, that shock of blue-black hair, those intensely blue eyes that she'd fallen in love with at first sight, and despite herself, a trickle of excitement stirred under her anger. If she softened and smiled at him, he would pull her down on his lap and kiss her, and then he would take her into their bedroom, lock the door against intrusion from the boys, who were playing outside, and they would make love—but no, she couldn't do that. If she hoped to convince Tad that she was right, she had to keep her head and not succumb to the sexual excitement he could arouse in her so easily.

"What would really ease the pain is having someone to share the responsibility of raising our boys for the next year," she said. "You have to admit that my parents have changed. It isn't as if we'd be living under the same roof, so there's no danger that the boys would be spoiled—and besides, Mother promised not to interfere with my discipline. They both understand now how we feel about those expensive gifts—"

"I don't believe their promises. What they want is to get you and the kids to Colorado so they can give you a big dose of luxury—and I don't like the way your mom keeps after you to go back to school. I know better than to suggest that you go stay with my parents. You've made it very plain how you feel about that, although . . . well, I did think you had a good time when we went home last year."

Shelley thought back to their visit with Tad's parents, and it was all she could do not to tell him a few truths. Oh, she was very fond of Tad's mom, but she still felt uncomfortable around the rest of his family. For one thing, she hated his father's cursing and his off-color jokes, and then there were Tad's brothers and their wives with their buttoned-down minds and their gossip and their small-town nosiness. A whole year of that would drive her crazy.

As for staying with her own parents, it wasn't because she craved luxury, no matter what Tad thought. But she would like a little time, a little space, to pursue her own interests. After all, she'd only been eighteen when she married Tad. When had she ever had a chance to stretch her wings a little? To be able, for a while, to shed responsibility and have someone else watch the kids and do her laundry—any woman would jump at the chance. It wasn't as if it were forever. It was only for a year—and Tad was being so unreasonable.

The doorbell rang and she went to answer it, thankful for the interruption because it gave her a little time to simmer down. The mailman handed her a special-delivery form to sign, and she carried the envelope inside, her eyes on the return address.

"What is it?" Tad said from the kitchen doorway.

"Special delivery—from Crystal," she said. "I wonder if something's wrong. I haven't heard from her since her divorce—"

"You might as well open it, honey. If it's bad news, it won't go away."

A few seconds later, she was reading the words embossed on a creamy white card—a wedding invitation. A note, written in Crystal's bold, angular handwriting, was enclosed; it was stapled to a round-trip airline ticket to Honolulu.

"I do hope you can come to my wedding," Crystal had written. "It's been ten years since we were all together, so it seems the perfect time to have that reunion we talked about. What better time to get together than at my wedding, right? I hope you won't be insulted that I've enclosed an airline ticket, but it occurs to me that you might not be in the position to accept my invitation without it. Do, do come! I want the three of you to share this very happy occasion with me."

Silently, Shelley handed the contents of the envelope to Tad. Her first impulse was to rush to the phone to call Tai and Shelley, but she wanted to get Tad's reaction first. He read the note, examined the invitation, then studied the ticket before he commented, "First class. Your friend isn't cheap, is she? If you want to go—why not? You could use a vacation away from the kids—but I pay for the ticket. We don't need your friend's charity, even if she *is* marrying a four-star general."

Crystal's wedding invitation came at the wrong time—but then, Bobby Jo thought, when would have been the right time? In fact, the timing on everything seemed to be a little off lately. True, Josh had kept his word, and the incident when he'd struck her hadn't been repeated. In fact, he seldom spoke to her and Vicky these days, which was a relief—and also unnerving.

Since he'd been permanently grounded following a back operation last year, he was more and more difficult to understand—and to cope with.

So there was several things that made the idea of a vacation attractive to Bobby Jo. Josh wanted sex all the time now, sometimes at the most inconvenient times. After supper, he would fall asleep on the couch in front of the television set, and when he woke up at ten or eleven, he was ready for sex, right there and then. He didn't even bother with preliminaries before he was going at her—and when she protested that Vicky might wake up and hear them, he shrugged and told her to grow up, that kids these days knew all about sex. As a result, she was always too tense to enjoy it. Sometimes she found herself wishing he would get an unaccompanied tour overseas for a year, like Shelley's husband, just to give her a rest and the chance to get her head together.

Their social life had deteriorated, too. Even before he'd been grounded because of his back—in fact, ever since he'd washed out of test pilot school—he'd stopped seeing his old buddies. She knew it was his pride, and in a way she understood—but she did like to be with other people once in a while. Once, she had invited a former coworker and her husband over for dinner and cards, hoping Josh would enjoy it. He'd been reasonably polite that evening, but he'd made no effort to hide his boredom when the conversation turned to real estate, and nothing had come of it because the other couple hadn't returned the invitation.

With Josh's promotion to major that spring, there was more money, of course. Not so much that they could live in luxury, but yes, in that respect, life was easier, even though Josh had gone out and bought that big, expensive sports car.

So when the invitation had come from Crystal, there wasn't any reason for her not to go. Only . . . well, the airline ticket bugged her. It was sort of insulting, as if Crystal were saying that Josh couldn't provide for his wife and kid.

Josh didn't share her annoyance. He just shrugged when she voiced this opinion and told her, "If your friend wants to spring for the plane ticket, take her up on it. On the bread her old man pulls down, she can afford a dozen tickets. Besides, it can't hurt to get in cozy with a general's wife. In this man's air force, you never know when you'll need a favor."

"Then you don't care if I go?"

"Why should I? I can batch it for a couple of days, and Vicky can stay with her friend—what's her name? The little blond kid?"

Bobby Jo had vacillated a while, but after she'd talked to Tai and Shelley on the phone and discovered they were going, the opportunity to see them again was too tempting and she accepted the invitation.

Her next worry was clothes. She wanted to look as nice as the others, of course, which was a problem since she'd picked up those extra fifteen pounds in the past two years. Tai would look like an Oriental doll, as usual, in her simple, tailored clothes, and Crystal would be decked out in her wedding finery, something expensive and showy, no doubt. It didn't matter what Shelley wore—she would still be the prettiest woman at the wedding. So Bobby Jo's pride demanded that she look especially nice, which was why she spent far more than she could afford for a summer suit for day wear and a cocktail gown for the wedding reception. At the last minute, she added a pretty summer dress, too.

Of course, Josh had complained about the expense of her new clothes. She'd had to bite her lip not to remind him of the expensive new sport jackets he'd brought back from England when he'd gone there on an exercise just before his back operation. These days, she was very careful what she said to him. It wasn't that she was afraid Josh would hurt her physically. It was just that . . . well, he said such cutting things when he was mad at her. It was best not to argue with him, even when he was being unreasonable—*especially* when he was unreasonable.

Not only did she hate quarreling, but she owed Josh something because of the son she'd robbed him of. When there hadn't been any more children, she had taken fertility tests at the base hospital. The doctor had talked about scar tissue, and he'd given her treatments, including a D&C, but he hadn't been hopeful. There was little chance that she would bear another child. When she'd told Josh, he had looked at her as if she were damaged goods, and that's when he'd stopped trying to please her sexually.

Sometimes she found it hard to function under the burden of knowing that a botched-up abortion of another man's child had robbed Josh of the son he wanted. She still couldn't bring herself to go to church, so even that solace was lost to her.

And when Josh's temper flared up over some minor thing and he flayed her with his biting, hurtful remarks, she kept away from him until he was over his anger. After all, she owed him—even if he didn't realize how much.

The morning of the wedding, when he took her to the airport, he kissed her perfunctorily and then said, "I hope you don't go blabbing your private business to your friends. Just remember—the air force is one big closed community, and it's best to keep your mouth shut."

"I'm not a gossip."

"You could have fooled me. I thought you gals told each other everything."

"Not everything," she said, and thought of Shelley, who was the only one who knew her secret.

C H A P T E R
✦ 43 ✦

THE WEDDING OF GENERAL ARNOLD KRAUSE, COMMAND-er-In-Chief of Pacific Air Forces, to Crystal Moore Norton would be one of the year's major social events—to quote the *Honolulu Advertiser*.

After all, how often did a four-star general, especially one rumored to be slated to become chief of staff, get married? Crystal reflected as she sat at the dressing table in the master bedroom she would legally share with Arnold when they returned from their honeymoon.

She had consulted Arnold on every detail of the wedding, had scrupulously followed his recommendations for the guest list—with a few additions of her own. The mayor of Honolulu and the governor of Hawaii would be there, and she had even captured a real plum in Senator Ching, the Islands' senior—and socially elusive—congressman. Admiral Moran from Camp Smith, and Admiral Kildare from Pearl Harbor, plus the army's ranking general in Hawaii, General Muench, had accepted their invitations, and even the marines and the coast guard would be represented by senior officers.

Crystal's personal list had included her parents, of course. How else could she get the maximum enjoyment from the day if Janet wasn't there? She'd also invited several ex-classmates and three of her teachers from Punahou, and half a dozen senior officers whose wives she'd once toadied to so assiduously when she was married to Grant. They were undoubtedly preening themselves for being included, but she couldn't help that. It was important to her that they be there on this particular day.

And finally, there were her three "best friends" from high school. Tai, who had been class valedictorian, an honor that should have been hers. Bobby Jo, who had cheated her out of being homecoming queen. Shelley, who'd been born with everything that Crystal had coveted and who had thrown it all away so stupidly. Oh, yes, they would be here today.

Crystal rose from the dressing table where she'd been applying her makeup and went to stand by the window, staring out at the well-kept lawns and elaborate tropical plantings, the thick, impeccably trimmed hedge that gave these quarters the illusion of being isolated from the rest of the base. How ironic that this was the same house that Shelley's parents had occupied when General Pritchard had been commander of PACAF, ten years ago.

She had sent a wedding invitation and a brief, friendly note to the Pritchards, but Mrs. Pritchard had begged off, citing ill health. It was just an excuse, of course. That stiff-necked bitch simply hadn't wanted to witness the wedding of a woman her own daughter's age who would now be equal to her in rank. But that was okay. Other women would soon find out that snubbing Crystal when she'd been Grant's wife was going to cost them now. Then there were the three friends who had lorded it over her at Punahou, and her mother, who never in her whole life had given her a word of praise.

Now they would know how wrong they'd been.

Because look who had landed on top of the heap. . . .

Crystal turned back to the dressing table to give her face and hair one last examination. In the past ten years, her appearance had changed—and she wasn't sure it was for the better. She knew all the tricks of makeup, how to give her sallow skin the illusion of beauty, how to make her eyes look larger, more brilliant. But wasn't there a sharpness in her features that made her look years older than she was?

Once she was married to Arnold, of course, she could afford all the massages and treatments she needed to preserve her looks. She would start making yearly visits to the best of the beauty farms—and later, when she really needed it, she would have a face lift and an eyelid tuck. She didn't doubt for a minute that Arnold would pay the bill to keep his wife well preserved. In fact, he had been surprisingly generous with the

wedding expenses. It was only when she told him what her
gown would cost that he'd balked a little.

"You'll only be wearing it once," he'd pointed out. "And
why white? After all, you can't very well pass as a virgin.
Everybody knows you've been married before. You can't just
brush poor Grant under the rug. Don't you think white is a
little inappropriate?"

"The gown isn't really white. It's ivory."

"That's even worse. It's not your color, old dear."

He was right, of course. "I'll have it made up in light blue,"
she said.

"For three thousand dollars, it should be made from gold,"
he grumbled.

He'd finally agreed to pay the bill after she'd reminded him
that everybody of importance in the Islands, including the governor and a United States senator, would be there. But he'd
balked again when she told him she wanted three matrons to
attend her.

"That's ostentatious," he'd said bluntly.

"It's sort of a sentimental thing with me, Arnold," she'd
said, her voice coaxing. "The four of us were best friends at
Punahou—how can I choose one over the other two? Besides,
we made a pact to hold a ten-year reunion in Hawaii—and it's
been ten years since we graduated."

Arnold's shrewd eyes had appraised her for a long moment.
"You continue to surprise me, Crystal. I never suspected you
had a sentimental streak."

"Maybe you don't know me as well as you think," she'd
retorted.

"I know you keep my glands working overtime. I also know
you're a great hostess, that you know your place in the scheme
of things, and that you'll be an asset as my wife. Which is
why I'm marrying you. The sex is just a bonus."

Crystal had dredged up what she hoped was a credible smile.
"I think you're great in bed, too," she'd told him.

The brush she was holding fell from Crystal's hand and
clattered onto the dressing table. Great in bed—what a laugh!
Arnold was a miserable lover, even when he made a feeble
attempt to satisfy her. But he was the only game in town, the
means to an end. Which was why she was willing to put up
with Arnold, to please and appease him, even though sex with
him was increasingly tiresome.

Well, today would make up for everything—and nobody was going to rain on her parade. She'd made sure of that.

Crystal's smile held a feline satisfaction as she put on her robe. She had told her three friends that if they sent their measurements, she would arrange to have their gowns made for the wedding because there wasn't time to consult them about every little detail. "Trust me," she'd added. "You know I'll take as much pains with your gowns as I do with mine."

They had accepted, of course. What else could they do? And she'd kept her promise. She'd taken great pains with their gowns.

For Tai, she'd chosen yellow—to give her tawny skin a sallow cast. Pink for Bobby Jo, who had picked up weight, just as Crystal had once predicted she would, to clash with her auburn hair and make her look like Miss Piggy. And for Shelley, who looked like a princess even in a cotton sweat shirt and jeans, she had chosen a pale chartreuse that only one person in a thousand could get by with—and certainly not a silver blond. So no one else would outshine her, and by the time it was over, there'd be no doubt in anyone's mind, including her mother's, that Crystal had pulled off the coup of the year.

The first inkling that everything wasn't going as she'd planned came from her father.

One of the stewards brought her word that Maurice had arrived half an hour earlier than expected to escort her to the ceremony. When she went downstairs, still wearing her robe, she found him in the living room. As handsome as ever, even though he'd put on a little weight since retirement, there was a hangdog expression in his eyes that alerted her that something was wrong.

"You look like a princess," he said with a little too much heartiness. He kissed her on the cheek, then took a long gulp from the drink in his hand that the steward had provided.

"Where's Janet?" she said.

"She's sick as a dog, hon. Woke up this morning with one of her headaches—nausea, the whole bit. She says to tell you how sorry she is, especially since you went to so much trouble, arranging to have that dress made for her and paying our plane fare and making reservations for us at the Illikai. Here—she gave me this note for you."

Crystal opened the note, but she turned her back on her

father and went to the window as if she needed more light
before she read it.

> *Dear Crystal,*
>   *So sorry to miss your current wedding. But then you
> wouldn't want Arnold to be afflicted with a sick mother-
> in-law, would you? And thanks for the gown you sent.
> You really shouldn't have gone to so much trouble and
> expense. I have any number of things that would have
> been suitable—we do lead a very active social life in
> Huntington Beach, you know. However, I'll keep the
> gown. It'll come in handy for quiet dinners alone with
> your father. Oh—I'll try to make it to the reception, but
> if I don't, go ahead without me. Ta-ta.*

The notepaper rustled in Crystal's hand. It was all she could
do not to tear the letter into tiny pieces, to scream and pull her
hair. The light from the windows blurred as a jagged line began
to pulsate at the perimeter of her vision. She blinked several
times, forcing it to go away. It was a minute before she felt it
was safe to turn and face her father.

"Too bad," she said lightly. "Just about everybody of importance in the Islands is going to be there—including the governor
and Senator Ching. Be sure to tell Janet all about it, every little
detail, when you get back to the hotel."

"About the hotel bill, hon—your mom wants to stay over
a few days, and it's only fair—"

"Arnold will pay for it. Our treat. In fact, he's already
arranged to have the bill charged to his account." She glanced
at the tiny jeweled watch on her wrist. "Can you amuse yourself
for a while? Just call the steward if you want another drink. I
have to finish dressing."

She hesitated, then added, "My friends from Punahou will
be here shortly. I sent Arnold's car and driver to pick them up
at the airport and take them to their hotel to get dressed. I'd
planned to have Janet attend me—I'll need some help with my
dress—but since she couldn't make it, will you send up my
friends when they get here?"

She realized that her voice sounded strained, so she was
glad when Arnold came into the room. He was already dressed
for the wedding, and she forgot her disappointment as she
examined him. He did look . . . well, important. Not distin-

guished like Grant or handsome like her father, but still . . . yes, he did have an air of command. There was no mistaking that he was a man to be reckoned with.

"Well, father-in-law," Arnold said, his voice booming, "are you ready to give the bride away?"

"Yes, sir," Maurice said.

"Come, come. We're family now. Call me Arnold."

"Arnold, then," Maurice said, beaming.

"So how do you like living in Huntington Beach—"

Crystal listened to their polite exchange for a while, then excused herself and went back upstairs. But instead of getting her gown out of the closet, she sat on the edge of the bed, breathing deeply, hoping to ward off the headache. When that didn't help, she took two of the pills the doctor had prescribed, washing them down with a shot of whiskey from the bedroom's small portable bar. As a final precaution, she got the oxygen cylinder she'd had installed in the dressing room on the recommendation of her doctor and fitted the plastic tubes into her nostrils, careful not to mess up her hair.

Only when the quivering at the edge of her sight faded and the pounding in her head diminished to a small echo did she take her wedding gown from the closet. Mind over matter, she thought. You had to be strong to make it in this life.

The sound of women's heels, clicking on the hardwood floor of the hall, alerted her that her three Punahou friends had arrived. A moment later the room was filled with women, all talking at once. Tai, her jet black hair gleaming like a mynah bird's wing, looked striking in chartreuse, while Bobby Jo's statuesque figure showed to advantage in yellow, and Shelley looked angelic in pink. Crystal was so caught up in the flurry of greetings that it was a moment before she realized they were wearing the wrong gowns.

Bobby Jo explained the change. "You don't know how close we came to a disaster, Crystal! They delivered the wrong gowns to our hotel rooms. We compared notes and finally figured out there was some kind of mix-up because you'd never order a pink gown for me, not with my skin tones. I looked just like a tomato in that gown Shelley's wearing. You wouldn't believe what a whiz Shelley's become with a needle! Shelley's gown is a little short, and mine is too tight around the waist, but if I don't bend over, it should be okay. I love this shade of yellow—it's my favorite color. Doesn't Shelley look awesome in pink? And that chartreuse is perfect for Tai—but then, you've always had the best clothes sense of anyone I know."

The headache came raging back. Crystal turned blindly and groped for the bourbon decanter. She poured herself a glass, downed it quickly. Later, she told herself, she would have a screaming fit, but right now she had to salvage the rest of the day. . . .

The wedding, an hour later, almost made up for her thwarted plans. As she came down the aisle with her father's hand cupped around her elbow, Crystal was haunted by a feeling of déjà vu. She and Grant had been married in this same chapel. How long ago it seemed now. What was Grant doing at this very moment? Even before their divorce he had dropped completely out of sight, and she'd had to deal with his lawyer. Had he moved to San Francisco? Was he living it up with a lover? Had he taken that job with the Hoover Institute? Once she was married, he would start drawing his full pension—and of course he had his trust fund.

What would he say when he found out she'd married Arnold, that she was the wife of a four-star general? Or maybe he already knew. If so, she hoped it had pricked that pride of his— but she doubted it would. She'd never been able to penetrate his thick skin—not even with a bullet. How ironic that it had merely broken a vase before he'd wrestled the gun from her hand.

It was strange that he hadn't shown any shock or fear. In fact, she'd had the crazy idea that he might have welcomed the bullet. Well, she hadn't killed him, but at least it had brought things to a head. He had been, in his own way, a gentleman about the incident, telling the military policemen who had investigated the shot that he'd been cleaning his gun when it went off.

Later, he'd allowed her to file for divorce on grounds of incompatibility and hadn't contested it. Everybody had assumed that he was at fault—which damned well was the truth. When she'd left Grant and moved into an apartment in Honolulu, Arnold had contacted her to tell her that if she wanted to resume their relationship, he would set her up at a luxury Waikiki residence hotel and pay her a generous allowance.

Of course she had accepted. She wasn't equipped to live on Grant's half pension or to earn a living—not and maintain any kind of decent life-style. What she hadn't expected, two

months after her divorce was final, was Arnold's proposal, that
cold-blooded businesslike proposal. . . .

Her step must have faltered because her father's hand tightened around her elbow. She elevated her chin a quarter of an
inch and stared straight ahead as she moved slowly down the
aisle. Everything in her life for the past ten years had been
pointed toward this moment. She meant to enjoy every minute
of it. She would show them, all those losers who had tried to
put her down, what it meant to have power. Before she was
finished, they would all jump to her tune—or face the con-
sequences.

The reception, at the Hickam Officers Club, was lavish,
every detail carefully orchestrated—from the caviar canapes
to the champagne, which had been special-ordered from France.
The guests, from the noise and the amount of food and drink
they were consuming, were having a wonderful time. When
the governor, a transplanted coast haoli, complimented Crystal
on the reception, she was tempted to tell him that without her
supervision, they would have been served the Officers Club's
usual tired canapes and domestic champagne, that the flowers
would have been tropical, so trite in Hawaii, instead of spring
flowers flown in from the mainland. But instead she smiled
sweetly and told the governor that he was more than kind, that
she hoped he and his charming wife had a good time.

To her irritation, her father had gotten over his first awe and
was monopolizing Arnold. Well, Maurice was always one to
toady to those he considered his superiors, so she shouldn't be
surprised. Which made it all the more strange that he'd bombed
as an air force officer.

She accepted another glass of champagne from a passing
waiter and sipped it while she listened to two women, wives
of senior colonels, who were vying for her attention with compliments about her gown, the reception, the whole ball of wax.

How sweet it was—and how she was going to enjoy being
Arnold's wife. If he became chief of staff, they would move
to Washington, the hub of power. Of course he would have to
retire someday, but . . . well, she'd think about that when it
happened. "You did a good job with the reception, Crystal,"
Arnold said in her ear. "They'll be talking about this spread
for the rest of the year. I just hope it doesn't turn the Honorable
Senator Ching off. He's not the military's strongest ally on the

hill, you know. He's always bleating about overruns and military spending."

"Maybe this will mellow him," she said.

"He seemed very curious about you when I was talking to him. Have you ever met him before?"

"No. We don't—didn't exactly move in the same circles," she said dryly.

"Well, he's coming this way now—no, he's stopped to talk to that little Chinese friend of yours—what's her name? Tai something?"

"Tai-Ching MacGarrett—no, it's Henderson now," she said absently, her eyes on Tai.

She stiffened when Senator Ching and Tai, still talking, moved slowly toward her and Arnold.

"Crystal, I'd like you to meet my uncle, Senator Ching," Tai said.

Crystal felt the shock, like a bolt of electricity, all the way to her toes, but somehow she managed to smile and murmur something appropriate.

"I've heard a lot about you from my niece," Senator Ching said. "I was telling Tai how proud I am of her. She's a Ching, through and through."

He smiled at Tai, who looked a little embarrassed. "We Chings are stubborn to a fault. Tell us we can't do something and we'll prove you wrong if it kills us. We also have too much pride—our ancestors probably called it 'face'—which can be a lethal combination. Fortunately, Tai has more than her share of courage. It took courage to make it through the academy and flight training. Now she tells me she wants to be a fighter pilot—if Congress will only change their stupid rules, to quote her own words. She just might do it, too—provided she can convince enough male chauvinists, like me, that it's feasible."

Arnold beamed at Tai. "So you're related to the senator. Crystal never told me."

"Maybe it slipped her mind, sir," Tai said.

A white-jacketed waiter, carrying a tray of champagne, passed. Blindly, Crystal set down the empty glass in her hand and snatched up a full one. She drained it, ignoring Arnold's frown. "I'm sure Tai will get everything she deserves," she said; she had trouble enunciating her words because her tongue felt so numb.

Her father came up, and she introduced him to the senator,

who chatted with him politely. Arnold was soon deep in conversation with Tai, who seemed unawed by his rank, and Crystal slipped away, heading for the ladies' room. There was a strange taste in her mouth, as if she'd just inhaled ashes, and she wanted to scream and cry—or do both. Instead, when she reached the women's lounge, she took several deep breaths, renewed her makeup, and tucked a few stray strands back into her elaborate hairdo before she returned to the reception.

The next hour was an ordeal, but she endured it stoically, smiling and acknowledging compliments and best wishes, consoled by the knowledge that no one watching could possibly guess the turmoil that was boiling up inside her. And then, finally, it was time to return to Arnold's quarters so she could change into her traveling clothes.

Arnold's driver snapped to attention when she appeared and quickly opened the door of the staff car. He was very young, hardly more than a boy, and his deference was a balm to Crystal's jangled nerves, even though the opinion of an enlisted man held little weight with her. Still . . . he was extremely attractive. Yes, very attractive indeed, with that broad forehead and curly hair and those ingenuous eyes. . . .

The house was quiet when she let herself in. From the back of the house, she heard the stewards' voices as she went upstairs to the master bedroom. She took a bottle at random from the portable bar, poured a double shot of amber-colored liquid into a glass, drained it in one gulp. The jolt of alcohol steadied her. It would all be over soon. Arnold was taking her to Hilo for a brief honeymoon. Later, when he could get away longer, they were planning a tour of the East—Japan, Hong Kong, Thailand, Australia.

Footsteps sounded in the hall, and someone knocked on the door. When she called out an impatient "Come in!" her three friends entered, looking like butterflies in their pale dresses.

"We saw you slip away and thought you might need help," Bobby Jo said. "Or would you rather be alone for a while?"

"Oh, do stay." Crystal waved them toward four chairs that formed a conversation group in one corner of the spacious bedroom. "I still have about half an hour before I have to change—why don't we have another drink? You all look like you could use one."

Without waiting for an answer, she splashed bourbon into four glasses, not bothering with mixers. When they each had a glass in their hands, she raised her own glass in a toast. "Here's to marriage—and other disasters," she said.

All day, Bobby Jo had felt out of sorts, and she wasn't sure why. It wasn't the wedding. It had gone like clockwork, although she'd noticed that for all her smiles, Crystal didn't quite look the happy bride. No, the trouble lay elsewhere, within herself. It was strange to remember how she'd once loved weddings, even the austere ones favored by the members of her father's church. Her own, to Josh, had been something out of a fairy tale with all the trimmings, including the raised swords of Josh's friends. How could she have known that a day would come when she'd wish she had gone off and had her baby alone— disgrace or no disgrace?

Of course, she had put a good face on it today. She'd talked to the other guests, laughed at the right times, responded as best she could to the festive atmosphere. And when her friends asked how Josh and Vicky were, she'd said that they were both fine, thank you.

That wasn't true, of course. Josh hadn't been fine since he'd washed out of test pilot school. What would they say if she told them that he was sullen and morose most of the time, that he was drinking much too much these days? Sometimes, when they were watching TV she would look up to find him staring at her, his eyes brooding. That's when she was very careful to walk softly and not do anything to draw his ire.

So this trip to Hawaii should have been a welcome change, a real holiday. And she did enjoy visiting with Tai and Shelley again. It was just that . . . well, she felt so depressed when Tai talked about her husband. When she said Steven's name, her eyes lighted up and there was a smile in her voice—how sure of herself Tai was! She had always envied Tai because she was so—so on top of things.

And Shelley—how could she be so calm and look so lovely with all she'd gone through in the past ten years? It didn't help that she felt so ashamed every time she looked at her friend that it was hard to talk naturally to her. Well, when she got back home, she intended to change her ways and start writing regularly again. After all, it wasn't Shelley's fault that she knew about the abortion.

As for Crystal—she hadn't changed much. She had been pleasant and certainly generous, the way she'd paid for everything. In fact, Bobby Jo still felt strange, having Crystal's husband pay her hotel expenses as well as her plane fare. But when she'd changed her mind at the last minute, Josh had insisted that she go.

"It's your chance to make points with your friend's old man. You never know—maybe he can do something to get me back on flying status," he'd said.

Another thing that bothered her was that she kept comparing Arnold, Crystal's new bridegroom, with Grant, her ex-husband. From the snapshots Crystal had sent her from time to time, Grant had been . . . well, such a distinguished-looking man, more like her idea of a general than Arnold Krause, who reminded her of the frog prince before he'd changed back into his human form.

The truth was that she didn't like him—not at all. The way he'd looked her over—and she'd been really shocked when he'd brushed his hand against her rear. It hadn't been an accident, either. She was sure of that. So she didn't envy Crystal, not at all. Josh wasn't the man he used to be—or the one she'd thought he was—and he liked women too much, but he wouldn't make a pass at one of her friends—at least she didn't think he would.

As Bobby Jo sipped her drink, she watched Crystal covertly. How thin she was—and it wasn't becoming. By the time she was forty, she would look like a witch with that sharp nose and long upper lip. That was her third drink in the past few minutes, too. If she wasn't careful, she'd end up drunk on her own wedding night.

"—so when the governor's wife invited us to dinner, I said yes, of course, although I rather dread having to attend one of those boring political affairs." Crystal's voice was slurred, and her eyes held a glitter, as if they were made of glass. "Of course you know all about political figures, don't you, Tai. Why didn't you ever tell us your uncle was Senator Ching?"

"I thought I had," Tai said.

"You know you didn't." Crystal wagged her finger at Tai. "Kept it to yourself, you did. Is that how you got your appointment to the academy?"

"Uncle Ching nominated me—but I had to pass all the tests before it was official," Tai said.

"Oh, *of course* you did." Crystal's voice dripped sarcasm. "Well, I don't blame you. I'd do the same. Use what you have to get what you want. That's how the system works. I do hope you plan to get out of the air force and go into something else. Arnold tells me that service couples who marry each other have several strikes against them when it comes to promotions and such."

"There are a few problems, but Steven and I think the advantages outweigh the disadvantages."

"And I always thought you were so practical. The truth is that one man is just like the next—in bed, I mean. They all have essentially the same equipment. It's what they can do for you that really counts."

Crystal waved her glass in Shelley's direction. "Look at Shelley. She married for love, and what did she get? Tied down with two kids and living on enlisted pay—and nothing better to look forward to. Is it worth it, Shelley? If you had it to do over, would you still elope with your precious Tad?"

It seemed to Bobby Jo that Shelley was a long time replying to Crystal's attack. "I love Tad. We have a good marriage," she said finally.

"Well, you have to say that, don't you? How can you admit you made a mistake when you were dumb enough to burn all your bridges behind you?"

"Knock it off, Crystal," Tai said before Shelley could answer her. "You have your ideas about what's important—but the rest of us don't agree. You can't expect other people to live by your standards."

"But we can learn from other people's mistakes," Shelley said unexpectedly. "Lately, I've been going through something of a—a personal crisis. I'm human, and I hate always worrying about finances. But you can't live and sleep with money. It only buys *things*. What matters is people—and whether there's love in a marriage. And there's plenty of love between Tad and me. So—to answer your question—yes, if I had it to do over, I'd still marry Tad. That doesn't mean that I don't have problems."

Crystal's mouth twisted into an ugly smile. "And I think you're a damned fool—or a liar. You threw it all away. You gave up a great future for—what? Intellectual conversation? A meeting of stimulating minds? Or was it a big cock that got to you? Didn't anyone ever tell you that you can get all the sex you need without marrying for it? What you don't have is guts, Shelley. Well, I've got guts—and now I have the power—"

"Secondhand power," Tai said, her voice cool.

Crystal whirled on her. "And you—what have you done that's so great? A half-assed career as a pilot—and even that isn't going anywhere. You'll end up being a housewife, just like Shelley and Bobby Jo, and then you'll feel sorry for yourself for the rest of your life. Even if you hadn't married your—what is he now? a major?—it would be the same. The big boys are never going to let a woman into their club. You blew it, Tai. You really blew it."

"And you haven't? If power and position are what you want—how about when Arnold retires? How old is he? Certainly old enough to be retiring in the near future. Then what will you be? The wife of a retired general officer. Nobody's going to give a damn about your opinions or cater to you then. And you'll still be a young woman—what will you do with the rest of *your* life? Divorce Arnold and marry someone else? You could make quite a career for yourself out of marrying old generals and staying with them until they retire, then divorcing them and marrying another one."

Crystal's eyes were so murderous that Bobby Jo said quickly, "Oh, please—we're all tired. Why don't we talk about something else?"

Crystal gave her a contemptuous look. "Always the little peacemaker, aren't you? What about *your* marriage, Bobby Jo? Why do I have the feeling that you're covering up something? Could it be because you change the subject every time your husband's name comes up? What happened? Did he finally get tired of little Miss Dumbo? Did the sex wear thin? I heard a rumor that he got in a little trouble at test pilot school—something about being caught fooling around with some instructor's wife, wasn't it? That doesn't sound like a marriage made in heaven to me. So don't act like I just grew horns. You're all jealous as hell—you'd love a chance to be in my shoes."

Tai eyed Crystal, her face without expression. To Bobby Jo, her friend had never looked more Oriental. "We don't envy you, Crystal. We feel sorry for you. To marry a man for what he can give you would be hell on earth."

"I agree," Shelley said, but there was no anger, only weariness, in her voice. "The thing that matters is having one person in the world who puts you ahead of himself. The rest is all garbage."

Crystal's nostrils flared. But instead of attacking Shelley or Tai, she pointed her finger at Bobby Jo. "And you? You agree with these two losers?"

"I—I guess I do," Bobby Jo said slowly, trying to be honest. "Maybe I haven't always. Until today, I probably would have said that the important thing is doing your duty. But you can't hide the way you feel twenty-four hours a day, can you? If you don't love someone anymore, they know it even if they try to fool themselves. In the end, they hate you, hate themselves."

"I don't know what the hell you're talking about—but then you're always been a little short in the brains department."

"And you're so smart?" Tai snapped. "If you've got it all together, why the hell are you drinking so much on your wedding day?"

"Listen, I don't have to listen to your crap—"

"No, you don't. But you started this discussion. Which makes me wonder why you invited us to your wedding. Was it because you wanted to lord it over us? Well, you made a mistake. Marrying an old man, one who was pinching my ass half an hour ago, is not my idea of marrying well."

Crystal snatched off her shoe and jumped to her feet. She flung the shoe at Tai, who dodged it easily. She looked so ridiculous that Bobby Jo had to stifle a giggle. "Get out, you bitch—I want you out of here before I call the stewards to throw you out. You're a loser, and that's all you'll ever be."

Tai went to the door and opened it. "I'll send your dress back by messenger," she said.

"I think it's time I left, too," Shelley said, getting to her feet.

"Get out—get out, all of you!" Crystal's face was distorted with anger. "But before you go, think about this. Arnold will do anything I ask. I've got him right in the palm of my hand. If I tell him how the three of you insulted me, he'll see that none of your husbands ever get another promotion again in the air force. And don't think he can't. So don't start planning any promotion parties!"

"And you think about *this*," Tai said quietly. "I've never asked my uncle for anything except for a chance to compete for an appointment at the academy. But to protect myself, to protect my friends, I'm going to repeat this conversation to him. Don't do anything you'll be sorry for, Crystal. Take out your spite on someone who won't fight back—and be very careful, even then. You could get a big surprise."

She stalked out of the room, followed closely by Shelley. Bobby Jo stood rooted to the spot. She wanted to leave—but then Crystal would be all alone. She met Crystal's frenzied eyes, and she backed away, suddenly afraid.

"Get out, you dumb bitch!" Crystal screamed. "You make me want to puke—you always have!"

Bobby Jo fled through the door, along the hall, and down the stairs. Tai and Shelley were waiting for her in the foyer. They both looked a little sick.

"I think she's crazy," Bobby Jo said weakly.

Tai shook her head. "She's full of hate. Lord knows how long she's kept it bottled up inside her. In a way, I'm not sorry it happened. It gave me a handle on something that—on a personal problem. After I've had time to think it through, I'll write you both about it, okay?"

Bobby Jo nodded. "I have some decisions of my own to make," she confessed. "It's not easy—I've never been very good at thinking for myself."

"Which makes it unanimous." Shelley's lipstick was smudged; her hair looked more silver than blond in the brilliant sunlight. "It's funny how we all cover up, isn't it? How we go on living with things instead of bringing them out into the open."

Bobby Jo was glad when the taxi Tai asked one of the stewards to summon came quickly. She had so many things to sort out in her mind—and she didn't want to be distracted. By unspoken mutual consent, they were all silent as the taxi drove them to their hotel. When they parted in the lobby of the Illikai, they were still subdued, although they made arrangements to meet for dinner later that evening.

Bobby Jo realized that, like her, her friends needed time to evaluate what had happened. Alone in her room, she examined her conscience and couldn't think of any reason for Crystal's attack—unless it was that homecoming queen business. And Crystal *had* wanted to be class valedictorian the worst way. She might still harbor resentment toward Tai for that—but what about Shelley? Shelley had never competed with Crystal for anything.

That evening over dinner, the three of them talked about everything except Crystal's wedding, then went to their rooms early. Although they were booked on the same plane, they didn't ask for seats together, something for which Bobby Jo was grateful. She needed more time alone to think.

Later, at San Francisco International, before they went their separate ways, it was Tai who voiced the thing that was on all their minds.

"We took a beating emotionally from Crystal, but we can't let it interfere with our friendship with each other. I'll be writing to both of you as soon as I get my own life in order. I want your promise that we won't lose touch with each other."

Although Bobby Jo and Shelley only nodded, Bobby Jo was sure they would keep their promise. There was one good thing about the incident with Crystal—she no longer felt embarrassed that Shelley knew about the abortion.

And wasn't it strange that it had taken her so long to realize that Shelley was one of the most unjudgmental people she'd ever met?

CHAPTER

✦ 44 ✦

CRYSTAL WAS STILL SITTING IN THE LOUNGE CHAIR, STILL dressed in her wedding finery except for the shoe she was holding in her hand, when Arnold came through the door.

"Why aren't you getting ready, Crystal?" he said, irritation edging his voice. "And where are your friends?"

"They were tired—they went back to their hotel." She dropped the shoe on the floor, stood, and moved to the dressing table to pick up her hairbrush. Her back to Arnold, she began brushing out her elaborate coiffure.

"What the hell are you doing?" he demanded. "The hairdresser was here three hours this morning, fixing your hair."

"I want to change my look. This hairdo wasn't the real me," she said.

"Okay, what happened? Weren't your friends properly impressed with your big triumph?"

That got her attention. She turned to meet his ironic stare. "I don't know what you're talking about, Arnold."

"Come on. You didn't invite them here out of nostalgia for the good ol' days. You wanted to throw your four-star general catch in their faces. And I'm not knocking it. It's a natural instinct. Why the hell do you think I go home to the Bronx every year to see my relatives—especially my stinking uncle, who treated me like garbage as a kid and who said I'd turn out just like my old man?"

515

Crystal met his hard eyes. "Why are you telling me this now? You never talk about your family."

"To let you know I understand. I even approve—as long as you keep it in perspective. Just don't expect other people to play your game. Because they won't. I've got one cousin who asks me every time I go home when I'm going to make captain."

Crystal found herself smiling. "That's a joke, right?"

"No joke. The bastard's always hated my guts. He used to beat me up regularly when we were kids. But since he goes to such lengths to put me down, I figure these stars must really get to him. You should figure the same about your friends."

"They don't envy me. They feel sorry for me."

He shrugged. "That's their problem. Why should you worry about a bunch of losers like that? The redhead's husband, for instance—do you know what happens to gung-ho fighter pilots who get grounded? The gravy train stops. When they put in their twenty years, out they go. Wing commanders have to be rated—and that's the road to higher command. Besides, the air force needs young pilots, not old men. And your friend Tai—she's a gutsy gal, but she's a female in a man's world. When she figures out the odds against her, she'll drop out."

"Not Tai—damn her," Crystal said, venom slurring her words. "She's too bullheaded."

"Then she's really in for a letdown. Your friend Bobby Jo—she's the opposite, isn't she? A weak willow. She strikes me as the camp-follower type."

"You're right. Bobby Jo's never had an opinion of her own in her life."

"And the other one? Curtis Pritchard's kid? She really messed up her life, marrying a grease monkey. She could've done a lot better."

Crystal discovered her good humor had been restored. "My thoughts exactly."

Arnold came up behind her and began unbuttoning the row of tiny buttons down the back of her wedding gown. "If you know all this, why did you let them get under your skin?"

"I didn't," she lied. "It was just that . . . well, it's been a long day and I'm worn out. And I don't see the point of this conversation—"

"The point is that I want you to start thinking like a winner. Your trouble is that you think small—and you don't understand power. Getting some puerile revenge on people who put you down is kid stuff. Power is being one of the boys in the back room, someone who's in control."

"And yet—you go back to the Bronx every year."

"I have my weaknesses, but I don't kid myself that they matter. I keep them under control."

She looked at him closely. "You knew all along why I invited them, didn't you?"

"Oh, you aren't so hard to figure out. And I don't object to a little bitchiness in my wife. Just don't use it on me. And maybe this is the time to put our cards on the table. I know you think I'm pretty crude, and you're right. I got rid of my Bronx accent, but I'm still an old street fighter and always will be. But we're two of a kind, Crystal. We want the same thing—and don't care how we get it."

"I'm ambitious for you, of course—"

"Let's cut out the shit. I'm telling you how it's going to be from now on. For one thing, you're going to keep your nose clean. A man in my position can't afford any scandal. So there'll be no more high jinks with young boys. That's a little too kinky for most honest citizens to stomach."

Crystal was silent for the reason that she'd lost her voice. How long had he known about Jason—and how had he found out?

"The rewards will make it worthwhile," Arnold was going on. "In another three years, I'll be retiring—"

At her gasp of dismay, he smiled thinly. "That shakes you up, does it? Well, don't sweat it. The perks don't have to stop with retirement. How would you like to be a senator's wife?"

"A—what?"

"I have friends in the Bronx—important friends. They need someone to combat the Republicans on their own territory, someone who won't be tarred and feathered for being too liberal—and what could be more conservative than a retired air force general?"

"Are you saying—"

"I've been courted, felt out, approached. First, I do my stint as chief of staff—that's already in the bag—and then I retire and we move back to New York. I give out a few nostalgic interviews about my boyhood in the Bronx and tell the good citizens how much I want to return to my roots. Someone will

appoint me to a nonelective government job, and then—away
we go."

"What are your chances of making it in politics?" Crystal
asked, her interest fully aroused. A senator's wife—that would
put her in very exclusive company. . . .

"As good as making it out of the Bronx in the first place.
Do you know the most difficult thing I ever did? Getting that
appointment to West Point. The rest of it has been a snap
compared to that. Back then, the appointments went to upper-
class kids. Officers and gentlemen—with the emphasis on
gentlemen. Which is why I opted for the air force after I'd
graduated from the Point. I knew I wouldn't have to take the
crap I would in the army because to be a pilot you don't need
a pedigree. So I made the switch, and here I am. I've made
mistakes, of course. For one thing, I married Sophie, who
turned out to be a weak vessel. Couldn't take the hurdles without a drink in her hand. I would've divorced her except a
divorced man has more than a couple of strikes against him in
the military—at least until recently."

"And you think I can take it?"

"I know you can. You're hungry as hell. Of course you're
screwed up emotionally, but that's okay. Who isn't?"

She stared at his grim smile. "So what if I turn out just like
Sophie?"

"I'll dump you so fast you won't know what hit you. But
that won't happen. I never make the same mistake twice. You'll
work your ass off, backing me because you want just what I
want. That's why I married you."

"That and other reasons?"

"Oh, you're good in bed. I'm not knocking that."

"I think you're great, too, lover," she murmured.

"You don't think any such thing. You're a cold fish sexually,
but that's all right with me. The best prostitutes are frigid.
You're good—really good. Inventive, too. But that isn't why
I married you."

He moved so quickly that she didn't have time to evade
him before he'd seized her face between his thick fingers,
squeezing until she gave a cry of pain.

"You're going to toe the line, sister. No more sex games
with little boys—not if you want to stay healthy. You understand what I'm saying? No slipping around, not even with men
your own age. And from now on, you're permanently on the

wagon. Do you understand? You don't handle your liquor well, so no more drinking for you."

Crystal stared into Arnold's hard eyes, and she knew that he meant it. If she didn't measure up, he would discard her without compunction.

"Okay," she whispered.

"Just so we understand each other." His grip on her still painfully tight, he kissed her, his open mouth wet and too soft. "And I think there's time for a little romp in the hay before you change clothes. How about showing your new husband just how grateful you are that he decided to marry you instead of just paying the rent on your apartment?"

Automatically, Crystal put her arms around his thick neck and moved her hips against his, hiding her distaste. After all, the rewards he offered were irresistible. She was a realist—and she'd always known that anything worth having came with a big price tag.

Of course, it wasn't a sure thing. Arnold knew how to play the military game—but politics had its own rules. It could go either way—but however it turned out, she intended to land on her feet. In fact, she was looking forward to the fight. Who knows, she thought as Arnold propelled her rapidly toward the bed, she might even end up First Lady someday.

It seemed so strange to Shelley that she had only been gone two days. Tad had said much the same thing when he'd picked her up at the airport. As they drove toward home in their five-year-old Ford, it seemed impossible that so much had happened since she'd left home. How was it possible that a brief encounter with three old friends—no, make that two old friends and one old enemy—had put her own life back on track?

In fact, she felt a little smug when she compared what she had with Crystal. Tad would never be able to provide her with luxuries, but then he loved her—and that made all the difference. Tad's ways were different from hers, and in so many things they would never see eye to eye. Sometimes it almost seemed as if they spoke a different language—and yet the two of them were two parts of a whole. Which was some kind of miracle.

Yes, it was a miracle that they'd found each other—and how could she have forgotten why she had married Tad in the first place? How had she allowed outside problems to erode that feeling she'd had from the day they'd met of being wanted, needed, loved?

The past ten years had been rough—but the feeling was still there, strong as ever. Not just sex. Sex alone could never hold two people together. But caring could. And Tad cared for her, put her first, even above his loyalty to his family—wasn't it about time she did the same?

The problems would remain, of course. Although she'd never told him how she felt about his father or his brothers, he sensed their dislike, and it made him defensive. In turn, she felt defensive when he criticized her father—which didn't make much sense. Both of them knew the imperfections of their own families, had rebelled against it—how could she have forgotten the years that her parents had sent her off to school because they didn't want to bother with her? And this recent concern for her—it was all a sham. It was their grandsons her parents wanted because they hoped the boys would fill the void Tony's death had left in their lives.

Tad's hand squeezed her knee. "You're awful quiet. What's cooking in that blond head of yours?"

"I was thinking about the wedding."

"Not much like ours, I'll bet."

"No, not like ours. We had a wonderful wedding. This one was pretty grim."

"Grim? I thought the governor and a couple of mayors and—who was the other big shot?"

"Senator Ching. Who turns out to be Tai's uncle."

Tad whistled softly. "Well, you do have influential friends. How come she never mentioned it?"

"That's Tai. She keeps her own counsel."

"Whatta you know. A woman who doesn't tell everybody her business."

"That remark is going to cost you," she said darkly.

"Uh-huh. Well, if it costs more than . . . uh, five hundred dollars, which is what we've got in the bank, forget it."

She groaned. "Back to earth again."

"Right. It'll get better, but first we have some bad times to get through—such as being separated for the next twelve months." Although his tone was neutral, she sensed the question he wanted to ask her. "We have to start thinking about college for the boys in a few more years—and maybe it's time for another baby, too."

Shelley was silent. This was something that couldn't be brushed aside easily. She had no desire for another baby—but Tad did. It was one more problem to add to the others—so why didn't it seem to be all that important?

"Okay, spit it out," Tad said. "You've got something on your mind, and you're going to spring it on me eventually. Since the boys will take you over when we get home, let's talk about it now."

"I was thinking about—about something in the past that I'll bet you've forgotten."

"Something good?"

"Very good."

"That's easy. You were remembering that time at Camp John Hay when I got the sex thing right for the first time."

She gave him him a surprised look. "How on earth did you do that?"

"Just because I've got grease under my nails doesn't mean I'm—what's that word everybody uses? Insensitive?"

She laughed at his wry tone. "What am I thinking about now?"

"You're wishing we were home and the boys were in bed so we could fool around."

"Wrong. I was thinking about that day in the Philippines when I had that run-in with Mrs. Blackwell in the prego line. I'll bet you don't remember what you said when I asked you if you were mad at me."

"I don't think I said anything, did I?"

"You said, 'Hell, no, I'm not mad. You did the right thing.'"

"And you still remember *that*? Women are crazy."

"We remember the important things—most of the time. I forgot a lot of things, such as being the world's loneliest kid the first seventeen years of my life—until I met you."

He was silent for a moment. "Does that mean what I think it means?"

"It means I'll be staying in Shreveport while you're gone. If my folks want to see the boys, they can come here for a visit."

"Folks—you called them your folks. Do you know you always called them your parents before?"

"So?"

"So I'm nuts about you, Shelley. I know you think I was

way off base, wanting you to stay put while I'm gone, but I'm afraid of losing you. Crazy, huh?"

"Not crazy. Intuitive."

"Right. I'm one wild and intuitive guy." Tad steered the car to the side of the road and killed the motor. When he put his arms around Shelley, she kissed him—hard. Sure enough, the old magic was still there.

"God, Shelley—you were only gone two days, and you wouldn't believe all the weird things that've been going through my head. Like maybe the plane would go down over the Pacific, or maybe you'd meet some guy you used to know at Punahou and fall for him, or maybe you'd take a good look at what you gave a guy up to marry me and decide not to come back. How can a guy get so screwed up?"

Shelley thought of Crystal, of Arnold Krause with his hot eyes and wet mouth. "I have what I want right here," she said.

It was late, after they had put the boys to bed and had made love and Tad was sleeping beside her, that some of the euphoria wore off. Because there were still so many problems—God, were there ever!

There was the long separation to get through. There was the business of trying to stretch Tad's pay to make ends meet—and her parents weren't going to go away. Neither was Tad's family. Then there was another worry, inherent in any long separation. She was a sexually active woman. With no outlet for her needs, she would be tempted to stray—and so would Tad, who attracted women as if he wore some kind of magical charm.

So there was jealousy to cope with—and a dozen other things.

But maybe, if they were very lucky, they would make it together into old age. God help them, they just had to make it.

Bobby Jo heard Josh's voice through the screen door as she came up the walk. She had taken a taxi from the airport because the phone had been busy when she'd called. She could have dialed again in a few minutes, but she'd been too impatient to get home. Now she wished she'd waited because she'd just discovered that she didn't want to face Josh yet, not until she'd had more time to think.

She paused outside the door, wondering who he was talking

to in that too loud voice. Not Vicky. She was staying with her friend Georgette. Did Josh have company? No, it was a one-sided conversation, which meant he was talking on the phone.

"—can't make it. My old lady's coming home sometime today and I have to be here when she calls. . . . Hell, no, she doesn't tell me what to do. Where'd you get that idea? Okay, I know I haven't been sitting in on the games like I used to, but everything gets a little old after a while." There was a long pause, followed by his laugh. "No, not that. But even sex needs a little variety. . . . Yeah, sure, we'll get together soon. And keep the faith, big buddy."

Through the screen door, she caught a glimpse of Josh as he moved away from the hall phone, heading for the kitchen. She took a deep breath and pumped cheerfulness into her voice.

"Anybody home?" she called.

Josh turned to stare at her. He was wearing jeans and a soiled T-shirt; it was obvious he hadn't shaved since she'd left. She wondered if he'd planned to come to the airport to pick her up looking like that.

"So you're home. How come you didn't give me a buzz?"

"The phone was busy, so I decided to take the Airporter and save you a trip."

"Yeah, well, the phone about rang off the hook today." He opened the screen door, took her suitcases from her, and gave her a quick kiss. "First there were a couple of calls for Vicky, which I referred to her friend's house, then someone called about an energy survey—one of those damned hype jobs. And a woman called, wants you to take some job for the wives' club. I told her you'd call her back, but I forgot to get her name. Then Jim Connors asked me to sit in on a poker game with some of the guys. I told him I was waiting for you to call me from the airport."

"Well, I'm home now. Go ahead if you like."

"You sure you don't mind?"

"No, I don't mind. I'll go pick up Vicky—"

"Why don't you leave her there for a while? I can think of something interesting to do right now."

Bobby Jo considered him for a long moment. "I think we'd better have a talk instead, Josh. This may seem pretty sudden to you, but I've decided to go back to work."

"You've what?"

"I'm going back to work. We can use the money, and

besides . . . well, I was doing so well, you know. My sales record was one of the highest in the office." She discovered that her heart was beating very fast, that she was having trouble breathing. "Mr. Shoulders says I'm a natural salesperson—"

"What the hell—I thought we thrashed this all out? I want you at home, taking care of the house and the kid—"

"Vicky. Her name is Vicky, Josh."

"What does that mean—no, don't tell me. What happened to you while you were gone? Those friends of yours fill your head full of garbage? Well, forget it—and forget the job, too. We already decided that your place was at home."

"*You* decided—just like you make all the decisions around here. Which is partially my fault. It's too easy to give in and keep things peaceful."

"You're weird—you know that? What's that dyke friend of yours been saying to you?"

"Are you talking about Tai?"

"Who else? What's with you and her, anyway? Were you getting it on in high school? Everybody at the academy knew she was a lesbian. She never fratted with anyone—and she was into martial arts, too. But I never really thought you were involved with her, not the way you let me crawl all over you on our first date."

Bobby Jo was aware of a rush of anger—but also of a feeling of relief, which she couldn't pin down. Why was she glad that Josh was being his most obnoxious?

Because it makes it easier for you to leave him, Bobby Jo. . . .

The thought was so startling that she lost her power of speech. Of course—that's why she'd felt so strange, ever since she'd left Crystal's house—fearful and yet elated. Subconsciously, she had known that she was going to leave Josh.

And why had it taken her so long to come to this decision? Was it because she knew how hard it would be, trying to earn a living for herself and Vicky? Or was it fear? Telling Josh that she didn't want to be married to him any longer wasn't going to be easy. He might even get ugly. Would he try to get custody of Vicky, just for spite? Well, she'd face that if it happened. In a strange way, she would even miss him. She had loved him once—and you didn't live with someone for ten years and not have it hurt like hell when you busted up.

But that wasn't going to stop her. She was fighting for her life, for her freedom—and if she had to pay a big price, so be it.

"I have something to say to you," she said carefully. "It's very important."

"What if I don't want to listen to you?"

"You'd better listen—not that it matters in the long run. I came to a decision while I was gone—something Shelley said brought it all to a head. She was talking about something else, but she could've meant our marriage. She said we have to keep remembering what's really important. And that's what I haven't been doing. Which is why I'm leaving you, Josh. You don't need me, you never have. I'm just a warm body to you, someone to sleep with, to fix your meals and make your bed and bring you a beer when you want it—"

"You're out of your fucking mind—"

"No, I'm finally sane. I should have left you years ago. I've wasted so much time, trying to salvage something that was never there. But it isn't too late. I'm going to start all over again—"

"Who's the man? You've got someone on the string or you wouldn't be talking this way. Who is he?"

"I'm not leaving you for another man. I don't need a man to be happy. If I did, I'd probably stay with you. My only chance for happiness is to pull out before it's too late."

"You dumb broad—you couldn't get along five minutes without some guy to support you." Josh's face was distorted with anger. "That job of yours was a laugh—you really believed all the crap that Shoulders guy handed you. All he wanted was to get into your pants—"

"I can see why you'd believe that. You don't want a wife who thinks for herself—and don't get any ideas about man-handling me, because if you do, I'll go to the police. And how would that look on your record? That you're a wife beater?"

"You bitch—"

"No, I'm not a bitch. That's the point. I thought I was, and I chose my own punishment—staying with you. But I finally saw the light. You've always made fun of me, mocked my accent, criticized my taste, and laughed at my opinions, so how come you didn't divorce me? Didn't you ever wonder about that? It's because you want someone around you can look down on—it makes you feel big. And did you ever wonder what's wrong with someone who only feels like a man when he's putting someone else down—or screwing some woman?"

She thought he would hit her then. He took a step toward her, but she didn't retreat. In the end, he was the one who backed off.

"So get out. I've been sick of you for a long time," he said. "The only reason I stayed with you was because of the kid."

"No, *you* get out. This is my house. I'll even pack your things for you."

"You'll never get one red cent from me!"

"Oh, you'll pay child support for Vicky. But I can support myself. All I want from you is to be left alone."

Josh stared at her, and unexpectedly, she felt a stirring of pity for him. He didn't love her—but he did need her. The thing was—she didn't need him, not anymore.

"It's that Shoulders guy, isn't it? He's been sniffing around— he put you up to this. What did he promise you? A fancy apartment somewhere? Money? Don't tell me he offered to marry you? Have you had sex with him yet? Maybe you should— I'd hate to think you'd give up a good sex life for a wimp like that."

"Where did you get the idea that we have a good sex life? You don't make love to me—you're too concerned about your own satisfaction. I don't know why you bother—masturbation would be a lot less trouble," she said wearily.

Josh's face turned dark red. "I don't have to listen to this crap," he snarled. He turned and went pounding off down the hall. A few seconds later, she heard the storage room door open and knew he was getting out his flight bag.

Feeling weak, Bobby Jo leaned against the wall. The worse part was over, but there were so many problems ahead. Telling Vicky that her parents were getting a divorce. Going back to work—and this time knowing that she had to make good in order to support herself and Vicky. Facing her friends, her family, with the news that the marriage that had seemed so happy from the outside had been rotten to the core.

And Josh would be back. She'd said some terrible things to him, and right now his instinct was to slam out of here and move into the BOQ. But the fact that she'd asked him to leave would rankle, and his pride would demand that he talk her into coming back to him. Oh, yes, she knew him so well. So it wasn't over—not yet. She would be assaulted on all sides by advice and other people's ideas of what was right for her—including those of her father, who considered divorce a mortal sin. But she would face it step by step, day by day.

And she wouldn't make the mistake of taking the easy out—going from Josh directly into another man's arms. But oh, it was a temptation. All she had to do was pick up the phone, call Sam, and he would be here in minutes, offering her his shoulder to cry on, possibly a new marriage eventually, one that would be safe and secure.

But if she did that, what would she have proved? What would happen to the strength that had been so long in coming to her? Maybe in time, it would work out with Sam. He was the kind of man she should have married—or was that true? Maybe, in his own way, he would be as bad for her as Josh. Well, it was too soon to worry about that. Like everything else in life, it would work itself out.

At last she had taken one giant step.

Tai finished her wine and then nibbled a piece of cheesecake, finally pushing it aside. Across the table, Steven had already finished his dessert and was looking very pleased with himself.

"How about that cheesecake?" he gloated. "I found it at that little Jewish deli in Old Town. It's every bit as good as New York cheesecake—right?"

"Hmm . . . very good," she said absently.

How was she going to tell him—how even approach the subject? For the past two hours, ever since he'd picked her up at the airport, they had talked about a dozen things, but she still hadn't been able to broach the subject uppermost in her mind and, she was sure, in Steven's.

She had to ease into it, of course—why was that so difficult for her? She was half Chinese, wasn't she? And everybody knew the Oriental mind was subtle. So why was it so hard to find the right words to tell Steven that she'd figured out a way they could both have what they wanted and still stay together?

And wasn't it odd that it was Crystal who had given her the answer to their problem—if it *was* the right answer—when she'd made that snide remark about her ending up as a house-wife like the others. Just another of Crystal's barbs, and yet it had triggered off a whole new line of thinking, another view of their problem.

She thought of Crystal's tirade—and the venom that had

prompted it. Where had all that hatred and resentment come from? Some of it was the liquor Crystal had been drinking, but the rest—she really hated them all. Well, it was out in the open now. Better to know who your enemies were so you could be on guard. Not that she was afraid of Crystal.

In fact, she felt sorry for her. The price of getting what she wanted, being married to someone like Arnold Krause, was too high for anyone to pay. There had been no mention of Grant, no explanation of why that marriage had failed. It had been so sudden, too. One day Grant was retiring and the next they were getting a divorce. Then, a few months later, the wedding invitation had come. . . .

"You've been awfully quiet since you got back," Steven said.

"And I thought you hadn't noticed how little I had to say about my sojourn in Paradise."

"You've been stewing inside like Mount Saint Helens getting ready to erupt. What's bothering you?"

"I'm not sure how you're going to take this, Steven—which is why I keep putting it off, I guess."

She saw his eyes change. Funny—brown eyes were supposed to hide emotion, but Steven's were a barometer to how he felt. When they turned dark like that, it meant he was deeply moved or sexually aroused—or afraid.

"I hope you aren't going to tell me something for my own good," he said. "If so, I don't think I want to hear it."

"It's for both our good. You know we can't go on like this. Living apart most of the time with the possibility of another long separation hanging over us because I'm due for an overseas assignment, then coming together like strangers. We even have different friends we see when we're apart—and balancing a bankbook in tandem is the pits."

"And then there's the kid we want—or that I want," he said quietly.

"I want your baby, Steven. But until we can provide him with a real home and two full-time parents, I don't want to bring a kid into the world. But I may have the solution. What I'm suggesting is drastic, and once it's done, it isn't reversible."

"Are you trying to tell me that you want to resign when you get your mandatory service in? Are you sure? I know how crazy you are about flying. You'll never be happy grounded."

"No, that's not what I mean. The one who should resign is

you, Steven. I think you should leave the air force when your time is up."

"Me? But that's asinine!"

"Why asinine? Suppose you were the one who was crazy about flying, who wanted to be a pilot for as long as possible. And what if I had other interests, such as a fascination with computers and a yen to create the first workable artificial intelligence program, and couldn't care less about flying? Then I'd be the natural one to resign and follow you wherever you're assigned. And no one would turn a hair."

"But what the hell would I do? What kind of career could I build, following you from base to base?"

He paused, staring at her. "I see your point. If the reverse were true, I wouldn't even ask that question. So you want me to be a—a house husband, is that it? To stay home and take care of our kids—if any? You sure you don't want me to have them, too? After all, if you get pregnant, you're grounded for nine months."

She absorbed his sarcastic tone without flinching, knowing that it was a natural reaction. "No, not a house husband. That works for some couples, but not for us. Besides, it would be such a waste if you didn't use your training to the fullest, just as it's a waste when it happens to a woman. But there is a way out—if it sounds right to you."

"What is it?"

"What do you do when you're home between flights?"

"Aside from pulling you under the covers every chance I get?"

"When you're here alone—how do you spend your time?"

"Well, I've been working on a new software program, that Ada variation I told you about. Is that what you mean? What does that have to do with this?"

"People can make a very good living out of putting together new software programs, can't they?"

"Sure—if you work your tail off, and if you get lucky."

"But you *could* make a career of it, right? The thing is, it takes a long time before it pays off sometimes. I heard you talking to Chuck Breland about it the other day. You said it was chancy as hell—like trying to make it as a writer or an artist. You need time—big hunks of it. And space, lack of pressure—just what you'd have if you quit the air force. Part of the time, I'd be gone on flights, and without me to bug you,

you could work undisturbed. You can also work anywhere in the world that had an electric outlet."

She stopped because Steven's face had undergone a complete wipeout of expression. Either he was deep in thought, or he was fighting hard not to blast her with a few truths about ball-busting women. Because for all his tolerance and sweet reason, he was also a man. A man who'd had it pounded into him for four years at the academy that he was the best, the greatest, a prime specimen. . . .

Steven got up and came around the table toward her. He shook her hand solemnly. "You've got it," he said. "How the hell did you come up with this?"

In her relief, Tai began to laugh. "Oriental ingenuity," she sputtered just before he kissed her.